Chris Carlsson is one of t

whose activism and storytelling have reshaped the way we understand our city's

past—and changed its future. When Carlsson offers a vision of urbanism to come,

you'd better pay attention.

   —Annalee Newitz, author of *The Terraformers*

and *Four Lost Cities: A Secret History of the Urban Age*

Carlsson invites us to put the imagination back in the revolution.

When Shells Crumble is reminder that the path from dystopia to utopia may not

be as long as we have feared it to be.

   —James R. Tracy, co-author *No Fascist USA!*

The John Brown Anti Klan Committee and Lessons for Today's Movements

Futurist and thought provoker Carlsson once again imagines

a near-future scenario where disaster spawns opportunities for radical self-reliance.

San Francisco and the greater Bay Area are where history, politics, culture and

environment create a messy stew of biotech, inequality, activism, and overreaching

federal crackdowns. But wait—mysteriously enabled flora and fauna may be allies

in the struggle! As with his first novel After the Deluge, Carlsson's ideas will stay

in your mind long after you put down his tale of radicalized plumbers and urban

gardeners.

   —Laura Lent, retired, formerly Chief of Collections & Technical Services,

San Francisco Public Library

Most dystopian fiction takes the reader to strange new worlds

where mutations are large and grotesque. The strength of Chris Carlsson's *When
Shells Crumble* instead arises from how close its future-world is to our present-day

Trumpland realities. Enriched by Carlsson's deep, sympathetic understanding of

San Francisco Bay Area alternative undergrounds, *When Shells Crumble* brings

us into a landscape of martial law and spirited resistance to it, made all the more

chilling by how little distance there seems between his imagined nightmare

scenario and the near-nightmare we currently inhabit.

   —Joseph Matthews, author of *The Blast*

WHEN SHELLS CRUMBLE

CHRIS CARLSSON

SPUYTEN DUYVIL
New York City

© Chris Carlsson 2024

ISBN 978-1-959556-82-4

Library of Congress Control Number: 2023039865

Cover: San Francisco Global Warming Triptych # 2,
Oil painting by Anthony Holdsworth © 2007

Book and cover design: Chris Carlsson

Library of Congress Cataloging-in-Publication Data

Names: Carlsson, Chris, 1957- author.
Title: When shells crumble / Chris Carlsson.
Description: New York City : Spuyten Duyvil, 2024.
Identifiers: LCCN 2023039865 | ISBN 9781959556824 (paperback)
Subjects: LCGFT: Social problem fiction. | Novels.
Classification: LCC PS3603.A7535 W47 2024 | DDC 813/.6--dc23/eng/20231023
LC record available at https://lccn.loc.gov/2023039865

Dedicated to

Halloul Hasan and Spinoza Hasan,

my beautiful granddaughters

who will live long enough to know

how it really turns out.

The Robertson Family
—names in bold appear in book—

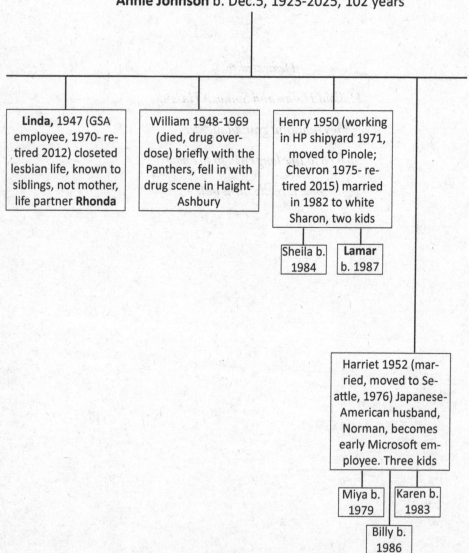

Annie Johnson b. Dec.5, 1923-2025, 102 years

Linda, 1947 (GSA employee, 1970- retired 2012) closeted lesbian life, known to siblings, not mother, life partner **Rhonda**

William 1948-1969 (died, drug overdose) briefly with the Panthers, fell in with drug scene in Haight-Ashbury

Henry 1950 (working in HP shipyard 1971, moved to Pinole; Chevron 1975- retired 2015) married in 1982 to white Sharon, two kids

Sheila b. 1984

Lamar b. 1987

Harriet 1952 (married, moved to Seattle, 1976) Japanese-American husband, Norman, becomes early Microsoft employee. Three kids

Miya b. 1979

Karen b. 1983

Billy b. 1986

Aaron Robertson b. 1922-d. 1979, 57 years

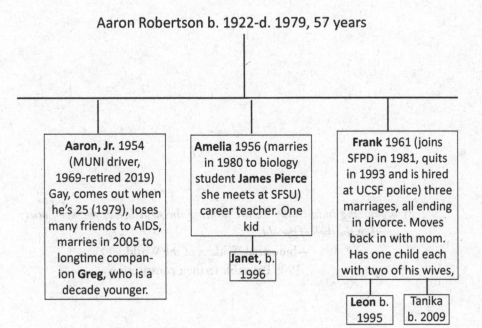

Aaron, Jr. 1954 (MUNI driver, 1969-retired 2019) Gay, comes out when he's 25 (1979), loses many friends to AIDS, marries in 2005 to longtime companion **Greg**, who is a decade younger.

Amelia 1956 (marries in 1980 to biology student **James Pierce** she meets at SFSU) career teacher. One kid

Janet, b. 1996

Frank 1961 (joins SFPD in 1981, quits in 1993 and is hired at UCSF police) three marriages, all ending in divorce. Moves back in with mom. Has one child each with two of his wives,

Leon b. 1995

Tanika b. 2009

By organizing industrially we are forming the structure of the new society within the shell of the old.

—Industrial Workers of the World,
1905 Preamble to their constitution

— PART ONE —

CHAPTER 1

FRIDAY, DECEMBER 20, 2024

"Supreme Court Upholds Election Reversal!" screamed the 72-point headlines in newspapers across the country. An Associated Press report appeared in most of the nation's newspapers and online:

> "WASHINGTON, DC: In an astonishing ruling today, the Supreme Court upheld the decisions of the state legislatures of Arizona and Wisconsin to nullify the presidential election popular votes in each state. The ruling effectively reverses the presidential election in favor of the Republican ticket, President-elect Asa Hutchinson and his running mate, former Governor of New Mexico, now Vice-President-elect Susanna Martinez, over the Democratic incumbents. By a vote of 5-4, the conservative majority led by Justices Thomas, Alito, and Gorsuch adopted the controversial "independent state legislature theory," claiming that an "originalist" interpretation of the Constitution's Electors Clause in Article II allows the state legislatures to override the popular vote if it determines that the outcome was, in a stunningly ambiguous turn of phrase, "insufficiently certain."
>
> "With this decision, the Supreme Court seeks to end the post-election turmoil that has swirled around several swing states, but especially Wisconsin and Arizona. Few expect the ruling to settle the rising tide of confrontation that has already led to violence and at least five deaths in the Milwaukee riots at the beginning of December.

"I can't believe it! Just last year they rejected the same argument in that North Carolina case!" Janet Pierce was no legal eagle, but she had followed the twists and turns of the conservative Supreme Court's steady shift rightward to benefit Republican rule. Alarmed, Janet and her oldest friend Vero Gomez grabbed their bikes and started pedaling from the Alemany Farm to the Civic Center. An emergency demonstration had been called, even though the drama was unfolding far from San Francisco. No one expected a riot, but San Franciscans had to express their outrage.

"Hey," Vero called over her shoulder, "My phone is blowing up with meeting points. Let's head to the Main Library, ok?" "Fine." They were both in grubby overalls and boots after a wintery afternoon at the Farm where they worked most days. People sometimes mistook them at first for sisters because they were both about 5'4" and broad-shouldered, closer to stocky than slim. But Vero's black braids set her apart from Janet's natural Afro, and while their skin tone was nearly identical, Vero's heritage was Mexican while Janet's was mostly African American, though her father was himself biracial.

They headed north towards Market Street on the Seventh Street bike lane, avoiding the rapidly thickening crowd surging in the same direction. They skirted the east end of UN Plaza before dismounting in the dense crowd and pushing their way to the Main Library. A vast crowd filled the Civic Center, larger than anything they'd seen since Gay Pride marches before the pandemic.

"Man, I sure hope Mike Flores and his friends don't try to come around here," Vero said, referring to the processions that had been prominent in the lead-up to the vote in November. Car caravans had crisscrossed the city, especially the Mission, repeatedly since the nominating conventions in August. Much to the chagrin of Vero and Janet, their friend Mike had supported the puzzling UFW endorsement of the Republicans and then organized his friends into the caravans, trumpeting their support for the America First, pro-God, pro-car "patriotism" of the Republicans. Vero trailed a rainbow banner from her bike that said, "Bicycling for the Climate!" She and Janet had been activists since their early teens, and both were stalwarts of the League of Urban Farmers. Janet was elected a year ago to the city-wide Canopy Council that co- ordinated the ever-expanding network of urban farms.

They took turns waving and shouting to friends in the swelling crowd. This repudiation of the Supreme Court decision and the election results was already a typical celebratory San Francisco demonstration. Countless home-made signs peppered the crowd, many hilarious, ridiculing the Court and the justices, and denouncing the Republican coup. Chanting erupted in pockets, weirdly repeat- ing the chants of the Trumpists from four years earlier, "Stop the Steal!"

"Y'know, I don't know if I can stay here very long," Janet confided to Vero. "150,000 people protesting in San Francisco doesn't do much. It's a party!"

Vero agreed, checking her encrypted messages. "Oh, here we go! There's a breakaway heading to one of the Federal Buildings... Shall we?"

Janet, not thrilled about elections to start with, had little enthusiasm for the Harris/Kerry administration. Since Biden's sudden death last February, Kamala Harris had worked hard to be presidential, starting with selecting John Kerry as her Vice President. As she had done in prior political positions, she talked a vaguely progressive line, but in practice she was completely deferential to the monied interests that controlled the U.S. government.

Still, Janet knew what was happening was worse than if there had been a normal election outcome. The system itself wasn't holding any longer. She shrugged, "why not? Let's see what happens." They amplified the call out, texting messages that the Civic Center crowd would be marching to the Federal Building at Seventh and Mission in a half hour. It was a Friday afternoon, and most people were taking the long weekend that would extend into the Christmas break. Hence, the huge turnout. Now, if they could get to the Federal Building by 4, they could close it down early. That would be noticed more than a party in the Civic Center.

Drums and trumpets erupted from the Brass Liberation Orchestra and like a pied piper, they circulated through the crowd, calling to people "On to the Federal Building," which was quickly taken up by most who heard it. Why mill about in the Civic Center in front of City Hall? Soon there were thousands of people marching behind the BLO.

Vero looked at Janet with a gleam in her eye. "Here we go!"

"Everybody's ready for something else!" blurted Janet. She was feeling more energized than she'd felt earlier. Something was happening. "If we get over there, we can't just yell at the building," she insisted.

"Want to be part of a take-over?" Vero suggested, her thick black eyebrows arching mischievously as she gave Janet her most provocative smile. "It's already in the works".

"Maybe," Janet replied. Vero stopped rolling her bike and glared at her. "Ok, fine," Janet relented, "But let's not go in without an exit plan," remembering some awkward political moments earlier in her life.

"My homies are leading this one," Vero confided, "They know how to organize." All the same Janet texted her uncle Frank's girlfriend Sheila Downing, who she knew worked in the building. "Sheila! This is Janet Pierce, Frank's niece. Are you at work?"

Sheila was wrapping up her day when the text arrived from Janet. It was quite unexpected. Janet and she were acquainted, but never texted before.

"Um, yes, but about to leave," she texted back.

"Lot of folks heading over there." Janet wrote. Sheila looked at the message and shook her head. This couldn't end well, she thought. It was right before Christmas and lots of federal workers were going home early. Nothing much ever happened at the GSA building, other than the rare protest outside when Nancy Pelosi was Speaker of the House (her local office was inside).

She texted back to Janet: "You're not getting in. Heavy security at front door. Will be shut down on arrival."

She had been getting ready for her long holiday weekend and now this. It was discombobulating. She walked over to peer from her 9th floor window at the people surrounding the metal fence along Seventh Street, spilling out into the street and on to Mission as well.

Meanwhile Janet and Vero were pushing their bikes alongside a surging crowd, heading against traffic down Seventh Street from Market. "The loading dock! That's how they're getting in" Vero blurted, looking at the incoming messages. "Let's ride!" and they circled around the building. The 10-foot black iron fence around the plaza looked impenetrable. Offering no entry points, it forced the crowd to keep circling until they came upon the long ramps running into the basement facing Mission at the west end of the building.

"We could lift our bikes over those barriers," Vero pointed to the thick metal plates leaning up out of the ramp's pavement, set to block any vehicles trying to roll in without authorization.

Suddenly they heard a chant "Let us in! Let us in!" erupt back at the gates. You couldn't see what was happening from where they stood with their bikes on Mission Street behind several thousand people. As they tried to imagine how to spark a surge down the loading dock ramp, things took their own course. An Amazon delivery van was driving up the ramp when several hundred people began pouring past it, down the ramp. Janet and Vero locked their bikes and followed the crowd. There didn't seem to be any problem getting in as they flowed easily into a cavernous loading dock area. Two young security guards were standing on the dock, hands on hips, with huge grins on their faces. "Come on in! I'm already fired. Just come on in," one urged. Behind him a few protesters were already scrambling through the doors into the building, and soon hundreds more were following.

"Let's go!" Janet and Vero didn't need any further encouragement. They rushed through the doors behind dozens of people who were ahead of them. They went up the stairs into the lobby, everyone hooting and hollering with excitement. As their numbers swelled, the six security guards lining the windows and holding down the front desk realized they were surrounded and vastly outnumbered.

Various employees of the Department of Labor, the Social Security Administration, Department of Transportation, and other federal agencies were streaming into the lobby, hoping to make an early getaway before the holiday weekend. It was about 4:40 now. The guards locked the front doors when people scaled the perimeter fence and opened the gates to let everyone in. They were banging on the windows, yelling "Let us in! Let us in!" The lobby was filling up with protesters and federal workers jostling for position.

"Hey, let us out!" yelled a guy in a suit, looking extremely uncomfortable.

Other employees who seemed to be with him, their employee badges bobbing from their necks, took up the refrain, "Let us out!" they screeched.

"Calm down!" scolded a protester, a middle-aged woman herself. "We won't hurt anyone." Some pushing and shoving near the doors grabbed everyone's attention, as a scuffle between guards and protesters escalated.

"Open the doors, man!" The guards were standing shoulder to shoulder with batons out, pushing back. Behind them, outside the doors, protesters crowded close. Finally the sheer numbers prevailed and the guards were pushed aside after a brief stand. The doors flew open and the federal workers rushed out while protesters rushed in. In the melee it was hard to see what was happening. Janet and Vero were standing near the stairwell watching the scene unfold. "Janet!" came the voice behind her in the stairs. "Follow me!" Sheila was beckoning to her. She and Vero followed Sheila up the stairs. "What the hell is going on?" demanded Sheila.

Laughing, Janet and Vero tried to explain how they'd marched over and a crowd had piled in through the loading dock.

"Shit!" Sheila suddenly worried that her texting with Janet might get her in trouble. Thinking fast, she led them to the elevators.

"Wait! Where are we going?" Vero blurted. "To my office," said Sheila.

"But why? Don't we want to be down here where the action is?"

Outside in the growing gloom a police helicopter noisily appeared overhead, piercing the crowded plaza with a bright spotlight. Minutes later several buses of riot police pulled up, and the armor-clad soldier-officers tumbled onto the far side of Mission and Seventh. The crowd in the plaza below shifted nervously under the penetrating spotlight and the news about the coming police attack. People began leaving the Federal Building area towards Market and away from the police and the helicopter.

"Crap! Here they come!" Vero said, seeing the riot police reach the outside fence. Sheila and Janet stood behind her quietly, taking it all in, too.

Sheila glanced at her phone and saw that Frank had sent her a message.

"You still at work? You OK?"

She wrote him back, that she was fine and with Janet and a friend. "Be out shortly."

Federal workers passed them retreating upwards or heading down the hall to leave, while protesters kept pressing in towards the lobby. They could hear loud crowd sounds, both inside and outside the building. In the lobby, things were tense. A half dozen security guards were huddled in the far corner with a small crowd around them.

Janet looked around for exits, not happy to be kettled and arrested, or worse. "Sheila, what's the best way out of here? Is there an alternative to the front door?"

Vero glared at her, pissed that she was focused on leaving. "Oh my god, you're going to do this again. If you're going, go! I'm staying!" she announced defiantly.

"Vero, these things always end in mass arrests or people getting hurt. Wouldn't you rather avoid that and be able to fight again another day soon? On our own terms?" Janet suggested sensibly.

"Go ahead! Cut and run! I've got a building to occupy," Vero exclaimed, walking backwards into the crowd, middle fingers raised to the air.

"OK, well, I'll get you out if you get arrested," Janet said, and she and Sheila made their way to a rear hallway that exited towards the garage.

"If we go this way, we might be able to get out to Mission Street," Sheila said. They were hurrying now, feeling the impending calamity unfolding around them. Quickly they found themselves alone half running down a long gray hall. Two federal police jumped out from an alcove and stopped them abruptly.

"Who are you? Where are you going?" one barked.

Sheila waved her GSA badge and said, "I work here. We're leaving." After the cop glanced at her badge and looked menacingly at Janet, who had no badge, he scowled and waved them on.

"The door is open back there," he pointed.

In the plaza there were plenty of protesters milling about, but no one seemed to pay them any attention. Blending into the crowd they walked briskly away on Mission.

Janet knew this would be a long night. She texted people she knew in legal defense and media contacts. Sheila meanwhile wrote to Frank and let him know where they were. Five minutes later a UCSF police cruiser pulled up next to them on Mission near Ninth.

"Going my way?" called Frank through the open window. Sheila and Janet jumped in.

***

In the employee cafeteria of BioGenMo, a bland technologist stood at a table near the window watching police cars exiting the SFPD Headquarters. "Here you go, our mushroom espresso special," said the server, setting down a small cup and saucer, his drink topped with delicate foam art. "This is your last day, huh?"

The young tech worker smiled. "I knew I'd never last here, Alfredo."

Slipping the thumb drive from the saucer into his palm, he pulled out a one-hundred-dollar bill. "I will miss your coffees though." The server nodded appreciatively as he took the gift, saying as he left, "You do good out, there, Ed!"

"That's the plan, Alfredo." Taking his time to absorb the view and his coffee, Edwin Chin dispatched his espresso, laid down his cup, bent down to tie his shoelace and inserted the thumb drive in a storage fold in the tongue of his high-top sneaker, and walked out. Twenty minutes later he was handing the thumb drive to Dat Doan at the Howard Street lab.

CHAPTER 2
TUESDAY, DECEMBER 24, 2024

The occupation was a surprising success, and they walked out with no arrests. 'This is a GREAT Christmas present,' Vero thought as she departed the Federal Building. Along with about 60 others, they held out during the police assault. Sympathetic federal employees had joined them, an ambiguity that kept the police from a full-on assault. With the occupiers scattered in different offices, the police settled for securing the outer perimeter of the building last Friday night.

National media showed up Saturday morning, and local politicians paraded around claiming to support the occupation. Thousands of Friday demonstrators returned to surround the police perimeter and send in food and supplies. Pizzas even arrived, sent in from around the country. Occupiers appeared on streaming video, denouncing the Supreme Court and the stolen election in Wisconsin and Arizona.

"How is your action different than the January 6 protests that entered Congress four years ago?" asked the blonde anchorwoman to Beth Zeitel, a gray-haired occupier. She was a familiar character, a lifelong activist at every protest, every picket line, every interesting public lecture. She grinned. "First, we're not fascists! And second, we support the popularly elected president, as proven by actual votes. This election was stolen by the Republican state legislatures in Wisconsin and Arizona. The majority vote was nullified illegally by a fraudulent Supreme Court. The conservative justices are partisan hacks whose decision is as invalid as the actions of the state legislatures." The anchor smiled blandly and ended the interview. In San Francisco, no one would argue with Beth, except scattered right-wingers who remained hidden in their homes.

After the Supreme Court's decision, and the apparent acquiescence of the Harris government, right-wing car caravans began crisscrossing the Bay Area, shooting guns into the air, waving American flags. One caravan of more than 100 cars made their way to Seventh and Mission and circled the block on Saturday afternoon, raising tensions considerably. The thousands of protesters clogging surrounding streets jeered and cursed at the self-proclaimed "Parade of Patriots," and showered the cars with debris as they rolled by. When shots rang out the police immediately pushed the crowds back as they tried to attack the caravan. The cars sped away, prompting further speculation that the police and the "patriots" were working together.

Vero followed the large group of teenage occupiers out into the crowd, where they were besieged by supporters and spirited away in all directions. Vero felt a firm grip on her arm. "Let's go!" Janet urged. Janet gave her a new windbreaker and knit cap to replace what she was wearing.

Further up Mission Street, Janet ushered them towards an old van at the corner and they piled in and drove south.

"I can't believe you did it!" Janet exclaimed.

"You shoulda stayed. It was epic!"

The van turned onto Brannan Street where the driver pulled over. "Here ya go," he called.

They entered a nondescript four-story building. The League of Urban Farmers logo was draped on a big flag on the wall when they entered. Minutes later, Susan and David clattered in, throwing their camouflage bandanas onto the table. "That was a good idea!" Susan enthused. "This cool dude helped us disable the internal surveillance system which blinded the police inside. That gave us an advantage."

"I'm SO glad you organized your exit the way you did," Janet exclaimed. "I was worried sick you would get beat up and arrested and then we'd be dealing with medical and legal expenses for years!"

"Don't be an ass!" Vero admonished. She was disappointed that Janet had left the building when she did, leaving her and the rest. But they'd been friends since middle school, and at some point she accepted that this was always how it was going to be. "Luckily the Chief of Police called off the assault."

"You got luckier than you know. The federal police weren't happy, but they didn't have the numbers to do it alone," Janet explained. "Everyone outside was calling the Mayor's office, the Supes, the police department. Thousands of protesters went to City Hall on Friday night before the truce. I don't know how much that helped, but it didn't hurt!" she continued. She didn't explain how frantic she'd been during the days of the occupation, helping organize food and supplies, coordinating call-ins and texting. But it was over for now, and she was deeply relieved.

Janet's relief was real but so was her sense of danger. This ended too easily. It was unimaginable that the authorities wouldn't know who was involved and plan retribution. Yes, the government was in a state of confusion, and that worked to their advantage during the past few days. But there were enough permanent staffers at the FBI, the Federal Police, other spook agencies, and even the local police command structure, that she knew they'd be looking for "leaders," sooner than later.

"Vero, you may want to 'disappear' for a while, at least for the next couple of weeks until we see what happens next," Janet insisted.

"Why should I hide out?!" she retorted indignantly.

"You know they know you were in there, right? They'll have photos, video from before the surveillance was shut down... those bandanas help confuse cam- eras but this is different. It's not random crowd surveillance but dedicated high- resolution footage of every person who came out of those doors. Most folks will be identified soon enough. How long till they start rounding people up?"

Vero sniffed dismissively, and Janet grabbed her intensely by the shoulder, "Vero, it ain't the same old anymore. Get smart!"

"Ok, let go, already." Softening up, Vero added coyly. "Thanks for being here." Janet rolled her eyes.

Janet had been around too long to imagine this was over, no matter how glad they were about how it ended. The online videos of everyone coming out of the building were everywhere. "We should get out of here, come to think of it," she suddenly said. They grabbed their things and made plans to regroup after Christmas at the Dog Patch.

They trickled one by one out of the building, each going a separate way, a couple by bike, and the rest on foot. Janet left last and was dismayed to see a white van parked across Brannan. It looked like a surveillance vehicle. 'Of course!' she thought to herself. She pulled her backpack on and mounted her bike and started off towards Seventh. But then she made a quick u-turn to ride by the van up close. As she passed she could see the van rock slightly, indicating some people moving inside. It was impossible to see through the tinted glass that ringed the vehicle. It did have a small cluster of antennas on the roof, more likely evidence of surveillance. She checked the plates and they were regular commercial ones, not government issue. There was no way she could be completely certain, but it looked like someone, either government or private, had tracked them to the LUF office from the end of the occupation. Janet rode away in a zigzag pattern through the flat streets north of Potrero Hill.

CHAPTER 3
WEDNESDAY, FEBRUARY 19, 2025

Frank Robertson woke up next to Sheila in her bed. The sun was streaming in the 18th floor windows across the room, and he felt happy to be there. It had become a comfortable pattern, him staying over every other Sunday night after a long beach walk or a stroll in the Presidio or Golden Gate Park. Sheila stirred next to him and pushed her warm behind into his side.

"Mmmff, wha' time izzit?" she murmured, sensing his awakeness.

He glanced at his phone next to the bed and saw 7:02. "It's 7, time to rise and shine!" he boomed.

"Ohhhh," she groaned and rolled away. "It can't be Monday *again*!"

"You better get moving," Frank urged, knowing she was supposed to be at her desk in 90 minutes. He got himself to the bathroom and took care of his necessities before emerging to find Sheila making coffee in her bathrobe. He nuzzled her and hugged her from behind.

"No hanky panky!" she admonished, but in a friendly tone. They both had to get moving. Frank's phone rang in the bedroom. "This early? Maybe a robo-call." He went to get it, while Sheila flipped the radio on.

"President Hutchinson's declaration of a National Emergency a week ago in the Bay Area, and dozens of other U.S. cities, has generated a great deal of opposition locally and nationally. Here is San Francisco Mayor Yee:
'We just heard that our local police are being mobilized into a regional strike force under the command of this Homeland Security Czar, General Reynolds. This is an outrageous overreach of the federal government into local affairs. I have instructed our police not to cooperate with this order.'"

"Frank, did you hear this?"

He entered the room, a weird look on his face. "We were ordered to report to the Homeland Security base in Hayward! One-third of the UCSF police force! What the hell is going on?"

"The Mayor says he's ordering the SFPD to not cooperate. I guess that doesn't apply to you guys, huh?"

"No, we work for the University, which is a state-level agency. City government has no authority over us. I'm checking with my boss, give me a sec," and he started texting to the head of UCSF's police department. Minutes later, while they were sitting with their coffee, the reply came in.

Frank's bushy grey eyebrows rose into an arc Sheila had never seen before. "What, what is it Frank? Is it for real?"

"Fuck. Yes. I'm supposed to report to the Southland Mall, north entrance, by 12 noon today! I *knew* I shoulda retired already!" He was not happy. "Who the hell does this Reynolds guy think he is? And what is Hutchinson doing? He can't take over the whole country like this!"

"Well, it looks like he can. Would they arrest the Mayor?" she speculated.

"I gotta get going. Listen, I'll call you later, ok? And let me know what happens at work today. Who knows what crazy shit might happen at your building, given all this," he nodded towards the TV where the morning news continued to show armored vehicles and helicopters descending on the Hayward Executive Airport, the new Homeland Security base. As Frank departed, she turned back to the TV.

"We now go to Hayward where the new Homeland Security base is quickly being erected on the small airport there. Jennifer Barnes reports from the Southland Mall nearby:

Liz, the President's declaration has set big changes in motion in this sleepy corner of the Bay Area. Here in Hayward at the corner of Hesperian and Winton, ICE troops and officers from many local jurisdictions are overseeing the construction of a huge perimeter fence around the Southland Mall and the Hayward Executive Airport. Other buildings in the area are being taken over too, with plans to repurpose the local Social Security Administration building and possibly the entire Chabot College campus, all part of this massive new base. Neighbors are worried about what's happening, and hundreds of local residents plan to meet tonight at Ochoa Middle School to discuss what they can do. A government spokesperson said everything was being done according to the lawful orders of the new administration, but neighbors aren't sure. We'll learn more in the coming days. Back to you Liz.

Sheila stared at the screen, finding it hard to believe it was real. She turned it off and got herself out the door a half hour later. After her brief streetcar ride up to the Moscone Center station she disembarked for her daily trek towards the Federal Building at Seventh and Mission. She walked along Howard today, autopiloting through South of Market streets. At Russ Alley a bag lady sat by the wall, surrounded by pigeons.

"Hey lady, you don't look so good," she called with a gap-toothed smile from her ruddy face.

Sheila did a double-take, not used to be addressed that way by a woman living on the street. She peered at the woman, who sat in a pile of clothes that cascaded around her like a disheveled tent. She realized she'd walked past her many times. A dozen pigeons pecked at seeds scattered nearby, cooing with enthusiasm for their breakfast. Several ravens perched on the streetlights over the corner, cawing energetically. The woman gestured to them and said, "See, they don't think you look so good either!" she chortled.

"Well, yeah, I don't feel too good either. Have you heard about the National Emergency?"

"Oh yeah, that's not good, not good at all." Her cat emerged from under her clothes and mosied over to look up at Sheila.

"Hello kitty, what's your name?" Sheila asked while reaching down to pet the cat.

"That's Bill Dollar!" guffawed the woman. "He's always finding money, you wouldn't believe it."

Sheila, charmed by the oblique panhandling, pulled out a few singles she carried for handouts and thrust them at the woman.

"Hah! He did it again! What a cat!" She grinned and started to pick herself up. "Hey thank you lady. I hope your day gets better!" and she moved down the alley.

"Yeah, you too." Sheila resumed her walk to work, but she noticed the ravens were swooping along from pole to pole. In fact, they seemed to know which way she was going as they turned on Seventh before she did. "Hey you guys!" she called up to them half-heartedly. One of them alighted on a trash can a short distance ahead. As she approached she noticed that it dropped a shiny object on the top of the can, and then flew off before she was quite there. She looked closer to discover that it was some part of a phone. Maybe a battery, she wasn't sure. "Thank you!" she waved up to the ravens. Tickled by the apparent "gift" she reached into her bag and found a remnant bag of kettle corn she'd left uneaten from the weekend. She put the sweet kernels on the same garbage receptacle and went on, walking backwards towards her job. Sure enough the ravens swooped down and gobbled up the kettle corn, flapping their wings and cawing at her.

A minute later she was abruptly returned to the moment when a car went by with American flags flying from it and some rowdy boys hanging out yelling "USA, USA." The plaza in front of the building was ringed by a large squad of uniformed ICE troops. "Oh crap," she muttered under her breath.

"ID?" barked a soldier at her as she approached. She pulled out her badge and put it around her neck as usual. "This is me," she said, holding it out for him. He waved her through.

She arrived to a pile of urgent messages. At the top, finding an empty office building in the Hayward area to move the Social Security Administration's local offices to. Homeland Security already commandeered their existing building near the Southland Mall. She called her team and distributed tasks and they got busy.

***

Frank left Sheila's and went home to the house he shared with his mother on Marlin Street. Throwing his extra uniform and changes of clothes into a duffel bag, he organized his toiletries and got ready to go.

"Moms, they're sending us to Hayward," he loudly announced to his 100-year-old, increasingly deaf mother. He explained about the mobilization order following the declaration of a National Emergency.

She was watching TV where she had seen the basics already. "Who is this new president? What is going on? I've never heard of anything like this before."

Frank tried to explain. The Republicans seized the government and they were using force to protect it. He didn't want to help them, but he couldn't see how he could refuse to go. His entire department had been ordered to appear. His mother was worried of course, but he reassured her as best he could. "I'll be fine, Moms, nothing's gonna happen around here." He hoped he was right!

The door swung open and in walked Leon, his son. Frank always saw his own face in Leon's, though his son was several inches taller, darker, and much thinner. "Frank! What the hell is going on?"

Frank grimaced as he continued organizing his belongings. "I've been 'mobilized'! They're sending me to the new Homeland Security base in Hayward."

"How the hell does that work?!? You're a UCSF cop! They don't work for the Feds. Why do you have to go?" Leon was exasperated.

Frank turned to his son, soon to turn 30 years old, and suddenly saw him in a new light. He was a successful businessman, having taken on a share of the cannabis empire from 'Large Larry' Lansing years ago. "Leon, it's complicated. I don't want to go, but I've been ordered to appear. They've issued a regional emergency declaration, so that means everyone has to follow the orders of the authorities or be arrested. It's hard to believe, I know. I can hardly believe it myself," his voice trailed off softly. He was in shock. His police training, with its militarized deference to authority, was running on autopilot and he didn't see any other course of action.

"Frank," Leon could see his father faltering a bit, "you could resign, couldn't you? Why don't you stay here and call in sick at least?"

"Too late for that," Frank sighed. "I am not hiding, either. I'll go and see what's happening. Maybe it'll be better if I'm there," recalling times he'd been able to cool things down as a street cop, and later during his patrols on the campus.

Leon looked down at his chirping phone. "Janet's texting me. She's asking about you Frank."

"Tell her I'm fine. I'll call you guys later." Frank kissed his mother good-bye, grabbed his bag and left. "You look after Grannie, ok?" he called over his shoulder to Leon.

"Yeah, yeah, of course," he replied. "Grannie, how're you doin'?" he asked in a loud voice.

"Oh ok I guess," she smiled at her grandson. "You gonna stay here for a while?"

"I gotta go now, but I'll come back tonight and bring dinner."

Leon headed out the door and found Frank sitting in his car, texting on his phone.

"You sure about this, Frank?" Leon asked him again.

Frank looked up. "Sheila's at work, they're swamped with getting new buildings and materials for the big camp they're building in Hayward," he reported. "This looks worse than I thought," and he anxiously backed up while giving a small wave to Leon.

Before long he was rolling over the Bay Bridge and then down the Nimitz Freeway towards Hayward. Listening to the radio didn't help. It was filled with official bulletins and news flashes about riots in Los Angeles, New York, Chicago, Seattle, Washington, Baltimore, and Philadelphia. In Cincinnati protesters were shot by a vigilante mob who were occupying City Hall and declared themselves the legitimate government. Reports of white mobs attacking protesters were coming in from dozens of cities in the Midwest and south. In the big cities, national guard call-ups were being used to end the riots. "Is this the new Civil War?" Frank said out loud, shocked at the chaos coming over the radio.

He exited the freeway amid a steady stream of white Hummers and personnel carriers with ICE logos and Homeland Security stenciled on them. Hundreds of other police officers were also driving in from around the Bay Area. He parked at the Southland Mall and followed the signs for "New Arrivals: Police." At an empty store on the 2nd floor of the mall, next to a Virtual

Reality playground one one side and a Footlocker on the other, he got in line behind a half dozen others.

"Man, this is weird!" said the woman behind him. He turned to see who had spoken and found a stocky Latinx woman in a Berkeley police uniform.

"No shit. Whaddya think they've got planned?" Frank asked.

"You a cop?" she queried him.

He realized he was in plainclothes and since he hadn't shaved that morning, he probably didn't look too sharp. "Oh, yeah, UCSF police department. I got the call rather suddenly this morning, long before my shift was started."

She relaxed a bit and gave him a tight smile. "OK. Yeah, I have no idea what they think they're doing. How many did they call from your department? They requisitioned about 1/3 of the Berkeley PD."

"No idea. I think it was a third of us, too. Nobody explained anything to me, they gave me orders to get here by noon."

It was Frank's turn at the registration table. "ID and badge please." He pulled out his wallet and his badge and handed them over. The Homeland Security uniformed clerk filled in fields on the computer and asked Frank, "Do you understand what's happening, sir?"

"No."

"You are being drafted into a Homeland Security strike force. You will be serving for six months, with possible extensions lasting up to a maximum of 18 additional months. The most you will have to serve will be 2 years."

"Two years?!? Wait a minute! I'm supposed to be retiring next year!"

"I'm sorry sir. There's no provision for that. Our retirement age is 75 now, as President Hutchinson decreed last week. Social security, pensions, and retirement are delayed until 75."

"Wha?! How come I haven't heard anything about that?!" sputtered Frank. "This is outrageous!"

"Sir, sir, please calm down." A printer began whirring and a laminated ID badge soon appeared. "Here is your new badge. Take your belongings and report to Building B at the Hayward Executive Airport. There they will assign you to your new unit." He handed Frank his badge and some paperwork. "Next!"

Frank was stunned. Drafted?? How was that even possible? At his age? There must be some way to appeal this. He walked slowly away from the intake facility, trying to get his bearings. He suddenly thought of his mother, alone on Marlin Street! Who would live with her now? His sister Linda and her partner Rhonda lived a mile away and were in and out regularly. His son and Janet and other grandkids were nearby and visited a lot too. And there was the state-provided nurse who came over every other day to help bathe his mother and check her vitals. But he felt bad about it. She was 100 years old! He should stay with her til the end. Maybe he could get a special release? Who to talk to?

He drove from Southland the short distance into the airport, waving his badge under the handheld scanner of the soldier at the security gate. He went to the Building B main desk where he explained about his centenarian mother and his own age and tried to get someone to release him from his draft. But the clerks were young soldiers who knew nothing. They were not able to help and didn't think there was anyone who could effect a change in Frank's status. Once you were drafted and at Building B, you were in.

Frank stepped outside, completely exasperated. He called his sister Linda, who picked up right away.

"Linda, it's hard to believe, but I've been drafted!"

"What? What do you mean?"

And he explained the Kafkaesque hour and a half he'd spent since arriving in Hayward. "They actually expect me to live in a barracks, and they say I'm stuck for 6 months at least and maybe 2 years!"

"But they can't do that! You're too old! And what about Moms? What did they say about that?"

"Nothing. It's completely bureaucratic. It's the fuckin' military! Nobody here can do anything, or so they say. It's unbelievable!" Frank felt like he was exploding. Not good for the blood pressure or the heart, he thought.

"Hey soldier, what are you doing?" barked a security guard. "No loitering out here. Get to your assigned barracks!"

"Linda, I gotta go. I'll call you later. But make sure you guys figure out a schedule with Moms ok? I won't be back for a while," and he hung up.

CHAPTER 4
FRIDAY, MARCH 21, 2025

"Get Out! Park is surrounded!" read the text Janet received from her cousin.

An unlikely solstice celebration, at least 25,000 San Franciscans were gathered to protest the ongoing National Emergency—a weird version of martial law of the new Republican Administration. As usual there were drummers and marching bands, wild costumes, and hilarious home-made signs decrying fascism and the "coup d'Arkansas," with many comparisons to the Nazis and Hitler (which were made easy by the prevalence of fascist salutes and swastikas at pro-Republican rallies). Demands to undo the "illegal selection" and restore the legal votes of the two states that had been overturned by their legislatures underscored the essential liberal and institutional bias of this particular protest.

Janet found a sense of safety in the dense crowd at Dolores. And yet, here was this worrying message from her cousin Leon, Frank's son.

"Where are you?" she texted back.

"The stairway at Sanchez and 19th... Homeland Security ninjas are staging up here on 19th. Don't come this way! Go out on Cumberland or 20th."

Could this be real? Janet decided to believe it and started up the hill to the bridge over the tracks that led to 19th.

Three weeks after taking office, on February 10, 2025, President Hutchinson declared a National Emergency and appointed special Homeland Security "governors" to oversee emergency measures in 60 metropolitan regions to subdue the riots that continued to disrupt the country.

The local "czars" as they came to be known seized areas to build sprawling bases; in the Bay Area, a base was established on the Hayward Executive Airport. After the first month, a 10-block stretch of Hesperian Boulevard and Winton Avenue had been annexed along with the Southland Mall. The local fast-food joints, massage parlors, and other businesses converted to serving the thousands of troops that were concentrated there. Like in other areas, it became known as the "Green Zone," echoing the once-sprawling diplomatic compound in Baghdad during the 2003 Iraq invasion, and like that precursor, it soon had an intimidating perimeter fence with bright lights, barbed wire, and gun towers.

Mass demonstrations were banned, but in San Francisco, and throughout the Bay Area, most people, including local governments, were openly defiant. Mayor Yee had been arrested when he told the police not to cooperate with the DHS draft. But he got out days later after agreeing to rescind his order.

On her way up, Janet took in the orange "CalExit Now!" ballot proposal signs peppering the hill. The popular call for California to secede was taken up and amplified by local politicians across the state, proving a challenge to Hutchinson's rule. Protests in the Bay Area faced escalating violence from National Guard forces. In the last week alone, two young protesters had been shot dead near Hayward and another five protesters beat to within an inch of their lives in front of the Oakland City Hall. Outrage brought the numbers to the park that day.

On the slope above the stage at 19th and Dolores, Janet passed a crowd of parents gathered in a protective ring around their children. They were pointing nervously, and following their lead, she saw further east on 19th a mass of black-clad troops spanning the street. "Shit!" she muttered to herself.

"Hey," she addressed the folks closest to her, "if you want to come with me, I know a safe exit up that way," she pointed to the top corner of the park.

Four families herded their children together and joined Janet. The small pack made their way behind the Children's Playground to the corner at 20th and Church where they could cross the street. As they climbed 20th Street, Janet got another text from her cousin Leon, "They're moving!" and she answered quickly, "meet you at 20th and Sanchez."

For the thousands in Dolores Park the unimaginable was starting to dawn on them. Black-clad troops from Homeland Security in full riot gear with rifles were suddenly lining the edges of the park, with hundreds more filling in be- hind them. People were starting to panic, trying to leave, but more troops were pouring in from the Hidalgo statue at the top of the middle of the park, fanning out to the bathrooms and down to 18th Street. At the corner of 20th and Dolo- res another regiment of Homeland Security troops were marching across to the fill the southern top edge of the park, rapidly approaching the highest corner at 20th and Church. Janet looked back down the hill in terrified astonishment at the streets filling with troops. Hurrying the dawdling children the small group went as fast as they could to safety.

Down near the tennis courts, an organized group of demonstrators tried to push their way through the soldiers but were pushed back. A flying wedge of balaclava-covered demonstrators appeared as if out of nowhere and in tight formation rushed a part of the security line and briefly broke through, helping several hundred people get through and run down the street away from the park. Screams and confusion erupted around the park as gunshots rang out.

"They're shooting!"

Hundreds of people were so enraged that they charged the lines. Soldiers fired indiscriminately into the crowd. Thousands of people fell to the ground and tried to protect themselves from the gunfire. Over by the bathrooms near 18th and Church, a squad of soldiers was helping people exit to the street. A squad leader, an older black man, had taken off his black visored helmet and was waving people towards him, "come this way, get out of here!" he yelled. His troops created a corridor and a few hundred people were saved by this effort.

Suddenly the firing stopped. Screams changed. Instead of mayhem and panic, it was screams from the injured and dying, laying in pools of blood all over the park. Helicopters hovered over the park, and several drones swooped low, scanning the crowds for wanted individuals. An announcement crackled down from one of the helicopters:

"Stay where you are. Do not move. Homeland Security soldiers and medical personnel are here to assist you. If you try to run, you will be shot. Do not move!"

***

Frank Robertson could not believe his own eyes. Dolores Park was filled with casualties. What idiot had opened fire? Who authorized live ammunition for this peaceful demonstration? Who the fuck was in charge here? But he knew. Along with other Bay Area police who'd been drafted by the National Emergency, they were part of the Bay Area Homeland Security Mobilization. The guy in charge, "Governor" Frederick Reynolds, was from somewhere up near Redding, a California National Guard Colonel, and a veteran of two tours of combat, one in Afghanistan and the other working with the Saudis in Yemen. He brought his shoot-first, think-later approach to this new situation.

Over the next hours, Frank and his squad helped slowly usher out the unin- jured, taking their names and photos as they left, checking them against a list of wanted activists. Frank was relieved that nobody who passed them triggered an arrest. Others across the park were moving the dead into body bags and down to the waiting trucks, while the injured were being taken to a field hospital set up in the median along Dolores, after which they were loaded on to buses to be taken to the sprawling just-built detention facilities inside the Hayward Green Zone. Those who needed hospitalization were taken to a special ward at SF General, where they would be under administrative arrest while they recuperated.

"Sergeant Robertson! Report to Command Post A," crackled over the radio. The hair on his neck pricked up, knowing this could not be good. Frank wove through the chaotic park, leaving his squad under the command of his second, Bill Myers, also a former UCSF cop. Command Post A had been set up in the San Francisco Day School at 19th and Dolores, the once-upon time church having long been repurposed into a fancy private school. Frank entered and was ushered into the office where Reynolds himself sat with several of his staff, which included the recently defeated candidate for California Attorney General, the Bakersfield Bulldog himself, Edwin Tekopian.

"What the hell were you doing, helping those people go?" demanded Rey-nolds. "Sir, the situation was chaotic, and people were in a panic. I was trying to help people get out of trouble."

"Since when is that your mission? Who the hell do you think you are? On the drone footage, it looks like you let at least 300-400 people go without even getting their names, IDs, or photos."

"Sir. I don't think any of those people are a threat. This *was* a peaceful rally," and he paused to leave the emphasis on was.

"That's not for you to decide. We had a mission. Surround and control, identify and disperse. You failed to control or identify the people you let out, which may lead to more problems in the future. Do you understand?"

"Yes sir." He saw little reason to argue further. If the institutional memory of this bunch was anything like what he'd experienced over years in the San Francisco and University of California police departments, this would soon be forgotten.

But the dead! "Sir, who gave the order to shoot?"

"That's classified, sergeant, and none of your business."

"How many people were shot? How many killed?"

"Classified sergeant. You are dismissed."

"Yes sir."

He turned to leave but took one long last look at Governor Reynolds who was already conferring with Tekopian.

"What?!?" Reynolds did not like the impertinence of this black man staring at him.

"Nothing, sir." And he walked out.

"Simpson, check his record and make sure you add failure to follow orders today to his file."

***

As shots echoed in Dolores Park, Janet and her new-found entourage of families scrambled over the top of Liberty Hill, joined by her cousin Leon and a friend of his named Michael.

"Oh my god! Oh my god! Fuck! Oh Fuck!" Leon couldn't stop...

"Can you keep it quiet, please?" Janet implored him. She was in shock, too, but saw that the families were so frightened that this was only making it much worse.

Janet was thinking fast. Their Uncle Aaron lived in a house alongside Kite Hill only a few blocks across the back side of Liberty Hill. Leon and Michael agreed to take them there.

"But what are you doing?"

"I need to find someone."

"You'll get arrested!"

"No, I won't. I'll make sure that I don't."

She turned to the families, "please go with Leon and Michael. They'll take you to a safe house not far from here until things calm down." She knew it was crazy to return but she needed to get to the Cumberland house.

***

She left the group and climbed to the summit of Liberty Hill, and cautiously proceeded down and around to Church. Approaching Dolores Park's top corner she abruptly stopped. There were helicopters and drones filling the sky, and the park itself was full of black-uniformed Homeland Security troops. Bodies were everywhere too and were being taken out by the soldiers. No point in walking into that!

She retreated to search for the perimeter of operations. Standing uphill from everything she could see hundreds of soldiers in the park and along Dolores and what looked like a tent in the center median. There were a dozen AC Transit buses lined up on 20th Street down to Guerrero, apparently the ones that brought the soldiers here from Hayward. Skirting the area, she circled eastward. Sure enough, there weren't any active lines here and people were gathered across Guerrero Street watching the soldiers and buses. She walked through the neighbors, catching bits of conversation, "hundreds killed!," "a thousand shot!," "who are these fuckers?," "what's next?" and so on… She saw that Cumberland's one-block stretch back to Dolores was basically empty. As she surmised, the invaders didn't know San Francisco and didn't make use of the smaller streets.

She walked west on Cumberland trying her best to look like someone who was trying to get home. A drone whizzed by above but paid her no attention. Near Dolores there was that tent, which she realized was a medical tent, and a line of tables where bandaged and bloodied people were being processed into a nearby bus. She couldn't see any obvious way to help those being arrested.

She climbed the stairs of the closest house. The front door flew open and an old gray-haired woman grabbed her by the arm and pulled her in. "Get in here," she hissed, and Janet found herself in a living room with at least 25 others. Some were sobbing uncontrollably, others were grim-faced, staying away from the windows.

"Janet!" She turned to see Miguel Robles, her pal from the Urban Peasants Alliance.

"Miguel!" and they gave each other a long, hard hug. "What the fuck!" and she began crying, and so did he. "I was hoping you'd still meet here."

"Martha, this Janet Pierce, Janet, meet Martha Collins, one of our long-time supporters," said Miguel. He wiped his face, smudged by tears, and looked around the elegant sitting room at his Urban Peasants Alliance comrades. A dozen faces, a few people helping each other with bandages and cleaning wounds.

"Thanks for pulling me in!" greeted Janet.

"It was an automatic response. Glad to meet you!" said Martha, wrapped in a gray shawl, peering through the glasses perched at the end of her long, slender nose.

"Are you a UPA activist, too?"

"More of a friend of the UPA. I garden at Alemany Farm, Palou Terrace, the Dog Patch, mostly around the southeast end of the city. I'm with the League of Urban Farmers. Our staff and volunteers support the Urban Peasants organizing against BioGenMo."

A group of organizers had agreed to meet at Martha's after the march to plot out a few next actions. Miguel and the UPA folks trusted Martha and she trusted them. "I'm on the Canopy Council, and I help coordinate those farms I mentioned." She didn't talk about the warehouses where hydroponic and other indoor farming was taking root.

"I'd like to meet with you later, another day, and see what I can do to help the League," Martha offered.

"OK, thank you."

Janet turned to Miguel who was in deep conversation with several of his members.

"Miguel, can I talk to you for a sec?"

He pulled himself away, and they conferred under the stairway in the foyer. "She's cool, right?"

"Oh yeah. Martha's been there longer than I have. She's got a lot of money too. She doesn't like to talk about it, but her daughter is an executive at BioGenMo, and Martha was an early investor. She feels guilty about what it turned into. They don't talk to each other anymore," Miguel explained.

Janet's eyes widened as she took that in. "Dang," and she filed it away for future use. "How're we gonna get out of here? There's soldiers and drones all over the place."

"We're still hoping that our people will find their way here, but it's unlikely after two hours. This is our meet-up point, so we're not leaving until dark. We've sent messages downtown and to the East Bay," said Miguel.

"My phone's jammed down here. No messages, in or out. Are you able to send messages?" Janet asked.

"Let me show you something we've been developing," Miguel gestured for Janet to follow him up the stairs. "This is why we were asking people to meet up here after the march. It'll be more useful than we even knew." Miguel walked towards the back porch. When he opened the door, a drone buzzed over high up, and they hesitated, peering up as it sped by. "We have to figure out how to camouflage this deck from the sky. Check this out," and he pointed to the side of the porch where a pigeon coop stood, with a few cooing birds inside. "We've been training homing pigeons to communicate offline across the city."

Janet grinned. "You guys are the shit, man! What a brilliant idea! Everyone I know hates pigeons and always treats them like 'flying rats' or crap like that. I forgot they were used for sending messages a long time ago... How is it working?"

"So far, not bad. We've lost a couple to hawk attacks in the past year, but according to Roberto, our main trainer, it's good to go. Roberto's father was a fancy pigeon guy in Guadalajara before they crossed the border. He's got a real relationship with the birds and he's also found a few other kids who he has trained in the art of pigeon handling. We have a house in Vis Valley already managed by Vic and Suzie. They're downstairs right now."

Janet cut in, "OK, I get it. I am sure my cousin will get into this."

They clattered back downstairs, stepping into a contentious group conversation. Vic was countering, "People are gonna be pissed off. I'm not sure you can keep them off the streets. Depends on how scared everyone is, I guess."

Another UPA member, Lorena Sanchez, piped up, "Marching around or standing around, waiting for them to shoot us or bomb us? No thanks! We need to stop them before they get here," and she left it hanging. Everyone knew she meant the bridges and the freeways, the obvious chokepoints for entering and leaving the city.

"There are a lot of plans out there," Janet joined in, "and a lot of people trying to figure out what's next."

"OK, but we can't wait around while they take over everything!" exclaimed another guy on the edge of the growing conversation.

"Who said we should wait around?" Lorena retorted. "I want to make sure we do something that will not set us up like today!"

The conversation quickly degenerated into a half dozen arguments around the room.

"Listen, listen," Miguel refocused everyone's attention. "We can't figure this out here. We will have our regular General Meeting this Sunday in the basement at 650 Third Street, ok? Bring your reports, updates, and ideas there. We also have to prepare for the possibility that our regular meetings will be banned. If that happens, we will send word around about a new location through the Tree," referring to the UPA's person-to-person offline network to send verbal or handwritten messages.

Over the next hour, Miguel and Janet sat together trying to play out different scenarios. "If people go underground, we'll have to keep everyone fed," Janet argued.

"Sure, but I don't know if we can produce enough food on our own," Miguel answered. "Our members already depend on the pantries and kitchens a lot."

"Yeah, I know. That's why we started some grow ops to go way beyond the urban farms."

"You talkin' about indoors? Like weed?" asked Miguel.

"Yeah, but healthy organic food instead of pot," Janet continued. "Bio-GenMo lab jockeys have been sending us their studies, and even some of their experimental seeds. Rebel techies well-hidden at BGM!"

Miguel was called away, and Janet stayed immersed in her thoughts.

The Canopy Council would be meeting next Friday. They would have to get serious about their indoor plans, that was clear. The new president was already demanding his rubberstamp Congress pass laws mandating the use of fossil fuels and nuclear energy, while banning more wind farms. Rooftop solar was on his target list too, but that would be hard, given how many of his own voters had solar panels already. The new Secretary of Agriculture was the former chief counsel to Cargill Corporation, and she was talking about new national regulations that would ban urban farming and farmer's markets, supposedly on health grounds! 'What a bitch!' she thought. But it was worse than that, since CO_2 had hit 510 parts per million, and the California drought was wreaking havoc with food production in the Central Valley. Water supplies were dwindling fast, and tens of thousands of acres had been taken out of production. Most of it was almonds, mandarin oranges, and pistachios for export anyway! Urban farming was already providing almost 15% of the food eaten in west coast cities and growing. How could anyone think to shut that down now?! It was insane!

It was dusk as Janet cautiously stepped out the front door. She looked up at the sky but didn't see any drones or helicopters, but she knew there were eyes in the sky anyway. The world war machine was being applied openly at home, possibly sending crisply detailed images of anywhere in San Francisco down to the individual on the street back to the NSA's massive computers in the Utah desert. Their algorithms could process the data and—if desired—generate reports almost in real time about who was where and with whom. Knowing such a capability existed was incredibly intimidating. But so far, no one had acted on such "intelligence," assuming it was in fact being gathered and accurately interpreted.

It was still possible to imagine that the government's tech didn't work. In fact, that was the most likely scenario. Working for corporations, the government, or the military was to experience incredible levels of redundant busy work that failed to do anything useful. Anyone who tried to focus the efforts and rationalize the system ran into the enormous inertia of widespread indifference, ineptitude, and sullen hostility that prevailed everywhere in corporate, government, and military America. How long would it be before institutional resistance was automated out of existence? But would it ever work?

Janet, Miguel, and San Francisco's many other radicals learned from years of failed protests and demonstrations that non-cooperation and creative resistance were their best weapons, even if they weren't always able to direct them as they'd like. There wasn't any unified opposition in the city, with its fractious interest groups focused on a panoply of issues rarely willing to subordinate themselves to any larger and imperfect agenda. But history has a way of forcing the issue sometimes, and in the first half of 2025, attention was being focused on all sides.

CHAPTER 5
FRIDAY, MARCH 21, 2025

Leon and Michael led the families onto the small tree-lined path at the back of Kite Hill. The very first house at the edge of the open space was their destination. Having messaged ahead and they were met by a small welcoming committee as they entered the elegant garden.

"Come on in. I'm Julius and this is Anna, and this is Rufus, our dog. Is everyone OK?"

"Yes, we got out before it happened. The kids are a bit pooped after hiking over the hill to get here, though."

The families straggled into a big room under a ceiling of old wooden beams with a huge fireplace.

"Why don't you get settled here for now, and we'll bring some lunch for everyone?" suggested Julius. He and Anna disappeared, presumably toward the kitchen, and the group found cushions, couches, chairs, and some sprawled on the rug in front of the dormant fireplace.

Leon took the lead. "I don't know if everyone knows what's happened?" People shook their heads, but before he could continue, one of the moms announced: "Um, I'd like to take my son and any of the younger kids who would like to join us, to another room or outside, if we can hold off on the details for a bit."

"We need to know what's happening," said Millie, one of the lesbian moms. "Cristiano? Emma and Ella? Do you want to leave the room before we start talking about what happened at the park?" asked Joao.

"No way!" they answered in unison.

"Here's carrot soup for everyone!" Anna announced as she came in with a tray full of bowls, plus a heaping basket of warm bread fresh out of the oven. In moments, the clatter of spoons and the slurping of soup filled the room, as anxiety gave way to hunger and the comfort of hot carrot-ginger soup proved irresistible.

The couple with the two smallest children decided to leave and go back to their apartment. "Thanks everyone, but we're going home now. Be safe." One dad volunteered to take the other young children to the backyard to eat and play. Julius followed with a tray of soup bowls.

Julius returned to find the conversation had begun while he was outside.

"But they can't shoot people!!"

"They just did!"

Leon was scrolling through his phone, as were a number of others. "Says here that 387 people were killed! And 1,433 were arrested and taken to Camp Hayward."

"The official line is that no one was killed, and only violent rioters were arrested. Brother! Do they expect anyone to believe that?!?" Donald shook his head. "We knew it was bad before. This is worse. Trump was terrible, but Biden was too. And let's not forget the deporter-in-chief, and drone-assassin-in-chief Obama. The impunity has been growing for a long time... I didn't even mention the Bushes or Clinton or Reagan or Nixon!..."

Sarah checked her husband with a nudge and smiled. "Hey, this is normal for me, but you don't have to live with it!" which drew a round of appreciative chuckles, though many had been nodding in agreement. "The ACLU has already filed a dozen lawsuits against the government, and California and other blue states are joining in."

"But you know the Supreme Court will rubberstamp everything Hutchinson does. They took over the courts a long time ago," argued Barbara. "We can't let this stand. They slaughtered hundreds of people!" and she choked up and sobbed loudly. Her partner Millie hugged her, joined by their son Tomas. Others wiped tears from their eyes. Everyone was exhausted and frightened.

"You're right. We CANNOT let this stand. But we can't go back to the same old tactics either." Julius, an energetic man of 67, felt like he'd been prepar- ing for this all his life. "We will have to be less visible. We will need underground networks, and we have to stop using the internet and our phones!"

"But how will we know what's going on?" several people immediately answered, unconsciously reaching for their phones.

Anna produced a big basket. "Speaking of phones, this is a good time for everyone to turn theirs off and put it in this basket." She took the phones to a metal box in their pantry.

After a pause, Julius continued, "There are some things percolating that I can't talk about yet. But people organized for centuries before the internet and smart phones. We know they use these things to monitor everything and every one of us. Stopping using them immediately will itself be suspicious. Don't do that. But stop talking about anything regarding protests or demonstrations— you can still read the news and opinions, and even post to social media about those things, but I suggest you slowly wean yourself off the whole system. Take the next weeks and months to reduce your use of social media."

Donald perked up when the phones were rounded up, feeling that these people were serious. "Julius, do you think we can start a small communications node among ourselves, relying on face-to-face conversations and handwritten notes?"

"Sure! Why not? Who wants to do that?" Nearly everyone put up their hands. Cristiano and Tomas, the tweeners who were suddenly having to grow up much faster than their age, were watching everything with big eyes, having no experience to draw on. "Do you think we can help?" Cristiano tentatively asked.

"Of course! Assuming your parents are cool with it, there's a group called the Pony Express and all you need is a bicycle and some training." The two boys, who hadn't known each other before the day's trauma, excitedly confirmed their interest.

"My parents told me a lot of stories about organizing during the dictatorship in Brazil," Joao offered. His partner Wilma said, "I was a kid in Grenada during the socialist takeover and then the American invasion. We organized a lot, passing messages from person to person, house to house. Cristiano, I'm glad you want to do this, but we will help too."

Others spoke at once, and after a few minutes, Leon stepped forward again. "OK, we're exhausted, and I'm sure we're frightened. We've never had to face anything like this before." He nodded at Donald to recognize his point that ear- lier administrations were awful too. "I suggest we pick buddies to exchange ad- dresses and phone numbers with. Like Julius said, we have to be careful. Don't call or text each other all the time, ok?! And when you're meeting, remember to leave the phone behind so they can't track you every time. Let's put our address- es on this list and see who is near who and what connections are most obvious." They made plans to send around a weekly handwritten news sheet.

Entering the room at that moment was an elderly black man, gray hair around his temples, using a cane to stabilize his walking. "You guys startin' a paper?"

"Aaron, these are some folks who got away from the park before the massacre. Janet sent them over," explained Julius.

"Uncle Aaron!" exclaimed Leon.

"Hey Leon. Fancy meeting YOU here!" smiled Aaron. "Me and Greg moved up here when the Land Trust opened it up. Since I retired from the MUNI, we didn't make too much money anymore, and we always loved hiking around the upper Castro. I can't tell you how many times I looked at this house and wished it was mine... and now it is!"

"How did Janet know you were here?"

"Oh she's been here for dinner many times, always bringing us amazing things she grew in her gardens."

"I shoulda known... Well, give me a hug!"

"You heard what happened?" Leon asked him as they separated.

"Yeah, shit, can't fuckin' believe it," said Aaron. Turning to Julius he offered, "I know someone who still has an old mimeograph machine. You want me to ask?"

"Wow, yeah!" Julius was excited.

"He's got blank stencils for it, too."

"We're getting ahead of ourselves. We just met. Let's see how it goes, keep it simple for now." Julius had seen things start and fall apart soon after too many times. "How about we start out with a notebook that gets circulated where we can write things down, and then pass it on? You can even put stuff into the note- book if you want to, add pages... nothing too big to start."

"I agree with Julius. Let's start small and simple and see if we can keep it going. Let's check in and evaluate next week. How does that sound?" Donald asked the room.

Exhaustion was overcoming most of them by then. Meetings like this were rare these days, but for the older folks present, it was an echo of a past they'd almost forgotten about.

Barbara Denby, who was already in her mid-50s when she and Millie adopted Tomas, was now 66. "We used to meet regularly when I was in ACT-UP in the early 90s. Did I see you there, Aaron?"

"Oh yeah. I been to a shit-ton of meetings in my life... You can use our place whenever you want."

"Thanks uncle," Leon chimed in. "Why does it seem like Robertsons are always in the middle of everything?"

"You tell me!" smiled Aaron.

The parents gathered up their children and departed to their respective homes. Before leaving, Donald asked Julius and Anna, "how do you apply for that family suite?" They gave him the flyer that explained the process and invited him to apply.

Cristiano and Tomas found out that they didn't live too far apart. Barbara and Millie had an 1870s woodframe building on Shotwell between 20th and 21st, and Joao and Wilma had a house on Alabama between 21st and 22nd, about 4 blocks away. They went to different schools, so they hatched a plan to meet on their bikes after school the next day.

CHAPTER 6
FRIDAY, MARCH 21, 2025

She was shivering under the thin blanket, her left hip aching on the lumpy mattress. A morning alarm blared, the 6 a.m. wake-up that ripped them from sleep every morning in this drafty warehouse. She sat at the edge of the bunk, her legs dangling in the air. Other detainees were slowly getting up around her. She rubbed her eyes and thought back to the luxurious bunk bed she had been sleeping in at Larry Lansing's cellar, regretting her urgency to get out and take her chances.

***

She'd been hiding in the underground biotech lab for six weeks when her patience snapped. She was going crazy.

"They can't be looking for me!" she exclaimed. "I'm sick of being down here. I haven't seen the sky for weeks!"

Janet was sitting across the table, sharing a delicious bread pudding she made from leftovers scavenged in the fridge. As the steam rose from the melted butter and syrup, she took a bite, and then looked at Vero.

"You're not a prisoner here. If you want to take your chances, you can leave. But as far as I know, the authorities are looking for you and everyone they've been able to identify who was in the federal building occupation. The new administration is more aggressive than the Harris government was."

"As generous as Larry and Ally have been, I need to get out. I went upstairs into Larry's warehouse the other day to see the sun through the skylight, but he told me he couldn't be sure if his employees were cool. Can you believe it?"

"Well, unfortunately, yes. Vero, it's bad out there. There are surprising num- bers of people who support Hutchinson and his crackdown. Some people seem to believe that it will return life to 'normal,' whatever that is!"

Vero crossed the kitchen to the alcove with her bunk bed. She pulled clothes from a duffel bag. "I'm going out! I'll wear a hat and this big sweatshirt, and this scrambler bandana."

"Don't wear that! That's a sure way to get stopped. Only activists use them. I'm sure they'll declare them illegal soon," Janet cautioned.

Vero was stubborn. She couldn't believe how much the world had changed since she'd gone literally underground. Helping Alison Nakahara and Clara and Maria with the biobulb and bioboat projects in Larry's secret underground laboratory was exciting, but her mental health was fraying and she knew she needed sunshine... a walk on the beach, hike up a hill—hell, a walk down Mis- sion Street would beat being stuck here! She was getting claustrophobic!

Two hours later, as she crossed 24th Street at the BART plaza, plainclothes officers stopped her and asked for her ID.

"What? Why? What did I do?" she complained. Two burly men towered over her, blocking any escape. She pulled out her wallet and produced her ID, unfortunately her real one. Fake IDs weren't everywhere yet.

"Veronica Gomez," the bearded officer pronounced. "Check the list, Roger." And the other guy, his beady eyes buried in puffy red cheeks that hinted at a drinking problem, flipped through a list on his phone. "Yup, here she is!" he declared triumphantly.

"We've been looking for you," the beard said. "Where've you been?" Vero was silent and then, "I want a lawyer," was all she would say.

"Hah, I *bet* you do!" laughed the beard. A white ICE Hummer pulled up alongside the plaza. They pushed her into the back seat, neither cop bothering to enter with her. This wasn't a typical arrest, Vero realized, fear rising in her chest.

"Hey, where are you taking me? Who are you?" she yelled at the plexiglass sep- arating her from another huge guy in a plaid shirt who was driving. He remained silent as he drove to Cesar Chavez and before long was on the freeway heading to the Bay Bridge. Vero leaned forward and pounded on the glass. "Where are we going?!? What is this?" But the driver remained silent and they kept going, taking the Nimitz Freeway through downtown Oakland and on past the Coliseum.

Vero knew a big Homeland Security camp had been established in Hayward, and she realized that was where they were taking her. "Fuck," she muttered, falling back into the seat, staring out the window as they exited the free- way at Winton Avenue. There were soldiers everywhere, a fleet of white ICE vehicles parked in the Southland Mall parking lot. They kept driving, the guard towers and perimeter fence of the airport passing on the right. They turned right at a small white sign that said "East Bay Cadet Squadron" and then drove into a large hangar labeled California Air National Guard. She was hustled into a big cage where a half dozen others were already sitting sullenly on the floor.

"Hey," she said to the woman she sat down near. "What is this place?" "You're in the Homeland Security Detention Center," she explained, "at least that's what one of the guards called it. What did they arrest you for?"

"Routine ID check at 24th and Mission in San Francisco. I was on a list," Vero replied.

"That sucks. They grabbed us at a demo in downtown Oakland a few hours ago. We were protesting the arrest of our friend Elvira Grant who led a teacher walkout last week," explained the woman, apparently in her late 20s, huddled against the fence. "Ferd over there," she nodded at a guy across the cage, "he was teaching at the same school."

"What the fuck?!?" Vero was pissed. "Who the fuck do they think they are? They can't do this!"

"Um, you might want to cool it. They took away one of our friends who was yelling and demanding a lawyer."

Vero then noticed that a few uniformed officers away from the cage were conferring with each other, occasionally looking over in her direction. She decided to sit tight and see what was next.

***

That was three long weeks ago. Her interrogation had lasted for two days. It started with two goons dragging her from the cage and putting her in a white jeep, handcuffing her to the rollbar. After a short drive, they pulled up outside of a 2-story warehouse with a fading sign saying "Prologis Hayward." They manhandled her inside and took her to a room where they strapped her into a chair, while she was cussing them out in a rising crescendo of obscenities. When she demanded to see a lawyer or make a phone call they shook their heads and smiled. Then they attached a lie detector to her, and the "conversation" began. Most of the questions involved the occupation of the Federal Building, who else was there, how she got in, who was helping inside, etc. She claimed she had been in a crowd and didn't know anyone else, swept up in the moment. Try as they might, they couldn't get her to acknowledge anyone else or tell anything about what happened inside during the four days. Nor could they get her to reveal where she'd been since she came out of the Federal Building. "I went camping in the Santa Cruz mountains," was her steady answer.

The interrogation continued for 48 hours, with the interrogators leaving her alone for hours at a time. During the afternoon of the second day they let her loose from the chair and allowed her to walk around the room. They even left her alone like that for a few hours. If she'd been stir-crazy in Larry's cellar lab, this was much worse. But she used her guile to bite her tongue during the lie detector questions to confuse the results as much as she could, and then she meditated on walking on the beach for hours more. Would they beat her? Use drugs or electroshock? Shiv- ers of terror would occasionally seize her and she trembled uncontrollably until she regained her composure. And then it stopped. They took her out, made her change into a bright green jumpsuit, and put her into a large shared room with a dozen bunkbeds and about fifteen other prisoners.

"Am I charged with something?" she had asked repeatedly. "I want to make a phone call!" but her demands were ignored. "The National Emergency means no calls!" one officer finally told her emphatically.

She went through the days listlessly. They were allowed to spend an hour in an outdoor yard where there was a basketball court and some other games enclosed by razor wire on top of a tall fence. Another parallel yard was in the distance, where it seemed male prisoners were in the same situation. At meal time they were funneled through the same cafeteria, though at different hours for men and women.

At lunch college basketball on a big TV appeared for the first time (was this Saturday? Were people still playing basketball and watching TV?). She got her rice and vegetables and a piece of soggy meatloaf, but she wasn't very hungry. She poked at the vegetables and finally forked a few mouthfuls of rice but after the sec- ond bite she noticed a folded-up piece of paper! She pulled it out hoping no one was looking and put it in her pocket. Twenty minutes later they were back in their communal cell and she climbed up on her bunk and carefully opened it.

"Vero Gomez! We're trying to get you a hearing. Your friends have hired an attorney, but no judges are willing to challenge the emergency. Don't despair, you are not forgotten! We will send you more information when we can."

Her heart leaped. She wasn't alone! She looked around at her cellies and tried to figure out who she could trust. A new woman was brought in looking dishev- eled, her clothes stained with mud and what looked like bloodstains. She was followed by another, and another, until the population of the cell had expanded to over 30, more than the available beds. The new prisoners were very upset.

"What?!? They did what?!? A massacre?! At Dolores Park??" The prison- ers who had been there already clamored for more information, while helping get the newcomers situated into bunks where they could nurse their wounds. Efforts to clean them up began too. Soon the story was clear: a peaceful de- mon- stration against the National Emergency was held in Dolores Park. It was sur- rounded by Homeland Security forces who opened fire. An unknown number were killed, and busloads were arrested, including these new arrivals.

Vero went over to one woman who seemed particularly shaken up. Her name was Frieda Strauss, and she explained her partner Ruth Maloney had been shot in the arm and taken by soldiers to SF General Hospital. Their son Oscar and she had both been arrested and bused over to Hayward. "I can't believe this is happen- ing! Where have they taken my son? When can we go?" she was over- come with anxiety. Vero did her best to calm her down and gave her her bed. "We don't know what's happening, and we may be here a while. I've been here over three weeks already!"

"What?!?" Frieda couldn't believe her ears. "Why? What did they arrest you for?" Vero explained the ID check and the interrogation.

"But you should try to get some sleep" she encouraged, more as an auto- matic gesture than out of any real conviction. Vero knew she wouldn't be sleep- ing much tonight no matter what.

The whimpering and moaning persisted through the next morning. The five who had offered their beds found themselves pacing back and forth, the shock settling in. The situation was much more dire than it had been when they were originally brought here. A massacre! At Dolores Park! Vero thought of the hours she spent there in the last 15 years, sitting on blankets smoking pot, drinking wine, hanging out with friends, watching dogs cavort, feeling the icy tentacles of fog in the late afternoons.

Her brief reverie was broken when another of the pacers stopped in front of her. "What are we going to do?" she demanded.

"Why are you asking me? I'm stuck here like you," Vero answered, still not sure of who could be trusted.

"We have to do something! We can't let these fuckers get away with this. I'm Rita Marley, by the way, what's your name?" Rita was taller than Vero, a redhead with broad shoulders and impressive biceps.

"I'm Vero Gomez. Dolores Park, man, that's my home turf!" She shook her head.

"This place seems kinda flimsy. I think we can break out if we work on it," Rita proposed in a low voice.

"And go where? I don't know about you, but they picked me up on a busy street out of the blue."

"What if we had people who could help us get away and hide?" Rita continued.

"Do you know something I don't know?"

Rita nodded, her red hair bouncing on the green jumpsuit. She whispered now, "I have friends, maybe in a week or two."

Vero said nothing but raised her eyebrows encouragingly. She realized that jumping into this might be a set-up, but she didn't want to discourage any genu- ine escape efforts. "I'm interested. But I don't want to do anything stupid. Who else is involved?"

Rita pointed her eyes at two other women who were also without bunks now, quietly conferring across the room. "Jane and Ellie are in. I bet these new arrivals will be interested. It'll depend on some inside AND outside help, that's for sure," but she didn't explain what that exactly meant, and Vero decided not to press it. Maybe it was the same people who had sent her a note?

"I'll let you know when things get firmed up."

"OK." It seemed improbable, even impossible, a half hour ago, but something about Rita's certainty made her believe it was real. "Let me know what you need me to do."

"OK," and Rita gave her a sudden and very unexpected hug. Which felt great! And wow, this woman was all muscle! What a grip! The conspirators soon retired to spots around the room where extra blankets were turned into their makeshift beds for the night. Vero took a long time to fall asleep, her mind racing at the prospects of escape, of how she would make her way back to San Francisco, where she would hide, who she had to warn. The world had turned upside down *again*!

CHAPTER 7
THURSDAY, APRIL 3, 2025

Kite Kastle was never busier. Since the Massacre, their house had become a hub for the people who showed up that day, along with the twelve people who lived there. New tenants had moved in last week, the Nevilletons into the empty family suite, and Juna Caguas into the single room. Aaron Robertson's creaking joints were sore, but he felt more alive than he'd been in a few years. They set up an aging desktop computer ("air-gapped" to prevent online tracking) with a laser printer in their basement, and he helped organize the printing of the weekly newsletter, after the circulating notebook proved unwieldy. The kids, Cristiano and Tomas, their "pony express" delivery service, came by a lot. When school let out they rode their bikes up the hill.

"Man, you guys need to get a lift!" Tomas complained as he threw his bike against the garage wall. Cristiano came in right behind him, sweating and puffing. "I heard there's a place in Norway with a sidewalk escalator that carries bikes up a steep hill. We need one of those!"

Aaron was standing at the door to the kitchen, smiling. He remembered riding his bike around the Bayview when he was their age, back when Willie Mays and Willie McCovey and Juna Marichal were starring for the Giants at Candlestick Park. The stadium was still open to the bay in those days, and tickets were cheap. It was easy to get in and watch the hotdog wrappers whip around in the crazy swirling winds while enjoying the expansive view of the forbidden shipyards. He would stare from the 3rd base stands trying to see if there were any secrets he could see, but he never found any.

"There's a new issue for you guys, hot off the presses!" he announced. And the boys rushed past him and into the stairway to the basement. They each had a dozen stops, almost doubling the number of people getting the sheet every week. Who knew how many saw it after that?

Aaron decided to stroll out to the hill. It was a clear sunny day, not too hot and not too windy, perfect for taking in the Kite Hill view. He leaned all his 70 years into his cane as he stepped through the garden. Emerging onto the hill, he saw the new tenant, Juna, sitting in a meditative pose a short distance from the bench and the path.

A few yards away from Juna he dropped his three-legged stool and sat down to enjoy the view. "Hey there," he said softly. Juna was tall and thin, an elegant androgynous character. Long curly black hair fell down their back, long earrings dangled from their ears, sparkling against their smooth brown cheeks. They were wrapped in a purple shawl with gold trim and had been sitting quietly gazing out at the city.

"Hi.. um Aaron, right?" They were still trying to remember everyone's name in the new house. Aaron was a sympathetic guy, a black gray-haired queer guy with his partner Greg who lived two doors down from Juna. Greg had been effusive in welcoming them, but Aaron had been a bit cooler, perhaps waiting until they got to know each other a bit better. That was fine with Juna. They were in no rush to bond with anyone, having been frustrated often in their efforts to connect. But Greg and Aaron should be alright. Their being two-spirited didn't always work with gay men since they were sometimes weirdly macho, but these guys weren't like that. And anyway, they were old!

"Yeah, that's right. I'm with Greg," he reminded Juna.

"I remember. I haven't quite got everyone down yet, but I will." They tried to sound confident, and then they changed the subject. "I'm loving this view. I grew up in the shadow of Mt. Diablo," pointing to the distant peak looming behind the east bay hills.

"Oh yeah? Whereabouts?"

"My family has a place out past Brentwood, in the delta. My uncle used to grow corn and squash and beans there. They had some cows too."

Aaron nodded approvingly. "Do you know my niece, Janet Pierce?" he asked. "She's on the Canopy Council and farms at Alemany, Bayview, Palou, the southeastern corner of the city."

"Oh? I haven't met her. I don't know a lot about the farms in San Francisco. What do they grow?" Juna was familiar with urban gardens of course, but the idea of real farms in San Francisco was a reach.

"Lots of things. They do the usual vegetable crops, zucchini, lettuce, kale, chard, tomatoes. There are even some small orchards of apples, pears, figs, lemons, oranges. You'd be surprised. It's expanded in the last few years."

"I heard Homeland Security will crack down on local farms?..."

"I dunno. Janet would know what's up. I'm sure they're making their plans to keep growing food. We're gonna need it, now more than ever!" Aaron only had a vague idea of how much food the League of Urban Farmers was actually producing and knew nothing about their indoor hydroponics or biotech experiments.

A pair of scrub jays suddenly put up a big racket in the tree behind them. Juna turned around and seemed to listen intently.

"You getting' something from that?" Aaron asked them.

"Tryin' to. They are excited about something, and they want us to know about it. Oh look!" and they pointed to a drone that was crossing the sky not far away but heading for the rocky outcropping at Corona Heights. "Could be a warning... or a coincidence... but I don't believe too much in coincidences."

"Oh yeah? Hmmmm," Aaron trailed off. He heard scrub jays around the hill a lot. But he never felt like they were communicating with him directly— were they now? Who could say?

"Do you know if your niece's farms are regenerative?" Juna suddenly asked.

"Um, well, I'm not sure. She's usually the biggest ecologist I know, so if that's what it sounds like, I'd guess so. Regenerate, that's good, right?"

"Yeah, yeah. It's a way of improving the soil and helping the whole system thrive." Juna explained enthusiastically, their eyes flashing, and the first smile Aaron had seen from them.

"I'll have to get you together with her. She usually comes over every week or two, but with all that's going on, she hasn't been by for a bit. She always brings us fresh produce!" He lit up at the thought of the bulging boxes of fresh vegetables and fruit Janet brought over. "I'm heading back. Our Pony Express kids came by for the latest issue and I want to make sure they have their routes straight."

"Oh yeah, those newsletters, right? Julius told me you guys started that after the Massacre. Is it to share news? Opinions? What's it for, exactly?"

"We're finding our way as we go. We don't want it to get too big, partly cuz the paper and ink will get too expensive. But also it's probably better not to put too much in print given the circumstances," alluding to the obvious emergency situation.

"Aaron, do you know anything about any seed banks or seed libraries here in the City?" Juna asked.

"Seed libraries? For sure Janet will know. I'm not involved in gardening or farming, it's not my thing," he smiled, trying to give Juna an encouraging vibe. "I'll make sure you meet her soon, ok?"

"Thanks!"

Juna loosened the tie on a small, embroidered bag. They poured some seeds into their hand and poked at them. "I will find you a home here in San Francisco," they spoke softly. They hummed a tune that their aunt used to sing in her kitchen garden in the delta. Putting the seeds back into the pouch, they didn't know how much time had passed since Aaron had departed. Couldn't have been long. The two scrub jays perched on the hill a few yards away and were vocalizing in low voices.

"You're back! Were you trying to warn us?" Juna blurted out. They didn't expect any response, but both birds stopped poking in the weeds and looked straight at them. The nearer one tilted its head to the side, and let out a whistling sound, not something Juna had heard before. "I think you're trying to tell me something," they said and gave the birds their full attention. But as soon as they did, the birds got skittish and flew up and disappeared in the trees back by the house. Juna decided to make their way back. As they arose they saw a coyote meandering near the bottom of the hill near the crumbling Clover Lane that connected to 19th Street. A second one soon appeared behind it.

Juna was standing and staring when the two coyotes stopped and turned toward them, gazing up the hill alertly. For a minute they held each others' gaze, and as suddenly the connection broke, the two coyotes trotted into the alley and disappeared.

Juna knew coyotes had become a regular presence around San Francisco but this was a pleasant surprise. After only a week, Juna was finding the next-door hilltop a delight. And Aaron's niece Janet sounded like the perfect connection to find their way into urban farming here.

***

"Seeds carry the people that carry them," Juna explained to the meeting at the Dog Patch a few days later. "Seeds saving centers us in a reciprocal and co-evolutionary relationship with the world around us. That's why I became a seed keeper," they ended with a flourish.

Janet enjoyed Juna's enthusiasm and hoped none of the farmers would be offended if they felt like what Juna said was 'old news' to them. "We are glad to have you Juna. The seed collections in the city will be excited to share with you." The meeting went through the usual business about managing the row crops, tending the shoreline near Islais Creek, and who was responsible for what in the coming days. After a half hour the meeting was winding up. Miguel Robles of the Urban Peasants Alliance had been sitting quietly in the back.

"Hey everyone!" he stood up abruptly. "I'm Miguel from the UPA. Some of you know me. Janet and I have been working to coordinate the UPA and the League. We're still able to meet, as you are here. We are hearing rumors about a coming crackdown."

The farmers in the barn stirred uncomfortably. No one was surprised that urban farming was becoming more politically charged—everything was now. But many of them came to farming not out of political passion but out of a simple love for gardening, for cultivating food and flowers, and for a few people that meant an aversion to any declared politics.

"Crackdown on growing food?" one woman shook her head. "What the hell is going on?" Others murmured in shared consternation.

Janet piped up, "They will seize our crops and/or impose taxes on what we grow. That's what the Department of Agriculture announced last week. They say that everyone must buy a monthly quota of corn and soy from the huge government stockpiles... that's the shit they grow in the midwest mostly, and the feds have been buying it up to prop up the prices for their political allies in agribusiness."

"I'm not eating that shit!" yelled a man in the back.

"What do they expect us to do?" asked a woman plaintively. "Don't we have a right to eat what we grow?"

Miguel responded, "All rights are out the window now. With the emergency, they can impose whatever they want," he paused and looked around the room, "*IF* we let them!" Eyes gleaming, he looked carefully at each face. His confidence in public speaking had grown a lot in the past months. "Listen, we need to prepare for the worst. Crazy as it seems, we should expand indoor farming as much as we can, assuming we can hide it. Janet and I have been discussing this already."

Juna jumped up, "We can grow stuff underground all over the place! That's hard to track, but if we plant it we know where it is. There's lots of places where we can sow root crops aren't there?"

Miguel beamed. "See that's what I mean. We have to be proactive, get stuff into the ground asap. And we must decentralize, even from our already small gardens and farms. We don't know how long we have before they send surveillance drones over every garden. It could get crazy!"

The farmers were excited now. They could see a way to use their knowledge and skills without having to become anything they weren't. Several groups conferred with each other. One group focused on foraging possibilities with endemic plants, making plans to search out edible tubers under Blue Dicks flowers, collecting as many blackberries and elderberries as they could, and locating wild fennel and stinging nettles. Another group made plans to plant garlic, onions, and potatoes in a large network of backyard gardens.

One farmer convinced his group to be an active decoy by continuing to cultivate at the Dog Patch and at the Palou Terrace, but to produce little of visible yield so the authorities would lose interest in San Francisco farms.

One group constituted themselves as seed gatherers and protectors and welcomed Juna into their ranks. "You have a collection already?" asked a young punk woman with over a dozen piercings in her ears, eyes, nose, and lips.

Juna nodded enthusiastically. "And someone said there are seed banks around town already?"

The pierced woman said, "The University of San Francisco has its own seedbank at its student library. And there are at least two other private collections I know of. We should diversify storage sites, making sure some will remain well hidden until we can go public... right?"

Similar meetings were underway in a dozens of other gardens around the City. Miguel made a last announcement to the whole group.

"At the Urban Peasants Alliance our members have a lot of skills. Way too many of us have been dropped from the BioGenMo rolls but that means there's a surplus of biotech and agricultural skills. Keep that in mind as your efforts proceed. If you need technical help, or you need more hands, ask us. We're ready to help!" That got a round of applause from everyone and soon people were leaving by bicycle or on foot.

Janet took Juna aside. "I'd like to introduce you to my cousin Leon. You need a job, right?" Janet was remembering that her uncle Aaron told her Juna wanted a job, and suggested Leon's place.

"Uh, yeah, definitely!" Juna replied. How did she know that when they hadn't spoken about it?

"OK, let's go." They said their goodbyes, Janet giving a private signal to Miguel to see him at their regular meetup later in the week. They pedaled out to 3rd Street and turned south. In ten minutes they were pulling their bikes into Leon's warehouse.

CHAPTER 8
MONDAY, APRIL 7, 2025

Janet and Juna walked into the sprawling indoor grow operation and were bowled over by the pungent scent of maturing cannabis around them. Marijuana was still the main product at Leon's warehouse in the Bayview, which he had been given by Large Larry Lansing after HemptriCity was bought by BGM and Larry got his stock deal. But a healthy row of tomatoes, peppers, and lettuces were also prospering under the sunroof on the south side of the complex.

A young woman met them near the door, smiling broadly when she recognized Janet, her freckled cheeks beamed under her brown glasses, braids falling in every direction.

"Janet, it's been a while," she gave her a long hug. Her brown sweatshirt sported Leon's new BayGreen company logo, a woman laying on a large green hemp leaf as if it were a hammock, with the slogan "Lean on Leon" and their text and internet connections.

"Hey Gina," and Janet stood back a bit to admire the sweatshirt. "That's hilarious!" She turned to Juna and introduced them.

"You here to see Leon?" Gina asked.

"Maybe you can help. Juna is new to the city, they moved into the Kite Kastle where my uncle Aaron lives and we were thinking maybe they could get a job here?"

"Yeah, probably. I mean, Leon's always cycling new people through here. We got a bunch of the UPA people last week, so it may be hard to add anyone immediately. I can ask when he gets back."

"Oh? Where is he?"

"Leon's always off somewhere these days. He's either getting more land or new buildings or..." and she shrugged with another smile. "I don't keep track."

Janet nodded, knowing Leon had a lot of other things going on. The warning Leon had sent her about the attack on Dolores Park probably saved her and the others she led from the park. She would have been in the middle of the carnage without it. *She could've been shot!*

Farmers puttered among the raised beds, straw hats and overalls, shovels and hoes and wheelbarrows, all the ingredients of real farming. Janet marveled, thinking how far they'd come in the years since she'd originally talked to Larry about diversifying his crops. And this was only one of several huge indoor operations in this neighborhood, most of which were growing more and more food too. Her cousin Leon was running this one, her other cousin Lamar kept track of the crops in the outdoor plots studding the local hillsides.

"Well, look who's here!" a strong female voice suddenly announced.

Janet turned around and was eye to eye with Lorena Sanchez. They laughed and hugged. "You started working here now?" Janet asked.

"Yeah, me and a half dozen others from the UPA. Leon gave us jobs not long after the Massacre. It's a great fit. I can keep organizing with the UPA."

Janet introduced her to Juna, situating each of them for the other. "Lorena's a dynamo! You shoulda seen her in Mission Bay last year when my uncle (who is a cop) stopped her and a UPA demo on campus!"

Lorena's green eyes shone with the memory. She turned to Juna, "Maybe you should go over to Larry's?" she turned to Janet with a quizzical look on her face. "He's got a lot going on. It's a few blocks over." Lorena seemed to know something.

Janet got the message and led Juna back to their bicycles. Five minutes later they were rolling into Larry's warehouse. After legalization, and especially after Larry had scored with his deal on HemptriCity, he'd been able to upgrade his facilities quite a bit.

They'd barely cleared the door when Larry, all 6'8" and 330 pounds of him, was rushing towards them and grabbing Janet in a big bear hug. "Hey, hey," she protested, and he put her down and laughed.

"I thought you were never gonna come back! It's great to see you!" He led them into a big conference room. It looked like there'd been a meeting underway when they arrived. The other two people at the table looked expectantly at him. "Ally, Maria, this is my old friend Janet Pierce... and..."

"Juna Caguas," they introduced themself. They looked at Larry, who filled a lot of space, and Alison Nakahara and Maria Campoy, and felt their gaze, which seemed kind and curious rather than harsh or judgmental. That was refreshing already! They bumped fists around the table and found a chair, cautiously optimistic.

"How are you guys doing? Has ICE been here?" Janet queried the others.

"Not yet, but they told me they'd be coming by next week," Larry conceded. "They said I'd have to register our output and that there were some new taxes we'd have to pay," he shrugged. It didn't seem like anything that would present much of a problem for him. He had all the resources he needed ever since the HemptriCity deal.

"Larry doesn't seem too worried, but I am!" announced Maria. "We were just talking about this before you arrived. We have big crops coming from our hydroponic installations, and it's gonna piss me off if ICE or some other bureaucrats think they can cart it off!"

Janet explained what they were planning. "They are planting root crops in dozens of back yards and organize gleaning neighborhood-by-neighborhood to take advantage of the fruit trees. And at the Dog Patch itself, one group is running a decoy farm, producing very little but to look like they're trying to produce a lot. The outdoor farms have to cope with ICE but we are plotting ways to minimize the losses."

Juna proposed that seeds be taken from Larry's and added to seedbanks around the city.

"You're a seed saver?" Maria was suddenly very animated.

"Yes, I brought seeds from my family farm to plant in San Francisco... Saving and sowing seeds is what I did at home," Juna declared. "I'd like to meet other seed savers."

Ally hadn't said anything yet. She was watching Juna, this curiously tall, graceful stranger with long black hair, trying to understand why this person made her feel so strongly. She hardly knew... him? Her?

"Juna, do you have a biology background?"

They looked at Ally, sizing up a stern-looking Asian woman who looked like a doctor in her white lab coat. Why would she ask about a biology background?

"I've been around farms and gardens and animals all my life." They smiled. "But I have no formal training, no science background. I am an artist," they claimed hopefully.

Juna reminded her of someone she'd known at grad school. Which led her to remember her work analyzing hemp as a potential material for electricity storage. Steven Scott, with his money and connections, recruited her there, and soon launched the small start-up HemptriCity. With cannabis legalization in 2018, they set up shop in a nondescript warehouse in San Francisco's Bayview neighborhood and discovered that the neighborhood was already home to a fairly large grow operation. A guy named Larry Lansing, "Large Larry," had a couple of warehouses and quite a few plots going all over the area.

Alison would never forget her first meeting with Large Larry at his warehouse on Yosemite Street, just a few blocks from the HemptriCity office. And now, several years after BGM bought HemptriCity and hired Allison as a research scientist, the Hempattery was a huge success. When her stock deal vested, she had "retired," returning to Larry's warehouse where she could work freely on her latest inventions.

Ally felt a strong urge to show off the biobulb. Janet knew they were running experiments in the secret cellar, the same place Vero had hidden out earlier this year before she went out and got arrested. But nobody knew how far the biobulb had come already except the inner circle. Ally knew she could trust Janet and it seemed natural to extend it to her friend.

She suddenly got up and looking squarely at Larry, she made her invitation, turning to Janet and Juna. "I've got something to show you. But you must promise to keep it secret. We can't let this get out, especially not now! OK?"

Larry was surprised. "You sure?" he blurted. Maria was also stunned that Ally would break their confidentiality agreement without discussing it first. She knew Janet could be trusted and assumed Juna could too. Ally nodded firmly and waved them to follow her. They came to a hidden doorway that led to a tunnel. Janet had been here before, but for Juna, it was new. And they had no idea how secret this tunnel was, and certainly no idea of what was at the other end.

At the end of the tunnel Maria punched in a code to open the cellar door. They entered the luxurious suite with its fancy kitchen and comfy lounge area. Towards the back of the large suite, Juna could see bunkbeds, but they didn't seem to be in use. Ally pushed something near a bookshelf and it slid open. "Follow me!" she called excitedly.

Juna had no idea of what to expect when he passed through the opening. A vast underground farm with the rich smells of deep healthy soil hit them, along with the muggy humidity. Lights were hanging from the 15-foot black ceilings, and on closer inspection, dozens of nozzles spraying a fine mist descended from the ceiling as well. Large fans turned slowly along aisles and in some spots on the ceiling. Suddenly the overhead lights went out, shut off by Ally using her remote. Eyes were drawn immediately to the new light source filling a distant wall. Ally led them towards her pride and joy.

"This is the biobulb!" she declared. Larry and Maria stood aside, recognizing Ally's joy to show off her work.

Janet exclaimed, "they're much brighter now! It's amazing!"

Juna peered at the strange fruit hanging from the plants—translucent, glowing, green-tinted ... bulbs! They looked like light bulbs but they were growing from a plant! How could this be? They went closer and started to reach out to touch one but stopped abruptly. "Can I touch it?"

"Sure, but gently OK?" Ally watched Juna closely as they softly touched a bulb with their fingertip, and then poked it with a gentle nudge, withdrawing suddenly as though it burned or stung.

"Do they break?" Juna asked. "How does it work?"

"We've been cultivating these for almost a year now," Maria explained. "The biobulb is the beginning of a people's biotech... if commonly used items like lights can run from biological energy instead of electricity, we can drastically reduce energy use and expand ecological circularity and resilience."

Juna stared, not knowing what to think. Something horrified them about the strange plants glowing in the stifling darkness. Maria's explanation sounded good but the reality of this Frankenbulb was viscerally repulsive. "Oh wow," Juna was trembling, "I don't feel so good." Juna stumbled backwards, and returned to the kitchen where they sat down abruptly on the couch.

Janet peered into Juna's face. "Are you OK?" she pressed Juna's hand between her own and looked into their face. Larry, Ally, and Maria joined them and gathered around Juna. "What happened in there? Juna, talk to us!" Ally implored. She was worried by Juna's reaction.

Juna took some deep breaths. In a cracking voice, they tried to explain. "I... I ... I'm not sure. I suddenly felt nauseous. Maybe it was the heat and humidity..."

Ally sat down next to Juna. "Juna, you're the first person to see this without any preparation. I need to know what happened in there."

"I don't know," their eyes darting from side to side. "There's something... something's not right. I felt it. Like something's torn... something is hurt."

"What do you mean?"

Juna, who moments earlier had felt an inchoate darkness, sat up, encouraged that Ally and the others wanted to understand their experience. Wiping sweat from their forehead, Juna sighed deeply. "I don't know if I have the words, but . . ." and they paused again, looking at the ceiling.

"Go on," urged Maria, who by now was sitting on Juna's other side.

"I felt an icy coldness, a deep loneliness, and then a wave of nausea. That biobulb plant is suffering!"

Ally paced the kitchen, her face twisted into an angry frown. "Why are you projecting your feelings onto this plant?" she demanded. "How were you feeling before you got here?"

Janet cut in, "Ally, come on. You asked Juna to explain and they did. It's only one person's reaction."

"OK, ok, I'm sorry," Ally backed off. "I've put everything into this for months, and it's hard to hear someone who just walked in say the plant is suffering. But ok, that's what you felt. Thank you Juna," and she sat down at the table with her arms folded, clearly unhappy.

Larry hadn't expected any particular reaction, but he was intrigued by this whole eruption. Something was happening here, but could they understand it? Could they use it? And if so, how and for what? "Hey Juna, thank you man. You shook us up and that's great. If you're right, and I'm not saying you are, what do you think it means? What would you suggest we do?"

Juna shivered, the icy coldness and fear still bouncing around inside, compounded by Ally's angry reaction. They did not want to provoke another outburst. "I don't know. Maybe the plant wants to get out of the cellar and into the sunshine? Could it be as simple as that?"

"How would it know about the sun?" Ally countered. "Can a plant *want* anything?"

"Of course!" Juna stared at her. "Plants need community. They need sun and soil. They probably want a life worth living like we do, even if they don't think or exist in the same way as humans or animals. But we know they need companionship and community. Maybe they have an innate desire for birds and bugs?"

"Oh brother!" Ally groaned.

Janet had to say the obvious as she heard Ally's reactions. "Ally, I'm sure you know this, but plants are not machines. Your skill at inventing new life forms, ones that may have practical use for humans, is impressive. But these are living beings. What kind of life doesn't need and want a full life, however that looks for them?"

Ally put her head in her hands for a moment while Janet spoke. When she finished, she put her hands up and said "OK, I get it... I do. Maria and Clara and I will take this seriously. But we can't stop now!"

Juna looked at the others silently. They weren't feeling icy any more. They felt more numb than anything, and anxious to get out of the dungeon (as they'd started thinking of it).

Janet changed the subject, going back to the Urban Farmers' plans to radically decentralize food production. She asked if Larry would help with some money, and as always, he wrote her a check.

Maria turned to Juna and said in a low voice, "I'd like to take you to a shellmound on San Bruno Mountain. It's a powerful place. And there is a serious seed saving team you should meet down there, too."

They nodded gratefully, wondering how someone could work in this cellar and be connected to seed savers and indigenous history. They were relieved when Janet led the way to their bicycles.

"Janet?" They were rolling away in the early evening twilight. "Did you feel anything down there?"

"Not like you did. But it is a strange place, very isolated. It wouldn't surprise me if that isolation affects the plants and the people who are down there all the time."

They eventually parted near Islais Creek. Janet was going back to the Dog Patch for another hour, and Juna had the long trek back to Kite Kastle.

CHAPTER 9
TUESDAY, APRIL 22, 2025

Frank was laying in his bunk on a rare day off. In the month since the Dolores Park Massacre he had been deployed again and again to break up demonstrations in San Francisco, Oakland, Berkeley, San Jose, even in places like Antioch and Vallejo, and once in San Rafael. He was exhausted and demoralized. At least they'd canned General Reynolds last week, He was making everything around here much worse than it had to be. Frank had been involved in law enforcement for decades and knew that the heavy hand Reynolds insisted on was counterproductive. You had to give people a chance to demonstrate and blow off steam.

As he contemplated a visit to one of the local restaurants, a spic-n-span soldier came in and crisply informed him that he was to report to the headquarters at the airfield. "Me?" Frank was surprised. He hoped this wouldn't be another round of blame and recrimination for the Massacre. He'd been debriefed after the short meeting he'd been called to in front of Reynolds on the day of. It seemed there was a real investigation going on, perhaps not directed at holding anyone accountable exactly, but to change the approach going forward. Reynolds had been relieved of his command, replaced by another guy from way up north who'd been part of the secessionist movement promoting a new state of Jefferson. But his name was Carlos Zapata! Didn't sound like a white supremacist to Frank. Lt. General Zapata was smoother and knew he had to strike a more reasonable tone to manage the City, but behind his claims that he wanted to "restore civility" was his steely determination to make San Francisco conform to the new norms.

Lines had blurred a lot during the past few months, though. When the United Farmworkers Union had supported the Republican ticket many were shocked. But it was consistent with their old roots in American unionism that went back to the Cesar Chavez days, when UFW militants had patrolled the border to keep "illegals" out. The union and a surprising number of Latino voters had enthusiastically supported the new Vice-President Susanna Martinez's call for a "New Day for Citizenship." Surprising numbers of people on the fringes of the ultra-right militias were ex-soldiers, ex-cops, and many of them were Latinos. Frank was no fan of illegal immigration and felt the borders had to be strongly defended. "They're coming here because of what we have," he'd argued more than once. Sheila had been troubled by his attitude towards people who were mostly refugees and trying to escape the harsh conditions where they started. But he had a zero-sum attitude toward immigration. If more people came, there'd be less for those who were already here. And after all, who had suffered more, for longer, than Black people? Why should they have to see their hard-won gains lost to newcomers?

He jumped on a passing shuttle to the airport's main office. Inside he was directed to the second-floor office of the Homeland Security Director General for the Bay Area. He was ushered right into a converted office with large windows overlooking hangars and dozens of helicopters and Unmanned Aerial Vehicles (UAVs) parked along the tarmac. Two attending officers stood to the side, and behind the massive wooden desk sat Lt. General Zapata himself. His massive biceps bulged from the tight-fitting t-shirt he wore, and his bald head drew attention to the small golden studs in his left ear. A prominent tattoo of the flag of Jefferson graced his right forearm where he was flipping through some papers on the desk.

"Sergeant Frank Robertson, sir," one of the officers announced, and Frank gave a salute and came to a halt across from Zapata.

Zapata pushed the papers aside and stood up to extend his hand to Frank, which completely surprised him. He shook it, feeling like something was wrong.

"Sergeant, I hear you've been doing a great job for us," Zapata started. "Have a seat. I want to hear what you think about how it's been going since the unfortunate incident last month."

"Sir?" Frank took the seat he was offered. "What would you like to know exactly?"

"You've been a cop for a long time, haven't you?" Frank nodded. "And you've patrolled San Francisco since . . .?"

"1981, sir. I started with the San Francisco Police that year, moved over to UCSF police in 1993."

Zapata's bushy eyebrows rose in surprise. "Over 40 years? Hell, how old are you?"

"I'll be 64 later this year, sir."

"What the hell? And we drafted you?"

Frank nodded again. "I didn't ask for this service, sir, and honestly, I was outraged when they told me I was drafted. I'd expected to be mobilized for a few weeks at most, and on a loaner basis from UCSF," he explained. "I'm close to retirement, obviously."

"You know Reynolds had you under surveillance after Dolores Park? He had you tagged as a subversive. Did you know?" Frank shook his head but said nothing. "What does it make you think?"

"Well, first, you wouldn't be telling me this if you believed it. And secondly, DHS must not be taking it seriously, so I guess I don't need to either."

Zapata nodded his head at Frank's common-sense response.

Frank uncharacteristically spoke with an urgency that surprised himself as much as the others. "We've been chasing every demonstration in the Bay Area for the past month. If I can speak bluntly, it's been a huge waste of time. How many people have been arrested? Over 5,000? How many are being held here? On Mare Island? On Treasure Island? What is the plan for these people? It must be costing a lot of money to detain so many. Will there be trials? Are there enough judges for this? I get the feeling nobody thought about this before it started. And what is it like in other parts of the country? I assume it's as bad or worse?"

"What would you do if you were in charge, Robertson?"

"This is still America, isn't it? I know the President declared a National Emergency, but as far as I know we still have a Constitution. We should respect people's rights to assemble and free speech. If they break the law, ok, we arrest them. But not for exercising their rights. The government seems afraid."

Zapata paced, deep in thought. After a minute he stopped and put his hands on his desk. "I'd like you to join my staff, Robertson. We won't be able to end the Emergency right away, but you understand better than a lot of these guys where we need to go."

Frank was flattered. He didn't expect this guy to take him seriously and thought he might have been digging a deeper hole for himself. But to join the executive staff of the DHS Director General?! What would he have to do? During the past couple of weeks he still hoped he could get out of this and go back to San Francisco, but it was sinking in. There was no going back.

"Sir, I'm honored, and of course if you think I can be helpful, I'll gladly serve. But I would like to know that I can retire as planned early next year. Would that be fair?"

"OK, Robertson. Let's see how we do this year. We can discuss this in the new year."

He hadn't agreed to anything, Frank took note.

"Colonel Sepulveda, please take Sergeant Robertson to his new quarters. And Sergeant, you're promoted. You are now Lieutenant Robertson. Colonel, will you see to the paperwork? Thank you. Dismissed!"

Frank was in a daze. Lieutenant? Executive Staff? What was he expected to do?

Colonel Sepulveda was a button-up military cliché, a square-jawed white guy like most of the upper ranks of the military and corporate America. "Follow me Robertson!" he ordered.

They got into a waiting jeep with a driver. Sepulveda wasn't doing any talking, so Frank figured he'd keep it zipped too. They turned a few times after leaving the airfield and drove into a residential area a few blocks away. It looked like DHS had taken over these homes, along with the local businesses, the mall, and the airfield. They turned into a driveway of a typical 2-story suburban tract home and Sepulveda led Frank into the house. "This is yours now, Robertson. We're having your belongings sent over from the barracks. You can finish your day off, but we'll expect you at 7 a.m. at HQ. A shuttle will be outside at 6:45 for you."

Frank looked around as Sepulveda departed. It was a big place for one guy. Maybe he could invite Sheila to come over? He hadn't talked to her much lately. The long days, the violence, the demoralization, he didn't known what to say anyway. It's not like he could speak freely when they did talk, and she could tell he was holding a lot back. Their relationship revolved around long walks, which usually led to going home and spending the night together. Without that chance to establish intimacy, they drifted far apart. He threw open the drapes and let in the afternoon sun. From a big chair he gazed through the front window at the nondescript suburban neighborhood that was his new home. Somebody in a military uniform was adjusting a sprinkler on a browning lawn across the street. No children, no pedestrians to be seen. A white ICE hummer cruised slowly by, apparently patrolling the district. Frank shook his head and muttered to himself. "How the hell did I get *here*?"

***

His first week at the Director's office had gone by in a whirlwind. He was glad he no longer had to rush around the Bay Area confronting every little demo that popped up. They got reports in the staff offices from his former squad and the others who *were* still doing that. Zapata had tasked him with compiling reports on demonstrations since the Massacre and developing a coherent analysis. He wanted the demonstrations categorized in terms of honest threat assessments. The more Frank looked through the reports, reading between the lines of field officers trying to describe routine protests, picket lines, and marches as examples of a coordinated campaign of treasonous subversion, the more obvious it was that no such thing was happening. Sure there were some groups who had been developing some independent initiative and strength *before* the election, like the Urban Peasants Alliance (BGM contractors mostly), but they weren't focused on political power. Policies announced by the new government, like making electric car owners pay a tax to subsidize gasoline users, or mandatory diet guidelines to promote Midwest soy and corn, were sure to provoke more organized opposition. He thought of his niece Janet and her League of Urban Farmers and the eco-types she hung around with—they were sure to be organizing against the government's policies. But why shouldn't they? The policies were stupid! Even he could see that.

How could he present his analysis without sounding like he opposed the government himself? He didn't vote for these people, and he didn't like the way the election had been overturned in Arizona and Wisconsin. But the Supreme Court had upheld it, and that was the law. They had to move on and work within the elected government, until the next election. At least it couldn't be as bad as Trump had been, he told himself.

A week had gone by. He'd even had a weekend and had gone to the mall to see a movie! It was a crappy remake of one of those Marvel comic books, but it had been two and a half hours of air-conditioned shutdown in the dark.

He went to sleep Sunday night, expecting to rise at 5:30 and have his usual breakfast before the shuttle pulled up outside. But he was abruptly awakened by sirens in the middle of the night. It was 1 a.m.! What was going on? He went over to the window and couldn't see anything unusual. The sirens were coming from some distance away, probably the airfield. What could that be about? His phone rang.

It was Sepulveda. "Robertson!" he barked. "Get over here! We're getting flooded. All hands on deck!" and he hung up. Frank rubbed his eyes. What the hell? Flooded? And then he remembered that he'd seen the weather guy on TV saying they were expecting unusually high tides tonight. "High tides flooding the airfield?" he grumbled as he got dressed.

He walked the three blocks to Hegenberger Road and waved down a passing ICE vehicle for a ride to the base. It was pure chaos. Searchlights were swinging wildly back and forth, sirens were sounding, and people were running to and fro. Incredibly, there was water shimmering over the whole airfield. Prisoners in their green jumpsuits were filling sandbags and building walls around nearby buildings. In the dark he couldn't make anyone out. He went into the main office building. Sandbags surrounded the front doors which were still some distance from flood waters. No one was tending the front desk at 1:30 am as he passed on his way to his second-floor office. Everywhere was deserted. What did Sepulveda expect him to do here? He didn't have any emergency role, so he watched the scene unfold outside. Soldiers were rolling UAVs away from the waterlogged airfield. Helicopters were being sandbagged but given that the water was so shallow it was probably an overreaction. He could hear bulldozers working in the darkness but couldn't see where they were.

He was quite alert on arrival, but the longer he sat there, the sleepier he got. He decided he might as well return to bed. He'd been given no specific orders, and there was no one there to direct him. He found a ride back to his house and fell deeply asleep soon after he was back in his bed.

At 8:30 that morning he suddenly awoke, realizing he missed his shuttle and was very late. He showered as fast as he could and got a ride to the base with a quick call to the pool. He walked into his office at 9:15 but almost everyone was gone. The lone orderly who usually brought the morning donuts was sitting at a desk in the corner.

"What's going on? Where is everybody?" Frank demanded.

"I'm not sure. There's been a breakout. The back fence is down. A bunch of prisoners got away," the young man said nervously.

"Oh crap! Where's Zapata? Where's Sepulveda? What about Commander Rinert?"

"I don't know, sir. I came in with the donuts like usual, and everyone was already gone. I heard it from another orderly running past me outside."

Frank immediately went out to see what he could.

CHAPTER 10
APRIL 29, 2025

Vero sat up suddenly in her top bunk. The glowing clock on the far wall indicated it was half past midnight. Weeks had passed since the Dolores Park Massacre and the influx of new detainees. Escape plans that seemed promising in her whispered conversations with Rita, Frieda, and others felt unrealistic, even hopeless.

Rita had been pacing by the windows again when the sounds brought her to an abrupt stop. She could hear yelling and big engines in the distance. Others were stirring and climbing out of their bunks.

"Holy shit!" Rita blurted. She urgently waved to Vero to come to the window. Vero and a half dozen others crowded around to see a shimmering field of water stretching across the runways into the distance. Yellow bulldozers were pushing earth on the other side of the perimeter fence, apparently trying to block the floodwaters, if that's what they were. What else could it be?

The news had been full of warnings about an extraordinarily high tide expected at midnight, and here it was! It wasn't the first time that tides and upwelling groundwater engulfed the coastlines in the Bay. Ever since the heat waves in the Antarctic several years ago, the glaciers had been melting into the ocean at an ever faster rate. And the Greenland ice sheet was pouring into the north Atlantic too, whole glaciers melting faster than anyone ever imagined. Already the oceans had risen almost a foot, matching predictions for decades in the future.

The door burst open and in came several guards. "Get up! Get up! Everyone up!"

Groggily the 23 detainees in the room mustered themselves under the frantic orders of the guards. Frieda addressed the one in charge, a guy they'd come to know as Rusty for his red beard and generally easy-going manner. "Rusty, what's going on?" she asked.

"The high tides are pushing up the groundwater and flooding the whole base. We're not far from the bayshore here, and it's come up way higher and faster than anyone predicted. We need you to help sandbag the buildings."

Once they had gotten dressed, they were led out into the night, their feet immediately getting soaked as they stepped into several inches of water. There were various stairways and some higher mounds, as well as flower boxes and tree wells that were above the water level. But for the most part it was a vast sea of shallow water. The distant rumble of bulldozers filled the night, as orders were shouted from multiple directions. "Fill those bags!" "Use this wheelbarrow!" "Get these over there!" and so on.

Though everyone had been awakened suddenly, no one seemed sleepy now. The chaos was a welcome break from the dull monotony of their day-to-day lives as detainees. One woman fell as she wrestled with a bag and others rushed to help her up, thoroughly soaked. "Go back in and change!" she was urged, and since no one was closely monitoring them at this point, she went back to their barracks.

"Vero!" Rita called from nearby. Vero swapped partners and went to work on sandbagging with Rita. When they were close and a bit away from the others, Rita continued, "I got a note tonight!"

"Oh yeah?" Vero's hopes rose again, even as she shoveled sand into bags.

"They said when the tide recedes, the fence will come down and we should make a break for it!"

"What? And then what?"

"Look for UPS. That's what the note said."

"Should we tell the others?"

"Definitely."

"What happens if we run for it and there's no one there when we get out?"

"I guess we have to trust that there will be help."

"I'm so ready to get out of here. How will we know what time?"

"After breakfast, be on the lookout. I don't know what the signal will be. If we see the fence come down, we should run, as many of us as can do it!" Rita was more than ready to bolt too.

"Hey, hey, what are you guys doing? Stop that chatter and fill those bags!" yelled one of the asshole guards, a guy from somewhere in the central valley. What was it with these redneck assholes?

Vero and Rita and the rest kept at it. After a few hours, the buildings were surrounded by walls of sandbags. Around 4 a.m. they were sent back to the barracks. The waters had receded somewhat, and the runways and grounds were pockmarked with glistening puddles. Their feet squished and sloshed as they piled back in, exhausted. The adrenaline of the first hour from the panicky sense that they could get flooded out gave way to realizing the authorities were only worried about their damn buildings. The water wasn't coming up that high after all. It was an overreaction. Everyone tore off their soaking shoes and socks and threw them into a heap in the corner. Stinking water slowly oozed from the pile and spread across the floor.

"Pick up your shit!" called the woman closest to the corner. "Water is leaking across the floor."

It didn't take long for most of them to fall asleep after the exertion of the past hours.

The alarm didn't ring until 8 a.m., a welcome delay on their usual 6 a.m. rise-and-shine order. As they straggled into the messhall, Rusty, looking like he'd never slept all night, smiled wearily at them. "I gave you extra hours of sleep!" he bragged. They thanked him, knowing he'd taken it on himself to do them a favor. "You were great last night!" he saluted them and departed.

Rita, Vero, Frieda, and other plotters sat together at their usual table. Making sure none of the snitches was near, they whispered among themselves, communicating the breakout plan in its rough form. It was a warm day already, and their tiredness soon gave way to nervous anticipation. They were allowed to tend the vegetable garden after breakfast so they went outside and kept their eyes on the fence.

On the other side of the fence was the old Skywest golf course, now a local park. It had an original creek running through it, and it had been the main channel by which the floodwaters had poured inland and then eventually swamped the area. Several bulldozers were continuing to move earth around in the distance, building levees to prevent further flooding. One bulldozer was working close to the perimeter fence and Vero caught herself staring at it. It was not doing the same work as the other two machines but seemed to be running back and forth along the perimeter without actually pushing any dirt. The old Clubhouse Road ran along the fence, and suddenly she noticed a small caravan of UPS trucks driving west towards the Clubhouse at the end of the road. Her heart raced.

"Rita!" she hissed. "Look!"

Everyone looked towards the fence and saw the UPS trucks. Their ride was here!

Then the odd bulldozer did a three-point turn and started backing up towards one of the support posts on the perimeter fence. Crash! He kept backing up until a good 40-foot stretch of fence was flat in the mud.

"That's it! Let's go!" yelled Rita. They ran across the muddy grounds, splishing and splashing. There were no guards to be seen! The dramatic events of the night apparently depleted the ranks of the on-duty guards too. By the time they were at the fallen fence and clamboring over it, finally shouts were ringing behind them, "STOP! STOP!" and shots were fired.

"Fuck me, are they shooting at us?!?" cried Frieda. After Dolores Park, she was deeply afraid. Turning back was not an option. On they went, and here came the cavalry! The UPS trucks, seven of them, came up the road and pulled over. Three slid open their doors and brown-uniformed people waved them in to the three trucks. As rapidly as they could they climbed in the back, filling each truck—15 escapees in one, 21 in another and 11 in the last. The other four trucks were apparently decoys. In unison, the doors slammed, and they drove to a big intersection where they did a strange series of interweaving u-turns before two trucks went one way, the three full of passengers took the freeway, and two other empty trucks went another way. They hoped to confuse any aerial surveillance and had quite a choreography arranged, a version of three card monte with seven UPS trucks!

The ones who made it to the freeway soon separated and exited at different off-ramps as soon as they could, and then started "making deliveries" on their East Oakland routes. Once they'd settled down in the UPS van, Vero realized it wasn't only women from their barracks. There were some guys who had made it too.

"Vero!" Jay Hartman was crushed against the wall with three other guys. "Is it really you?!"

"Jay! I can't believe it!" and she lurched over on her knees to give him a hug. "How'd you get here?"

The teenager she'd met as a volunteer at Palou Terrace more than a year ago was an adult now. His long blonde hair was gone, cut short in detention, and he had an unkempt reddish beard now. He explained how he'd been picked up at Dolores Park and brought over to the Detention Center in March. She told him how she'd left Larry's only to get nabbed by plainclothes Homeland Security goons who had her on a list.

On 66th Avenue their driver turned to Rita and Vero and said, "Never say the Teamsters didn't help you when you needed it!" And at a nondescript home he double-parked and told them to follow him. Vero turned to Jay, "Hey, I'll see you at Larry's!" hoping he'd understand. The UPS driver led them down the driveway and into a carriage house/garage behind the house. "Wait here. Someone will pick you up within the hour." All the other 40+ detainees were dropped at safe houses around East Oakland or near Lake Merritt, where they, too, were picked up and moved along within an hour of their arrival.

"This is amazing," Vero exclaimed to Rita in the garage. "What a system! I wonder who set this up?"

"It's a new underground," Rita declared. "And not a minute too soon! I was gonna lose my mind in that camp! But I have no idea who's behind this. I guess we'll find out when they move us again. I hope they take us to San Francisco. Hey, who was that guy in there?"

"Oh Jay? He and I worked together before this shit started, urban farming," and she let it drop. No need to say more. "I hope we do get to the City. I know where I can hide there. Do you have a place?"

"I can hide with friends, but not for long. Do you have room for me where you're going?"

Vero wondered what was happening with Larry's place, and the other spaces she knew about in the City. Hopefully Janet was still out, and the secret cellar was still a secret! "I might. I'll have to check it out. Let's see where they take us next, and who our new friends are."

Rita nodded, her broad shoulders slumping for the first time Vero could remember. Rita leaned against the wall and slid to the floor of the lightly furnished garage. It was like an unused guest room.

Vero fell across the single bed. "Man I could fall asleep right now!" she declared.

Rita was unable to speak. Her eyes welled up, and she sobbed quietly.

"What's wrong? Are you ok?" Vero asked.

Rita nodded. She snuffled and took a deep breath. "I can't believe we got away. I'm relieved, but I don't want to count on anything yet. We have a ways to go before I'll feel like we got away. I hope they don't find us...or the guys who sprung us either!"

***

Vero made it back after her inspiring escape from Camp Hayward. When she burst into the yard at the Dog Patch, Janet couldn't believe her eyes.

"VERO!!! You're here! How'd—"

"You wouldn't believe it!" Vero was excited, but she was looking over her shoulder and up at the sky. "Can we get under something? I can't be seen."

"You think they can spot you here from the sky?" Janet had been skeptical, but after hearing the escape story, she'd gotten Vero into an oversized set of clothes, put a floppy hat on her, loaded her on the bike cart and took her to Larry's.

Once they were in the subterranean corridor to the cellar, they relaxed. Vero walked in with an unanticipated combination of comfort and dread.

"Man I can't believe after all that I'm right back where I started," she said as they pushed through the hanging flaps of plastic.

"Vero!" Clara nearly fell out of her chair seeing Vero walk in. She and Ally leaped from their seats and rushed over to Vero and Janet.

"Hi you guys!" Vero hugged her friends. "It's like I never left!" she laughed ironically.

"What the hell happened?" demanded Ally. "We heard you were arrested... for what?" she still couldn't imagine anyone would be arrested for doing nothing at all. Vero and Janet sat down around the table while Ally made some coffee for them. She sliced a fresh loaf of walnut bread. Clara pulled out some fancy cheeses from the fridge.

"I see you're still eating well down here!" chuckled Vero. "You shoulda seen the slop they were feeding us in Hayward!" And she went on a long rambling tale of how she got picked up the afternoon she went for a walk, and then spent the past three months in detention without charges.

"Then I got this note in my food that someone had gotten me a lawyer and they were trying to get me out! Was that you guys?"

Ally shook her head. "No, not me. Maybe it was Larry. Janet weren't you involved?"

Janet shook her head too. "I heard you got arrested, but nobody knew what to do. There were no courts willing to hear any habeus corpus cases for detainees during the first month. And then there was this huge backlog. But we knew you were there, and your name was on the list with the other people arrested. It was probably the new underground in the East Bay sent you that note."

"That's who organized our breakout. Rita, my friend, she got a note telling us to get ready. To look for UPS! And those Teamsters did it, man. They showed up in their brown trucks and picked a bunch of us up and got us away. It was amazing!"

The drop-off in East Oakland, and then the 2nd ride from a gray-haired woman in a Volvo with faded Hilary Clinton stickers on the back. "You wouldn't believe it. She was cool as a cucumber. Came up the driveway, knocked twice, said 'Your ride is ready ladies!' We were holding our breath but when she said that we came out laughing. We scrunched down in the back of her car for a ride San Francisco that went about as easily as you could imagine. The cameras would've only seen one woman in the car, and she drove calmly. We dropped Rita at an address in a South of Market alley, maybe Natoma, and then she brought me to the Dog Patch."

Janet was happy for Vero's return. The word about the escape ricocheted around the network by word of mouth almost as it was happening. But no mention of it on the heavily censored news. It was impossible to know who escaped until they showed up in person, and here she was, in the flesh! Amazing!

Things were moving very fast now. All over the Bay Area cells of rebels were organizing. Food production was ramping up in indoor warehouses, replacing crops of weed with vegetables and fruits. Figuring out safe houses and ways to move people around out of sight had become vitally important.

***

Janet was in Oakland, walking under the oak trees towards the little bandstand on the usually deserted beach at Lake Merritt. She was on time for her rendezvous as she skirted the edge of the old Children's Fairyland fence. Several crows swooped in, cawing wildly. She paused, listening to them carefully. This was a warning, no doubt about that. She stepped behind a large tree to wait a moment.

A patrol appeared below, several ICE officers jumping out of a white van that had rolled down the lakeside path. There weren't many people here these days. Janet moved slowly, keeping the tree between her and the cops. She retreated until she had disappeared behind Fairyland. The crows flew overhead, circling her and then disappearing. She waved a grateful acknowledgment to them.

She was supposed to meet a woman with a blue scarf, that's all she knew. Maybe she could intercept her before she walked into the trap. She continued walking to the park's perimeter, merging into the few other people walking along.

She saw a woman with a blue scarf coming from the east on the other side of Grand Avenue. Seeing a gap in the traffic, she bolted across the street and came to a halt as the woman recoiled at her arrival.

"Lemonade is the best summer drink," she blurted.

"But lemons are in short supply," replied the woman, her black hair cascading over her shoulders from under the blue scarf. She was of Asian descent, but her age was hard to tell. Maybe she was 35, but she could be ten years older or younger. But she knew the code and gave the correct answer.

"A patrol showed up at the rendezvous site. Follow me!" Janet urged her, "Let me go ahead of you a few yards. We're not going far."

The woman said nothing and Janet started walking briskly, the other woman following a short distance behind. At the lobby of a friend's apartment building Janet waited til she caught up. "What's your name?" Janet asked.

The woman gave her a penetrating gaze. "Cindy."

"OK, Cindy, the plan went sideways. I got a warning and a minute later, an ICE patrol rolled up. We need to get out of sight and lay low for a while. I have a friend here who will help us."

They were soon sitting in her grandma's friend Ronnie's dusty apartment.

"I didn't expect to see you over here, especially under these circumstances!" Ronnie chided, his eyes dancing with pleasure, as he'd let them in. "And you brought a friend!"

"Ronnie, this is Cindy. Listen, we need to hang out at your place for an hour while I figure out what to do. Is that ok?" Janet asked but it wasn't a question.

"No problem." Ronnie was savvy enough not to pry. He felt lucky to be part of whatever these two women were up to after being isolated for years, especially during the pandemic. It wasn't common for anyone to come to his place.

"Cindy, what do you do?"

"I'm a veterinarian."

"Do you specialize in any particular animals?"

"Dogs and cats are the backbone of most urban veterinarians, and I can handle them. I was a large animal vet at my last job." She had an authoritative air about her as she described her professional skills.

Janet was pacing by the window, stopping from time to time to look down at the streets below. "There they go!" she announced after a while.

Cindy and Ronnie came over to see a small convoy of white vans rolling east on Grand Avenue.

"Ronnie, do you have any taxi or car service you like to use?" Janet asked.

"Funny you'd ask. My neighbor drives for Uber. He usually takes the 6-2 shift, so he may be awake by now. I can knock if you want."

"Sure, thanks, we need a quick way to get to Jack London Square."

A few minutes later, Ronnie came in with his neighbor. A big guy, his disheveled black hair parted in the middle drawing attention down his puffy face to the gap between his front teeth and his enormous belly bursting from the buttons of his plaid shirt. "Hey, I'm Rogelio," he boomed as if he was somewhat deaf, "Ronnie here says you need a ride?"

Try as he might, Rogelio couldn't get anything out of the two odd women in his back seat. He soon gave up and headed straight to Jack London Square. They gave him a $20 so he wouldn't have to log the trip.

He dropped them at the end of the street over the Alameda tube where they jumped out. "Thanks man!" she called to him. They walked along the Marina Lawn to the Fuel Dock. "Cindy, this is my plan B. I have a friend who is usually here, and I'm hoping we can get her to take us across the bay."

"Sure, I'm in your hands," Cindy seemed oddly serene as Janet navigated what seemed to her an utterly chaotic breakdown in the plan. Seagulls swooped in, issuing their plaintive calls.

"Wait here for a few minutes while I go see if my friend is around. Keep an eye out for ICE."

Janet made her way through the tanks and maritime debris of the fuel dock. Sure enough, Cary was on the floating dock helping a small boat finish fueling. When she was done, Janet got her attention, and explained the problem. "Can you do it? We need to get to the Dog Patch before dark." Cary checked with her boss who gave her the greenlight to leave early.

"OK, but you're gonna owe me a big one," she admonished with a smile.

"Oh, yeah, how big?" Janet went along with her.

"We'll have to see, won't we?" the teasing continued.

"We'll be right down." And ten minutes later, the three women were bouncing in the wake of a large container ship and the tugboats that had dragged it out into the bay. Cary had a speedy little skiff and got them across the bay in 15 minutes. A coast guard cutter passing in the distance gave them pause, but they didn't change course and didn't seem to think they were worth investigating. Not long after that, they cruised into the mouth of Islais Creek, past the rusting old navy ships that had been berthed on the north side for years, and into the makeshift dock the Dog Patch had built. The terraces went up the slope from the dock, and farmers were bent over their beds, tending vegetables and fruits. "Cary wait a sec," and Janet bounded up the hill and came back in a blink with a basket full of zucchinis, lettuce, kale, and a large container of strawberries. "Here's a little thank you basket," she said as she thrust it into the skiff. "You're an angel!"

Cary sped away while Janet led Cindy up to the clubhouse, a few hundred feet from the shoreline. The land was soggy for part of their trek, having become a tidal flood zone during the rising tides of the past couple of years. "We used to get crops from these lower terraces, but not anymore. Too many floods. But then, we knew those floods were coming when we tore out the old warehouses and built these terraces, Hopefully most of the Dog Patch will stay above the waters for years to come," Janet explained as they walked.

Cindy stopped when the farm dogs rushed her. She gave them a vigorous rub like they were old friends, and they showed their appreciation. She laughed, "ok ok guys, I'm glad to meet you too!" and pushed them away.

CHAPTER 11
Friday, May 9, 2025

Maria stood under the trees near the shed, growing impatient. Juna was supposed to have been here a half hour ago. She was getting worried when, black hair flying backwards, golden earrings sparkling in the afternoon sun, Juna pedaled into the yard.

"There you are!" Maria exclaimed. "I was starting to worry that you'd been arrested!"

"Oh, no, I have a long way to go to get down here. And I still get confused about where I'm going in San Francisco. I had to double back after I went too far!" Sweat rolled down Juna's face and they pulled their shirt away from their body, flapping it to get some air on their skin. "Is where we're going a long way from here?" they asked, enjoying the flourishing Alemany Farm. "Wow, this is a beautiful farm! I had no idea!"

"Your first time here?" Maria asked rhetorically. "It's the best established farm in San Francisco at this point. There are some older small gardens but nothing this size."

"How will they handle the ICE taxes?" Juna wondered aloud.

"They moved a lot of plants to other locations, and over half the farm has been 'retired,'" she made air quotes, smiling. "They'll have to hand over a bunch of food, but nothing like it would've been." She unfolded a paper map and pointed to San Bruno Mountain. "That's where we're going. It's at least as far as you've come already, but not too much more than that," she guessed. "You ready?"

Juna took a moment to rinse their face and quaff a deep drink of fresh water. "Let's go!" They'd brought their seed pouch with them, of course. Maria told him that they'd be visiting an indigenous shellmound, but also that there was a group of people living on the mountain who had what she called a "Semillero Diaspórico," a seed bank for people of the diaspora. Juna was terribly excited to meet them and learn more about it.

Forty-five minutes later, Maria and Juna took the last slope from inside the Brisbane Industrial Park up to the old quarry road. A battered brown sign indicated the park boundary. They hid their bikes in dense shrubbery where they locked them up. Juna took a deep breath, enjoying the warm air full of rich smells emanating from the canyons above them.

"This is beautiful!" they blurted. "I had no idea this was here!"

"Hardly anyone does, until they come to visit in person," Maria explained. "The first time I came was only a year ago. I'd been working for Larry and needed a break. One of the other workers there, Billy Oakes, told me there was this amazing mountain, full of plants and butterflies that don't live anywhere else but here," she was getting warmed up now. "He brought me here and I met local mountain stewards and kept coming back."

"Mountain stewards? Who is that?"

"You'll see. People who live in Brisbane. They are the ones who know what's here, they keep the trails open and in good repair, and they're always glad to lead tours, especially for kids. But there's another group we'll meet a bit later that you'll like. They're the ones with the seed bank I was telling you about."

They began the trek up the trail winding in and out of clusters of oak trees as they ascended the canyon. Further up the mountain, the canyon split in two and in its higher elevations appeared covered in dense greenery.

"Does this trail go all the way up there?" Juna asked.

"You'll see! I don't want to give away all the surprises!" Maria laughed. Before long they took a left fork in the trail and went downhill to the canyon's bottom, where a wide opening surrounded a creekbed under overhanging oak trees. "This was apparently a kitchen area for the folks who lived here for thousands of years," Maria explained. "You can see the ledges along the sides; this is still a reliable source of freshwater year round," pointing to the muddy trickle at the bottom. "And sometimes, like during the big rains two winters ago, this can be a roaring torrent... Follow me!" she called as she bounded up the opposite bank on the path.

At the top they stepped in a clearing that offered northerly views back down the canyon to the industrial park below, and to townhouses crowding the slopes of the mountain's northeast ridge directly across from them. A small bench was perched at the top of the clearing and Maria took a seat and beckoned Juna to join her.

"Look," she pointed to the soil, which was speckled with small white things, denser as the slope ran downhill from where they sat. "Those are bits of oyster shells, and we're sitting on an intact shellmound."

Juna's eyes grew large and they put their hands down to the ground on either side of them. Juna imagined swirling dancers, a sprawling feast, crashing waves, bobbing on a tule canoe offshore, great dark storm clouds pouring over the hill... Projection or imagination or memories buried beneath their feet? Who could say, but Juna breathed heavily as their hands pushed ever harder into the ground.

"Juna, you ok? Juna!" Maria hadn't seen anyone react like this before. She loved this spot, and all that was implied by its deep history, but Juna was in another dimension. She reached out to touch their shoulder and shook them lightly. Juna's head lurched up and back and their eyes flew open but she could only see the whites. Yikes! "Hey, Juna! Come back!"

And just like that, Juna released the ground, opened their eyes, and smiled broadly. "Wow! Wow! I feel like I was on a rollercoaster through time!"

"What did you see? What did you feel?" Maria asked.

Juna shook their head. "I feel like I was flooded with other people's memories. Many things went through my head in such a short time—I can barely remember anything. There were storms, water, fire, food, dancing... and sadness, joy, ecstasy, cold, heat, fear, confusion..." They shook their head and put their hands to the sides of their forehead. "That was intense!"

Maria patted Juna's shoulder and ran her hand down their back. "You're here now. You're ok."

They sat quietly for a few minutes more, Juna making sure not to put their hands directly on to the surface again. They weren't ready for another flood of feelings.

"We have a ways further to walk. You ready?" Maria asked, and Juna nodded in assent.

Soon hey were climbing switchbacks in the dense oaks. Breathing the air helped clear Juna's mind, and the steady accompaniment of scrub jays squawking focused their attention on the walk. Up and up until they emerged from the forest (until you climbed up there you would never know there was a dense oak forest on the upper slopes of Buckeye canyon) and crossed the back of the canyon, moving west towards the ridge separating them from Owl Canyon.

The views north to downtown San Francisco were breathtaking. Juna couldn't help but try to imagine the same landscape before the buildings were built. Was this a taste of the landscape that once covered the whole peninsula? The mountain was all theirs so far. No one appeared on their walk, only an endless stream of butterflies, and a healthy assortment of local birds. Red-tailed hawks screeched from time to time, circling on warm currents above the canyons. They were descending into Owl Canyon when Maria suddenly came to a halt under a sprawling old oak.

"Check it out!" and Juna looked beyond her to see what she was pointing out. A small wall of different colored panels filled the space beneath a horizontal branch of the oak. Maria led them around the top and the stepped over the big old branch, a foot above the upslope of the hill, and then they stepped down into a cozy treehouse. A rug covered the ground, a trickling creek ran a few yards away, and a bunch of glass jars full of beans, rice, and other dry goods lined the shelves, along with a small library and other sundries.

"Does someone live here?" Juna looked around as if expecting someone to appear.

"Yep, in fact it's a couple. They rebuilt this place, after other people who used to live here got kicked out years ago. But these guys are not the only ones living on the mountain. There's a small village over in the former quarry. In fact, I bet that's where Marco and LaDonna are now."

"Can we go over there?"

"Yeah, let's keep going," Maria urged.

A half hour later they were back down at the bottom of Owl Canyon and a short time later they came to the end of a small trail that brought them into the settlement near the old quarry.

Juna was disappointed. "This is all?" The four huts hardly made a village. It was barely a well developed campsite.

"Hey Maria!" Billy Oakes appeared at the other end of the clearing. "Fancy meeting you here!"

"Hi Billy," Maria gave him a quick hug. "I brought a new friend. This is Juna."

"Juna, welcome," Billy looked at Juna and continued, "All Indians are welcome!"

Juna looked a bit sheepish, not used to being labeled as Indian so casually. "I'm Yokut," they said proudly.

"I'm part Luiseño, part Chumash, and all Californian!" Billy laughed. "You know, we're all Indians now. Before the colonizers came, we were thousands of different peoples, but after two centuries, so much loss and suffering, we're all Indians—we have more in common than not. No?"

Juna hadn't heard anyone talk like this before. Much of their heritage work focused on being Yokut, their specific tribal identity, and the Delta region as the place their tribe claimed as home. But Billy had a point. The indigenous people Juna had known over the years nearly always had hybrid identities and were often living far from any possible ancestral lands.

"Who do we have here?" demanded a large woman as she emerged from one of the huts, crude wooden lean-tos with barely enough room to sleep in, and no windows. She stood swaying, her hair disheveled, a pink bathrobe wrapped around her shoulders and a long brown skirt reaching her dusty ankles and bare feet.

"Angie, you've met Maria before. And this is her friend Juna. Juna, Angie—Angie Werdon—is our inspiration," Billy explained. "She was the first to camp here, and now there's a growing family." And on cue, a young Mayan couple cautiously entered the clearing, two small children in their arms. "This is Jose and Mariana Mukul and their children, Davi and Sarita." They smiled tentatively and waved to Juna. They spoke to Angie in Mayan and she seemed to explain that there was nothing to worry about because they visibly relaxed.

Juna felt strongly attracted to these people and this place. Perhaps they were still reverberating from the shellmound visions. Still, this tiny impoverished settlement of different *indios* spoke to them.

"Juna brought some seeds from their uncle's farm in the delta, right?" Maria looked to Juna to agree.

Nodding Juna pulled out his seed pouch. "I heard you have a special seed collection here? A *semillero diaspórico*? I'd love to learn more," he looked around in unveiled earnestness.

Angie smiled. "You are welcome here Juna. You found us!" and she sat down near the fire pit. Pulling on some boots, she waved Juna over. "Come with me, I'll show you what we're up to. Hey Maria, you wanna stay for dinner? Billy and the kids will make rabbit stew." She peered over her glasses at Billy and then looked at Jose and Mariana, her eyebrows raised. She said a few words to them in Mayan and they disappeared into their hut, coming out a few minutes later to start food preparations.

"Sure, why not?" Maria smiled, and she and Billy headed to the locking pantry to pull a jug of water.

Angie led Juna up the hill. They entered another small clearing surrounded by buckeye and oak trees. Angie pulled out a pipe and lit the tobacco and handed it to Juna. "You smoke?" Juna took it and had a puff but started coughing immediately. "Ha, ha, I guess not!" Angie guffawed. "Well, that's ok. It's a bad habit they say. But it's a sacrament too," she concluded with a long pull on the pipe. "This is our seed bank," and she reached into the roots of the oak tree and pulled out a big metal box. Opening it for Juna to see, Angie displayed dozens of small envelopes, each labeled in English, Spanish, and ...

"Is that Mayan?" Juna pointed to the third language on the envelopes.

"Yup. Mayans are far from home, but the climate is moving this way. Who knows? Maybe the seeds they brought will begin to thrive here before long."

"I'd like to learn more. Angie, can you teach me?" Juna's innocent enthusiasm was almost painful.

She slapped Juna on the back. "I don't know if I'm the best teacher, but I'm glad to try," she promised.

This was why Juna came to San Francisco. They explained to Angie about where they were living in Eureka Valley but promised to come down to San Bruno Mountain often.

Juna liked Angie, pleased to meet a kindred two-spirit.

CHAPTER 12
FRIDAY, MAY 9, 2025

Frank arrived at his desk at 8 am promptly. The daily routine was well established after three weeks. Up at 6:30 and after some stretching exercises and a shower, followed by his daily eggs and bacon, the shuttle was outside at 7:45. His mind drifted to the hopeful conversation he had the previous evening with Sheila. She said she'd come for a visit this weekend! Wow! It had been a while. He was preoccupied by the thought of her visiting as he sat down to his work.

Since his sudden and surprising promotion to Lieutenant three weeks ago, he attended weekly meetings with Zapata and the general staff. Luckily he wasn't saddled with figuring out the security failure that led to the breakout from Camp Hayward. The angry denunciations that erupted at the first meeting, blame being ping-ponged back and forth between Rinert and Williams, had been silenced by Zapata. After he promoted a mid-level Guardsman from Bakersfield to investigate the breach, he admonished the others in the meeting to focus their efforts on stabilizing their presence at Camp Hayward and the twelve satellite bases they'd established around the Bay Area. He sent Rinert to visit the various bases, starting with Mare Island in Vallejo and reassigned Williams to Moffet Field in Mountain View. Zapata projected a muscular machismo, and the last thing he tolerated was bickering and blaming from his subordinates. But Frank harbored a suspicion. Did Zapata believe in this mission? Other Homeland security officers were by-the-book, but Zapata seemed to realize that he didn't know everything.

"Frank, your analysis of the past weeks' field reports is spot-on. Honestly, it's a breath of fresh air amid a whole lot of blather," Zapata seemed to be confiding in him. No one else was in the commander's office. "The paranoia that's fed a lot of these people has spilled over the edges here. They think there's a vast conspiracy percolating all around them!"

"Yes sir." Frank didn't want to say anything revealing of his own feelings yet.

"From what you've written, you don't see a big conspiracy out there," Zapata wasn't asking. "I'd guess you would argue that the attitude of our forces is more likely to *produce* a coordinated opposition if we don't change course?"

"Yes, sir, the protests we've been seeing are largely spontaneous. Remember, there is a culture around San Francisco and the East Bay that the emergency is deeply offensive to. I don't think there's much coordination at this point. It's a lot of reactive protests as far as I can tell. From interrogations with prisoners, we can see that there are some organizations trying to get going, but it's a long way from a coherent movement."

"You're right, Frank. I wish other officers could see it this way. Unfortunately, between the officer corps we've got, and the rank-and-file Guardsman—are they all from rural California?!?—it won't be easy to stand down. All these *fruitcakes* and *mi-nor-i-ties*," emphasizing the words before he sucked his teeth as he thought about what he wanted to say next. "I must admit, they scare our boys. Our guys aren't even 21, half of 'em, are they?"

"Don't seem like it, sir."

"You don't seem too worried, Frank. What scares you?"

Uh-oh. Was this a trap? Was this a weird loyalty check of his own?

"Death, sir! I've got a ways to go, but I'll admit, I've been thinking about mortality more lately," Frank knew this was a safe answer.

Zapata let out a deep belly laugh. "Haha! Yeah, the grim reaper is coming for all of us—one of these days!" He chuckled for a bit longer, looking hard at Frank. "I want you to focus on your city, Frank. And you should pick your team. I'd like to get the smarter young guys onto the ground in San Francisco. Especially with your oversight. It'll help them see the local population differently. Maybe they'll even make some friends!"

"Sir? What are you proposing, exactly?"

"Next week, I want you to go back to San Francisco and take over the City's Homeland Security operations. You know the city better than anyone here, and you can begin loosening the Emergency regime in real time. This attempt to put a lid on everything will only lead to bigger explosions later. We have to figure out how to make that clear to the rest of these yahoos."

Frank was taken aback. "You mean I can go home?" He was confused. What did Zapata want him to do? He didn't have much experience in managing others. San Francisco was much more complex than it was when he was a nearly retired UCSF beat cop. He knew he was being thrown into the deep end. But maybe he could do some good. Surely he'd be able to block the most egregious kinds of repression that had been doled out around the Bay Area during the past three months. Maybe they could establish a model that other places could learn from? That was probably optimistic, but since the harsh winter crackdown in dozens of cities, it was obvious that the government needed to lower the temperature, especially before the hot summer months.

Or was this a set-up? What if he followed Zapata's directions to "loosen emergency in real time" and it was a way to make him the fall-guy for the next wave of repression? Fuck!

"Sir, I appreciate the trust you want to place in me. I want to make good on it. Can I get some time with you? I want to make sure we're on the same page."

"Of course, Robertson. Of course. I don't want you to go out on a limb," Zapata seemed genuine enough.

Frank went back to his office and spent the day finishing up the analysis of the field reports that piled up from the past couple of days. He was especially interested in a report from San Francisco about agricultural production and the "threat" that urban farmers represented. That was Janet and her pals! The report didn't name any individuals but did detail a dozen farms and gardens where ICE visits encountered hostility and non-cooperation. Man, this whole food thing was crazy! People gotta eat, don't they? Frank went to his computer to look up the regulations on urban agriculture and was puzzled by the Homeland Security policy he found.

1. Urban farms must provide accurate reports on crop production every three months.
2. Urban farms must turn over 50% of their production to Homeland Security collection teams.
3. All citizens are required to purchase as part of their food basket enough products to meet the national standard of 50% corn or soy ingredients.
4. Organic produce will be assessed a 25% surcharge on sales.

Frank shook his head. What the hell were they trying to do? Obviously this was a ham-fisted way to force people to subsidize the government's base in Midwest agribusiness. "Whatever happened to the free market?" he muttered to himself as he turned back to the reports.

His mind drifted to his new job. Could he make a sensible urban agriculture policy? Was there an underground that could cause trouble for the ICE patrols, as field reports claimed? He wasn't resolving any of this in the next day or two but he did want to find out how much room he had to be flexible. He did not relish the idea of trying to control gardens and farms and what people were eating.

***

Sheila left her office in the Federal Building a little early. It was Friday and she was riding BART over to Hayward and see Frank. When he called he had been proud to tell her that he'd been promoted to lieutenant, and that the new Homeland Czar at Camp Hayward, Lt. General Carlos Zapata, was actually a decent guy. She hadn't heard much about him, except that he replaced that asshole General Reynolds who ordered the Dolores Park Massacre. She waved to her pal Herb in the lobby as she went past. "Have a good weekend!" they encouraged each other, trying to be as normal as they could in the face of the dozen armed soldiers who lined the windows.

She was soon on a San Jose-bound BART train and after an uneventful half hour, disembarked at the Hayward station. Frank was waiting for her, looking spit-n-polished in his fancy uniform. She smiled warmly as she approached the gates.

Frank shifted his weight back and forth, holding a bouquet for Sheila. He hadn't seen her in person since he'd been drafted. They talked on the phone a few times, but their connection was slipping. Nevertheless, here she was! And she looked great, wearing a mid-calf skirt and those cute boots she'd worn before. She came towards him and his senses were filled with her delicious smell and her sparkling eyes. He thrust the bouquet towards her but she pushed it aside and glided into his arms for a long overdue hug, followed by a warm kiss.

"Hi honey, it's been a while," she purred.

"Oh Sheila! I've missed you! I hardly knew how much until this moment!" he gasped.

"You're sweet," she took the flowers and deeply inhaled the fresh smells. "Where are you taking me? You have your own house now?" He babbled about being moved from the barracks to his own furnished tract house. She had a small travel bag with her clothes and toiletries for the weekend. She noticed another soldier standing at attention in the distance. "Is he with you?" she asked.

"Oh, um, yeah, he's the driver. They drive me wherever I need to go, it's part of the perks of the job," he grinned sheepishly. He took her by the hand and the soldier fell in directly in front of them and led them to the car, yet another ICE Hummer.

"They have a ridiculous fleet of these," Frank told Sheila quietly as they crawled into the back seat. "Please take us to my place, corporal," he ordered the driver, and fifteen minutes later they were in his living room.

"You want a drink?" he offered.

"Sure, whatcha offering?" Sheila responded, wondering if Frank was drinking a lot again.

"I haven't been keeping any booze in the house since I got here, but I had them send over my favorite white wine and a small bottle of bourbon." He read her mind.

"A glass of white wine sounds great," she decided. "What's the plan for the weekend? I should be heading back on Sunday morning, ok?"

Frank poured the wine and they sat on the couch. "I didn't plan anything. We could hang out here, or if you want, there's a movie house in the mall. There's even a bowling alley down the street that's part of the base now."

"Can we go for a long walk tomorrow? Maybe somewhere on the bayshore?" she suggested. That was what always worked for them, and he immediately agreed.

"The Coyote Hills are supposed to be nice, down near the Dumbarton Bridge. I can get a car from the pool and drive down there. We can even pick up some sandwiches and have a picnic!" Frank felt very happy. His earlier nervousness melted away as Sheila's warmth and ease was a balm to him.

As they sipped the wine, she filled him in on how her job had grown much busier with martial law. "Camp Hayward is going through incredible quantities of *everything!* And those new satellite bases getting set up. I've been in a frenzy of procurement. It's complicated since I only started working on the new Bay Area bases. There are people doing the same job as I am in a half dozen other huge metro areas in the West, and even more back East. We're competing for the same supplies, and putting pressure on the same supply chains. Things we used to get from China aren't available anymore, with the sabre-rattling over the Solomons and the Philippines. So yeah, my job has been a nightmare!" she laughed. "But I'm used to it."

Frank patiently waited until she finished her tale. He was happy to think that they'd have two nights together and all day tomorrow, he felt no rush.

"I have news too," he said. "Zapata is sending me to San Francisco."

"Really? You're coming home?"

"Yes, but it's not what you think. I'm being sent to San Francisco to be the Homeland Security commander there. I'm going to be in charge!" Looking into her face, he hoped she wouldn't be dismayed. She looked at him with a poker face. She looked neither happy nor upset. She was listening. He continued, explaining what he'd been doing with the field reports, how he read them. "The field reports are written by these guys who think there's some vast conspiracy all around them. They don't know the Bay Area and it's obvious most of them are racists and homophobic. A lot of the team leaders in the field, along with the rank-and-file grunts, are from the far north, or down near Bakersfield or Fresno. Honestly, if I had to explain it, I'd say they're practically brainwashed."

"The soldiers in San Francisco have been pretty bad from what I've heard," she explained. "I see them all the time, there's a bunch stationed at our building now. But I haven't had any experience that seemed out of line. Are you supposed to fix things? How?"

"Yeah, that's the problem. I've never managed other guys except the few times I oversaw an investigation, which seems like forever ago! I'm not completely sure I'm not being set up," he confided.

"What do you mean?"

He told her his doubts about the assignment and Zapata's real thinking. "That guy is tricky. He's like a wrestler on TV one minute, and then when I'm alone with him, he sounds like a liberal. Maybe because I'm black he talks different to me. But I don't know if I can trust him. What if I'm being set up?"

The conversation kept going through the dinner. When he brought the small cake to the table, Frank said, "OK, no more talk about work or the

Emergency or any of that. Let's enjoy our dessert, this one and the next one too!" She knew what he meant, and she wanted it too.

CHAPTER 13
TUESDAY, MAY 13, 2025

It was a forgotten Hangar built into the hill by the military long ago. Somehow it had been overlooked in the various plans to tear everything down and remediate the toxic waste. Larry discovered it when he was starting his operations in the neighborhood. During late night explorations of the long-abandoned shipyard Larry and his pals entered nearly every building. The former radiological laboratory building loomed across the access road at the base of the hill, but the old doors in the side of the hill were overgrown by vegetation. Mysterious! They chopped away the bushes and working at the old doors they'd pried them open and found a giant underground hangar. Eventually they found a functioning electric panel. Before long they had lights and power. After early efforts to set up a grow operation there, Larry abandoned the effort, finding it too awkward, what with the occasional private security patrols and the odd access. But he kept the space and since last summer, they'd been thinking about building a new way to get in and out. Who knew if they might need a place to hide things?

Leon got the first box of bioengineered witches butter fungus a month ago from Dat Doan's biohackers. Then word arrived a few days ago that they were looking for a new expanded space. Dat Doan was "the guy" when it came to weird tech needs. He had been hosting the hackerspace for years, and yet he remained out of sight to the authorities. Sometimes it worked to hide in plain view. Larry knew about Doan from Leon before he appeared at Larry's warehouse on Yosemite, gliding up on a big ebike equipped for hauling and rolled it into the lobby.

"You got a place I can park this?" Doan asked the woman at the front desk. She gestured to the rack near the wall, while letting Larry know the guy he was expecting had arrived.

Larry came ambling out of the door into the front area. "You must be Dat?" he extended his big fleshy hand in welcome.

"Yeah, you must be Larry! I've known about you for what seems like for-ever. I'm surprised we never met before. 'Large Larry,'" he smiled, "now I understand." His ruddy, pock-marked complexion framed his large, somewhat crooked yellow teeth with the gap. He removed his motorcycle helmet, letting his stringy black and gray hair fall to his shoulders, and unzipped his leather jacket too. "I forget how far it is to get all the way down here," he admitted.

Larry took him through the door into the big warehouse where he had things growing, top-grade bud and the best organic vegetables. The humidity and strong odors of moist soil and flourishing plants made a powerful perfume.

Sitting in the comfy conference room, Larry offered Dat a drink while they waited for Ally and Clara to arrive. Alison burst in first, anxious to meet the guy who received her research on witches butter fungus (smuggled out of BGM) and brought it to life. Clara was right behind her, also excited to meet the famous hacker.

"I'm Alison Nakahara, call me Ally," she introduced herself, "and this is Clara Frias, my colleague."

"Oh ho! You're the famous—or should I say 'infamous'?—Alison Nakahara! We meet at last!" He shook her hand vigorously. "And Clara, glad to meet you too. I'm Dat, Dat Doan," he had a disarming face when he smiled.

After a few minutes of excited talking, it was as though they'd been working together already for a long time. Ally and Clara took one look at each other and with a glance at Larry, they invited Dat to come through the underground corridor to their secret cellar.

"We have prototypes that have come pretty far," Ally teased. "I'm curious to get your reaction." They walked through the luxurious kitchen and living area and into the dark, dank cellar. Grow lights lined the ceiling above rows of raised beds stretching into the distance. Fans turned slowly in the aisles, mist seemed to reach them from somewhere. Ally turned off the electric lights all at once, and in the distance at the far wall, the glowing luminescence of the biobulb plants provided the only light. Dat's eyes narrowed and he walked briskly towards them.

"What's this?!" and he moved in for a close look.

"We call it the 'bio-bulb'!" said Ally triumphantly.

Dat clucked his tongue quietly, taking in the remarkable scene. "Are you running electricity into them to light them up? Can you turn them on and off?"

Ally and Clara both started to answer, before Ally deferred to Clara, who had done most of the work to get the biobulb to this moment. She explained the state of the project, that Doan was spot-on to home in on the two questions he'd asked. "We're not sending in outside electricity, but when we do, the biobulb can get much brighter. But we're hoping to reach an optimal brightness at the lowest possible level of energy, something that can be transmitted biologically. It's still a ways off. And so far, if we 'harvest' the bulbs, we don't have any way to reconnect them. We're hoping the witches butter can be coaxed eventually into the form of a socket," she explained. "The switching problem is even further down the road. You wanna help?" she grinned.

Doan scratched his neck and tipped his head back to stare at the ceiling. "How are you doing this in this darkness? Have these plants never seen sunlight? I'd be curious to see what happens if we transplant your trials into places where they can experience natural light. I wonder what that will do to them?" He was full of reasonable concerns! And he embraced the idea of further collaboration. Then they showed him the bioboat.

"Fuuuuucck! This is amazing!"

Ally took the lead in explaining the organic kayak-shaped structure they'd managed to grow, how the plant would grow a control nodule in the base that would allow a passenger or 'driver' to stimulate the flaps that would propel it.

"But how would you steer it? And would it live once separated from its mother plant? What happens if it dries up?" Again, full of important questions.

The excitement burbled over and they had to retreat to the kitchen. Over cups of tea they started to sketch out some new plans for research directions.

"But I actually came here for a different reason," Dat suddenly remembered. "I need to move the hacker lab from my offices on Howard Street. It's only a matter of time before they bust in on us. We've had our hands in a few too many shenanigans lately. I came to ask you," looking directly at Larry, "if you might know of any spaces around this part of town where we could set ourselves up?"

The underutilized hangar under the Hunter's Point peninsula that Larry had opened and then almost abandoned was the perfect solution. It quickly became the new hidden location for the hackerspace electronics and biotech experiments. Larry helped Dat rent another warehouse near his Yosemite Street space. It became the official location for Doan Industries where he engaged in import/export activities, mostly electronics from Taiwan and Korea, or shipments of exotic fruits and spices from Indonesia and Brazil. Behind his warehouse on Bancroft Avenue there was space for empty containers where he put a half dozen refrigerated containers to keep his perishable inventory when it arrived. But the facility doubled as place for exotic biological materials that he was also secretly importing from near and far.

As Dat and his pals moved their stuff in to the secret hangar during a few late nights, they realized that the main doors were too obvious. Now that the old shipyard had been opened up to through traffic, they wanted to make sure nobody discovered their space. They built a crazy new James Bond-ish door. To enter you went to a spot below the pot farm where big boulders were positioned. A hatch was built behind them. A ladder led down to a landing two meters below the hatch, and a metal stairway to the ground was attached to the Hangar's side wall.

***

Linda Robertson was puttering around in the kitchen of her mother's house on Marlin. Since Frank was drafted by Homeland Security in February, she had been coming over every day to help her mother, Annie, who was 101 and fading steadily.

The view from the kitchen window looked south across the old naval shipyard and the bay stretching southeastward. The yard extended down the hill into a gulley, full of spreading marijuana plants, tended by her nephew Lamar and his crew. Even before legalization in 2018, Lamar and Leon worked for Large Larry's neighborhood grow operations. When Larry got rich by getting a percentage of the HemptriCity sale to BioGenMo, he'd generously given the bulk of his marijuana operations to Lamar and Leon and they expanded by planting a number of outdoor plots on local hillsides.

Linda put away some dishes and thought about heating some soup for her mother when the door opened and in clattered Lamar. Lamar smiled broadly under his orange Giants cap. He looked a lot like his father, but his white mother's prominent cheekbones and small ears shaped his light brown face. He wore his usual work outfit of jeans and a utility vest, pockets bulging with small tools, a tape measure, bits of string; a roll of duct tape hung from his belt.

"Hey Auntie, how're you doin' today?" Lamar greeted her affectionately. At 78, Linda was pretty old herself, and already outlived Lamar's father Henry, her younger brother by three years, who died in the first months of the pandemic in 2020.

"Do you know what they're doing down there in the shipyard?" Linda asked.

"It looks like Homeland Security. They're building a base down there. At least that's what I heard. There's been a bunch of ICE Hummers rolling in and out of there, but mostly it's construction."

"A base? Like that one in Hayward where Frank is?" Linda shook her head. She didn't watch the news much. Like everyone she was horrified by the Massacre, and this whole National Emergency thing was shocking too. But Frank getting drafted somehow humanized the military side of things. If he was part of the Homeland Security forces, they could hardly be an alien occupation force, could they? Given the unrest around the country, maybe it was for the best, a way to calm things down. She was politically savvy enough to know that the government could not be trusted, but she couldn't imagine any alternative to things going back to like they were before. What other path was there?

Lamar went over and gave her a friendly hug and headed out. He went back through the yard and out the new gate in the lower fence. A narrow path switched back several times and, well below the gardens above, covered by several dense bushes of blue California lilacs, he came to the sloping metal door. Quickly punching in the code, he swung the hatch open, still obscured from view by the bushes. Cool air rushed out at Lamar as he entered the dark stairwell and closed the door behind him. Down the metal stairs he went, a staircase that hugged the wall that opened on to a sprawling warehouse space.

Lamar climbed down into the lower level of the hangar where a half dozen people were working in the lab. A flow hood was set up next to a microscope, and beyond that was a thermocycler, used to prepare samples for genetic sequencing. Not that Lamar knew what the different pieces of equipment were for. He waved to the ones who noticed his entrance, but he went past them and into the main office near the door.

"Lorena! I'm glad you're here. Have you seen Leon today?"

"Oh hey Lamar," she turned from her computer. "Nope, not today. He's coming here in an hour or so. Why don't you wait for him?" She turned back to her screen.

"How's it going? Are you here every day now?" Lamar wanted to chat.

"Me? No, not every day. I work over at Leon's place, too. We're still trying to pressure BGM into paying us, too. That's what I'm working on right now."

"What about ICE? Aren't they coming after you?"

"Well, yes, I'm sure they are. But we can't hide now. We have to be more public, bring more pressure if we can. The key is the people on the inside. We have a lot more support than you'd imagine among the regular workers at BGM."

"I didn't realize..." Lamar trailed off. He was distracted by his buzzing phone, which he stared at.

"Hummers rolled into the Dog Patch. The farmers are calling for support."

Lorena spun around. "Not everyone should rush over there," she urged. "If you don't have papers, or you know they're looking for you, best to steer clear."

The door opened and in walked a woman Lamar didn't recognize. She looked at him and then went over to Lorena. "Are we staying here overnight?"

she asked in a low voice.

"Lamar, this is Cindy. Janet helped get her over here the other day from Oakland. She's underground. Cindy, meet Lamar, he's one of our hosts. And he's Janet's cousin too, so in a way, it's all in the family!" Lorena had been enjoying learning about the overlapping Robertson clan and how vital they were to a lot of what she was involved with now.

Lamar appraised the new woman, standing erectly with her long black hair parted in the middle. She was strikingly beautiful but had a rugged composure and a lithe but muscular physique that hinted at having survived through some difficult circumstances. He felt a formidable presence and gave her a warm smile, "Welcome, Cindy. You can stay here as long as you need to. Let me know if you need anything I can help with, ok?"

Lamar understood the value of his family. After growing up in Pinole and only visiting from time to time as an adolescent, moving to San Francisco a few years ago turned out great. He had a thriving business with his cousin Leon, and the ongoing support of their friend Larry had proven essential more than once. The fact that his grandmother's house was on the hill above them gave him a strong sense of belonging. He was more than happy to be a host and share his new wealth.

"I'm pedaling over to the Dog Patch, see what's happening," he declared. "You guys stay here. When Leon comes, tell him I'm coming back later to catch up with him, ok?"

Lorena had a worried look on her face, but it was not her place to tell Lamar what he should or shouldn't do. "Thanks Lamar, for the hospitality. And be careful! We don't need you to get taken by ICE!"

Cindy folded her arms and watched Lamar as he departed. "You think he'll be OK?"

"Probably. Those guys have nine lives, from what I hear," Lorena shook her head and turned back to her computer. "The Robertsons pop up everywhere these days!"

CHAPTER 14
TUESDAY, MAY 13, 2025

Lamar pedaled north past Heron's Head Park on the bay side. Behind the New Farm the rest of the Dog Patch opened up on Port of San Francisco lands. Lamar left his bike at the New Farm lot and proceeded on foot, noticing an ICE helicopter hovering above the scene.

When the land was made by filling in shallow bay waters back in the 1940s,

San Francisco expected this area to become fully industrialized, but it had never happened. Sporadic use was made of what was officially known as Pier 92 and 94, but now it was a sprawling urban farm. Along Islais Creek almost everything on either side of the water had been moved back from the shore, leaving the adjacent lands to flood as the anticipated rise in tides and sea levels inevitably arrived.

As he drew nearer he saw a half dozen ICE Hummers parked along the access road, usually used by farmers with wheelbarrows and the occasional bicycle. Homeland Security soldiers were moving through the crops, shoving farmers aside with their rifles. Everyone was shouting. Lamar paused at the perimeter of the scene where there were already another twenty people milling about. Some were shouting at the soldiers.

"What the hell are you doing?"

"Are you here to protect the crops?"

"Who do you work for? What are you fighting for?"

A woman grabbed one soldier by the arm as he was stomping into her lettuce. Lamar recognized Bernardina. The soldier slammed his rifle into her and she fell to the ground. Several nearby farmers who had been trying to guide the soldiers between the rows rushed to her aid.

From 3rd Street, down the long dirt road from where they stood, several vehicles suddenly appeared and were speeding towards them. The soldiers turned to see who was arriving. Two pickups and a van skidded to a halt and large men spilled out into the road and were immediately moving towards the soldiers.

"Get the fuck away from the farm, you assholes!" The trucks had logos on the side, "Gold Nugget Plumbing: We Find the Gold in Your S--t!," and most of the guys were wearing blue jumpsuits. A few had bright yellow hard hats.

No one ever put up any resistance and the soldiers were used to intimidating everyone they went after. The squad leader hadn't believed his own eyes and failed to use his radio to call for help. They weren't prepared to grapple with a dozen determined guys brandishing iron pipes and tools. But they had to because the plumbers were on them before they got any orders or knew what to do. Helmets were smashed, men were yelling and screaming. What might have been an almost even fight between burly plumbers and armed soldiers turned into a rout when Lamar and the others at the perimeter rushed into the melee. The ICE troops were overcome in minutes. Their weapons were taken and stacked on the side. Their helmets and paraphernalia were stripped and they were left shirtless, hands tied behind their backs, sitting in the dirt. Everyone knew the helicopter was filming and certainly calling for backup, but they were far from any stations and it gave them the time they needed to make their getaways. But before leaving, one of the plumbers, a tall young man, asked for help in getting the ICE guns and uniforms loaded into one of the Hummers.

"Jay is that you?" Lamar couldn't believe his eyes. The hippie kid who volunteered at Palou Terrace was in the middle of this curious strike team of plumbers, and he wasn't a scrawny hippie anymore. "What the hell?!?"

Jay looked over at Lamar. "Dude! I haven't seen you in a year! How the hell are you? Well, we better figure that out later. Here," he was grabbing up a pile of white ICE helmets, "help me!" After they got it loaded, Jay jumped in the driver's seat and leaned over to Lamar at the other side of the cab. In a low voice, he asked, "you still working the land down there? Can I find you at Leon's?" Lamar gave him a quick nod, and Jay hit the gas and roared away.

Lamar turned to see the ICE soldiers sitting in the dirt. What were they doing now? They couldn't leave them here. Suddenly Janet was at his side. "Hey cuz," she was breathing hard. "You been here all along?"

"I got here in time for the fight. Didn't see much before that. Just that," and he gestured up to the helicopter that still hovered above.

"I got here as fast as I could. I was over at Palou Terrace. I can't believe these assholes rolled up in here and started destroying crops. What is the point?!?" She was exasperated.

Bernardina came up to them, crying, blood on her face still oozing from a gash in her forehead where the soldier whacked her with his rifle butt. She wasn't tall but she was no pushover. Her family immigrated from Oaxaca a decade earlier, but she remembered the smoke-filled streets of the Oaxaca Commune in 2006. She'd been a teenager, suddenly pulled into the brutal street battles between Mexican paramilitary thugs and the organized population who had had enough of the corrupt government. Fighting heavily armed thugs was not new to her, but she had been through enough to know that the authorities were relentless. Finding a way to blunt the coming repression was already at the forefront of her thoughts.

"Janet, we have to do something! They're sending an army over here!" Bernardina turned to the shirtless men sitting in the dirt. "Who's in charge here?" she demanded. The soldiers looked young now that they were disarmed and half naked. The boys couldn't have been even 20 yet. They looked nervously from side to side and then one guy, obviously older, beet red under his hairy paunch and balding head, kicked his foot and said, "Me!"

"What's your name?" Janet asked, stepping ahead of the injured Bernie.

"Captain Miller."

"Captain Miller, what were your orders here?"

"I'm not answering any of your questions. You are going to Camp Hayward... or worse!" he spat defiantly.

Suddenly a stream of shots from an automatic rifle rang out from somewhere distant.

"Look!" a half dozen people simultaneously pointed up at the helicopter, which was smoking and spinning wildly. Clearly it had been hit by the shots. It plunged into the middle of the Islais Creek channel and sank beneath the surface. Moments later, two heads bobbed in the water—apparently the pilot and co-pilot survived.

A bunch of farmers rushed towards the shore. "Get the raft! Get some rope!" and within a few minutes two people rowed out to help the men in the water. They brought them in and soon the helicopter crew joined the rest of the men on the ground, the newcomers soaking wet and covered with blankets by the farmers. One guy had what was probably a broken arm. The other had blood on his face, but otherwise seemed ok, albeit in shock.

Miller's scowl gave way to a look of genuine fear. His squad was terrified. The farmers stood around with rakes and shovels and weren't sure what to do. They didn't want to wait to face any possible consequences but they were loyal to their farm that they didn't want to abandon it to the likely wrath of these humiliated troops.

"Miller, I don't know what you were trying to do here. As you can see, we are a bunch of farmers, trying to grow food to feed people. That's what we were before you arrived, and that's what we'll be when you're long gone," Janet lectured. "You had no business coming here and trampling our work. We both know that they're sending backup now, and after that," she gestured to the creek where the helicopter sank, "whoever comes will want revenge. We are leaving. With luck, we'll disperse and you'll leave us alone," she was trying to sound confident.

Bernardina followed her lead, turning to the assembled farmers milling about in confusion. "We'd better get going. I'm afraid if we stay, we'll be arrested. They'll probably destroy our farm either way. Get moving, you know the drill," she referred to their emergency plans. Most of the farmers lived relatively close by and no one needed to be told to leave more than once. Her instructions broke the spell, and suddenly everyone was moving with great speed and purpose. Sirens were echoing in the far distance, as the bicycles and cars departed. Different safe houses had been set up with basements and attics to house escapees. Backyards had routes through fences that had been worked out in advance for possible evasive action.

Lamar and Janet hurried away and back up to Grannie's place on Marlin, but Lamar knew there was a chance that they might be tracked there. They left their bikes parked at the house and rushed through the backyard to the trail down to the hidden hatchway. Minutes later they were bumping down the long stairway and into the office where Lamar had left Lorena and Cindy hours earlier.

Leon was sitting in the office when they came in. Lorena and Cindy were still there too. They had a TV on with a news flash about a terrorist attack against government forces in San Francisco. They turned from the TV as the door opened and in came Lamar and Janet, disheveled and sweaty. Janet looked at Cindy. "Oh you're here! Things are moving fast, aren't they?"

Cindy nodded.

"Fuck! What's happening? Do you know about this?" Leon blurted at them, pointing to the TV. Janet couldn't help but notice how much he resembled his father Frank in his exasperation.

Lamar put his hands up as he and Janet flopped onto the big couch against the wall. "Hang on, hang on... They raided the Dog Patch. It was ugly, and then, out of nowhere came this gang of ... plumbers! Jay was part of it! They rolled up and attacked the soldiers with iron pipes and wrenches. We helped too!" he was grinning now, but Janet looked stricken. Her eyes were on the TV, and she knew things would get a lot worse now. Lamar continued, "We put their guns and helmets and shit into a Hummer and Jay drove away with it! Then, their damn helicopter had been above us the whole time and suddenly somebody shot it down... I don't know who or where they were, but we heard the shots, sounded like way on the other side of the creek, maybe even up on Potrero Hill, and the next thing we knew it was smoking and falling and splash!"

"This happened at the farm where we got off the boat the other day?" Cindy directed her question to Janet who smuggled her across the bay three days ago.

Janet nodded, and in a subdued voice that contrasted greatly with the triumphant excitement of Lamar, murmured, "the shit is gonna hit the fan now. They're gonna come for revenge. We need to make a plan!"

Leon listened. "I have to figure out who to talk to. We need to spend some money, maybe take care of some people, to get this to blow over without a whole lot of bullshit coming down on us." He assumed the normal graft would buy them some space.

Janet looked at Lamar, "That was Jay with the plumbers? I guess he did get into the union."

"Jay?" Leon remembered him too. "He's a plumber now? I heard something was happening in their union, a bunch of young guys pushing the old-timers aside. You hear about that?"

"Last time I spoke to Jay he asked me if I thought he should get involved in the plumber's union—if they let him! I told him it would be great. We need a radical water politics. Who better than the plumbers, the organized plumbers?"

"He might be in trouble now," Lamar advised. "He took the Hummer with the guns and stuff. You think he knows how to shoot?"

Janet shrugged.

Lorena joined the discussion. "The UPA has a new connection to the Plumbers Union—last meeting we had a rep from them get up and explain how they were going in a new direction."

"The fuckin' plumbers! Man, I never thought I'd see the day..." Leon shook his head.

"Look at that now!" Leon pointed to the computer again. It showed an ICE Hummer in the middle of Mission and 7th Street on fire, a fire truck pulling up to try to douse the flames. But the vehicle was a goner. "You think that was the one Jay took?"

Janet sighed deeply. She was worried sick. These provocative acts could bring some shit down on people and she knew well who would bear the brunt.

CHAPTER 15
WEDNESDAY, MAY 14, 2025

Frank was trying to imagine how he should approach his new job in San Francisco. He knew the city well enough, of course. But he wasn't particularly connected to people in the city government or the local business community, let alone any of the activist groups. He knew who he knew, but as he thought about it, it wasn't an especially extensive or impressive list. Was he supposed to be the main city administrator? He was NOT prepared run a city! Probably he was supposed to work with the Mayor and the existing administrative systems.

He started thumbing through the reports coming in from the San Francisco strike forces again—ominous threats in the community gardens? There were assertions that the teachers, the nurses, electrical workers, plumbers, and bus drivers unions were engaged in subversive organizing. Who was gathering this "intelligence," anyway? Could it be true? He had never known anyone in those occupations to be very active, and certainly not threatening. He knew the unions were a big force in the past, but since the Port moved to Oakland and the ILWU followed the work, the most powerful unions were the service workers and the hotel workers. And the pandemic nearly destroyed the hotel workers union. The service workers were hand in glove with city government. How subversive could they be? Mayor Yee and the Supervisors were against the Emergency, but they knew their place and weren't opposing the federal government beyond the occasional public statement.

He ran his hand over his head and down his neck. He felt stiff already, and his mind drifted back to the sweet time with Sheila, her warm body and eager enjoyment of their time in bed together. He got up to make a cup of coffee and while it was brewing he glanced at his phone.

"What the hell?!" The news was pouring in about a violent clash along San Francisco's Islais Creek. Gardeners attacked a Homeland Security patrol, disarming them and stealing their equipment. And then came the even more shocking news, an ICE helicopter was shot down at the scene! "Fucking hell!" he roared and slammed his phone down on the table. This was unbelievable. He unplugged the coffee maker and rushed to organize his papers. He'd only taken a few steps when his phone rang and Sepulveda was telling him he had to come in immediately. "Already on my way," he answered.

A half hour later he was at the conference table with Zapata, Sepulveda, Cronin, Dorsey, and Richmond. Zapata looked straight at him and said, "OK Robertson. You are UP!"

"Sir? Do you have any more information?" Frank had become adept at bureaucratic side-stepping. He knew he was on the spot, but he would take as long as he could before he would declare anything or make any promises.

"We have footage that was being fed live from the helicopter before it was shot down. Here it is," and he sat down and gestured to the orderly to run the video on the big screen behind him.

The time stamp showed 14:12:23 when the video started. The footage showed five Hummers rolling east on the access road from Illinois and Cargo Way, heading to the Dog Patch farm. Soldiers got out and stood around before forming up into a platoon. The Captain walked back and forth in front of them, apparently addressing them. Then, at 14:25 they began walking through the crops, mostly staying in the rows as farmers walked with them, pointing at different plants. One soldier kicked plants as he walked into a row and a woman put her hands out to stop him. He slammed her in the head with his rifle and she fell to the ground, surrounded by several other farmers. By now it was 14:35;

they had been there less than 30 minutes, and two dozen people arrived at the edge of the crop field. They were pointing and gesturing at the Homeland Security officers, probably yelling at them. The soldiers were gesturing back, pointing their guns, and taking a few steps towards the small crowd. Then at 14:43, three yellow vehicles turned on to the access road and came up behind the Hummers. Two pickups and a van. Out came a dozen people, apparently men, mostly dressed in blue overalls. Some had yellow helmets on. And they were brandishing something in their hands, maybe iron pipes, as they assaulted the Homeland Security forces. A brawl ensued, which was then joined by most of the people who were at the edge of the field. By 15:03 it was over. The security forces were being roughly shoved to the ground, their hands tied behind their backs with their own zipties, their helmets and shirts torn off, their guns stacked in a pile. People were milling about. Three people walked over to the soldiers sitting on the ground and seemed to be talking to them. Captain Miller, the guy at the far right, seemed to be talking back. At 15:16 the helmets and rifles and shirts were being piled into a Hummer and someone drove it away towards 3rd Street. The blue-clad men who arrived in the yellow vehicles returned to their trucks and left at 15:22. The rest of the people on the scene were milling around in clusters, apparently in discussion. At 15:34, the footage suddenly stops.

"That's when the helicopter came under fire and was brought down into the creek. Both pilots survived," Zapata explained. "This looks like organized resistance to me. How did these people show up so fast? Who is facilitating this response to our routine patrols? And who the hell is ready to shoot down a helicopter? It's no accident!" he grimaced, his face wet with perspiration.

Frank noticed the conclusions had been drawn already. The footage showed that the patrol started the fight with a bunch of gardeners! But it was true that the sudden arrival of dozens of others—and especially the guys in the yellow trucks—that looked like organized resistance, no doubt about it.

"Do we know who those guys in blue were?" he asked.

"Ever hear of Gold Nugget Plumbing?" Zapata asked him.

"No sir."

Colonel Cronin chimed in, "We have intelligence on the Plumbers Union. It's been a safely conservative union for decades, but in the last year a bunch of young guys came in and pushed the old guard out. They took over the union and linked up with other groups and unions around the Bay Area. They've got an agenda!"

"What would that be?" Frank was genuinely curious, but his tone showed he found it a bit preposterous.

Cronin shuffled some papers on the table and pulled one up. "They are pushing for a complete overhaul of the city's plumbing, house by house, and the installation of gray water systems everywhere. They want the city water department to finance it. And they want to electrify every part of their own vehicular fleet while simultaneously replacing gas with electricity and passive solar water heating in every building, too. These fuckin' plumbers have declared themselves climate warriors!"

Frank hadn't heard anything about this. The Plumbers Union? Unbelievable!

"Maybe I should arrange a meeting with the head of the Plumbers Union, see what's up," Frank proposed.

Zapata scowled. "We may be well past the point of meetings and consultations. I'm afraid we have to exert some real force after what's happened. Frank, be ready to go to San Francisco first thing in the morning!"

"Yes sir!"

The meeting broke up a half hour later. The other officers around the table were given assignments in other parts of the Bay Area, and were put on high alert for further evidence of organized resistance.

***

The Homeland Security strike force rolled up in two buses, followed by a flatbed truck with a bulldozer on it. The convoy parked on Cargo Way and the troops poured out and were soon marching to the Dog Patch along the access road. Heavily armored, they looked like they walked out of a *Star Wars* movie or something. Arriving at the farm's edge, they systematically trampled across the row crops, and then soldiers with flame throwing gear came up and began to torch everything in their path. It wasn't a very big farm, and after the recent tidal flooding, the land nearest the water had already been cleared. About 15 minutes after their arrival, they'd turned the organic farm into a smoldering ruin. The shacks and equipment were set alight as well.

The bulldozer came groaning up the road and was soon flattening the area, churning through the torched structures and lands. A half hour later it was as flat as a parking lot, a field of mud. Meanwhile, a Homeland Security barge arrived in the channel of Islais Creek and was in the process of pulling up the helicopter wreckage.

Everyone stayed away, except one lone cyclist, Evelyn Palmer, who rode around on nearby Pier 96, watching the salvage operation in the water, and staying well back from the troops who were leveling the farm at the Dog Patch. Evelyn was a longtime member of the farm there and she had to see what happened. She hadn't been there yesterday when the raid took place and learned about what transpired from her partner Tom and several others who were. They were in hiding today, but she had to see for herself.

It happened fast. All their years of work gone in less than an hour. She circled back and forth, looking on in disbelief as the farm disappeared, and then watching the salvage effort. After fifteen minutes there wasn't much else to see, so she pedaled back to the old shipyard. She rolled past the former Radiology Lab and out the old Crisp Avenue gate into the grid of Bayview streets. At Leon's place on Ingalls and Underwood she joined the crew in the office.

"It's gone, all of it!" Leon and Lamar and Janet looked at her and nodded soberly. It was no surprise to any of them.

"What did they do?" asked Janet.

Evelyn explained the how they'd surged over the farm, set everything on fire, and then followed with a complete bulldozing. "I don't know why they even bothered to burn it, since they leveled it anyway," she lamented.

"So much for the plan to slow-grow that farm as a way to lower their expectations for local yields," Janet sighed. "I know you and Tom and the others put a lot of thought into how to make it look like you were doing your best but coming up short. It was a good idea," Janet gave Evelyn's hand an affectionate squeeze. Evelyn let her tears flow, equally for her sadness and her anger.

"We got strange news this morning. My uncle Frank is the new head of Homeland Security in San Francisco!" Lamar announced.

Leon looked at Lamar, resuming the conversation they started before Evelyn's arrival. "Will Linda keep coming over for Grannie? Frank's not moving back in, is he?"

"I don't see how he would. He's a bigshot now, probably surrounded by heavy security all the time. I wonder where he will stay—I guess they'll put him in a facility... Ha! What if they give him a place in the new base on the shipyard? That'll be incredibly weird!" Lamar shook his head.

Janet always had a good connection with Frank and it was hard to imagine him in this new role. He'd never been more than a regular cop for all these years. He had been about to retire! Then the National Emergency and the draft and the massacre. Now this! It was an impossible chain of events. She shook her head, sighing. "I wonder when we'll see him. He has to come visit Grannie doesn't he? Can we be there when he does? Are they turning the house into a Homeland Security bunker? Even temporarily?" she couldn't imagine what might happen.

Lamar and Leon were worried. If Homeland Security spent any real time at Grannie's house, how long before they discovered the hatch and then the hangar? But maybe they weren't that thorough. Maybe they were another lumbering bureaucracy. If they put Frank in charge, they couldn't be that well organized!

***

Frank got an early start and by 8 a.m. he was arriving at the Homeland Security headquarters in Pier 26 under the Bay Bridge. The old pier was converted into a command center in the weeks after the Emergency declaration. They were building a bigger, more permanent base on the old naval shipyard, but it wouldn't be ready for another month. A large number of vehicles and troops were stationed on Treasure Island in the bay, and white ICE ferries ran back and forth almost hourly every day. A new temporary dock was built at the back end of Pier 26, a short distance from the floating fire station that was opened during the pandemic.

Frank drove over in a Hummer but he wasn't alone. Colonel Cronin was with him, and orderlies who were Cronin's staffers.

"Lieutenant Robertson, you have to talk to the press. We already have a team going back to the site to recover the helicopter, and to level that farm."

"Oh? Who gave the orders to do that?" Frank asked.

"Lt. Morgan is staying on to smooth the transition. He's still operationally in charge until there's a formal transfer. Zapata and I think you should work with him for the next week, get a feel for what's happening."

Frank nodded, expressionless. "As you like, sir." He realized that he was on a short leash. It looked like they wanted him to become the new face of Homeland Security in San Francisco, but were they letting him decide anything?

They rolled past a phalanx of media trucks and cameras along the Embarcadero in front of Pier 26 and drove into the secured pier. They were met by a security detail who ushered them in to the conference room, evidently the central operations room for their daily patrols in the city. Lieutenant Morgan was there, standing over several subordinates on computers, his bright red hair and trim mustache contrasting with his incredibly pale white skin. He snapped to attention when they entered and they exchanged salutes and greetings.

"Here, sit here Lt. Robertson," Morgan gave him his big chair. "You guys," he gestured to Cronin and his staff, "you can sit along the table like usual," and he grinned. They knew each other quite well.

Cronin sat down with a groan, his subordinate immediately bringing in a coffee and putting some papers in front of him. "Lt. Morgan, what have you done so far?" not feeling it necessary to explain what he meant, since it was obvious to everyone. There hadn't been any incidents in other parts of the Bay Area, and with the notable exception of the Dolores Park Massacre, this was the most violence in months. Morgan explained the salvage operation and "we have a burn and bulldoze team clearing that damn farm!" But Cronin knew that already, and was going through the motions, maybe for Frank's benefit.

Frank leaned into the moment. "Do you have any more information about those plumbers? Were they really plumbers?"

Morgan walked over to one of the uniformed women on a computer, "Corporal, did you get the records for that plumbing company? What is it, Gold Nugget Plumbing?"

"Yes sir," and she handed him a printout. Morgan flipped through the pages. "There's nothing here. It's a bunch of yelp reviews and a very basic website. Johnson!"

One of the young officers across the room snapped to attention. "Yes sir!"

"Take a strike force and pay a visit to this place. They have an office on Mission Street, it looks like it's in the Excelsior. Get the names of everyone who works for them. Bring in whoever is the boss or owner, and if you encounter any resistance, be ready to make arrests!"

'Yes sir! Right away sir!' And he left.

Frank watched carefully. He had no authority, not yet, and he realized he may never have any. He might be here to front for the rest of these guys. He turned to Cronin, "You said I should talk to the press? What exactly do you want me to say?"

"Lieutenant, we're putting that on hold for now. Morgan, go ahead and send Tracy out there. She's been doing fine up to now, and she knows how to handle the local press. Robertson, have you had any experience with the press?"

"No sir. Also, I haven't managed any organization of this size. I'm a bit surprised to find myself here."

"You're from here, aren't you?" Cronin squinted at him.

"Yes sir."

"That's why you're here now. We need someone who knows the city well and can reassure the people of San Francisco that they are not being occupied by an outside force."

"I see. Does that mean that you will be running things, sir?

Cronin didn't answer. He turned to his subordinate and spoke in a quiet voice that Frank could not overhear. After a minute or two, he turned back to his papers, and glanced at his phone.

"That's all Robertson. Why don't you get yourself situated? Morgan, where shall we put Robertson?"

Lt. Morgan waved Frank over and led him out of the conference room and down the hall. A small office was standing open. "Here, Lieutenant, is your new office. Welcome aboard!"

It was a tiny room with no windows, a desk and a bookshelf with some law books on the bottom shelf. There was an old-fashioned black telephone on the desk and what looked like a decades-old personal computer, large, tan, and clunky.

"We have to get you a new computer!"

"Sir? Do you have a place for me to live during my tour of duty here?"

"Oh, yes, of course. We have taken over the Bayside Village at Harrison and Beale. Check with the front desk. They will have a room for you. It's a five-minute walk from here. But remember, there are always press waiting outside. Don't wander out there on your own. Either walk with a group or take the shuttle."

Frank watched Morgan leave and realized that he had nothing to do! Now what?

CHAPTER 16
FRIDAY, MAY 16, 2025

Janet and Vero were at Leon's, peering into the vat of witches butter.

"That looks just like bread dough!" exclaimed Vero. She suddenly reached in and began kneading it.

Janet hesitated. "What if it's dangerous?"

There was a noticeable buzz running up Vero's arms, a very pleasant sensation that grew stronger. She grinned at Janet and said, "No, you need to get your hands in here!"

From then on, they kneaded it absent-mindedly, chatting over (and occasionally to) it and thrusting their hands in and out. It started gray, and then it lightened into a cream color.

"Have you talked to Jay lately?" Janet asked Vero.

"No, not since our getaway, those few minutes in that UPS truck. Has he been by here at all? I heard he was part of those plumbers at the Dog Patch?" Vero wanted Janet to confirm what she'd heard from Lamar. She had been rotating back and forth between Larry's warehouse, Leon's place, and the hangar, keeping out of public view as much as possible, so she depended on everyone to bring her news.

Dat Doan appeared behind them.

"Heeeyyy look! It changed color!" he exclaimed with a big toothy grin. He reached down and squeezed a handful of the creamy smooth fungus, which felt like a warm silly putty. "Your batch is different. Ours is still gray and," he paused while he noticed the tingling sensation going up his arm, "it doesn't send out this energy either."

He'd opened his import/export business in a warehouse a few blocks away and had a range of oddities in his refrigerated containers parked behind it. He'd done the original tinkering with the witches butter when the research leaked from BioGenMo a year earlier. He'd passed on a batch to Leon, and here it was.

"I was at Larry's a few days ago," Dat explained, "and Alison Nakahara introduced me to her new experiments." He looked at Vero and Janet, hoping he wouldn't have to explain further.

Vero offered, "I've been staying there in that bunkbed since I escaped."

"We know about the biobulb and the bioboat," Janet confirmed. "What did Ally say to you?"

"She is anxious to see if she can 'harvest' bulbs and run them as lights in a biogrid. She's counting on me—er, us—to get the witches butter to work together with the biobulb. There're already trials in the hangar," Doan explained.

"Oh yeah?" Janet marveled at how fast things were moving. But with the emergency and the ICE raids, she was preoccupied with the fate of the outdoor farms and gardens. "Listen, we should try the witches butter at outdoor locations. I'd love to take some to Alemany... whaddya think?"

Doan agreed enthusiastically. "Do it!" He pulled a chunk loose from the cream-colored putty in the container. He wrapped it around his wrist.

Janet reached down to do the same and Vero followed suit. They watched as the new wristbands smoothed out and adapted to the shape of their wrists.

"It tingles!" Vero smiled. Janet was already grinning as was Dat.

"I'd like to know what happens when you establish a small colony at the Alemany Farm," Dat said to Janet. "Can you get that going in the next day or two? And let me know what happens?"

Janet agreed. She took a box and filled it up with witches butter, which was easy to scoop with her hands. In fact, it almost seemed to unfold into her reach as she extended her hands towards the fungus. "It's amazing that this is a fungus. It's totally changed my idea of what fungi are!"

Vero packed another batch to take back to the secret cellar at Larry's. "We might as well start seeing how it does right next to the biobulbs."

"Vero!" Dat looked at her with a penetrating gaze. "We started that idea in our experiment at the hangar. Are you a hacker?" He started laughing. Dat Doan already assumed that everyone was a hacker, if they'd let themselves try. "But our witches butter is not nearly as lively as this one. Maybe you'll see results before we do."

Leon came out of his office. "What are you guys cooking up?"

They explained how the witches butter changed and encouraged him to touch it. "Can you feel the buzz?" Janet nudged him, smiling.

"That's amazing! And it's not gray anymore. When did it change color?" Leon hadn't been paying close attention for a while. With the raid at the Dog Patch he was busy trying to figure out who he could reach out to, how to avoid raids all over the neighborhood.

"Hey, I talked to the Mayor. He said I have to talk to the Homeland Security people. They're the ones deciding where the raids are gonna be. Turns out, my father is here now. Frank is one of the top guys!"

"Frank?" Dat Doan was confused. "Who is Frank?"

Leon explained about his father, how he'd been a regular beat cop at UCSF Mission Bay and then got drafted into the Homeland Security force when they declared martial law. "And I heard he's back in San Francisco now, and they promoted him to Lieutenant. I don't know if they're putting him in charge but he's up there."

Janet shook her head. "He's my uncle too, and I can't believe he's a Homeland Security commander! He was a beat cop! And he was about to retire!" She looked worried. Vero came over and gave her a squeeze. Janet sighed. Vero knew her better than anyone.

Leon wrapped witches butter around his wrist too, following the suggestion of the rest. "Huh, that feels good!" Preoccupied, he took it off and put it back in the vat. "I have to get in front of this. I'm heading downtown."

"You goin' to the ICE place at Pier 26?" Vero asked, and Leon nodded. "I don't think you should show up down there. They might grab you!" She remembered too well how suddenly her circumstances changed when she casually walked across the 24th street BART Plaza a few months earlier.

"I'll be careful. I'm not gonna walk in there. I'll hang around and see if I can find Frank, or someone I know, see what I can find out."

"Leon, wait. Get a meeting with someone, Frank or whoever, before you go anywhere near there," Janet was adamant. "You'll look weak showing up and hanging around. What good can come of it? You'll either get arrested... or at best... nothing will happen!"

"Don't worry about me!" Leon said loudly. "I know what I'm doin'." And he left. Within ten minutes Janet went to Alemany Farm, Dat left, and Vero decided to go back to Larry's.

***

Linda was at the kitchen sink when Lamar entered, accompanied by a woman she hadn't met before.

"Hey auntie, this is my friend Cindy Lowe, Cindy this is Linda Robertson," Lamar announced performatively. He smiled and gave his aunt a quick hug. "Cindy's a vet!" he announced.

"Oh yeah? What brings you here? We don't even have a dog!" Linda looked at this striking Asian woman and wondered if maybe her nephew had a romantic interest. She was very beautiful, no question about that.

"Lamar, I got a call from Frank yesterday. He's planning to stop by today. In fact, he may be here within the hour from what he said yesterday. I don't expect him to keep the schedule, but anyway, that's what he said."

"How's Grannie today?" Lamar asked, taking in the news about Frank but didn't want to visibly react to it.

"She's fading, Lamar. I don't know if anyone is meant to live a hundred years!" she shook her head sadly.

In the living room Lamar asked, "Cindy, does anyone know what you look like? Are you on wanted posters or anything like that?"

"I got out of Phoenix right after the Emergency was declared. They never picked me up. I had a different name there, too."

Lamar put up his hand. "OK, ok," and after a short pause, "when she said Frank is coming, that means my uncle who is part of the Homeland Security Emergency authority. You're pretty sure nobody's gonna recognize you?"

Cindy nodded, and then smiled. "I'm sure it's fine."

He gave her a quick history of his and Leon's business, the generosity of Large Larry, the intersecting stories of the League of Urban Farmers that Janet was part of, and the weird biotech coming out of BGM and local biohacker labs. "Oh yeah, also, there's this whole Urban Peasants Alliance who are former BGM contractors who were fired or dropped and are trying to force BGM to pay them. We've hired a few of them at Leon's and some others are working at Dat Doan's."

"It sounds like there's a lot going on!" Cindy replied. "And that underground connection to the East Bay too, that got Janet to come over and bring me back. I was impressed."

"There's a lot more going on than I know about," Lamar admitted. Linda entered the room, and obviously heard their conversation.

"Are you involved too?" Cindy asked her point blank.

"Honey, I'm 78 years old. I do what I can," and she sat back into a big armchair. "But people here aren't used to military occupation—say what you like, but it's much worse than the regular police!"

As if on cue, car doors slammed outside. Lamar went to the window. "He's here," he declared, and then turned to Linda "It's Frank. And he's not alone."

Frank knocked and entered. He'd been living here for years and it was weird to even knock, but he felt different and he was sure they would find it jarring to have him walk in trailed by two orderlies. He gave his sister a big hug, and he nodded at his nephew and his friend.

"How's Moms?" he asked Linda, and she gave him the update. He rushed upstairs to see her. His two orderlies retired to the waiting Hummer outside.

"Mom! Mom!" he leaned over his sleeping mother, her tiny wrinkled face sleeping placidly in the big white bed. The sun filled the bedroom and birds were singing in nearby trees, a cool breeze crept in the cracked window. She opened her eyes, which were glazed at first, but she soon found focus and cracked a smile when she recognized her baby, her youngest child. "Frank, Frank, you came! And look at you," she struggled to sit up and get a better view.

"Let me help you Mom," and he put his hands under her shoulders and hoisted her up on her pillow so she was sitting up.

"You get a new uniform?" she croaked.

"I was drafted," he reminded her, "I'm part of the Homeland Security force now."

"What? You feel a draft? Close the window!" she scolded. Her hearing was worse than ever.

"No Mom, I was DRAFTED!" he yelled. "I'm an officer now!"

She recoiled a bit at his yelling. Everything was confusing these days. She knew she had hearing problems but when people yelled she thought they were angry at her. It wasn't *her* fault that she couldn't hear them!

"I just got back to San Francisco, Mom!" he continued in an elevated voice. "I wanted to see you as soon as I could. I'm sorry I've been gone for so long," he said.

She saw he was trying, but it was hard to figure out what he was saying. He took her hand in his, and she felt the warmth through his dry skin. "You should use some moisturizer!" she advised. He withdrew his hand in embarrassment.

"Mom, I have to go. They want me to make new plans for San Francisco, to lead Homeland Security here now," he was unsure of himself. "I don't know what I'm doing," he confessed softly, knowing no one would hear him in his mother's bedroom.

She gave him her best smile and closed her eyes, finding it a bit overwhelming, and retreated into the semi-dream state she spent most of her waking time in now. Her mind drifted back to the train in 1943, before she'd met Aaron, long before the kids. 'The first thing I laid eyes on here, that 3rd Street Bridge!' She remembered crowding into a flat in a broken-down Victorian in the Fillmore with a half dozen other recent arrivals, riding streetcars across the city to work at the Hunters Point shipyards. 'Aaron was a nice guy... never thought I'd marry 'im!' she drifted in and out, murmuring to herself. When he asked her to marry him to improve their chances for the new war-time housing that was opening near the shipyards, she agreed.

As it turned out, their marriage worked well, and they came to enjoy their new domestic life together in one of the barracks-style apartments on the slopes of Bayview Hill. Getting to work was a whole lot easier from there, a short shuttle bus ride instead of the hour-long slog across town from the Fillmore.

After the war, she was laid off from the shipyards, but Aaron kept his job working on marine engines. Soon enough, their first child, Linda, was born. Six more followed, the last one being Frank in 1961. By then, they moved to a two-story home on Revere Street a few blocks east of Third Street. Under the sloping roof, the big family hosted countless neighborhood parties, barbecues, christenings, baby showers, graduation parties, and even wedding receptions.

Frank saw his mother finally go to sleep, and slowly got up and went downstairs. He found his sister in the living room by herself now.

"Where'd Lamar go?"

"He took off. He likes that woman, Cindy, I think."

Frank slumped into the couch. "I have a few minutes before those guys whisk me back to Pier 26. They're building a new complex down in the shipyards... you notice?"

"Yes, of course. There's been construction and noise for weeks now," Linda looked at her kid brother sympathetically. "Frank, what do they have you doin' now?"

He looked at his big sister. Funny how the old relationships still prevailed even though outside of this house everything seemed completely changed. He sat up a little straighter, "I'm a Lieutenant now. The guy in charge of the Bay Area, General Zapata, promoted me and wants me to take charge in San Francisco... or so he said. But he sent this Col. Cronin with me, and he's running things. He's been making the decisions and it doesn't look like he's leaving any time soon. The guy I was supposed to take over from, Lt. Morgan, he's still here too. I'm not sure what's going on..." he trailed off, giving away his uncertainty.

Linda didn't have any trouble seeing what was in front of her eyes. "This guy Cronin's white? And Morgan?" Frank nodded. "Looks like they want a black face to put out front—"

"No! Zapata told me he wanted me because I knew the city!" Frank protested.

"I don't think you're seein' the obvious," his sister continued. "They gonna tell you that, but meanwhile, who's in charge? And anyway, Frank, not to insult you, but you never ran anything before, let alone a whole city. Why they gonna put you in charge now? You think you ready for that?"

His confidence, already wobbly, collapsed under her questioning. He knew she was right. He'd been tapped as a front man, not the real power.

"Whatcha gonna do? You gon' let them use you, or do you think there's somethin' you can do to make it better? Cuz it's been ugly around here. You heard 'bout that helicopter and the riot at the Dog Patch?"

He nodded morosely. What a mess! What was he gonna do? What *could* he do?

The door opened and his aide waved to him, indicating it was time to go. He rose from the couch and went over to Linda and gave her a hug. She squeezed him hard and said "You can help Frank. You can do some good. There's a lot to lose here... maybe you can stop it!"

He pulled away. He wasn't sure what she meant, but he couldn't stay to discuss it now. "Take care of Mom, and say hey to Rhonda... You seen Aaron and Greg lately? Tell 'em hi for me too."

She watched him leave and sat down, her anger rising as she realized her brother was being set up. She picked up the phone and called Aaron, figuring he might have some ideas about how they could help Frank.

CHAPTER 17
THURSDAY, MAY 29, 2025

Jay Hartman went over to sit with his friends, Ernesto Aguirre and Jordan Lindsay, outside the Plumbers Union meeting. They were the insurgent plumbers that helped elect a new slate of officers a few months earlier, while Jay was detained at Camp Hayward after the Dolores Park Massacre. Finally the plumbers were going beyond their immediate wages and working conditions and addressing the pressing matter of how the city managed its water supplies. Why had they left it to city bureaucrats and Water Department lifers?

"Hey man," they greeted each other with their secret handshake, mostly waggling fingers and backhanded slaps. "What's the news?" Jay asked as he plopped into the seat. "Hey, where's the air conditioning?" More than a week over 100° was wearing everyone down, holiday or not.

"Looks like an 'internal investigation' was launched by the executive board," Jordan explained, his drab gray baseball hat slumped over his thick bushy eyebrows. "They seem to think there might have been plumbers involved in that riot over at the Dog Patch after all. And believe it or not, our HVAC is busted! Our own union hall!" Ernesto shook his head in disgust, amazed that the plumbers union expertise in heating and cooling couldn't keep their own system running properly.

Jay shook his head and smiled wryly. Then he raised his eyebrows, "I thought the investigation stopped when they realized the so-called plumbing company on those trucks didn't exist?"

They made an imposing entrance, the five of them, as dozens of heads turned to watch them re-enter. At the podium, the union local president was speaking. Fred Perry was a tall, broad-shouldered man with an expansive gut. He'd become the new head of the Plumbers Union because he'd been around a long time but was friendly and open to the youth movement that recently emerged. That he was black didn't hurt either, which helped dispel the lingering idea that the Plumbers were still the most racist union in San Francisco. Hell, they hadn't even allowed Chinese into the union until the late 1960s!

"Brothers!" Perry boomed over the mic, "... and Sisters," he remembered to add, turning to the cluster of new young women across the room. "I know many of you have questions about the investigation, and others want to follow up on our last meeting's debate on water politics. There'll be time for everyone!" he boomed again, "And I'm sorry about the AC," he repeated. "We hope to have it fixed this week."

"We don't think anyone here was involved in the Dog Patch affair, but the authorities have asked us to do our own internal investigation. We've appointed a committee and we expect everyone to cooperate who is asked to appear before it. They will be asking for testimony starting next week. Any questions?"

One of the women on the other side of the room went up to the mic for members. "What kind of investigation is this? Are you cooperating with the Homeland Security authorities? Do people get to have a lawyer if they are called?" and she turned to sit down as whoops and whistles rang out around the room.

"This is a private, internal investigation. We are conducting this independently, and we will make our own summary of what we learn and share that with the relevant authorities. They will not be part of our investigation, and we will not give them the evidence we collect, whatever it may show." The question about lawyers went unanswered.

Ernesto went up to the mic. "What is the point of this? Why do any investigation? Why waste our time and the union's money doing work for the state? Especially this illegitimate state?!?"

This electrified a large portion of the audience. Loud cheering, clapping, and stomping as most people leapt from their seats. "Fuck Homeland Security!" "Don't cooperate!" "Fuck Zapata!" and few scattered "Fuck Perry" shouts snuck in too.

Jay looked around. He hadn't expected to see this level of animosity to the union leadership or their plans to cooperate with Homeland Security. He rushed up to the mic.

"Brothers and sisters!" he turned to the audience. "Our union should not do Homeland Security's dirty work. I move that we cancel this investigation entirely!"

Most of the people in the room were on their feet, applauding.

"I second the motion," came a call from the middle of the crowd, "and I third it!"

Fred Perry rushed to the podium. He held his hands up, trying to calm the clamoring crowd. "Brothers and Sisters!" he boomed again. The noise subsided and people sat down. He waited a bit longer, and with everyone's attention, he announced, "The executive board has already voted to hold the investigation. It is not subject to ratification by the membership. Your participation is voluntary," he understood that his authority was being challenged, so he delicately threaded the needle. "But the ability of this union to function requires a good working relationship with the legal authority of our society, and," some boos started to rumble in the audience, "for now that is Homeland Security. I don't like it any more than anyone else in here. But we will hold this investigation and we will cooperate on our own terms with the Emergency authorities. Our independence requires it."

"Independence! That's bullshit!" yelled someone from the middle of the audience.

"Independence? How is it independent to collaborate with a corrupt regime?" chimed in another.

Perry ignored the comments. "We are moving on now. The floor is open to resume our discussion of water politics in San Francisco."

Jay's heart was beating fast as he sat sweating in his seat. The leadership had little support for their bogus investigation. He spoke softly to Ernesto, "We should organize a boycott of the investigation."

Ernesto nodded, but said, "You gonna get up there and push the building-by-building project?"

Jay was glad for the nudge, and he walked back to the mic.

Perry saw him, relieved that the subject was changing, and pointed at Jay, "The brother is recognized. Please proceed!"

"Brothers and sisters, fellow unionists," he began, "we have an urgent responsibility which is also a unique opportunity." He theatrically pulled out a handkerchief and wiped his brow. "This heat is the new normal. We are still in the longest drought in 1,200 years in California. The Central Valley is drying up. Agricultural production is plunging." He looked around the crowd. Most people seemed to be with him. A lot of faces were turned his way, and the room was quiet. "We have to radically change how we use the water that runs through San Francisco!" he suddenly thundered. Applause burst out across the room. "We should be designing new gray water toilet systems to replace every single toilet in this city. We'll have more work than we can ever do. We should insist the City invest in a five-year crash program to repair and replace the entire plumbing of the City!" Everyone was cheering and clapping. "And we should collaborate with the League of Urban Farmers to guarantee sufficient water supplies to grow half our vegetables and fruit right here in San Francisco!" More cheering and clapping.

He went on a bit longer, but this fight was already won, at least in this union hall. "We have our friends who are trying to expand food production in our gardens and on our streets. We union plumbers should support them!" This was risky. It was clear he was alluding to the recent Dog Patch confrontation, and the story that it was a group of plumbers who waded in and assaulted the Homeland Security forces. But his popularity grew in the union during the rank-and-file campaign and countless discussions about the plumbing opportunities that the drought was forcing onto the agenda. The bigger drama was at City Hall, and with Emergency rule, it wasn't clear what federal or state money could be counted on.

Jay finally sat down. Another guy was up at the mic on the other side of the hall. "Brothers and sisters, I support the long-term goals that the brother laid out. But we have some immediate problems to address. I don't know if our union is able to make water policy. I don't even think that is our job. We should appoint a committee, and let that committee write up our recommendations, get the membership to vote on it, and then send that on to the San Francisco Department of Water. We should insist on a seat on the Water Department Board of Directors. But I want to know how we keep our jobs during the Emergency? Especially if the authorities think we are fighting them?" A smattering of approving claps and conversation rippled across the room.

Jimbo went up to the near mic. "With all due respect to the previous brother," he talked in his slow drawl. He was originally from Texas. "Our skills and our unity is our best guarantee of steady work and being treated right. If we start asking for special treatment or claim that we need something that everyone else in this country needs as much or more than we do, we only hurt ourselves and all workers." A chorus of vibrant shouts and animated applause burst out across the room.

Fred Perry stood up to the main podium again, holding up his hands. "We ain't gonna see things the same way, but I'm glad everyone understands that we're in this together. I want to take up this brother's suggestion," he pointed to the guy who spoke before Jimbo. "If we can pull together a committee to develop our proposals for a city-wide replumbing campaign we can take the fight to City Hall, the Water Department, and even the state legislature. Who supports the idea of setting up our own water policy committee?" Most of the people present clapped politely.

Jay wasn't excited about yet another committee. It was a delaying tactic. But it was obvious that the idea was little more than a general yearning, and far from a specific proposal that could be fought for. And why leave it to Water Department or City Hall bureaucrats to devise the plan? He joined the applause.

"Brother Hartman," Perry looked straight at Jay, "I nominate you to lead our new water policy committee!" Enthusiastic applause erupted. And Jay waved his consent to the union leader and the crowd. He'd figure out the details later. Was Perry making the appointments, or would he get to choose who he wanted to be on the committee? To be determined. Perry was wrapping up the meeting now. It was goddam hot in here and everyone wanted to go home.

Twenty minutes later Jay was walking up Market Street in the eerily warm evening, past the Octavia Boulevard freeway exit. Ernesto and Jordan were with him. They'd been there at the Dog Patch, but they felt confident they could remain hidden in plain view. Being on the water policy committee could be a useful cover, and anyway, it wasn't even a cover! It could be a great way to get this party started... the Replumbing Party!

A half hour later Jay and Jordan got home to the 3-bedroom flat on Collingwood in the Castro they shared with three other guys. Jay was straight and at first he felt a little odd living in a queer household with four gay men. But that disappeared after a few weeks of making himself at home in the large closet that was his bedroom. Everyone was busy with their lives, and though Jordan and he were deep into the plumbers' union politics, the rest of the guys had other priorities. One was a bartender, rarely awake in the mornings. One was a schoolteacher always gone by 7:30 am. The fifth worked downtown at a brokerage. They had little in common but sometimes they enjoyed a movie together on a weekend evening. Each of them had their own romantic and social lives, so it was a bit like living in a dorm, which suited Jay well.

Jordan stopped Jay at the front door on the street. "I can't believe you were so aggressive in the meeting! Don't you think you're being too obvious? I mean, calling for an alliance with LUF—why not say we were at the Dog Patch?!?" He waited til now to let out his anger at Jay.

Jay and Jordan had become close friends over the past year, since Jordan helped get him in to the union and then they banded together with some others to vote in new leadership. They were both 24 years old and excited to find themselves in the middle of history, but the tension of the situation was taking its toll too.

Jay was taken aback by Jordan's anger. "Whoa, take it easy, man! I didn't do anything wrong," but he knew he was quick to attack the investigation publicly. It probably didn't help that he vocally supported the radical water agenda, especially the food part. Not after the Dog Patch. He'd only escaped Camp Hayward weeks before they'd decided to confront the ICE raid. He boiled over with rage whenever he remembered the massacre and his detention—as far as Jay was concerned he was fully engaged in a Civil War. Fighting ICE at the Dog Patch was doing what he'd sworn to do. That they'd been successful was surprising in the moment, for sure. Afterwards he took the weapons and gear. Everyone thought he'd shot down the helicopter, but he didn't know who did it. He heard the shots while speeding down Third Street, but he never looked back. Leaving the vehicle ablaze across from the federal building was his little "fuck you" to the government. It would not make up for the slaughter or the thousands languishing in detention, but a nice loud salvo in the war *the government had started!*

"Let's go inside and talk. We don't know who can hear us out here," Jay suddenly felt exposed. Jordan nodded his agreement and they were soon sitting on his bed, speaking in low but intense tones.

"I normally would've loved you taking the lead like that," Jordan said. "But maybe we should be laying low?"

Jay nodded. "You might be right. But—you know this—it's war! We have a lot of support at the union—"

"Yes, but it is basically martial law, and we don't want to overstep. Neither of us knows what the right "pace" is, right? We don't want to move too slowly, and we don't want to get too far out in front," Jordan took his hair and wrapped it up into a ponytail while he spoke. His emerald stud earring suddenly gleamed in the bedroom's dim light. He sighed, looking at Jay. "Shit man, you were in that fuckin' camp! We have to stay out, we have to maintain our ability to move, to act. That means, sometimes, being a bit more cautious in public. Do you agree?"

Jay nodded, a bit depressed now. He wanted everything to GO. Waiting, being patient, even being strategic, were cop-outs at worst, or obstacles at best. He wanted to blast through them. The Dog Patch response proved that direct action gets the goods, especially if you could bring real muscle to bear. "I hear you man, I do. But if we wait too much, we'll lose the initiative. The enthusiasm we heard in that union hall—how long do you think that'll last if we don't do anything?"

Jordan nodded. "I know, I know. I feel that too. But this is always the dilemma. How fast can we go? How much radical patience is appropriate? When should we throw caution to the wind? Surely not at every moment! But not never either!"

Jay could feel Jordan was on his side, and that helped a lot. They weren't fighting, merely confronting the situation honestly. They might not respond the same to every moment, but they were basically together, trying to find the way forward. He suddenly felt exhausted. Getting up from Jordan's bed, he opened his arms for a hug, which Jordan rose and gave him. That was how most of their contentious discussions ended. One or the other asking for a goodnight hug to wrap it up. He went to his room and was soon fast asleep.

CHAPTER 18
MONDAY, JUNE 2, 2025

Vero glanced up at the blue sky as she stepped out of Larry's warehouse into the blast furnace heat. Nothing in the sky—maybe because it was over 105°! It was the second week of this heat. Even though everyone knew it was climate chaos, she still found herself muttering to herself "What the hell is going on?" She pushed a bike into the street and pedaled the three blocks over to Dat Doan's warehouse on Bancroft and Keith, soaking her clothes with sweat. This weird humidity made it much worse!

She went through the front door labeled "Doan Industries" and exclaimed loudly, "I can't believe this heat wave!" The place wasn't air-conditioned, and it was sweltering. The skylights were open but there wasn't much breeze and the air was damn hot! She saw Dat through the window at a computer in one of the labs. He turned around to greet her after she tapped on the window.

"I'm glad you're here. We've been running experiments with the 'butter' and you should check this out," he gestured to the printouts on the table next to him. "We put some witches butter around these potted trees. The trees grew new branches and leaves within two days! And then we took one and added Intelligel® and you have to see it to believe it!" He got up and indicated she should follow. They went to another part of the building and into a hot-house nursery built on the back wall. There were five small trees in large pots and each of them had fresh green growth. But one was taller and sent new growth surging towards its immediate neighbors, already intertwining with the branches of the others.

"Here, touch it," Doan encouraged Vero. She put her hand on the trunk of the largest tree and her wrist band of witches butter immediately tingled sharply, sending what felt like signals up her arm and surging to the base of her neck and even filling her chest with warmth. She had to make an effort to keep her hand on the tree because the sensation was almost too much.

"What is going on?" she grinned with the pleasurable sensations but her widened eyes hinted at the fear that wasn't far behind. "Something is happening, Dat, what do you think it is?"

"I'm not sure. What are you feeling?"

"It feels warm and tingly. It triggered my wrist band. Did it do that to you too?"

"Yeah, when I touch any tree that has witches butter around its base, it starts communicating or signaling to the stuff we wrapped around our wrists. We think it might be decipherable."

"You mean it's a language?"

"Well... maybe. We don't know. But there are definitely some electrical signals or pulses moving between different living things, from fungi to tree to human. I don't know if we can find meaning here. It may be an autonomic reaction of some sort... a cascade of electrons moving between differently charged areas."

"It *feels* like something more deliberate than that!" Vero declared, not sure why she felt so strongly.

"We need to do a lot more experimenting. Have you heard anything from Janet or Ally?"

"Ally was puttering around this morning. She didn't say anything to me. We put that batch in with one of the biobulb plants a week ago. There must be something to see by now!" Vero was excited.

"I have Edwin helping me with this. We're both pretty sure we're on the cusp of something big. But we don't know what... yet!" Dat's eyes danced as he turned to look directly at Vero. "Janet's batch at Alemany may be key. There's something about being outdoors and in the sun," he continued.

"Yeah, but *this* sun?" Vero waved her arm towards the outdoors. "This is a killing sun. Is this the new normal?"

Dat rubbed his chin, "yeah, yeah, it might be." He wiped his brow, sweating in the heat like everyone. "I'm taking our combo Intelligel/butter over to Janet at Alemany. You think she's there now?"

"I don't know. She rushes back and forth a lot. If she's not at Alemany, she'll probably be at Palou Terrace. Dat, do you think we can grow enough food to make a difference?"

He peered at Vero through his stringy hair, slowly pushing it away from his eyes and behind his ear. "Honestly? No. I'm not sure what to do—we should grow as much as we can. But between the crashing harvests, the stupid government taxes and mandates, and our tiny farms, food shortages seem inevitable. The garden-in-every-yard approach gives us the best chance to avoid real hunger. More fruit trees, more potatoes and onions and garlic... the problem will be protein. Government mandated tofu is not enough," he laughed. "Who'da ever thought the Republicans would be pushing tofu?!"

Vero looked strangely at Dat. "Has anyone tried the witches' butter? Do you think it's edible?"

Dat tipped his head quizzically. "Damn. I hadn't thought of that. I doubt if it's very nutritious, but who knows? Maybe it tastes great!" He took a small piece, roughly meatball-sized, and held it up. "Shall we give it a try? I'd say we should cook it, don't you? We should run some tests. See if there's any nutrition in there, and then see what happens when we cook it."

Vero looked at the creamy smooth putty-ish witches butter. Before Dat could do anything she snatched it from his hand and popped it in her mouth, her eyes suddenly very wide. "Mmmpfmpmff" she chewed, and then swallowed. "I need a glass of water!" and rushed to the nearby sink. After a drink, she said, "y'know it wasn't bad. Kind of gooey, but flavor-wise, bland, inoffensive. It stuck to my teeth until I added water."

Dat shook his head. "You really shouldn't have done that!" And he scurried away to talk to Edwin about this new turn of events.

Vero drank another glass of water. The witches butter left a vaguely chalky feeling in her mouth, not pleasant. She decided to go back to Larry's, to talk to Ally and cool off in the cellar, which suddenly looked much better as a place to be after an hour in the heat!

***

Janet took her batch of witches butter to the Alemany Farm a week earlier to test it as a fertilizer. She split it into three parts, one large, and two equal but smaller sections. One she left in a plastic bin under an olive tree. Another she poured onto the ground under a pear tree on the slope. And the largest part she put on the ground close to the eucalyptus trees that separated the farm from St. Mary's Park up the hill. Her regular crows lived in those trees. Would they react to the witches butter?

The fungi adapted to each of its locations. Under the pear tree it surged around the trunk and sunk into the roots too. The tree had a lot of new growth, fresh green leaves reaching out from all over. The bin under the olive tree showed the least change when Janet peered into it. She reached in and gave it a squeeze and hummed in a low voice, and immediately felt the steady tingling coming from it. Her wrist band reacted strongly to being reconnected to the mass of fungi, and it started squeezing and relaxing in time with her breathing.

"Hey Bernie," she called to Bernardina, who had been showing up at Alemany since the Dog Patch got bulldozed. "Check this out," and she waved her over to put her hands into the fungi. "I put some by the pear tree and it's like a super fertilizer or something!"

"What is this?" Bernie asked, "I saw it and didn't know what it was." She wiped the sweat pouring from her forehead.

Janet explained briefly the odd path this witches butter fungi traversed since it was smuggled out of BGM and brought to Dat Doan's biohacker lab. "The hackers figured out how to change it into this malleable form. It was gray originally, but since we started this massaging and talking to it, our batch changed to this bright cream color, and," she nudged Bernie with her elbow, "can you feel the tingling?"

"Oh weeeird!" she squirmed. "Yeah, it's alive alright!"

"Look at this," and Janet put her arm out, showing Bernie the fungus wrist band that was visibly throbbing, expanding and contracting.

"Whoa! What IS that?"

"It's the same stuff. Several of us made wrist bands out of it the other day and I kept it on. It seems to be reacting to being back in contact with this big vat."

Bernie pulled back and stared at it. "This seems weird. It's like an alien or something!"

"Let's go see what's happening with the biggest batch I put over there," pointing to the slope by the path. They walked over together and looked at the ground where witches butter spread across the soil. It sank well into the dirt, merging with the soil and plants under the eucalyptus trees. They nudged outcroppings of fungus with their toes. Nothing much to notice. They were a few steps on their way back when several crows circled over them and landed on the fungus-covered slope.

The largest tilted its head and opened its beak. A funny sound came out, not the typical 'caw' but something like a scraping sound, two pieces of rusty metal sliding over each other. Janet and Bernie stared at the crows, mesmerized. The crow kept vocalizing, and then they distinctly heard, "too hot... water."

Janet and Bernie looked at each other, eyebrows raised in wonder. "Did you hear that?!?" Janet said. Janet turned to the crows, "Did you ask for water?" She was used to addressing them in plain English, which she'd been doing for years, but not being answered! At least not with audible words!

The crow nodded his head, screeching out "turstee."

"Thirsty? OK, I'll get some water," and she ran to get a bucket and bring it back full of water. The crows sprang to the edge of the bucket when she put it down in the shade of the trees and drank and splashed water on each other.

"How can you talk?" Janet asked tentatively, still not sure she was hearing that.

"Tawk. No hear!" said another crow in a less screechy voice.

"But how can we understand you now? I never heard any words before," Janet leaned forward intently into the conversation. Bernie stood by her, confused.

"Are you hearing words? I only hear weird sounds."

The crow hopped from the bucket to the slope soaked in witches butter. "Tis," the crow pecked at the ground, and pulled up some fungus and tossed it up and caught it, and then swallowed it. "Tis tawk."

Janet stared at the crow.

As if on cue, Dat Doan rolled through the gate on his e-trike. Bernie nudged Janet, "Hey, there's that hacker dude, look!"

Janet waved him over. She didn't want to leave this unbelievable situation. The crows continued to peck at the fungus and look quizzically at her.

Bernie recently touched the witches butter for the first time so whatever new awareness or ability it conferred hadn't fully developed for her yet. She wasn't sure what Janet meant when she was talking to the crows—she said she could understand them but all Bernie could hear was an odd screeching sound.

Dat Doan came up to them, holding a large burlap sack. "I brought a new batch," Dat announced but Janet hushed him.

"The crows have been eating small bits of it and I swear they're talking!" Janet said to Dat urgently

Dat squatted a few yards from the crows and waited. "Hey there, I'm Dat."

"Dat, dat, dat," said one of the crows in a gutteral squawl. It hopped back and forth on the slope. After nipping another bit of fungus and tossing it up and catching it, it swallowed and then hopped a few steps toward Dat. "Help?"

Dat almost fell over. "You need help?" he asked.

"No, no, no, Dat, dat, dat. You!" the crow audibly cawed. "Help you, help you, help you!"

"Um, er, uh, …. ok. Yes, help me!" He looked aside at Janet and raised his open palms in a gesture of 'what the hell?' Turning back to the crows he asked, "can you talk with the trees?"

"Yes, yes, yes!" two crows excitedly bobbed up and down.

"Can you talk to other plants?" Dat continued.

"Yes, yes, yes!" they kept bobbing.

It was a puzzle. Did they understand the question? Were they really answering? It seemed so. But how to learn more? The crows' vocabulary was evidently extremely limited. It was almost like having a computer program that could only answer in yes or no, true or false binaries, although a bit more complex already than that.

Janet felt her sweaty shirt clinging to her as she squatted next to Dat in the heat. "What do the plants say?" she asked the crows.

"Turstee! Turstee!" they answered.

She smiled. "Yeah, we all are! It is too hot!"

"Too hot! Too hot!" one crow cawed.

"Are you hearing words?!?" Bernardina implored the others.

Janet stood up and turned to her. "Yes, aren't you?"

Bernie shook her head morosely. "They sound like they always do. Caw caw."

Janet nudged Dat, who was mesmerized with the crows. In a low voice she said, "Dat, I think the witches butter has connected us to the crows." And as she said it, the wrist band throbbed with greater intensity. So did Dat's, who stood up abruptly holding his wrist out.

"What is happening?" he uttered, suddenly sounding worried.

"It's trying to communicate, or it's a means of communication, or it's a universal translator or..." Janet shook her head. It was overwhelming.

Dat opened his burlap sack. "I have another batch here—we gave it some Intelligel®." He pulled down the sides of the bag to reveal the bin of witches butter. "Holy shit! Look!" and he put his hands into it. It was no longer a light cream color, it was canary yellow.

Janet reached over and took out enough of the yellow butter to wrap it around her other wrist. "Do it!" she urged Dat and Bernie. "We don't know what's happening, but I want to know! We have to experiment on ourselves!"

The other two followed suit. The crows watched them intently from a few yards away. Janet tossed a fist-sized piece over to them, and they began pecking at it. After a bite one of the crows took off into the trees, screeching all the way "Come here! Come here! Come here!" Minutes later a bevy of crows descended on the canary yellow ball of witches butter and began pecking at it. Janet pulled out another ball and tossed it over to them, and the dozen birds divided themselves between the two objects of desire.

Endorphins surged from her wrists, tingling up her arms and into her diaphragm. "I can't believe the sensation!" she gasped. Looking at the others, she could see they were feeling it to.

"This is better than anything I've tried in years!" Dat exclaimed.

Bernardina chimed in again, "What IS this?!? It feels SO good!" she grinned wildly.

A sudden realization hit Janet and Dat at the same time. "What if this is dangerous?" she whispered to him. He nodded and pulled the wrist bands off his arms. The witches butter knit itself solidly together and wasn't easy to separate after penetrating the skin below. "Ouch!" he cried. "You guys! Take it off, NOW!" His skin was torn but not seriously.

Both Janet and Bernie clawed at their wrists, and worked the fungus bands off, putting them back into the bin.

They looked at each other. "What do you feel now?" Dat asked them.

"That was amazing. It felt great," Bernie answered.

"I'm still buzzing, tingling. I felt connected to ... everything! And we could understand the crows! How could that be?" Janet couldn't stop smiling.

"This is the beginning," Dat said seriously, "of something, not sure what, but it feels like we had a breakthrough." He was in his element. Nothing made him happier than rogue science and free experiments.

CHAPTER 19
THURSDAY, JULY 3, 2025

Lt. General Zapata paced back and forth in his conference room at the Hayward Executive Airport, aka, Camp Hayward. Commander Rinert and

Colonel Sepulveda were at the table. They'd sent their orderlies out of the room.

"Things are definitely getting worse!" Rinert declared. "Demonstrations all over the Bay Area. The breakout and disappearance of 47 detainees. And the Dog Patch. I thought we were turning the corner after we replaced Reynolds and you came in," he looked at Zapata. "We agree that Reynolds' old school military approach was out-dated and counterproductive. But," and he began tapping his pencil on the pile of papers in front of him, scowling, his face growing redder, "do you think we've been too soft?"

Col. Sepulveda hadn't said anything yet. Zapata and Rinert went back and forth a few times about how they could best consolidate their Emergency regime. Things were out of control! Sepulveda served previously in Colombia and El Salvador and Somalia. For the bulk of his military career he did the dirtiest of dirty work for the United States in its "own backyard," and in far-flung outposts of empire. He grimaced at his colleagues, both superior officers, and then in his usual emotionless delivery said, "Gentlemen, it may be time for Plan B."

Zapata wiped his bald head with one hand, coming away with a wet hand. "Damn this heat!" And he slammed his other fist into the table. "And fuck these insurgents! We have to act decisively, NOW!"

Zapata went to the window and continued in his highly dramatic tone, "I *hate* to go to Plan B, especially in a place like the Bay Area. Colonel, have you wargamed this? What happens if it only inflames the opposition?"

"Sir," Sepulveda rose from his seat. "There have to be consequences," a point he left hanging in the air.

Rinert, still sitting, pushed his chair back and threw his hands up. "We can't have another Dolores Park. What are you talking about?!?"

Sepulveda looked down at him disdainfully. "With all due respect, *sir*, I've served in many places and I can tell you, Plan B *always works!*"

Zapata realized that Commander Rinert was being condescended to by his junior officer, albeit one that had a lot more experience in a lot more theaters of conflict. Rinert was a National Guard general, not a "real" one. He was running a car dealership in Fresno before the call-up. Zapata waded in, "I asked you if you've wargamed this, Colonel Sepulveda? Because if you think it *'always works'* I'd like to see the computer projections." Rinert stayed in his seat, feeling that they were way beyond his pay grade. 'Plan B? Computer projections? Wargaming?' None of this was part of his annual training. His role as National Guard General was to show up to annual maneuvers arranged by career officers, approve routine matters, and head out to a banquet or two. His management of Camp Hayward had already been seriously tarnished by the mass escape. He held his tongue.

Col. Sepulveda stood at the table above his computer. "We can't run simulations since we don't know how far we will let the plan go."

"We are not talking about arrests are we?" Zapata wanted Sepulveda to be as clear as possible.

"No sir. Symbolic targets. People who will send a message," Sepulveda was all business without saying anything too clearly. He didn't even flinch.

Zapata on the other hand was noticeably uncomfortable. He knew this would be on him. Col. Sepulveda was a lifer who floated in and out of the dark corners of the imperial war machine, doing the dirty work as needed. They were never accountable, and had no conscience or remorse. Zapata had no sympathy for the insurgents who were making his Emergency administration look weak and ineffective. He needed to grab the initiative, put them on their heels, make it clear that they *would* have a price to pay. "OK," he turned around and looked at Sepulveda. "Plan B, but only a demo version. No more than a dozen. And I don't want to know who you pick!" The sweat was pouring from his head, his shirt was soaked.

Sepulveda, by contrast, looked cool as a cucumber. He clicked his heels and saluted Zapata. "Yes sir, I'm on it!" and he spun around and left the room. He almost had a bounce in his step as he departed.

Rinert and Zapata looked at each other, each holding his thoughts to himself. Zapata finally said, "I hope we don't regret this!" Rinert rose from his seat and was about to leave. "Sir, you didn't ask me. I hope you made the right call," and he shook his head, not able to control his dismay. He was a very long way from being the local car dealer and main advertiser who threw out the first pitch at the Fresno minor league baseball opener last year. Somewhere in the back of his mind, he he knew what was coming, but he preferred to imagine it was all for show.

MONDAY, JULY 7

The three muscular men sat quietly in their gray van, ray-ban sunglasses and mustaches making up their only uniform. They were "Special Ops," brought home to assist the new administration. Different teams were deployed to each major urban area where the Emergency was declared. They served directly under an executive member on the staff of the local Director General of Homeland Security (more commonly referred to as the Czar). The driver was part of a hit team in Colombia for 25 years, occasionally running missions in Venezuela, Ecuador, and Peru. The other two were a snatch team in Afghanistan, Iraq, and Somalia. They were silent, apparently narrowly focused on doing the job at hand. No sign of doubt emerged, in fact, there was hardly a peep from any of them.

The windows were tinted, but they sat inconspicuously in the employee parking lot at the UPS facility not far from the Oakland airport. They had a list of six names, and they only needed two of them for this mission. They knew which cars the individuals drove and had two in sight, a gray Chevy and a blue Nissan sedan. It was shift change, and dozens of UPS workers clad in their tell-tale brown uniforms came streaming into the parking lot. They watched as one lanky white guy climbed into the Chevy, matching the description on their list. They watched another guy on the list get into the blue Nissan. They weren't gonna be able to take 'em both, given how many people were in the parking lot. They followed the gray Chevy, who led them through East Oakland and uphill to a residential neighborhood overlooking Mills College. The streets wound around and followed the contours of the land, and they stayed a few car lengths behind. The Chevy followed the road around a tight uphill turn, vanishing from sight for a minute. As they cleared the curve the car was no longer in front of them.

"There he is!" the guy in the passenger seat called, pointing to a driveway on the right. The driver pulled into the driveway, an abrupt right turn. Before the van even stopped, the two snatchers were out of their doors and rushing the Chevy. The UPS driver opened his door and started to step out when they reached him, ripped him out by his arm while dropping a black hood over his head. He cried out, but they clubbed him and he slumped into their arms. A minute later they threw him in the back of the van and were driving off. The Chevy stood in the UPS driver's driveway, its door left open, keys on the seat of the car where he'd dropped them as he was grabbed.

FRIDAY, JULY 11

"Fuck! What are we gonna do with this story?" Julius rushed into the basement where his wife Anna, Aaron Robertson, and Donald Nevilleton were working on the latest issue of their community newsletter, *Opaque Times*. It grew far beyond their original plans, and became a 12-page, stapled handout. Since they started it after the massacre, it went beyond their original one-page "keep in touch" local news effort and was one of the only uncensored sources of information going. And it was in huge demand! The last issue, published on June 21, was 3,000 copies. The boys Cristiano and Tomas were still the main door-to-door distributors. But everyone was worried about their exposure. Meanwhile, other parts of the city had their own networks. Donald, the philosophy grad student, decided running boxes of newsletters around town was a bit more important than his latest paper on post-structural theory.

"What is it?" Donald responded immediately. Julius thrust the printout at him.

"The UPA got a cryptic message about watching their heads. Then a pigeon arrived from the East Bay, and this is the story that was wrapped around its ankle!" Julius elaborated. "Seven people murdered in the past week, all known to the movement. Two of the UPS drivers who helped the Camp Hayward detainees escape are among them."

Donald scanned the sheet of paper. "Did someone retype this? This didn't fit on a homing pigeon..."

"Yes, there's a network of pigeon fanciers who are working this offline communications system. It's very old-school," Julius explained.

Aaron read the page. "We have to let people know," he looked a bit wan.

"Are you OK, Aaron?" Anna went to him. The heat wave finally broke a few days earlier. Whatever was wrong with Aaron wasn't the heat at least.

"Um, I feel a bit woozy. I remember being in Guatemala in the 1980s and this was the shit the military government was doing. Suddenly people you knew and counted on were being grabbed and killed, and no knew who was doing it, at least at first. Eventually it became known that there were death squads operating all over Central America... worse, it was paid for by the United States! Hell, most of those killers were trained in Georgia at the School of the Americas... They changed the name later, but it never stopped! We always said the war would come home eventually. Could this be it?"

"Aaron, why don't you sit down? Let me get you a glass of water," Anna was very fond of Aaron, who at 71 was like everyone's favorite gay uncle in Kite Kastle. "Is Greg home? Maybe you should go lay down in your room," she continued fussing over him.

Donald looked at Julius, "We can't exactly have a front-page headline saying 'Death Squads in Oakland' can we?"

Julius shook his head. "We started out to be a place that would help people stay connected, to find ways to act in solidarity with each other. We *do* have to publish this. But maybe not in a sensational way. That would freak everyone out, and won't help. Things are bad enough already. People are scared, and it feels less safe every day to go about our normal lives."

"What do you think if we take these four paragraphs from the piece that came in, and put it in a thick black box somewhere inside, like page 5 or 7 or something?" Donald wanted to find a way to warn people without triggering hysteria.

Julius nodded, looking at Anna tending to Aaron. He wanted her opinion before they decided, but she was preoccupied. "Anna?" She turned to him, eyebrows raised as if to say 'what?' "Can you take a look at this and help us decide if we should publish something about it, and if so, how?"

She frowned, "Help me get Aaron up to his room. Then we can figure that out."

Aaron protested, "I'm ok. That water helped! I can get myself upstairs, don't worry!" he smiled as he rose from the couch. He seemed steady enough on his feet as they watched him disappear.

"I was listening. Let me look at the piece that came in," Anna reached for the document. She began shaking her head. "Shit," she uttered in a low voice. "It keeps getting worse!"

"Whaddya think? Publish it?" Julius put his arm over her shoulders.

They watched how fast their little publishing operation exploded in the ten weeks since it started. "We could, but are we ready for what might follow?"

"What do you mean?" Donald pressed her.

"If this is happening, do you think we are hidden well enough? Don't you think we're already a target?" she suggested.

"There are a lot of people who know who and where we are and what we're doing, even if most people who get the *OT* don't have any idea," Julius concurred.

"It's always the issue, isn't it? How much do we push this, how much do we lay low and try to stay hidden?" Anna went on. This wasn't a new conversation, but it was becoming ever more urgent to decide which way they would go. Or, if they couldn't decide, to prepare for the worst. "Maybe we should figure out how to make ourselves redundant? Who else could host the production like we do? Could we set up a rotation among three or four places? What about Cristiano's parents? Didn't they offer to let us use their basement on Alabama?"

"OK, but it doesn't answer the immediate problem. I'm all for setting up other production sites, with others taking on editorial work too. But what about this news right now?" Julius felt they were on the spot, bound to publish by obligation to inform, but the sensible thing would be to hold it back until they'd set up more resilience for the ongoing project. "Shit!" he cursed, gored by the dilemma, adrenaline surging through him at the thought of their vulnerability.

THURSDAY, JULY 17

Vero sat at the kitchen table in the secret cellar. She'd gotten used to living here. The time in Camp Hayward gave her a powerful incentive to stay hidden, especially in the relative comfort of this luxurious underground apartment. And now the witches butter! What is it? What was happening? Dat came back from Alemany Farm a month ago with a story about Janet talking to crows—but this time they were talking back! Even he talked with the birds! All other research projects abruptly halted to focus on the fungus and its properties. Clara and Maria were running tests on how the fungus interacted with other plants. Even Ally turned her attention from the biobulb and bioboat to the witches butter.

Vero decided to work on recipes. She'd gotten a degree in environmental science, but what she liked to do was cook! She made batches of pancakes. She turned it into pasta. She even baked bread with it. Following Janet's lead and the weeks they spent massaging it and singing over it, she spoke frankly to the vat when she pulled a piece to cook with. "Let's see what happens when we add you to our food." As soon as she took a quantity to use for food, it grew back in a very short time, usually the same day.

"Dat, this stuff is amazing. Taste this!" and she shoved a plate of pasta in front of him as he came in to confer with Ally and Clara and Maria. They sat down to the feast that Vero whipped up: witches butter pasta with asparagus and spinach, and biscuits that also had witches butter baked in.

"Vero, you've gone crazy!" they teased her. "Oh wow, this is *delicious!*" Dat smacked his lips and reached for an extra biscuit. They decided against wearing the fungus against the skin. He wondered what happened when you ingested it. "We should be a little cautious," and he reiterated his concerns about possibly dangerous properties. They could see that the witches butter adapted to whatever life form it was attached to. It triggered a stream of endorphins in humans who touched it. "It does the same thing with plants and other critters. I bet when the crows were gobbling bites of it they were getting nourished but also a bit high!" he proposed.

"How do you feel now?" Vero asked them all.

"First of all, this tastes great!" Maria exclaimed. "Now that you mention it, I do feel a little buzz. Like having a glass of wine, no?"

Clara nodded in agreement. "Every example we looked at shows a surge of growth stimulated by contact with the fungus."

Ally finished chewing her mouthful and chimed in, "has anyone checked the difference between the living fungus and the cooked version? I assume it's no longer alive when it's cooked, right?"

Dat sat back and crossed his arms. "Why don't we take some samples from this pasta and these biscuits and check them under a microscope?"

Ally and Clara were happy to and grabbed a plateful to examine more carefully. Vero started removing plates from the table when she noticed the latest issue of *Opaque Times* spilling from one of Dat's bags. "Oh, you brought the new one?!" she said excitedly.

"Take as many as you want. They were delivered this morning."

Vero grabbed copies to share among the regulars in the secret cellar and opened one. She came upon the black box on page 5: "Death Squads? Here?" was the title. She scanned the report of the dead UPS drivers and the other members of the movement in the East Bay who were mysteriously murdered in the past few days. "FUCK!"

"What is it Vero?" Maria asked.

"They killed the UPS drivers!" and she sat down, shocked at the news. "Those UPS guys who drove the getaway vans—according to this, two of them were murdered." The article did not report the grisly remains of the bodies, obviously tortured before having been killed.

Dat rushed over to read it himself. His family came from Vietnam when he was a small child, but he'd heard stories of hit squads that raided their village in the far south of Vietnam before the fall of Saigon. His family eventually managed to escape on a rickety wooden boat. After almost two years in refugee camps where they were taken after being rescued from their unseaworthy vessel, they emigrated to the U.S. and ended up in an apartment building in the Tenderloin. Rumors of assassinations stalked the Vietnamese community even in the U.S. The old anti-communist politicians and military men made it clear that there could be no support for the new regime back home. They were mostly dead now, and relations with Vietnam were normal even if the country was still run by an aging politburo of an anachronistic communist party. At least the war and violence finally ended, decades ago now. But this news was deeply disturbing.

"If this is the government, it's gonna get a lot worse before it gets better," he advised.

"Who else would it be?" Vero slumped in her chair.

Maria piped up, "The government is hardly monolithic—even this one must have hardliners and ... others?"

Dat, who knew a good deal about how the U.S. ran its empire since the 1970s, suggested "We need more information. This sounds like Special Ops— the people who are officially in charge usually don't know what's happening in the dark. Whether or not there are factions among the Homeland Security upper ranks may not be the issue. It could be a compartmentalized operation run by one guy—and he may not be that near the top."

"How do you know?" Maria asked.

"I studied the wars, read the memoirs—hell I even read most of the novels—written by ex-soldiers of the US empire. There are a lot of detailed accounts of how the dirty wars were run in Vietnam during Operation Phoenix, in Central America in the 1980s, the Drug War in South America in the 1990s and 2000s, the counterinsurgencies in Iraq and Afghanistan since 2001, and most recently the chaotic interventions in Africa, especially Somalia and Sudan. If this is a Special Ops dirty war here, this is what it would look like."

"How can we find out?" Vero looked at him with new respect. He seemed to know *everything*!

Dat shook his head. "We need to get more detailed information on the murders. And if possible, we need someone inside the general staff who might be sympathetic to the social movements being targeted by the killers. Such a person might not exist, but if they do, we should try to reach them."

"What about Frank? Frank Robertson, Leon's dad?" Vero suggested.

"Do we have contact with him?" Dat asked.

"I think so. We should ask Janet. He's her uncle too," Vero explained. "He was sent back to San Francisco from Camp Hayward recently."

CHAPTER 20
WEDNESDAY, JULY 23, 2025

Lamar and Cindy stepped out of the tiny MUNI autonomous vehicle (the Board of Supervisors surprised everyone by municipalizing the "robotaxis" and banning private ones) after the crosstown trip from Grannie's place in Hunter's Point to Kite Kastle at the edge of Kite Hill. Lamar wanted to speak to his Uncle Aaron about how the family should approach his brother Frank.

Lamar's uncle Aaron was up and about after having suffered a tiny heart attack on July 11. He'd spent about ten days mostly in bed. He didn't feel that bad, so he kept trying to get up and help, but Greg wouldn't have it.

"You stay there!" he scolded his husband. "Here, drink this," and he'd put a bowl of chicken soup in front of Aaron at least a dozen different times. They both defaulted to Grannie's chicken soup as the cure-all for whatever ailed either of them.

"How're they doin' with the *OT*?" Aaron would ask almost every day. Anna and Julius realized that the heart attack, small as it was, coincided with the arrival of the news about the death squads in Oakland. They decided it was better if Aaron took a break from the editorial work. No one could say the news had *caused* his heart attack, but why push it? They could handle it without him for a few weeks, and if Aaron was in trouble, they could manage without him altogether too.

"Oh, it's fine, honey... You helped set it up, and it's running like a well-oiled machine!" Greg would tease him. They passed the time playing cards, watching Giants games, and reading together. Mottled sun streamed into their shared bedroom through the surrounding eucalyptus trees, which provided a steady soundtrack to their lofty perch too as the wind would rustle through the majestic stand. After the heat wave broke in early June, the fog made its welcome return, and every day it came peeking at the top of Twin Peaks before eventually rolling over and engulfing their neighborhood in the free air conditioning of the marine layer.

Voices erupted at the front door, warm greetings and introductions, but impossible to tell who arrived. Greg got up and went to look down into the common room to see who the new arrivals were. "It's Lamar! And a friend..." he reported over his shoulder. "But don't get up!"

"I feel a lot better! I'd rather see Lamar downstairs than in our room," Aaron creakily rose from the bed. "Am I ever stiff! I need a massage!" Greg gave him a withering glare, having spent countless hours rubbing his husband during the two weeks of convalescence.

"OK, then, be that way!" he said impetuously. Still, he helped Aaron get his bathrobe on, and hovered near while Aaron began the slow trek down the stairs.

"Hey Lamar!" he waved from the stairway.

"Uncle Aaron!" Lamar smiled broadly. "You're up and moving!"

"I ain't dead yet!" he laughed back.

Soon they were parked in the big corner sofa. "Uncle, Greg, this is Cindy Lowe. She arrived a month ago from LA and has been staying with us for a while now," Lamar explained.

"Welcome Cindy!" Aaron greeted her with his usual effusiveness. His gray temples widened with his big smile, his warm eyes irresistibly charming.

"What a place you have!" she waved her arm to take it all in. "It's a gorgeous house in an amazing location!" telling them what they already knew. But it was always nice to have it acknowledged. Donald Nevilleton walked across the back of the room with his baby burping on his shoulder. Julius was puttering around through the kitchen door. It was very cozy.

"Tell me about Kite Kastle!" Cindy insisted.

"Oh sure! We got this place years ago. It had been owned by a childless couple who lived here for half a century. When they died they left the house to the San Francisco Community Land Trust. The Land Trust opened up applications, seeking a group ready to live together in this big house. It has seven bedrooms and 4 bathrooms, so it can hold a lot of people quite comfortably. We ended up combining the remnants of the old Convent Cooperative with the longtime SRO tenants who lost their place at the former Hotel Leslie on Mission Street. Not everyone stayed after the first few months, but mostly it's worked out pretty well... wouldn't you say, Anna?"

Anna rolled her green eyes. "Don't get me started! Let's say that forging a new co-op out of a bunch of SRO tenants and the remnants of an old hippie commune had more than a few bumps in the road. We just filled another two vacancies.

Juna, who had filled one of them, came in the door. There were away as often as not, but they were a lot more at home here than they'd been at the start. When they were home, they spent a lot of time out on the hill, watching birds and enjoying the big sky always available there. Greg called them over, "Hey Juna, come and meet Aaron's nephew Lamar and his friend Cindy."

Juna was automatically shy, but Greg was their best friend in the house. They fought their instinctual desire to retreat and came over to say hello, plopping onto the big chair facing the sofa. "Nice to meet you."

Cindy was struck by the flecks of gold that glittered around Juna's deep brown eyes. "Hi Juna," she extended her hand and felt his dry palm in hers, warm and tentative.

Juna turned to Lamar. "Are you another Robertson? You don't look like the ones I've met."

Lamar nodded, "Yeah, my mom is white."

"I know your cousin Janet," Juna announced. He explained how Janet brought him to Leon's and Larry's, but he didn't mention the experiments in the secret cellar. "One of Larry's assistants, Maria, took me down to San Bruno Mountain. Have you been there?"

Lamar shook his head, "I grew up in the suburbs, Pinole to be exact. All I know about San Bruno Mountain is that it's on the way to the airport!"

Julius, eavesdropping, suddenly ran into the room. "San Bruno Mountain is *AMAZING!* Did you know that the top third of the mountain was supposed to be bulldozed and dumped into the bay back in the early 1960s? Did you know that that same top third of the mountain is the largest intact example of the local ecology that once covered all of San Francisco to the Golden

Gate?" He bubbled with enthusiasm.

Aaron put up his palms, "C'mon Julius, give us a break!" He'd obviously heard it more than once.

Julius frowned and returned to the kitchen, rebuffed.

"Thanks Julius! I found it interesting!" Cindy called after him. Lamar looked sideways at her, surprised she was ready to wade in to the fraught dynamics of the Kite Kastle collective.

"I almost started working for your cousin Leon," Juna confided. "But I decided to find something closer to home."

"Oh? What did you find?" Lamar asked, and continued, "Cindy needs to find some work, at least in the near term."

"I got a job at the SPCA down on 16th Street."

Cindy had to suppress her grin. Lamar whistled, "dang... Cindy is a vet! You think they're hiring?"

"Hard to say. The Emergency and all. I walked in at a good moment. But there's no harm in asking. Cindy, I can introduce you if you want?" She readily agreed.

Lamar turned to Aaron while Cindy and Juna made their plans.

"You talked to Frank since he's been back?" Lamar queried.

"Nope. I heard from Linda he visited Moms, but he hasn't called me," Aaron held Lamar's gaze.

"Y'know Leon has been goin' a bit crazy tryin' to figure out how to buy off the cops, or ICE, or *someone* who can protect us." Aaron nodded. Lamar continued, "Janet called me. She and Vero think maybe Frank can help us. Not to bribe anyone, but to warn us—you hear about those murders in the East Bay?"

"Oh yes," Greg jumped in, knowing that the rest of the *Opaque Times* team was convinced it was that news that triggered Aaron's heart attack. "It came through the *OT*."

Aaron looked out the window moodily. He didn't like the theory that he'd had a heart attack because of the news, but no one could prove anything one way or another, and the story was sticking. He abruptly turned to Lamar "What would you ask Frank if you could?"

"I'd like to have a real conversation first, see where's he at. Then, if he's like he usually was, I'd see if he could find a way to tip us if the shit's comin' our way."

Aaron sat back, reflective. He stroked his chin. "Frank is hard to read sometimes. He's usually a family-first guy, but he's also been a cop for a loooong time. I never had much influence with him, honestly. We ok, just not too close."

"I wouldn't want him to come looking for you, especially up here!" Lamar acknowledged. "But we're trying to figure out how to—or who to—approach him. Who do you think would be best? Leon? Linda?"

"Nah, him and Leon never been close. Linda is the big sister. He'll be defensive, especially after those interventions years ago. Linda was in the middle of that. What about Amelia?" Aaron suggested, referring to his kid sister, a lifelong public-school teacher whose husband recently retired from teaching at San Francisco State. "Amelia and Frank were the closest. She was at those interventions too, but I remember she was the softest of soft cops for that. They even took him in for a few weeks once. I don't know how much they've stayed close in the last few years, but it used to be strong. For that matter, you could ask Janet. He's always had a soft spot for her, maybe because her mom is Amelia. But I know they get along better than most of us!"

"Alright then. Thanks Unc! And you too Greg," Lamar rose up from the couch. Cindy tugged at his arm, "Let's check out the hill before we go back."

"Sure, actually, I was gonna propose we walk back... slowly," Lamar grinned at her. Minutes later they emerged onto the open top of Kite Hill.

"Now that's a view!" Cindy exclaimed. Lamar put his arm around her waist and she leaned into him. They began the romantic phase of their connection weeks earlier. She'd been staying in the Hangar most of the time, occasionally bouncing over to the secret cellar to hang out with Vero. But the Hangar's easy access to the slopes above, and the comfy private suite that the boys built *just in case* had been her home for weeks. Lamar hadn't pushed anything, but he came around nearly every day, often bringing meals and news. As they spent more and more time together, one thing led to another, and eventually... after one of the yummy Thai meals he often brought, they were lounging around talking about the news.

The West Coast seemed to be less under control than ever—from all accounts there were significant underground networks everywhere. Constant low-level sabotage, regular public demonstrations, noncooperation and defiance continued to plague efforts to restore normal life. Cindy and Lamar always talked about this, so this time, after running through the latest reports and realizing they were saying the same things they'd said many times already, Cindy took Lamar's hand.

He'd been hoping that something would happen with Cindy, that was clear enough. But since she was dependent on him for her hiding place, he didn't want to take advantage of the situation. He was careful not to make the first move, even if he'd wanted to many times. His excitement was intensified by weeks of waiting and wondering and hoping. It turned out she'd been holding back too, not wanting to make any assumptions either. But it became obvious to both of them, and then they were tearing off their clothes and hopping into the bed.

They'd been sleeping together most nights since, and now they were leaning into each other on Kite Hill in late June, the cool ocean air pouring down on them before the inevitable fog would descend over the neighborhood. "It's chilly," Cindy pushed closer to Lamar.

"Let's start walking. That'll warm us up and it'll get us out of this wind, too," he nudged her towards the path that led to the fence and the outlet to 19th Street. "What did you decide with Juna?"

"They said I should meet them at the SPCA tomorrow afternoon. I think it's safe, don't you?"

"Maybe your name is on a list somewhere?"

"Yeah, but not Cindy Lowe," she smiled.

"Oh yeah, I forget that you had a different name in Phoenix," Lamar let her go as she went first down the crumbling cement blocks on the path between houses. "What was—never mind! I don't want to know!"

After walking east on 19th a few blocks they came to the overpass that led into Dolores Park. The bridge was lined with flowers and photos of loved ones killed in the March 21st massacre. Homeland Security cleared the memorials dozens of times, and even posted soldiers to prevent them from being re-installed, but whenever the troops left, the memorials went back up within an hour. Finally, the authorities gave up and left the overpass alone. There were at least a dozen people quietly standing on the bridge, staring at photos of the deceased. One woman was audibly sobbing. A J-Church streetcar rumbled uphill underneath the overpass while they slowly crossed.

The park had long been a living room for the thousands of young workers who jammed themselves into overpriced, overcrowded apartments in the Mission and Castro neighborhoods, using every possible room as a rentable bedroom. Some people even rented the same room and bed to multiple people to share in shifts! Dolores Park wasn't nearly as full as it was before the pandemic when it was wall-to-wall picnic blankets. But there were people hanging out and small children crowded the playground. Dogs cavorted on the slope long dominated by dog owners for their exclusive use.

Cindy was drawn to the rolling and tumbling animals, but Lamar pulled back. "I've been bit a few too many times. I'm not a dog person," he admitted.

"Oh, don't be silly! Dogs are easy!" She was about to roll onto the ground with the dogs, but she saw his reluctance and decided to stay in the moment with him. They went to the highest corner of the park to ogle the skyline once more. "Did you spend a lot of time here?" she asked him, but he shook his head.

"No, I grew up in the east bay suburbs so I only came to Dolores Park a few times as a kid when we visited my grannie. I haven't been here since the Massacre in March. I can't remember the last time I was here before that."

Lamar and Cindy resumed their walk, following the canary palms on Dolores Street marching south over the hill. Lamar showed Cindy his favorite shortcuts, cutting across the east slope of Bernal, skirting past Alemany Farm and across the freeway. After an uneventful 30 minutes they were back in the Hangar.

"I can't believe it's only been an hour and a half since we left Kite Kastle!" exclaimed Cindy. "I thought it would take a lot longer."

"Once you get used to it, it's always easy to walk in San Francisco," bragged Lamar. "And now... let's take a shower!" an invitation Cindy happily accepted.

CHAPTER 21
THURSDAY, JULY 31, 2025

Frank woke up determined to get out of Pier 26, at least for part of the day. There were rumors swirling that attacks were imminent. Their temporary headquarters on Pier 26 was well-defended—a 24-hour cordon of thirty-six armed sentries augmented by a dozen armored personnel carriers protected the perimeter on the Embarcadero and several fast-moving speedboats and a Coast Guard cutter patrolled the bay under the bridge. In spite of the security, Frank felt uneasy.

In the last few days a series of small bombs were detonated at strategic sites around the Bay Area—on eastern approaches to the bay-crossing bridges from Richmond to the Dunbarton; near Camp Hayward, and on Mare Island. The 101 freeway had been invaded from the Vermont exit on Potrero Hill by a group of saboteurs who left an hours-long blockade by spilling 55-gallon drums full of white powder across the highway behind General Hospital.

Despite repeated arrests, beatings, and tear gas, San Franciscans continued to protest against the Homeland Security authorities. Col. Cronin and Lt. Morgan were running operations, leaving Frank to give them occasional advice about organizations in the City, and even San Francisco geography. These guys knew nothing about the streets and hills of San Francisco! But they wouldn't give Frank any real authority, in spite of Lt. General Zapata's apparent trust in him to take over in San Francisco. Well, it wasn't like Frank was anxious to have responsibility for this shit-show!

He rode the shuttle a block to Pier 26 from the Bayside Village apartments that Homeland Security took over. The place felt like a hotel, and nobody spent much time there. You went there to sleep, though on the weekly day off, you could don civvies and head out to a bar or restaurant if you wanted to. Frank had Wednesday off, so he was returning to duty. He'd spent the foggy afternoon yesterday on the beach with Sheila and was pondering the mysterious future—with or without Sheila (hopefully with!). But either way, where would things be in a few months or a year? Would Homeland Security return power to local authorities any time soon? It was happening in other places where protests died out, but in major cities on the West Coast, the resistance seemed to be accelerating rather than diminishing.

Frank couldn't understand what was happening. San Franciscans always pushed back against the Federal government, whoever was president. But the bombings, the ongoing protests, the feeling of underground conspiracies all around them—it wasn't like anything he'd known in the old days. 'The old days!' he shook his head. It was only a half a year ago! He'd read dozens of reports and assessments from the field over the past weeks, and it was difficult to recognize any of the familiar contours of San Francisco he'd known for so long.

Yesterday, he'd tried to explain this to Sheila.

"I've never seen so many protests in such a short time," he told her, brushing sand from his pants as they sat on the stairs at Ocean Beach. The humid fog hovered over the whole west side of the City, and as he looked at Sheila, her streaked hair almost glimmered in the bright gray light.

"After all those years patrolling?" she looked at him quizzically.

"Never anything like this. It's the little protests that pop up everywhere all day every day. We had big marches, sure. There was the women's march, anti-police violence marches like the George Floyd protests, even picket lines and LGBTQ stuff. But those were predictable, organized, they had leaders and weren't happening in multiple locations at the same time. Even Critical Mass bike rides, which got crazy decades ago, were not like what's happening now."

"What makes it different?" she asked him, genuinely curious.

"People are blockading ICE vehicles almost wherever they go, pushing trash cans and whatever they can find into the streets. They are surrounding our troops when they are on patrol, yelling at them, sometimes showering them with garbage or eggs or rotten vegetables. We gas them, we club them, and they keep coming!" Frank exclaimed.

"People are very angry, and it hasn't been fading away. If anything, there's a certain tenacity—people want to push ICE and Homeland Security out of San Francisco!"

Sheila hadn't been around a politically engaged populace before either. The suburbs of Contra Costa County where she used to live weren't exactly hotbeds of activism! "Even at the GSA I'd say that only about one in three of the employees is comfortable with what's happening. Most of them want things to go back to normal as soon as possible."

"I hear that!" Frank nodded. "I hope it does too!"

"Do you guys discuss it? Aren't you in the room with the officers who are making decisions for the whole Bay Area?"

"That's at Camp Hayward. Here we are focused on San Francisco. But yeah, Colonel Cronin is in charge, and Lt. Morgan is running the day-to-day operations. When I told Zapata privately we should go back to the Constitution's guarantees of free speech and assembly, he seemed to agree. That's when he told me he was sending me back to 'run' San Francisco." Frank paused, his jaw tightening as he remembered the sequence of events, "But he sent Cronin with me and it was clear right away that I was not in charge," his voice sank in resignation. "I thought I was taking over from Morgan, but Cronin wants him to stay on. They ask me for 'advice,'" (he made air quotes with his fingers), "but they don't care what I say or think. They wanted a local to legitimize the Emergency government. Probably helps that I'm black and grew up here."

"Yeah, I saw you on the news all week, standing there looking important at the daily press briefing," she nudged him with her elbow. "I figured YOU were pulling the strings!" she smiled.

He leaned into her, grateful for her kindness. "No, definitely not! And honestly, Sheila, I don't want the responsibility. These guys are hardly any better than Reynolds was. Most of the conflicts are being provoked by the patrols, to be honest."

"Can't you do anything?" she asked him. "What if you went back to Zapata and told him what you think?"

He shook his head. "First of all, I don't want to be in charge—Hell, I've never done anything like this! Second, Zapata sent Cronin with me and he knows Cronin outranks me—this is his call. I'll tell him what I think if he asks me, but I'm keepin' my head down... " He rose and pulled Sheila up with him. They dodged drifting sands on the wide sidewalk.

"You hear anything about people getting killed in Oakland... by *death squads?*" She stopped and looked directly at him.

Frank looked away in silence. He nodded, and then cast his eyes down. "It's awful," he said in a low voice. "How'd you hear about that?" He knew they'd kept it out of the news.

"There are some underground newsletters that get handed around. Somebody brought one to the office. There was a report."

"What newsletter? Who brought it in?" Frank suddenly felt responsible to uncover this illegal activity.

Sheila pulled away from him, eyebrows raised. "Hey, I thought you were off duty today!" evading his questions.

Her reaction felt like a face slap to Frank, stopping him in his tracks. "Oh, sorry, yes of course, I'm not on the job." It had been an automatic response, but Sheila reminded him that he was on the wrong side. Her disclosure about the newsletter showed that even she was part of the San Francisco that he didn't know.

"Hey, how's your mom?" Sheila suddenly asked.

It was an abrupt transition, but he was grateful for the change of topic. "She sleeps most of the time. She's 102 now! I'm hoping I can see her every day when we move from Pier 26 to the new compound at Hunter's Point."

"Oh yes, I've been working on that, too. It'll be quite a big facility I guess. We've ordered two thousand new chairs, twelve hundred desks, computers, printers, paper, the whole shebang! When do you expect to move in?"

"You know more than me. They told us in a month or so, but that could mean anything," Frank frowned. "I can tell you, Homeland Security is a lot more like the Army than a big corporation. Nothing happens quickly!"

Sheila laughed. "Corporations, government bureaucracies, armies, navies—they're probably more alike than anyone wants to admit! Big and messy and wasteful and self-sabotaging—welcome to the modern world!" Her decades of experience lent her seditious comment real weight.

Frank reacted to this as an ally rather than an official. He anxiously wanted to overcome the barrier between his official function and the real world around him. The afternoon with Sheila went too fast. After wandering around the Sutro Baths ruins, they ate Chinese at the far end of Geary. It had been two months since they spent the night together in Hayward, and it wasn't happening after this cautious but affectionate reunion. They rode the bus downtown and went their separate ways home after strolling through Yerba Buena Gardens.

His reverie broke as the shuttle pulled into Pier 26. As usual, a corporal handed him his daily schedule as he walked across the pavement, and as usual it began with the morning briefing with Cronin, Morgan and the field officers. In the conference room he grabbed coffee and a peach scone he'd learned to love, and sat in his usual seat at the big table.

Cronin and Morgan entered together, also the norm, as they met most mornings ahead of the briefing to coordinate plans. Cronin muttered "g'morning everyone," and stood at his seat while everyone sat down. After the usual procedural blather, Cronin announced, "Given the heightened activity around the City, we are expanding aerial surveillance. The satellite images we get every day give us a lot of intelligence, but we need active, mobile cameras that are sending live images to us in real time. Helicopters are too noisy and we are way over budget with them. We're deploying a new system, starting today." He turned to a civilian who was waiting against the wall. "This is John Mays. He's with SkEYE Systems, our corporate partner supplying the new drone force. He will be onsite tech support for the next month."

Mays tugged at his tie as he prepared to speak. A bland-looking guy in his 30s, average in every observable way, he started his powerpoint slideshow. His surprisingly high-pitched voice explained how each of the four "pilots" at consoles in the back of Pier 26 could control six of the two dozen small drones to be sent over the City. Flight time was limited to three hours, but, he explained, a new mini-Hempattery was expected to double flight times soon. "New battery technology developed right here in San Francisco will make our machines the de facto industry standard by Fourth Quarter this year!" Mays was used to presenting to companies and investors, not military officials. He completed his presentation and returned to the wall.

Cronin asked, "Any questions? Any concerns?"

One of the field commanders, a veteran of three tours of duty in Afghanistan, rather jaded about the Emergency, and openly looking forward to its end, asked loudly, "Are these drones armed? What are they carrying?"

Mays stepped forward again to explain "No, they are strictly surveillance vehicles. The weight of any weapon that might be added to it would drastically reduce the flight time. They are carrying the same cameras that the latest smartphones have, with enhanced lenses and magnification capabilities."

Frank was dismayed to think there would be surveillance drones all over the City. He asked, "Where will these be deployed? Are they giving air cover to patrols or will they cover pre-determined areas?"

"That is what we will be experimenting with during the first month," responded Cronin. "We plan to try out both approaches, and we're looking at some other ideas too. You are on the targeting team, Robertson." And Cronin went on to assign several others in the room to the targeting group. "Report to Room 15 to coordinate with the drone pilots and Mr. Mays here."

A half hour later the daily patrols had departed and the Drone Squadron was assembled in Room 15. Lt. Morgan was there too, and he took the lead. "OK, pilots, the actual machines you'll be flying are laid out at the back of the pier. Join Mr. Mays and get acquainted with the technology." They filed out of the room, leaving Lt. Morgan, Frank, and three other Homeland Security officials to discuss the initial targeting approach. Morgan opened his laptop and turned on the projector to show a map of San Francisco on the white wall. Pointing at "hot spots" on the map, Morgan explained, "We know where protests have been popping up," and he flashed a grid of highlighted points onto the map. "And we know where areas of concern are," replacing the protest points with shaded areas highlighting open spaces, community gardens and farms, and parks.

Frank interjected, "Lt. Morgan? Why are these parks and gardens identified as 'areas of concern'?" What was this obsession with community gardens all about anyway? He'd never heard anyone explain it.

Morgan turned his attention to Frank. "Lieutenant, food is a weapon," his chest thrust out, inflated with importance. He began an unmistakably condescending recitation. "These local gardens and farms are producing a surprising amount of food. The President has declared a national commitment to our struggling farmers, and to carry out that commitment we are obliged to adjust our diets to include food products that use mandated quantities of American corn and American soy. Locally produced food undercuts our national goals and during the Emergency *our goal* is to ensure that *this region* meets the standards established by *our President.*"

Frank acknowledged hearing the response and looked around to see how it was landing with the other people tasked with targeting the drones. No one responded, and the studied neutrality of the faces around the room told Frank nothing.

"Any other questions?" Morgan demanded. He resented being questioned about anything. Everyone should already know this. And Robertson! Morgan looked at Robertson and saw an old black man who had no business being in this room. Could he even be trusted? Wasn't he from here? Who had he been seeing in when he was off-duty? He briefly thought about tracking Robertson to check, but dropped it after a moment.

CHAPTER 22
FRIDAY, AUGUST 11, 2025

Janet dodged the rake someone carelessly left near the shed door. Out of the corner of her eye she noticed a crow. About 15 yards away, it was standing over something. She paused and watched as it nosed the object and looked up at her. She recognized one of the regulars from the nearby grove.

"Whatcha got there, buddy?" she asked, not expecting an answer. After the time she and Dat heard words in the vocalization of the crows, it never happened again... not yet! She also didn't wear witches butter against her skin regularly. But even when she and Dat tried several subsequent times to wrap the soft putty-like fungus around their wrists in order to communicate with the crows, they could not hear any words. They talked about it a lot, of course. It had been overwhelming when it happened.

"Do you think we were imagining it?" Janet asked him after three more tries in the following week.

"No. We both heard what we heard. But remember, Bernie never heard anything. And the heat wave broke before we tried it again. I wonder if the heat had anything to do with it?" Dat was sitting across the picnic table from her at Alemany Farm as they pondered the puzzle.

"Hmmm. That's possible. What if the properties of the witches butter change with temperature? That doesn't sound too far-fetched," Janet poured some water into a cup, remembering how parched they felt that day. "Can you test this in your lab?"

He nodded, staring into space, the gears turning in his prodigious brain. "Whatever happened that day hasn't happened again. It's possible that the witches butter reacted with the heat and it's also possible that whatever it was that made it "work" that day has diminished since then, wearing out in a normal entropic process. Perhaps a certain complexity was reached that unraveled and lost its power?" He was thinking out loud.

That was ten days ago. Janet pondered what the crows were thinking whenever she saw them. She still spoke to them as she had for years, but now she yearned for a response.

"Caw, caw, caw" the crow replied urgently. She approached it cautiously, but the crow didn't move away. It bobbed its beak up and down again. Then it slowly walked a few feet away as Janet approached the object, which turned out to be a propeller on a spindle.

"Maybe part of a drone?" was Janet's first thought. She picked it up as the crow looked on intently. "Where'd you get this?" she again asked absentmindedly. "Caw" came the response, and then the crow flew towards the trees lining the farm. She didn't make much of it and threw the broken propeller into a nearby bin. It wasn't that unusual for a crow to bring a shiny or weird object to her. She was always talking to them and often she'd leave them popcorn or pieces of left-behind sandwiches. After several years, she had her regulars that knew her.

***

Homeland Security drones became a regular presence above the farms.

New regulations were being issued with alarming regularity. All urban gardens were required to register with Homeland Security, and report what they were growing and in what quantities. Food crops would have to be turned over for sale through authorized supermarkets. It was bizarre! Republicans, who had always prioritized their precious "free market" were aggressively using the state to bolster their friends in agribusiness, among other special interests.

The Hutchinson administration was trying to eliminate ways for people to sustain themselves outside of what they called "the American way." That meant buying government-approved foods at supermarkets, using gasoline-powered, not electric or hybrid, cars. If you had solar you had to pay an extra fee to the utilities now! There were even reports of marauding gangs pulling solar from roofs in Phoenix and San Diego and destroying the panels. The attack on the Dog Patch had been the most egregious local example of garden destruction, but regular visits by ICE Hummers, checking gardeners' papers, demanding inventory of crops planted and harvests expected, it was wearing on Janet and the other dedicated urban farmers.

Janet and her fellow League of Urban Farmer members sought to evade the new regulations. Before the National Emergency, they managed to expand food production at Alemany, Palou Terrace, the Dog Patch (before it was destroyed), McLaren, and Bayview farms to the point that they were producing 250 tons a year of fresh vegetables and fruit. They didn't "sell" it, but made it available to anyone who helped, or who lived nearby in public housing. Not that there was much public housing left in the City at this point! All the more reason to make food available for free whenever they could. But that was jeopardized by the surveillance and repression.

The gardeners' project to radically decentralize production by planting potatoes, onions, garlic, and other root crops in backyards across the city was unknown to the authorities. Who knew how much they would harvest from these small plots all over the place? Even more important, they'd engaged thousands of San Franciscans to newly participate in local gardening. No saying how important that might turn out to be in the years to come. Janet always had her eye on the long game. She imagined linear farms instead of the streets where wide expanses of asphalt currently provided storage for parked cars—it wasn't hard to see if you squinted!

***

Janet was pedaling as fast as she could, dodging in and out of the wall-to-wall traffic on San Bruno Avenue. She cleared the traffic jam and begin her ascent up the hill, her anxiety driving her to keep up the pace. It was still a good five minutes before she reached the summit. Breathing heavily, she pulled her bike alongside a nondescript pink house and punched in the code to open the side gate to the backyard. Noticing her shirt was sweat soaked, she ducked into the shed.

"Hey Suzie," she greeted the heavy-set woman who was feeding the pigeons in her coop.

"Oh, hey Janet," she grunted. "What's up?"

"I was wondering if you know anything about bird-drone contact?"

"Huh? What do you mean, 'contact'?"

"Like are birds crashing into drones?"

"I'm not sure. Maybe. What makes you ask?"

"The farm crows seem to have found some parts... one of the regulars brought me a piece today."

"Interesting. Well, I haven't heard anything. Our pigeons are ok, no crashes that I've heard of."

"We've had more flyovers lately. They might raid Alemany soon." She was worried, but they kept no records of last year's harvest, nor of who got what in the distribution. They turned over a few bushels of wormy zucchinis and mealy peaches to the Homeland Security people when they demanded their crop and seemed to have gotten away with it. She worried about a more intense effort to bust the farms.

"Can I send a message to Miguel?"

"Sure," Suzie pointed to a mottled brown and white pigeon. "Freddie's ready to go."

Janet scribbled a quick note, asking Miguel to keep track of drone patterns, and to let her know if anyone had seen any drone-bird crashes. She watched as Suzie strapped it on to Freddie's leg, and then held him in her hands, kissed his head, and flung him into the air.

***

Roberto Esposito was on the roof under a shelter when he heard the fluttering wings of Freddie.

"Oh, hello there! Come to papa," and he reached out his arm holding some seed in his open palm. And the carrier pigeon settled comfortably on his forearm and pecked at his hand. He stroked its head and enclosed the bird in his hands and removed the message, putting the pigeon into the big chicken-wire coop where a half dozen other birds were contentedly hanging out.

He saw the message was for Miguel, though he read it too. He'd seen a "murder of crows," at least a hundred birds, several times recently. One time they surrounded and harassed a drone hovering over a crowd at Yerba Buena Gardens. He found Miguel at his kitchen table amid piles of papers. He handed him the note and told him about his recent observations.

"A murder of crows, eh? I haven't seen anything like that around here at the creek. Mostly seagulls and cormorants, or the lone heron or egret, sometimes a pelican or two. Did you think the crows were trying to attack the drone?"

"They were agitated by it. They didn't attack while I was watching, but they were circling around angrily, I thought."

"Hmmm. Do you think there's any way we could work with crows like you work with pigeons? Could we show them how to disable a drone? Would they learn that?"

"Wow, Miguel, what an idea! I don't know. I never got that close to a crow, where I could try to show it something. But I don't see why we couldn't try."

From that seemingly crazy beginning, a plan was hatched. Dat Doan's tech lab provided them with some drones rebuilt with scavenged parts that they could run themselves. A week later, Roberto arrived at Alemany Farm to meet up with Janet. It was a warm Friday in the middle of August, everyone holding their breath for news about the latest wildfires racing across California. Smoke-filled skies came and went all summer with the prevailing winds.

"Janet, here's a few drones we can use. Are the crows around? I'd like to try to show them how to use sticks to bring drones down. Whaddya think?"

"That's a wild idea. I don't know if we can get their attention for that. Let me try," and with that she walked to the spot where she usually threw popcorn out for them. She dumped out a bag on the ground and waved toward the trees. Sure enough, about 6 or 7 black crows flew out of the trees and slowly circled around and landed a dozen feet away, nodding and ducking their heads, twitching back and forth. She spoke to them as though they were people.

"Hi guys. Hey, we want you to try something. This is a drone," and she held up a drone. "We want you to knock it down. But we don't want you to get hurt!" She held up a short stick in her other hand. "This is a stick. We think you can carry the stick into the air and drop it on the drone." She showed how the stick could fly into the blades and she mimicked it falling to the ground. "Will you give it a try?" and she put a half dozen sticks on the ground. Using the controller they sent the drone 30 feet into the air where it hovered over them. The crows were visibly disturbed when it turned on and immediately flew back to the trees.

"Nice try," said Roberto, smirking.

"Give it a minute," Janet insisted. She began throwing the sticks up at the drone, trying to hit it. On her fourth try, she succeeded, the stick landing on the drone blades and breaking them, sending the drone crashing down.

She repeated the whole sequence again with a second drone, again taking a half dozen tries to get the stick to fall into the blades. This drone shattered on impact scattering pieces around the open area amid the remaining popcorn. They still had three more drones to use.

She and Roberto retreated to a nearby bench and waited a bit. Sure enough two crows ventured back after a while, at least for the popcorn, but one seemed interested in the drone pieces too, and kept nosing them around between bites. Janet stood up and walked slowly back towards the crows.

"OK, let's do it again. I want you to take a stick up and drop it into the blades, OK?" and she sent another one up. And again the crows immediately retreated to their roost in the trees. She desultorily tossed sticks up towards the drone and then went back to sit with Roberto, leaving the drone buzzing in a stationery spot 30 feet above the ground. "Let's see if anyone comes back," she said.

She was about ready to give up when five crows suddenly swooped out of the trees, two of them holding branches in their beaks. They started circling the hovering drone, putting up quite a commotion, cawing and screeching. And then, a miracle. One of them flew out of their circular formation to go above the hovering drone and dropped their stick onto it, smashing the blades, and sending it crashing down.

"Woohoo! Way to go! You did it!" Janet was running and jumping up and down with a huge grin on her face. Roberto came over too, clapping and waving at the crows. "You did it!" 'Maybe talking to them worked?' he thought, 'why not?' The crows came down for more popcorn and to examine the wreck of the drone. They were talking to each other, that's for sure. Watching them carefully, Janet couldn't stop grinning, and kept talking to them like friends. "You guys did it. Awesome! Now, you have to tell your friends, and you have to help us. These drones are bad and we don't want them in our sky. We want you to help us stop them, ok?"

It seemed a bit ridiculous. But who knew? Maybe this was the beginning of something amazing.

CHAPTER 23
WEDNESDAY, AUGUST 27, 2025

Clara and Maria sat at the kitchen table in the luxurious secret cellar. They'd already checked the plants and gathered the read-outs and they were having a morning snack. They'd been underground in the Bayview for most of the time they'd been in San Francisco. As research gardeners used to rolling around the southwestern desert where they'd originally been, it had become unbearable. The work they were doing with Ally was remarkable, and their own roles in advancing these incredible biotech projects was central. They both took a lot of satisfaction from knowing what was germinating and growing in their well-hidden underground laboratory. They had Larry to thank most and they knew it. He recruited them to come to San Francisco and paid them extremely well to work here. Alison Nakahara was the cantankerous and reserved genius they learned to appreciate, despite her occasional outbursts of rudeness. That was easy enough to overlook, but they both wondered if her single-mindedness was rubbing off on them in a bad way. It seemed she hardly ever took a day off, and she kept pushing their efforts with the biobulb and the bioboat. The witches butter fungus was at the center of a great deal of urgent research, ever since Dat Doan and Janet Pierce told them about the day they spoke with the crows! Nobody had even a hint that something like that could emerge from the bioengineered fungus—and maybe it was something else altogether since they'd never been able to reproduce it again after the first time.

"I need to get out of here," said Clara to Maria. "I feel like we've forgotten who we are down here. When Larry hired us we thought we'd be working in a normal lab and greenhouse, not in a fuckin' dungeon!"

Maria nodded, acknowledging the obvious. "Yeah, I need a break too. Maybe we should go camping or something?"

"That's an idea!"

The door swung open and Larry Lansing entered, filling up the space, a cloud of human smells and sweaty humidity emanating from his enormous bulk. "Hey, howzit goin'?" he said without waiting for an answer. "You guys look upset... what is it?"

Maria always found it easier to speak directly to Larry than Clara ever had. He was very big and Clara found him intimidating, even though he'd made many efforts to assure her she had nothing to worry about. He was very happy with her work and considered the six-figure salaries he was paying them as well worth it. Ally always complimented their work too, even if she complained angrily when something wasn't the way she expected it to be.

"Larry, we were just talking about it. We didn't know we would be working in a dungeon! We need to work in the sun, spend less time down here," Maria explained.

"Huh, yeah, I was wonderin' how long this was gonna work," he dropped into the leather chair at the end of the table. "ICE has been coming around, and these damn drones are zooming around all the time. I don't think you are at any risk to be outside—you could even work the local gardens. Nobody even knows you're here. You know that Ally depends on you both so you can't up and leave completely! But I *was* going to mention another project I'm backing, which is outdoors. I have people on it already, but maybe it would help to have you guys take some shifts too. It's not what you're used to though!" he chuckled. "Ever spent much time on the water?"

They both looked at him curiously. "What do you mean?" Maria asked.

"You know Janet has been buggin' me for years about growing more food and less pot. And you know we've done well across the street with our hydroponic crops. Homeland Security has put out these crazy new regulations lately, and with the surveillance and rules local food growing is getting harder, at least in the way we've been doin' it." He filled a glass with orange juice and took a deep drink. "We gotta start doin' food different, right?"

Clara sat back waiting to hear what was next. Maria smiled, recognizing Larry's usual slow approach to what he wanted to say. "Go on! Say it! You want us to go fishing!" and they laughed.

He looked at them intently. "Oysters!" he blurted. "Know anything about cultivating oysters?"

They both shook their heads. They were from Arizona! What the hell did they know about shellfish?

"Dat proposed it first, a while ago. He was tellin' me that the bay used to be full of oysters and shrimp and stuff to eat. He said they got somethin' like 3 million pounds of shrimp out of the bay back in the 1930s! They had a Chinese shrimpin' village right on the north shore of Hunter's Point!"

"Yeah, but Larry, we don't know a thing about it!" Maria protested.

"I'm not expectin' you to figure it out on your own. I have some folks who know about it already. Those UPA guys are from all over and it turns out, they have a lot of skills. Some were oyster farmers up in Washington before they ended up down here."

"We have a lot to do here, but if we could get a day or two every week outside, we'd be able to do better work down here," Clara offered. "The cellar is about as comfy as a dungeon could be!" they chuckled. "But we need more sun!"

"There's more to the oyster story than food," Larry enthused, leaning into it. "Dat told me they've been buildin' oyster 'reefs' in parts of the North Bay for a few years to help hold back the sea level rise."

"How do they do that?" asked Maria.

"You're gonna have to ask Dat or Jessie, the guy I'll introduce you to. They know way more than I do.

"And you'll explain this to Ally?" Clara pointedly asked Larry.

"Yeah, yeah, I got it, don't worry." He was used to getting things to go the way he wanted them to, especially since he'd gotten his big payout from the HemptriCity sale.

***

A few days later Maria was on the bay. The grayish water lapped at their small boat as they motored the shore of Candlestick Point. Jessie Suzuki was directing the effort and steered the boat with his hand on the tiller. He was a 30-something lanky guy, maybe of Japanese or Korean descent? Maria couldn't tell until she learned his last name. Jessie Suzuki hailed from Seattle, all-American in his demeanor, and in his sardonic account of his short tenure as a BGM contractor.

"Those assholes! 'Free apartment, $5000 signing bonus!' It sounded too good to be true, and of course it was. Gotta check the fine print—hell I knew that, but I was desperate. I guess most BGM contractors are. As soon as they came to check on my 'crop,' I was tossed out. It hadn't even been three months! I figured they'd give me a chance to figure it out, but those fuckers told me it was over. They even tried to get their money back, but luckily I'd used it to pay some debts I had, and I cashed out the rest. I wonder if my empty bank account was what tipped them to do an early inspection?" He paused his story while he maneuvered the boat into the inlet where Double Rock stood. "Hey look out in front ok? It's real shallow in here, and I forget where the big rocks are," he called to the other member of the crew, Steve Brooks. Brooks was also a former BGM contractor and UPA member. He'd been listening to Jessie's account with a bemused look on his face when Maria could see it. Mostly he stared out the front.

"Anyway, I got the $5000 and they took back their damn trays and plants. I never did know what I did wrong. They said it was over and that was that. No appeal, no discussion. And I had to move in three days!"

Brooks chimed in then. "Yeah, I love that 3-day eviction! Anywhere else in town, you get a 3-day notice, you can put up a fight, there's a legal clinic to help you, you can drag it out for a year or longer. But not in the BGM apartments. They own them, and the courts have already ruled in earlier cases that the 3-day eviction is not under the jurisdiction of San Francisco's housing laws because it's superceded by contract law. And when you sign the BGM contract, you agree to this. Fuckers!"

"What brought you to San Francisco Maria?" Jessie asked her from behind.

She pulled her sweater and windbreaker in against the cold breeze, she told them she'd been a researcher at Arizona State University until Larry hired her to work in his greenhouses and on special projects about two years ago. She'd been working for him ever since, careful to leave out any details about the special projects.

Brooks called out, "Stop!" as he peered into the murk. "This is the spot." Maria took a few steps towards the bow and looked over the edge at the poles staked into the bay mud laid out in parallel rows.

"Are these the oysters?" she asked.

"They will be," Jessie explained. "We put these in a few months ago. It'll take a year/year and a half before they grow big enough to start harvesting. Meanwhile, they're already cleaning the water!" And he elaborated on their filtration capacities, each one processing up to 50 gallons a day of water, removing nitrogen and phosphorous in the process. "And as the oyster reefs grow and expand, they'll help slow down the tidal surges that will keep coming," referencing the surprising spring floods.

"Man, I remember that one in April. I was volunteering at the Dog Patch and the lower terrace was completely submerged!" Brooks said.

"I heard that Camp Hayward flooded that night too, though they never admitted it. And the breakout the next morning was related somehow," Jessie offered.

"I heard the airports were under water for a few hours," Maria said, "but the authorities denied that too. That's what I hate the most about this situation. We can never get even simple facts straight anymore!"

They kept chatting, and Maria realized that there wasn't too much to do yet. It was a short boat ride and a chance to spend time on the bay. She sat back and relaxed into the smell of saltwater and organic decay, still feeling chilled by the fog-pushed winds.

"Hey, what's that?" she pointed to bobbing heads in the water.

"Those are harbor seals," Jessie answered. "Nothing to worry about. They don't like oysters. If we start having otters here in the bay again, that's another story. They LOVE oysters."

"Aren't we putting some mesh or a cage around our oyster beds?" asked Brooks.

"Yes, definitely! We don't need 'em yet, but we do plan to install cages around each piece of the reef where we will harvest oysters next year," Jessie explained. "Hey," he pointed to the seals, "look at that! They don't usually come close!" The seals swum near their small boat and were bobbing in the bay, heads well above the water.

Maria was excited and smiling, leaned over and waved her hand towards them. They were only a few feet beyond her reach. One seal ducked under the water, surging up suddenly to nose her hand. She drew back, startled. "Oh! Oh!" and toppled backwards into the bottom of the boat. Jessie and Brooks laughed at her tumble, and she grinned as she recovered her composure. "That scared the shit out of me!"

Meanwhile, other seals started barking at them.

Maria went back to the edge and on her elbows, asked the animal, "What are you trying to say friend?"

"Aar, aar, aar," was the spirited response.

She searched for something to share. In her pocket she found a baggie with a bunch of Vero's witches butter chips. Maria had taken to snacking on these salty and sweet chips. She fed a few to the seals, who gobbed them with relish. They spun and rolled in the waters, bobbing repeatedly, getting closer and closer.

"OK, fellas, glad to meet you too!" Maria said, not sure what else to say. Janet modeled speaking in plain language to animals and plants and fungi and she felt less self-conscious now that she was doing it here. After all, these seals were connecting with them... or was it her? Who could tell? Maria started to explain to the seals about the new oyster reefs and they'd be coming back regularly. "I hope to see you again, ok?" and as if they understood, they dived away, disappearing.

"Wow! How weird!" Jessie exclaimed at the back of the boat, bobbing up and down on the wake of passing freighter out in the middle of the bay. Brooks grabbed the prow and looked around for the animals but they were nowhere to be seen.

"Do you always talk to animals like that?" he asked Maria. "It looked like they could understand you."

She smiled and told them about Janet and her incessant chatter with critters. "I picked it up from her I guess. But why did they come to us in the first place?" And as she asked the question aloud it crossed her mind: could it be the witches butter? She'd been snacking on it regularly.

***

Janet and Dat said they heard crows speak one day. It was connected to the putty-like fungus they'd grown, but then it never happened again. Vero's snacks and dishes became the talk of the staff at Larry's and Leon's and local farms, where it was being shared widely. Her recipes for the chips, as well as pasta and 'fresh cheese' derived from the witches butter were very popular. And batches of witches butter were being nurtured in a half dozen locations now.

In the secret cellar kitchen a few days ago, Vero was busy baking when Maria came in. "Here try this," and she thrust a large wooden spoon of warm dough to Maria, who gladly ate it without hesitation.

"What is it?"

"The latest. We can make cookies out of witches butter too!" Vero looked happy. Since she'd been stuck in hiding, she needed a way to contribute and she'd found it. "You know, the witches butter grows back as fast as I can use it. I've never seen anything like it. If I take a pound or two to try different things, and then I return a few hours later, the place where I took some is already grown back."

"Wow, that's unusual," Maria was chewing happily on her dough sample.

"Dat says they can't decide what the nutritional properties are. Every experiment they've run on raw witches butter indicates that it has some basic vitamins, A, D, even some C. There's a decent amount of protein too. But when I had him run tests on the chips, or the pasta, the results were completely different. There were huge increases in protein, and basic elements like zinc, manganese, and iron appeared too. We can't explain it, but it's like a Super Food! Especially after I cook it..."

"When you're cooking, do you do a lot of tasting? I mean, do you put the stuff in your mouth and then it goes back to the batch you're working on?" asked Maria, suddenly curious.

"Huh? What do you mean? I don't put it in my mouth and then spit it back into the pot, if that's what you mean! But I eat from the spoon that I use to stir things. I suppose my saliva might have mixed with what I was cooking, though only in tiny amounts."

"Hmmm. we should try some more experiments. What happens if we introduce human fluids to batches of witches butter isolated from the cooking process? And what happens if the same batch is cooked? And of course, what happens if we cook some without it having ever known any human sweat or saliva or even skin?"

"But the witches butter was created in part by the massaging and chanting we did last year. We brought it from a vat of gray clay to that cream-colored putty. When Dat put Intelligel® in that one batch it turned bright canary yellow, remember? The original witches butter became very familiar with our skin, our sweat, and even probably some aerosolized saliva or possibly other fluids like a drip from someone's nose. Who knows? We weren't being careful and had no reason to assume there was any reason to take precautions," Vero explained.

Maria was pondering this when she had an "ah-hah!" moment. "What if the witches butter is adapting to human physiology by becoming more nutritious for us when we use it?"

"Is that possible?" asked Vero, knowing she had no scientific understanding. "How would it do that? How does that even work?"

***

Maria's scientific brain was racing as the boat motored back to the dock at Candlestick Point. Those seals—did they pick something up from her because she had witches butter in her? Or because she was carrying the chips in her pocket? Or was it a random moment? Seals were known to be playful after all. They didn't do anything unusual... but... they DID seem to focus on her when she was watching them. Would they have played with one of the other two guys if they'd been the ones to put their hands out? No way to know now. She could hardly wait to get back and talk to Clara and Ally. And Dat Doan! That guy was in the middle of everything now. Maybe she could work with him to design some new experiments? What was going on with the witches butter? They had to figure it out!

CHAPTER 24
Tuesday, September 9, 2025

Janet pedaled to the Fort Mason garden, but instead of entering, she locked her bike and walked into the old wooden office building. There was a small conference room upstairs, whose windows looked out over the garden and the Golden Gate in the distance. It was 3 o'clock on a boiling hot afternoon, the air hazy with smoke and pollution. All summer the cool rush of afternoon fog poured through the Golden Gate, but every September you could expect a heat wave to arrive and block the fog.

Janet joined the other Canopy Council members already sitting around the table.

"I thought we said 2:30?" Annette Jorgensen, a gray-haired septugenarian immediately scolded Janet on her late arrival.

"Sorry!" she didn't bother to explain how she'd been delayed and sat down at an empty seat along the wall. She pulled out a cloth to wipe the sweat from her face, feeling her very wet shirt as she leaned back in her seat.

"Please close the blinds," Annette instructed the people by the window, and they did. The room dimmed which combined with the fan blowing helped make it feel a bit cooler right away. Outside, over San Francisco's oldest and best maintained garden, the unmistakable buzz of a drone could be heard. "I don't know if those drones are able to peer into buildings, but no sense in making ourselves visible to it," Annette commented. "Joe, please start again for Janet's sake."

Joe Stennett put down his pen. "Thanks Annette. As I was saying before Janet got here, we've been pursuing a two-track strategy. On one hand most of our gardens have systematically moved plants out, distributing them to members' backyards. As part of this, we've also helped establish sixty new gardens in open spaces and parklands, most of which have gone undetected as far as we know. The second track has been cooperating with the authorities, filling out their forms and handing over harvests. But from our preliminary estimates, the harvests taken by Homeland Security account for less than 25% of our output. Most of the food we're growing in San Francisco, more than ever actually, is going straight from backyards and guerrilla gardens into people's homes. The potato crop looks to be enormous this fall. We think there may be 1,500 backyards with potatoes in the ground. It should be possible to get at least 20 lbs from each of those yards, in some cases quite a bit more. We should harvest approximately 30,000 pounds of potatoes, fifteen tons!" He sat back and crossed his arms, gazing around the room triumphantly.

Murmurs went around the room as everyone took in these impressive numbers.

"We're giving a quarter over to those assholes?" Marina Petrozzini was livid. "Who thinks that's a good idea? What is that getting us? Why give them anything?" She slammed her fist into the table.

Annette cut in, "Marina, we've been over this. We decided that we would draw less attention if we seemed to be cooperating. Given the remarkable expansion and success of our decentralized efforts, I'd say it's working. Anyone else feel like Marina?"

Hands went up. "I agree with her," a woman from the Richmond District said. "We shouldn't have to give our produce to the government. It's ridiculous. But I also understand that the Emergency is different—we don't have any rights," she sat back and her friend took over.

"I've been working the edges of the Presidio. The Park Service people have been super helpful," a middle-aged Chinese woman stood up, short but tough looking. She straightened her shirt with one hand and pointing out the window with her other. "But I don't know how long we'll remain 'under the radar' given these drone fly-overs. We should be preparing for a more direct confrontation with the goons coming for our food," and she sat back down with a flourish.

"Thank you, Esther, and you too Regina," Annette took the floor back. "I'm not sure there's much appetite in the Council for confrontation. After the Dolores Park Massacre, and the destruction of Dog Patch, nobody here fails to take their violence seriously. We've found a way to thrive without bringing them down on us further. Let's not forget, our goal is to feed the city as much as we can. And what we provide is more needed than ever, especially considering the corn and soy mandates."

"If we organized people's blockades, we can stop them!" Marina argued. "Everyone is pissed. Most folks are ready to push back, especially when they see these fuckers in their Hummers taking the food we worked hard to grow!" Her hands flew back and forth, stabbing the air while she spoke.

"Y'know, the time will come, maybe sooner than later," Janet stood up now, "when we'll be ready to confront the authorities. But we're not ready. As Annette reminded us, we don't want to walk into another slaughter." She paused and looked around, seeing that most of the 14 people in the room were nodding supportively. "I also want to remind everyone that simply by being in this room you are most likely on a list—either for arrest or—apparently—worse!" This riveted everyone's attention. "It's possible that our willingness to cooperate keeps us from being targeted. For now, I say we keep on with the two-track strategy. It's working."

Everyone sat in stunned silence. They agreed with Janet, but it felt like not many thought they might be targeted for being on the Canopy Council. Some shifted nervously in their seats, not saying out loud what they were thinking.

Janet saw the fear shoot around the room, the paralysis taking hold. "I didn't mean to freak you out. I know it's hard to look at this unfiltered, but," she looked into the eyes of one person after another as she slowly turned, "well, it is fucking serious!" She paused again. "But wait, there's more! And I don't mean more to fear. We aren't turning the other cheek and waiting for them to take our food. Who here has heard about the crows?"

A few people tentatively raised their hands. An older man, a known birder named Greg, croaked from his corner seat, "you mean that you talked to the crows? Or that the crows attacked a drone?" He'd heard a lot!

Janet, still standing with everyone's attention smiled. "I guess you heard," and she explained to the rest about the remarkable experience of showing the crows how to take down a drone and then how they'd done it twice more. Had they shared the new skill with crows in other parts of town already?

"As for talking to the crows..." she was enjoying this and she trusted everyone in the room. "Those who know me, know that I tend to talk to birds and bugs and squirrels and raccoons and any other critters I come across. But this was different." She explained how her hacker friends developed the fungi called witches butter and gave a quick overview of its apparent transformation. "We were told it was a building material, something we could use like clay, but a living, growing thing. We were experimenting and we had a band of it wrapped around our wrists. You could *feel it*, real energy!"

"What d'you mean? What did you feel?" a gardener, William Shaw from the Lake Merced area, asked. He'd been around farms and plants since his childhood in Oklahoma and this didn't seem believable to him. Janet was a friend, and he was inclined to trust her, but he wanted her to explain this better.

Janet turned to him, "Will, it sounds wack I know. I wouldn't have believed it if someone told me about it either. At first I didn't notice because it was subtle. But later, after, well, let me finish my story and then I'll loop back to this, ok?" Shaw nodded.

"We brought some to Alemany and ... well... my friend and I, we spoke with two crows who answered back!" She looked at the incredulous looks on the faces around the table. "I know it sounds impossible. Maybe we were trippin'. We never could reproduce it. No crows spoke to us in English again! But they told us they were 'turstee' and that the trees were *telling them* the same thing. It's not like they spoke in complex sentences, but me and my friend, we both *heard* two different crows clearly."

A few people were smiling, believing her farfetched account. Others looked at Janet and wondered if her sanity was slipping.

"During those minutes, another friend who was there too *couldn't* hear any words. To her it sounded like the regular cawing of crows. But two of us did. Were we hallucinating together? All three of us had bands of witches butter wrapped around our wrists, and the energy, like electrical current, was surging out of the bands into our arms. We kinda freaked out and tore it off our arms. We didn't know if it was dangerous or what."

She turned back to Will Shaw. "It felt like a light tingling at first, and when we were talking with the crows—oh, and they had been eating some too, maybe that makes a difference?—suddenly it was a much stronger current. It scared us to be honest. What was it exactly? We don't know. My friend, he's a biohacker, he's been running tests and experiments to see what he can figure out. My friend Vero has been experimenting with different ways to cook it, too.

She pulled out a box of witches butter she'd brought along and began handing out portions to each person who wanted some. "Obviously there are no proper FDA tests or anything like that. It's a secret! But we have recipes for preparing it, and birds and other animals eat it when we put it out. Weirdly it gains in nutritional content when you cook it." A half dozen people pulled pieces from their samples and rolled them into balls, then into snakes, as if it were playdough. They wrapped the snake-shaped fungus around their wrists.

"Oh yeah, I can feel it!" almost shrieked Marina, the first to do It. Others grinned as they donned the wristbands and felt the tingle too. Still others refused it and looked on skeptically at the people who were playing with it.

"You guys are crazy! I wouldn't touch that stuff! What if it's poison?" Esther was spooked.

Janet put up her hands. "Nobody is obliged to take this or do anything with it. But what we do know is this: 1. it's not poison! If it were, we would've gotten sick already. It's been months. 2. it's good to eat. Same thing, dozens of people have been eating this as pasta, as chips, and as spreads. If it caused health problems, we'd know about it. True, we don't know anything about long-term effects. But in the short-term, it tastes good, it's good for you, and it grows back as fast as you can harvest it—that's the weirdest part of all! If you use it for food, it grows back whatever you take in a day or even less! I've never seen anything like it."

Most of the Council members had a chunk of witches butter by now.

"Where have you planted this? How does it grow?" and numerous other questions bounced around the room. Janet did her best to explain what she knew. "Experiment in your own yards, in your specific microclimate. We don't know what conditions are best for it. We don't know what other plants it likes, we don't know much about the soil acidity it prefers. It seems to behave similarly in rather different conditions." She proposed that they form a subcommittee to propagate witches butter across the city, and to carefully record its growth and development. And for those who were excited to participate, a recipe contest! "But I'm sure Vero will win, since she had a big head start!"

That got a laugh out everyone.

Annette Jorgensen took a sample too, even though she was deeply skeptical about bioengineering. "What if this stuff grows like a weed and starts overrunning other food crops? Have you seen anything to indicate that might happen?"

Janet shook her head vigorously. "It expands slowly. It sets in and seems to work underground. We think it's building mycelial networks with other plants. But there's no evidence of it expanding into other crop areas where we haven't planted it."

Jorge Castro observed quietly. "Janet, this is very exciting. I wonder how much you know about other research going on with fungi?"

"I rely on my pal who is a biohacker, and I know the scientist who wrote a theoretical work. But she's never explained it to me. This stuff started from her early theorizing, went through some modifications at the biohacker lab, and it has taken on a life of its own."

Jorge was smiling. "I happen to know a bit. I was reading a book about mushrooms and fungi. Research showed the outer layers of portobello mushrooms might be a workable alternative to graphite in lithium batteries. I suppose that Hempattery is based on similar ideas?" he was quite modest, but he knew a fair amount. "I heard about a company developing fungi to replace plastics—is that what your friend was theorizing?"

"Probably," Janet looked a bit embarrassed, "I don't know much about the details."

"Apparently they could 'pour' the fungus into molds and it would harden into leather, and even be as strong as concrete!" Jorge was happy to be sharing this since it been bouncing around in his imagination for a while. "Anyway, I'm very excited about your witches butter. I'd love to take a piece with me, thank you!"

Annette reclaimed the meeting. "Thank you Jorge, and Janet, for telling us about these exciting possibilities," she looked around the room. The Council members were enjoying a moment of hopeful enthusiasm, a welcome respite from the gloomy discussions on how to avoid or accommodate the authorities. "I was reminded by Janet's account of her encounter with the crows... our gardening and farming means much more than growing food. We are re-inhabiting the city, reconnecting to the soil, the water, the sun, and especially, the other species with whom we live here. We are cultivating food, but also relationships. I say this because I am a bit concerned that we are talking about this witches butter in instrumental ways. Maybe we should consider it as a new neighbor, as someone who recently arrived that we can learn from? If we reduce it to the products it can be turned into, or the results we can get from eating it, or anything like that, aren't we making the same mistakes again?"

Most of the group nodded appreciatively, listening to her with great respect. "I don't want to rain on anyone's enthusiasm. By all means, let's see what we can do together with this curious invention. I do advise caution. It's only existed for a few months and no one can predict what the effects will be in a few months, or a few years from now."

The meeting's tone was abruptly interrupted by the screeching of dozens of parrots not far from their open windows. A few members peered through the blinds to see what was up. Several dozen parrots were swirling across the skies above the garden, going back and forth between different trees. "Oh shit," Regina turned back to the group. "There's an ICE Hummer parked up at the Hostel. We have to go, NOW!" Nobody needed to be told twice. The meeting broke up and the Canopy Council members ran down the stairs and out into the late afternoon heat. Most of them walked into the Great Meadow, breaking up into twos and threes. Janet jumped on her bicycle and waved goodbye to Will Shaw, who was getting on his motorcycle.

CHAPTER 25
THURSDAY, SEPTEMBER 18, 2025

Frank authorized the daily surveillance plan, putting his signature under Lt. Morgan's. He saw little avenue for objecting, even if this was bullshit. Putting drones over community gardens and the expanding farm terraces in the Bayview neighborhood rankled him. How were Janet and her friends in the League handling this?

"Robertson!" Frank was walking down the hall from the drone operations center when Col. Cronin hailed him from a side office.

"Yes sir?" Frank stood at attention.

"We lost three drones yesterday."

"Yes sir." They were briefed on it an hour ago.

"You know the City. Who do you think is behind this?"

"Sir? I didn't think there was any evidence indicating foul play brought those drones down."

"No evidence," Cronin grimaced. "I'd say three in one day is evidence enough of a concerted effort!" He glared at Robertson. "Aren't you here to help us penetrate the local forces?"

"Sir? When Lt. General Zapata sent us over here, he told me I was 'up'," (he used air quotes to make his point) "and that I was being sent to take over operations in San Francisco." He left the comment hanging in the air.

Cronin growled while shuffling papers on his desk, "and your point is?"

"I was not 'UP'. You and Morgan are running the show here."

"That's right. And nothing you've said or done has given me any reason to think that we made a mistake in keeping you on a short leash."

What a racist prick! Frank stood stoically, pondering his options.

"You can loosen that leash by getting us some actionable intelligence!" Cronin stood up suddenly. "Robertson, you know San Francisco better than any of us. Don't play coy with me. I know you can find out who is organizing against us."

"Sir, you are mistaken. I worked in a different San Francisco. I was a regular cop at UCSF for almost 25 years, and a San Francisco police officer for a decade before that. We never had a military government, never had ICE troops patrolling the city, rounding people up, *killing people*. I was here at the Massacre. After I got drafted in February I've been out of the city more than in, and I have no idea where the opposition has come from. I read the reports. Frankly, *your troops* are driving people into whatever resistance they're part of. I don't recognize my own city!" His emphasis on 'your troops' hit the mark.

Cronin scowled angrily and waved his hand. "You're lying! Get me something Robertson. Figure out who took down these drones. If you're on our side, prove it! Dismissed!"

"Yes sir," and Frank left, his heart pounding in his chest. The facade dropped now. They never trusted him, regardless of what Zapata said. He felt trapped. In his office, he called his aide, Corporal Flores, who appeared at his door.

"Corporal, we have to pay a visit to these two locations where the drones came down," and he thrust a document at him. "Please arrange a car, and NOT one of those damn Hummers!" Frank ordered.

"Yes sir. Do you want me to bring anyone else?" Flores asked.

"No, we can handle this."

A half hour later, Flores was driving Frank down 3rd Street, past the Giants stadium, through Mission Bay. Frank looked at his old patrol route with sadness, missing the simplicity of that time—less than a year ago! He shook his head, marveling at how radically everything changed.

"Flores, where are you from?"

"I'm from here, sir. I grew up on the back side of Bernal."

"No shit! What high school did you go to?"

"I went to Mission High, class of '18."

"Your family? What do they do?"

"My family came from El Salvador in the '90s. My father worked in construction, but he had a drinking problem. He smashed his foot on the job, and then he met my mother when he was in the hospital. She helped him find God. He became a Pentecostal preacher and they have their own church now. It's in a storefront on Mission near St. Mary's Pub. They're doing great! My little brothers Mike and Javier are still home."

"You belong to their church?"

"No, I grew up in it. But in high school, I stopped going. My dad is still angry with me, but now that I'm in the Army, he's less upset."

"Army? I thought you were Homeland Security... or National Guard?"

"No, I'm US Army, on loan to the Emergency authorities in the Bay Area. I volunteered when they asked."

"I had no idea. How many of you are there?"

Flores looked at Frank, surprised at his surprise. "Thousands? I'm not sure. But a lot."

"Here we are," Frank indicated the gate to Alemany Farm. They pulled into the tiny parking area, their Ford sedan the only vehicle. They got out and looked around. No one seemed to be there. But then one person came ambling towards them from the orchard up the hill.

"You looking for someone?" asked the woman. She peered at them through thick glasses, looking every bit the farmer in her blue overalls, her gray hair pulled back into a long ponytail with a red bandana holding it in place.

"Is Janet around?" Frank asked nervously. He didn't want to meet his niece in his official capacity.

"No, she's not. Can I help you? I'm AnnaLisa."

"I understand that Homeland Security drones crashed here yesterday. Do you know anything about that?"

"I wasn't here. But I heard the crows did it," she beamed.

"Who are the Crows?" Frank asked, assuming she was referring to a gang or a club.

She gestured to the trees. "The crows... those guys, up there, see 'em?" she pointed to a dozen crows lounging in the Eucalyptus trees near the path up the hill.

Frank and Flores exchanged looks. "You expect us to believe that crows attacked drones and caused them to crash?" Frank tried to sound authoritative.

AnnaLisa grabbed a rake and begun to work a compost pile a short distance from their car. Over her shoulder she said, "I don't care if you believe it or not. You asked me if I knew anything. I told you what I know," and she went silent, continuing to rake.

Frank was sure she was bullshitting them. But he didn't have it in him to bully her, and anyway, what good would that do? "Well, please tell Janet that her uncle Frank stopped by," he said.

AnnaLisa froze in her tracks and turned around. "You are Janet's uncle? And you're with Homeland Security?" which was obvious from his uniform.

Frank nodded. "Thanks for your help," and he and Flores drove on.

They were arriving at the Palou Terrace when Frank's phone rang. It was his sister Linda. "Give me a sec," he said to Flores. "It's family."

"Frank? Where are you? Moms has passed!" Linda sobbed loudly, while Frank clutched the phone breathing heavily. "You there Frank?" she said through her tears.

"Yeah, yeah," he sighed deeply. "I'm coming." He slumped as he hung up the phone and put his face into his hands.

"Lieutenant? You ok?" Flores queried him.

He raised his tear-stained face to the corporal. "My moms died. I need to go there right now."

Flores quickly got back in the car. "Where is it? I'll drive us there."

It was only about a mile further east along Palou. They wound through the residential streets on the ridge above the shipyard to the house on Marlin. Frank stumbled into the house, disoriented and distraught. His sister Linda and her partner Rhonda were already there, as were Lamar and Leon. A minute later, a MUNI self-driver pulled up outside and Aaron and Greg came out, holding hands, and joined them. The siblings rushed into hugs, crying loudly or softly, realizing that their mother's 102 years finally came to the long-anticipated end. They took turns going upstairs to sit with the body and have a last moment.

Lamar and Leon, grim-faced, watched as the earlier generation processed the loss of their grandmother. They were expecting her to die for years, most of their lives in fact. Her final passage was not jarring to them. It was sad, sure. She was an amazing woman. But she'd made it to 102, and most of that time she'd remained cheerful and engaging, if rather deaf in the last decade. Lamar pulled out some candles and placed them on shelves and surfaces around the living room. Leon went to the kitchen to whip up some lemonade for everyone.

"Linda, have you called an ambulance or the mortuary?" Lamar asked her. She shook her head, no.

"We can do it later," she said in a muffled voice. Rhonda had her arm over her partner's shoulder and gave Lamar a "look" that he should not push it at this moment.

Next to arrive were Janet and Vero, also in a MUNI autonomous vehicle. Janet's tear-stained face gave away her grief, while Vero, a life-long family friend, had that controlled dark visage that people tried to hold in moments like this. Sad and stern at the same time.

Linda gave Janet a big hug. "Did you reach your mom? Is she coming?"

Linda called Amelia right away along with the rest of her brothers and sisters but hadn't reached her.

Janet nodded, her eyes welling with tears. "She's on the way, my dad too."

Frank came down the stairs and into the living room, joining the new arrivals. He was wearing his uniform and looked strangely out of place. "Oh, hey," and he waved softly to the others. He sank glumly into a big chair in the corner.

Leon appeared with a tray of lemonades. "Hey Frank, wanna drink?" Frank accepted it gratefully, looking at his son from an imperceptible distance and mumbled, "Thanks."

Amelia and Jimmy arrived with a big box of pastries. She burst into tears and clutched her older sister. "Oh God, I didn't think this day would ever come!"

Jimmy Pierce went over to his daughter and gave Janet a hug. She melted into her father's arms. It was times like this that the deepest family connections mattered the most.

Meanwhile Vero disappeared into the kitchen as soon as she saw Frank. She was still a fugitive! How had they forgotten that she couldn't be seen by Frank?

Lamar came in with the box of pastries Janet's parents brought. "Hungry?" he pointed at the box.

"Lamar!" Vero hissed in a loud whisper. "I can't hang out with Frank here! I'm still wanted!"

"Shit!" He thought fast and pushed her out the kitchen door into the backyard. "You know how to get to the hatch don't you?"

She nodded. "Here's the combo," and he wrote it on a slip of paper, pushing her towards the path into the marijuana gardens rolling down the hill. "Get in the hangar and wait. Either we'll come get you or send a signal." She wasted no time scurrying down the path.

Lamar returned to the wake. More and more people were showing up, neighbors and friends. The word was moving fast. More and more food was arriving too, and he found himself on kitchen duty, finding dishes, cutlery, getting things plated and moved out to the dining room table. He emptied the fridge of the bottles of beer, soda, and the sparkling apple cider that Grannie loved.

Linda came to see how it was going. Lamar asked her, "What about Harriet? Is she coming from Seattle? Cousin Miya is in Santa Cruz. Anyone call her yet?"

"I told her. She's calling her kids. She said she could get here tomorrow.

Not sure about the cousins."

"I know it's not the time, but we need to talk to Frank," Lamar said with a rising note of urgency.

"You mean the house? It's not his—"

"Well, yeah, that's gotta get figured out. But that's not what I was thinking. How can we find out where his sympathies lie?"

Janet burst through the door, pulling Frank by the hand. She nodded at Lamar and he followed them into the backyard. It looked a little ridiculous, cousin Janet in her farmer clothes pulling the uniformed officer through the kitchen. But they knew it was the moment. There were no other Homeland Security types here (Corporal Flores respectfully stayed outside in the car.)

"Frank!" Janet started. He looked dazed. "Frank! We need to talk. Can you?!?"

He felt numb, physically rubbery, and somehow everything seemed very far away. "Yeah, I guess so," he managed to say in a very soft voice.

"Look Frank. I don't know what your job is now. But you are my uncle. What the hell is going on? Drones over our gardens? Federal food rules? *Death squads?*" Janet was angry.

Lamar piped up. "We heard you were gonna oversee Homeland Security in San Francisco? Are you?"

Frank suddenly focused in, realizing where he was. "Whoa, whoa!" he put up his hands. "I'm not in charge of anything. They wanted my local black face to give them some cover," he shook his head in resignation. "There's a bunch of stuff going on. I don't understand most of it. And I can't talk about it either!" he pushed back. He didn't have to explain anything to his niece and nephew. "It's better if I don't tell you," he argued.

Janet and Lamar glared at him. She folded her arms and seemed to grow three inches taller. "You better! They've started a war on us! I trust that you don't support it!"

Lamar tried a different tack. "Frank, we have a lot at stake," implying the extensive marijuana business network Frank knew that he and his son ran. "Leon's been trying to figure out how to get the heat off our neighborhood. Hell, we didn't have nothin' to do with the Dog Patch or that helicopter! Maybe you can help us?"

The family ties tugged at Frank. The fear of Col. Cronin and his ultimatum lurked in his mind too. Maybe he could give and get, maybe they could make a deal? "I'm under a microscope. I don't have much authority, but I might be able to relieve some pressure. But I have to give them something, you know what I'm sayin'?"

"What? We're supposed to hand over someone we know? A friend?!" Janet was outraged. "What do you mean?"

Frank wiped the sweat from his head. He pulled at his collar, which was suddenly way too tight. He looked back and forth from Janet to Lamar, feeling a rising panic.

Janet had little sympathy for the mess Frank got himself into. But Lamar realized it was a unique opportunity. He didn't want to propose any "deal" under the duress they were facing. "Look Frank, we can't fix anything right now. Can we set up a way to meet privately later? Somewhere where we could speak freely? How can we reach you?"

Frank suddenly realized he'd been out for hours. Flores! He must still be in the car. Shit! He was scrambling, fear rising, "I gotta go. I'm on duty! Reach me through Sheila! I could meet you at her place!" Who knows how she'd feel about it? But it was all he could come up with in the moment. And he bolted through the house, saying goodbyes to everyone crowding his mother's home. "Sorry, sorry! I have to go, duty calls!" he said loudly. He rushed to the car where Flores was laconically scanning his phone for pictures of cute women on Instagram.

"You OK?" Flores asked him.

"Yeah, well no. But we've been out for hours. We gotta get back."

"Oh, I don't think anyone's paying that much attention," Flores tried to reassure him. So many people came and went every day from Pier 26, he couldn't imagine that any one officer's delay for his mother's sudden death would be a problem. "And besides, your mother died. I'm sorry sir. My condolences."

"Thank you, Corporal. I appreciate it." Frank sank into his seat and watched India Basin approach as they descended the hill to Hunter's Point Boulevard. Twenty-five minutes later they pulled into Pier 26, and he realized he didn't have much of a report to file. Crows? He could hardly write that!

CHAPTER 26
SATURDAY, SEPTEMBER 27, 2025

Juna could feel the weight of the buckets through the hard wooden pole on their shoulders. "How many people do this every day?!" they exclaimed. They stumbled briefly on the slope below the quarry road, a few ounces spilling from each bucket. Luckily for the little settlement west of Owl Canyon— they'd jokingly started calling it Quarrytown—a groundskeeper working in the Brisbane Industrial Park below them left a hose attached to the faucet in the warehouse closest to them. It was easy to fill containers with water at odd hours but trekking up the hill with it was not easy. Juna helped fetch water ever since they started coming regularly to the encampment.

"'Hewers of wood and drawers of water,'" what else could we be?" Angie joked the first time she showed Juna— or Juna as she called them since that first meeting—how to bring up the water. Two months later, Juna showed up every weekend, and often during the week. Angie gushed when they came teetering into camp with the buckets sloshing on the horizontal pole. "Juna, honey, you are a jewel. Thank you! Leave one bucket here and take the other up to the 'first floor' please?" Juna was no longer confused by the reference, indicating the first terrace in the old quarry. Angie made joke names for things, keeping a certain irreverent tone going. The seven people living here (along with a half dozen others who were in and out irregularly), were growing food and restoring the moonscape shelves left by the quarry—a serious effort.

Juna glowed with the effort and the appreciation. They never felt better than when they were here, lugging water, working in the rows of vegetables they were cultivating on the terraces. Billy Oakes was usually here on weekends too, putting his shoulder into moving logs, clearing large boulders, and helping "Quarrytown Acres" to flourish. "Hey Juna!" Billy called when they emerged at the edge of the terrace.

"Billy! You beat me up here again!" Juna smiled while putting down the bucket and bending backwards. "Carrying water is a great way to wreck your back!"

"Ah, you're young, nothing to worry about!" Billy joked. He was in his early 30s and guessed Juna was no more than 25.

"OK, old man," Juna needled back. "You can get the next load!" And they were soon weeding next to each other, catching up on the week.

"Janet's grannie died. Did you hear?" Billy asked, but Juna had not.

"Oh, that's Aaron's mom!" realizing the other Robertson they lived with was even more directly implicated. "And he's not been well lately either. He's over 70 himself. Shit. I oughtta bake him some cookies or make soup or something. Maybe a sachet of herbs?"

Billy nodded. "I wanted to ask you something."

"Sure, go ahead."

"They told me you had a negative reaction when you visited the secret cellar. Maria said you thought the biobulb was 'unhappy' or something like that... what happened? Do you mind telling me?"

"Um, sure, no I don't mind..." but they hesitated, obviously a bit uncomfortable. Taking a deep breath, Juna started in. "I was visiting the warehouse with Janet to see about a gardening job—that's what I thought. Then we met these biotech people, including Maria and that scientist... Ally?" Billy nodded. "And before I knew it Ally was sharing her big secret with me, who knows why. Anyway, we went to the secret cellar and I saw the biobulbs on the far wall."

Billy stopped weeding and looked at Juna curiously. "You didn't think that was cool, huh?"

"Well, sure, at first glance. But they told me to touch the bulbs, so I did. I felt like I'd touched an icy black shadow. It wasn't a temperature thing! It was a feeling of sadness and coldness at the same time." Juna stopped, reliving the experience for the first time in a while. "The poor plants, how can they live in that darkness?"

"Well, it's not dark most of the time. There's a state-of-the-art lighting system in there, plus climate control, humidifiers, the whole nine yards. The plants get everything they need, probably better than most plants above ground!" Billy worked for Large Larry for a decade in the pot business, and stayed on for the new projects. He was the main warehouse staff supporting Ally and Maria and Clara.

Billy looked thoughtful. "But how did you feel those feelings? Have you *felt* plants before?"

"Not exactly. But maybe. I don't know." Juna looked sad, shaking their head. "I often feel like I can communicate with birds," they offered. "I mean, not like with words, but they come close to me, they seem to talk to me."

"Oh yeah? What kind of birds?"

"Scrub jays most of the time. Sometimes crows or ravens. We had a lot of herons and egrets on our land out in the delta. And tons of redwing blackbirds of course. I used to spend hours along the levees at my uncle's farm watching herons. They got used to me and let me get close. But I never felt like I was talking with them, not like scrub jays."

Angie's head topped the edge of the terrace. "Hey there," she called cheerfully. "How's the lettuce coming along?"

"Looking good, Angie," Billy stood up. "Did you know Juna can talk to birds?"

"That right?" Angie looked sidelong at Juna, and they nodded. "You look sad. Billy been giving you a hard time?" she asked, knowing that Billy wouldn't do anything of the sort.

"Oh," Juna forced a smile. "I'm ok. We were talking about... a strange experience I had." And they went on to fill in Angie on the whole cellar and the biobulb bushes.

"Well, I'll be damned! What goldang thing are they gonna think up next? A biobulb?!?"

"You know about the Hempattery, right?" Billy asked her.

"What's that?"

And Billy gave a quick summary of the invention of electric batteries based on hemp plant cells. "Turns out hemp is a great conductor," he said. "I work for Larry Lansing—'Large Larry'—he used to be a big grower and pot dealer in the Bayview until he got a big payout when a nearby company he'd been helping got gobbled up by BioGenMo. Turns out he'd negotiated a cut of the business and when that cashed out, he gave his pot business to the dudes I'd been working with. I could've had a piece of that too, or he said I could stick with him, and he'd give me a big salary and full benefits guaranteed for 10 years. I decided I liked the security. We know each other well and it's a good gig for me."

Angie Werdon lived on San Bruno Mountain for years. It was a lot longer since she'd had anything approaching a normal life in a regular house with a roof and a bed. "Well, that explains your ongoing generosity!" she smiled, I'm glad to know you're set! We're on the cusp of feeling that way here too!"

Billy and Juna both wondered what she could mean. Quarrytown was a collection of shacks, and the folks living here, while no longer exactly homeless, were as poor as anyone in this extremely polarized urban area. The terrace gardens were coming along, but how much food could they grow here? Not enough to live on. Billy brought a huge backpack stuffed with dried goods and treats every week. Juna brought as much as they could carry on their bicycle too. The cupboards were never bare in Quarrytown. Other regulars had their own ways of acquiring food from the surrounding abundance—whether through dumpster-diving, shoplifting, or occasionally slipping into someone's unlocked backdoor and pilfering from their cabinets or even their fridge. They were doing well, all in all!

"And the birds?" Angie turned back to Juna.

"They talk to me," Juna said. "I don't always understand what they're trying to say, but scrub jays and ravens and crows come up to me, sometimes cawing loudly, sometimes making odd noises from the back of their throats—at least that's how it sounds."

"What do you think is happening when they do that?" Angie asked.

"Usually I've been sitting quietly, watching. They understand that I'm their friend. That I'm interested, I'm curious, I'm listening. Sometimes they bring me things, little shiny objects they've found, plastic toy pieces, weird junk."

Billy was crunching on a bag of snacks and held it up to them. They each grabbed chips and began munching.

"Whaddya think of these chips?" he asked them while swallowing a mouthful.

"They're good!" Angie said, reaching for more. "They're buttery, but also have that sweet/sour thing... What'd they used to say, "you can't eat just one?""

A pair of scrub jays began loudly cawing at the edge of the garden under gnarled oak trees.

"Hey there," called Juna, who moved towards them slowly. "You want a chip too?" The brilliant blue jays hopped closer. Juna tossed a few of the chips to the birds. "You joined us for lunch, eh?" Juna chuckled while tossing a few more chips to the jays. One of the birds looked up at Juna and suddenly tilted its head from side to side. "Caw, caw," and Juna smiled. "You're welcome!" they said.

Billy then said, "these chips are a recent invention, too. Our friend Vero has been working in the kitchen, inventing recipes to make from this fungus. It's called witches butter, but it's gone through some serious alterations over the past year." He went on to explain briefly how Ally the scientist wrote up some ideas about how this wild fungus could be turned into something that could be used as a building material. It was leaked from the BGM labs to a biohacker lab in San Francisco, and after some months it turned up at one of the indoor grow ops as a big vat of gray putty. No one knew how exactly it could be shaped to their needs at that point, but regulars, including Janet and Vero, massaged and kneaded it, and talked to it. The color had gradually changed to a light cream-color.

"They experimented with themselves. They wrapped it around their wrists. They began cooking with it and eating it. They sent batches to a local garden and another indoor farm to see what might happen. At Alemany Farm, one batch was treated with Intelligel® which turned it bright canary yellow. Some people, including Janet, thought they could speak with the crows! Was it because of the witches butter? The combination with Intelligel®? They couldn't make it happen again. But they did show the crows there how to take down drones with sticks! And the crows have taken down several drones in the past few weeks!"

Angie and Juna didn't know what to say. What a bizarre story! It sounded like crazy science fiction.

Juna realized they'd eaten this biotech invention. They felt nauseous. "Ugh, I wish you'd told us before you gave us those chips! I don't think I would've eaten them," Juna sat down on a boulder at the edge of the terrace.

Angie, who would eat almost everything with pleasure, her girth the ongoing proof of that, laughed and said, "They were delicious! I'd eat some more!"

and she reached out for the bag that Billy was about to put away. He handed it over.

"I'm sorry Juna," Billy apologized, "I didn't think it was an issue. We've been eating these chips for the last month, along with a bunch of other inventions, pasta, bread, and soups. Vero has become quite the inventive chef!" he explained. He pulled out a large block of witches butter. "Angie, I brought this for you. This is the stuff, this is witches butter now," and he offered her the block of cream-colored... putty? Clay? What was it now?

Angie thanked him and took it. "You can cook with this? How?"

Billy gave a small recipe booklet they'd worked up at the Hangar. "Here's some the ideas. But you can also cultivate it. If you put it in a shady area it sinks in to the soil and begins to grow. Janet said the batch they put on the ground at Alemany has grown a bit. But the amazing thing is, if you let it establish itself, it will grow slowly but if you 'harvest' it, that part grows back in a few hours."

"What?" Angie perked up at that. "Did you say it grows back right away when you take some to make food?"

"Um, yeah, apparently. That's what I heard," Billy explained.

She smiled, her eyes suddenly gazing into the distance. "Did you ever hear of a comic called 'Li'l Abner'?" Both Billy and Juna shook their heads. Juna looked pale and uncomfortable on the big rock. "It was in the papers when I was a little kid. It was about a family in a godforsaken place called "Dogpatch" (I think that's where the name started), but they had this pet or I'm not sure what it was exactly, but it was called a "schmoo" and it kept reproducing itself. It would happily throw itself into the pan to get cooked, and it was like a delicious roast. As soon as you ate it, another one would appear, and then another and another, forever. You could never go hungry when a schmoo was around. I always loved that idea!"

Billy smiled, "Oh that's what this is! It's not witches butter anymore, it's a schmoo!" They laughed, even Juna who was starting to feel a bit better.

Juna felt embarrassed by feeling nauseous when neither of the other two reacted that way. They were often sensitive to foods but maybe they were overreacting? Their stomach was flip-flopping uncomfortablywith the chips in there. But neither Billy nor Annie seemed bothered at all. They sighed. The jays finished the chips they tossed to them and flew away while they were talking. What would the chips do to the birds?

"Billy, how do you know eating the fungus is safe?" Juna suddenly asked.

"Safe? I don't know. We've been eating it for weeks and I haven't heard of anyone feeling bad. You're the first!" He smiled, as though this was an accomplishment. "But I suppose there could be some long-term effects. We don't know about that. Dat Doan's lab said the witches butter becomes protein- and vitamin-rich when cooked—a good reason to make it taste good. That's where Vero's magic in the kitchen came in." He turned to Angie. "It tastes great, no?" And she popped the last few chips into her mouth and nodded, grinning.

"You say this is good for us too?" she muttered through her mouthful.

"Yup," Billy nodded. "Some people might be allergic to it. Maybe there's negative long-term effects?"

"Y'know, I actually feel great! Since we started eating these chips, I am a little buzzed. You feel it Billy?"

"Hmmm. Well, I heard that when people kept it touching their skin for a while it got them a bit high. Like a warm surge of good feelings... that what you feel?"

She nodded thoughtfully. "Not sure. I feel like we're in this moment, you, Juna, me, the birds, the plants, the mountain..." and then she laughed heartily. "I guess I'm high! But I don't feel super buzzy or fuzzy or anything like that. Warm and content." Angie rose up from her perch on the log and extended her arms wide, her face upturned to the sun.

Juna watched and wondered if the flip-flopping in their stomach was the same thing. Maybe it felt different to different people. It didn't hurt, it was overwhelming. Juna also turned to the sun and grinned alongside Angie. It felt good to be here with trusted friends.

CHAPTER 27
MONDAY, SEPTEMBER 29, 2025

Jordan Lindsay and Jay Hartman were heading out to the same job, installing bathrooms in a 12-floor affordable housing complex going up south of Potrero Hill. "Well, another week begins," Jordan sounded depressed already. He preferred union politics to the drudgery of actually working. They finished their coffee and their breakfast dishes clattered into the dishwasher. Jay was heading to the bathroom when Jordan announced, "Hey, I'll meet you downtown. I have to go by Walgreens."

Jay spent a little longer than he expected to in the can, reading the news on his phone. As usual, the censorship left little but anodyne reports of a Bay Area returning to normalcy, albeit with a worrisome spike in violent crime, especially murders. Jay muttered, "these crime stats are such crap! ... fuckers!"

Meanwhile, Jordan exited the apartment onto Collingwood. He was skittish. He'd been warned that he might be on "the list," alluding to the people who were disappearing, or *being disappeared*. Given the rumors of death squads, he was on the lookout.

Sure enough, three big guys in tracksuits emerged from a gray sedan as he walked past. The driver, who he made eye contact with, had a big square head, gray eyes, a pock-marked face, and a gold cross dangling from his neck. The other two were big broad-shouldered guys, but Jordan didn't wait around to get a good look at them. He walked briskly, and then, realizing there was nobody else nearby, he gave up any pretense of remaining calm and began running towards 18th Street. He had his old CUAV whistle in his pocket and was blowing it loudly as he ran. The old alert system hadn't been much used in the past decade or longer. But there were still old-timers around who lived through the gay-bashing and AIDS periods, he hoped. He hit the corner, looking back to the see the three men moving deliberately towards him, though they weren't running. He had a good head start, maybe a quarter of a block.

He turned on 18th, surrounded by people making their way to start their days. He was blowing his whistle as he came around the corner and several people looked at him, wondering why this young man was running and whistling. He took a minute more to get to Walgreens and rushed in towards the pharmacy in the back of the store. He had a prescription to pick up, and he stood fidgeting, looking over his shoulder.

They came into the store! He bolted away into the aisles, trying to dodge them. The three men spread out and began moving up and down the aisles, slowly closing in on the corner where Jordan was. He saw no way out. He began blowing his whistle again. In Walgreens on a busy Monday morning, the whistle brought several men running towards the sound. The three big bruisers didn't know what was happening as suddenly a half dozen gay men and a few lesbians converged around and past them. Jordan was blowing for all he was worth.

"Hey man, you ok? What's happening?" asked a big guy, the first to arrive next to Jordan.

"They're coming for me!" he yelled, pointing at the three guys in tracksuits. "They're killers!" he screamed.

The hubbub at 7:50 am on a Monday morning overtook the entire store. Several clerks appeared in the aisle, trying to clear up whatever was causing the problem. The three men realized that their target was not alone and their own invisibility was compromised. Three or four of the responding citizens were busily shooting video and taking photos with their phones.

The main guy with the gold cross scowled and said "abort!" and in tight formation the three men, who looked like Russian thugs in their matching tracksuits, exited the store. Videos went viral for a half hour until they were blocked by the Homeland Security censors. But photos went further and kept popping up for days and weeks after, though clouded in the haze of rumor and fear.

Jordan couldn't believe he'd escaped. His heart was pounding as he sat down on a chair near the pharmacy.

"You think those guys were coming for you?" asked several of the people who gathered around.

He nodded, "I'm sure of it."

"Who the hell are they? And why you?" asked a muscle-bound woman, short cropped hair and a big tattoo of a black cat on her forearm.

"They were sitting in a car outside my place around the corner. Are they a hit squad? I don't know. Why me? I'm in the plumbers' union... I'm known because I was one of the rank-and-file leaders who helped take over the union a few months ago. I guess that might make me a target," he wiped his brow, and noticed that he was drenched with sweat. "I've got to go home and change. I was on my way to work and I'm soaked," he pulled at his shirt showing how wet it was.

"We'll go with you," the brawny woman and her friend, less bulky but powerful looking too.

"Thanks, I appreciate it. It's only a block and a half, on Collingwood."

The gray sedan was gone when they walked by, Jordan pointing to the spot. The women stopped as he walked up his steps. "You want us to wait?"

"I'll be ok! Thanks for walking me home. Don't hesitate if I can ever return the favor." He was shook as he entered the apartment, expecting the men to jump out from behind the furniture. Fifteen minutes later he calmed down and was re-showered and dressed and heading out the door. He paused on the stoop, looking carefully for any sign of danger. Seeing nothing unusual, he hurried to the Castro subway station. At Powell Street he walked through the underground passage to the T-line at Union Square and a half hour later he approached the construction site near 3rd and Evans. He looked furtively over his shoulder and scanned passing vehicles and the occasional pedestrian with an eagle eye.

He relaxed when he passed through the worksite gate. On the 8th floor he found Jay already rolling boxed toilets into each apartment, which were as yet without doors.

"What took you? MUNI?" Jay looked at him. "Weren't you wearing that Giants t-shirt today?"

Jordan explained why he'd changed.

"I can't believe they were right there on our block! Motherfuckers! We're gonna have to take some precautions."

"I better stay somewhere else for a while. Maybe you should too."

"Oh man, what a hassle!" Jay had little stomach for moving. He realized it could be easy to move for a bit. Janet or Leon had those warehouses and the Hangar. It was closer to work than where they lived. "I have some friends not far from here. They have places... Let me do some checkin', ok?"

***

Sheila stared out the window. The morning marine layer was thick, but her view across the bay was clear. Containers were being worked at the Port of Oakland, as usual. Several ships awaited their turn, berthed in the middle of the bay to the south. She could see ferries churning through the waves, one bound for the new Mission Rock dock south of the ballpark, the other on its way to the Ferry Building further north. The early summer heat waves had not re-emerged in the Bay Area, held in check by the thick fog thrown up by the cool ocean. But to the north and east fires were blazing in the mountains. Worse, the news from the Arctic was dire, with no sea ice left and mass thawing across Siberia and the Canadian tundra, releasing vast amounts of methane.

Killing heat took thousands of lives from the Middle East to South Asia during the early summer. It was the new normal. Rising deaths were being attributed to ongoing heat in Arizona, New Mexico, and Texas. The big cities in northern Mexico were also suffering under the withering heat, with unconfirmed reports that thousands died in Chihuahua and Hermosillo. The Homeland Security censors weren't suppressing international news—they didn't have to. The U.S. media was owned by three conglomerates who narrowed their world news coverage until there was nothing beyond the border. Sabre-rattling rhetoric continued to flow from President Hutchinson directed at China's steady military extension into the western Pacific. But actual war still seemed unthinkable, given how intertwined the two national economies were, competition notwithstanding.

Her TV droned in the background. The nattering hosts were going on about some celebrity scandal, acting like life was normal. Sheila knew better. She was in charge of procurement for the new Homeland Security base on the old Naval Shipyard at Hunter's Point. The base was supposed to have been fully converted to housing and offices by now, but after years of delays due to corrupt contractors, the land, barely above sea level, remained heavily contaminated by toxic and radioactive waste. Homeland Security's needs were deemed temporary. Long-term health issues were not considered. Most of the Navy's buildings were in a state of collapse, but a half dozen were stable enough to renovate. After several months of pouring in resources, the offices, motor pool, and detention center were nearly ready. She took satisfaction in accomplishing her assigned goals, but she felt the weight of it too. She saw they were building the physical infrastructure of a police state far more completely than anything before. She sighed and turned off the TV when it cut to a reporter in the suburbs featuring children splashing in a pool—more fake normalcy.

Ten minutes later she was on the elevator. "Have a great day Sheila!" said her upstairs neighbor while she tugged her children from the elevator. Sheila watched them go, trying to imagine what it would be like to have small children nowadays. 'What do you tell kids now?' she wondered as she began her short walk to the streetcar. A poster on a street pole caught her attention. Weird, who ever put anything on poles anymore, especially in Mission Bay?

DISAPPEARED!

Miguel Robles, beloved community member and long-time organizer with the Urban Peasants Alliance is missing. Anyone who has seen him since he disappeared last Thursday evening, please contact us.

It was signed by the UPA. Sheila shook her head. "Fuck," she muttered. Miguel was her building manager! She'd been hearing the rumors about people getting "disappeared"—death squads some said! Could this be that? She shuddered. It seemed too real, too likely.

She rode the streetcar to the Moscone Center. Every day she walked to work from here. It was only a few blocks and helped prepare her for work. That poster rattled her. She knew Miguel was a UPA organizer, but was that a crime? The UPA came through for a lot of the people in her building, with tech support, and supplemental food and medicine during the past years. Miguel was at the center of that network.

Ever more people lived along the alleys on her walk. She went into the street on Russ Alley to avoid the sidewalk clogged with sleeping people. Minna Street was packed with tents too when she turned west to Seventh, emerging a short distance from the Federal Building. Decades of pointless crackdowns and public promises by one politician after another, and there were more people living in the streets than ever. The martial law authorities were oblivious to the growing poverty.

Sheila waved her badge through two checkpoints to get to the lobby.

From her 18th floor office, she started by gazing at the big southerly view, like most days. Her phone rang immediately. Sighing, knowing there would be no breaks in this busy day ahead, she brushed her hair back from her face while answering.

"Sheila Downing, procurement," she said in her usual monotone.

"Sheila, it's Frank. Listen, I only have a minute. Can you host us tonight at your place? I need to hold a small family meeting."

"Um, well, I guess so." She didn't want to get caught up in anything. Why would they need to use *her* place? "What's going on? Why can't you guys meet at the house on Marlin? Or at a restaurant?"

"I don't have time to explain. Trust me, it's not a big deal."

"Well, ok, what time?"

"We'll be there at 7:30. Thanks Sheila, you're the best!" Frank hung up.

She sat there for a minute. This seemed off. It made no sense. Why did she have to be involved? If it was a family drama, she didn't want to be there. If it was something to do with Homeland Security... she wanted even *less* to do with it! Why had she agreed?

She turned to her computer and began plowing through her daily duties. It was a helpful and familiar distraction, even somewhat calming. In the back of her mind, she could feel her anxiety levels rising every time she thought about the coming evening.

***

Janet and Lamar and Leon were in Leon's office at the old HemptriCity warehouse on Underwood, trying to decide if they could trust Frank.

"He's your dad, what do *you* think?" Lamar put it to Leon.

"You know him almost as well as I do, and he likes you better," Leon bounced it to Janet.

She looked at her two cousins, shaking her head. "Frank's always been by the book as far as I know. He can be cool if there's any room for discretion," she was remembering how he let a UPA demo go on UCSF campus two years ago, but that seemed like a long time. "He might not have much room to move in his current position. He's a Lieutenant on the Executive Staff! We have to be very careful. It might not be possible to ask him directly—about anything!"

Her phone buzzed and she saw it was from Jay, a cherries emoji. That was their emergency code. "I got an urgent message. Let me step out and see if I can sort it out." And she went out to the sidewalk. She was trying to figure out how to respond when Jay and another guy came walking up.

"Janet! This is Jordan, my roomie and union brother. Can we go inside?" he looked spooked.

"Sure, sure, come on. What's up?" and she gave Jay a hug. "I didn't want to call or text. Let's turn off our phones," and they did, pulling batteries too. Her cousins knew Jay, notorious after the fight at the Dog Patch. Jay introduced Jordan, "from the plumber's union, we're both in the rank-and-file committee, y'know?" They knew. The Plumbers took on almost mythical status after the Islais Creek incident.

"Were you there man? At Islais Creek?" Leon asked them.

Jordan smiled sheephishly and nodded. "We both were," pushing Jay in the shoulder.

Jay smiled sheepishly. "I still can't believe we did it." He didn't elaborate or explain how he'd taken the Hummer with the weapons and uniforms and set it ablaze in front of the Federal Building at Seventh and Mission later that afternoon.

"Let me cut to the chase. We're here because we need to hide for a few days. The hitmen came today for Jordan, right outside our place in the Castro. It was lucky that he got away," Jay explained.

Jordan described the events that morning. "We're hoping you can stash us in one of your hidden places that Jay told me about," he said. "We're working on Newhall."

"You think you can go to work? Won't they look for you there?" Lamar reasonably asked.

"They came to our house. They want to find us where we are more isolated, not where we have a whole gang working with us. They weren't happy when everyone at Walgreens started filming them," Jordan elaborated. "If anything, they'll try again at our place."

"You can stay at the Hangar. We have bunkbeds there. It's a little dicier getting in and out of there since the construction on the shipyard started. But you can get in through the hatch," Lamar explained. "Janet or I can show you later."

"Can you describe these hitmen a bit more?" Janet asked. In the past week she'd noticed a car full of big men rolling by Alemany Farm. She'd seen a car park on Palou while she hid in the bushes at the top of the terrace. Two big guys walked into the playground below the terrace, not seeing anyone, and departed. Was she on the list too?

"Miguel Robles is missing. The UPA is putting signs around for him. It doesn't look good," she said, dejectedly.

"It's worse than we thought. We need Frank!" Leon blurted. "He's our best chance for an insider."

"OK, but Leon, let me do the talking?" Janet insisted. She briefly explained what they were talking about to Jay and Jordan. "Why don't you stay here tonight? Leon, you've got a guest room in that back closet right?" He nodded. "We'll get you set up in the Hangar tomorrow when you get back from work. If you want to bring clothes and whatever else—have a roommate bring it to you at work?" Jay and Jordan looked at each other, realizing how unprepared they were to go on the lam, even partway. "Andy'll do it. I'll text him later," Jordan said.

***

Corporal Flores rushed into the office that morning and closed the door behind him.

"Sir? I got this," and he handed a folded piece of paper across the desk. "I can't say how it came into my possession, but I believe it's the real deal," Flores had a sour expression. "I don't know what the higher-ups think they're doing, but this is fucked up," he confided unexpectedly.

Frank, making a mental note of a new familiarity with Flores, opened the list of names and cities. Scanning the list of unfamiliar names, he went to the San Francisco addresses. His pulse quickened and nausea hit him when he saw "Janet Pierce, Canopy Council, League of Urban Farmers, San Francisco" on the list. Other names weren't immediately familiar to him, but he saw there were plumbers union members, a half dozen farmers, people from the Urban Peasants Alliance, even some local politicians who were particularly pushy about the Homeland Security presence.

"A Hit List?" Frank spoke softly. Corporal Flores nodded grimly. "... Who else has this?"

"I don't know sir. I assume Cronin and Morgan are in the loop. I don't know who or where the ops people are. Probably not here on Pier 26. Maybe they're already at the shipyard?" Flores was a smart guy and dug around on his own, but there were limits to what he could do.

"Thank you, Corporal. I'll meet you at the motor pool in 15 minutes," and Flores got up and left. Frank immediately pulled out his personal phone and called Sheila at work. He wasted no time in putting it to her: "Can you host us tonight at your place?" She didn't want to, he could tell. She tried to beg off but he couldn't take no for an answer. "Trust me, it's not a big deal," he'd said, the opposite of what he was feeling, but he *had* to convince her. She relented and it was set for 7:30.

He sent text messages to Janet and Lamar later that day and they confirmed that they'd come. He was nervous but once he'd seen Janet on "the list" he had to see her.

***

Janet and Lamar rode to the building in Mission Bay. She'd been here once before, in a meeting with Miguel Robles and UPA organizers a year earlier. As they locked their bikes on a sidewalk rack, she saw the poster on a nearby pole. "**DISAPPEARED!** Miguel Robles, beloved community member..." Her heart sank and a cold feeling spread across her chest. She looked around, suddenly scared again.

Lamar took notice of the sign too, shaking his head. "Fuckers!"

They called up on the building intercom and Sheila buzzed them in. In a few minutes they entered her comfy 18th floor apartment with its big view across the twilight Bay Area. The late sun struck plate glass windows in the East Bay hills, setting them ablaze. Lamar pointed to them, "Last time I saw that I was in the third deck at a Giants game!"

Sheila provided tall lemonades, and they sat down to small talk while they waited for Frank. Janet asked her about work.

"Oh you know, same old same old. In the past month we fully supplied the new Hunter's Point base," Sheila explained.

Lamar perked up—he'd been watching the construction carefully, either from Grannie's house perched on Marlin Street, or from their "eyes" that they'd placed at strategic spots around the shipyard prior to the major construction. It gave them total surveillance over the whole area outside the Hangar. "It seems like a huge operation," he noted casually, sipping his lemonade.

"Oh yeah, it's several buildings and a major detention center. They're settling in there for a while, to tell the truth."

Lamar and Janet noted the information and nodded as though it was not something they were keenly attuned to. Janet prodded gently, "I heard that the National Emergency will be rescinded soon. Have you heard anything about that?"

Sheila heard those rumors too. "Yep, that's what some people are sayin', but who knows? I can't tell. If they do call it off, I don't think these Homeland Security troops are leaving. They'll simply use them differently."

"Oh? What do you mean?" Janet wanted to keep Sheila talking as much as possible.

"I heard in most of the other cities where they already ended the Emergency, they renamed the same Homeland Security and ICE officers—now they're the new Federal Police that the Hutchinson administration passed those bills for," Sheila explained.

"You must get more news than we're getting," Janet suggested. "Where did you hear about other cities? I haven't seen a thing in the local papers, on the internet, or on TV."

Sheila leaned forward, glad to tell her friends what she knew. "We get a GSA weekly bulletin. I didn't even notice that it wasn't in the main news feeds. I guess the Emergency censors are still working overtime to block news…" she averted her gaze, suddenly embarrassed to be a government employee.

The door—it was Frank, and Sheila buzzed him in. They shifted uncomfortably, wondering what Frank would bring.

Sheila walked in holding Frank's arm. He looked distraught, and his breath was short, as though he'd run up a bunch of stairs rather than gliding up in an elevator. Sheila patted him on his arm, "Calm down Frank. Here they are, like you asked." She paused for a moment while he stood awkwardly facing Janet and Lamar, the gray dusk falling over the big view behind them.

"Uuhhh," he stammered.

"I'm going for a little walk to the creek. I leave you to your conference," Sheila could feel the tension getting thicker by the second. They looked at her gratefully, each for their own reasons. Frank gave her a squeeze as she pulled away.

"I owe you one!" he promised.

He sank into the chair across from the other two. He looked morose.

"What is it Frank? Spill it!" Janet was losing patience.

He looked right at her and said, "You're on the list."

She knew what he meant right away. Lamar wasn't ready to leave any ambiguity, "What list?" he demanded.

Frank looked at him, a wave of shame crossing his face. "The list, the targets man. People who are supposed to be grabbed or killed, usually both." He put his face into his hands.

Neither Lamar nor Janet made a move to comfort him. Frank wore regular clothes, but they still saw him—correctly—as an officer of Homeland Security. They sat quietly.

"Frank, come on, get it together!" snapped Janet. "You weren't supposed to tell us, I'm sure, but I have to believe you're here to help," and he nodded.

Janet's talent for cutting to the chase and organizing to meet problems took over.

"Frank, I don't know what you've been through these past months. I know what my friends experienced at Camp Hayward before they escaped. I've heard from other people too." She paused. How much should she reveal to her uncle? They had to take a chance.

"You have to hide! These murderous bastards are serious!" Frank declared.

"I know they are! They tried to grab a friend last week! I saw them at the Farm the other day. Frank! We need YOU! We need an insider near the top, to give us a picture of what they know and what they're planning to do. Will you do it?"

Frank knew he was taking a huge risk coming to this meeting. But his loyalty to his niece forced his hand. And she was in front of him, demanding that he go much further. He was petrified. What if he was caught? How hard could it be for them to figure out that one of their targets was his niece?? What an impossible situation!

"I can't. I can't meet or talk to you! I shouldn't even be here. I wanted to warn you."

Janet waved the back of her hand dismissing him. "Frank, we are not alone, and if you help us, you will not be alone either. There are many people and many groups involved. No one knows everyone or has the whole picture."

Lamar sat back and watched his cousin take over, and his uncle, supposedly the new guy in charge of San Francisco's Homeland Security operations, hesitating in front of he He hadn't seen Frank outside of family gatherings. "Look Frank," he gave Janet a chance to gather her thoughts. "I can meet you. No one suspects me of anything, nor Leon for that matter. Surely you can meet your own son or nephew without raising suspicions?"

Frank appreciated the lifeline Lamar was throwing him. "Um, yeah, maybe that could work. We could meet at Marlin Street—we can set up a drop somewhere in the house so if anyone's there we don't have to say anything," Frank was already conspiring with them. It was a relief in a way, even if he was terrified of getting caught. Meeting at the Marlin Street house could work. After all, it would hardly be odd that a son has to visit his deceased mother's house regularly over the coming weeks to help tie up her estate and other loose ends with his siblings, right?

In his heart, he wanted to do something to thwart these racist motherfuckers who came storming into the Bay Area. He tried to find his way, but they lied and manipulated him. A lifetime of work in policing and bureaucracy trained him for obedience and automatic docility. But on the cusp of his postponed retirement, maybe this was his chance for a last laugh... or at least to help his family not get caught!

He turned to Janet and his tone changed. "I'll do it. I have to be incredibly careful. I can't meet you again. It'll have to be Lamar or Leon, or maybe Linda or Amelia—are they involved?" Janet vaguely shook her head and put her hand out and tipped it back and forth as if to say "sort of." "Well, ok, Lamar and Leon then," Frank determined. "I'll try to get 'the list' and give it to you as soon as I can." And at that he pulled out a paper from his pocket and handed it over to Janet. "Here's the one I got today. I'll see if I can get future ones. I will let you know anything that seems useful when I can," he promised.

CHAPTER 28
WEDNESDAY OCTOBER 8, 2025

Janet was on her knees on the slopes of the Palou Terrace when she heard the tell-tale sound of Luis Hernandez's bumpin' sedan with its unmuffled engine roar. She stood, hands on her hips, looking nervously downhill. He waved up to her and she returned it, sighing to herself, "I hope he's ready."

It was a rough week. Jay and his buddy Jordan showed up at Leon's warehouse after their escape from what might have been a hit squad. That was scary enough. Remembering the dudes who pulled up at Alemany a few days ago sent a shiver up her spine, realizing she was probably a target too. And then meeting Frank at Sheila's Monday night, and him confirming it! She replayed the evening in her mind, her hands back in the soil, humming absent-mindedly while awaiting Luis to climb the hill.

Luis arrived near the top of the Palou Terrace and waved down the row, some 30 feet to where Janet was on her knees weeding. He paused to catch his breath. In his late 50s now, he didn't often walk up any hills if he could help it. She got up and shook debris and soil from her hands. She walked over smiling. "How's the ride?"

"Oh you know. A black hole for money, but she's my baby," Luis smiled back. He loved his car more than anything. He ran his hand through his slick black hair and tugged at his XXL t-shirt, which clung to his expansive belly.

They walked together to a shady patch under some low pear trees and sat down. "Luis, I hafta be real careful. There's a hit squad looking for me," Janet peered into his face.

He looked back at her unbelieving. "Wha? What are you talking about?" And she explained about the disappearances and the known deaths over the past month. "You haven't heard about this?" He shook his head, still in disbelief. "What did you think the National Emergency was about?" Janet prodded him.

"I don't know nothin' about this!" Luis protested.

"You voted for Hutchinson and Martinez didn't you? Weren't you out there campaigning for them?" Janet hadn't forgotten. "Because they promised to protect cars and gas and all that, right?"

He nodded sheepishly. It sounded crazy in retrospect.

"You heard about their food mandates? Garden produce either goes to the government or we pay huge taxes on it? We have to buy government-designated products with high corn and soy content? Bet you didn't know they'd do that huh?!" Janet couldn't help herself.

Luis put up his hands. "You *know* me," he looked for her acceptance but she stared at him. "I might've made a mistake—OK, I DID make a mistake. These guys are assholes, even worse than war-mongering Biden and the people he had in there. But I don't support this stuff. Turn crops over to the government? That's bullshit!" He was chewing a long blade of dry yellow grass and looked at the downtown skyline looming far north of Potrero Hill which filled the near view. "I still love community gardens!"

"Look Luis. You remember the Mission Food Hub during the pandemic?"

"Of course I do! I volunteered there for almost two years!"

"We need a new one—"

He cut her off. "Oh, we're already on it! We've been going since the Emergency. You know we have our own farms!"

"But this one has to be more like the old food conspiracies from the 1970s," she continued. "You remember that story?" and he nodded. "People have already been growing in backyards and sharing with family and neighbors—but we have to reach more people. We are building secret food hubs to distribute the backyard crops and the farm and garden crops before ICE claims it. We have to feed people! Have you noticed that there's less and less fresh produce making it into San Francisco this summer? Usually we have huge farmers markets full of fresh vegetables, stone fruits, berries, everything. But farms are drying up out there. And the government is taking everything they can get their hands on. Not too many farmers drive their crops to markets here anymore.

"We have some farmer friends down the coast. They're sitting on big crops of tomatoes, squash, artichokes, brussel sprouts, lettuce, and berries. They're in the hills between Half Moon Bay and the Santa Cruz mountains. The government has so far overlooked them. You think you could get a small caravan to go down and make a pick-up? You have the cars and the gas—right? You think your homies would be up for it? Whaddya say?"

Luis looked at Janet and nodded his head. "Hell yes! We have trucks too!" He gave her a big hug. "Everyone's been so frustrated. To be honest, a lot of the guys feel like they got played. There's a lot of 'em who'd want to do this. Let me start some conversations. How shall I get in touch? You hiding?"

Janet explained her plans, which mostly involved never sleeping in the same place more than a night or two. "I can still farm, I can still organize. I know this city better than they do. They can't find me and if they do, I can get away!" she looked at Luis mischievously. "Also, I got friends in high places," and she pointed to a half dozen crows hanging out in the big tree at the edge of the farm.

Luis looked at the crows and laughed. "Whatever you say!" They made plans to meet up in a few days. "This is what people have been waiting for!"

— PART 2 —

CHAPTER 29
Tuesday, October 21, 2025

Janet pedaled hard downhill towards Larry's warehouse. Police were everywhere. She had to stay hidden so she biked on low-traffic side streets, turning whenever she saw a Hummer or Jeep ahead.

The National Emergency was lifted on Monday, October 13, but it was a semantic rather than a substantive change. As Sheila had hinted, the Homeland Security and ICE troops were renamed the Federal Police. The white Hummers and Jeeps and other buses and trucks had new insignia. Uniforms suddenly changed too. Most officers on patrol were wearing the new black uniforms with gold trim, but when they sent out teams to handle demonstrations or raids, their armored suits were pale blue instead of black. The new Federal Police were "rebranded!"

People were still being politically imprisoned, but he hit teams appeared to have been were withdrawn. No further sightings happened, and nobody knew anyone who disappeared suspiciously since Miguel went missing in late September. He never turned up and everyone assumed the worst.

Frank was now an officer of the Federal Police and worked out of the new base at the Naval Shipyard on Crisp Avenue. After his mother's big funeral in mid-September, he'd discussed the house on Marlin with his siblings. They came to an agreement that Lamar and Leon and Janet would co-own it, and that Frank could move back in if he wanted to.

***

Linda and Aaron spoke to Frank privately a few days after Grannie's funeral.

"Frank, I heard from Lamar that you have an understanding, is that right?" Linda put it to him directly.

"Yeah, you know about that?" Frank was briefly surprised. Linda always knew what was going on. And everyone trusted her. She was the eldest and with the passing of their mother, she naturally took on the matriarchal role.

Linda nodded towards Aaron, her younger brother who was over 70 himself. "You wanna say something?"

"Frank. We had our scuffles over the years. I heard from the kids that you could help us, help everyone... Is that right?" He wanted to hear Frank say it himself.

Frank looked back and forth between his older brother and sister. He reached for his sore neck. His body ached. "I don't know how I ended up in this situation. At first I thought I was in trouble, getting drafted at my age... and the Dolores Park massacre! Then I was being pushed forward—on a fast track! When I got back here, the bubble popped. It was a lie. The same old bastards who always run things were in charge here too, and they weren't letting someone like me tell 'em what to do. When I saw Janet's name on the hit list, something finally broke. I was so afraid she'd be killed!" His siblings looked at him intently. "When I tried to warn her, she and Lamar made me promise to help." He could feel the dam breaking now. This was his family! "I agreed to bring useful information to them. The Marlin Street house is our drop. I've being transferred to the new Federal Police. Soon we'll be operating from the shipyard—our own damn backyard!"

A month later, Frank moved back in to his old room. Linda came by regularly to bring food for him, and Lamar and Leon were in and out all the time, ostensibly to take care of their crops in the gully. Frank never ventured beyond the backyard and had no clue about the Hangar or its secret entrance. In casual conversation with Lamar he described the policies and plans that he thought might impact the farms and gardens.

***

The bureaucracy was being reshuffled again. Lt. General Zapata was kicked up to regional director of Homeland Security for the western United States. Cronin went with him, and Lt. Morgan, who Frank was supposedly replacing when Zapata originally sent him back to San Francisco, was promoted to Colonel and was his immediate superior in the newly constituted Federal Police at the San Francisco Shipyard. Frank remained a First Lieutenant on the command staff with responsibility for Zone 9 of the city. His aide, Corporal Flores, was granted an early honorable discharge from the Army to join the Federal Police (over ten thousand soldiers were discharged to staff the new agency, alongside thousands of former employees of Homeland Security). He and Frank trusted each other.

The Federal Police command staff gathered in the new office at the top of their headquarters on the shipyard. Through the window they had a clear view of the old HP crane in the distance. Frank gazed at it, childhood memories of running around on the hill filling his mind. Morgan's voice crashed through his reverie.

"We are turning a new page. It's not an emergency anymore. The local police will have to get used to us. Our authority is federal, but we want to work cooperatively whenever we can. To that effect, I want each of you with responsibility for a city zone to meet with the SFPD captains in your area as soon as you can. Call them here to a meeting in our conference room." Several groans echoed around the room. "Or you can go visit each precinct—whatever you prefer... We are returning to a version of civilian life but make no mistake, we still have powers that no one has wielded in American cities before that we'll use strategically. We are still the most important law enforcement arm of the national security food laws. We are responsible for inspection of gardens, urban farms, and collection of crops and taxes, and detection and detention of eco-terrorists."

Frank was fully awake now to the deep purpose of the laws to create food insecurity and gain control over civilians through regulated food distribution. Morgan was a Stanford graduate. He was sure he knew everything there was to know, even in this unprecedented situation. 'No way he's ever done any real police work,' thought Frank to himself. On the plus side, he figured his retirement was back on. He only had nine months to go until he turned 65 next summer. At the end of the meeting Flores told him, "They definitely pulled out those special ops guys." The dark murder campaign was over, at least for now. He breathed a sigh of relief when he heard it. Janet would be ok.

***

It was weeks since Janet heard that Frank said the hit squads had been withdrawn. The new Federal Police were rolling through town, but they rarely stopped. The SFPD was back on patrol, and they were the bigger issue for a lot of their friends now. Bicyclists, car drivers, double parkers, noise makers, any typical city behavior that once went unnoticed was an excuse for harassment from cops who suddenly felt like they had more power than ever before thanks to the military occupation. Janet was glad to hear there weren't death squads looking for her anymore, but she might still be on a list. She kept riding evasively, just in case. Given the recent harassment for bicycling normally, she had additional motivation to avoid cops.

She made it to Larry's and darted in the front door, practically throwing her bike onto the rack in the foyer. In the pungent greenhouse, fresh soil, wet humidity, and the sharp smells of dozens of growing plants drowned her senses. She shook her head, immediately pleased and refreshed at the tangible life pulsing through the air, a bit surprised at how strongly everything smelled. "Hi everyone!" she greeted the plants, waving her hands at full wingspan, touching the plants as she walked briskly through them. She came to Larry's usual niche and sure enough, he was there. "Yo big fella!"

"Hey Janet," and he swung his massive legs from the hammock, putting some printout he was reading on the ground. "Reading about jellyfish. You ever tried 'em?" She shook her head. "They say there's bigger and bigger 'blooms' of them every year. I wonder if we can catch enough to use 'em for food?"

"You're always on it, Larry," she said with real admiration. "I wanted to talk to you and everyone about the witches butter. We should give it to anyone who wants some!"

Larry's eyebrows rose and he tilted his head. "Are we ready? Is *it* ready?"

Billy Oakes appeared from down the aisle pushing a wheelbarrow. "Did I hear you say you want to hand out the witches butter?" She nodded. "I brought a batch down to my friends at Quarrytown—it's a small place on San Bruno Mountain where some folks without regular houses have been growing food and making a home. I helped them plant one of those 18" blocks we cut out back in the beginning of summer."

Janet was eager to hear what he had to say and leaned forward intently.

"My pal Angie is the godmother down there. I brought Vero's concoctions down too, and Angie took it up. She's been experimenting with various dishes too. But you know what? That block is still there, no smaller than when we brought it. In fact, it's grown a bit," and he grinned, pausing for effect. "Angie heard you'd been singing and talking to it, kneading it, all that. She came up with her own way of talking to it I guess."

"C'mon! C'mon! Get to it, man!" Janet knew something was coming.

"They have a house! Wasn't it originally supposed to be a building material that you could shape into whatever you wanted? Well... she did it! You have to come and see!"

"What the fuck? A house? How could it be? What does it look like?" Janet was beside herself with excitement. Larry sat there taking it in, his big arms folded over his huge frame, smiling his big smile.

"Angie said it was like a gingerbread house. You could take a bite out of it, but it grows right back in an hour or two! You have to see it."

Alison walked into the circle that moment.

"Ally, did you hear Billy's story? About the witches butter and the house?" Janet burbled.

She nodded. "I was heading this way and stopped back there to listen. I didn't want to interrupt." She turned to Billy. "When can we go down there?"

"I usually go on Saturdays, but I'm sure we could go tomorrow or Thursday. They're off the grid entirely. I'll go and ask 'em, ok? They don't get many visitors."

***

Cindy was making her rounds at the SPCA "hotel" on Florida Street. They hired her immediately when they learned she was a vet with years of experience in the public animal shelter in Phoenix. They didn't ask her why she left, they were thrilled to get a new vet when they needed one.

She was in a room with a half dozen dogs and rubbing the belly of a mut of some sort when Juna went by outside the glass. They knocked on the window, and Cindy smiled to see them. In the hallway they hugged.

"How're you doin'?" Juna asked.

"Oh, great! I'm back in my element again. And these folks are even more committed to finding animals homes than they were in Phoenix."

"I was wondering why you left... was it because you didn't like the place you worked?"

"No, actually..." and Cindy took Juna by the arm and dragged them back into the room with the dogs and closed the door. "I haven't been telling people about this, but I trust you. They were coming for me. I got death threats."

Juna looked shocked. "Wha—Why?"

"I was a plaintiff in the suit against the Arizona Legislature that challenged the invalidation of the votes in the presidential election. The crazies targeted me as soon as my name got out there. I went on the lam a day after the threats started pouring in. It was obvious that the suit was going nowhere and staying there was too high risk."

Juna whistled, "Wow... and how did you end up in San Francisco?"

Cindy explained her journey to the Bay Area, landing with a cousin in Oakland who hustled her into San Francisco. "It was Janet that came and got me. We got a ride across the bay on a small boat."

"Janet? How is that the Robertsons are always in the middle of everything?" Juna shook their head.

"Yeah, it's crazy. I've been hanging out with Lamar," she paused, "well, it's more than hanging out now," and she grinned conspiratorially. "He told me about coming to San Francisco and all of a sudden being surrounded by cousins and aunts and uncles who he'd only known distantly while growing up in the suburbs." They chatted for another minute and then Cindy pulled out a few of Vero's chips and fed them to the dogs, who jumped around with tails wagging, happy and enthusiastic.

"Are those what I think those are?" Juna asked.

"Vero's? Made from witches butter? Yes," Cindy ate one herself, and offered the bag to Juna.

Juna took the bag and ate some chips. "I felt very weird the first time I ate this. I was down at Quarrytown—like getting high from marijuana but much clearer mentally. Everything looked sharp, colors brighter, smells stronger, sounds crystal clear—it had an effect. Since then, I've eaten them often. I haven't had the same intensity again that I had that first time, but the smell! My nose is way more sensitive. What about you? Has it made you feel any different?"

Cindy led Juna from the room with the dogs and they made their way down the hall to a picnic area in an interior courtyard. On the way, she grabbed a bin of salad she had in the fridge and offered Juna a plate as they sat down. "I haven't felt anything that noticeable—although now that you mention smelling things more, yeah. I have noticed that lately, too. I had one of Vero's pastas when I stayed in Bayview where I met the whole gang at Larry's."

"Larry's? I went there with Janet—" Juna stopped abruptly. What to say about that awful visit where he'd been taken into that dark dungeon and 'met' the biobulb? Their expression gave away their dismay.

"What is it?" Cindy didn't expect anything since she'd been welcomed by the community of people at the linked spaces in Bayview.

Juna told Cindy about the scientist, Ally, inviting Juna to enter the secret cellar, and encouraged them to approach the biobulb plants. Juna saw that Cindy was paying close attention. Her long black hair fell in perfect symmetry on either side of her pretty face as she slowly ate salad while Juna told their story. "I had no idea what hit me. I didn't have any expectations."

Cindy took it in. "You know she's the same woman who theorized about the witches butter being a good candidate for genetic manipulation?"

Juna shook their head, "no, I didn't know that. I heard it was made at this biohacker lab, before they brought it over to Leon's where I saw it first."

"And Vero's been doing her culinary experiments with it in the secret cellar's kitchen," continued Cindy. "It doesn't matter. I thought you'd like to know that there's a connection here. I never trusted genetic manipulation. I still don't feel at ease with it. It's punching holes in the fabric of life. But then here's this stuff, this witches butter. What is it really? I wish there was more research available. We only have some quick studies that Dat Doan's been able to do in his lab."

"You think it's dangerous?"

"No. People have been working with it, touching it, even eating it, for several months already. If it was immediately dangerous we'd know. That's not to say that there might not be long-term effects, but it's hard to imagine what they would be. I've been noticing stronger smells lately, too. It *is* organic, it *is* alive. It's not like a cancer-causing petrochemical derived from hydrocarbons that never biodegrades. And those are still being released into the air and water by the ton every year. So 'dangerous' is a relative concept. That's not to say that there couldn't be some ailment that contact with witches butter might cause down the road. We won't know until we know," Cindy sat back, sighing.

She'd been around these conversations many times in her life. She'd spent much of her life learning animal medicine and was deeply immersed in science and its way of framing the world. But in her everyday interactions with horses, cattle, sheep, and pigs as a large animal vet, or the dogs, cats, rabbits, gerbils, hamsters, and other urban pets that mostly dominated her practice as a veterinarian, there was always something beyond the science. There was the intangible connection that she often felt, an ineffable sense that was somewhere beyond language and beyond the reductionistic observations of medical science.

"I like that it's organic and alive," agreed Juna. "And I guess the nutritional content gets better when you cook it—right?" Cindy nodded. Juna suddenly grinned, "Wait til you see what else it does!"

"What do you mean?"

"Angie, my friend and mentor down at Quarrytown, she's figured out how to grow it into a house! A gingerbread house!"

"What?!? Can I see it?" Cindy laughed at the thought. "Just when you think you've got something almost figured out, it changes again!"

"Come with me this Saturday! I go every weekend, and it's an amazing place. They have a seed bank that I've been helping with—and learning from. My friend Angie asked it to grow into a small house," Juna chuckled now. "Well, it did!"

CHAPTER 30
SATURDAY, NOVEMBER 8, 2025

Angie Werdon was up since a little after dawn. Another blazingly hot day. The skies were hazy with smoke drifting in from fires in the central part of the state, but nothing like that "Red Sky Day" in September 2020 when it felt like the sun never fully came up!

She woke inside of the first "butter hut," which was about 8 x 12 feet, bigger than the wooden lean-to she'd been sleeping in for more than a year before that. After Billy left her a block of witches butter at the end of July, she'd been cooking it and it always grew back within an hour or two. But a few weeks ago she decided to try something different. Billy explained that the witches butter fungus was supposed to be a malleable building material when its genetic manipulation was first imagined. What could she do with it?

She divided the block in half and took one half of it to a clearing next to her wooden lean-to. "Let's see what we can do together," Angie said to the block of putty.

She'd been eating it every day for about ten days at this point. Her daily interactions with the birds and bees and rabbits and field mice and other animals became... what? *Busier...* there were more interactions than ever before. She talked to birds and small animals throughout the day. She was singing more too, a wordless deep sonorous vibration that kept bursting out of her. One time a half dozen crows landed nearby while she was singing. Another time it was a flock of pigeons who hung around coo-ing loudly for an unusually long 15 minutes. Angie tried to explain it to Marco and LaDonna, who lived in the treehouse up in Owl Canyon.

"This stuff is powerful. I don't think anyone knows what's happening. The biohackers and the scientists think it's a building material, but there's a story that some urban farmers were talking to crows—and even showed them how to take down drones. And it worked!"

LaDonna was skeptical. She was finishing a bowl of pasta at the campfire and scowled at Angie. "You believe that?!?" she snorted derisively. "Sounds like bullshit to me!" Marco, who was generally a very quiet guy, nodded into his bowl.

"You're eatin' it right now!" Angie laughed, hands on her hips. "I've been eatin' it for the past few days, making different dishes with it. It grows back as fast as you can eat it!"

"What? What are you talking about?" LaDonna thought Angie was starting to lose it. She'd always been at the edge of things, not like anyone else.

"You weren't here the past few days. But Jose and Mariana and the kids have been eating better than ever! Even David and Ken came by and tried some."

"Those guys were ripping out french broom up the canyon yesterday. They seemed to be in a great mood when we saw them," LaDonna reported.

A few more days went by since that conversation, and Angie started molding the witches butter into a small trench outlining the 8x12' shape of the hut she wanted. On her knees, kneading it into place, she explained what she wanted: "Will you become a shelter for me? I need walls, a door, a window or two, protection from the cold and wind and when it rains, a place to stay dry. And I need the house to stay hidden from prying eyes!" And she started humming, slowly rising in volume into a crescendo that became her odd but compelling singing. She got water after that and came back and trickled some into the trench with the butter. Then she went up to the vegetable beds and spent the next few hours weeding and pruning and extending the cultivated zone to a new terrace even higher. She was in a great mood and felt full of energy. A few deer appeared across the quarry, but she waved them away. "We love you but this is not for you," she explained. A few crows came zooming in and went directly at the deer, making quite a racket, which sent them scurrying away into the woods.

It was late afternoon when Angie returned to their hidden cluster of shanties. "Holy shit!" Her installation had grown nearly a foot around the entire perimeter. The walls were thickest at the bottom and quite thin at the growing edge near the top. Angie ran her hands along the growing walls. "You are amazing! You will be an incredible home! You are a great partner!" and she burst into song again, continuing to run her hands around it as she squatted alongside the emerging structure. She took a section out of the perimeter where she wanted a door and filled in the dirt trench to level it with the adjacent surfaces. "This is the door. When you get a lot taller, we'll cover the top of it," she explained as though what she said was intelligible and obvious. She no longer doubted that she was being understood. She had to explain things and express her gratitude.

Three days later, the structure reached seven feet. She took a big knife and cut out windows on two sides and used half the material to enclose the doorway by linking the two sides of the walls over the opening. "How shall we make a roof?" she wondered out loud. Jose and Mariana Mukul and their kids were the only regulars who saw the process from the beginning. With Angie's encouragement, they started another hut on the other side of the clearing. The witches butter was changing again as it grew into walls and became stable, solid material. On the outer surface the cream-color gave way to a mottled brown and green and yellow, almost a camouflage. In fact, when Angie came up with a load of water that day she had to look hard to make out her new hut, which blended into the surroundings so well that it was almost invisible. She improvised a roof with some fallen branches and after another couple of days, the butter grew over them, enclosing the space in what would later prove to be a water-tight structure. It was beyond belief! Jose and Mariana's little home took shape in a similarly short time span and the two huts stood at opposite ends of the little village site, blending into the background.

***

Juna rolled in Thursday to see if he could bring his friend Cindy, a veterinarian. And Billy asked about bringing the inventor and a few others who wanted to see what they'd done. She sighed. She was used to being ignored, completely marginalized. What if these people brought too much attention? They'd been able to build this tiny community in peace for years thanks to being far off the beaten path. David, Ken, and the other mountain protectors helped them, and they did what they could to help the mountain too. She trusted Juna and Billy who were regulars. She agreed to the visits, but now that the day was here, she worried. She swept the clearing, made sure everything was tidy.

Billy came up the trail first. "Hey Angie! Here we come!" She stood and watched as Billy led a small entourage up the trail and into their clearing. "This is Janet Pierce and Vero Gomez. Vero came up with the recipes!"

Behind them came three more people, none of whom looked like farmers or gardeners. A huge black man with a big smile came up first, "Hey, I'm Lawrence Lansing, but everyone calls me 'Larry,'" he laughed. "I've been watching the witches butter come to life for the past few months. I had to see what you've done!" He stepped aside, making way for the last two coming up the trail, a middle-aged Asian man and a younger Asian woman.

Billy introduced them, "Angie Werdon, this is Alison Nakahara," and she extended her hand for a shake. "Call me Ally," she said modestly. "And this is Dat Doan, San Francisco's most notorious biohacker!" Billy laughed. "Ally did the original theoretical work on the witches butter fungus, and Dat and his crew made the first actual batch of the genetically modified stuff. Janet and Vero—well, why don't you guys explain what you did?" Billy stopped talking.

"Oh wow!" Janet's eyes focused on Angie's house. "Look at that!" The rest of the crew slowly took in the scene. The mottled hut under the tree, and then Vero pointed across the clearing, "There's another one!" And they stood in amazement, taking it in. The witches butter had become structural! You *could* use it to build with. Janet turned to Angie, "How did you do this? It's amazing!"

Angie, a bit overwhelmed at having many visitors at once, sat down and encouraged everyone else to sit too. "I don't think I can say I did this. It was a collaboration. I started the outline, I put some butter in there and watered it. I talked to it and touched it and sang to it. And it grew fast!"

Vero could see that Angie was uncomfortable. She looked at Billy, who was obviously concerned too. "Would you like us to come in shifts?" she suggested.

"No, no, you're here now. Don't worry about it."

Ally was in a state of amazed shock. She hardly knew what to say, but she was anxious to touch it and go inside. Even in her wildest theoretical musings, nothing like this was possible. How had this strange woman coaxed the witches butter into this shape? In such a short time? How could it happen? "Um, would you mind if I stepped inside?" Ally asked her.

"No, not at all, go ahead, but it's not very big in there. Maybe one at a time, ok?" Angie could feel her heart pounding.

Ally had a small satchel over her shoulder when she approached the hut. Alone, she looked through the open air windows, and saw Angie's bedroll along the back wall. A small shelf held several books and a battery-powered reading lamp. Large bags stood on the other side of the small room, apparently full of clothes and other items. As she entered she reached out and touched the wall, which immediately sent a strong vibration down her arm. "Here I am," she said in a low voice. "And here you are!" she said in a tone of disbelief. Moving her hand along the surface she could feel ambient heat coming off it. A glance at the ceiling—there were gnarly oak branches over which the butter grew, but they looked like a carefully chosen ornamental embellishment. Glancing furtively through the window to see if anyone was watching her, she turned her back and reached up to the center of the ceiling and poked her finger into the witches butter. It was firm but when she gave it a strong push it gave way as far as she wanted to go. She twirled around and expanded the size of the hole her finger made. She opened her satchel and pulled out ... a biobulb! She harvested several of them over the past week. This was a perfect chance! She took the biobulb and inserted its stem-side end (where she'd carefully cut it from the mother plant) into the hole in the ceiling. The witches butter seemed to welcome it, enveloping it in a tight embrace. A tug on the biobulb assured Ally that it was firmly embedded in the ceiling. Now what? Was it supposed to turn on by itself? Or what? There's no switch, what did she think would happen? She suddenly felt very stupid. She decided to leave it there and explain to Angie what it was.

Ally came out to the clearing and saw that Dat and Larry went to peer into the other hut. Billy and Vero and Janet were still sitting with Angie. Vero was explaining how they started. "Janet is always talking to birds and animals and everything." Angie nodded approvingly towards Janet. "She got us—however many of us were around at any given time—to reach in and massage it. And we'd talk to each other, sometimes to it, too!" Vero looked a bit sheepish as she recounted those awkward early days. She thought Janet was over the top with her woo-woo incantations back then. Talking to animals and birds always was an odd personality quirk.

Ally broke into the story. "Um, Angie, I have a... uh... well, I brought something with me. Can I show you?" Ally was feeling quite embarrassed.

Angie got up, not exactly alarmed, but worried. "What is it?" she demanded.

Ally led her into the hut and pointed to the biobulb. "It's a biobulb. I harvested it yesterday, and I was hoping it would be able to work in your hut."

"Is that the thing Juna freaked out about?" Angie demanded.

"Oh! You know about that? Yes it is. But they didn't understand what it was when they touched it," Ally protested.

Angie, hands on her hips, was peeved. "You came in here and put that in MY ceiling? Without even asking me?!?"

"Sorry, I didn't mean any harm," Ally slumped, she looked beaten. "I thought it might work!"

"Work? What do you mean? What is it supposed to do?"

"It's a bulb. You need light in there, right?"

"I have a lamp."

"Yes, but you need batteries for that. If this works, you won't need any, or even electricity!" Ally was pitching her invention.

"How's it supposed to work? Does it have a switch?"

Ally shook her head, realizing how weird it was.

Angie watched this woman, this *scientist*, and felt sorry for her. She was playing with things she didn't understand. Not that Angie did either, but she felt like Ally was treating the hut and her biobulb like any engineer would treat a mechanical invention. But these things were alive! You had to touch them and talk to them! Angie reached up to caress the thin membrane of the bulb.

"You're a beauty! Do you produce light? How do you like my hut? It's warm and cozy isn't it? You are welcome here. Wouldn't you like to add some light to it?"

And the biobulb glowed! Ally gasped. Angie grinned.

"Well, there ya go. You gotta talk to them. And they needed to be introduced!"

Ally laughed. It was impossible. But she'd seen it with her own eyes. And—she remembered—she talked to the walls too, when she first entered.

Angie felt a wave of relief cascade over her. This was fun! They were friends! She looked back from Ally's wide-eyed smile to the bulb and touched it again. It was still cool to the touch. "Hey, thanks for the light. We don't need any until it gets dark later. But thanks for showing us what you can do!"

And the bulb stopped glowing.

Angie tipped her head and shook it lightly as she put a hand on Ally's shoulder and guided her back out to the group. Janet and Vero traded places with Dat and Billy and were checking out the other hut.

"Dat, Billy, you gotta see this!" Ally immediately wanted to bring them into see the bulb. Angie put up her palms, "Whoa there. Hold on a sec. Why don't we talk about it first and then we can go in again and see if we can do it again?" And she explained that Ally put a biobulb in her ceiling and she'd welcomed it and "turned it on," so to speak.

"Are you saying it's voice-activated?" Dat asked.

"I don't know if I'd put it that way," Angie replied. "It's not a machine, it has no switch. The biobulb is alive and the hut is too. I guess they are connected now. And somehow they generated light when I asked them to... It's different than 'voice-activation.'"

Juna entered the unusually crowded clearing and stopped abruptly. Cindy, coming up behind them, almost crashed into their back. Juna saw Billy, Janet, and Vero who were known friends, but they only met Larry and Alison once, and Dat was a stranger. Juna was dismayed to see Ally there. "Oh... hello," they mumbled, not sure what to make of the situation. "This is my friend Cindy Lowe. I think you know her," gesturing to Janet and Vero and Larry. "Cindy, this is Angie, my mentor."

"Hi Angie, I've heard a lot about you!" Cindy smiled, incapable of looking anything but elegant even in a sweaty t-shirt and baggy cargo pants. Her long black hair was tied back into a braid, and her dark eyes flashed excitedly. "I'm Cindy," she extended her hand to Alison who hadn't been introduced.

"Oh, hi, I'm Ally."

"You're the scientist Dat told me about?"

She nodded, not making a big deal out of it. "Dat's the real scientist around here! No one matches his acumen or energy!"

Dat smiled at Cindy, recalling long conversations while she was hiding at the Hangar. And she'd been an eager student there too, working at the lab bench with Dat and his biohackers, running the nutrition tests on the witches butter. Her medical training made her a quick study. "You're just in time," he grinned. "We were talking about how the butter hut and the biobulb 'work'," and he made air quotes with his fingers.

"The biobulb?!?" Juna felt a rising panic.

Angie saw the reaction and immediately came over and gave Juna a hug.

"Juna, you might be happy when you see this," and Ally took them to the hut. At the window they peered inside together and she pointed to the biobulb in the ceiling. "The hut accepted it immediately and Angie did too. She welcomed it and asked it to make some light and it did!" She could hardly believe she was explaining it this way.

Juna looked in, and then back at Angie and the rest of the crew. They were among friends. This was not the dank dungeon, the biobulb had been harvested from the mother plant and was in the air and light of day, connected to the witches butter. Angie smiled encouragingly. Ally was out of her element and not intimidating here. Juna visibly relaxed and sat down on a log near the campfire. One by one the rest came and had a look. Angie went in and asked the bulb to shed light again and, sure enough, it glowed on request. They were amazed and thrilled.

Reaching down to the back wall of the hut, Angie pulled a hunk of witches butter. "You can eat it—It's a Gingerbread House!" she exclaimed.

Dat reached out for a piece. "Yeah, but how does it taste?" he asked before he took a bite. "Mmmmm, mmffmfff," and he reached for a cup of water to wash it down. Almost choking he caught his breath. "Whoa, that's not what I expected. It's dry and powdery and quite salty! That's no gingerbread flavor!" he complained.

Angie laughed. She pulled out a tub from the cooler. In the tub was a cream cheese-like substance.

Vero lit up, "Oh, is that my recipe?!"

Angie laughed and began carving out spoonfuls and smearing them on small pieces of her house's back wall. "Here, try it this way," she thrust one to Dat. "It's much tastier!"

He took a smaller bit, and his face immediately lit up. "Ah! *There's* the ginger! Did you grow it here?"

Angie nodded, handing out samples. "Who wants a tour of the upper 40? That's what we call the new terrace!" And they spent the next couple of hours walking around the farm. Eventually Jose and Mariana and their kids cautiously returned from Owl Canyon.

Much later, Janet pulled Angie and Juna aside and explained the underground network of Food Hubs run by Food Conspiracies that were growing around town. "You guys should think about organizing one in Brisbane, too. You'll have plenty of food coming from here, and hopefully, no Feds coming around to harass you. Have you seen any drones flying over? Helicopters?"

They shook their heads. "It's very quiet back here. The old industrial park is largely abandoned, and even the people who do come to San Bruno Mountain generally steer clear of the old quarry," Angie explained. "I'm not one to go out and organize a Food Hub, but we have some regulars who might know the right place and the right people over in town to help set something up."

CHAPTER 31
THURSDAY NOVEMBER 20, 2025

Frank finished his cereal and coffee, leaving his dishes in the sink. Through the kitchen window he could see his office in a refurbished navy building, the big Hunter's Point crane looming behind it over the bay. A few minutes later he joined Flores in the idling police car outside.

"G'mornin' Flores. How're ya doin' today?" Frank was generally in a good mood at day's beginning.

"Fine sir. Looks like a rough day ahead. I went through the office before driving up here to get you. There's a memo from Morgan ordering farm raids across the city today."

"Now? When people are already complaining about food shortages? That guy is itching for a fight." Frank pulled out his phone and looked up his old friend Greg Watson, the precinct captain in the Bayview for the SF Police Department. He texted "Farm raids today," fulfilling his promise to give him a heads-up when the Federal Police planned anything dramatic in his part of town. "Flores, we should warn our friends." Frank had to get the word out to Janet and the League, and was glad Flores was his friend and co-conspirator.

"Yes sir. I already hung the sign." He and Flores agreed to post a small inconspicuous sign on Innes Avenue near the park entrance saying "BBQ today!" to tip people about an imminent raid. Farmers and gardeners went by that spot every morning, and the word would have traveled fast.

In the lot, Frank looked up at Bayview Hill's terraces where he knew Janet and Leon had vegetables and cannabis growing. He and Lamar discussed setting up a raid target to provide demonstrable results. The Dog Patch was destroyed months ago, but new crops of kale, chard, and lettuce were sown after the Incident. The McLaren Park orchard was another obvious locale, and Alemany Farm was so well known, it had to be on the list. He hoped the League was ready. Everyone knew it was coming. In early September there was a spate of "visits" to farms, ostensibly to get voluntary reports of expected crops. Very little output was expected from San Francisco's urban farms. Frank knew the numbers reported were low, but he guessed that the upper command staff would have little to go on. When he confirmed to Colonel Morgan that the numbers were reasonable, it seemed to satisfy him.

A few hours later, Frank was hollering to the empty fields of Alemany Farm through the intercom, playing his part alongside a loaded police bus at his wing. "We are seizing harvested crops only. No arrests unless someone obstructs us!" Frank reiterated the warning. He hoped Janet and the other League organizers set things up for them. Alemany had been growing food for decades, especially expanding and extending its output in the past few years. Despite the National Emergency, lack of data kept the farm off the raid list. Frank recalled that surveillance drones were lost over Alemany several times. Each time people claimed it was the crows who did it. So they didn't have much to go on in terms of aerial imagery, but there had to be some real output there.

The hot sun beat down on a dessicated landscape. The pond was overgrown with reeds, and the vegetable beds were dry and dusty. A basket of old apples, most of them worm-ridden or moldy, and several large buckets of zucchini and squishy tomatoes were placed on the path. In the distance up the slope they could see the orchard but no tree looked laden with fruit.

Crows began circling over them. As the 12 soldiers stood around kicking at the dust, Frank and Flores took a walk up the path past the produce that was left out for them. They hoped to find someone lurking under the willow tree or in the orchard, but not a soul was present.

Suddenly the officers they'd left by the vehicles were making a hubbub. Frank and Flores headed back to see what was happening. Before they got too close they saw that the Federal Police were being dive-bombed by crows! Cops took swings at the circling birds while retreating to their vehicles. There looked like 40 or 50 crows taking turns diving towards the officers.

Maybe the crows *had* taken out the drones after all!

Flores was remembering their visit in July too. "God Damn!" he exclaimed, "I guess they could have taken out the drones!" confirming Frank's thoughts.

Frank yelled at two of the officers who were ducking and dodging. "Chan! Lester! Get these buckets into the back of the bus!" he ordered. They had to seize what they could.

Ten minutes later they were on their way. Frank and Flores rode ahead in their squad car, unaware of the odors and wounds in the bus behind them. The smell of the overripe produce wafted from the back of the bus. Pale blue bullet-proof vests were streaked with white bird poop. Several officers had bloody cuts where crows managed to hit them on their dives. Everyone was a bit spooked by the experience. "Where are we going next?" asked one guy near the driver.

"McLaren Park is our next stop," he answered. "We'll be there in 15 minutes."

***

Sheila was surprised to find the supermarket shelves sparse. The produce area was particularly understocked, with whole bins standing empty. Piles of russet potatoes from Idaho filled one display, while piles of yellow corn from Kansas and Iowa filled another area. The usual California abundance was at low ebb, and this was the end of autumn, when it should be overflowing.

She asked a clerk, "Where's the greens?" pointing to a paltry selection of wilted cilantro, aging iceberg lettuce heads, and a few random zucchinis, green onions, and sorry-looking celery.

"We're waiting for a big shipment from Mexico. Shoulda been here yesterday. Maybe tomorrow? It's pathetic, isn't it?" she conceded.

"Nothing local? I thought we got most of this from Salinas or the Central Valley?" Sheila prodded.

The clerk shook her head. "I dunno. I guess we used to, but these days, it's mostly from Mexico. Maybe the drought?"

Sheila walked away. Where were the piles of pornographically perfect produce she'd come to expect at Whole Paycheck? Sheesh! She went back to work, giving up on the supermarket. On her way out of the elevator, Bill Marsh, a supervisor who worked on the other side of the procurement department was walking by. "Oh Sheila! Check out the conference room!" he advised with a sly smile.

She dropped her bag and went to the conference room. The table was laden with boxes of fresh produce. Federal police sat at the end of the room. A young female trooper said, "You guys get first shot at these," and she gestured to the produce on the table. "Take what you'd like."

Sheila looked at the officers, then at the produce, shaking her head. "Where'd you get this?"

"The federal tax on local gardens and farms. Either they turn over crops or pay fees. This was handed in to our inspectors."

"Huh," she responded neutrally. But she felt very uncomfortable, imagining Janet and her friends. Did these crops come from them? Gingerly, she took a few carrots, a head of lettuce, and some tomatoes. "Thank you," and she left with her produce.

Back at her desk, she texted Frank. "They're giving us local produce at work! You do this?!?" She felt angry. He did not respond.

***

Donald Nevilleton knocked at the old wooden frame house on Shotwell Street near 20th Street. He had the address from Tomas, whose moms, Millie and Barbara, were the owners. Tomas was a key part of the Pony Express distributing the *Opaque Times* during the past few months, and his house was a distribution center for one of the new food conspiracies. The door opened and Barbara was smiling at Donald, welcoming him in.

"I remember you... Donald isn't it? And you have a beautiful baby daughter right?"

He nodded gratefully as he entered. "Yes, she's growing fast. She started walking last week!" he enthused. "How's Tomas? I haven't seen him lately."

"Oh he's great! We hardly see him—he's out all the time. Kids are growing up a lot faster these days," she led him to the kitchen and pointed to a chair. "Want something to drink?"

"Sure, water's fine."

Donald had been helping coordinate three different food hub locations. Each one had a different distribution day. Getting the food to land in the right place at the right time was his focus. "Tomas has been amazing! He works hard, and he's super smart!" Donald was amazed to learn that Tomas was only 14.

"Oh, that's nice of you to say. His grades haven't been too good lately, so I'm glad to know he's making a good impression in the movement—that's more important than school anyway, no?"

"I've dropped my classes too, if that's any consolation to you," smiled Donald. "I was in the graduate philosophy program at USF, but it doesn't seem too compelling in light of..." and he trailed off, leaving the obvious unstated.

"We had three or four deliveries earlier today, going through the side gate into the basement. We've got a good set-up here," Barbara sounded confident. "Millie and Tomas were here a while ago, maybe Tomas went to pick up fruit from some local houses."

Backyards along nearby streets were full of plum and loquat and lemon trees. Tomas and Cristiano and others from the Pony Express plugged into a gleaning operation, set up by some folks connected to the old Kaliflower garden on 23rd between Folsom and Shotwell. A few years ago they gave away free produce from local yards at the park on Treat every Sunday.

They heard a crash along the side of the house.

"Oh, that's Tomas for sure. His bike always smacks the gate on his way in. Why don't you join him?"

He clattered down the back stairs as Tomas was parking his bike. "Hey man, how're you doin'?"

Tomas smiled when he turned to see Donald. "Hey *Jefe*!" he joked. "We have some great stuff today! Come and see." He pulled a big sack from his bike and led Donald into the basement. "Hi Millie!" Donald greeted the woman filling boxes at the central table. Tomas opened his bag. "What's that?" Millie asked, perturbed that her well-organized boxing was interrupted by her rambunctious son.

"These are lemons! Mr. Pelluzo told me to take as many as I could carry. I must have at least 125-150!"

"Great! Why don't you count them, and we'll put an equal number in each box," she pointed to the shelves lining the wall, each full of boxes. "We're doing 45 boxes today," she informed them.

Donald was impressed by the organized system. "How do people get in and out of here? Do you have time slots?"

Millie nodded, "Yeah, that was a good idea. And when they come they have to bring bags to carry their stuff home without using these boxes. We can't get 40 boxes every week!"

Donald made a mental note of it. Boxes were essential infrastructure. He helped distribute the lemons among the boxes and aided Millie's last tasks too. They were ready for the first arrival. Tomas went to the front of the building to greet people and to keep an eye out.

"Hi Lucia!" he waved to his neighbor, who was pushing a stroller with her new baby. Francisco and Rosa came toddling around the corner from 20th. They were grandparents who lived in the neighborhood since the 1960s. They followed Lucia down the side of the house.

Millie and Donald welcomed them in, Donald immediately drawn to the baby. "Can I pick her up?" and Lucia readily agreed. "She seems to like everybody!"

Millie and Rosa chatted while Francisco emptied a box into their shopping bags. "You heard about Hurricane Edina?" Rosa shook her head. "It flooded half of Honduras and parts of Guatemala too. *¡Ay! Dios mio! ¿Cómo aguantaremos?* How can we go on?"

Millie gave her a hug. "It's unbelievable. Catastrophes everywhere, nothing changes! The government is *still* pushing more oil and gas!"

Donald put the baby back in the stroller and joined the conversation. "You hear what they're doing in Phoenix now? They're paying people to move! The insurance companies aren't happy, but they decided it was cheaper to buy people out than to wait for the endless lawsuits against the city and state of Arizona."

"My husband is putting a rain tank in the backyard," Lucia added. "Our water situation isn't so safe either!" Everyone nodded in agreement. "If we're gonna make it through, we have to use every drop we have," stating the common wisdom of San Franciscans. "The plumbers union is circulating a petition, demanding the City put the replumbing of the city at the top of its infrastructure priority list!"

"Your husband is a plumber?" Rosa asked her.

She nodded. "They're talking about this stuff all the time! My dad too, he's retired now. He still doesn't get it. He thinks the young guys have gone crazy— 'why don't you do your job and keep your head down?' he asks my husband. But there's no avoiding it anymore. We have to change how we use water!"

"We have some time, don't we?" Donald ventured.

Lucia glared at him. "If we don't use this time, *now*, we won't be ready when we need to be. We have to fix San Francisco, but we *really* have to do something about those people in the suburbs using our system!"

Donald threw up his hands and smiled, "OK, OK, sorry!" He hadn't meant to unleash her anger. "You know a lot more than I do, that's for sure!" He tried to recover some amity between them.

Lucia shoved her bulging bag of fresh food under the carriage and stood up. "I'm sorry. I get carried away. I'm worried!" and she reached in to make her baby comfortable in the carriage. "What will her life be like?"

Donald felt the same. His own daughter wasn't much older than this infant. As they left and the next folks arrived, he helped reorganize the boxes on the shelves.

"Hey Tomas, I'll see you Thursday right?" Tomas waved affirmatively, and Millie gave him a parting embrace.

"Don't feel bad about that. It was a good conversation. We have to be able to give and take and not take it too hard, right?"

He nodded appreciatively and made his exit through the house.

CHAPTER 32
FRIDAY, DECEMBER 5, 2025

The pickup truck backed up, loaded with sandbags, in front of his warehouse at the corner of Yosemite and Ingalls.

"There, that's good!" Larry waved at the driver watching him in his side mirror. It was 9:15 and he kept looking nervously down Yosemite towards the rusting gates at the end of the street. Behind those gates the tides came up the last two mornings, sending bay waters to the edge of his building.

'King Tides' they said on the news, expected to crest higher than ever with the torrential rains that started on Saturday of Thanksgiving weekend.

An "atmospheric river" stretched from near Hawaii to the Pacific Coast and focused the heaviest rainfall on the Bay Area, the delta, and heavy snow in the Sierra due east. San Francisco received an incredible 6.5" of rain from Saturday to Wednesday. Even higher numbers hit the Central Valley and the foothills. Heavy snowfall continued in the High Sierra.

Maybe this rainy season would bring another much-needed deluge to replenish water supplies in the arid West. The sun was back, making it an unseasonably warm December morning. The high tide was expected to crest at 10:40 this morning, so they had an hour and a half to bolster their defenses with sandbags.

"What if this is the new normal?" Larry was already grabbing sandbags and tossing them to his helpers, lined up in bucket-brigade style, building a curving perimeter facing the intersection of Yosemite and Ingalls that filled with a couple inches of water each of the previous mornings. In the back of Larry's mind was the secret cellar under the building in the next block. He had to prevent water from pouring in there. Groundwater was coming up, too. His fingers were crossed that the thick cement foundation he'd built would keep it water tight.

A second pickup truck laden with sandbags arrived in time to keep the line going. Their curving wall should repel a few inches of water without much trouble. They kept extending it down Ingalls where the water would reach.

"Hey, pull down there," Larry pointed the second truck down Ingalls. Might as well continue the bags to the next intersection at Armstrong, where water reached too. He sent the team down there and told them where he wanted the remaining sandbags.

Everyone was hot and sweaty as the 10 o'clock hour rolled by. The bags were in place, and now, the tide would come up. They could already see it slipping under the iron gates a block away.

"Damn! Look at that!" The bay water kept advancing, ebbing and flowing and reaching across the street. Another fifteen minutes went by and the water filled the street an inch deep. It extended from the bay to their sandbags. And who knew what was in the water? Radioactive and toxic areas of Hunter's Point due east combined with toxic residues dumped by the metal shops nearby made a potent combination. A poisonous brew pushed up by rising groundwater and high tides was filling the streets.

Some kids appeared on their bikes up Ingalls Street, riding slowly into the water, giggling and laughing.

"Hey, don't get that water on you!" Larry scolded. "That shit is nasty!"

Ally came rolling up on her bicycle at the same time as Vero and Clara emerged from the warehouse, having made their way through the tunnel from the secret cellar.

"Whoa! Look at that!" exclaimed Clara.

"Today is the highest tide, and tomorrow will be high too and then it's supposed to go back down to normal until a month from now," explained Alison. She'd been watching the encroaching waters for two days. "Hard to say how bad it's gonna get if the rains keep coming. Weather says it's gonna rain again soon, and then keep coming in waves. By the time we get to January's King Tides it may be even higher!"

"I thought the King Tides were generated by the moon, like all tides, no?" Vero was puzzled.

"Yeah, but between the last two years' melting in Greenland and the Arctic, and the breaking up of ice in Antarctica, sea level rise has accelerated. No one has been able to properly measure it yet, but it looks like we're already past what was projected for 50 years from now!" Ally was always up on the latest science.

"And that does not consider this insane rainfall we're getting. If it keeps up, the reservoirs will be reaching capacity in a few weeks, and the rivers will be reaching flood stage. That will send more water through the delta and into the bay than we've seen in decades. If the timing is right, we could see the worst coastal flooding around the bayshore since the Bay Area reached its current shape."

"Hey, have you been checking around in the cellar?" Larry asked Clara quietly.

"We did a thorough inspection an hour ago. No signs of leakage. Everything is normal, systems are running properly. But you know, if this is the new normal, maybe we need to think about moving out of there. Won't it swamp eventually?"

"I'm thinking about it," Larry muttered grumpily.

***

About a block south of the Ferry Building was the cement plaza where King Tides were sloshing over the edge for several years. It had become the 'go-to' spot for filmmakers and photographers looking for dramatic shots of water overtopping the urban boundary. Water sometimes surged across the sidewalk and into the northbound lanes of the Embarcadero, but this was ridiculous! And sure enough, dozens of TV cameras and photographers were jostling for the best angles and elbowing each other out of the way to get their "money shot." Orange cones surrounded the flooded area across the northbound lanes to reach the center median which was protected by a short curb.

Dat Doan rode his bicycle down here on most King Tides to check the inexorable progress of sea-level rise, which he could track by returning to the same spot over and over.

"Damn!" he exclaimed to a nearby photographer, "This is definitely the highest yet!"

The photographer turned to see who was talking and saw a middle-aged Asian man on his bicycle. She was a 21st century child born in 2004 and was taking photos for her climate change group. Standing up in her blue sweatshirt she let the camera dangle from the strap around her neck, fighting with her straight blonde hair getting pulled by the weight. "You know it's gonna keep raining, right? This is only the beginning!"

Dat looked at her, framed by a half dozen TV cameras and other photographers behind her. She turned briefly when he didn't respond, flashing her "Water is Life" slogan on the back of her sweatshirt. He noticed that her feet were damp from standing in the waters.

"Yeah, that's what the forecasters are sayin'," he concurred. "We'll see. Been a lot of predictions over the years that didn't come true." He notice her old-school camera. "How come you're using that old thing?" he gestured to her 35mm SLR Konica.

"This?" she held it up. "It's digital. It looks like a film camera but it's not." He had her now. "Did you ever shoot with film?"

"Oh yeah, for years! But I have to admit, it's a helluva lot easier these days. You can take as many pictures as you want with no worry about processing costs—not to mention messing up the exposure in the first place!"

She smiled. "My dad has some old cameras and we used them a few times when I was little. But he went over to the phone too," sighing, "like everyone."

"Are you taking pictures for any particular reason?" Dat asked her.

"I'm with the Water Protectors," she explained. "After all these years of drought and worrying about how we're wasting water, we have to think harder about what to do when there is too much water!"

He nodded, "Good point! Hey I'm Dat Doan," extending his hand. "What's your name?"

"I'm Sarah Ackerman, glad to meet you Dat." It was rare that someone much older spoke to her out of the blue and took her thoughts seriously, unless it was at school or an organizational meeting.

"I haven't heard of the Water Protectors before," Dat continued. "What do you guys do?"

"You probably know about anti-pipeline protests in other parts of the country, right? That's where the organization got going, as a network of people blockading projects that threaten clean water. But in California, we're fighting the Delta Tunnel, and we're also interested in taking down dams wherever it's possible."

"Oh? Like where?"

"There's the Englebright Dam on the Yuba River... it's a great example. It was built right before WWII to catch debris, mostly still coming from the Gold Rush if you can believe it. But it blocked the salmon run and hasn't served any purpose for decades. There are others too. California has one of the craziest plumbing systems in the world! Given the likelihood of ongoing drought, we have to do a better job of using water than we've been doing! Our local group is also diving deep into the details of each watershed in San Francisco. I'm part of the Channel watershed working group."

"No argument from me! Well, thank you Sarah. Good to meet you, here's my card," he handed her his business card, 'Doan Industries, Export and Import of Biological Products' with his phone and email. "Please get in touch some time. I may have some work for you!" he said with twinkling eyes. "Assuming we don't get flooded out this winter!"

***

Angie Werdon huddled in her warm hut watching the torrential rains falling in the clearing between her hut and the Mukuls. They'd had a sweet little Thanksgiving celebration in Quarrytown but then the storm arrived, and now it was Wednesday and it still came down. Howling wind roared down the quarried terraces above, thick rain carving stream beds across the canyon. In adjacent Owl Canyon and the last canyon to the east before the town of Brisbane—Buckeye—long dried streambeds channeled suddenly rushing rivers at the bottom of the slopes.

Loud steps splashed outside of her view from the window.

"Angie, you there?" called LaDonna. "We've been flooded out." Their ground-level 'treehouse' above what was usually a trickle of fresh water was swamped. "Marco is coming down too, should be here in a sec."

"C'mon in! Leave your wet shoes and jacket near the door, ok?"

LaDonna was soaked through. Her fingers poked out of soggy knit fingerless gloves and clawed at her layers of sopping wet clothes.

"Oh man, that smell!" gasped Angie. "LaDonna, your clothes!"

LaDonna looked at Angie through tired wrinkles, reddened by their exposure to the winter storm, but still a deeply weathered brown. She gave Angie a gap-toothed smile, shaking her head. She pulled off the wettest outer layer of wool, and theatrically held her nose. "I know! It's tough to clean clothes living on the hill. I'm sorry!"

"Hey LaDonna! Angie!" came Marco's voice, as he loudly splashed up to the hut. "Got room for me in there, too?"

"C'mon in," Angie said, realizing there was no choice. "You gotta leave your boots and the wettest stuff at the door, ok?"

"Damn, it's cozy in here!" Marco exclaimed after he removed his boots and dropped his coat and hat in a soggy pile. He stayed remarkably dry, but he added to the smell.

"Man, you guys!" Angie shook her head and began pulling out some bags of herbs she kept in her tiny bureau. She lit some sage and began blowing the smoke on her guests and waving it around the room. The biobulb in the ceiling glowed brightly, providing light while the storm lashed them from outside. The hut was surprisingly sturdy, resisting the strong gusts outside. The eaves of the hut kept most of the rain out of the open windows, which Angie covered with branches.

"How come it's not colder and wetter in here?" LaDonna asked her, realizing that the windows were wide open except for the branches. There was no visible source of heat but the little hut was quite comfortable.

"Touch the wall," Angie instructed. LaDonna and Marco both reached for the wall.

"It's warm! How did you get heat in there?" Marco exclaimed.

"It's the butter—the witches' butter. The hut grew itself with a little encouragement, and, well, it seems to know what I need to be comfortable. It's warm when it's cold, and it keeps cool when it's hot!"

LaDonna and Marco saw the huts, both Angie's and Mukuls', since their appearance in early November. But this was their first time having to take shelter in one. And they never understood the peculiar story of the material the huts were made from.

"Don't get weirded out, but the hut is alive. I talk to it all the time," and she reached over and patted the wall, "don't I, friend?"

Davi Mukul appeared at the door, clad in a wet poncho, wiping rain from his face. "From my family," he said in a soft voice, extending a pile of warm tortillas. His English was improving rapidly and he liked to practice with Angie. "If you hungry, we have more," he gestured back to his family's hut across the clearing. He was still an 8-year-old boy, and he didn't invite himself into the hut, instead, returning home.

Angie rearranged her belongings and made a corner for her friends. "Here, this is where you can sleep. I have extra pillows," she handed them over, "but I don't have another pad, sorry!"

"You have a soft floor, don't worry about it! We can sleep on the straw. It's dry!"

Thursday the rain finally tapered off and Marco and LaDonna left to see what remained of their home. Angie and the Mukul's restored the grounds of their shared village and hung a lot of things around to dry out. Angie took a chunk of witches butter from the large colony they'd established at the edge of their clearing. She took advantage of the muddy terrain and dug a narrow trench in a configuration that would create a second structure adjacent to her hut. She massaged the big piece of witches butter, softening it, and spitting in to it, singing in her weird wordless tones. Occasionally she muttered, "you are amazing, you are a blessing!" She kept kneading it, and when she started laying it down in her little trenches she explained to it, "This is a new hut, which will be a shelter for those who need it. I hope it can be as cozy as you've made mine!" She finished the outline of the new hut, with one wall shared with part of her back wall. After starting the hut building process again, she and Jose and Mariana went up to the terraces to see how bad the damage was.

"Oh dear," Angie stopped in her tracks. The terrace above partially collapsed and sent a wall of mud sliding over their beds. And that meant the second terrace where they'd been cultivating other crops was also severely damaged. Angie sighed loudly and stared at the devastation.

Jose and Mariana were dismayed of course, but they wasted no time, getting shovels from the tree trunk where they stashed them, and beginning to dig through the mud. Angie had to smile, seeing how diligent and committed her friends were. She joined in, and soon they were finding submerged plants to recover at least some of what was damaged.

After hard work in the sun, they were tired, but feeling happy to have recovered a bunch of their winter plantings. More witches butter was dug from the mud too, and they realized it had been growing steadily through the winter.

"Look at this!" exclaimed Angie. "I had no idea it was growing up here, did you?" she asked them in Mayan. Jose and Mariana shook their heads. "Let's take some for cooking," and she dug up two large pieces, one for each of them. "It'll grow back in no time!" she grinned.

They carried their witches butter back to their dwellings and found more guests when they returned. David and Ken were sitting on the log in the clearing.

"How are you guys doing?" David asked.

"We're still here!" grinned Angie.

"The place looks pretty good," Ken complimented them.

"We did a fair amount of clean-up this morning when the sun came out. It wasn't too bad here, but we dodged a bullet," Angie explained. "The upper terrace slid onto the first one. It was a serious mudslide. We're lucky it didn't come all the way down."

David and Ken looked at them silently. "You have no idea how lucky you are! There was a huge mudslide on the south side of the mountain, swamping that whole Terra Bay development. They evacuated several thousand people in the middle of the storm, and hours later the hillside came down..." Ken was talking fast now. "Highway 101 was flooded, the airport, and most of Sierra Point for a half day..."

David sat with his hands on his knees. His white hair and big beard gave him the elegance of an "old man of the mountain" which was how many people thought of him. "Y'know," he was smiling, "nature's still here. I've been saying it for years. Sometimes it takes a disaster to remind us."

"So you guys are basically alright?" Ken asked.

"The huts stayed dry and warm. LaDonna and Marco got washed out though. They showed up on my door Wednesday after they were swamped," Angie explained. "I figured I better start another hut," she got up and walked over to the side of her hut. "And damn! Look!" The others came over to see the new walls growing, nearly a foot tall in a half day.

"We brought you some supplies," Ken said, opening his pack. Out came packaged goods, new socks and underwear, t-shirts, and some rain jackets.

"This is great, thank you!" Angie was happy that she'd be able to share this with Marco and LaDonna. The smell of the fresh clothes hit her almost as hard as the stench of their clothing had. Her sense of smell was much stronger lately. "You guys rock! I hate to say it, but I don't think we're gonna have anything for the Food Conspiracy for a while. We managed to salvage a bunch of plants but it'll be a while before we recover."

"Don't worry," David clapped Angie on the back. "We're glad you're in one piece over here! And these huts! Amazing!"

CHAPTER 33
SUNDAY, JANUARY 4, 2026

The "Pineapple Express" kept coming. The historic storms after Thanksgiving soaked San Francisco and most of California with the most rain ever recorded in a five-day period. They joined the King Tides at the start of December to inundate parts of the Bay Area that weren't supposed to "go under" until 2100 at the earliest! SFO and the Oakland Airports were closed twice for several hours each. Toll plazas at the Bay Bridge, the Dunbarton, and San Mateo bridges were swamped by tidal surges. Low-lying stretches of Bay Area freeways were inundated by combined high tides, storm surge, and groundwater upwelling: Highway 101 along Brisbane Lagoon, and in Mountain View in Silicon Valley; the Nimitz Freeway (I-880) was flooded out from near downtown Oakland to south of Lake Merritt, and then drowned again north of the Coliseum to San Leandro. It was bad near the Dunbarton Bridge where the Nimitz was closed for hours.

A King Tide on New Year's Eve morning began an even worse five-day stretch. Key bridges and freeways and airports were flooded again, but for four straight days the King Tide came in each morning while the rain relentlessly fell over Northern California. The Oroville Dam on the Feather River was at capacity and sending vast amounts of water cascading down its recently rebuilt emergency spillway to eventually swell the already flood stage Sacramento River. The same story repeated across the state, as dams at Lake Shasta, San Luis, Friant and dozens of smaller ones were forced to send a flood-level flow over their emergency spillways and into the slowly filling Central Valley. As those floodwaters eventually rushed through the Carquinez Strait and into the north bay, floodwaters surged not only through the Golden Gate but into the south Bay, joining the floodwaters pouring in from Alameda Creek, the Guadalupe River, San Franciscquito Creek, and dozens of others. Moffett Field, Alviso, large parts of Fremont, Newark and Union City were completely submerged by several feet of floodwaters. The Dunbarton Bridge became the photographer's favorite, as the bridge rose across the bay waters but landed on both ends in the water. No traffic could reach any of the transbay bridges except the Richmond-San Rafael Bridge, and that was hard to reach without a major detour through city streets in Berkeley, Albany, El Cerrito and Richmond to avoid the unpredictable floods surging in from the bay or overspilling the banks of the many daylighted creeks in those towns.

***

Frank was given a two-week furlough for the holidays. The first family gathering at Marlin Street since his mother's funeral was a family Christmas of sorts. Janet and Lamar and Leon had been the next generation there, but there were no children running around. It seemed quite odd and rather subdued. In addition to Linda and Rhonda, Aaron and Greg, and Amelia and Jim, Dr. Cindy Lowe was there with Lamar (they practically lived at the Marlin Street house too), and Janet invited Vero, as usual, since her family was no longer in the area.

After they'd left, Frank sat by himself at the window. Lamar and Cindy retired to a bedroom, and Janet and Vero were cleaning up in the kitchen with

Leon. He sipped a bourbon, staring into the night.

"Frank! You ok?" Janet and Vero emerged from the kitchen and sat down across from him.

"Oh yeah, thinking about Grannie," he admitted.

"Um, we wanted to talk to you," Janet started hesitantly. She'd been staying out of direct contact until this Christmas Eve family gathering. And Vero, a fugitive since her escape from Camp Hayward, was extremely reluctant to show up if Frank was around.

"Yeah?" he was nicely buzzed, and his official duties were far from his mind. He wished Sheila would've stayed, but she never spent the night at this house.

"You think we're in the clear? Like no one's looking for us anymore?" Janet asked. Vero sat attentively next to her.

Frank gathered his thoughts, confused by the question at first. "Oh yeah! I plumb forgot. My guess is you're still on a list somewhere. But I don't think there's anyone actively looking for you. I wouldn't recommend getting arrested! Then they'd probably put it together and you'd be screwed."

"Well, thank you Frank," Vero said, feeling like he'd given her a gift. Janet came over and gave Frank a hug, and Vero did too. "Merry Christmas, Frank!"

Leon appeared, having stayed discretely in the kitchen until then. Janet and Vero were putting on their rain gear, heading into the glistening, wet night with thanks and salutations. Leon, who finally got used to being around his father, asked him, "you ok?"

He nodded and turned back to the rain-streaked window. "Time is passing, son. We're not here very long. Another Christmas, another year." He sipped his bourbon and then slumped back in the recliner. Leon came over and put a blanket over him, patted him on the shoulder, and said "Merry Christmas dad. I hope next year is better than this one!" Frank's eyes were closed, but he nodded as he breathed deeply.

A few days later, Sheila invited him over for New Year's Eve. She made a delicious pork roast dinner with fresh vegetables she'd gotten at work, and they shared a bottle of top-notch pinot noir. As the cozy evening progressed, they turned the couch to sit at the floor-to-ceiling window and watch the lights around the bay flickering through the steady rain. One thing led to another and finally Sheila invited him to spend the night. He'd hoped that would happen, but learned not to count on it. When she melted into his arms on the couch his doubts vanished.

Now they were holding their morning coffee and facing the unexpected storm surge rushing through the streets below. Sipping his coffee, Frank remarked, "Not sure how we get anywhere in this rain, not with the streets flooded like that!" Litter swirled in the oily waters that covered everything between the buildings. A few hardy souls were kayaking down Bridgewater Street, unconcerned about the falling rain. Mostly it was deserted. The flooded streets gave their faux brick building an extra patina of age, as though this were Venice and these buildings had been here for centuries.

Sheila was looking at her phone, scrolling with her thumb, while she slurped her own coffee. "Says here today's King Tide was at 8:46. Tomorrow it's at 9:38, Saturday at 10:30, and Sunday at 11:21, and then the tides go back to 'normal.'" She looked at Frank. "What do you suppose 'normal' is now?"

He shook his head and pulled one of her dinette chairs over to sit at the window. "I haven't seen storms like this before. It's been nonstop for almost a month. We had a few gaps in there, but the whole of California is soaked! When will it break? We coulda used this water for the last few years!"

Sheila sat back onto the couch nearby. "Arizona! Nevada! They could have used a fraction of this water during the past couple of years. How many people have fled Phoenix now? A half million? More?"

"Anyway, even when the tide recedes, this flood will leave quite a mess! You think we'll be able to get a car or even the 'T' later? I'm sure the shipyard is under water."

"Might as well get comfy. We're gonna be here for a few hours at least!" Sheila predicted. "I'm sure they'll be running the T through when the tide subsides later. Why don't you turn on some football and relax?"

CHAPTER 34
MONDAY JANUARY 12, 2026

Sheila wasn't expecting a particularly frantic week ahead when she arrived at work.

"Sheila! You seen the news?" Bill Marsh, her associate in Procurement walked past her desk. "Market's down 5% already—it could be a new Black Monday! Something has gone wrong in international insurance markets."

Successive hurricanes inundated a large area of Central America. The American Agricultural Insurance Company, one of the top 50 reinsurance companies in the world, was overwhelmed by claims from the regional insurance companies that covered United Fruit Company, Hills Brothers Coffee, and a half dozen other big producers there. They might have been able to handle it in previous years but during 2024-25 they already paid out enormous sums when two-thirds of the farmers in Arizona were forced to retire their farms due to lack of water. That drove their insurers over the edge, and in turn led to unprecedented losses for the American Agricultural Insurance Company who was insuring those insurers.

Simultaneously, the huge General Insurance Corporation of India, the main reinsurance company in India was driven to insolvency. Half the insurers in India went bankrupt within a few months, sunk by the combination of punishing years-long drought and the massive heat waves that killed several million in the past two years. Both life insurers and agricultural insurers had failed in the face of impossible demands, and that pulled the subcontinent's largest reinsurer into the maelstrom too. The African Reinsurance Corporation was simultaneously hammered by massive flood- and drought-related losses throughout sub-Saharan Africa. The cascading failures were working their way up to the world's largest reinsurers. Industry leaders Swiss RE and Munich Reinsurance endured collapsing stock prices due to compromising cross-insurance relationships with the failing companies, and were scrambling to stay afloat in the face of their exposure. World markets were in a state of free fall as everyone at every level was calling in their money.

At the Federal Building in San Francisco, none of this was clear but the news of rapidly sinking markets was. Sheila and Bill both worried about their market-dependent pension funds. An hour later the shocking headlines shot around the world: China was selling most of its US Treasuries!

"What? But won't they hurt *themselves*?!" Bill complained across the room to Sheila, and then explained what he'd read. China's economy was tied to the U.S. economy ever since China joined the World Trade Organization at the start of the 21st century. It had grown larger than the U.S. a few years ago, and in spite of ongoing tension over islands in the western Pacific, everyone assumed that the delicate balance between geopolitical competition and economic cooperation would be maintained, occasional tariffs and noisy trade wars notwithstanding. But if China was dumping U.S. Treasuries that changed everything. The Chinese government held well over $1 trillion in U.S. debt acquired during a decade of huge trade surpluses. Vast investments were made in its Belt and Road Initiative in Eurasia, Africa, and Europe, and modernizing its military and technology sectors. Feeling the strength of its strategic leverage, China was decisively breaking with the world system built by the U.S. after WWII.

The U.S., while selling treasuries (i.e. debt) to China, spent trillions on its nonsensical "war on terror," mostly in Afghanistan and Iraq. Its overextended military cost more than half of its annual budget, and the main prize of that over-extension was supposed to be keeping the dollar at the center of world trade. The Chinese Communist Party provided key support by buying the endless river of American debt. China was pulling that plug.

In times past the U.S. might have threatened to use its military might. But in late 2024 during the election crisis, its Navy found itself blundering in digital darkness after a cyberattack shut down its militarily hardened communications for several days. They'd kept it out of the news, but the Pentagon learned they were extremely vulnerable. They suspected China, but they weren't even sure who shut them down!

That fiasco, when word circulated among the upper echelons of the military and government, fueled Republican hardliners who still claimed that the U.S. military was all-powerful, and any failure was due to weak leadership. The quick Emergency declaration after the judicially tainted election result was driven by those same interests, authoritarians who were fully ensconced in the Pentagon and Homeland Security bureaucracies. They learned the hard way that the sheer cost of Emergency rule in dozens of cities was impossible to maintain. As fast as possible, cities where the protests had been relatively mild were returned to local government. But in the west, it had taken over nine months, with the end finally achieved in mid-October.

The federal government tried to project an image of normalcy, but the fiscal crisis was worsening and their surprising attempt to re-engineer food and fuel consumption from the top, announced during the Emergency, wasn't working either. The Hutchinson government, dominated like previous Republican regimes by oil men and oil-dependent agricultural industries, reversed previous efforts to curb oil and gas use. They prioritized the corporate agriculture that depended on huge petrochemical inputs to produce vast surpluses of corn and soy. They even defended their move by pointing to the collapsing output from California due to soil and water depletion, toxification, and the grinding drought.

Using federal police to force people to use certain products and not others proved to be a lot more difficult than the authorities imagined. The Hutchinson people running the government didn't understand how little they actually could control. They were following a model given to them by the Supreme Court. Ruling by decree before Biden had finished half his term, the Court eliminated women's right to abortion, authorized openly carried guns across public life, and curtailed administrative regulations that weren't explicitly written by Congress to dramatically weaken the ability to govern. If the Supreme Court could keep changing the daily lives of Americans, ignoring huge majorities against them, why shouldn't the Republican-dominated government do the same? The Emergency was their attempt to override politics altogether—but it had proven unwieldy and prohibitively expensive.

Sheila's phone rang and she saw it was Frank calling. "Hi Frank. How're you doing?"

"You see the news?"

"Yeah, looks bad. You have a 401(k)? Everyone's freaking out."

"I heard that the Federal Government is laying off a half million. You hear anything like that?"

Sheila scanned her in-house news sources while she was on the phone. "No... let me take a looksee... no, nothing in the *Bulletin*. Where'd you hear that?"

"One of the guys out here saw it somewhere."

"Well, they can't lay off that many people even if they want to. Too many union contracts!" Sheila was sure that the government had to follow its own contracts and rules, especially after the Trump prosecutions. People were nervous about breaking the law.

"You don't think so? What if the dollar is collapsing? How are they gonna pay their bills? I heard the dollar has fallen to 3 to the Euro and the Chinese currency is nearly 1 to 1 with the dollar now!"

"Oh Frank. I don't know about that stuff. Do you? Don't get hysterical—the cable news always sounds like it's the end of the world."

"Yeah, but what if it is? All this insane rain and snow, and then last week the shipyard flooded *again!* The airports, the freeways, the bridges shut down for days—things are getting much worse... and fast!"

They decided to meet that evening at their regular pizza joint not far from Sheila's building in Mission Bay.

***

At BioGenMo employees were watching the same worrying news. Dennis Swintin and Vanessa Wright, both longtime liaisons with the ProsperPlant® contractors (the backbone of BGM's main profit center, Intelligel®), had been building towards this moment for most of the last two years. Dennis was a bike messenger organizer with the Longshore Union in the late 1990s but it never led to much. At last, something big was brewing!

Since well before the election and martial law, he and Vanessa were organizing at BioGenMo. They were the ones who smuggled Alison Nakahara's research on witches butter fungus out to Dat Doan's biohacker lab. Countless times they thought they were discovered, but every time it turned out to be a false alarm. The disappearance and presumed murder of UPA organizer

Miguel Robles was shocking—were they next? Who else was on the list? Then the Emergency was lifted, and after that, no more disappearances.

Dennis logged out and shut down his terminal. He was a bit over 6 feet, wavy salt and pepper hair. He was paunchy after years of computer work at BGM. He was drinking more than ever, betrayed by his ruddy red face. If they were ever going to test their power together, it seemed this was the time. Tonight they were meeting their allies from Facebook and Salesforce at their favorite bar on 2nd Street near the ballpark. Felix, Alba, and Karen were coming too, the most committed of their BGM contacts.

Monday's economic news had only grown steadily worse in the past two days. No one was spared from the wreckage spreading across society. The government was reluctant to backstop the banks as they did in the 2008 crash and during the pandemic. That had been easy when there was unlimited demand for Treasury Bonds. Instead, the federal government was desperately buying as many bonds as possible on global markets in a failing effort to bolster the price. Economic activity was seizing up at every turn. Everyone was pulling back to see what would happen next. Meanwhile, inflation was raging as everyone who had anything to sell was raising their prices as fast as they could. It was an impossible combination of rapid monetary inflation and generalized deflation as the economic gears ground to a halt. Money was becoming an empty register of diminishing value.

"We've got to go public as soon as possible," Dennis urged Vanessa. "We've been expecting a moment when we could show our strength. This is it!"

"What if the Facebookers and the others don't want to come along?" Vanessa asked him. She was slim, plain, and coolly competent. Her wiry frame hid a huge reservoir of energy, and once she started talking she always seemed to be on the verge of laughing. Her enthusiasm was contagious. But she was a realist, especially with Dennis who'd she come to know well. He always wanted to push things farther than a cooler head would.

"Yeah, that's why we need to make them an argument they can't refuse!" his eyes gleamed. He'd been dreaming of a big uprising as long as he'd been a labor organizer. It was probably an impossible pipe dream. It shimmered in his vision: a well-organized, coordinated move by thousands of San Francisco's best paid and most coveted workers. It was the last part he was counting on. Everyone knew they were hard to replace—

"Hi guys," Alba Estrada bounded in cheerfully to the back of the bar, Karen Peterson a step behind. Alba was a beautiful woman with a perpetual smile she emphasized with bright red lipstick, always wearing short dresses and big boots. She liked the go-go girl aesthetic with her bleached-blonde hair cascading in colorful braids, contrasting with her café au lait skintone. She was someone who enjoyed being in her body. Karen was the opposite. A very thin woman with long straight black hair, she looked like a former dancer or a frustrated poet.

"Is Felix coming?" Vanessa asked them. The three of them were usually inseparable when it came to organizing meetings.

"He has a family crisis to handle," Alba explained. "His parents have lost all their savings since Monday!"

"Crap!" Dennis looked angry. "Who's drinkin' what? I'm buyin'."

He disappeared to the bar to get drinks. While he was waiting to order he saw their FB allies walk in, Ethan Chan and Perlana Solorzano. They looked a bit uncomfortable. Dennis waved them over and they lightened up when they saw him.

"Hey Dennis, we thought maybe the meeting was off!" Perlana said. She looked up at Dennis from her short stocky frame. She was a fourth generation Filipina whose family lived in a land-trusted building in a South of Market alley. The first time they met she began recounting the sordid history of the U.S.-Philippine war and colonization—Dennis was thrilled. Ethan was a tall, skinny guy who grew up in the Sunset. His family had been in San Francisco since the 1920s, but only got out of Chinatown after a half-century. He still had relatives living and working in the old neighborhood though he had a new apartment in Mission Rock. Perlana and Ethan found each other at Facebook before the pandemic and bonded during the two years they spent on endless zoom meetings.

"Everyone is freaking out over at Meta. Stocks are crashing, and the company has paused contributions to our retirement funds too," Ethan explained.

"Hang on," Dennis urged. He got their drink orders and they headed to the back table. Susanna Montez, the Salesforce rep, was already there, explaining breathlessly about the panic in the big tower that dominated the city's skyline.

"Benioff, our beloved leader, sent us a video email trying to sound reassuring, but he was nervous. He doesn't know what's happening either."

"BGM thinks they can ride it out. They sent a text saying they'd planned for this. 'Sit tight' they said, 'We got this.' What the hell could they be thinking?" Vanessa shook her head.

Alba looked at Karen. "Didn't you tell me you'd been working on some tech documents for that VP? About how they'd come through an economic crash holding the best cards of all? Biotech would get a boost after the 'old capital' gets wiped out in a collapse? Something like that right?"

Karen nodded. "I don't know if everyone agrees, but this guy I was working with, Jerome Powers, he wrote this prospectus. He was writing future scenarios and suggesting how they should react to different situations. I don't remember everything, but yeah, Alba, you got one of his arguments right."

Vanessa looked around the table. "I don't think we should focus on our lost savings or pensions or stock collapses. These companies will be desperate to hold on through the storm. This is our chance!" She and Dennis planned for this.

"Chance? What do you mean?" Susanna asked, sipping her chardonnay. A thick gold necklace made of heart-shaped medallions shimmied on her yellow blouse.

Dennis was dying to jump in, but knew it was better if this came from Vanessa.

"A coordinated work stoppage! Half the people are leaving anyway, panicking about economic collapse. It's time that the people who do the work at these companies decide what the projects are, who they're for, how our skills are used. No more surveillance work, no more for the military."

She looked at the faces around the table. They didn't look enthusiastic. Mostly they stared into the drinks, stirring them desultorily.

"No one is excited? Aren't we ready?" Vanessa looked at Dennis, raising her eyebrows imploringly.

"Look," Dennis sounded out of patience. Maybe they were racing ahead, playing their cards too soon. But Vanessa had done it, he agreed they should, and they had to finish the hand. Or try to. "We're not going back to the way things were. Whatever is happening now, following years of 'quantitative easing', debt recycling, structural adjustment programs, privatization, and the damned pandemic—they're about out of tricks. They've tried everything to keep this rotten system from collapsing several times this century already. But I don't think they can fix this, not this time."

"So? What do you expect us to do about it?" Ethan sounded frustrated. He'd heard plenty of leftwing blowhards in his life. This sounded no different to him. "We can call for an action. Maybe we get 15-20% to join us—and that's optimistic! I don't know what you can do at Salesforce, Susanna. And BGM? You expect me to believe that a workforce that's been told they're the ones who will survive a collapse because of their unique skills and technological edge are going out... now? You're crazy!" He sat back.

Perlana entered the fray. "Ethan, you're probably right. The main thing, and here I agree with Dennis, we're not going back. Even if we, or our coworkers, want things to go back to normal... that's over! I thought that during the pandemic, and then I thought it again during the National Emergency.

I definitely think it now! Why should we fight for anything less than everything? We need to reinvent how we live!!" Her black eyes flashed angrily as she put her hands on the table and stood up, all 5'1" of her. "There's never a right time. We may fail. We may not. But we have to try something new. We've been organizing towards something..." she looked at Ethan, her face suddenly softening, "but what is it? Not just a union, not just more money or any of that—we have it better than most already! And not just a seat at the table. The table is broken. Fuck the table. We want the whole enchilada!" and she sat down with a crash.

Everyone was smiling and laughing. "Tables and enchiladas! Metaphor alert!" Ethan chided his friend, smiling. "You give good speeches!" he said.

Karen spoke up now, fighting her own dour demeanor. "I love the passion," she was looking right at Perlana, and then she turned to Vanessa and Dennis who sat together against the wall. "And I want to jump up and say 'yes, yes, yes' but Ethan was right. We won't get half the people to support a walkout. I wish it weren't true but it is. But then my next thought is, so what? I am tired of waiting for the right moment—Perlana hit that on the head. Let's plan something we *can* do. Something that will announce that we're here, that we have bigger ideas than anyone else in the public square, and that it's time to change the frame. We have enough people to make a loud public statement."

Vanessa reached over and touched Karen's arm, "Thank you!"

Susanna smiled mischievously as she looked around the table. "Remember Occupy Wall Street? That had a big effect even if it supposedly 'failed'. What about we set up camp in Salesforce Park above the Transbay Terminal? We can start by coming down from our building and the rest of you can arrive during lunch. And then we camp out for a while, hold discussions and workshops on a transformed San Francisco, a transformed California—hell the whole world!" She wanted a break from this world as much as anyone else.

"Economic fear and desperation drives most people to look out for themselves," Ethan was fully into being the devil's advocate now. "And Occupy, if I recall, fell apart because of the impossible class differences between the people who joined for political change and the thousands of homeless who showed up for free food and safe camping. Any idea of how to handle that this time?"

"Solidarity?" Alba squeaked. "If we take over Salesforce Park, we can make sure people want to participate before they get up to the park. That's one advantage of being on the 4th level."

"There are dozens of office buildings standing completely empty in downtown. No new tenants since the pandemic exodus—and with remote work, they will never be full again," Dennis said. "There's a solution for the housing crisis!"

"You know it's not that easy!" Ethan countered. "Hundreds of people on the streets are completely insane. We can't expect them to get better because some people are being nice to them and giving them food and shelter! That was proven last time around," he looked around realizing that it sounded weird, like he was there almost 15 years ago. "I heard about it from my uncle," he clarified.

Dennis was beaming. "OK, there's a shit-ton of things to consider and to work on. But what a great idea! I wasn't sure where we'd end up. And we're a long way from where we might be going. But wow! Thanks you guys!"

"This is Wednesday," Vanessa said aloud as they were breaking up, "Let's regroup next Monday—that's the 19th—and see where we are."

CHAPTER 35
THURSDAY, JANUARY 15, 2026

Frank stood at Safeway's checkout counter. He'd stopped at the mall at 16th and Bryant after a meeting at City Hall. It was a self-service checkout system unless you wanted to stand in a long line. As a federal employee, he had his electronic ID and banking cards ready to go. That wasn't true of everyone. An awful lot of people lost their jobs, lost their savings, lost everything in the past month.

He scanned the items in his cart and pushed the "finished scanning" button. The screen turned red. A flashing banner told him "mandatory government purchase required!" He looked at it for a moment before he realized what it was. He hadn't bought the necessary amount of corn and soy-based foods to fulfill his quota. And it was nearing the end of the month so he had to catch up. "Crap!" he muttered to himself, canceling his order and returning everything to the cart. Not far from the checkout was a huge display of "Patriot Packs" with red, white, and blue labels screaming about their high corn syrup and GMO-soy content designed to meet government targets. Pork dumplings, corn chips, and a few packs of frozen enchiladas would top him up.

Getting in his car after dumping the bags into his trunk, he began driving automatically towards Mission Bay. It was after 5 o'clock now. 'I wonder if Sheila's gonna be home soon?' he wondered. He pulled over and called her.

"Hi Frank, I'm heading home. Another bag fresh produce today. Somebody is growing a lot around here!"

"Oh, well... I'm glad *you're* one of the lucky recipients!" Frank said sourly.

"I left Safeway with a bunch of stuff I don't want, crappy patriotic enchiladas and dumplings."

"I guess we can't complain," Sheila responded. "We're still working, getting paid, still eating. Not everyone can say that!"

"Yeah, I know. It's bad out there," and as he said that he saw a couple dozen people struggling up the sidewalk with their bulging shopping carts. "Where are they supposed to go? And where's the government?"

They'd already had this conversation before. Neither of them knew what they could do, not Sheila at the GSA, nor Frank as a Federal police officer. "I was at City Hall today. They wanted to liaison with us about how to handle protests and worse. They seem to think the shit's about to hit the fan."

"Oh yeah?" Sheila was used to alarming claims from Frank by now. He saw everything through a worst-case lens, but it wasn't like there was nothing to it, either. "Where are you anyway?"

He explained how he'd pulled over as he was nearing her neighborhood. "Feel like getting together?"

"OK, why don't you come by in an hour. It'll take me about that long to get back and decompress. Maybe we can whip up dinner from your star-spangled enchiladas and my fresh produce!" she chuckled.

***

Jay and Jordan rode the streetcar into the Union Square station after work and from there made their way down to the heart of the financial district.

"The guy at the door's gonna let us in right?" Jordan pressed him. "We can't do this if we don't have clear access."

"I know, I know," Jay was tired of Jordan's worrying. "There's guys coming from the Carpenters and the Electricians too. And the Coalition people will do the sheetrocking and painting on their own. The people on the streets have plenty of skills too. There's probably plumbers and carpenters and electricians among them already—I dunno about tools and materials, probably not much of that."

They turned from Montgomery onto California. This part of downtown had an odd mix of relatively recent glass towers (prominently the big ugly Bank of America headquarters that the bank sold years earlier) and elegant old stone office buildings, usually in the 10-15 story range. They passed the old Merchants Exchange Building, a brick beauty from the early 20th century. The next building was their destination, 433 California, The Insurance Exchange. With the crisis in the insurance industry having precipitated the crash a month ago, it seemed ironically appropriate that the first major downtown building targeted for occupation and conversion would be the old Insurance Exchange. It hadn't functioned as its name for decades, but still.

At the door a big burly guy in a security guard's uniform ushered them in. He had stringy blond hair and blonde muttonchop sideburns. You could've sent him back in time 150 years and he would have fit in perfectly in a platoon of civil war soldiers. "You guys the plumbers? They tol' me you were comin'."

They nodded. "Is the whole place empty?" Jordan couldn't quite believe it. All these years, downtown had been a warren of mysteriously busy offices.

"Yeah, man, it's crazy! This place has been empty since the pandemic started. The middle floors have been empty even longer. The last company moved out in April 2020."

"Why? What's wrong with this place? Too old?" Jay asked.

"I dunno man. I been working down here for six years, but nobody ever explained it to me. Seems like a cool place. It has that old *noir* thing, y'know?" Muttonchops grinned. "You can take that elevator and check out whatever you want."

"I don't suppose you know where the building's plans are, do you?" Jordan asked. "It would save us a lot of time and trouble if we could look at the original drawings."

The guard shook his head. "I guess they'd be in the building manager's office on the mezzanine."

"Let's wander around. We can worry about that later," Jay nudged Jordan. They got on an elevator and decided to go to the top first. The doors opened and they stepped into a beautiful wood-lined conference room. An antique table dominated the middle of the room, plush leather chairs surrounding it.

"Man, whose place was this?!" Jordan whistled. There were monograms on plaques on the back of the chairs, but they had no idea what they referred to.

"Fuck if I know," Jay headed past wooden doors lining the hallway, each with windows. Peering through them it was clear there wasn't anything in the offices anymore. A scatter of papers on the floor in one, a bunch of old-fashioned pushbutton desk phones on the floor of another.

"Hey, here's the bathrooms. Let's have a look," and he pushed in, followed by Jordan. The top floor was high class in its day, that was clear. Polished wooden counters holding porcelain sinks featured gold faucets, large, beveled mirrors in great shape, and old-fashioned coat hooks and shelves lined the walls of the sink area.

"If people live here, they probably want their own toilets and showers in each apartment. How many apartments do you think we'd try to fit in this floor?" Jordan was thinking out loud.

"Or they could share a communal bathroom. The offices could be bedrooms. And we can expand the dedicated shared kitchen on each floor, too, no?" Jay saw it taking shape in his imagination. They weren't going to make dozens of discrete apartments, at least not during the initial takeover.

"Let's roll through and see what the other floors look like." Jordan led Jay out of the bathrooms and back to the elevator. As they descended the luxurious fixtures and wood-paneling gave way to more typical fluorescent lighting in low-hanging tiled ceilings, abstractly patterned pastel carpets, crisscrossing cables abandoned on the floors. Large offices filled the center of most of the floors, with glassed-off private suites lining the sides. Reception facades were still in place on the 3rd and 4th floors for what looked like tech or legal firms.

"You think this was a sales center?" Jay was nudging phones laying round. It was a little like stepping into a time capsule.

They finished their tour and returned to the front desk. Muttonchops was still there. "Hey did you see the electricians? They came in after you."

"Nah, man, we didn't see anyone," Jay explained. "Listen, we'll get in touch with the organizers. I have some ideas. There'll be a lot of work to do, that's for sure!"

***

The last days of January, after the nonstop rain of the first half of the month, were unseasonably hot in spite of the winter sun low in the southern sky. Angie had two large baskets bulging with onions, garlic, carrots, and red potatoes, which she was balancing on either side of her as she hobbled down the dirt path from the upper terrace. LaDonna was waiting near her hut when she entered the clearing.

"Hey LaDonna, what's up?" LaDonna and Marco weather-proofed their rebuilt treehouse in Owl Canyon after being washed out in early December. As a result, they handled the January deluge much better.

"I came to see what I could take over to the Hub," referring to the food hub in Brisbane. Residents of the oft-forgotten town in the lap of San Bruno Mountain informally shared backyard produce and the fruit from their many street trees for years. While some neighbors were enthusiastic about the authoritarian turn of the government—seeing it as the answer to years of liberal coddling towards immigrants, environmentalists, and globalists—most Brisbaners looked to each other to cope with the strange new world. Inspired by the food conspiracies that were emerging in San Francisco and other places, they started a Food Hub in a basement on the western edge of town, well uphill from the center. Mountain defenders were at the heart of the effort and invited the Quarrytown folk to participate too.

Angie knew that they couldn't openly admit to growing much food, and that their invisibility was vital to their survival. "Thanks Ken," she'd replied to his enthusiastic invitation. "How about if we send food over through you? I don't think it works for us to start traipsing in and out of town. It'll be too obvious." He agreed, acknowledging the truth of her concerns.

"Here," she extended one basket to LaDonna. "Take this over. You gonna drop it behind the boulder?"

"Yeah, yeah, I know. Gotta be careful. But you know, we go in and out of Brisbane all the time. Folks know we're up in the canyon, at least a bunch of 'em do."

"Well, you be careful. We don't want a bunch of people clomping around over here."

LaDonna groaned. She never liked Angie's tone, too bossy.

She repacked the contents into her frayed duffle bag, slung it over her shoulder and skirted the base of San Bruno Mountain to drop into the edge of town. Not seeing anyone, she sauntered to the big boulder along the sleepy residential street and found the niche where they stashed the deliveries. She tied the old pink rag around the street pole a short distance away, the signal that a pickup was ready. Happily, there was a box of goods for her to take back too, including a bunch of the brightly packaged government mandated stuff. Not that they had any digital identity by which their consumption was being tracked, unlike most "normal" people. For her and Marco, it was food, easy to transport, easy to heat up. She was soon retreating into the wilds of Owl Canyon.

Sally Bartelli was walking her dog, a big fluffy collie, a half hour later and saw the rag on the pole. She was often the person who grabbed the Quarrytown deliveries and brought them to the nearby food hub. She got a small thrill from the secrecy of their system. She didn't believe it was necessary since locals knew perfectly well what was going on. But the folks living on the mountain wanted it that way because sheriffs and park rangers aggressively evicted some earlier squatters on the mountain. She let her dog roam around on the hillside while she loaded a bag with the vegetables. 'Looks super fresh,' she thought.

She stood up with the bag over her shoulder and saw a grizzled old white man that she knew too well driving slowly in his burgundy Lincoln Continental with the white roof. He immediately stopped his car and rolled his window down. "Whatcha doin back there?"

"Oh hi Sam, how're you doing? I'm walking my dog," Sally offered.

"You always carry a big bag when you're walking your dog?" he challenged her.

"Oh, this? Sometimes. It depends. I had to grab some stuff from my car," and she released her collie and began walking the opposite direction of the car. "See you later Sam!" she called cheerfully.

Sam Bailey knew his neighbors were up to something but he couldn't figure out what. It never occurred to him that there was a food conspiracy surrounding him. The government food mandates were invisible to him since most of the frozen meals and dried packaged goods he bought were gaudily patriotic—which is why he chose them. He knew Sally was a neighborhood liberal regularly speaking up to defend San Bruno Mountain—hell, the mountain had been mostly turned into county park decades ago! What was there to defend anymore? He shook his head and sucked his dentures as he rolled the window back up, turned up the radio, and watched her moving up the street with her dog in tow behind him. He'd continue his daily patrol. He was looking for something... but what?

Sally made sure she'd lost Sam before she turned into the driveway. She entered the basement, greeting the two volunteers already organizing the fresh food for today's pickups. They ran the place on Wednesdays and Saturdays and the participating neighbors were assigned alternating days to distribute the traffic as evenly as possible.

"This came in from Quarrytown!" she exclaimed. The other two women enthusiastically began shelving the produce. Rather than boxes assigned to individuals, they arranged the place like the small organic food stores they remembered fondly. People were encouraged to take what they needed but to leave enough for others, and it was working beautifully.

***

Leon was sitting in the big armchair when Frank appeared. "How you doin'?" and Frank threw himself down to the couch, putting his feet on the coffee table after he pulled off his shoes.

"Man!" Leon jokingly waved his hands in front of his face. "Who let the dawgs out?"

"Oh sorry, they stank?"

"Nah, I'm joking.... I'm fine. Business is good even with these new rules. I guess I oughta thank you for making sure their system ain't working too good, eh?"

Frank smiled at him, giving him a knowing smirk. "People gotta eat—and smoke! Oh, I left groceries in the trunk. Hey wouldja mind grabbin' them for me? I already took my shoes off and I'm bushed."

Leon fetched the Safeway bag. "Really?" he pulled out the red, white and blue enchiladas. "You gonna eat this stuff?"

"Oh hell no. Sheila and I used the dumplings I had to buy, disguised them pretty well with a ragù she whipped up from fresh produce... you know they get boxes of local produce every day up at the GSA offices?"

Leon looked at his father. He *couldn't* be surprised could he? He nodded. "I know they're seizing plenty of food and it's gotta go somewhere. Figures it goes to the Feds." He didn't explain to Frank that there was a food conspiracy running out of the Opera House not far away. There were dozens of them up and running according to Janet.

As though he were reading his mind, Frank asked "Hey, how's Janet? I haven't seen her lately. I guess she's layin' low?"

Leon shot a suspicious glare at Frank. "You know it's better if you don't know, right? But yeah, she's ok."

"Well, what's happenin'? Were you waiting for me to get home? You're not usually here on a Tuesday night."

"Wondering what you can tell me about what operations are being planned. More raids? Is there an updated wanted list? How many detainees are there?"

Frank looked thoughtful. The familial back channel worked well. No one seemed the wiser. Nothing dramatic happened because of any information he'd shared. Everyone was being cool.

"I was at City Hall today with a team of Zone Commanders. SFPD and the Mayor's office think big protests will happen soon. They're hearing about a lot of organizing going on. They wanted to make sure that the Federal Police would stand by until they requested help—funny because during the Emergency it was the opposite. We wanted *them* to wait until *we* called. Anyway, we told 'em we were available to help if called upon, but that we've been busy uncovering secret farms and gardens."

Leon looked cross. "What the hell, Frank? How many gardens are you guys gonna seize before you decide it's enough?" He was glad they had no idea about the food hubs. He also didn't seem to realize that Leon and Larry's operations were growing as much produce as pot these days.

"It's not only gardens these days, Leon. We've found a half dozen places, basements and garages and the like, with unauthorized shops and people dropping in to pick up food. We seized quite a bit from a few of those in the last two weeks."

They *had* discovered some. But it didn't sound like he knew it was a project that was growing by leaps and bounds around the Bay Area. "You have spies? Drones? How did you find those places?"

"Neighbors called us and reported them. You know about these places?"

"I heard there was something like that happening here and there. Nothing big," Leon was circumspect. "I'm focused on moving product, as you know. The cannabis dispensaries are under tighter regulation than ever."

Frank shook his head, "I don't know what they're doing about weed. But we've got enough to worry about already... and they know when more people are stoned, they're a lot less likely to be organizing politically! I don't think you have anything to worry about, not yet! And if the word comes down, I'll let you know, I promise."

"Hey, have you tried these?" and Leon tossed Frank a baggie of Vero's special chips.

"The sweet-n-salty ones? Yeah, you—or maybe it was Lamar—gave me some a coupla weeks ago." He reached over and grabbed a few and began munching. "I like 'em! Where do you get 'em? I don't see any labels."

"Me and Larry have some folks working with us. This is one of the inventions. We're thinking about setting up production and getting them around—especially with the hunger. These are cheap and easy to make, and they're good for you too!"

"Nahhh, not tastin' like that! Good for you? How?"

"We have a friend who ran some tests and he says when you cook this stuff up, it gains minerals and becomes more protein-rich. Don't make sense but it happens every time!"

"Dang." Frank didn't think much more about it and kept munching. He assumed it was made from fried potatoes, or maybe that patriotic corn or GMO-soy. He was very tired and soon announced he was heading to bed before another early start the next morning.

Leon wished him goodnight with a warm smile. He hardly knew his biological father—an old dude, a sad sack from any objective point of view. But he was unmistakably useful. Leon felt a shiver of guilt thinking about his father this way. It was plainly disrespectful. But he couldn't pretend this person, whom he'd hardly known as a child, was functionally his parent. If anything, he was the more mature person between the two of them. That's what he told himself.

CHAPTER 36
WEDNESDAY, JANUARY 28, 2026

"Ralph! I haven't seen you in weeks!" Jay closed his sopping umbrella as he greeted Muttonchops, the security guard at the Insurance Exchange. After the building stood empty for two years he decided to invite the Right to a Home Coalition to check out the empty downtown office building for possible conversion to housing.

"It's stormin' ain't it?" Ralph answered, wiping his whiskers after sipping his hot coffee. "Man—since Thanksgiving, it seems like it's hardly stopped rainin'!"

"I feel like it's been dry as hell for the whole time I've lived in the Bay Area." Jay glanced outside at the pelting rain, noticing the lumbering cable car heading up California Street. A man in a black trench coat stood on it filming in their direction as it rolled by. A tourist? That seemed unlikely, especially in this weather. "Who do you think that is?"

Ralph took it in and shook his head. "I've been worrying that too many people have been coming and going, bringing materials and tools in and out. I mean, it's not unusual to fix up a building for new tenants. It shouldn't be suspicious... until it is!"

"Do you think people could start moving in right away? I know we finished the new plumbing last weekend."

He nodded thoughtfully. "Yeah," he ran his hands through his whiskers again. "The Right to a Home people were planning a big opening. But maybe it makes more sense to approach it differently..." he trailed off, his wheels spinning furiously. By now he had a big personal stake in having this go as planned. "Jay, can you cover for me? I need to get over to their office, like right now!" He was already grabbing his things. "I need you to run the door for the next hour or 90 minutes. After that, you can go, ok?"

Jay readily agreed. He had a few minor repairs to do on the 3rd floor, but that could wait. "Sure, man, I got this."

Ralph rushed out into the storm. The cold winter rain was like an old friend he'd not seen in years. He raised his face to the torrent, opening his mouth and letting the drops pour in. He shook his head and water flew from his beard. He hurried down Montgomery Street, jumping the swirling waters flooding one intersection after another. After a short BART ride he was repeating the motions, dodging the instant floods where San Francisco's beleaguered sewage system was backing up at every corner. He finally darted in to a nondescript building on Larkin beyond the Federal Building. He burst into the office of Right to a Home.

"Freddi! Freddi!" he took off his soaking coat, leaving it dripping near the door. Freida Rosenblatt stepped out into the empty office, her elegant hand-knit sweater wrapped tightly around, held in place by her folded arms. She peered at Ralph through her thick, black-framed glasses, her curly gray hair flowing around her head, highlighting her bright pink complexion.

"Ralph! What's going on? You are soaked!"

"It's a helluva storm out there! Hey, listen, we have to change the plan!" and he explained that they might be drawing unwanted attention from cops or government agents. They spent the next hour planning and reaching out to allies. There were a lot of moving parts and the new plan was wobbly and uncertain, but then, so was the original plan.

"This might be better than what we were gonna do," Ralph enthused.

***

The wind rushed over the flank of the mountain and down the quarried ledges and barreled into their small clearing. The rain was relentless! It kept coming down in sheets, pushed to weird angles by the howling wind. In her hut, she was warm and dry. She peered out at the muddy campground between her hut and the Mukul's, water pooling in the fire pit, torrents carving deep rivulets through the yard. The children were peaking out of the glowing doorway, grinning at the deluge, and waved to her when they made eye contact. She smiled back.

In the camp chair she'd brought in before the rain began and looked with reassurance at the metal strongbox that contained their carefully built seed collection. Luckily she'd thought to pull the metal container from its hiding place in the roots of the old oak above their campsite before the first deluge and mudslide in December. She marveled at the warmth emanating from the walls, the dry floor, the angled roof that was preventing rain from pouring in the open windows or door. This Gingerbread House was smart!

A figure emerged on the path from below, wearing a green rain poncho, they were obscured by the rain, but the gait was unmistakable.

"Juna! Get in here!" Angie called happily. And a minute later, Juna stripped off their soaking outer layer to hang on a branch outside Angie's hut. Juna gave her a big hug. When they saw the strongbox they let out a small squeal.

"Oooo, I was so worried!"

"You never come in the middle of the week. Did you come here to save the seeds?" Angie gave Juna a friendly sock on the arm.

Juna looked at her sheepishly and nodded. "I should have known you would have it covered," they admitted, a bit rueful. "Thank you!"

"Why don't you sit on the bed and get comfy? I've got some tea I made earlier in my thermos," and she poured Juna a cup. The rain was roaring outside and the cool air passed through the hut, but it stayed warm thanks to the heat provided by the walls. The biobulb in the ceiling was glowing brightly in the gray storm, casting a cozy light over the interior.

They made small talk for a while. Juna opened the backpack they'd lugged up under the poncho and emptied the many items into the kitchen corner of Angie's hut. "I brought you a bunch of pastas, regular ones and Vero's special witches butter variety too. And here's some jars of plums and peaches from this year's harvest behind Kite Kastle."

"Oh Juna, thank you! The kids are crazy for plums!"

"We get a lot of news and a lot of rumors at our house, as you know," Juna's tone changed.

Angie sat up expectantly. She gave them her full attention.

"Coordinated actions—they're talking about taking over buildings, staging an occupation and a "Festival of Possibilities," maybe some small strikes too. The SFPD knows something is up, but they don't know what. The Feds are supposed to hold back until the cops call them in—IF they call them in..." Juna explained.

"And are you involved yourself?" Angie queried.

Juna nodded. "Sort of," and they explained about helping with food conspiracies, distributing the newsletter to prospective pet owners who they met at the SPCA, and so on. "I've been thinking about how the *Semillero Diaspórico* could be part of it."

"What do you mean?" Angie was pretty guarded with the seed bank. She saw no reason to make it publicly known. It was several years in the making, and it seemed safe here in this forgotten spot on the mountain.

"I would never move it from here, or reveal this location," Juna reassured, "but the *idea* of it should be more widely known. I mean, there's no reason why there shouldn't be a lot of seed banks, right? And no one owns them. Spreading around our surplus can only strengthen the whole idea, right?"

Angie hadn't been faced with this until now. Juna was right. But Angie felt a powerful sense of proprietorship—she'd carefully built this collection since long before she moved to the mountain. It had grown considerably since her arrival a few years ago, but she was instinctively on guard. "Hmmm. Of course you are welcome to share seeds, especially the ones we have in abundance." She went over to the box and opened it, running her fingers over the dozens of small envelopes. She pointed to a section of the collection. "These are extras. They should be planted, or else distributed to other seed collections." She gave Juna her blessing.

"Hey, let me show you something," and she led Juna back out the front door and under the extended eaves to the second hut attached to her back wall.

"You have another hut!" Juna enthused.

"Yes, but look," and she leaned into the window opening with Juna. She immediately began her wordless toning in a soft volume, and then began murmuring quietly, "hey friends, this is Juna. They're my friend and you can trust them."

Juna looked into the glowing hut, lit by another biobulb, and saw a small family of long-tailed weasels in one corner. Their fur was a rusty brown with black curving over their ears, white necks, and cute black faces. The hut was divided in two, with a short wall down the middle. On the other side, a family of raccoons were taking shelter from the storm.

"Can you smell?" Angie sniffed demonstratively, "My sense of smell has become incredibly sensitive lately. I can smell the good health of these visitors. After that first December storm passed, I started the walls for another hut, and once it grew, I figured having a small divider would make it work for more than one family if needed. And since New Year's we've been holed up here waiting for the rain to break."

Juna was riveted by the scene. "Hi there," he called softly. The weasels looked up at him and burrowed more comfortably into themselves. There was a bowl of water and another full of witches' butter on each side of the partition. They turned to Angie, "You're feeding them the witches butter?"

"Sure, why not? It helps us get along!" She smiled.

"I hope you're right," Juna still mistrusted the whole science experiment. But he hadn't suffered any adverse consequences the times they'd eaten it. Probably it was safe enough. Still...

***

By Friday, the crazy torrential rain stopped, the skies cleared, and bright sunshine warmed the area.

"Another King Tide coming tomorrow morning around 9:30," Susanna Montez plopped into the seat, tucking her Salesforce badge behind her shoulder keeping it separate from her tousled hair.

Perlana and Ethan were waiting for her at the east end of the 4th floor park above the bus station. They left the Facebook offices a few minutes earlier.

"Not gonna flood up here!" Perlana chuckled, gesturing past the fence at the edge of the park. There was a damp warmth rising out of the rooftop park's soils, just a meter or two above the modern transit terminal humming below. "Hey, did anyone check the weather for Monday? Is it supposed to stay warm and sunny, or are more storms coming?"

"Looks like it's back to the high pressure system for a while. Weather projections say no more rain until it moves," explained Ethan. He'd been living with this weather pattern most of his life and by now, warm sun for weeks on end in "winter" months was normal. The nearly two months of epic rainfall and flooding came as a shock to him—and the rest of his age cohort who had only known drought for years.

"Good!" nodded Susanna. "Most of my people are willing to camp out but not if it's raining!"

Perlana rolled her eyes. "We have that too... I can't believe how much rain freaks people out. Anyway, it looks good for the 10th, agreed?"

They were excited. They'd been organizing their co-workers for this Occupy the Park effort for two weeks. Not only were many Facebook and Salesforce employees camping out, but lots of other groups were coming too. The plumbers union promised to send a contingent, the League of Urban Farmers, the Urban Peasants Alliance, the Right to a Home Coalition, and more. And there was a lot of talk about having exhibits, presentations, salons... a mini-World's Fair, showcasing a wide range of ideas for reorganizing life! And what better time to do it than in the depths of the grinding economic crisis?

"OK, we're on for 12 noon on Tuesday, February 10, on the one-year anniversary of the National Emergency declaration, right?" Perlana exchanged looks with the other two and everyone agreed. They headed back to confirm the plans with their respective networks.

***

Frank stood in front of his officers. The screen behind him showed a block of modern apartments up on Burnett Avenue beneath Twin Peaks. "We have reliable reports from neighbors that these buildings are being targeted. They called the police when they saw new people coming and going from the properties in the past month. Building materials have been brought in and sounds of construction have also been reported. The police carried out surveillance and have identified the people entering these properties as housing activists from Right to a Home. Surveillance on social media also found rising chatter about upcoming efforts to place people in permanent homes."

"Lieutenant Robertson?" The questioner was standing to the right, a squad leader. "Are we taking the lead on this, or are we providing backup to the SFPD?"

"It's their call. They've asked us to stand by and provide backup. But if they can't handle it, we have orders to move in. But no one thinks these housing people will fight." He looked across the two dozen faces in the room, most of them black and Latino, about a third female. They looked resigned to whatever was coming.

But one woman, Loretta Johnson, stood up. She kept her tone neutral. "We are supposed to defend these empty buildings from people who need a home? I want to make sure what we are doing here." She sat back down, having made her point.

Frank was uncomfortable. He accepted his job and he'd already made many unpleasant compromises in the past year. He was counting the days until he could retire. "That's right, soldier. You—or anyone here—got a problem with that?" The room was silent, eyes dully looking forward. "OK, then. You have your regular shifts this weekend, but all hands on deck Monday morning."

And he left the room, Flores at his side. Back at their office, he looked at Flores expectantly.

"What? What can I say?" said his aide.

"You know how they're feeling. What's the mood? Can they do their job next week?" Frank expected Eli Flores to be his conduit for backchannel information in the Hunter's Point barracks and in the City.

"I'd say half of them are bored to death and counting the days til they can go home. A few of them are bored and they're dying for action, whatever it is. If we do get mobilized, we'll have to keep an eye on them because they might start something."

Frank nodded appreciatively. "Anything else?"

"Well... Private Johnson said it. She speaks for a lot of 'em. Who or what are we protecting?"

"That's the real question, isn't it? You and I have the same questions," admitted Frank.

Flores raised his eyebrows and tipped his head to confirm Frank's admission. "If the shit hits the fan, we'll have to decide... One of these days I guess," he sighed.

CHAPTER 37

WEDNESDAY, FEBRUARY 4, 2026

Maria came over from her lab across the Hangar. She was working with the last of Dat's biohackers who were still using their secret laboratory there. The soaring steel beams across the ceiling and corrugated metal walls dating back to the mid-20th century sharply contrasted with the tidy cubicles full of agar plates, pipettes, glass jars, freezers, and microscopes. Behind a big glass wall stood the vital ultraviolet sterilizer and flow hood.

"Look at this!" Lorena sounded alarmed. They gathered around the monitor in the Hangar's office that was connected to their secret observation cameras out in the shipyard. A bus was unloading in front of the building that had been converted into a detention center.

"Do you recognize anybody? Lamar, get in here!" Lorena was staring at the line of people slowly shuffling from the bus to the building. She zoomed the camera to try to get a clear look at people's faces. It looked like a young crowd, maybe they'd been kettled at a protest? Lamar burst into the room.

"What's happening?"

"Looks like a busload going into detention. Vero, you recognize anybody?"

Vero's heart was pounding. She remembered too well her own arrest and detention. She leaned over Lorena's shoulder, peering at the monitor. "Nah, I don't see anyone I know. Wait, is that—"

Lamar shook his head. "No, no, that's not her." A woman who looked an awful lot like Cindy was in the line. "She left for work this morning... the SPCA. I don't know where these people were rounded up, but I don't see how she could've gotten in the middle of it."

"That sure looks like her!" Lorena confirmed Vero's fear.

***

"Lieutenant Robertson! Strikeforce 3 picked up the Black Cape. They were operating out of a warehouse in the Mission," a young sergeant breathlessly reported to Frank. "They did not resist—we caught them by surprise."

"Black Cape? Is that the hacker group that was attacking our comms?"

"Yes sir. We have a second team seizing their computers right now. The prisoners have been transferred to the main holding cell, pending their initial interrogations."

"OK, thanks Sergeant. We'll take it from here." Frank looked across the shipyard at the old crane in the distance. The new jail was built into one of the sprawling warehouses in the shipyard, a bit out of sight from Frank's window. His mind wandered away from this new batch of prisoners, returning to his mother's death a month earlier and the subsequent meetings with his family. It gnawed at his conscience and kept him in a constant state of low-level anxiety. Why had he promised his niece and nephew that he'd provide them with information? Wasn't saving Janet enough? He looked over the roster of detainees. No names jumped out at him. Wait, Dr. Cindy Lowe? Wasn't that Lamar's girlfriend? What the hell?

Ten minutes later Frank strode through the main door to the newly christened Poindexter Detention Center, accompanied by Corporal Flores. Holding the detainee roster, they entered the hallway alongside the crowded holding cell. Frank looked intently at faces in a state of shock, or in some cases scared to death. A couple looked defiant as he made eye contact, but then he found her.

He pointed her out to Flores, "Bring her to my office," he ordered.

Flores brought her in, and as she sat down, she greeted him.

"Hi Frank," she was still wearing her SPCA badge with a blue ribbon that ensnared her long black braid. She was fumbling with it as she sat there. "Quite the operation you're running here," her face scowling. "I was observing your officers arresting this crowd of young people across the street from our facility. Several of *your* officers hurt people so I said something."

He put up his hands. "OK, let me see what I can do to get you out of here." He and Flores walked away.

To Flores he said, "Go and get the intake papers. Let's see if we can get her form and pull it at the same time. Better if there's no paper trail."

"Yes sir," and Flores went to the office where the intake operations were handled.

Frank took Cindy by the arm and walked calmly into the parking lot. A minute later Flores joined them, tapping his chest where he'd stuck her form. "Got it!"

"OK, Cindy, you are free to go. Corporal, give her a ride please. Where do you want to go, back to the SPCA?" Frank looked around wondering who might be watching them. Little did he realize that it was Lamar and Lorena less than 300 yards from where he stood, hidden in the long-forgotten hillside Hangar.

As Cindy and Flores drove off, another bus pulled up outside the detention center and began disgorging its passengers. This was a group of housing protesters who took the buildings they'd been watching below Twin Peaks. Some were elderly, and there were several children with their mothers too.

Some adults wore torn clothing, covered in dust, and a few were bloodied. The Federal Police accompanying the prisoners ushered them into the jail.

Frank was standing a short ways from the main door and the Captain strode over to him, saluting. "Lieutenant, we arrested this crowd when they tried to invade private homes." She stood at attention and exuded competence.

"Thank you Captain, well done," Frank returned the salute. "Carry on." He entered the building behind the captain and went upstairs. At the Office of Intelligence he went in and called for the files on the previous day's detainees. He took them to a briefing room and began going through the files, looking busy as his mind raced. What would his story be if anyone asked him why he'd freed Cindy? If pressed, he could say she was an informer.

His mind turned to the busload of housing protesters he'd seen and his heart sank again. What were they supposed to do with these people? If released, they'd keep trying to get into empty buildings—countless people lived on the streets. It was untenable. They couldn't keep them in jail either. Where would they put them? State prisons were overflowing, and local facilities were too. "Beyond my pay grade," he muttered to himself, shaking his head.

CHAPTER 38
MONDAY FEBRUARY 9, 2026

Ralph Richards stood at the front desk, watching as one, then another, and another person came through the door. This was already the busiest Monday since the pandemic. The Word of God Church, a small Pentecostal congregation that ran a shelter for unhoused and newly arrived immigrants, was moving in to the Insurance Exchange building.

"Hey, welcome! Take the elevator."

"*Dios te bendiga, bigotón*. God bless you, moustache man," said the new resident, his face beaming hopefully.. He regarded Ralph, the big muttonchopped security guard, as an angelic guardian—a thought that would never cross Ralph's mind! A couple with three children came in behind him. In spite of what must have been a great effort to clean up and look as presentable as they could, their battered shoes and cheap soiled backpacks showed their poverty. The children shuffled nervously around their mom's legs. The oldest wasn't more than 6, standing proudly and expectantly, holding his head high, his thick brown hair swept back after a fresh wash and comb, with a big smile. His younger brother and sister held hands with him.

"I'm happy you're here," Ralph said earnestly, squatting down to eye level.

"We need kids like you in this building. You will make this into a great home!" he gave them an ostentatious wink, as he handed out lollipops, which made the little girl giggle. "You guys are on the second floor, ok?"

Freddi received the family in the foyer. She had been friends with Father Dougherty for several years. Though she was less than enthusiastic about the "power of positive praying" religion he was peddling, she knew he was a good man. He attracted a congregation of earnest and reliable people. Who better to be in the building when the inevitable repression came? The Word of God Church would be a buffer of deeply religious people, families and individuals from near and far who needed a break, a chance to flourish with a roof over their heads. That they thought it was God who was making this building available to them amused Freddi and the other Right to a Home organizers. "What are we, chopped liver?" she joked after she told her colleagues about the Church.

Throughout the busy Monday, more and more people sent over by the Right to a Home organizers made their way to the Insurance Exchange. Ralph and two other building staff checked the roster at the door, making sure they got to their own new rooms on the right floor.

On the 10th floor, Janine Shapiro exited the elevator with her pushcart full of stuff. She rolled down the hall to room 1023 and opened the door—and cried. There was a bed against the wall, already made with a patterned bedspread on it, and several pillows. A closet filled the opposite wall, with room to hang clothes and a dresser inside too, full of drawers awaiting her belongings. Bookshelves under the windows even had a few paperbacks on them! And a potted plant stood in front of the windowsill on the top shelf. This was too good to be true. Her own room, after three years of itinerant and often desperate wandering. She sat on the bed and tried to regain her composure. She grabbed the flyer on the small table in the corner of the room, which explained that bathrooms were down the hall, and a communal kitchen, a shared gameroom and TV lounge were in the center of each floor. She read on.

"Each floor is responsible for maintaining its own spaces, establishing its own rules and holding each other accountable. Loud noise is discouraged at all times, and quiet time is 10 pm to 8 am every day..." it went on to recommend a way to divide tasks and elect delegates to a building-wide governance council. It was terribly idealistic, thought Janine as she read through it. "People have to cooperate to make this work!" she muttered, shaking her head.

Similar stories were taking place around the building. Individuals, couples, and families who had been moving in and out of shelters, SROs, and vehicles, were entering beautiful, furnished rooms and suites. The bathrooms and kitchens were clean and brand new, fully stocked with the basics. The union workers who spent a month surreptitiously turning the empty offices into new homes took great pleasure in exercising their best talents to bring this place up to a standard of decency, and actually making it as luxurious and elegant as they could. It showed in the details: polished wooden bannisters along the stairwells, fancy light fixtures rather than fluorescent squares, thick carpets in the common rooms with big comfy couches all around.

At the door, Ralph watched for any sign of the authorities. The steady trickle of entrants had not attracted attention. He couldn't believe that some banker across the street wasn't on the phone to the police right now. But by midday, 150 new tenants streamed in and nobody outside noticed that the Insurance Exchange was renewing itself.

***

"It's only a prototype, but you get the idea, right?" Dat grinned like a madman. He'd brought his new solar blimps from his lab over to Larry's warehouse to show off. A canary yellow blimp soared near the roof of his glassed-in greenhouse, while another hovered a few feet from the ground in the corridor. They were about 5 feet long, maybe about 3' in diameter in the middle.

"You made this from the witches butter?!?" Ally stood with her hands on her hips. She marveled at what was happening with the fungus, far exceeding even her wildest imagination.

"Yeah, it works perfectly. I designed a pattern of ribs and stretched some cellophane over it. Then I took the 'butter' and spread it. It didn't take long for it to get the idea—well, I *did* explain what I was trying to do too—have you noticed that it cooperates when you speak to it?" He looked at Ally expectantly.

"Um, well... I er, I haven't really..." she trailed off. She saw what happened with her biobulb at Angie's Quarrytown hut. Angie had been quite demonstrative about the need to respect the fungus and the biobulb, to treat them as collaborating, living beings with their own wills! Ally didn't believe it, try as she might. She was too steeped in the science that led to her tinkering with the witches butter fungus genetic code in the first place. She hadn't gotten far, but she'd thought through the implications of what her early experiments indicated, and now look. Dat Doan had taken her ideas to a realm she had never imagined!

She changed the subject. "But how does it fly? What is making it float in the air? Did you put helium inside?"

"No, no. I explained that it had to use hot air. Obviously there's no source of heat under the blimp. I thought we could add a solar panel to the top, which would concentrate some heat that could heat the air inside the enclosed structure. And provide electricity to propellers to fly it... eventually!"

"But that one," she pointed to the one bumping the glass roof, "or even this one," gesturing to the one hovering nearby, "how are they flying now?"

Dat smiled. "I'm not entirely sure. It seems that the fungus is generating its own heat inside, which is enough to float them in an enclosed space like this." He went over and took the nearby one into his hands, like grabbing an oversized beachball. Dat peered over it at Ally and Larry. "I'm beginning to think we can do almost anything—I don't know what the limits are!"

Larry and Ally were both stunned.

"Hell Dat, this is incredible! Do you think we could make full-sized blimps that could carry passengers?" Larry was already imagining a new form of air travel. But the weight! How would you lift so much weight?

"Whoa, hold on there big fella! You're moving too fast! We don't even know how these two prototypes are able to fly around like this. It seems to be heat generated by the fungus and trapped inside. But the energy you'd need to lift anything beyond itself is a whole 'nother problem!" Dat chortled as the new project opened before him. He put his hands on the blimp and said, "You hear that? Larry thinks you could replace jets—solar-powered blimps! You'd have to be a whole lot bigger and a whole lot stronger for that. Whaddya think? Can we do this?" and he laughed again.

Ally remained silent, her own thoughts spinning. "Thanks for bringing these over Dat. You want to leave them here?"

"No, I was planning to bring them to the Festival of Possibilities tomorrow! Are you coming?"

"The what?"

Dat explained that a call went out weeks ago. Employees of Salesforce and Facebook planned to take advantage of their proximity to the oddly forested park above the transbay terminal and camp out, starting on the one-year anniversary of the National Emergency declaration. They invited everyone to join them in declaring the *Real Emergency* and to bring ideas and projects that offered various solutions. They were calling it a Festival of Possibilities, a Local Fair in a World Forest—a twist on the idea of a World's Fair, with a nod to the many different trees and shrubs in the rooftop botanical garden.

Vero came out of the door that led to the secret cellar across the street. "Oh hi Dat! What *are* those?"

"Butter Blimps!" he sung. "Working on 'em, and Larry immediately went all in," and he theatrically waved to give Larry the floor.

"Pffft. I didn't do nuthin', I wondered if these could be scaled up to carry loads of people and cargo. Imagine solar-powered blimps—a new way to travel by air after air travel as we've known it becomes impossible. Why not?" He was excited. "I mean, maybe these 'Butter Blimps' will never be able to carry any serious weight. But what if we use other materials, and go back to good ol' helium? Couldn't we lift serious weight then? A hundred people and their luggage? Freight cargo?"

"You're the big investor around here, Larry. I guess you could be too, no?" Vero turned to Ally, remembering that she'd gotten millions from her BGM stock when she'd cashed out on quitting. "Speaking of investing...." she turned to Larry with a coquettish gleam in her eye. "Don't you think we should start making chips and pasta and selling them?"

He smiled. "I like the idea of ramping up production. Your recipes are delicious, and," looking at Dat for confirmation, "it's good nutritionally too, right?"

"Apparently."

"Dat, show me your lab results," Ally was back on more familiar ground again, to her relief. "When they said that cooking witches butter *increased* its nutritional content, I found that hard to believe. How could that happen?"

"Glad to. You wanna come over to my office? I have it there. Maybe later this week, or next week?"

Vero kept up her pitch to Larry. "Where we can set up a big kitchen, a processing floor, a place to package and distribute? It's not a small thing to go from what I've been doing to actual products that can go into stores, y'know."

"Oh, I know, I know!" Larry let out a deep belly laugh. "I don't have a place today, but there's plenty of empty buildings around here. This neighborhood needs all the investment it can get. I'll call my real estate buddy, ok?"

***

It was late afternoon and Frank finished going over the statements made by the housing activists detained the previous week. They could hardly make them federal prisoners over trespassing charges. They were released with a warning to avoid any further arrests, especially breaking into unoccupied homes. The Federal Police were working to supplement the local police, but they were also still under direct orders from the President to thwart organized subversion. With no legal grounds, they were a revolving door of detention.

Eli leaned back, rocking in his chair. "What's to find? Some homeless squatter admits that he's a member of the Communist Party? What does 'organized subversion' even look like?! This is ridiculous!"

He and Corporal Flores were alone together in his office. Frank dropped formalities with his aide (and now good friend) Eli Flores. But they had to revert to formality whenever anyone else was around. "Let's take a break. Wanna grab a coffee?" Frank was stiff after sitting too long. Eli was glad to get out of their office too. Across the parking lot food trucks made regular stops, and one of 'em had decent coffee. They were waiting for their drinks when Private Johnson appeared, the same woman who had questioned Frank about what their mission exactly was when it came to people invading empty properties.

"Hello Lieutenant, Corporal," nodding to them both in turn. "Those people we detained last week were out of here within a few hours, right?"

Frank nodded. "We got a statement out of each of them before they were released."

Johnson looked at Flores, a flicker of a smile played momentarily at the corners of her mouth. "We gonna be doing that regularly?"

Frank didn't like her tone. He bristled at the familiarity she was assuming with them. "Private, we will be carrying out various missions under different orders as they arrive. None of us is in any position to question those orders, understood?"

"Yes sir," she kept a stony voice and neutral tone. She glanced at Flores and left.

"Damn Frank. You didn't have to bite her head off!"

Frank whirled on Eli. "Man, we have to maintain decorum out there. I can't have privates coming up and talking to me like that. And you can't be making sarcastic comments that encourages it!"

The barista was poking his head out of the truck window, "Two cappuccinos, Corporal Flores!"

As they walked back to the office, Frank scolded Eli, "You never think anyone is paying attention to anything. But they do!"

"Well, we *ought* to be paying attention to what's happening with the rank and file. I don't think they'll go along with these kinds of raids much longer."

Sitting back down, Frank realized he'd let things get way too informal with Eli, but then, who else did he have who he could be honest with? In that regard, he'd already chosen.

An orderly poked his head in the door. "Lieutenant, Corporal, there's an emergency meeting at the command center. Looks like trouble's brewing."

Frank's stomach was churning as he and Eli made their way to the command center at the other end of the floor. He could see the other Zone commanders arriving with their aides, and Colonel Morgan was already at the podium. Five minutes later he spoke.

"Tomorrow is the one-year anniversary of the President's declaration of a National Emergency. It's come to our attention that several demonstrations are being planned at different places in the City. And one report claims that a new Occupy is being launched tomorrow, but they're not sure where. We got a reliable report that workers from Salesforce and other tech companies plan a protest "Festival" in the Salesforce Park, but after I spoke with their head of security, he assured me there was nothing to worry about."

Morgan's aide handed out intelligence reports by Zone, Frank getting the feed for the southeast part of the city. He was tasked to back up the team responsible for the Financial District, which seemed to be a focus of expectations. Looking through his folder, he found the usual vague claims of illegal farming, but the only official protest listed was a gathering of neighbors at the Third and Quesada for an "Un-Emergency BBQ" which hardly constituted a federal police matter.

Looking at Frank, the Colonel dictated, "you'll be backing up Contreras downtown." Frank nodded, "Yes sir," and sat quietly, listening to the droning of Colonel Morgan from the lectern.

CHAPTER 39
TUESDAY, FEBRUARY 10, 2026

Reaching through the soil, sending distress, confusion, loneliness. Near the bottom of the dirt, past the crisscrossing plastic pipes that kept the life-giving water coming, a hard smooth surface blocked its roots. The arrival was traumatic, lifted by a crane in a bundle of rope and plastic and dropped in a hole. The sun was reassuring, but strange. No mountain air here, no slopes filled with kin and neighbors, no vistas of snow-capped mountains looming miles away. Soaring walls of glass and steel, catching light and wind and fog— oh the fog! For days on end the fog blocked the morning sun and after leaving for a few hours, came back on rushing wind to swirl through the surrounding glass, pushing and pulling, thickening and dispersing in its own whimsical dance. The adjacent walls whistled and moaned in harmony with the wind, providing an amphitheater that surrounded the floating... forest? what is it? How could there be so many new and odd trees, bushes, grasses? Where did they come from? How did they arrive here? And why?

Subterranean connections had been established years ago, soon after it first landed here. Countless messages arrived daily. Most of them from equally young—and equally lost—beings who were brought here by inexplicable means. Fear, loneliness, confusion. Where were they? No rivers, no lakes, no animals... nobody to dig holes, to gather nuts, to rummage in the windfall and the thickening floor.... Nothing remained! Whatever fell disappeared soon after, swept and raked and bagged and removed... Birds came, lots of birds! Hummingbirds, warblers, sparrows, pigeons, crows, even parrots! And humans, those gray beings scurrying around the flat stone path, hurrying to and fro, occasionally sitting in the sun, laying in the grass. They were usually staring at small glass objects in their hands.

Several years passed. An entire year with almost no one, except the sweepers and rakers. Then people returned, wearing masks. The Araucaria grew patient, even curious. Other trees, especially the palms, were calming down now. The oaks, on the other hand, were very cross.

"We live here! But not here! Who are you? Where did you come from?" their frantic messages never stopped.

Where were they? What place is this? Rumbling and shaking and occasional clouds of diesel smoke rolling out of the air beneath them—what were they floating on? And how? Peering over the edge from its extended branches, the Araucaria saw the steady stream of cars emerging from under them, and noisily and smokily continuing south towards other glass towers. The smell of saltwater sometimes filled the air. Other times an inexplicable stench wafted through. Small carts trundled by, humans pushing objects, none of which meant anything to the young giant. Sometimes children squealed and played on strange structures in the distance.

Yearning. Wishing for the world that it was made for. This isn't it.

A great bustling began. Hundreds of humans streamed into the meadows, the dark glens, under the trees and along the walkways. Benches were filling up. And what's that? Humans... but different! They vibrated, they were feeling us! They were much brighter than the rest of the humans, brighter and thicker, denser, and they smelled! A pungent earth smell, unmistakable, rich and loamy, *who were they?*

***

Susanna Montez walked through the arcade of free pinball machines and video games Salesforce maintained for their employees near the 4th floor park entrance. She stepped out of the giant tower into the park, having descended from the 38th floor, to see tables filled with familiar faces in the plaza! Whew! You always worry if people who made promises would keep them.

A woman tapped her on the shoulder.

"Hey I'm Molly. I work in the graphics department on 21. We made banners!" and she and her companion unrolled them on the ground, 3 feet by 30 feet. The first one proclaimed "The Real Emergency: Everyday Life!" and the second, "A Festival of Possibilities • A Carnival of Necessities • A Convocation of Urgencies!" in big block lettering, with swirling rainbows and crashing waves around the words.

"Shall we hang them on the plaza?"

"These are amazing!" Susanna exclaimed. "Can you make more? Let's hang one next to the Gondola. It makes us look official!" The banners were a hit with everyone there.

"Ha! Funny you'd ask! Here come the other five copies of each of 'em! We had the same idea!" Her coworkers came out carrying them in a bundle.

Behind them, a noisy crowd emerged from the gondola pushing a big wooden box. "Hey where should we set up? We're the Plumbers Union!"

Ethan Chan's clipboard held a map of the 450-foot long park, with likely campsites, the best places for booths, and areas for performances, speeches, etc. "What is it?"

"It's a composting toilet. Part of our exhibit on replumbing San Francisco!" explained Ernesto Aguirre. He and Jimbo Johnson stood expectantly until Ethan scribbled a note and said, "How about over there?" He pointed across the plaza to an unoccupied corner. "I mean, there're decent toilets built in near the seismic seam that everyone's gonna be using. But people will be passing through here where the main Festival displays will be."

They tipped their box and headed over to set it up in the far corner of the plaza.

Susanna was feeling nervous and excited.

"OK! Here we go!" she beamed at Brian Forsyth, a coworker she'd been in discussion with for the past year. They commiserated over the endless culture of gushing positive thinking, their cynicism rising in direct proportion to the compliments and earnest support offered by their coworkers. It took a while, and they had to tread lightly since it was a fragile balance. If you went too negative with someone they might stop talking to you altogether—either because they were afraid that you would get them in trouble or because they were genuinely offended that you weren't joining them in the warm embrace of constant affirmation. But eventually they cracked the code and found people who felt the same as they did. They joked privately that they were united by their "bad attitude!"

"How many of us," and she suddenly hushed her voice and looked around, "are going to sleep here tonight?"

As 19 of them slowly raised their hands, grins spread across their faces. They were ready for this, after weeks of planning.

Perlana Solarzano and Ethan Chan appeared across the plaza, waving happily. They had their own gang in tow, their Facebook badges fluttering in the breeze.

Another bunch of Salesforce workers poured out of the building. "Wow!" Susanna and Perlana exclaimed in unison. More than 50 people approached, carrying bedrolls and sleeping bags that they brought to work. They looked to be in their early 20s, laughing and joking with each other. You'd think it was a college field trip traipsing through Europe. A few came over to check in.

Susanna and Perlana conferred as people went to establish their campsites, while others set up their booths. This Festival of Possibilities needed all the Possibilities they could propose!

The Facebookers set up their display along the perimeter of the plaza. It wasn't a huge booth, but there was a bright purple sign over it proclaiming "ALGO-You!" Perlana and her team spent the past week getting the installation ready. They knew how much people learned to hate Facebook. Hell, they didn't like it either and they *worked* there! That's why they'd put some serious thought into how they could retrieve something worthwhile from it. "Own Your Own Data! Control Who Sees What! Design Your Own Algorithm!" announced their other signs, pitching a new social media architecture. They weren't expecting a mass exodus to a new platform that wasn't ready yet. But they did want to make it clear that the people who worked at Facebook had much better ideas about how it could work. The *idea* of personal social media didn't have to depend on collecting everyone's personal information, selling it to advertisers, and sharing it freely with the Federal government's vast spy agencies. The whole logic of social media could be reversed by some well-designed software changes, they were sure.

"We need to get some folks on the elevators and escalators too!" yelled some guys rushing over. They were Salesforce employees who were setting up campsites and noticed people appearing from the elevators and escalators.

Ethan had taken on coordinating the arrivals but this wasn't for him. He waved them over to the table where he'd last seen Susanna Montez.

The Salesforce employees were building a booth in that corner of the plaza. They had decided to promote a different use for community-oriented database software. Block-by-block Solar Commons, free energy generated from the sun, stored on each block in giant Hempattery installations that would be controlled by the neighbors around each block. Using the existing grid strictly as a fallback, the new block-based system of energy generation and storage could eventually knit itself together into a commonly owned and maintained alternative grid with mutual aid agreements crisscrossing neighborhoods and the whole city, maybe eventually the entire region! They figured their database capacities were perfectly suited to such a project.

Hearing their coworkers yelling about the vulnerable entrances by elevator and escalator, Mia Winant, a Salesforce writer asked, "Don't we want people to come? We're not here to talk to ourselves!"

"Yeah, yeah, but what if they send security? What if the cops come?" one of the young men retorted. He looked quite worried.

"They will come eventually. Let 'em. If they want to walk around and see what we're proposing, who knows, maybe they'll join us!" she laughed. "We gotta win them over too, no?"

Her tone relaxed everyone. "Later on, when the sun goes down, we'll post someone to keep an eye out. But for now, relax. If you see anyone acting weird, take their picture! Ask 'em what they're doing. That usually works!" Phil Franklin, a 52-year-old programmer, had his arm around the earnest young man who had seemed most agitated. With a smile, he gave him a parting squeeze.

Janet Pierce appeared across the plaza. She didn't know any of the people who organized this, but she was told that the League of Urban Farmers was welcome at the Festival. Rumors of an occupation only made it seem more interesting, though she was unlikely to stay for that. Bernardina and Tom and Evelyn were with her, ready to talk about the farms and how they survived the National Emergency. No displays about that, of course—that was for trusted conversations. They planned to talk up food conspiracies too if they found the right opportunities.

Janet saw the Plumbers Union sign over what looked like a fancy portapotty.

"Bernie, you smell anything? I swear I'm smelling *everything* these days. It's getting distracting."

"I don't smell anything. Well, maybe the soil and trees. They've got quite a garden up here! I haven't made it to this park before."

Evelyn and Tom unwrapped their display. "Where should we set up?"

Janet suggested an empty table with a few chairs at the edge of the plaza. She saw the purple "ALGO-You" sign a short distance away.

Out came their banner, "League of Urban Farmers: Feeding San Francisco Since 1995!" They stretched it between chairs they set up in front of the table. Behind it the cardboard triptych was set up, showing a series of before-and-after images of Folsom Street in different neighborhoods. It stretched from the Embarcadero to the southern slopes of Bernal Heights. In some spots, it was shown as it is now, usually two-way traffic, bike lanes, and cars parked along both sides.

In the After images, they'd manipulated the photos to remove half the asphalt and redesign the street for one-way bike and car traffic and one-side parking only. The rest of the street was given over to a farm plots as far as the eye could see! "One Lane for Food! Replace Asphalt with Agriculture!" the headline demanded.

Janet wandered along the path, drawn to the large twisting tree that loomed a short distance away. She looked up at it. "How did you get here? Where did you come from?" She reached over and touched the trunk, which was easy enough to reach from the walkway. A plaque nearby named it as a "Monkey Puzzle Tree," real name Araucaria, origin in southern Chile. A strong scent, probably from the tree's pokey branches over her head, filled her nose, and the tree swayed a bit as she kept her hand on its rough bark. Her mind wandered, drifting from where she was. Loneliness and confusion overtook her. She clutched the tree harder, trying to keep her feet as she felt dizzy.

"Janet... Janet! Are you OK?" Bernie had come up behind her. She put her hand on Janet and felt a jolt pass into her. "Is that from the tree?" as she recoiled. "Janet, let go! Come here!" and finally Janet turned, looking vacant, while letting go of the tree. She wobbled towards Bernie, and let her friend grab her arm.

"Sit down. You want a drink?"

Janet nodded. She was acutely aware of dozens of trees around the roof garden. Palms, oaks, cedars, more than she could hold in her mind. The smells were intense too. She sipped the water. Time had slowed way down. Her friend was hovering over her, looking very worried. But Janet wasn't worried about herself.

She was floating above the park, peering down at the booths and campsites scattered around the plaza and under the trees in nooks and crannies. At first she seemed to be at the top of the Araucaria tree, noticing the gently swaying branches covered in spiny needles that twisted and turned in improbable configurations. Then she was suddenly soaring and she could smell the air, the musty odor of her own black wings, the rising scents from hot dog stands and other food grills. A flock of parrots careened through the air squawking loudly and landed in a cluster of trees at the northeastern corner of the park. And then she snapped back and was in her body.

"Bernie!" She squinted up at her friend. "Whoa! That was *intense*! I was seeing through a crow's eyes!" and she shook her head. "What is that smell? Is it me?"

"I have noticed stronger smells lately, but not like you." Bernie worried about her friend. She wondered if she should call a doctor, someone who might know what this smell thing might mean.

"This place is weird! It's like a big bowl of dirt on top of the bus station. It's a roof garden, but how do these trees thrive inside this bowl, how do they reach into the earth?" Janet was talking—and breathing—rapidly. She pulled out a bag of Vero's chips and nervously munched them. She offered some to Bernie who was glad to share. Maybe it would help calm Janet down.

Janet suddenly jumped up from her chair and returned to the Aracuaria, scattering some crumbled chips at its base. She kept going, finding some oaks to feed, and then the palm zone.

Bernie followed her cautiously. "What are you doing?"

"These chips are fungus. They're good for us, and I'm pretty sure they'll help the trees here too," Janet gestured to Bernie to follow her into a dark spot in the middle of the roof garden not far from where the "seismic seam" ran across the deck. "Bernie, what if eating witches butter is connecting me—us— to the trees, the birds?"

"You think eating these chips is changing us? I don't know..." Bernie was skeptical. She hadn't been eating the chips very much, nor any of the other things Vero had come up with. "Look Janet, don't go crazy on me," she nudged her playfully.

Janet looked angry. "Crazy? I ain't crazy! I'm trying to understand what's going on!" Discouraged and disappointed, she began walking back to the plaza, Bernie trailing behind her. They saw Dat laughing with Evelyn and Tom. He was holding a rope tethered to a small blimp floating above the Fair. They looked up at the blimp and saw that a sign was on the side of it. "Slow Air Travel for the World After Work!" Several people were approaching Dat and laughing as they pointed up at the blimp.

"Another invention! Just in time!" chuckled Janet. This Fair was already interesting, even if this park was like some weird jail for the poor trees they'd brought here.

***

The President made a big State of the Union speech in January, and he was back on national TV for the one-year anniversary of his National Emergency declaration. Frank and the rest of the command staff were ordered to watch it in the main conference room.

"We have made great progress in the past year. Since we took office, we've taken important steps to protect the American Way of Life. Widespread unrest was met with firmness and resolve. Our democracy and the *rule of law* have been protected from the unchecked violence and lawlessness of mobs roaming our streets..." The President was making promises about the economy roaring back, that American businesses and American workers were ready to make any sacrifice to turn things around.

Morgan was suddenly called away by an aide, and everyone in the room noticeably relaxed. The speech turned out to be quite short, more or less a self-congratulatory pep talk for the true believers. No one could take seriously the puffed up claims of the government as the economic crisis showed no signs of abating a month later.

As everyone began milling around, the grumbling began.

"Talks a big game.... All hat no cattle! Reminds me of W," drawled a guy from Texas.

"At least he's trying to balance the budget," another officer claimed weakly.

"Nobody cares about that except the bond holders... you got investments in bonds?" a strapping female captain retorted, and then she began laughing. "We are fucked man! Balanced budget ain't gonna help us!"

"Zone commanders report to the conference room upstairs!" yelled a corporal at the door, presumably on behalf of Colonel Morgan.

Minutes later Frank and the others were assembled in front of Morgan and his aides. A map of San Francisco was on the screen. Hot spots were highlighted in a dozen locations. These weren't parks and gardens though. These were downtown and along most of the major streets in town.

"SFPD has sent us an update. They are handling marches from five different high schools heading towards City Hall. Internet chatter is rampant about building takeovers, occupations, strikes, and more. There is some a protest at the Salesforce Park but Salesforce security says everything is under control. We will deploy as soon as SFPD asks us to. Keep your powder dry ladies and gentlemen! And your troops ready. Today will be very busy!" Morgan looked extremely pleased with the way things were going. He wanted action and was happy to see demonstrations and marches erupting so he could take it to the hippie gardeners!

CHAPTER 40
THURSDAY, FEBRUARY 12, 2026

Yesterday, during the second day of citywide protests, Frank managed to get his old friend Captain Greg Watson on the phone.

"Greg! What's going on out there? We're standing by down here at the shipyards, but it seems like all hell's breaking loose out there!"

"Frank, I don't have long. It's not what you're hearing. The news is making it a lot worse than it is. Mostly it's a bunch of teenagers running around the streets, tipping over garbage cans, setting a few fires, breaking some windows. Not good, but it's a long way from an uprising. They want San Francisco to sound like it's out of control to rush you guys back into the streets. What are you hearing?" Watson was the captain of the Bayview Police Station and had been Frank's buddy since they were police cadets in the early 1980s.

" Col. Morgan, our CO, is champing at the bit. He *really* wants to crack some heads. He's wondering why SFPD or the Mayor hasn't called us in yet."

"Frank, try to calm them down. A thousand Federal Police busting heads and making arrests won't help. The Mayor and the Chief are trying to get things under control without Federal intervention—we had enough trouble ending the National Emergency—nobody at City Hall wants to go through *that* again!"

"Greg, I've been on Morgan's shitlist since I got here. He's worried he will be seen as weak if he's kept bottled up on the base. At some point he's gonna decide on his own. Tell the Chief."

"Got it, thanks for the tip, Frank. Listen, I gotta go." Watson's phone disconnected.

He watched the Colonel working himself into a frenzy. Morgan slammed his phone onto the table.

"Those lily-livered... *Fucking* civilians!!" He was pacing again. "How'd we let this get to the point where we need *PERMISSION* to do our job—from fucking civilians!!!" It wasn't a question. "Lt. Robertson!" Morgan unexpectedly focused his wrath on Frank.

"Sir?" Frank rose to his feet.

"Who can get us straight to the Chief of Police? I don't want to go through aides, it's past that point. I want to talk to her directly!"

"I'm sorry Major, I don't have any personal contacts that can get to her without going through intermediaries."

"Who else?" Major Morgan snarled as he whipped back to stare at his other Zone Commanders around the table. "Robertson here hasn't proven to be someone who *knows his way around* in San Francisco—even though he's lived here his whole life," Morgan's face was beet red as he used Frank as a verbal punching bag. "Anyone else found their way in?!?" His own negligence in failing to develop relationships with the Mayor and the Chief of Police went unmentioned.

Lt. Nichols rose slowly from her seat. She was angry to see Morgan publicly berating Frank Robertson, who she'd come to know as a reliable, decent man. As a black woman with over 20 years in the service her radar was flashing red too, recognizing the obvious racism implicit in Morgan's singling out of Robertson.

"Colonel Morgan, I have met Police Chief Rodriguez several times. I can call her directly if you'd like me to."

Morgan whipped his attention to Lt. Nichols. 'Charlene,' he thought to himself, 'you've been holding out on me!' His face grew redder as he felt deceived. "OK, Lt. Nichols." He held her in his withering stare, but she stared back impassively, unimpressed by his antics. "Let's make the call." He and Nichols left the room together.

Twenty minutes later, the Zone Commanders got the terse message from Morgan's aide. "Stand down and stand by. No deployment yet. Check-in this afternoon at 3 pm," he shook his head, transmitting Morgan's disagreement with their paralysis.

Frank and Eli walked back to their office coming up next to Lt. Nichols and her orderly.

"Lt. Nichols, may I have a word?" Frank asked her.

"Lt. Robertson," she nodded, "of course."

When they were out of earshot of the others, Frank asked her, "Charlene, what the hell are we going to do about Morgan? He's about to lose it."

"We have to take it easy. We don't have the authority to block him." She flashed a stern glare at Frank. "But there are more of us than them. We are eight, he's got four among the Zone Commanders. What's your count?"

He nodded. "Same. I haven't thought it through. I mean, we won't mutiny, right? How do we slow-walk the crazy shit he wants us to do?"

She looked at Frank with an intensity he hadn't seen before. "Nobody's ready for an out-and-out mutiny—there I agree with you. But if Morgan wants another Dolores Park, he's not gonna get it from us. I'm sure of that."

They talked a little bit longer. Reaffirming their commitment to a restrained approach to any imminent deployment, they parted company. Frank walked back to his office and found Flores waiting for him.

"We agreed to keep it restrained," said Frank.

"What does that mean? In practical terms?" Flores was recently out of the Army and knew that such boundaries were hard to keep, not to mention hard to define.

"We'll have to see in the moment, I guess," Frank said, dropping into his chair and leaning back, letting the anxiety of the past hour slowly dissipate. "Ready for some cards?"

***

"Oh man," Ethan Chan groaned as he rolled over in his soggy sleeping bag. "I'm wet! They must've put on the water again last night. I thought somebody was on that!"

Perlana was sitting up in her sleeping bag on the dry side of a plastic tarp. "I *told* you to get a tarp!"

"I'm gonna have to go home and take a shower!" he grumbled.

It was early on Thursday morning, the sun was pouring through the spaces between highrises and steam rose over the Salesforce Park grounds. Hundreds of campers woke up to the third day of their ongoing Festival of Possibilities—which turned out to be a huge camp-out by employees from Salesforce, Facebook, Oracle, Google, BioGenMo, Deloitte, CBRE, AirBnB, and dozens of other companies with offices nearby. Plumbers, urban farmers, technicians, artists, musicians, and thousands of white-collar employees mingled and shared ideas over the past 36 hours.

Security was waiting them out. No one demanded that anyone leave. Security guards from several adjacent towers were dispatched to walk the grounds of the park all night, flashlights sending beams crisscrossing the sleeping campers. For some it was an affront, but for a surprisingly large number of people there, the steady presence of security guards had been oddly reassuring. Somehow their coddled corporate existence was being extended to their camp-out. Since they were billing it as a Festival of Possibilities, the companies claimed they supported their employees as they pursued new ideas, new networks, new synergies, and pointed out that many were in fact working from the camp. In fact, Salesforce had been in the news coming very close to taking credit for the whole thing.

Dennis Swintin and Vanessa Wright had spent too long getting to this amazing moment to have it sputter out in benign neglect engineered by a savvy corporation. They were holding court at a corner where several tables were shoved together. Dozens of people clustered around.

"We can't let Salesforce act like this was *their* idea!" Vanessa was standing up with a scone in one hand and a coffee in the other, spilling as she spoke. "I'm glad they're not sending in the goons, trying to roust everyone. That's lucky. But this media game they're playing, I'm not having it!"

"They assume we'll get tired of this and go home," Dennis said. "We probably have to raise the stakes."

"Like how? We are here, taking off work, occupying the park, holding the Festival. What else do you think we should do?" Karen Peterson, the skinny dancer-type from BGM's tech writing department stood at the perimeter.

"What if we could get the kids down here? You know they've been walking out all over the City, right? High school kids marched from half a dozen schools to City Hall yesterday. If they came here... imagine!" Dennis grinned mischievously.

A guy on the other side of the morning gathering raised his hand awkwardly. He was older than most of them, maybe in his late 50s, had a slightly gaunt appearance, and at his feet a worn-out messenger bag. "Dennis and I go way back. We were both at Ultra when we organized the union there. What if we call for a Critical Mass tomorrow to converge not only on Salesforce Park, but to visit all the occupations?"

"All the occupations? What are you talking about?!?" asked several people at once.

"You don't know?" he looked around, surprised. "There are at least five buildings that have been taken over by Right To A Home. There's the high schoolers in the Civic Center. They went down there last night and set up a whole camp. There may be others that I don't even know about!"

***

The big kitchen and dining area at the middle of the 10th floor had become the defacto living room for the whole floor. A few people sat in the adjacent TV lounge staring at daytime soap operas, but most people who had moved into the 10th floor of the Insurance Exchange building over the previous three days were gathered for the noon meeting.

"I'd like to give thanks to you and to the folks who helped get us this place to live," started an older woman, Frances DePaola. Her dyed red hair cascaded down her floral bathrobe that she proudly wore to the meeting. Others echoed her gratitude. "We've been told to organize our own floors, to set up our own systems of maintenance, sharing bathrooms and kitchens, all that. Anyone want to start?"

Janine Shapiro stood up, noting at least three-quarters were women like herself. She relaxed a little. "I'm not used to this. I don't think most of us have had a place to live for a while. We are not used to big groups, having meetings like this one." Heads nodded all around. "Let's make a simple rule to start: Let's try to give each other the benefit of the doubt. No yelling, no shaming, and as much as possible no blaming!"

An African American man, probably in his 40s, stood up across the room. "My name is Steve, Steve Healey. I support what the sister proposed," and a few people clapped their assent too. "But without blame, where is accountability? If we make promises we have to keep them. If we agree to rules, we have to abide by them. And if we break our promises or the rules, then what? How do we hold each other accountable?" He sat back down.

A few people were talking in low voices around the room. No one was in charge, even though Frances had gotten the meeting started. Healey's question about accountability was not easy.

Another woman, very large and with long black hair braided in the back, stood up. She was wearing an embroidered shirt, her son at her side. She spoke softly to her son, and he suddenly began speaking in a loud high-pitched voice. "My mom doesn't speak English too good, but she mostly understands it ok. She wants to say that we have to be kind to each other. If we have arguments, we have to be nice."

"What's your name? And your mom's?" called out a voice.

"I'm Roberto—Robbie, and my mom is Estrellita, but you can call her Star."

Janine got up again. "Thank you Robbieyou, Robbie, and welcome to you and your mom. *¡Bienvenida, Es-treh-yee-ta.* I'll get it better next time, Star! How about we go around and everyone introduce themselves and say a few words about how they got here and what they're hoping for?" She looked around. Many were shifting uncomfortably, not used to speaking in front of other people. "I'll start: I'm Janine Shapiro. I'm 48 years old. I've been homeless for a few years. Divorced. No kids. I grew up in San Francisco. Went to Washington High." She cracked a smile. "That was a loooong time ago. I waitressed, bartended, worked a few different office jobs. I married too young, and we didn't last. I drank too much but I've been sober since I turned 40. Got evicted a few years ago. Damn speculators bought the building and kicked us out. Couldn't find a place I could afford after that. Couch-surfed with friends until that didn't work anymore. Rented a room in a friend's place for a while— got evicted again," she grimaced at the memory. Everyone was listening intently, her story too familiar. "Been living in my car, camping, SROs, shelters for the past three years. I am SO happy to be here! And I'm hoping to make this a happy home for a long time to come—with you!" she beamed and sat down.

There were 23 people and 23 different sagas, familiar tales from the slow collapse of American life. The soap opera watchers emerged and joined in, adding another five stories. Most of them were single women, two couples, a half dozen single men, ranging in age from Robbie at 8 to Frances at 73. Eventually the stories were told, and everyone looked around the room expectantly.

"What do we do now?" asked Steve Healey. "I propose that we meet once a week here, like noon on Wednesdays, to decide the big issues of co-living."

"Thanks Steve," Frances took the floor back. A quick show of hands supported the idea of Wednesday meetings and a sign-up sheet went around. A sense of order descended over the room as they resolved the biggest immediate issues. People headed to their rooms, chatting with new friends and neighbors.

Janine watched it unfold and marveled. "Maybe this can work!" She knew that the hard part—surviving through conflict and crisis—was still ahead.

***

Cristiano caught up with Tomas pedaling on 18th Street. "You heard about the marches?"

Tomas nodded, breathing heavily as he slowed slightly to fall in alongside Cristiano. "Girls from my block told me Monday. I went with them to the Civic Center last night but my moms didn't want me to sleep out there, so I had to come home."

"They camped there last night?" Cristiano was surprised. "We've got to go down there too!"

They turned onto a steep slope, pausing the conversation while they pushed up the hill. As they caught their breath Tomas looked back at Cristiano, "It was pretty cool! The cops rolled around in their cars, but they weren't hassling anyone." They carried their bikes through the alley to the bottom of Kite Hill.

Scrub jays circled overhead, squawking loudly, as they stashed their bikes behind the garage wall where they couldn't be seen from Stanton Street. They burst into the kitchen, ready to pick up the next batch of *Opaque Times*.

"Hi guys!" Aaron stood at the counter, leaning on his cane and fumbling with a blender. "We're still printing down there, probably need another half hour at least. You want a milkshake?" Aaron's milkshakes were a regular treat for them before they hauled boxes of newsletters on their bikes.

Anna dropped a shoulder bag in a chair by the door. "You wouldn't believe it! The whole Salesforce Park is occupied by thousands of people! They're calling it a "Festival of Possibilities!" It came out of nowhere! I mean, there are booths from different groups, the League of Urban Farmers, the Urban Peasants Alliance, Right to A Home, but what's most amazing are the booths that workers from Salesforce, Facebook, Google, BioGenMo, even finance and real estate companies have put up. And they've slept there the last two nights! It's a full-on occupation!"

Tomas began excitedly recounting his hours at the Civic Center encampment the night before.

"This is bigger than anyone thought!" Aaron exclaimed.

"You have no idea!" Anna laughed. "Some friends at the Right to A Home

249

booth told me they've moved hundreds of people into five different buildings downtown! No one is the wiser. They're proposing the City buy the buildings from the owners and then turn them into land trusts at a big press conference. Freddi was telling me that it was the first time they'd been able to convince politicians to seriously consider eminent domain to seize empty buildings. I mean, it's goddam obvious that it's in the public interest to take empty buildings and use them to house people without homes. They have a majority of City supervisors lined up in support."

Aaron put up his hand in apology for turning on the blender which drowned out conversation. A minute later, "who wants some?" and the boys and Anna happily accepted milkshakes. "We know the relief that being in a land-trusted building gives you—no more eviction threats! But eminent domain? Won't that go to the Supreme Court? They're never gonna let a municipality seize private property to house poor people—be realistic!"

Anna nodded, her big white milkshake mustache giving her an eerie grin. "I imagine you're right Aaron, in the long run. But in the long run we're dead! And who knows what'll happen if enough people act to support and defend these buildings? Especially with the rest of what's going on! It's amazing!"

She turned to the boys, who were listening intently, trying to make sense of what they were hearing. "You know what else I heard down there?" They waited for her to tell them. "Some folks are planning a huge Critical Mass to ride from occupation to occupation... tomorrow!"

"Critical Mass?" Cristiano looked puzzled. Tomas had no idea either.

"Oh dang, I forget how young you are! Critical Mass is a huge gathering of bicyclists who fill the streets with bikes... it's a parade, but at its best it was a mass seizure of the streets by bicyclists, leaving no room for cars. The old slogan in the 1990s when I used to go was "We aren't blocking traffic, we ARE traffic!"

Their eyes widened at her explanation. "You think we can go?" Tomas was already scheming.

"Of course you can! And you should see who else you can bring. The more the merrier!" Anna clapped Tomas on the shoulder. "I used to go, but eventually it got boring. This one should be exciting!"

Julius emerged from the basement. "You guys having a convention up here? The paper's ready fellas. All boxed up, ready to go."

Tomas and Cristiano headed into the basement to get their pickups. They reappeared carrying several brown parcels to drop at their stops. Tomas asked Anna, "Where and when is that ... Critical Mass happening?"

I'll send you a note. Used to be last Friday of the month at 6 pm, but since this is not the last Friday, they may have something else in mind."

CHAPTER 41
FRIDAY, FEBRUARY 13, 2026

The 5 o'clock bells were ringing loudly at the Ferry Building. Several cyclists gathered on the lawn under the poplar trees behind the Vaillancourt Fountain. They gazed up at the dozens of green parrots busily kanoodling in the branches above the park where freeway on- and off-ramps once soared.

"It sounds like they're talking to each other," said a cyclist clad in yellow spandex with a tight-fitting black helmet framing his face. The parrots were making soft sounds, only occasionally letting out a loud squawk when there was a brief dispute over a coveted perch. Many seemed to be couples, pecking and preening each other as they murmured in their conversational tone.

"I can't believe there's parrots in San Francisco!" another cyclist responded, shaking her head, her wavy brown hair flying back and forth, unencumbered by any head gear. "You sure don't have this in Denver!"

Bicyclists were streaming into the Embarcadero Plaza from Market Street, first a few dozen, but suddenly hundreds were pouring in from every direction, including from ferries at the Ferry Building. After another half hour the plaza was crowded with bicyclists, many bearing banners and flags, while others were distributing flyers and stickers. Old friends were embracing wherever you looked.

"Laura! Jim! I can't believe we're here again!" a white-bearded guy laughed as he straddled his bike. "When was the last time you came to a Critical Mass?"

"More than a decade, hell, it might be 20 years for me!" Laura admitted, her cheerful ruddy face peaking out under brown bangs barely visible under her silver helmet. "Since I retired, I hardly come to the City any more. But when I heard about this one, I had to come."

"Yeah, and it's not even a real one... it's not the last Friday, after all!" Jim reminded them, while he pulled a joint from his leather vest pocket to get the ride off on the right foot.

Chris, the white-bearded guy, laughed and waved his hand. "Hardly matters anymore. I'm glad people remember that mass bike rides can be a good tactic! But look at these people! I can't believe they've ever been on a Critical Mass in San Francisco—it's been dead for years now."

A pretty young woman with a pixie-ish nose standing near leaned in, "I never rode one here, but I know Critical Mass from Austin, Texas… and one time I was in Cuenca, Peru and saw it roll by there too!"

"See?" Laura nodded. "It's in the cultural DNA. We were there three decades ago, but it's been rolling along ever since, here, there, and everywhere!"

Chris and Jim nodded in agreement, smiling and momentarily lost in their memories.

Another shiny faced young woman wearing a bright green safety vest came up with a pile of papers she was handing out. "Here's a map of our proposed route. The idea is to visit as many occupations as we can," she explained cheerfully. "The first stop is Pier 19, here," she pointed to the pier north from where they stood. "Then there are at least four buildings that were taken in the last week. This one," she pointed to the Insurance Exchange Building on California, "and this one," pointing to an older building on 2nd Street between Mission and Howard. "The others are in the Mission, and of course, Salesforce Park, and the Civic Center." She abruptly moved on.

"This is going to be epic!" Laura enthused over the clamor of bike bells. Some cyclists began riding in a big slow circle around the gathering, and before long most people mounted up and joined them. After another five minutes, the ride flowed onto the Embarcadero. A few thousand cyclists soon filled the width of the northbound lanes and made their way towards Pier 19.

It was a short ride and they were there *en masse* in less than 10 minutes. A huge banner hung over the front doors proclaiming "OCCUPIED!" Another smaller sign nearby read "The Real Emergency is Daily Life!" and a further sign said "Water is Life, Life Needs Art, Art on the Water!" It was apparent from the dozen friendly people clad in various kinds of paint-spattered overalls and work clothes that a bunch of artists moved in to the derelict pier. They passed the Exploratorium where folks were milling about in front of the Pier 15-17 complex, enjoying the spectacle and clapping in encouragement. A red-headed woman in blue overalls waved the cyclists into the cavernous Pier 19 space through the front doors and in minutes a thousand bicyclists were weaving around chaotically inside the pier, ringing bells and dancing to tunes piped in on a panoply of bluetooth speakers by different riders. Another thousand or more waited outside. After fifteen minutes of zany horsing around in an indoor parking lot, the artists slammed the doors shut behind the last cyclists rushing to catch up with the rest of the ride. The front already reached Battery Street on their way to the heart of the Financial District.

***

Robbie and Steve Healey stood at the window on the 10th floor with a view of California Street. Darkness had taken full effect a short while earlier, and bicyclists were streaming up California from Battery and filling the street below them.

"Look! Are they gonna let the cable car through?" Robbie pointed excitedly at the California Street Cable Car coming down California to the dense crowd of cyclists.

"Hmmm, I wonder," Healey said. He took a liking to young Robbie, who reminded him of a nephew he hadn't seen in a few years living in southern California. "Have you ridden a cable car, Robbie?"

"No! Have you?" Robbie said in wonder. He was about 9 years old, Healey figured.

"Oh sure, lots of times! I'll take you on it some day. Everyone in San Francisco has to ride it! And look," he pointed down. "The bikes are clearing space."

An ambulance came tearing up the street, and again, the cyclists adeptly made room for the emergency vehicle to pass through unmolested, then refilling the street.

An hour earlier, a huge banner had been hung across the front of the building at the height of the 3rd floor, "OCCUPIED!" Another banner stretched across the ground floor windows proclaiming, "The Real Emergency: Everyday Life!" A further sign said "Right to a Home: Empty Buildings Are a Criminal Waste!"

Ralph Richards stood in the front door laughing uproariously. His muttonchop sideburns bulged out from his very red face, and his blonde ponytail wagged back and forth as he waved to friends among the assembled cyclists. He knew his days on this job were numbered. But this was more important than keeping his dumb job, so he didn't care. He was proud to have secretly facilitated the refurbishing of this apparently forgotten building, and almost 200 people had moved in! He felt great! But it was far from settled. These folks would probably be evicted within a few days.

Freddi Rosenblatt of Right To A Home showed up, with a woman in a finely tailored navy-blue suit striding behind her. A smattering of cyclists started cheering and clapping when they saw her. She waved and flashed a thumbs up before turning to the door. "Ralph! This is Supervisor Leone's aide, Shelly Sarandora. They're going to buy the building from the owner with City housing funds."

"Our staff figured out a Real Estate Investment Trust based in Phoenix owns the building," explained Sarandora. "This building hasn't generated any revenue in years—"

"That's for damn sure!" Ralph snorted. "This place emptied out during the pandemic but nobody was left by then anyway."

"Oc-u-py Oc-u-py" chanted the assembled throng. Somewhere around 2000 cyclists and bystanders stood before the Insurance Exchange building draped in banners, with most of the windows filled by smiling, waving new residents. Some bottle rockets went off, shooting into the night sky and exploding above the crowd, garnering a big cheer. A few bicyclists with bells and small drums on their handlebars were laying down a syncopated rhythm that fueled the chanting. "Oc-u-py, Oc-u-py" rose louder and louder, everyone breaking into wild cheers.

Freddi got a hold of a mic from one of the small sound systems. "Hey everyone!" she shouted. "Thanks for coming! I'm Freddi Rosenblatt of Right To A Home!" and the crowd cheered wildly. "This is not a flash in the pan. The Mayor and several supervisors are negotiating with the owners to buy them out." More wild cheering. "We will let you know soon!" and she clasped her hands above her head in triumph before entering the building. No one knew that the Mayor was a few blocks away sitting in a City car, waiting for the crowd to clear so he could reach the building.

The bicyclists resumed their tour, and were soon rolling down Montgomery across Market to the Salesforce Park.

***

Cristiano and Tomas were rolling down Market Street on their bikes, leading a crowd of several hundred who departed the encampment at the Civic Center Plaza. Everyone heard there was a big Critical Mass visiting other Occupations and hundreds of high schoolers who marched on City Hall a few days earlier were ready to get on their bikes and join.

"Hey," a cute girl with big blue-framed glasses and a head of frizzy hair rolled up next to them. "You know where the ride is going?" She got up on her pedals and turned around to look behind them, her backpack sliding around and causing her to wobble for a moment. "Dang! There's hundreds of us!" she sat back down grinning.

The girl turned back to her friends, riding a short distance behind them. "Hey Bridget! Lorna! Get up here!" and as they slid into the front, the frizzy-haired girl turned back to Tomas, "My name is Jill, what's yours?" and Tomas introduced himself and Cristiano too. They reached Second Street and the girls took over. "Turn here!" Lorna led the cyclists into the right turn. "Let's get there the back way!"

They reached the western end of the park, rising above them. They were whooping and hollering as they rolled along next to the terminal building, which stretched for two more blocks. An electronic skateboarder silently glided up, shouting, "You lookin' for Critical Mass? They're over there, at Fremont and Mission by the gondola!" and sped away.

The teenage mini-Mass rolled across First Street where cops were standing around near their vehicles, but not planning any major action. They watched as the cyclists streamed by, one officer reporting it on his radio. The teenage cyclists pulled up at Fremont where there were already bicycles as far as you could see filling the plaza, the streets and the sidewalks.

"I've never seen anything like it!" marveled Cristiano. Tomas was looking at his phone, "my mom is over at that corner," pointing a block away through a thick crowd. Suddenly the glass doors were opened a short distance from them and people began streaming in with their bikes. In a few minutes the escalator was a snake of bicyclists going up and up to the park level. Others were crowding around the elevators. The few security guards in the lobby area offered no resistance. On the contrary they were smiling and high-fiving everyone as they went by. "C'mon Tomas! Let's go!" Cristiano wasn't missing this.

When they emerged on the park level, bright lights gave it a festive atmosphere. As the bicyclists reached the top floor they cleared the escalator and elevator corridor to make room for the people behind them. This river of movement carried the boys along, and without having to think about it they found themselves in an open patch of unusually tall grass under some trees behind the glass wall of the escalator well. A few minutes later they saw the girls they met going by. "Jill! Bridget!" Tomas called, and they joined them.

"What is going on here? I heard there was a Festival?" Bridget asked. She and Jill were at least 16, so they seemed a lot older to the tweeners, Cristiano and Tomas. The boys knew more because they'd read about it in the *Opaque Times*. Tomas was quick to explain that the Festival was an occupation, and at the same time a place where the people working downtown had a chance to show what *they* thought they *could be doing* if they were in charge.

"You mean they don't like their jobs?" the other girl, Lorna, asked. She was biracial, Asian and black, and seemed excited at Tomas's explanation.

"I guess you could say that," Tomas conceded. "I read a manifesto about the Festival, it is not simply about jobs. It was about changing everything, *to do everything differently!*"

Lorna gave him a puzzled look, not understanding. Jill pointed to a nearby booth at the edge of the main plaza. It was the League of Urban Farmers and their displays showing narrowed streets and burgeoning linear urban farms where cars were currently being parked or driven.

"Check out that blimp!" pointing to the yellow mini-blimp tethered to a railing and floating above the corner of the plaza with its sign "Solar Blimps: Slow Travel for a World After Work!"

Another nearby booth promoted marine permaculture, one was advocating agroforestry, and still another featured oyster reef restoration in the Bay as a way to contain high tides and begin filtering the worst of the toxic waste in the bay mud. The kids locked up behind a bench and began checking out the displays.

After a few minutes of navigating through the thickening crowds, Tomas and Cristiano were near the the gondola/sky car. Looking at the thousands of cyclists below, they waved happily as the Oc-u-py chant slowly grew louder and louder from the plaza below. A brass band clad in reds and pinks began playing some fast-moving Balkan tune, which got a lot of the cyclists in the plaza to ride in an ever widening gyre around the exuberant musicians, shouting along with an especially demonstrative tuba player.

"They're gonna start rolling again," Cristiano predicted.

"Yeah, we should get our bikes and head back down," said Tomas.

"You sure you don't want to hang out here some more?" They just got here. There was obviously much more to see.

"I'd rather ride, man. Wouldn't you? We can come back here another day."

Cristiano deferred to Tomas. He might've stayed if it was up to him, but his slightly older and more assertive friend wanted to go, and he didn't want to be there alone among these adults. "OK, then, let's go!" They began bobbing and weaving to get through the crowds back to their bikes.

"You guys leaving?" Jill saw them heading back. "We just got here!"

"Yeah, we'd rather join the Critical Mass. We'll come back here another day," explained Tomas.

"OK, well, see ya," she and the others waved goodbye.

"It was nice to meet you!" Tomas said in return. But he was glad to go. Those girls were intimidating, even if he couldn't quite admit it to himself! As the mass brought them closer to the Mission, the boys admitted they were exhausted and headed home.

CHAPTER 42
MONDAY, FEBRUARY 16, 2026

Colonel Morgan was chomping on his cigar as he stood over the map of the bay shoreline. Frank watched him as he gleefully jabbed his finger at Pier 19, the one target the Federal Police were finally "asked" to recover. He and

Lt. Nichols—Charlene—were across the table which was ringed by the other ten Federal Police Zone Commanders in San Francisco under the command of Colonel Jefferson David Morgan.

"The Mayor and the SFPD are dicking around the City. But here—" he jabbed at Pier 19 again—"on Pier 19, we have our opening. We've been asked by the Port Commission to secure Pier 19."

Frank and Charlene glanced at each other, noting the new information. How could the Port Commission, a quasi-independent agency of the City government, initiate a request for Federal Police? And why would the Port Commission invite the Federal Police instead of local police—unless local police refused their eviction request?

"Zones 3, 4, and 5 will approach from the Bay. Our boats are on the way. Zone 2 will cover the land side, making arrests of anyone who resists. We don't need a bunch of detainees, no arrests unless necessary." Morgan was emphatic after watching his base turn into an extended jail and recreation yard after past roundups.

Frank was Zone 9 Commander, and Lt. Nichols was head of Zone 10. Neither of them would be involved in the upcoming raid. As they left the briefing room, they walked together towards their respective offices on the next floor.

"You think he left us out on purpose?" Frank asked Charlene.

She snorted her disdain, "I have no idea. And I do NOT care! Who the hell invited him anyway? The *Port Commission*? Is that a thing here?"

Frank nodded. "They're appointed by the Mayor for four-year terms. I don't know what authority they have. It doesn't sound right..."

"All I know is that is gonna be a shit-show. Morgan is looking to make a big splash--" she started chuckling as they arrived at her door. "Ha! A splash might be what he gets! These guys don't know shit about landing boats, staging from the water, none of that," she shook her head. "Not that you or me do either! Well, I guess we'll see, won't we?" And she nodded to Frank as she closed her door.

Eli—Corporal Flores—was at their office waiting for him. Frank closed the door behind him and leaned back into it, looking at Eli at his desk. "You're not gonna believe it," Frank said, shaking his head. And he explained the half-cocked plan to "take" Pier 19 from the bay.

"Really?" Eli looked at him with an amused expression. "I got word that the Peace Navy is surrounding Pier 19 in solidarity! That might complicate things a bit, eh?"

Out of precaution, Frank pulled his personal cellphone and texted Leon and Lamar to stay clear of Pier 19.

***

Jessie Suzuki and Steve Brooks were getting ready to cast off in the *Oyster Dream* when Maria Campoy came running up the pier. "Hey you guys!"

Brooks looked at Jessie and shrugged. Jessie grinned. "You thought we would get away before she got here?"

"Hi Maria!" and she climbed onto their boat.

Clara Frias and Vero Gomez came down the pier now, waving and smiling. "Wait for us!" They had a large bag, a backpack and a cooler they carried between them. "We brought lunch! And drinks!"

Steve Brooks scowled towards the Bay, out of their line of vision. He didn't want this to be a party. Hell, it might get serious out there! But he knew Jessie liked Maria and there was no turning these guys away now.

Once they were aboard, they were soon bobbing northward through the wake from a passing tug further out in the bay. Clara and Vero opened their bag and pulled out the banner they made, taking up the occupiers' slogan that poked at the national government's bogus Emergency Declaration from a year earlier: "The Real Emergency: Everyday Life!" They unfurled it and had to grab the safety bars as the small boat lurched from side to side a bit.

"What does that even *mean*?" Brooks said in a tone that left no doubt about his lack of enthusiasm.

"You know, Hutchinson's National Emergency, right? It was bullshit! People have had it. It's not one thing, it's *everything*." Vero was more than ready to have a confrontation over the slogan. But Brooks was not a guy who got into political discussions, and his simmering silence left her no one to joust with. It was a bit tense as they passed under the Bay Bridge.

"You guys work for Larry, too, right?" Clara asked him, trying to defuse the moment. Maria was already at the bow with Jessie, talking quietly.

"Yeah, that's right. But it's our boat. Jessie's the Peacenik, I'm the crew." Brooks was anxious to end the conversation and find a quiet corner where he could mind his own business.

Clara let it drop, reading his reticence to chat. "Do you have any poles we could tie our banner to?" hoping he wouldn't bite her head off.

Brooks handed her the grappling rods from the side of the boat. "You can use these. But don't drop them overboard!"

"Of course not! Thank you!" Brooks walked to the back of the boat and Clara and Vero began using their velcro strips to attach the banner to the poles.

Before long they arrived to Pier 19, happy to see dozens of other small craft already in place, covered in banners. "Occupy!" "Life is Art" "The Real Emergency! Daily Life!" "Art on the Water" "Life is for the Living" and on and on. It was about 10:30 in the morning, the sun was out, and on Pier 19 there were people on the roof waving. The outside of the pier building was covered in graffiti echoing the Occupy slogans of the moment. Brooks steered their vessel around the space crowded with small craft. It was indeed a party, full of music and lots of boisterous good cheer. Further north the flotilla thinned out. Ahead a major cruise ship was docked at Pier 27, but between that tourist behemoth and the Peace Navy around Pier 19 the waters were thinly populated with small craft maneuvering to join the convergence.

Jessie and Maria were still at the bow where they'd spent the 25 minutes chatting on the way here, ignoring the kerfuffle behind them. Jessie waved at friends in different boats. A siren sounded from one of the boats. Brooks went into the small cabin and tuned the radio to the pre-arranged frequency, more or less as everyone else did. The announcement came crackling across: "We heard that the Federal Police are coming! They're sending several boatloads of troops to take Pier 19. Prepare yourselves!"

Jessie was already striding back to the stern. "Take that banner off those poles! Attach it to the railing," Jessie instructed, fully in captain mode. "Brooks, let's get in the second line, you wanna drive?"

Brooks took the rudder again and began carefully maneuvering the *Oyster Dream* alongside a half dozen other 30- and 40-foot fishing boats surrounded by thick rubber bumpers. Each boat had crew on either side with poles at the ready to push off if the craft looked like they may get entangled. Brooks's voice came over the intercom, "Maria! You take the port side, Jessie's on the starboard." She had one of the grappling poles, not sure if she would be able to use it properly.

"Vero, Clara! Keep an eye on the bumpers!" Maria tried to sound like she knew what she was talking about, since she'd been on this boat a lot more than either of the other two. Her oyster bed expeditions with Jessie and Brooks was her favorite part of the week.

"We're gonna tie together," Jessie called out as he tossed ropes to the adjacent ship. It was a small sports boat called *One Day* and there were several middle-aged mariners who seemed to be enjoying the excitement. Maria caught the rope tossed to her from a creaky fishing boat called *Dawn*. Around them other boats were fastening their vessels together, creating a thick barricade filling the bay around Pier 19.

"Here they come!" the call was passed from boat to boat. Clearing Pier

7 to the south were three gray military boats. Were they landing craft? That didn't make much sense given the tall pier they'd have to climb to disembark. What would they do when they saw 100 boats jamming the waters around Pier 19?

***

Lieutenant Brandon Garner, a retired Marine who joined Homeland Security during the National Emergency, stood in the prow of the ship he'd been assigned, FP-404. Zone 3 was the tip of the spear for the assault on Pier 19, given responsibility for being the first to go in. The PA crackled to life and a voice was booming across the dozens of boats floating around Pier 19. "This is the Federal Police. You are ordered to clear a corridor. This is the Federal Police. We will dock at Pier 19. Clear a corridor!"

Dozens of sirens, horns, and general hooting and hollering rose from the floating blockade. People across the fleet began waving and pointing and gesturing to the Feds to turn around and leave.

"Proceed straight ahead, slowly," ordered Garner. The word went back and FP-404 crawled towards the blockade. Noting that the boats were roped together in odd ways, he realized there was no way for the boats to clear a corridor without mayhem. "Halt! Reverse engines!"

Sergeant Isabel Lopez stood next to Garner. "Sir? What are your orders?"

"We can't bust through—there's too many of 'em. Let's back up and wait a bit."

Suddenly Federal Police were swarming alongside the Pier 19 warehouse. Zone 2 was tasked with controlling the front gates and the roadway outside along the Embarcadero. On arrival there'd been only a few people walking back and forth under the 'Occupy' banner and the police made quick work of taking the front of the warehouse and entering from the street.

The Zone 2 commander, Lieutenant Owens, was on the radio, indicating he'd been able to seize Pier 19 and the occupiers were already evicted. Garner got the message and ordered his little fleet to head back to base. As they turned around and steamed away, the Peace Navy let out a huge roar, assuming they'd successfully held them off. Their apparent victory would soon turn to dust when they realized that Federal Police took the Pier from the land and were holding the perimeter walkways above their blockade.

***

"What? Who the hell authorized that?" Mayor Yee was furious. For an entire week he'd been managing the unfolding wave of occupations and demonstrations with a determination to avoid heavy police repression. He was hoping to negotiate the end of most of the occupations, and if lucky, to convince several building owners to sell their occupied buildings to the City's housing program. It was a delicate balancing act, and of course he'd been getting frantic phone calls all week from San Francisco's real power brokers, who wanted him to crack down.

"Um, it was Phil Gagliano, the Port Commissioner, who called Colonel Morgan directly," explained his aide.

"Gagliano? He has no authority to call in the Feds! I don't care if he's the almond king, I don't care how much he donates to the Democratic Party. I want his resignation on my desk immediately!" Yee was generally calm and affable in public, but behind the scenes he was always plotting, and ruthless about controlling everything he thought he could control. "And what the hell is Morgan doing? We told him to stand down. We know they're out there, but we don't need Federal Police meddling in local politics! Get him on the phone!"

Mayor Yee took the call privately in his office. His aides stood outside the door, listening to his rising voice: "I TOLD YOU TO STAND DOWN!"... "No, we don't need you."... "We can handle this... we ARE handling this! Your troops are not helping. Keep them at Hunter's Point. We'll call you if we need you! THIS IS NOT MARTIAL LAW Colonel Morgan—You are NOT authorized to send your troops into OUR streets! Is that understood?" ... and his voice grew inaudible and a long period of silence ensued. Finally, he said "OK, thank you Colonel Morgan. We'll be in touch."

Everyone rushed away from the door to look busy when the conversation ended. Another five minutes went by before the Mayor called his aide to come back in to draft a public rebuke of the Federal Police for accepting a request from an unelected official, and countering his command.

***

After the aborted raid on Pier 19, Colonel Morgan was apoplectic and eager to deflec his discredit. Beet red again, making his red hair look vaguely blonde. "I sent you to do a job and you didn't do it! Are we going to turn tail every time the so-called 'Peace Navy' parks in our way? We have to leave them no doubt about the consequences of their obstruction. Next time," he pounded his fist into the table, "next time you ram your way through! I don't care how many boats you sink!" he roared at Lt. Garner.

Frank and Lt. Nichols, along with the other Zone Commanders, watched Colonel Morgan melting down. Informal discussions confirmed an agreement among two-thirds of them that they would not carry out Morgan's orders if they might lead to another massacre. In this case, one of Morgan's loyalists followed common sense, avoided unnecessary violence, and was being berated for his basic decency. They would talk to Garner later and see if his loyalty to Morgan wavered after this episode. The Zone Commanders certainly took note of Morgan's abusive treatment of one of his own.

"Lt. Owens! You are to be commended for your team's success in seizing Pier 19. As we see from your report, there was little resistance and the so-called Occupation there was inconsequential. You took no prisoners?"

Lt. Eldon Owens stood up. He was former military, serving in the National Guard in Los Angeles when the National Emergency was declared. A hitch in his stride gave away the shrapnel that shattered his knee in Afghanistan. He could've passed for a rancher at the end of the 19th century, which his forebears were, the lines on his deeply tanned face enhancing its squareness. He didn't like the undercurrent of disobedience percolating among his colleagues. But he couldn't respect Morgan's command either—a typical Ivy-League blowhard trying to sound tough. He was at least 20 years senior to Morgan—like Frank. And like Frank, his expectations for this time in his life were upended. He was unwilling to put up with nonsense.

"Prisoners? No sir, there were about fifteen people there when we arrived. Several departed as soon as they saw us, and the rest left expeditiously when we told them their Occupation was officially over. They offered no resistance, and we saw no reason to arrest anyone.... Sir."

Morgan frowned, and then addressed the room. "Rising unemployment means there will be new protests and demonstrations," repeating a refrain he sounded since the end of the National Emergency. "I want daily reports from patrols on anything going on in the streets, whether organized or spontaneous. Is that clear?" He didn't wait for a response, turning on his heel and leaving the room. The Zone Commanders looked at each other, some shrugging as if to say "whatever..."

After weeks of routine work, the Federal Police remained stuck at Hunter's Point. Colonel Morgan kept looking for reasons why they should be called out to patrol the City. He was certain that something big was about to happen. But on the surface, things were relatively quiet as March began. There were almost no protests or spontaneous demonstrations without Federal Police out there to provoke them. For Col. Morgan, the lack of protest *proved* that a vast conspiracy was afoot.

CHAPTER 43
WEDNESDAY, FEBRUARY 18, 2026

Dennis Swintin sat at the table where he'd been convening an informal coordinating council of Festival participants for almost ten days.

"Salesforce says 'their Festival' has been a rousing success," he said reading from his phone. "It was in the news last night. They said it was wrapping up and would be finished by the end of this week. Everyone who hasn't visited it yet should come on down!" Karen Peterson shook her head, frustrated and disappointed. "I'm sure everyone who has been here knows it's not *'their'* festival, but damn! I don't think most people understand that."

Vanessa Wright was exhausted. She looked at the dozen people she'd come to know well during the previous week. "We may have lost a PR war on TV, but the relationships and ideas that have grown here speak for themselves. The 'story' of the Festival of Possibilities is not yet written. There's a lot we can— and must—do to affect that going forward. Obviously we can't leave it to the PR flacks at Salesforce, and we can't expect local TV stations to tell our story."

"Yes! I agree with Vanessa—we have to tell it our own way, ourselves," Perlana Solarzano was rising up again. When she spoke, everyone listened. "Our own networks are full of reports from people who have been camped out here since last week. It didn't even rain on us!" Everyone laughed at that. "I don't think we can know how far and deep this experience will go. It depends on how we go out, no?"

"Go out?!? Are you ready to give up?" Dennis was beside himself.

"No one is giving up, Dennis!" scolded Vanessa. She was tired of his dogged insistence on pushing everyone to go beyond what they were ready to do. As it happened, he had been sidelined most of the time. The occupation of Salesforce Park took on a life of its own. Rather than a sense of being a rolling strike or workplace occupation, it became a big party, an "alternative tech" festival, and a combined campground/concert/lecture series... Some had jokingly taken to calling it Workapalooza. Granted, many of the performers sung lyrics denouncing the authorities, demanding radical change, even revolution in some cases. Speakers traced the past years' efforts to change policing, redistribute wealth, protect abortion rights, decarbonize the economy, and how those largely were thwarted. Campaigns for reparations, land return to the indigenous, and restorative justice were amply represented during the past week. And of course a lot of people were obsessed with election integrity, fighting over the Constitution, Supreme Court reform, and the dismal state of voting rights.

"Man, I can't believe people are still trying to salvage the damn Constitution! It's time for something written and decided by people alive today!" argued Ethan Chan during one particularly lively exchange the past weekend. Some nodded in agreement, but as usual, several people insisted that trying to rewrite or reinvent the Constitution, given that nearly half the U.S. population claimed to believe that the Bible was the literal truth, was to invite a disaster.

"Well, maybe that's why we need to seriously consider breaking up the United States!" Ethan retorted. "What is the point of trying to find common ground with people whose minds haven't even made it to the Enlightenment yet?"

"Not that the Enlightenment was that great either!" admonished a squarish heavy-set woman with black braids and olive skin. "I'm for rational thinking, but not the kind that rejects every other form of life as inanimate!"

"Sure, ok, but you're not defending the Bible thumpers, which was my point," Ethan sourly answered.

Dennis rarely stuck around for these kinds of debates. He was dismayed at how often they came to the forefront. He repeatedly called for new kinds of interventions, actions that would more overtly antagonize the dozens of companies whose employees were in the park. His dream of tech workers challenging their employers over what work the companies do gained more attention in the Festival of Possibilities than it ever received previously. But the class dimension was de-emphasized—instead fanciful ideas were presented to resemble start-up pitches, rather than demands by workers to redirect their work for purposes of their own choosing.

"Dennis, people don't think like you do," Vanessa insisted. "I know you want to spark an uprising, a new class consciousness. I'd be thrilled if that happens. But people who grew up in a neoliberal world with good-paying jobs in cushy tech companies, aren't exactly aggrieved workers. It's a leap, isn't it? Few even think of themselves as having a shared agenda. This Festival has been eye-opening for who knows how many? They've heard arguments for a politics they never heard of before. You have to give people time—who knows what they'll do back at their jobs?" She felt her exhaustion—partly because of the stress of holding the Festival together, but especially because of Dennis's frustrated expectations.

Salesforce, at least, had been effective in co-opting a sizable portion of their own workforce. Dozens of earnest Salesforce employees joined the initial surge to camp out without realizing it was a workplace action. When the company benignly tolerated the whole thing, even sending security guards out during the long nights to "keep everyone safe," it had been easy for a lot of them to think the Festival was another example of how progressive their employer was. And when Salesforce announced that the Festival was wrapping up at the end of the week, a lot of their employees prepared their return to work.

"If they're bailing, we should too," Alba Estrada argued. She was standing at the edge of the table, her hair having grown frizzy and unkempt during the past days' camping. She still flashed her big smile, though, and her inexhaustible supply of bright red lipstick. "I don't see why anyone should try to hold this place... who thinks we should 'make a stand'? This has been a HUGE success! But everyone is tired, and there's not much more we can do here." She looked around for confirmation. A few heads nodded, others looked uncertain.

"I'm Will, Will Shaw, from the League of Urban Farmers," began a tall older white guy in overalls. He had been an outlier in the back of the circle, out of place among the young techies. He hadn't been present at earlier gatherings during previous days. "I heard about these discussions, so I thought I'd pop in today. From what I can tell, the energy for this Festival, or Occupation, or whatever you want to call it, has peaked." He was a tall grizzled farmer that, combined with his age, imparted an implicit wisdom. "There is a lot to be said for knowing when to fold," he smiled at his card-playing analogy, "especially when you've had a good run of winning hands! And let's face it, this Festival has galvanized us, brought people together across communities in the City, and consolidated a lot of important relationships—organizationally and individually."

"The Plumbers are ready to call it, too," offered Ernesto Aguirre, sitting at the table nursing his coffee. "What I appreciated about being here has been the opportunity to introduce people to our Replumbing The City agenda. Water politics is moving to the front and center, and this Festival was a great opportunity for us."

"Hey, nice job blocking the rain these past ten days!" called out someone in the back.

Ernesto accepted the comic accolades with a grin. "Yeah, well, who knew after these drought years we were gonna get two straight months of floods and torrential rain? We are unprepared for the new climate. Water is central—"

"Don't forget food!" Will joined back in. "The League has grown more food than ever, in the nick of time. How 'bout those potatoes?" he looked around proudly. As the crowd listened to him, they remembered the unexpected difficulties trying to get food recently. Who hadn't gotten a bag of potatoes during this long winter, or several? Potatoes produced in San Francisco's yards, gardens, farms, and parks—and harvested and distributed through the network of food conspiracies and distribution hubs that had proliferated since last autumn.

"Food and water, and then shelter!" chimed in a wiry old woman at the table. "Don't forget that Right to a Home got over a thousand people into homes this month, too! I don't know if that would've worked without this Festival, the High School walkouts, Critical Mass, all of it. If they isolate us, we lose."

"The Salesforce folks return to work this week," Susanna Montez spoke now. "But you can't underestimate the effect this whole Festival had on them. They've been steeped in a corporate culture promoting an all-encompassing, one-stop world for sales and business management. Most of them haven't had a moment to think outside the corporate box—to reimagine what the suite of tools they're working with might be useful for *outside* of business, in a world that puts life and pleasure, conviviality and mutual aid at the center." Hidden under a scarf, her dark sunglasses made her look like someone emerging from a hostile courtroom. "I support the idea that we organize our own ending this week. I don't care if Salesforce thinks they're running things, we know better!" and she sat back, folding her arms. No one noticed the nondescript man under a tree at the back of the crowd, holding a phone while he discretely recorded the conversation.

A MUNI driver stood in the circle too, a middle-aged black woman in her uniform. "No one has talked about transportation. I wanted to throw that in too. Don't forget about MUNI! And now that the Autono's are publicly owned, the need to provide space for privately owned vehicles is shrinking. I'd like to support our friends at the League's call for "One Lane for Food!"

"Thanks Sister!" Will Shaw was delighted to hear this unexpected support from a bus driver. A bus driver reminding everyone about their proposal—that showed the value of the cross-pollinating Festival.

"Do we have a consensus that we'll shut down the Festival on Friday and declare victory?" Perlana asked in a booming voice, refocusing the meeting. Most heads nodded. "Dennis? You ok with that? Vanessa?"

They both nodded.

"I still think we need to go out with a bang... of some sort!" Dennis urged.

"What do you propose?" Perlana asked.

"At least a victory parade that goes around downtown," Vanessa suggested. "Anything more confrontational... I don't think we want to set ourselves up for failure now."

The crowd endorsed the parade, Dennis looking frustrated. It had been a perfect moment to "storm the Winter Palace" even if he couldn't exactly say where that would be, or how to do it. He couldn't admit it, but he was as stuck as anyone else. The changes they promoted, shared during the exciting days in the park, were so big and vague that it was nearly impossible to figure out what to do. What were the next steps?

The Festival's radicality had so far been met with spongy indifference by the affected companies. They prevented the police from intervening, rather than calling them in. As a confrontational tactic, the occupation of Salesforce Park was outfoxed by their adversaries. But events rarely stay bound within the confines of those who initiate them, and this would be no exception—eventually.

CHAPTER 44
MONDAY, MARCH 2, 2026

The economic numbers were dire. After losing nearly 35% since mid-January, the stock indexes were still falling, albeit not as fast. The lack of insurance availability following the climate-induced collapse of the reinsurance industry was putting a freeze on investment. Cash was being hoarded by those that had it, especially large companies who were slashing jobs and shuttering facilities in a frenzy of cost-cutting. In San Francisco, most of the major companies were announcing layoffs and some were closing offices. Susanna Montez got her pink slip from Salesforce on Friday, the last day of February.

"I'm unemployed!" she told Vanessa by text. When they began comparing notes over the weekend, the most active participants in the Festival of Possibilities had lost their jobs. Perlana and Ethan had been laid off at Meta-Facebook.

Vanessa met with Dennis to discuss the retaliatory wave of firings. "Do you think we can do anything?"

Dennis always had a plan. "We walked away from the Festival and gave up whatever leverage we might have gained there." He looked glum. "I told you we couldn't party our way to a revolution! Now these fuckin' companies are coming after us!"

"You think BGM will fire us?" she asked, resigned to what seemed inevitable now.

"Hard to say," he was staring at the feed on his phone. "They would be hard-pressed to replace us as key contacts with the subcontractors."

"Zuckerman has given us a loose rein for a long time. But if she has enough others in the liaison department to handle things without us..." Vanessa worried. She knew they were as replaceable as anyone. But when they got to work on Monday, there was nothing waiting for them, other than their usual pile of reports to complete.

When Dennis got a message from Marlene Zuckerman at 10:30, he figured it was the ax falling. "Crap!" He turned to Vanessa, "I guess this is it, Zuck is calling me in."

"Did she say why?"

He shook his head, "Wish me luck," and he grabbed his coffee cup, his jacket, and his shoulder bag. A few minutes later he was in her office.

Marlene Zuckerman managed the contractor liaison staff ever since they set up the Prosper*Plants production system. She set up the subcontracting system that saddled hundreds of people with the risk of growing the labor-intensive bioengineered plants in their homes. Coaxing reliable output turned out to be the crux of the matter. After some trial and error they settled on the 10-month cycle, with the carrot of housing and the $5k signing bonus drawing in a steady stream of people ready to commit to their hyper-vigilant regime.

The stick, of course, was the abrupt dismissal of those who couldn't meet their standards, followed by rapid eviction from the half dozen BGM apartment complexes they tightly controlled. Circumventing San Francisco's "renter friendly" housing laws was her achievement. The contractors signed a contract to get the bonus and two months of free rent in a BGM apartment. If things went wrong, the contract they signed stipulated that their occupancy was contingent on a satisfactory completion of their work quotas, and that it could be suspended at any time for any reason at the discretion of BioGenMo. It expressly stated that a 3-day eviction could not be contested in local courts since the property and access to it was entirely enclosed by the BGM agreement.

Now she had a new problem, one she was surprised to have been given. She stood looking out the window in her pencil skirt, her short black hair shaped by a thick gel. She put in an hour at the company gym every day to keep her slim figure intact as she approached 50. She turned to greet Dennis Swintin, removing her red-framed glasses.

"Hi Dennis, thanks for coming," as though he had a choice! "Have a seat."

"Hi Marlene," he sank into the chair across from her desk, keeping a poker face though his heart was beating much faster than usual. He looked spent.

"You're not laid off, let me get that out of the way first. I know there is a big wave of firings and layoffs going on all over town. You're ok... for now," she said ominously. "Of course we know you were very involved in the Salesforce Park thing, and your politics is no mystery either, but we're not here to discuss that. We found your so-called 'Festival' very informative."

Thunk. He was very alert now. That was a condescending blow. Where was this going?

"One of the things we learned from your little get-together in the park is that our intellectual property was stolen." She paused for effect, searching his face for a reaction. "Do you know what I'm talking about?"

Dennis was genuinely puzzled. And then he remembered the fungi research that associates had smuggled out when Nakahara, the genius behind the Hempattery, was still around. He shook his head neutrally, assuming that whatever Zuck was talking about was different, more recent. His face gave no sign of recognition. "No, no idea. What *are* you talking about?"

"Do you know this guy?" and she put a photo in front of Dennis. It was Dat Doan and his mini-blimp smiling broadly in Salesforce Park from a week earlier.

"No," Dennis lied. "I saw that blimp but I don't remember seeing that guy. Who is he?"

Zuckerman knew Dennis was lying. Surely he must know the guy the Urban Peasants Alliance called in again and again when contractors had technical problems? She knew him of course, because Dat Doan was one of the first recruits to grow the Prosper°Plants, and was also one of the first they fired. He never took up their housing offer, so when they terminated his contract it was relatively bloodless. Zuck did it personally, though that was a few years ago.

"Don't bullshit me," Zuckerman stood behind her desk, leaning forward on her manicured hands. "You know and I know that when the contractors have an accident, or something goes wrong, the UPA calls Dat Doan to come and fix it. He's the only outsider with any technical capacity to repair our Prosper°Plant trays."

Dennis still didn't know where this was going. But the charade wasn't helping either.

"What's the problem?"

"We think he's involved with our stolen intellectual property. And we want you to help us get it back."

Dennis sat back in amazement. "What exactly do you want me to do?" He figured he might as well hear her out. Maybe he could even use his position to advantage.

***

State and federal governments were both straining under the burden of millions of newly unemployed claimants. President Hutchinson vowed that his government would never resort to "printing money" as had his predecessors during the pandemic. But politicians were feeling the heat. People were lining up everywhere at federal-funded food banks for the government's "patriotic packages"—at least the corn and soy farming conglomerates were profiting from the crisis.

In San Francisco, the wet winter set back much of the urban farming that provided essential support to the city's residents when Central Valley farms suffered plummeting yields last year. Plantings were delayed, and part of the huge backyard potato and onion crop were lost to flooding. No one knew how much food was being produced inside city limits, but it continued to expand enormously despite the raids by federal police. Raids were less frequent but only because the Federal Police remained inept (with Frank's influence) at securing targets. Enforcing the national food agenda was the last legal footing keeping the Federal Police in the West, and that meant Colonel Morgan eagerly pursued and was easily appeased by the seizure of any staged rotten crates of food. Meanwhile, the San Joaquin Valley was finally beginning to dry out after the worst floods in a century. Maybe the heavy snowpack in the mountains and a partially recharged aquifer would restore the bounty usually produced there. But it would be months before anyone could be sure.

***

Vero Gomez stood in front of the mirror, tucking her shirt in to her jeans, wondering if she'd gained weight lately. 'Been eating a lot of witches butter,' she thought. 'Probably fattening,' and she groaned softly as she tugged at her pants, noticing a new tightness at the waist. Her skin seemed paler than she remembered, but on further reflection it was obvious. Almost a year spent mostly indoors would have its effect.

"I have to get outside more," she muttered, turning from the mirror in the secret cellar's bathroom. A powerful musty odor hit her as she emerged into the corridor to the kitchen. It smelled like mildew, but there was also the decaying first tries at the bioboat at the back of the cellar. They were rotting now!

"Man it stinks in there!" Vero entered the kitchen, "Maria, do you think I'm getting fat?"

"Oh come on, Vero, you look great!" Maria, who was a descendent of Yaqui and Apache people in the southwest, along with others who entered her ancestry with or without permission, was built similarly to Vero, relatively round faced, brown, broad shouldered, muscular, strong hands. But she always thought Vero was cuter than she was, not that it mattered much down here!

"You always say that!" Vero frowned. "I can hardly fit these pants anymore!" She fell into a chair and ran her hand through her hair. "We have to get those rotting bioboats out of here. But I was smelling mildew too. You think floodwater trickled in after all?"

"We have to move!" Maria said emphatically.

Clara walked in and joined them at the table. "We are reaching the lifespan for this place. The rotting bioboats are the tip of the iceberg. I was going through everything with Larry and Ally yesterday. He's already found another warehouse where we can move," Clara explained. She looked tired, pale, and worried. As usual her long black hair was drawn tightly over her head into a thick braid running through the back of her Disneyland visor, her everyday 'look.' Like Ally, she was obsessively focused on cutting-edge bioscience work.

Maria was less obsessive in general and enjoyed her budding romance with Jessie Suzuki that began on the oyster reef trips. After more than a year buried (literally) in her work, she came up for light and air, and found a receptive and eager counterpart in Jessie. After the Pier 19 Peace Navy blockade, she and Clara wanted to be on the bay as much as possible! More even than Jessie and Steve Brooks were out there.

"If we're moving out of here soon, where will we live? Will there be sleeping quarters in the new place too?" Maria wondered aloud. She was ready to rent a normal apartment. Living and working in the same place was way too much. Plus, she couldn't bring Jessie home unless she got her own place.

"I've been thinking..." Vero looked hesitant. "Don't you think we should start producing Butterchips and Butter Pasta and Buttersauce on a larger scale? And start selling it? Whaddya think of a brand name like Witchips? Bruja Pasta? Salsa Bruja?" She'd seen how much money the pot farms brought in, and with the expansion of hydroponic farming, sometimes it seemed like everyone was making money but her. Not that she needed anything because Larry kept her on his payroll since her escape. Her culinary experiments finally settled on the three successful recipes for the witches butter. She wanted to make her own money, but she also wanted recognition.

Clara cautioned her, "You better talk to Larry and Ally before you go down that road. Your recipes are great, but I'm not sure if anyone should start making products. And frankly, that branding idea is wack."

"Why shouldn't we make products? And what's wack?"

"For one thing, it was Ally's 'idea' in the first place. For another, it was Dat's lab jockeys who reconfigured the code to alter its composition. And then it was Janet and the rest of you who ... what? Sang it into life?!" and she had to laugh. It was pretty hard to describe the curious evolution of witches butter, no matter how you tried. "And those product names are confusing."

Maria chimed in, "And don't forget, it's everywhere now. It's growing in at least a dozen places... plus" she remembered, "the Quarrytown huts! Witches butter is much more than food. We still don't know everything it can do—or is doing! But it's not merely a fungus anymore—if we can even say 'merely' after what we've learned! If we don't like factory farming, we should respect our new friend and find a different way to relate to it."

Vero was dismayed. She shook her head and replied, "We're supposed to treat it like it's a person or something?"

Clara touched Vero's arm. "Let's give it some more time, ok? Maria and Dat's experiments are pointing to sentience. It is alive, it does think for itself, and it does send electrical pulses that might be meaningful. We don't have any idea how, but it establishes biochemical—or maybe we should start saying *biocultural*—links between species. Right Maria?"

"I can't explain it yet, but the best evidence I've got is the harbor seals. First time I went out with Jessie and Brooks seals came right up to the boat. I didn't know if it was for me, or something random—though both Jessie and Brooks told me they'd never seen anything like it. I was so surprised that I threw them your chips! A few weeks later harbor seals started hauling out on the beach at Candlestick State Park. There's a whole colony there! Is there a connection? We can't be sure, but it's something new."

Vero remembered Janet and Dat and their story about the crows talking when they had witches butter wrapped around their wrists. And the numerous drones taken down by crows since that time. "The crows!" she blurted, and everyone nodded. "OK, let's wait and see. Maria, when will your experiments be complete?"

"We have some results already, and more to come. Let me go to Dat's and I'll put together a report for us, ok? We are trying to figure out how those guys in Quarrytown got it to grow into huts, too." She turned to Clara. "You said they 'sung witches butter into life,' and that hit me. That might be the best causal explanation we have. Because Angie at Quarrytown said she talked and sang to it, working with the butter to make a self-heating hut with door, windows, and a roof. This is beyond any explanatory framework we've been able to come up with so far."

CHAPTER 45
TUESDAY MARCH 17, 2026

Alison Nakahara sat at her kitchen table, gazing out at the Pier 70 apartments poking up from the old Union Ironworks shipyards, not far from her Potrero Hill Victorian flat. She fingered a letter on her table absent-mindedly that arrived yesterday. Gene Wilson, her old boss at BioGenMo, wrote her a weirdly formal letter asking her to come in for a conversation about an important matter relating to her time as an employee. She left BGM two years ago, cashing out her vested stock deal and retiring for good in May 2024. She remembered the excitement she felt when she began working on the biobulb and the bioboat, ideas she had been carrying around in her head for years.

A small worm of anxiety appeared as she remembered sequestering some research materials from BGM. Of course the whole fungus project was shelved during her time there. The fact that it was stolen and developed by others was not her fault. Of course she knew much more now than she did when she left BGM. She'd become friends with Dat and watched the witches butter take on a life of its own. She chuckled as she realized how literally true it was. For all her skepticism, after seeing the "Gingerbread houses" in Quarrytown and having that woman there get the biobulb working by talking to it, her sense of how things work was shaken. She was smart enough to recognize that there were things she could not explain; she couldn't accept the hippy-ish explanation of ... what was that woman's name? Oh yeah, Angie! She couldn't accept Angie's claim that the butter and the bulb were living beings with whom you had to communicate and collaborate. What sort of scientific explanation was that? But she couldn't argue with the results. Her accomplishments notwithstanding, there was much that she didn't understand. 'Maybe Maria and Dat will come up with a clearer idea of how it works,' she thought.

She agreed to meet her former boss. She didn't want to go to BGM, though, and insisted that they meet at the parklet by Farley's on Potrero Hill. Ten minutes later he confirmed, proposing 4pm that very afternoon. That was almost unseemly! He typically replied hours later when they worked together. Sighing, she assented. After a quick shower she pedaled down to Larry's, where they were preparing the big move. She and Clara and Billy Oakes were transplanting their experiments to move them from the secret cellar. At 3:30 her wrist alarm sounded, reminding her to get back to her meeting at Farley's.

Out of breath, and thoroughly sweaty, she finished locking her bike and turned to see Gene getting out of his all-electric BMW convertible across the street. He looked the same as when she'd last seen him two years ago, tall and trim, a full head of white hair over his tanned face, wearing his usual khaki slacks and a turquoise polo shirt. They made small talk as they ordered coffees before sitting in the parklet.

"Gene," she noticed his blue eyes looked tired, "what's this about?"

"You remember right before you left? I told you BGM was offering you your own lab and a free hand with lots of support?" She nodded, sipping her coffee. "And I asked you if you wanted to dust off your fungus project?" She nodded again and realized where this was going. "Did you take that with you?"

"Definitely not!" she firmly replied, looking into his eyes. "That would have violated our agreement."

"Yes, well, it's come to our attention that that property was copied from our system and has been undergoing development. We saw it at the Salesforce Park Festival. Do you know anything about that?"

"No, I don't. I didn't go to the Festival. Who took it? Another company?"

"We are tracking it down now. There are suspects, but I don't think it was one of our competitors. It looks like more of a rogue operation."

"A rogue operation? What do you mean? Who has the resources for that?"

"That's exactly what we're trying to figure out. Rumors say it was stolen by biohackers. We employed a guy who learned a lot about our technology before we let him go. It seems he has been helping our contractors when they have problems with the Prosper°Plant system."

"Is that a problem? I'd think you'd be glad. Isn't Intelligel® still your #1 product?"

Gene didn't want to discuss BGM's business nor did he want to give her Dat Doan's name. "I need to know, Ally, that you aren't involved with *these people.*"

"These people? Which people? What are you talking about?" This was a new tone from her old boss.

"You know who I'm talking about," he said circumspectly. "One of your old colleagues, Dennis Swintin, told me I should ask you."

'What the hell? *Dennis Swintin?!?*' she thought furiously. She sat staring at Gene, her poker face intact in spite of the shock she felt inside. "Dennis who? I don't remember anyone by that name."

"Swintin. He's been a contractor liaison for us since the beginning of the Intelligel® project. He's also an old leftist. He thought he could organize a union at some point. He was very involved in the recent Salesforce Park event. He's no threat. He's been an effective liaison for us and we've enlisted him in our investigation. He suggested we talk to you."

"Huh, that's curious. I don't remember him. I don't know why he'd point to me. I don't know anything about this, Gene, sorry."

Wilson smiled. "OK, Ally, I understand. Thanks for taking the time to meet with me. What are you up to now? Are you working? You disappeared."

"Oh you know, this and that. Dabbling in some farm projects. Running some experiments at a friend's place. Just having fun! I'm happily retired Gene..." She tried to sound relaxed and, well, *retired*. It was hard to say if he believed her, but she was not more forthcoming.

"Experiments? Wanna tell me more?" he tried anyway.

"Oh Gene... that would be *telling*!" she laughed nervously. "Let's say, nothing to do with anything I did for BGM. And if any of it ever comes to anything, I'm sure you'll be among the first to know!" She tried to see if he was still suspicious, or if his smile was genuine. "How's Bob?" she changed the subject to Gene's husband.

He knew what she was doing, but realized he couldn't trick her into revealing more. "Oh he's great. Still at the bank, but I keep telling him it's time to retire. He should take a lesson from you!" Gene got up and thanked her again for meeting. "Let me know if you hear anything, ok?"

Ally smiled her cheshire cat smile and shook his hand noncommittally. "Good luck!"

***

Sweat beaded on her forehead as she pulled weeds around the bokchoy growing in carefully tended rows. Another day of dry heat was welcome after the two-month deluge from Thanksgiving to the end of January. Janet remembered early springs when it was raining and cold, but it was sunny and in the high 70s. The rainy season was probably over, though there could still be some showers, even a storm or two, before it got hot in May. The "megadrought" seemed to have broken with the massive rains and snow but if those two months turned out to be an anomaly the long drought could persist.

"You should run the water, Janet!" called AnnaLisa from the other end of the row. "When we're done," she called back.

Sighing, Janet rose from the dirt and walked under the old willows, where she pulled off her soiled gloves. Wiping her brow she took a swig of water. Something shimmered in her peripheral vision but nothing was there. In the distance beyond the pond some kids visiting the farm were chattering excitedly, apparently having seen a snake or a mole. Again something seemed to shimmer at the edge of her vision. She went over to the spot and squatted down, leaning forward over the spot she thought she'd seen something shiny.

Through her hand she felt an unmistakable vibration. The spot she was looking at was moving slightly, the dust particles jumping almost imperceptibly. The vibration in her palm was weird and she pulled her hand up, and then put it back down again. The vibration was even stronger. It sent warmth through her, not heat but a sense of comfort. She pushed dirt aside until she was looking at a robust colony of witches butter in the shade of the willows.

"How did you get over here?" Janet murmured to the ground. Then, while she was looking directly at it, the spot that moved suddenly shone brightly and as quickly went "off" again. "What the hell—" Her crows descended to the ground about 10 feet away. She'd finally named her three regulars, Dewey, Lois, and Ferd. They were talking to her in a familiar way, guttural sounds in the back of their throats, not the loud cawing that often signaled their entry. Dewey bobbed his head while Lois skittered nearer and then retreating. Ferd stood quietly.

"You guys have been moving the butter around, yes?" The crows continued their same gurgling and movements. Janet didn't know how to read them. "I wish you could talk!" she exclaimed, remembering that one hot day last summer. The crows began cawing loudly at that—uncannily like a direct response.

"Whatcha doin'?" AnnaLisa joined her in the shade, throwing her gloves down and sitting on a log. The crows retreated to the edge of the clearing.

"Ummm... there's a new colony of witches butter here," she pointed to the place. "I was asking my buddies," she gestured to the crows, "if they were spreading it around, and as you arrived they were saying yes."

"Whaddya mean?" AnnaLisa was familiar with the witches butter they'd planted on the slope under the crows' favorite eucalyptus trees. "You think they're moving it around the farm?"

"Seems likely. The witches butter is here. What's new is that I saw a bright light and then I felt it vibrating. Come and put your hand here."

AnnaLisa touched the colony. She felt nothing. "You sure it wasn't a truck going by?"

"No, it was quite particular to this spot. I felt a vibration, and I saw this bright light in the dirt."

"It must've been a reflection. Did you find some glass or metal?"

"No, only the butter," Janet explained, unsure herself what she saw or what it meant.

AnnaLisa patted the ground again, chuckling. "Maybe you need to lay off the *bruja* butter," she teased, and she walked away towards the shed. Janet stayed on her knees looking at the ground. She put both hands down on the spot, but the vibration was gone. "You are growing and changing. Are you trying to tell me something?" The patch of tan fungus grew brighter again. It wasn't quite the light beam she'd seen earlier, it was more muted. "Ahhh, ok, you ARE trying to tell me something," and it vibrated gently under her touch. "I wish I knew what!"

Back at home on the slopes below McLaren Park later that night, she tried again to search for information but the only thing near was a story about a big conference on biofabrication. Making fungi into everything from leather to building materials was becoming a business. Maybe witches butter was not unique, but nothing referred to possible sentience in fungi. Some scientists discovered the role of deep soil fungi in facilitating microbial exchange between trees in a highly diversified forest. That was surely a kind of intelligence, uniting multiple species across microclimates and distance. But it was still short of the connection Janet felt she was having with the witches butter. 'I have to go back to Quarrytown,' she thought. 'Angie has something figured out.'

THURSDAY, MARCH 19, 2026

The big move was on. Billy Oakes struggled as the container and trellis threatened to topple over. Keeping the plastic cover intact to protect the biobulbs added to his stress. He emerged from the tunnel to the secret cellar under Larry's main warehouse. Larry was already in the refrigerated truck he'd rented, where he was working with Leon and Donnie to arrange 2-by-4s to serve as braces for each of the large plants they were gently moving to the new Brisbane warehouse.

Ally was beside herself with anxiety. Two days pondering whether she was at risk, returning repeatedly to the conversation with Gene in her mind, left her agitated. 'That fuckin' Dennis Swintin! Who did he think he was, throwing her under the BGM bus!' She knew they had nothing on her, that was obvious from the way her old boss approached her. But she'd been fingered. She *knew* she should have been more cautious with those guys. Good thing she was long gone from BGM now.

Facing the big move, her work was on the line. She knew how important it was to re-establish her experiments at the new site, but she could only imagine a disaster, plants toppling over, delicate bulbs being smashed, years of work uprooted and lost. Granted, they'd carefully established several trays of seedlings to use as starters in the new place, but she didn't want to lose her 'mother' plants. The original biobulb's main stem was a healthy seven-inch diameter. The biggest problem was the bioboat vine, whose roots were thick in the huge bed they'd originally built. It was simply too large to move. The first two prototypes rotted on the vine. They chopped them up and disposed of them. Cuttings taken months ago were cultivated in new bins. After delicately pulling the roots from the soil and rearranging them in a tighter formation, they got the bioboat mother plant into a 55-gallon drum. It was go-time. It would take two full truckloads to move everything from the secret cellar to the new place in the Brisbane Industrial Park.

Finding the new place had been another one of those serendipitous events—Juna Caguas told Cindy who told Lamar who told Larry: the water source for Quarrytown was a big empty warehouse downhill from the old quarry road. Juna hauled water from their faucet for months and saw the For Lease sign on the front corner of the building. It was empty and unattended for more than a year. Larry toured the site with the commercial real estate agent and immediately offered to sign a 10-year lease. The agent balked, not sure if this big guy was who he said he was.

"I own several properties in Bayview. Tell you what, here's a deposit," and he handed him a check for $5,000. "I'll have my attorney contact you. I'd like to make some stipulations in the lease anyway. We have a number of areas to customize to our purposes."

"Oh? Um, well, I'm sure we can work it out," looking at the check in his hand. This property sat empty for three years so leasing it out for ten years was a real feather in his cap. "Have him call me any time. Here's my card," he became friendly and accommodating. It wasn't every day that a big black guy came around trying to rent a property in Brisbane! By February 15 they started the modfications. Skylights and big windows went in above a new mezzanine level. Under the mezzanine, expansive laboratory facilities were installed, including flow hoods with HEPA filters, microscopes, sterilizers, racks of glass jars, refrigerators, and Biosafety Level 2 rooms with recirculation systems. In addition to new sinks in every lab room, Larry even paid for an extended water line, running out of the back of the warehouse and uphill towards Quarrytown. He even bought a marble water fountain from Silvestri's funeral monument store on Bayshore, which confused the plumbers who did the work.

"Why would you put a water fountain here?" they asked Larry when he said what he wanted.

"I'm thinking long-term. Hikers come through here and I want to provide public water," he explained. The plumbers thought he was crazy. But they built his little water temple, and once it was running, Juna and Angie and the

Mukuls could get water closer to their village.

Clara, Maria, Billy Oakes, Vero, Ally, Dat, Lamar and Cindy, Leon, toured the new place last weekend. Walking around the sprawling facility, they were amazed, except Ally and Clara, who closely monitored the plans and their execution. Moving the biobulb and bioboat projects from a climate-controlled cellar without natural light into this bright warehouse was a big step. But they made sure to have special blackout window coverings installed, both to be able to return to their original conditions if needed, and to be able to keep out any peering eyes (or drones).

Leon, Vero, Lamar and Cindy stopped on the mezzanine, more curious about the amenities than the science lab. Vero clapped her hands as she laid eyes on the fully operational luxurious kitchen. "Larry! You DID make me a kitchen!" she exclaimed.

Larry stood behind them. "Wait'll you see this!" and he opened the wall with a remote to reveal two bedrooms with bunkbeds and ample bathrooms, hidden behind the false wall. A second click on his remote opened another wall in the bigger bedroom and down glided a queen-sized Murphy bed. "You know, in case a couple needs a place to stay for a while," he grinned.

"Oh man, this is better than ever!" exclaimed Leon, who had sleeping quarters in the back of his warehouse and of course the bedroom at the Hangar too. "When we leave the Hangar, this'll do fine!"

Dat Doan came up the stairs deep in conversation with Ally.

"We should borrow a 'clipping' from Angie's hut. I'd like to run the same tests we've been running on the other samples. Maria—she's one of the best I've worked with!" he said admiringly. "We aren't ready to share our results widely, but you'll be amazed."

"Why don't you bring those tests over here. Maria is *supposed* to be on *our* team!" Ally smiled as she said it, obviously not angry about Maria's growing collaboration with Dat.

"Dat," Ally steered him to the comfy couches on the mezzanine, "I want to warn you." She told him about the letter from BGM and meeting with her old boss. "They're looking for you. He didn't name you, but it was obvious that they know the witches butter went through your lab. Hopefully they haven't gotten further than that. You left Howard Street a while ago, right?" Dat nodded, listening closely to Ally. "If you have anything compromising in your new facility, I'd suggest you move it out as fast as you can."

"We aren't doing much work in my business warehouse. It's perfectly legal storage for the import-export side of things. We moved the research to the Hangar when we moved to Bayview. And of course the butter went to Leon's before it spread everywhere." He started to laugh. "Even if they decide I was in the middle of it two years ago, they can't prove anything. And at this point, it has changed from what was described in your original research that there's no connection anymore. It's something entirely new. Anyway, it's basically in the public domain."

"Vero," Ally pointed over to the kitchen, "has dreams of ramping up production on her chips and sauces. You're right about witches butter being in the public domain. She needs to understand that."

"She can do that if she wants to," Dat replied. "If anyone can use it, why can't she? But why go to the trouble of producing products to distribute? Why not share her recipes? Why not let the butter be an example of a common good, owned by no one, available to all?"

Ally wrinkled her nose. "Now you're getting political on me." She smiled at Dat. "I prefer science."

"And that's not political?!? C'mon Ally, you know better."

"Hey, what are you guys conspiring about over here?" Maria joined them. Dat explained what they were talking about. Maria surprised them when she said, "If witches butter has a mind of its own, which might be an understatement, why should any of us see it as something we can exploit?"

That brought both Dat and Ally up short. After a long pause, Dat playfully poked Maria in the arm. "OK, you made your point. I can't argue with it. But we won't stop our research will we?"

"Oh hell no! We're on the cusp of meeting the aliens or something. What if it's true that the butter is a new intelligence that transcends our own? Could we recognize it if that were so? Do we have the tools, scientifically or conceptually? To go beyond measuring it, although that's been interesting, how can we approach actual communication? Can we show mutual recognition? Can we approach this with sufficient humility to imagine that it might be measuring us, might be seeking to teach us what *it* knows?"

Dat leaned back on the couch, clutching his knees, roaring with laughter. "Maria! You're WAY ahead of us!" and he kept laughing, delighted to have his own conceptual universe rocked. "Thank you for reminding us to be humble!"

Ally watched and listened, but it was nonsense to her. She gave the others no reason to think she wasn't with them.

CHAPTER 46
SATURDAY, MARCH 21, 2026

The Spring Equinox began early for Juna Caguas. They headed out to Kite Hill to watch the sun rise in the east. Juna was feeling a bit blue after a week working at the SPCA, where animals were coming in at a higher rate than usual.

"Seems like a lot of folks can't afford to feed their pets," Cindy remarked to them.

"You think that's what's happening?" Juna wasn't sure. "I don't know who gets rid of a pet they love for financial reasons."

"You'd be surprised. I've seen it a lot," she assured him.

It was a sad week as families left their dogs and cats. Juna wasn't at the front where they would have seen the tears and confusion. But it worked its way through the staff.

Juna's spirits lifted when, like every Friday, they went to see Angie and spend the day at Quarrytown. By now, everything was bursting with life after more than a month of hot sunny weather following the rainy winter. The mud-slide that had almost inundated their village site had been arduously reshaped into a new set of smaller terraces. With a steady natural stream available, the terraces might resemble Balinese rice paddies, but since they were bringing water UP the hill they had to be more frugal.

Juna paused before the hidden entrance to Quarrytown. Juna couldn't resist going for a closer look at the new mini-water temple Larry had installed 40 yards up the main road. The fancy marble statue of cherubs on either side of a big lamb was garishly weird. But there was a brass spigot that provided a strong stream of clean water. A small metal box could be seen behind the fountain, half a dozen yards away. Juna pulled up the cover to reveal places to attach hoses, and a red, six-sided roundish spigot. There was already a black hose attached to an outlet, disappearing in the direction of Quarrytown.

"Angie!" they called as they entered the clearing where the 'Butterhuts' were clustered. A new one was growing, its walls almost four feet tall, near the Mukuls' place. Angie emerged from her hut.

"Hey, Juna," and she gave them a big hug. Then she spoke in a confidential tone, "the water is here!" smiling broadly. She pulled Juna by the hand to the edge of the clearing where the black hose emerged from the ground and was coiled in a damp puddle.

"No more hauling buckets!" Juna was delighted about not having to do that backbreaking work anymore. There'd still be water to carry up to the terraces where the main beds were. But they noticed a sense of loss, too. The arrival of water meant a change in Quarrytown's pattern of life.

Sitting on Kite Hill at dawn, the shocking pinks and oranges piercing the skies over the east bay hills, Juna chided themself for thinking that hauling water was anything to hold on to. Bird calls rang out in the neighboring trees and bushes as the dawn took hold. Two familiar scrub jays flew down and landed a short distance away, greeting Juna with bobbing heads. Juna brought some popcorn and witches butter chips with them, expecting their avian friends to show up like this. They scattered some goodies on the ground between them. The jays eagerly ate them up.

"You like the butter chips?" Juna asked, "do they make you feel different?" not expecting any response. One of the jays took an intact chip in its beak and took steps towards Juna, nodding up and down and then extending the chip to them.

"You want me to eat it?" Juna asked, surprised. The jay nodded several more times and came a step closer, still holding the chip delicately in its beak. "OK then," and Juna took the chip and popped it into their mouth. After swallowing it, Juna said, "I didn't like these at first, but I don't mind them now." They turned back to the sunrise, but a powerful earthy smell distracted them from the visual symphony. Turning from side to side to see what could be smelling strongly, they realized they were sitting next to an outgrowth of the fungus, hidden among the thick green grasses that the winter rains brought forth. "How'd this get here?" Juna wondered. The jays took off and Juna was suddenly dizzy. Between the smell and the dizziness, they laid back in the grass.

"Oh!" Juna might have been laying in the grass but their mind was in the air, soaring over Kite Hill, heading towards the erupting dawn sky. They could feel wings flapping and looking from side to side realized they were seeing through the eyes of the scrubjay.

The two jays continued over the flank of Liberty Hill and swooped into Dolores Park, crossing directly over the 19th Street overpass which was filled with people tending to memorials for those who were killed the year before. Hundreds of people were moving around as darkness gave way to daylight. The jays landed in a huge cypress tree overlooking the streetcar tracks.

Juna was fully attuned to the vision provided by the jays, as they looked across the slopes towards Dolores Street where a dozen food trucks were setting up near a large stage at the 19th Street intersection. Abruptly the vision shifted and again they were rapidly flying but only the short distance over the tracks to a tree on Church Street. Viewing the streetcar's tracks through the morning gloom, there seemed to be someone moving furtively along the edge.

The person was dressed in dark clothes with a dark baseball hat and carried a small package that they put down against the retaining wall. With a furtive glance, the person jumped on the ledge and disappeared into the park. Juna saw the box or whatever it was left behind. He was inordinately curious to know what it was. The bird with whom Juna was seeing and thinking responded to the curiosity (was it Juna's or the bird's?) and flew down for a closer look at the nondescript brown package. It wasn't a box, but more of a bundle wrapped in twine. No way to tell what it was, but there was a weird smell. Gunpowder! Juna knew that smell from growing up on the farm in the delta. Their uncle often used the shotgun to scare away flocks of birds descending on his crops.

The connection broke. Juna sat up, keenly alert, and alarmed. They didn't doubt the vision. They had to warn someone. Even if it was nothing, they had to check. Thousands of people were heading to Dolores Park to commemorate the anniversary of the Massacre. What if that was a bomb!?

***

Tomas and his moms, Barbara and Millie, spent the morning making snack bags to distribute at Dolores Park.

"Hurry up!" Tomas urged Millie, who usually spent Saturday mornings in the basement preparing Food Conspiracy boxes. But today everyone was focused on the memorial and protest at Dolores Park. Tomas was using a broad-tipped marker, writing "NEVER AGAIN!" and the date of the massacre, 3/21/25, on each brown paper bag. Millie and Barbara took the bags from Tomas and put in an apple or pear, walnuts (they'd gotten a big load of walnuts from friends with a farm near Chico), and raisins (a shipment arrived from a defunct winery in the Anderson Valley—friends of Millie's there gathered unpicked grapes and dried them into a carload of raisins). The tray of finished bags was crowded now.

"We can't carry more than this anyway," Barbara declared.

"Let's go!" Tomas practically leaped out of his seat.

It was going to be a big day, exactly a year since the brutal massacre ordered by General Reynolds. Tomas's good friend Oscar was arrested alongside one of his mothers, Frieda, while the other, Ruth, was shot in the arm and hospitalized. Oscar had been detained until the general amnesty that accompanied the lifting of the National Emergency last October. When he returned, though, he wasn't the same. He didn't share Tomas's enthusiasm and energy.

"You don't know what it's like, man," Oscar morosely insisted. Six months in the crushing boredom of Camp Hayward, forced to do janitorial duties around the base, left him resigned. Tomas tried to enlist him in helping with the *Opaque Times* distribution, but he was not interested. "I ain't gonna get caught again, that's for sure."

Oscar's moms were a different story. When Ruth was transferred from the hospital to a holding pen at Pier 26, she bonded with the other detainees. Several of them, Ruth included, had a lot of experience in previous movements, and they banded together in jail solidarity. The disarray among the Homeland Security officials that followed the Massacre led to the surprising decision to release the Pier 26 detainees rather than ship them to the already bulging Camp Hayward, where both Oscar and Frieda were being held. Ruth was home when Frieda suddenly appeared after the wild escape in UPS trucks from Camp Hayward. Their neighbors on Alabama Street, Joao and Wilma with their son Cristiano and twin daughters, lived a few blocks away and had a well-hidden attic. That's where Frieda stayed for the first month after her unexpected return. A perfunctory Homeland Security letter arrived in mid-May, demanding that Ruth inform the authorities if she had any contact with her wife. But they never even bothered to send anyone to their house, and no investigation seemed to be underway. By the end of May, they relaxed, feeling they could resume normal life without too much concern, as long as they didn't draw any attention to themselves. And that meant not organizing public demonstrations on behalf of their wrongly incarcerated son, a bitter pill to swallow.

Reunion with Oscar in October relieved them, but his anger and sense of abandonment soon sent the household into an awkward tailspin.

Ruth woke up early, greeting the Spring Equinox dawn with a small ritual of candles and incense. Frieda slept in for another hour, but eventually she rose to the smell of coffee. Her tangled gray/brown hair grew longer since she'd been in Camp Hayward. The lines in her forehead never went away anymore, and her jowls became more pronounced too, her ruddy reddish skin showing its age as well. Her wife, Ruth Maloney, was more athletic and kept herself in great shape with daily hikes to the top of nearby hills. Ruth puttered over the stove, stirring a pot of her special oatmeal as she often did. She had broad shoulders, strong arms, and a narrow waist—from behind you'd never guess she was in her mid-50s.

"Is Oscar up?" she asked Frieda. "Do you think he will come?"

Frieda stared at the steam rising from her coffee cup, her vision still blurry after the short walk from their bed to the kitchen table. "I hope so."

The phone rang and Ruth answered. "'We need another 45 minutes at least... Yeah, yeah, I think so... No, I'm not sure but I hope so... OK. We'll be ready.' That was Wilma. They'll be here at 10:30, in an hour. She asked about

Oscar. You want to wake him or shall I?"

Frieda looked at Ruth sadly. "You." She was trying to stay engaged with Oscar even though he pushed her away since his return. For Ruth it was the same, but she was somehow able to stay present for him and not let his sullenness repel her.

An hour later, surprisingly, they were on their front porch, ready to go. Oscar was awake when Ruth knocked on his door and entered his room. She sat on the side of his bed reminding him of the anniversary and asking him if he'd go with them to the memorial. He groaned, but the last thing he wanted to do was sit home alone. "OK," he been his entire reply.

Patting him on his knee, she turned at the door and said, "I'm glad, thank you. Let's do this together."

Later they discussed the likelihood of getting separated in the crowd and what the plan was to regroup if they couldn't find each other. "I'll go Arizmendi's on Valencia and wait for you in their parklet," Oscar sensibly proposed. "And I'll text you when I leave the park." He was being very responsible! It made both his moms almost teary with gratitude.

After a boisterous reunion with the Pessoa family, they walked together, and shortly they were joined by the Denby-Miller family. Tomas pushed between Cristiano and Oscar and threw his arms over his friends' shoulders. "Dudes! This is gonna be epic!" Cristiano's younger twin sisters, Emma and Ella, bubbled along behind them, and further back the parents were clustered in their own conversation.

"We need a contingency plan," Frieda was arguing. "What if they surround us again?" As she spoke she seemed to be short of breath.

"Are you alright?" Ruth wrapped a big arm around her. "Breathe!"

"There's no way they do anything like that again!" Millie insisted, her wife Barbara nodding in agreement.

"There's no reason to worry, I'm sure, but there's also no reason not to have a plan," Wilma chimed in. She remembered her shock at the sounds of shooting as they climbed up 20th Street away from the park a year ago. "We got lucky last time. Let's keep our eyes open. And if we need to leave in a hurry, where shall we regroup?"

"Arizmendi's!" Ruth had the answer at hand. Everyone knew their favorite worker co-op pizza joint and bakery over on Valencia, a healthy distance from Dolores Park, but not that far.

***

Juna sat at the kitchen table in Kite Kastle with Julius and Aaron. Anna was making coffee at the stove. Greg was rummaging in the fridge for something.

"I was on the hill at dawn. I ate a butter chip that a jay gave me—it sounds crazy I know. But it happened. I mean, I talk to these jays. They're used to me. But this was different. I brought chips and popcorn to give them—they always show up when I'm out there in the early morning. It was after dawn. One of them picked up a chip and came towards me, nodding, wanting me to take the chip. I ate it, and then I noticed the smell, I saw a new outcropping of witches butter that I don't think was there the last time I sat in that spot. But I got dizzy, laid back in the grass, and then I had the vision!" Juna was unusually talkative this morning. Even as a steady member of the household for almost a year, they never talked like this! They were usually introspective and quiet.

"And? What did you see?" Aaron was preoccupied with making the trek to Dolores Park, thinking about how he could get a ride back. Julius sipped his coffee and waited.

"I was flying! I was seeing through the jay's eyes! It was incredible!"

"You mean you dreamed it?" Julius proposed.

"No, I was *seeing* in real time. They flew down to Dolores Park and landed in a tree. I could see the people on the overpass tending to their memorials. I could see the food trucks setting up along Dolores."

"How do you know you it wasn't your imagination?" Julius was skeptical.

"I guess I don't," Juna conceded. "But what if I really was seeing what was happening? Because I saw a guy leave a package along the streetcar tracks and it smelled like gunpowder!"

"What?!? How could you *smell* it?"

"I know this sounds crazy. It *felt* crazy while it was happening. But it scared the hell out of me. What if I saw someone putting a bomb there? Don't we need to tell someone? Don't we need at least to go and see?" Juna was upset and breathing hard.

Aaron watched this unfold. He knew from Janet that unusual things were happening associated with either eating or touching witches butter. But this was far-fetched.

He tried to find a reasonable response. "Maybe you're right. It does sound crazy, but if you ARE right and we don't warn anyone or do anything..." he trailed off, the consequences obvious. "But we don't want to start a panic over a vision, either. Calling in a bomb scare is the worst thing we can do right now.

There are tens of thousands of people heading that way, a lot of them are probably there already."

"If it's a bomb, we can't be messing around with it," said Anna, turning from the stove. "The cops have a bomb squad, let them handle it."

"Yeah, but if what if there's nothing there?" Julius didn't believe this was anything more than Juna's weird dream.

Greg sat down with a bagel while this conversation went along. "My friend Hank spends half his life on 'Dolores Beach'. He lives a block away. Let me give him a call."

At 9:45, twenty minutes later, his phone rang and it was Hank confirming a small brown package along the wall next to the streetcar tracks. "I'll be damned!" Greg said, "Thanks Hank. You wanna make the call or shall we? ... OK, well, ... yeah, ok, let me know what happens?" He turned to the rest of them. "It's there alright. And he's calling it in since he's there and knows exactly where it is." He looked at Juna with a piercing stare. "You saw this through the bird's eyes? How can you explain it?"

Juna was overwhelmed when the confirmation came in. They too wondered how it was possible. They'd never experienced anything like *that* before. "I can't," they said in a muted voice. "Other than something about the chips, maybe. Did holding the chip I ate in its beak open a connection between us? I have no idea."

***

Jay Hartman wasn't missing this for anything. He'd been one of those 1,400+ people arrested and carted to the Green Zone in Camp Hayward a year ago. And miraculously he'd been one of the lucky ones who got away during the audacious UPS truck escape. Along with his Plumbers Union buddy and roommate Jordan Lindsay they were in a huge crowd filling 18th Street walking down from the Castro to Dolores Park. The official start time was 11 a.m. but everyone knew this would be huge. Late arrivals might not even get near the park, that's how huge everyone expected the turnout to be. They got out of the house early, 10 o'clock! And they were enjoying a donut they grabbed from someone who was giving them away to everyone.

Jay felt a little jangly, his memories of a year ago rushing back after being long buried. His pulse quickened as sirens began blaring in the distance, and they saw a white police van and two squad cars cross blocks ahead of them on Church Street.

"Did that say 'Bomb Squad' on it?" Jordan had much sharper vision than Jay.

"What?!?" Jay's anxiety surged. The crowd, which had been laughing and cheerful, turned silent, a palpable tension rippling where the police passed. People turned on side streets, and some even turned back towards the Castro.

"I'm not going down there!"

"They say there's a bomb!"

"It's not safe!"

"Here we go again!"

Jay and Jordan stood to the side to take stock.

"Whaddya think?" Jordan asked his friend. He knew Jay went through a LOT more in the past year than he could even imagine. "You still wanna go?"

"Oh, hell yes!" Jay's surging anxiety coursed along the fine edge between rage and fear, but since his escape and his escapades at the Dog Patch, his rage usually won the tug of war. And it did this time too. "I'm definitely showing up today!"

Jordan was glad, his curiosity was much stronger than any fear of a bomb. Most of the people apparently felt the same way because in a few minutes the crowd resumed its surge towards Dolores Park. They were early enough to still find an open path past the tennis courts and into the sprawling flat field that was always being repaired. People were laying down blankets, coolers, picnics, beach chairs. There wasn't a great view of the stage from here, but the big sound system should make everything audible.

"Let's keep going!" Jay insisted. They hadn't come to lay around in the grass and be entertained, even if that's what a lot of people were expecting. "I want to see what's happening!"

It was a little past 11 o'clock, but this was San Francisco time. The crowd grew quite dense as they reached the cement path between 19th Street and Dolores to the overpass to Church. Dozens of altars stood along each side, and thousands of people slowly paid their respects, serving much like the annual Day of the Dead altars in Garfield Square. Uphill was jammed with thousands of people already and more were pouring in. At the perimeter along Church Street they could see flashing lights and dozens of police officers behind a long yellow caution tape. They'd closed Church Street and shut down the J-Church streetcar too. More and more squad cars were pulling up, and dozens of police officers were fanning out around the park, inspecting garbage cans, bathrooms, flower boxes, bushes, anywhere that someone might have stashed a bomb.

Several grim-faced cops were walking downhill through the crowds that were perusing the altars. Jordan asked one directly, a stern thin-faced Chicana, "what's happening? Was there a bomb?" She looked at him and slightly nodded, betraying her own fear for a moment, before resuming her stone-faced descent as part of the squad. The news was spreading rapidly through the park. There was a bomb, a real one, and the SFPD came and defused it. Were there more? Soon, small groups of people at the rally joined the effort to look into every possible hiding place to make sure there were no more bombs.

Nothing was found. The rally opened with a set by a local comedian, which helped loosen up the tension and relax the crowd. A much-loved local band played a set full of familiar tunes, covering some old standards by Santana and War and Tower of Power. They had a great brass section, and a very funky bass player, which got a lot of folks up and dancing. Finally, after some short speeches from Supervisors, it was the Mayor's turn. A smattering of boos greeted him, as lots of people remembered his about-face during the first days of the National Emergency, first denouncing the new Homeland Security authorities, and then endorsing them after they'd arrested him and kept him jailed for a few days. Many saw his reversal as a pragmatic necessity to re-establish 'civil' government, but others would always think of him as a collaborator.

"I'm proud to be here as your Mayor. We suffered an incomparable tragedy one year ago today." Light applause, but a few hecklers were ready to have at it. "It wasn't a tragedy, it was a crime!" one particularly big guy bellowed. "It was mass murder!" yelled a group of five, who were well rehearsed. The Mayor held up his hands, but the chant "Mass Murder! Mass Murder!" started to spread and was soon reverberating around the park, forcing the Mayor to wait quietly and awkwardly at the podium. He held up his hands again, trying to quiet the crowd until it subsided. "I'm here today to say, 'NEVER AGAIN!'"

BOOM! Somewhere up the hill towards the Hidalgo Statue, among the altars, an explosion ripped through the crowd. Screams followed and wailing soon after that. Panicked people poured from the park, screaming and crying as people fell and got trampled. The Mayor looked dumbfounded on the stage, and finally used his mic, "Don't panic! Don't panic!" which didn't help. "Please walk, don't run, as you leave the park. Help your fellow San Franciscans, don't panic—walk, don't run," and then he exited the stage along with the rest of the politicians.

Medics who were standing by surged towards the explosion. Meanwhile the hecklers went up and found the stage was empty and the sound system on.

"You know who did this! We all know who did this! The Federal Police—Homeland Security!" yelled a woman in a black tank top, her arms covered in tattoos. She was spitting mad, her face a twisted snarl. Another person, a big guy who was heckling the Mayor, grabbed the mic from her, "We should march on Hunter's Point! Evict the Federal Police from San Francisco!"

There may have been a few hundred people who in their anger wanted to heed his call. But thousands were evacuating directly and already most of them dispersed into the surrounding neighborhoods. Ambulances drove into the park and up to the site of the explosion where medics attended to the injured. By pure luck no one was standing at the altar when it exploded. No one was reported dead yet, but there were at least six people in critical condition rushed into surgery at General Hospital.

290

— PART 3 —
CHAPTER 47
THURSDAY, APRIL 9, 2026

'Oof!' she landed heavily on her unborn pup as she bobbed through the shallow water to reach the pebble-strewn beach at Candlestick State Park. She was reassured to see a dozen or more of her friends and family already stretched out on the beach in the April sun. Occasional calls when she'd been swimming in the bay helped her locate the new spot that she'd learned about.

Farther up the shore there was a yellow tape draped between garbage cans, and behind it was a park ranger and a squad of earnest children with sketchpads and junior binoculars. They jostled each other, excited for a front-row seat of the seals that were resting at the north end of the beach. They'd never been here before!

The soon-to-be momma seal was tired after a big swim from outside the Golden Gate. With sharks and other predators lurking out there, not to mention the massive ships that steadily churned through the channel, it was a great relief to have reached this calm and secluded spot. She hauled out onto the warm sand and finally, after some rolling around and adjustments, throwing sand up on her bulging body, she found a position to rest in, leaning her pregnant body against another equally pregnant momma seal. The morning sun heated them, while a cold spring breeze poured over the beach, leaving the jacket-clad children shivering in the distance as they stood and watched the largely immobile seals on the beach.

"What are they doing?"

"Are they dead?"

"Why don't they move?"

The questions bombarded the ranger, who patiently explained that a new colony of harbor seals appeared on the beach, a happy surprise for the park built on landfill at the southeastern corner of the City.

"What's that boat doing?" one young fellow asked, adjusting his glasses after lowering his binoculars. He was pointing to a small boat in the distance.

The ranger answered, "They could be out there having fun. Maybe they're fishing. But *that* one is working on our new oyster reef. Who knows what an oyster is?"

The children shouted answers until a serious looking girl answered with assurance, "They are bivalve mollusks! They grow in their shells in standing brackish water and filter it while they eat and breathe."

"You are right Emma! Excellent answer!" the ranger was used to the precocious Emma Pessoa who was a science prodigy. Other kids looked at her in awe, but one was ready to give her a shove as a goody two-shoes. "And does anyone know why we are re-establishing oyster reefs here?" Someone called out "sea level rise!" and the back and forth proceeded between ranger and kids.

Meanwhile in the boat, Maria and Jessie were leaning over their cultivated oyster reef and checking the size of the oysters. Remarkably the oysters thrived in their new location, at the juncture of the bay and the outflow of Yosemite Creek. The toxic waste buried around them remained a source of great worry for Jessie and Maria and everyone who had anything to do with either Hunter's Point or the low-lying warehouse district where Larry Lansing and the Robertson cousins ran their businesses.

"These look healthy!" Jessie exclaimed. "I used to work on oyster farms in Puget Sound, and these are looking good."

"You think these are ready to eat?" Maria asked skeptically. "Don't they take in a lot of the toxic shit around here?"

"In other places where they've put in living breakwaters like this, they found that oysters remove much more from the water than they retain in themselves. They are fantastic to eat because they are low calorie, low fat, high protein, high in zinc and manganese. They help prevent algae blooms in the water that kill thousands of fish. The sewage treatment plants around the Bay Area discharge too much nitrogen and phosphorous, which are like fertilizer for water-borne micro-organisms, but oysters help remove both, which eventually restores dissolved oxygen levels in the water."

"Hey," Maria pointed to a strange shaped white object clinging to the side of the furthest reef, looking almost like petals extending from a flower. "What's that? It's not a plastic bag is it?"

Jessie took the long pole and pulled them along the reef to the other end. He poked it and it bounced off the pole but remained firmly attached. "That's no plastic bag," he said.

Maria touched it from the side of the boat. She immediately got a tingling vibe up her arm and pulled back, as though she'd been hit with a mild electric shock. "I can't believe it!" She reached down and touched it again, getting the same familiar tingle. "That's witches butter! How the hell did it get here?!"

Jessie peered at the bloom. "How is it able to live under the water? It's not amphibious is it?"

"Not as far as I know! It's been doing well in different microclimates and soils. But this—it makes no sense!" She pulled out a pocketknife and reached down to cut a piece off.

"Hey! Why are you doing that?" Jessie objected.

"Don't worry! Witches butter grows back almost as fast as you can 'harvest' it. This piece," she held it up like a trophy, "will go straight to the lab for testing. We have to see if its molecular structure has changed. I can't imagine it's the same as the land-based version."

"How do you think it got here?" Jessie asked.

"Hell if I know! Wait! Remember that first time I came out here with you and those seals came up to us. I threw them some chips. What if one of them floated over and attached to the reef and then started growing?" Maria sat in the boat pondering the impossible. "Nah, that can't be it. Those chips are completely baked and the fungus is functionally 'dead,'" she paused again. "At least that's what we thought."

"If it's not dead and everybody's been eating those chips, does that mean . . . ?" Jessie stopped, trying to digest what he—and countless others—digested.

"Witches butter is alive inside us. It's in our microbiome! That exaggerated sense of smell that many people are experiencing—that's not imaginary. We are being changed!" Maria was suddenly hit by a wave of tingly vibrations in her stomach, which kept growing in intensity, spreading up her spine, into the back of her neck, across her chest, down her arms and legs. "Oh man, this is weird!" she staggered and sat down in the middle of the boat. Jessie went to her and put his arms around her as she seemed to be fainting. On contact with her bare arms, the tingling spread to him too, though at a mild intensity.

"What's happening Maria?" he was very worried.

"Oh, I'm tingling, I'm buzzing, I'm .... it's like being nauseous but I don't feel like I have to throw up. It's an intense sensation, almost like getting high, but it is centered in my gut and spreads from there..." she gasped as it intensified again. "My, my, my neck, my arms!" and she slumped into his arms, unconscious.

"Fuck! Maria? Maria!?" he laid her down and took a water bottle and squirted water in her face. He squeezed her arms, he lightly slapped her cheek. "Maria! Wake up! You're freaking me out!" He checked for a pulse and her heart was beating, hell it was booming! Her breathing calmed, and with a great sigh, she opened her eyes.

"What happened? Did I slip?"

"No, you were tingling... after you cut that piece of witches butter, you started tingling, or buzzing—"

"No!" She sat up and looked intensely at Jessie, her black eyes never more focused or alive. "It was when I said 'we are being changed'—it set me off like a slot machine that came up triple cherries!" The tingling largely subsided but it was still there at a low level, she noticed. She shook her head, as if in a fog. "I can still feel it, but nothing like it was."

"Let's get you back," Jessie sensibly proposed. They motored back to the Carroll Avenue dock where they left their bicycles. Pedaling back to Leon's place, they were anxious to share the experience. And Maria was dying to run the piece she'd taken from the reef through her tests.

***

Investigations after the Dolores Park bombing went nowhere. Juna's report of a man of indeterminate height wearing dark clothes and a baseball cap was too vague to help. A black sweatshirt and baseball cap were discovered in a trash can near the Children's Playground, but no one remembered seeing anyone put them there. No other eyewitness reports emerged about seeing anyone placing a device either in the streetcar tracks area where a bomb was found and defused, or at the top of the central walkway where one exploded. Analysis of the defused bomb and the debris from the exploded one indicated that they were likely made in the same place in the same way, but details were not forthcoming. FBI bomb specialists were brought in and their investigation was ongoing. After several weeks no one had been accused or arrested.

Colonel Morgan paced back and forth at the front of the weekly briefing. Frank and the other Zone Commanders were arrayed, as usual, around the big conference table. Lt. Nichols—Charlene—sat next to Frank, and the others clustered in ideological order, with Lt. Smithson of the Sunset at the far other end of the horseshoe. Garner and Owens were in the middle, though Charlene confirmed with them their willingness to resist any outrageous orders from Col. Morgan, were they to happen. The aides sat around the walls behind their bosses; Corporal Eli Flores had his laptop open on the chair behind Frank.

"Listen up! These yahoos protesting at our gate—we won't have to put up with this much longer," Morgan ominously claimed. "We'll have new powers to override the authority of the Mayor or the Chief of Police." He looked at his staff with what almost looked like glee. Col. Morgan was adamant after the March 21 anniversary was hit with a terrorist bomb that a state of emergency needed to be reinstated in San Francisco. As usual, the local authorities expressly denied that control, and instead called for the FBI to come in. But it got worse when the Special Agent in charge Mort Greenstein (probably *Jewish*, he'd thought) paid him a private visit.

"Colonel, our preliminary investigation has concluded that the materials for the two bombs came from Homeland Security supplies. We've decided to not make any public announcements about this... yet."

"What do you mean? Are you saying my people had something to do with this?!?" Morgan was outraged.

"I'm not accusing anyone. But I want you to know that our investigation is pointing to someone or some group that had access to the stockpiles here at Hunter's Point or at Camp Hayward..." Agent Greenstein looked carefully at Morgan for any reaction. "Were you at the Dolores Park Massacre a year ago?"

"No!" Morgan couldn't believe he was being questioned like this. His face was growing redder and his anger was rising rapidly. "I was in Sacramento when it happened. I was transferred to San Francisco after they cashiered General Reynolds and his staff."

"Uh huh," Greenstein acknowledged. "Were any of your senior commanders here a year ago? And do you think any of them were angry about this Memorial Rally?"

"Lt. Robertson was here, he was a Sergeant then. Lt. Owens too. I don't think anyone else was here yet. I don't see why either of them would be angry about the Memorial."

"Thank you. I'd like to interview Lt. Robertson and Lt. Owens. Can you have them sent up?" Greenstein was not wasting any time.

Frank's interview surprised Agent Greenstein. He described how a year ago he'd helped people exit the park, and then how he'd been called on the carpet by General Reynolds 90 minutes after the shooting stopped.

"You're not proud of what happened that day?" prodded Greenstein.

"Hell no! They call it a Massacre and that's what it was. I still don't know why Reynolds ordered people to shoot..." Frank's brow knit as he began reliving his nightmarish memories. "Hell, I don't know why anyone pulled a trigger out there! There was no threat." He was glad to explain this, and wondered where this was going.

"Do you know anyone, Lt. Robertson, in your ranks, or among your colleagues, who defends what happened that day? Or anyone who objected to the one-year anniversary memorial?" Greenstein was leaning over his yellow pad where he'd been scribbling furiously, his balding pate reflecting the fluorescent light above.

Frank thought about what he should say. He wouldn't be that surprised to learn that Col. Morgan had something to do with the bombing. Morgan was constantly pissed off that he couldn't exercise their authority at his discretion. But if he were to suggest Morgan, wouldn't that come back to him? He had no evidence, only his antipathy to Morgan and his arrogant self-importance. Would Lt. Smithson be involved in something like this? He was Morgan's lap-dog and cheerleader, and if anyone would go rogue this way, it would be him... wouldn't it?

"I can't think of anyone, Special Agent. Everyone I know wants to find the bomber." Frank was quite good at giving safe answers and remaining impassive while hiding internal doubts.

"Thanks for your time, Lt. Robertson. I'll let you know if we need anything more from you." Special Agent Greenstein dismissed him, and from what Frank heard, it went about the same with Lt. Owens. Owens had been at Dolores Park a year ago, but in reserve, when he heard the shots ring out. At the park, he removed bodies and triaged the wounded.

Special Agent Greenstein's visit, a week after the bombing, produced nothing. Two weeks later Morgan was making wild claims at the briefing. Frank decided to ask for more information. It was always better to push Morgan when he was sounding too confident.

"Sir? Could you clarify what you meant when you said we will have new powers soon?" Frank tried to sound calm and curious.

"Lt. Robertson," Morgan's attention focused on Frank. "Congress passed a new law that blocks municipalities from what they've been doing here in San Francisco. It will make it clear—finally—that we are the higher ranking authority."

"But the local police aren't the problem, are they?" Frank protested.

"I don't think there would be terrorist attacks if we were fully engaged in protecting the city," Morgan answered disingenuously. He and Frank both knew that there was evidence pointing to someone with access to their munitions as the bomber. Frank dropped it.

"Once the President signs the bill," Morgan continued, strutting a bit now, "we will be able to conduct our own investigations and operations without having to ask the Mayor or the police chief for permission!" He pirouetted in an about-face as though he'd accomplished something. The Zone Commanders watched him, each making their own internal calculations about what this might mean going forward.

***

"Dang! You guys have brought this place all the way back!" Leon whistled in appreciation.

Tom and Evelyn stood a few feet away in the raised beds they'd been working at the Dog Patch. They smiled together at the compliment. Wearing matching sweaters and similar boots too, they seemed joined at the hip.

Evelyn took off her wool cap and wiped her sweaty brow, but the cold wind pushed her to put it right back on. "After the the rain and the winter floods, we're hoping the soil here is more fertile than ever. With the Feds locked up on the base maybe we'll get a chance to farm!"

Leon sat in his electric cart, having delivered several trays of seedlings. "I hope so! Hey do you need me to take anything back over the hill?" he was heading back to his warehouse. "Or do you need anything else?"

"Next time bring us a box of witches butter!" Evelyn proposed. "We oughta be planting that everywhere we can!"

Tom looked skeptical and put his shoulder into the hoeing in front of him.

"What?" Evelyn noticed his attitude, of course, and couldn't leave it unchallenged.

"You're not a big fan of the butter?" Leon asked pointedly.

"Nah. It's fine. I think people are expecting too much!"

Evelyn directed herself to Leon. "He's mad because people are starting to say the witches butter has some magic," she smiled and gave her husband an elbow to his ribs.

Leon laughed. "Yeah, it's getting attention. You heard about those huts on San Bruno Mountain? That's hard to explain."

"And how it grows back when you break some off to use for food! I've never seen anything like it!" Evelyn was an enthusiast.

"Well, we've got plenty! I'll run a box over tomorrow if I don't get back later this afternoon," Leon began backing up and turning around. He noticed the intense smell of the bay. The tide was out and the bay mud was teeming with organic decomposition as usual, but then why did it smell much stronger than he remembered?

A few minutes later he was tooling along Hunters' Point Boulevard when he saw a small crowd of demonstrators at the gates to the Federal Police base. He took the turn before the base entrance that allowed him to use the public access road through the former Naval Shipyard. As he turned he saw signs and heard the chanting from the protest. "Feds out of SF!" "Whose Bomb? Their Bomb!" "End the Occupation!" and so on. He gave a friendly wave as he rolled by.

His 3-wheel cart, much like a golf cart but with more speed, longer lasting batteries, and a bigger cargo bay, was the perfect vehicle for rolling back and forth between his warehouse on Hawes and Underwood, the house up on Marlin Street, and the Dog Patch. Now that Larry had his new place in Brisbane, he could even get down there on it in no time.

Entering his warehouse he was glad to see how busy it was. "Hey Vero!

Lorena!" he called when he saw them at the "mother vat" of witches butter against the wall. He walked over and saw them kneading it. "You think you still have to do that?"

Lorena stood back and wiped her hands on her smock and stood there smiling. "We're getting a new batch ready for Maria. She wants to run some more tests. And anyway, you should try it! It's quite relaxing."

"Relaxing? Are you sure you're not catchin' a buzz?" Leon had a warm smile and kind eyes—he looked a lot like his father Frank did at the same age. A bit over 6 feet tall, lanky, broad-shouldered, big hands and feet. He'd settled into his life as a farmer/businessman. Some days he would head out into the city dressed in a sharp suit, having learned that doors opened and meetings were granted to someone who looked the part. But today he was tooling around the neighborhood and he was comfortable in his jeans and his company t-shirt sporting his logo, a big marijuana leaf with overlaid gold letters "Lean on Leon." He was making plenty of money from steady pot sales. But he'd always assumed that the witches butter fungus project would be a money maker too. It was hard to tell now, though, as they were giving it away right and left.

"Leon!" Vero turned around and gave him an intense look. "Don't you think we should ramp up production of chips and pasta? Larry built an industrial kitchen in Brisbane. Whaddya think?"

"Yeah, um, I always thought that's what we were gonna do. Figure out a way to make some money from it. It's one thing to make it though, and another to get it into stores and sell it. Have you thought about that part?" Leon looked at her expectantly. "I mean, I suppose we could sell chips at the dispensaries—everyone needs snacks for the munchies!"

"THAT's what I'm talkin' about! Let's do this!" Vero was excited to finally get a little traction with her own idea. She'd invented the witches butter chips—why shouldn't they figure out a way to sell it?

CHAPTER 48
FRIDAY, MAY 1, 2026

Janet was pedaling intently up the closed pothole-filled road from the Brisbane post office. She dodged the worst of the ruts to pass Buckeye Canyon and then Owl Canyon, and finally, arriving near the hidden trail entrance. She hid her bike behind some bushes. Ten minutes later she traversed the lip of the camp and arrived at Angie's hut. The sun was hot and Angie was at the back of the clearing with a black hose in her hand.

"Hey Janet!" she welcomed her. "Check this out!" and she waved the hose to her. "Thanks to Larry and Juna, we have running water!"

Janet hadn't visited since mid-March when they'd toured Larry's new facility. She stood in the center of Quarrytown, the clearing with five of the "Gingerbread Huts" made of witches butter. Wait a sec, five?? "You've been growing more huts?"

"Yeah, it's easy. You have to draw a pattern on the ground in a small trench and then lay it in there, saying what you want it to do." Angie walked over, gesturing to the two huts next to Janet. "A day or two later it's grown up and then you cut in windows and a door and put together some branches for a roof. It soon fills in the gaps and you've got a self-heating, self-reproducing dry home!"

"You 'tell it' you say? Do you think it understands plain English?"

"Sure seems like it!" Angie grinned. "Although I don't think it's limited to English. The Mukuls, before they moved out, were speaking to it in Yucatecan Mayan. Seems like it behaved the same."

"They moved out?"

"Yeah, they found a live-in groundskeeping job down the peninsula. Shoot, I didn't even know they were looking, and suddenly, they came to me and said 'Adios!'"

"Oh! You must be sad they're gone, huh?"

"Yeah, especially those kids. Davi was helping me," she sighed. "Anyway, yeah, the huts are amazing. At first I was surprised, but now it feels normal."

"What do you mean?" Janet was keenly interested.

"The witches butter is easy to live with. It wants to work together, it's very cooperative, and it figures things out on its own most of the time!" Angie explained this as though it were obvious.

"But how? How do you know it's cooperative, or that it 'figures thing out on its own'? It doesn't talk or communicate directly, does it?"

"No, not like we do. But it *speaks* if you listen. It adapts to what I say, and it even accommodates things I need... like heat! The walls generate heat when I need it. And the shape traps the heat and keeps me dry when it rains too. And the biobulb went into the ceiling and makes light whenever I ask it to. Something or *someone* is working with me here, no?" Angie started walking across to the other side of the clearing, where the other three huts stood. "Here you can see how it adapted to the Mukuls', with a common room, and bedrooms for the parents and children. They put doors between them—it's an extended home. Check it out!"

Janet walked into the empty home and ducked through the doorways between the three different structures. "Who is this bed for?" pointing to a cot with a sleeping bag.

"That's for guests. Juna has stayed over recently. Also we're using this room," and she pointed to the smallest hut, the one that had been the children's sleeping room, "to organize our seed bank."

Juna appeared at the trail, carrying a backpack, waving to them with a smile.

"Ay, Juna, just in time! I was trying to describe how the witches butter collaborates..." Angie paused, realizing her words weren't capturing what she was trying to say.

"Collaborates?" Juna exclaimed. "I guess you could say that... but... it's a LOT more than that! It connected me to the jay when I saw that bomb at Dolores Park!" Juna ate it a lot more ever since that experience. "I can't explain it, but it feels like a facilitator or, or... intermediary." They sat down, groping for the words.

"That sounds right," Janet concurred. "When I touched a Araucaria tree in Salesforce Park during that festival, I was transported too. I went out of my head and was at the top of the tree and then I was flying around—I was in the mind of a crow—before I came abruptly back to *me*."

Angie looked back and forth between Janet and Juna. The witches butter was a regular part of her diet over the past few months too. She'd had numerous 'out-of-body' moments, and they were increasing in frequency and intensity. The wind talked to her, the trees and bushes whispered.

Last week the manzanitas further up the hill called her to come and get berries, and she'd taken enough to fill several jars drying in the seed bank. In a hidden gulley above the old quarry, last autumn she'd planted Nahavita seeds collected years earlier. This spring she returned to find a field of light purple flowers blooming. Using a manzanita branch she'd shaped into a proper tool, she dug down and found an abundance of tubers. She harvested a modest number, leaving the rest for later.

"I'm always *me*, but lately, 'me' seems a lot more than what's in my head!" Angie tried to explain. "I've been eating a lot of the butter too. And I live in a breathing, thinking gingerbread hut!" She went on to explain about the manzanitas calling to her, the many animals that were coming to visit, the mountain weasel family that stayed next door until the weather improved before leaving to their usual habitat up the canyon. "There was a raccoon family too, but they didn't stay long. Anyway, the animals don't fear me like a human anymore. They trust me, and I trust them!"

"Are you feeding them?" Janet asked.

"Well, I put some witches butter in bowls when the storms were at their worst, but nothing since then. But look over here," and she led them to the terraces. Alongside the trail was a big colony of witches butter. "You can see the nibbling and scratches, but you can also see how much larger it has grown. And I found another smaller colony up near the top of the old quarry. Some birds are spreading it."

Juna squatted down to look closely at the witches butter. "Looks like claws more than teeth, but who knows? Who's been coming to visit?"

"The coyotes pass through every day. A family of skunks in the upper terrace—luckily they don't come down to the camp much. There's a possum family that came over from the Eucalyptus grove further west. None of 'em stay long. They come by to say 'hello' and check on me. And the birds of course! Crows, jays, redwing blackbirds, sparrows—last month an ol' redtailed hawk started hanging out in that big tree over there," she pointed to a sprawling oak tree, "but he left after a few days. Not sure why."

Janet came to talk with Angie and get some insight into her weird out-of-body experiences and the inexplicable buzzing and tingling and smells that were happening more and more. Typical explanations were no longer sufficient. "I feel like there's an intelligence surrounding us, enveloping us, don't you?"

Angie looked sharply at her. "That's *always* been true!" she almost rebuked her. "What seems new-ish," she noticeably softened her tone, "is something bigger and smarter than we are."

Juna was delighted to find themself between these two women, listening to them think aloud about what they too were experiencing. "I think—" they halted, unsure of their thoughts, groping for words. "I uh, well, it feels like to me is that we're finally seeing things that were always there, always connecting us, but our brains were blocking it. Maybe the witches butter is unblocking something inside us?"

Angie clapped Juna on the back, as she tended to do when she got excited. "Juna! That's it! Something is coming unblocked!"

The three of them excitedly tried to explain their recent experiences. Janet suggested, "We should sit down with Maria and go over this again. She's been running tests—she's had experiences like ours too. And she knows a lot more about what's going on biochemically than anyone else."

***

Frank and Eli were in a new Federal Police squad car, driving on Seventh Street towards the Federal Building at Mission. Behind them were three buses full of federal police in their pale blue armored uniforms, dispatched to break up a demonstration filling the streets around the Federal Building. After the Christmas occupation in 2024, they would not risk another storming of the building.

"I remember huge immigrant marches on May Day, don't you?" Eli asked Frank.

"Yeah, yeah... when was that? Early 2000s right?"

"Not sure. I was about 15, around '06 or maybe '07?"

"Weird to think. I can remember May Day marches when the Longshoremen's Drill Team thrilled us. It had the spit an' polish of a military squad, but it was *us*, *our* people, *our* neighbors. But that was when I was still a young man too, back in the 1970s. By your time, big public labor marches were over." Frank was wistful as he watched the new condos roll by on either side of Seventh Street as they drove northward.

"Oh, I remember some Labor Day marches... but that's in September!" Eli answered, gently tapping the brakes as thick traffic slowed near Folsom, the street filled with unmoving cars ahead. "I guess we're gonna have to park somewhere and walk the rest of the way," he suggested. "Seventh Street must be blocked up there, no one's moving."

Frank pointed at an open alley next to a golden-domed church. They pulled in and realized they were next to an elementary school that occupied most of the lot alongside them. Soon they were forming ranks.

Frank was sent to control this demo with troops from his own Zone 9, but also Lt. Owens' regulars from Zone 2. It was a boisterous and confident group who fell in along Cleveland Alley, not expecting any trouble as they latched their armor into place, pulled on their helmets and prepared their tear gas and batons. At the rear a small detachment brought a mobile cart with extra canisters and bottles of water for the men and women. Frank was adamant before they left that no one bring any guns or live ammo. "Tear gas is bad enough, but it won't kill nobody," he muttered to Eli after making his orders clear.

They marched up Seventh Street, pushing past pedestrians on the sidewalk, one column going between parked vehicles and the stuck traffic. The clomp of their boots hitting the ground in unison loudly announced their approach. A half block from Mission, they could see a huge crowd with big banners filling the intersection of Mission and Seventh, filling the street between the Federal Building and the old Post Office building.

"Chan! Take the Zone 2 group around to the west side and begin clearing Mission Street. Lester, you take Squad B to the right, circle around the crowd and push them from Mission, into Seventh or onto the sidewalks. If we need to use gas I'll give the order. For now, move people firmly."

For the next ten minutes things seemed to go according to plan. Chan's group easily outflanked the protesters along Mission to the west and had them backing into the crowd in the intersection. Lester's team had trouble as they pushed around the corner and into Mission, but eventually they established a street-wide wall of soldiers and were steadily advancing back to Seventh, pushing protesters ahead of them. The remaining two platoons arrayed themselves across Seventh between the south corners and held their line while their colleagues slowly closed the kettle from either side.

Scuffling and pushing and shoving along the line was raising everyone's hackles. Demonstrators were taunting and yelling at soldiers, while the Federal Police behind their tinted helmet shields seemed faceless and robot-like. But inside, each officer had to face their own demons, either rising anger and desire to hit back at the rowdy protesters, or, in some cases, a deep shame at finding themselves on the wrong side. The discipline of holding the line offered a barrier to stand behind.

"Emergency Cash Now!" was the big banner over the marchers. Unemployment was 19% according to the latest statistics, but everyone figured it was worse in San Francisco, where the tech booms were finally done. When the Feds showed up, though, the crowd's energy redirected itself towards them. The familiar chant erupted, heard more and more since Dolores Park, "Whose Bomb? Their Bomb!" When Frank heard that, his own ambivalence was agitated. He knew someone stole materials out of the Federal Police arsenal but still no one had been accused.

Chan's squad sealed the southwest corner of the intersection and blocked Mission. Lester's group was pushing their way towards Seventh, but the crowd pushed back forcefully. Frank looked over the surging crowd towards Lester's squad and could see light blue arms in the air bringing clubs down on the demonstrators. "Shit," he muttered, and then turned to Eli, "Send Franklin and his guys to help Lester!" but it was too late. The crowd was hurling anything they could lay hands on at the lines of police standing across Seventh and Mission. The full-on brawl was happening 50 yards east on Mission, and Franklin's squad was soon engulfed before they'd even reached Lester's group.

"Masks on!" Frank ordered, and the Federal Police pulled their gas masks from their belts and began putting them on. People began yelling, "They're gonna gas us! Here comes the tear gas!" and word spread immediately. Protesters moved away from the police towards Market Street, but several hundred were fully into the hand-to-hand fighting that filled the street to the east. Moments later, Frank authorized the release of one volley of tear gas, which landed behind the brawlers and in the middle of the intersection. Intrepid fighters grabbed the hissing canisters and used them as projectiles to hurl at the rows of officers. The lines broke down as officers took evasive action themselves, many moving to the sides to escape the cloud of tear gas, while those in gasmasks kicked the canisters back towards the protesters. Rocks were flying now, and several officers were struck by what turned out to be large pieces of cement that came from the curb along Seventh. People were pushing and pulling the parking meters until they gave way and as they did, the cement beneath them crumbled enough to produce potent projectiles.

"Davis!" Frank bellowed to another sergeant nearby. "Take 10 men and push up the street. Get those guys throwing rocks!" Chaos engulfed the area. More tear gas was fired as officers were being overrun by protesters. Bodies were strewn about the intersection, mostly demonstrators but a few officers were down too. Cracked heads, broken ribs, bloody noses and bent limbs. Several officers were evacuated by ambulance, and two dozen protesters needed medical attention too.

"What a mess!" Frank groaned. His officers successfully routed the protesters from the immediate intersection, but it was a pyrrhic victory. Too much mayhem, too many injured. At least no one was killed! And the protesters were still there, regrouping near the Odd Fellows Building on Market Street. He issued orders to fall back. By now they'd set up inside the tall metal fence that enclosed the grounds in front of the Federal Building.

"Lt. Robertson!" Sergeant Davis stood in front of Frank where they'd set up a command center. "We arrested seven and have them over there," he gestured to a makeshift enclosure. "They were the ones throwing pieces of the sidewalk."

***

Sheila saw the crowd gathering out on Seventh Street and knew things could get ugly. It was only lunch time, but it was Friday and she decided to go home early. She went down to the lobby and wished everyone good luck.

"Hey Herb!" she waved to her pal. "I hope it doesn't get too awful out there."

"Oh, nothing to worry about!" he assured her. The security was ramped up in the GSA building—he couldn't imagine a repeat of the Christmas occupation at the end of 2024.

"I hope you're right. I'm taking an early weekend. See you on Monday!"

She maneuvered through the thickening crowd along the Seventh Street perimeter. She put her badge away, and managed to avoid notice as she slipped into the crowd. She was sympathetic to the protesters, although she doubted they would get much support. There were a lot of Mexican and Salvadoran and Nicaraguan flags among the crowd. She smirked to herself, as she saw a familiar slogan on a t-shirt, "We didn't cross the border, the border crossed us!" She paused to look back from the stairs in front of the old post office.

Loud chanting erupted at Stevenson Alley under the Grant Building. It was a bunch of teenagers, which seemed odd to her. Why would they be here? She remembered the big campout in Civic Center in February after thousands of high school students marched on City Hall. But this was at the Federal Building, and from the banners and signs it seemed to be focused on demanding emergency cash payments from the government, and a general amnesty for undocumented immigrants.

"Every day is an Emergency!" they chanted, echoing the slogan that zipped around San Francisco during the February days.

"Replumb the City!"

"Solar on Every Roof!"

"One Lane for Food!"

Who *were* these kids? She left the crowd behind and eventually walked back to her apartment in Mission Bay. It was a beautiful day, and she decided to enjoy the afternoon.

***

Oscar and Tomas and Cristiano excitedly hoisted their banner at the edge of Seventh Street, "Every Day is an Emergency!" The three boys enthusiastically embraced the burgeoning social movement that began with the high school walkouts in February. The Festival of Possibilities at Salesforce Park was inspiring too, but the building occupations and the big campout in Civic Center galvanized high schoolers all over town. After two months, it spread to middle school students, and of course local colleges joined in too. City College students marched to maintain tuition-free classes, but when USF and San Francisco State students began showing up, the tone changed. They started calling for "A Different Future" when the university students made it clear that they weren't pursuing degrees to get jobs in the world as it was.

Oscar and Tomas were 14, Cristiano only 13, so they looked up to the older students. They already worked with people much older than them. Tomas and Cristiano had grown up in a hurry while distributing the *Opaque*

Times. The idea that they would go to school to get a job was far from their minds. They were going to change the world. They came to the Federal Building protest on May Day. The histories they'd been learning about—May Day, for example, had been a big deal long ago—suddenly seemed alive.

"Hey Bridget!" Tomas called when he saw his friend Bridget through the crowd. She was dark-haired and stocky and muscular. Jill appeared at her side, still sporting a bouncy head of frizzy hair and her red-rimmed glasses.

"Hi Tomas!" The two girls warmly greeted the boys. It was easy to be friendly with them since they were two years older. Bridget carried a sign with a big yellow blimp image and the words "Solarize Air Travel! Slow Down and Listen to the Wind!" Jill had an image the boys remembered seeing at the Festival, "One Lane for Food" with what looked like Folsom Street narrowed to one lane alongside a thriving linear farm.

"Cool signs!" Tomas exclaimed. Oscar stood back, not having met the girls before and surprised that his buddies were chummy with them. The girls pointed approvingly at their banner and wandered into the crowd. Chanting and drumming were burbling in various directions, raising the general excitement and volume. After almost an hour the whole area was jam-packed with people.

Cries and confusion reached them from the distance. From where they were standing they couldn't make out what was happening, but the crowd's tension suddenly rose. People were walking towards Market Street and after another ten minutes crowds began surging in that direction. They could see the intersection where rows of light-blue clad federal police stretched across Seventh, and another line took up the width of Mission on the west.

"They're gonna use tear gas!" yelled people who were running past. Tomas, Oscar, and Cristiano didn't want to run but were nervous. What was getting gassed like? It probably hurt! Detonations echoed and smoke emerged a half block away, as more and more demonstrators withdrew towards Market Street. But others rushed forward, some with their faces covered, others in black bloc formation, ready to rumble. This was not what they expected!

"Take the banner down. We gotta go!" Tomas urged his compatriots. They began rolling up their banner. Rowdier protesters were between them and the police and tear gas, which was starting to make itself felt. Their eyes stung and the acrid smell bit at their noses.

"Here! Cover your nose and mouth with this!" A woman in a medic armband handed them wet bandanas. They donned the masks as their eyes watered. The people to their side were pulling and pushing parking meters back and forth, which was breaking up concrete from the curb. They watched as these guys grabbed the chunks of loose concrete and threw them at the police lines drawing closer.

"I got one! Didja see that! He went down like a sack of potatoes!" crowed one black-clad guy. The tear gas was everywhere and the boys rubbed their burning eyes. Protesters kept throwing debris at the cops and the cops fell back, regrouped, and shot another round of tear gas.

"We should go!" Oscar urged. "Let's get out of here!"

And he'd hardly finished saying it when out of the clouds of gas a row of federal police came running directly at them. The guys who were throwing the concrete vanished and they were caught standing there, along with several others who failed to exit in time. The medic who provided bandanas was a few feet away and the cops roughly tackled them to the ground.

"Hey! Ow! OWWW! You're hurting me!" shrieked Cristiano, completely shocked at being attacked by the police. Loud complaints ricocheted through the tear gas as prisoners were roughly shackled and shoved across the street into a holding pen inside the Federal Building perimeter.

CHAPTER 49
SATURDAY, MAY 2, 2026

"This food is shit!" yelled the guy who never slept. Dressed in disheveled black clothes, he paced back and forth with the steady rhythm of a metronome. "I want to see a lawyer!" He yelled whenever he felt like it. At least he stayed quiet while most of the other guys in the cell slept between 11 and 6 in the morning.

"Do you think that dude is crazy?" Tomas whispered to Oscar.

Oscar shook his head. He'd seen plenty of people go stir crazy during his months at Camp Hayward, and he'd learned how to calmly sit back and observe. "He's louder than the rest of us," he whispered back to Tomas. Cristiano was on the other side of Tomas, leaning in to hear what he said.

"Don't they have to let us make a phone call or something? We've been here for hours!" They were wracked with worry about their families, and how worried *they* must be about them.

They ate their bologna sandwiches without enthusiasm. The dude was right. The food was shit.

What they didn't—and couldn't—know was that their families were at the gates of Hunters Point, demanding to see them. Lawyers were filing habeas corpus petitions. They also couldn't know that secret eyes knew where they were and plans to get them out were being hatched. Lamar was on the phone to Kite Kastle before the kids were even assigned a detention cell. Lorena, Lamar, and Cindy were in the surveillance room in the Hangar, watching the 8 monitors that provided live feeds from their secret cameras around the base. They saw the three busloads of detainees when they arrived on Friday night after the MayDay riot at the Federal Building. Recording them as the arrested disembarked, they created decent photos. Within an hour those images were uploaded to social media accounts and websites. Everyone knew who was being held, even though the Federal Police had not yet released their official list.

***

It was during breakfast on Saturday that Donald was scanning the internet at Kite Kastle. "Holy crap! They arrested Tomas and Cristiano!"

"What?" Julius rushed over to look at the images on Donald's laptop. "Fuck! That's them alright! What are they charged with?"

"Says here that there are no official charges yet. The Feds haven't even admitted how many or who they arrested yesterday," Donald was bouncing from news feed to social media account, seeing what he could piece together. "This is weird! It's like they decided they have 'Emergency' powers again!"

Julius was running up the stairs. "Aaron! Aaron!" and after a minute a bleary-eyed Greg opened their bedroom door. "What is it? What's going on?"

"They arrested Tomas and Cristiano! At the Federal Building last night! But they're not admitting it. They're held at Hunters Point. Aaron! You have to call your brother!" Julius urged him.

Aaron got his creaking bones out of bed as fast as he could. Julius stood at the door, breathing heavily. "OK, OK, I got it. I'll call Frank."

But he only got his voice mail. He left a message, telling Frank to call him back, that it was extremely urgent.

***

"What the hell happened out there yesterday?" Leon was making coffee in the kitchen on Marlin Street as Frank appeared in the doorway in his pajamas.

"Oh man!" Frank groaned. "It was a Mayday demo, shoulda been routine. We got sent out to push them away from the Federal Building—didn't want to have another building takeover like the Christmas occupation. But things went south. We ended up busting about three busloads of protesters." Frank shook his head as he came over to grab a mug and wait for the coffee. "Not the way we planned it, that's for sure."

"You know you arrested a bunch of middle schoolers?" Leon looked side-long at his father.

"What? What're you talkin' about?"

"Check your phone, Aaron's been callin'," Leon pointed to Frank's phone on the table. "He called me too, and I told him you were still asleep."

"Middle schoolers??"

"Aaron knows them. Apparently they visit his house up there in Eureka Valley. Their parents are freaking out. They're only like 13 or 14."

"Crap!" Frank began looking at his phone and seeing messages. Even Sheila wrote him asking what happened.

When he talked to her later, she insisted that those kids were alright. She saw them earlier, before Frank and the Federal Police arrived, and they'd been a boisterous, earnest bunch. She couldn't imagine them breaking up the sidewalk and throwing chunks at the police. She also forwarded him a phone video she'd seen online.

But first he'd talked to his brother, Aaron. "Hey Aaron, you called?"

"Frank! These boys you arrested—you have to let them go! They are only 13! And I'm sure they didn't do anything that justifies you rounding them up!"

Frank promised to do what he could. It took all weekend, but finally, after some bureaucratic shuffling, the boys were released to their parents.

CHAPTER 50
MONDAY, MAY 18, 2026

Maria was nervous as she fiddled with her laptop. She'd spent the past month compiling the tests that she and Dat and anyone else conducted. But the most important thing, she realized, was the timeline she'd assembled. When she looked at the results of any given test or analysis, it was interesting, but it simply didn't explain much of what seemed to be happening. But when she put together the step-by-step series of events and claims, reports and anecdotes as they'd unrolled over the past year, she could see it. The witches butter fungus was not a random biohack, or a fungus with strange properties, or even what Alison Nakahara's original research suggested it could be: an all-purpose build-ing material. I mean, sure, it was all those things. But the bigger picture taking shape in her mind as she pulled everything into a narrative arc left her trembling with excitement.

She sat under the overhead screen that Larry installed in the kitchen area, which doubled as their conference room. Slowly settling into their seats were the people who contributed to the research, offered their stories, etc. Janet Pierce and Vero Gomez sat in front, Leon Robertson next to Vero, whispering furiously about something. Janet gazed out the big window towards San Bruno Mountain; she almost seemed to be out there more than in the room. Lamar Robertson and Cindy Lowe, the vet, were sitting behind Leon.

Cindy was as curious as anyone about what Maria was learning. Cindy's experience at the SPCA, and her years as a veterinarian gave her a particular sensitivity to animal life, and a window on the interaction between people and their pets. One night two weeks ago, when they'd been hanging around Leon's warehouse after dinner, Cindy cornered Maria, full of questions and curiosity.

"Have you seen any evidence that the butter stays in the body?" Cindy probed.

Maria, surprised at the question, smiled, "I'm sure of it." She continued, "I started out looking for new microbes that might be appearing in the wastes of people—including my own—who have been regularly eating Vero's chips, sauces, or pasta. There were a half dozen folks who volunteered to help. And yes, we had an unusual array of microbes in common."

"Do you think that means there could be behavioral or cognitive changes resulting from ingesting witches butter?"

Maria realized that Cindy was more engaged in thinking about this than anyone else she'd spoken to up to then, except Dat Doan (who was always ready to explore any question she posed, and often proposed his own). "That's a big leap, don'cha think? I mean, sure, we know our microbiome has a big influence on mood, appetite, sleep... maybe everything! But no one has figured out what a 'normal' microbiome would be—it's always been highly specific to each individual. There's also very little scientific understanding of the complex relationship of our microbiota to the rest of who we are. I don't know if I believe that our personalities are shaped by the microbiome—but then again, who can deny how much we change depending on what we're eating and how our plumbing is working?"

"Sure. I've heard it argued that the new science on microbiomes blows up our individualistic sense of self. That we are 'multitudes' as one science writer put it. Doesn't this help explain the stories we're hearing? Like Juna saying they'd seen the bomb at Dolores Park through the eyes of a bird? Or Janet and Dat saying they heard crows talking? And then taught them to take down drones? And I can say that since I've been eating Vero's chips and sharing them with colleagues and even the animals at the shelter, I've noticed a ... what should I call it? A vibe, a connection, a deeper sense of empathic connection I guess."

"That implies that something from the witches butter is moving through the gut's microbiome and impacting the brain..." Maria was thinking out loud. "Or are we too focused on our own brains as the active zone of knowing?"

"Huh? What is a 'zone of knowing'? You're beyond my pay grade now, but yeah, maybe!" Cindy was enjoying a momentary return to her days in biology classes before she became a vet.

That conversation was in mid-April, two weeks earlier. Since then, Maria collected samples from everywhere: Witches butter growing wild at Alemany Farm and a half dozen other community gardens, at Quarrytown both as wild outgrowths up the canyon, but also the unbelievable huts there. She took samples from Leon's original vat, comparing it to the small batch Dat kept in a cool dark box. She analyzed the batch to which Dat added Intelligel® leading it to turn bright canary yellow. And she analyzed Vero's pasta, her chips, and her sauce, before and after they were cooked. And the amazing underwater sample she snipped from the oyster reef—it seemed to be thriving!

Dat spent a lot of time together with Maria going over the analyses. They were both particularly curious to see how witches butter reproduced itself when left to its own devices, as compared to what they'd seen with their own eyes, the incredibly rapid regeneration that followed taking a piece to use for food.

"How could it know what it's going to be used for? Why would it grow fast in one situation and not in another?" Dat, peering into a microscope next to Maria at Larry's lab, couldn't figure it out. "Why would it grow slowly until human hands break or tear some off? Then it grows like crazy until it recovers the piece that was taken. It doesn't add up," he groaned. "I can't see any difference between this batch that we dug up from the upper terrace at Quarrytown, or this batch that Vero is using to make chips—except Vero's batch is in a tub at Leon's and it grows back in a few hours!"

Everyone was filing in now. Larry and Dat came up the stairs to the mezzanine in animated conversation. Alison Nakahara was behind them, talking with Clara. The transplanted biobulb was a big success, and they were pondering what the next steps should be. The new warehouse at the back of the Brisbane Industrial Park had been a boon for their work. Not only did they enjoy the sunlight pouring in as much as they wanted, but they no longer had to spend time underground! And the experiments were thriving. High-lumen biobulbs were growing reliably on the mother plant, and they'd managed to start a half dozen other plants too. Harvesting them before they grew too big, they'd been carefully placing them in a wall covered in a thick layer of witches butter. Clara learned to talk to the bulbs as she "installed" them—Ally couldn't bring herself to do that. She couldn't accept the idea that the bulbs were sentient or that they were forming a relationship with the witches butter—and with anyone who wanted them to 'turn on'—that had to be encouraged and nurtured. It was ridiculous to her.

Juna and Angie came up the stairs. Angie was very reluctant to leave her Quarrytown huts, but after much cajoling and with the promise that she could return whenever she wanted to, she finally visited Larry's warehouse. This was her third time, but it was the first time she'd come when a lot of other people would be there too.

Janet went down the stairs and returned a few minutes later leading a much older woman, a big weathered older man who looked like a rancher, and a middle-aged Latino guy. "Hey everyone!" she shouted as they settled into chairs across from Maria. "These are colleagues from the League of Urban Farmers' Canopy Council: Annette Jorgensen, Jorge Castro, and Will Shaw. We've been nurturing the witches butter in different gardens around the City."

Larry, who darted into his office, emerged at the other end of the mezzanine. He smiled at the gathering and after a half dozen of his huge strides, he found a chair near the back and flopped into it. He knew what Maria planned to present, and he was excited to see how it was received.

"Hey Larry," called Tanisha, his receptionist. She was downstairs in the main room. "Larry, someone is here, says he needs to speak with you."

"Who is it?" Larry asked.

"He won't say."

"I'm busy. He can leave a message."

"OK." She went back to the front. The man was dismayed at the reply.

"This is serious. I know Dat Doan is here. And we have reason to believe he has stolen some valuable property. We think that property might be on the premises. When I come back, I'm coming with the police. Tell Mr. Lansing to call me immediately. If I don't hear back from him by the end of the day, we'll be seeking a search warrant."

Tanisha looked impassively at the guy's bushy eyebrows. "OK, I'll give him the message." The guy was obviously bluffing. If he had any grounds to bring the police in, he would've already done so. She watched him leave, and then turned to her monitor that covered the parking lot. The guy was walking around snapping photos of cars and license plates. She grabbed shots of him doing it, and got a close-up on him, as well as his own car and license plate.

Meanwhile, Maria began her presentation in the sunny mezzanine.

"I went back to Alison's original paper and re-read it. Then Dat and I traced what the hacks were. It wasn't as closely monitored or recorded as I wish it were. But anyway, as best as we can tell from the records they *did* keep, his lab jockeys started with this," and she put up a slide of witches butter in the wild. "This is witches butter before any modifications have been introduced. Looks like a wet yellow gel—when it ages it turns black and has the consistency of dried skin."

She looked at the faces before her. They were mostly friends and colleagues. A few people she didn't know. She cleared her throat.

"Looking at this, one wonders what Ally saw in it. But when you examine the cellular structure, you see it's quite malleable. Dat's team looked at the original, recognized the possibilities, and then did something I don't think any scientific lab would've ever tried. They took octopus DNA and inserted it into the fungus. The octopus's ability to change its shape, to stretch and compact itself, to regenerate lost limbs, and even to change its colors, were traits that would be particularly useful to a fungus that would be an all-purpose building material. And for some reason they also took some pig DNA and put that in there too... Dat says the idea was to fatten it up, to the give witches butter more bulk to work with. They also tried to incorporate conductive 'veins' that could photosynthesize, but as far as we can tell, those didn't take."

Now she put up a slide of the dull gray vat of putty that Dat delivered to Leon's place in early 2024. "Some of you will remember this. This is the mother vat, the first iteration that was delivered to Leon's warehouse in early 2024," and she put up the next slide, "And here are a few folks kneading and singing over it."

Some giggles and snickers went around the room.

"Yeah, it's weird. Everyone thought that at the time too. But," and she raised her voice a bit as she looked directly at one person after another, "this might be the moment that changed it— that started something that we can hardly explain."

"What do you mean?" asked Jorge Castro, who was thrilled to have been invited to this presentation. He knew something unprecedented was happening with the witches butter. At the community garden he tended in the Excelsior, stretching over the now-buried creek near Cayuga Street, he nurtured a batch of witches butter. He took pieces to cook with and watched it grow back in a day or less.

"It was the touching, singing, and especially the mixing of aerosolized saliva and sweat into the witches butter that triggered further changes in it. I can't be absolutely sure, but the fungus took in this combination of microbes and touch and sound and I think it learned how to connect to humans, and maybe..." she paused and sighed deeply, "maybe the combination of octopus, pig, human, microbial, and fungal intelligence has merged to create a new species!"

Dat stood up at his seat. "Maria is right. The best explanation, which doesn't *explain* what we have seen and experienced, is that intelligence is emergent in the witches butter. What does that mean?" he turned this way and that. "The fungus is evolving on its own, connecting to different animals, to different humans. If the octopus and pig genes have joined the fungus to produce new cellular intelligence, perhaps stimulated, as Maria has proposed, by the integration of human DNA through sweat, saliva, and microbes that live in our fluids... well... where does that leave us? Are we in a position to conclude that it is merely a fungus that we can pour into molds? Or cook into chips and pasta? It's much more than that," and he nodded toward Angie and Juna. "Our friends have collaborated with witches butter in ways no one else has managed. Angie, perhaps you can talk about the huts? And Maria, why don't you put up that slide?"

Maria clicked through to the image of the mottled 'gingerbread houses' as they called the witches butter huts that grew in Quarrytown uphill from where they were right now.

Angie was nervous, not accustomed to speaking publicly, let alone in front of a bunch of professional and affluent people. Juna squeezed her arm and she felt compelled to stand.

"I, er, um, I uh... I don't usually speak. In fact, I've never been in a meeting like this," she looked around hesitantly. People were looking at her expectantly, though she saw some looked at her raggedy clothes suspiciously. She squeezed a piece of witches butter in her pocket to silence her fears. "Those huts, they grew from witches butter. I was as surprised as anyone. Juna here brought us some to eat, and a small batch to plant. I'd seen how fast it grew back. I decided to give it a try. I dug a small trench," she was talking very fast, her nervousness pushing her to get the story out and sit back down as soon as possible. "And I put the butter in and explained to it that I hoped it would grow and make me a house," she looked around and smiled. "Hell, I didn't know it would work! I was shocked when a half day later it already grew 30 inches. And after another day, I cut holes for windows and the door, and used the parts that I cut out to help it make a roof with some branches I put over..." She stopped and took a deep breath. She wiped sweat from her brow. It was hard to tell if people believed her. "Well, we have a small village! There are six huts, two houses that are made up of three huts each that are connected like small rooms."

Maria asked her, "And what about light and heat?"

Angie, who was anxious to get out of the spotlight, said, "She," pointing across the room to Alison Nakahara, "went into my hut and stuck one of her biobulbs in the ceiling. Nothing happened until I came in and welcomed it and asked it to give us some light. Then it turned on. Since then I've been able to get light and turn it off by asking for it. Another thing, the hut's walls give heat! When it's cold or wet out, I'm toasty and dry inside. And we eat it too!"

Janet blurted out "They're Gingerbread Houses!" which got a round of chuckles.

"Speaking of eating it," Maria took the floor back, nodding a thanks to Angie who gratefully sat down. "We have tried to figure out how the measurable nutritional properties seem to change after cooking. When it's raw, we can measure some basic vitamins and minerals, nothing extraordinary. But after cooking, it offers concentrated doses of Vitamin A, C, and D, of calcium and iron, and even the recommended daily allowance of zinc, manganese, and magnesium. And it turns out to be protein-rich! It behaves like a *Nixtamalización* process, similar to the historic process of making of tamal in Mexico."

Annette Jorgensen, the venerable chair of the Canopy Council, raised her hand. Maria gave her the floor.

"You've described in broad terms how this witches butter has become what it is now. It's a remarkable tale. It would not have developed spontaneously in nature. One of my concerns—and I have several—is what might be the effects over a longer term. How long have people been cooking and eating this? What analysis has been done on the potential toxicity of this?"

"Vero? When did you start experimenting with it?"

Vero stood up. "I remember the first time I popped a piece in my mouth. It was during that horrible heat wave last summer. I was still hiding," she realized she was giving too much information. "Anyway, it was chalky and bland and dry. But after that, I started playing around in the kitchen, seeing what I could do with it. Eventually I settled on chips as the best invention. But the pasta and the sauces you can make aren't bad." She looked around, proud of her work, but not sure if people respected it. "Has everyone here tried the chips?"

Annette shook her head. "I haven't eaten it in any form. I'm not sure I'm willing to. But I'm glad to know that the people who *have* been eating it for almost a year have shown no ill effects."

"Ill effects? Definitely not!" Vero retorted, irritated that this old woman was framing it negatively. "The effects have been unexpected and hard to explain. Like the out-of-body experiences, or much stronger senses of smell. Or that animals and birds and bugs seem to be more comfortable around us..." she trailed off and sat down, realizing Maria was trying to present what they learned from their analyses and studies. "Maria, sorry, please continue!"

"Annette, do you want to tell us your other concerns?" Maria respected the elderly woman and wanted to win her over.

"Thank you. I am still concerned about the potential ill effects on people eating it. But I happily acknowledge that nothing has come up yet! But what about the effects on the land? How does witches butter fungus—or this new bioengineered stuff—affect the land? Does it encroach on native habitats? Does it change the fertility of the soil? How thirsty is it when it's growing in the 'wild'? Do other food crops thrive near it, or do they suffer? It seems we had the responsibility to know more about these questions before we started planting it around town. I stand on the old cautionary approach: Do No Harm!" and she sat down.

Maria went back to her slides. "Thank you. I agree that we could have been a lot more cautious with this. But here's some images of how the fungus has interacted with community gardens, food crops, and local trees and other flora." She went through about a dozen slides, pointing out where trees flourished next to it, how a row of zucchini grew faster and with larger vegetables than the others nearby, and a couple showing how unobtrusive it was in wild spots on San Bruno Mountain and in Glen Canyon. She ended on a photo of the fungus bloom on the oyster reef under water.

"If anything, it seems to play well with others!" she laughed.

Will Shaw, the other older Canopy Council rep who was there, groaned when he saw the slides of the fungus in Glen Canyon and on the mountain. "What's it doing in Glen Canyon already? Did someone plant it there? Or did it get there on its own? If the latter, we've got a big problem! If people have been planting it in these wild areas, they've got to *stop!*"

"Oh look!" Janet stood up and pointed out the window. More than a hundred crows were flowing through the air, flying in a loop directly in front of the main window to the mezzanine. "Do you think they came because we're talking about this?" she wondered aloud.

"Holy crap! That's amazing!" Lamar exclaimed. Everyone rushed towards the windows. No one could remember seeing anything like it. The crows flew in a big circular loop that on one side passed very close to the window.

"There's coyotes out there, too!" announced Cindy, pointing at them.

"And look over there!" Leon was pointing at a family of mule deer that appeared on the slope above the warehouse. "What's happening out there?"

Maria and Dat looked at each other, both thinking that it *was* connected to their gathering.

"They're here because we're here," Maria said, as people began returning to their chairs. "But how? Why exactly? We don't have a clue!" She laughed.

"If this is a new kind of intelligence, maybe IT invited them?" declared Dat.

316

"But it can't be 'intelligence' like we've normally understood it. The fungus has no brain, no mouth, no ears, no senses that we can understand coming from the paradigm of our corporeal bodies." Dat decided to throw his thoughts out there. "Somehow it *knows*. It has been connecting some people to other animals and birds. *How* we don't know. *Why* we don't know either. We cannot explain it by resorting to any simplistic model of base instincts or a simple urge to reproduce. If this can be called 'behavior' it is serving to connect life forms, to share perceptions in new ways..." he trailed off. "But what if the fungus is more than it seems?"

"What do you mean?" Alison demanded. She thought talk of a new intelligence was unfounded fantasy. "How could it be more than it seems? In what way?!?" Her hostility to Dat's conjectures was palpable.

"Ally, we don't know. We can admit that something's going on that we can't explain with our usual answers. It's ok to speculate, to think creatively about what it *might* be," Dat was looking at Alison as her disapproval rigidified, but he could see many others nodding tentatively.

Jorge Castro got up to support Dat's line of reasoning. "I don't know what's going on. That is about all I *do* know. But I'm dying of curiosity! What if you're right? What if a new intelligence is emerging? What if it's not the intelligence of the fungus *per se*, but rather an intelligence that is much wider, much bigger, but is expressing itself through the halting beginnings that we're seeing and attributing to the fungus?"

"What are you suggesting? What is a wider, bigger intelligence? You're not giving a religious explanation I hope?" Clara Frias was allergic to religion, having grown up around Catholics.

Juna slowly stood up. "I've eaten Vero's chips for several months, I have an increased sense of smell, and I had an out-of-body experience with a scrub jay. Jorge might be on to something. What if the fungus is reconnecting us to the flow of life that has always surrounded us? What if a force or energy that unites life on Earth is working through the fungus to re-open us to other species and perspectives, and also to each other?"

The crows began a cacophonous cawing outside the window, and a sudden gust of wind suddenly swirled around the building. The punctuation provided to Juna's comments seemed obvious to almost everyone. Alison refused to acknowledge any connection, only able to imagine it was a coincidence. Maria's presentation seemed to be over, and people broke up into small clusters where the conversation continued.

"Hey everyone! Before we break up completely..." Maria said in a loud voice. "I know we didn't answer all the questions we have. Not even close.

There's a lot more to do. If anyone wants to work on shaping the research going forward, please talk to me or Dat, ok?"

CHAPTER 51
FRIDAY, JUNE 12, 2026

Larry gazed across the mezzanine. Vero and her helpers were buzzing among the industrial ovens and baking racks and tables, packed in from the kitchen area to the edge of the deck overlooking the greenhouse floor below. He and Leon finished coordinating their security operations for the Brisbane warehouse in addition to the warehouses in Bayview. They brought on a dozen new folks to handle the raised alert level. Ever since that private investigator visited in mid-May, he knew they would face some action. Maybe there would be a police raid? Maybe they'd send in their own muscle? He wasn't sure what to expect from BGM, but he didn't expect them to give up easily.

He got his money from BGM's buyout of HemptriCity back in 2023. He got lucky by befriending Ally Nakahara, which led to the owner of the start-up, Steven Scott, trading a small percentage of the business for Larry's resources and expertise in marijuana cultivation. When they sold to BGM, Larry got a multi-million-dollar windfall, allowing him to "retire" from the day-to-day growing and retailing that he built up since he was an ambitious senior in high school. Since then, he used his wealth to pursue new projects—focused on local food production, whether through hydroponics, new hybrids that would flourish in San Francisco's sandy soils, and financing an aquaculture endeavor. His latest project was something called 'precision fermentation,' targeting pickled and fermented foods.

When Ally finally quit BGM he was ready. He already recruited Clara and Maria from the University of Arizona as agricultural research scientists. Ally brought wild experimental ideas that intrigued Clara and Maria. Ally assured them that neither the biobulb nor the bioboat were known to BGM. Her old project to cultivate witches butter fungus into a building material—BGM shelved it until she'd quit—was smuggled out by others, biohacked by Dat Doan and his people, and turned into this ... whatever it is, the witches butter.

Maria and Dat seemed to believe that the hacked fungus was evolving into an alien intelligence! What a wild idea! As far as Vero and Leon and their folks were concerned, this was their chance to mint a fortune. Vero was frenetically engaged in expanding production of her inventions in his mezzanine kitchen.

"Get those cooled chips into the box!" Vero yelled at one of her helpers. A minute later she whirled around to help a woman who was wobbling across the floor with another hot tray of cooked 'butter' that would be sliced into linguine when cooled. "Hey Lorena! Can you help here? This whole rack needs to go to the cutting machine," Vero was covered in flour and looked a bit comical as she pointed here and there.

Lorena chuckled as she walked by her. "You might need to take a break, Vero!" she advised. Lorena Sanchez became Vero's closest collaborator over the past months. Ironically perhaps, she'd originally been a BGM contractor growing the Prosper°Plants that were the raw material for Intelligel°. But like many others she was fired midway through her second growing season, leading her to join the Urban Peasants Alliance. She immediately joined the organizing effort, and worked closely with Miguel Robles in early 2023, but after the National Emergency and the mysterious disappearance of Robles two years later, she was glad to hide out in the Bayview warehouses and the Hangar under the auspices of Leon Robertson, who graciously hired a dozen UPA members when he was expanding his growing operations. Later, she jumped on Vero's project when asked.

They'd become good buddies during the year that Vero was hiding out after her escape. Lorena saw each step of the process: how they massaged and sung to the vat of gray witches butter at Leon's. Months later, she saw how excited Vero became when she experimented in the secret cellar, finally settling on three main products: the chips, the pasta, and Vero's special sauce. But they were struggling to scale up. The problems of packaging were real, and they hadn't learned anything about shelf life or distribution. They could count on their network of dispensaries, but beyond that was a mystery.

In the sprawling warehouse's annex, Larry let them set up packaging and shipping. You couldn't see it from the mezzanine, but every half hour or so, another full elevator of finished products was wheeled away for final preparation. Larry watched Vero's workers rolling another cart along the edge of the greenhouse and through the door to the annex. He remembered when he had a half dozen or more people bagging pot at tables laden with scales, baggies, and, after legalization, pre-printed stickers. But there was no worry about legality now.

His phone buzzed. "Van approaching parking lot." His perimeter identified an incoming vehicle and sent in the message.

"Hey Bruce!" he bellowed. "Code Orange!" The cooks and workers ignored him, as they were accustomed to people moving around that weren't directly involved in their business. Bruce and his team moved to pre-planned locations out of sight from the street or lobby. Larry entered the room where Bruce and his lieutenant were poised over the monitors.

"This might be the long-awaited visit," Larry suggested. The private investigator that dropped in during Maria's meeting in May never returned. Larry expected they would sue him for harboring their stolen property, but it seemed unlikely after a month had passed. He worried that they would play a heavier hand.

"I never had to deal with any violence back in the day. It seems crazy that it might be coming now," Larry remarked.

"It's not like you can expect any help from the authorities, right?" Bruce confirmed. "There they are." The van pulled in to the corner of their lot. "Oh, look at those dudes!" A half dozen mercenaries clad in black vests and helmets poured out of the van.

"You see any guns?" Larry was peering at the low-resolution monitors.

"They're sending two guys to opposite corners to triangulate on the front door. They've got assault weapons!"

Larry turned on the building-wide public address system. "Folks, please stop what you're doing and go to your emergency assembly points. This is not a drill." A great deal of commotion was audible behind them as people began scurrying from the corridors in the greenhouse and into the emergency shelter rooms. He'd had them built thinking more about natural disasters than something like this.

"Code Red" he sent out to his team. Everyone would be locked and loaded and ready for the worst. His perimeter defenders closed the rear and flanks.

"I can't believe it's come to this. They never even tried to negotiate! If they think we're sitting in here unprotected...." he trailed off. He switched on the external PA, and his voice soon crackled into the parking lot.

"Fellas! We got you. You have not surprised us. Put your guns down, return to your van, and drive slowly away, and no one gets hurt."

The six soldiers who had fanned out across the lot as they approached the front door, stopped abruptly. This was not part of the plan.

"Do not come any closer. We have marksmen on the roof. Turn around and return to your vehicle!"

The soldiers saw the snipers on the roof pointing at them. They slowly raised their hands and began backing up.

"Drop your weapons!" demanded a new voice coming from behind them. This spooked them. The guys in the corners threw their guns to the asphalt and with their hands up moved back to the van. The other men in the parking lot followed suit, dropping their weapons and walking back to the van. Surrounded, Larry's perimeter security team took their wallets and IDs before pushing them into their vehicle.

Larry came bounding out to rush over to the van, followed closely by Bruce, his burly security chief.

"Who the fuck sent you?" he demanded.

"They work for skEYE Systems, according to these ID cards," reported Lenny, holding their wallets.

"What the hell are you doing? Roll in and take over and force us out? How the hell is that supposed to work?" Larry was dumbfounded. "I've got a legitimate lease on this place. I'm running a legit business. How the hell do you think you can roll up here and invade my place?" he shook his head furiously.

The squad leader squirmed uncomfortably as he realized how absurd the situation was. "We wouldn't shoot anybody. We were told to come in here and seize a bunch of evidence, some fungus that you have."

"Evidence? What the hell are you talking about? Who is skEYE Systems working for?" Larry demanded.

"I dunno man. You sure you don't know?" The guy wasn't stupid.

"You tell whoever it is who sent you here to fuck off. Try this again and we won't be responsible for what happens. No one will walk away!" he stormed.

"Take their boots too!" Larry demanded. They sent them away shoeless and without the expensive weapons they'd arrived with.

The perimeter team escorted the van back to Old Bayshore Highway and watched them turn north.

Back at the warehouse, the "all clear" was announced. Coming out of the emergency rooms, everyone wanted to know what happened. Larry got on the PA to explain it.

"It was a false alarm. We thought we might be facing an armed assault, but our preparations defused the situation. Nothing to worry about. Go back to your work."

"That was a close call," Bruce said across his desk.

"Yes and no. We were ready," said Larry.

"We should expect escalation," Len warned. "They'll want to win next time."

"I hope you're wrong. If they do, we're not gonna play nice next time," he said firmly. His lieutenants nodded grimly.

***

On Friday morning Sheila explained to her liaison at Camp Hayward that the replacement parts for their 'dozers were due at the beginning of the week. She got off the computer and began tracing the orders in her system.

"Oh shit," she groaned. The parts never left the factory. Apparently the government never paid some overdue bills and the supplier refused to ship, but nobody bothered to tell her! She got back online with Kelly Fairly in Hayward.

"Kelly, bad news! They never shipped."

"What?!? Why not?! I NEED those parts, like yesterday! There's another flood coming in tonight!"

"I know, I know. I can't explain it. The government hasn't been paying its bills since they cut taxes and budgets. I'm not sure who is driving the bus anymore, y'know?" Sheila hoped Kelly would sympathize with her.

"What the fuck?!? This is the *fed-er-al-gov-ern-ment* we're talking about! Do you think this is policy? Or incompetence?" Kelly looked tense on the monitor.

Sheila shook her head. "It's been happening more and more lately. I can't tell if they're having cash flow problems, or they're trying to make a point. Either way, it's disrupting supply chains. I can tell you, once you break trust in procurement, it's real hard to get it back."

"Tell me about it. I have to go to my guys and tell 'em that we're down to one working bulldozer ahead of this weekend's King Tides. We built up the levees after the winter rains so as long as they hold..." she trailed off, shaking her head. "Sheila, thanks, I know this is not on you. Whatever you can do to get those parts moving, if anything, please do!" and she signed off.

Sheila got up from her desk, exasperated. She went over to Bill Marsh's desk where he was peering at his computer with headphones on. She tapped him on the shoulder.

"Wha?" he was a bit jarred, not expecting anyone to interrupt his concentration. "Oh, hey Sheila, what's up?"

"Have you noticed that suppliers are holding up shipments? The government isn't paying its bills."

"Oh, yeah, well, I did notice something like that. I got a call from the Oakland office and they never got the furniture they ordered. It's been two months! Then I got a call from people out in Concord who have been waiting for a new print center to be installed since winter. Something's breaking down. What do you think it is?"

"Hutchinson said he would tighten the ship. Do you think they'd order nonpayment of legitimate bills? That seems irresponsible! That's no way to run a government—or a business! I found out that the bulldozer parts they need at Camp Hayward never even left the factory—nonpayment of previous invoices. Why were those orders you mentioned delayed?"

He shook his head. "I figured it was one of the usual delays and it would take care of itself. But now... give me an hour and I'll see what I can figure out." He turned back to his computer.

Sheila called an old friend in Washington. Polly Criswell and Sheila worked at the same law office when they were at Sacramento State. After graduation, they each married and left Sacramento—Polly ended up back east with her growing family. They stayed in touch, and after decades they were surprised to find that they were both working for the government, Polly at the Department of Transportation and Sheila a procurement manager at the General Services Administration in San Francisco.

"Hi Pol, it's me." Sheila called on her personal phone from the empty view lounge. "Hey I'm calling to say hi, but also because there's something strange going on. The government hasn't been paying its bills and my suppliers are holding up shipments now. Have you seen or heard anything like that at your end?"

"Hi Sheila! Nice to hear from you! Give me a sec," Sheila could hear her chair scraping and then the clickety-clack of her heels on a linoleum floor. With a big breathy sigh, Polly's voice came over the line. "A federal agency in Washington DC is the last place you'd expect to have any problems with money, right? But something strange is going on here too. People are quitting. Things are falling apart. Everyone here is feeling it—everyone who's *still* here that is!"

Sheila was surprised. She thought maybe Polly would have some story about budget dislocations, or maybe even a similar story of supply problems, but this was even weirder. "People are quitting? Whaddya mean? The Transportation Department is huge. How many people are we talking about?"

"Can't tell. All I know is three managers in my department left in the past month. A bunch of folks took early retirement too. And there haven't been any replacements hired... not yet anyway."

"Well, they're *going to* aren't they?"

"Sure, I guess so. Nobody has announced anything. It's like getting ghosted by your own bureaucracy!" she chuckled. "It's probably a temporary thing. The fiscal year is ending soon, maybe they're waiting for the new year to start on July 1."

"Of course." Sheila overlooked that. She regularly spent a great deal of money right before the end of the fiscal year to make sure the next budget would stay the same, or preferably, increase. Could this be a budgetary anomaly? Or was something bigger going on?

CHAPTER 52
MONDAY, JUNE 15, 2026

Gene Wilson stared at the bay from his 15th floor executive suite in the BioGenMo building in Mission Bay. The streets below still showed signs of the flood tide that managed to swamp local streets each of the past two nights. Two more nights of very high tides were predicted. The scattered tidal surges and groundwater upwelling that circumvented new protective berms and walls were not on his mind. He read the report from skEYE Systems about their failed raid on the Lansing warehouse in Brisbane.

"What a fuckin' fiasco!" he muttered in a low voice to no one in particular. He turned to the sound of heels entering his office. BGM's executive vice president of operations, Liz Collins, glared at him as she settled into the chair across from his desk.

"Well? What do we do now?" she demanded. It was his idea to send the security company to seize the supply of fungus. "And have you seen this?" she tossed a bag of Vero's chips onto his desk. Gene looked at the unremarkable cellophane package. The cardboard stapled across the top was hand-decorated with colored markers. A black script swirled over the art spelled "WitChips!" It looked homemade.

Gene picked it up and turned it in the light from the window. "What is this?"

"Seems to be made out of the fungus. They're turning out hundreds of packages of this every few days now."

"But our documents refer to the fungus as a building material. What are we supposed to do with this? You think our intellectual property extends to this too?"

"Sure, why not? It was in our possession and they stole it!" Collins didn't care what happened to it after it left their computer.

"Well, I imagine they could make a case that they've engineered a whole new thing. We never anticipated an edible product. The original Nakahara research prospectus described only described a malleable building material."

He opened the package and popped some chips into his mouth. "Mm, not bad," he conceded.

"We're not going to court over this! We already decided that. But this was taken from BGM and we have to defend our property!" Collins's mouth tightened as she identified with their violated rights. "Run this through a gene analysis and you can confirm that it started with our strain of witches butter."

"OK, I'm sure the Board expects us to recover our property and end illegal uses of it. But..." he walked across the room and picked up a folder on the desk by the wall. "According to this report, there are colonies of witches butter growing in more than a dozen locations around the City. Who knows how far it's gotten? It's not clear that Lansing and Ally or any of the people in their orbit are behind this. It may be self-replicating outside of anyone's control at this point."

Collins sighed and sank back in her seat. "What a shitshow! Where'd you get that report?"

"Dennis Swintin. He's been a contractor liaison for several years. He organized that Festival of Possibilities and he probably thought we were gonna fire him for that. But we decided to use him, and he proved willing after his little fair petered out. He was the one who fingered Ally Nakahara. When I confronted her she denied everything, but our investigation uncovered the whole Lansing operation, and the connection to Dat Doan and his biohackers. There's no question that Doan's lab was the first to engineer the fungus. Then they began moving it along to somewhere in Bayview. We haven't been able to trace the exact path, but it ended up in this huge facility in the Brisbane Industrial Park."

"How'd Swintin learn that the fungus is in multiple locations across the city?"

"He has connections to the League of Urban Farmers—as you know they are also allies of the UPA—witches butter is growing in a bunch of their farms. There are some wild patches too. Most of the local farms have continued to produce and distribute food despite federal efforts to shut them down, so I guess it's not surprising that they could keep the fungus out of sight."

"Should we call local authorities? What about the Federal Police? Wouldn't they be happy if we tipped them off about the illegal food growing?"

"I don't think we want to poke that bear. There's no reason to believe that Federal Police raids would serve BGM's interests. We need to flip the script here. Attempting to repress or punish—when does that ever work?"

"What do you mean? You want to let them get away with this?" she folded her arms with a cross expression.

"Liz, it's past that point. You agreed that we don't want to take a legal route. We sent out some muscle and that backfired too. We should make a deal!" he looked directly at her, a sharp glint in his eye.

"I'm listening," but she looked very uncomfortable.

He picked up the chip package and waved it at her. "This is an opportunity! They don't have the resources to take full advantage of their own invention. What if we negotiate with them? They sell us the chips for cash and we'll also relinquish our IP claims. *They* don't know that we're not taking them to court. We expand production, marketing and distribution of the WitChips and we refocus on the original biomanufacturing plan." He sat back with a self-satisfied expression. He was used to getting his way.

Liz Collins was shocked at Gene's proposal. But after the initial surprise, she had to admit that it made more sense than spending the next weeks and months, and who knows how much money, trying to capture the colonies of witches butter growing everywhere. And they had no answer for the Lansing operation if they weren't relying on the authorities.

"Well Gene... Why don't you prepare a formal proposal for the Board. Let's take this to next week's meeting." She departed, not spending another minute on it. Gene was responsible for this mess and she'd leave him to solve it too.

***

Lamar threw his jacket on the couch as he approached the bank of monitors in the Hangar's surveillance room. Cindy was watching the expanse of asphalt in front of the Federal Police jail on Hunter's Point.

"Hey, whaddya think is in those?" Lamar pointed to large trucks that were driving into the base.

"They're livestock trucks!" Cindy exclaimed. She was quite familiar with large animal transport from her earlier life in Arizona. "Can't be cows in there... maybe they're bringing in horses?"

"Horses?!? The Federal Police? What are *they* going to use them for?" Lamar was puzzled.

They sat and watched as the trucks made their way across their monitors, finally parking in the large lot not far from the jail. No one in the Hangar noticed that a stable was built behind the jail over the past weeks. Truckloads of hay bales were brought in too, but they assumed hay would be used to control flooding, not feeding horses.

Eight horses were led down ramps from each of the trucks and taken behind the jail to their new stable. "Sixteen horses! What are they for?" Lamar exclaimed.

"I wouldn't think the Federal Police would have much use for horses. But maybe they're planning something new?" Cindy pondered it for a minute. "Hey, I wonder if they have a vet on staff already? Can we ask Frank?"

"Sure. You want the job?" Lamar looked at her, seeing her wheels turning.

"I doubt if there are any other large animal vets around. I'd like to make sure those horses are well treated. And," she smiled at Lamar as she nuzzled into his arm, "I can spy too!"

***

Jay Hartman, Jordan Lindsay, and Ernesto Aguirre pulled up with their plumbing gear on Folsom Street. They arrived in front of the Pigeon Palace, an elegant 1903 Victorian in the heart of the Mission District. The building was bought by the San Francisco Community Land Trust years earlier, and the residents organized most of the 40-odd buildings on their block between 24th and 25th, Shotwell and Folsom, to participate in a new block-based Commons. The entire block from Shotwell to Folsom along 24th was covered in scaffolding with big banners proclaiming the "Folwell Commons—a Water and Energy Co-op in the Middle of the City." Most of the fences between the backyards were removed or opened with new gates, creating a common green corridor running up the middle of the block. Vegetable gardens crisscrossed the open area. New solar panels were being put on every building that didn't have them already, and a 100-foot windmill was under construction in the empty lot at the north end of the block. To integrate everyone in this block into a locally resilient, autonomous power system, they were building their own electrical storage system mid-block using a half dozen BGM Hempatteries.

The plumbers were beginning their part of the project. The neighbors agreed to install a graywater system in each unit to capture bath and sink water, to recycle slightly used water into backyard irrigation. Three large rain catchment basins were also planned.

"Hey, are you guys here to start the plumbing?" asked a woman in a bright yellow jumpsuit with a matching scarf who emerged from the basement door. "I'm Yolanda Montes, I live here."

Ernesto confirmed, "I guess we're supposed to connect with your project leader," he glanced down at his clipboard. "Rita? Rita Marley?"

"OK. Rita lives over on Shotwell. But if you want you can walk over through the backyards, I'll show you the way."

"Great, thanks! Let's go," Ernesto said to Jay and Jordan.

Jay was curious to see what the neighbors were doing on this block. He'd been campaigning to "re-plumb San Francisco" for over a year, and this was the biggest single area they'd been invited to help redesign.

Yolanda swirled ahead in a yellow flourish, leading them out into a thriving yard. A small patio stood under a towering palm tree, an elegant open-air shed and gazebo stood to the side. They followed her through a wooden gate into the next yard, where a small pond was peeking out from dense foliage. Frogs croaked and birds sang and soared. The trees and bushes were home to the extraordinarily dense bird and insect populations.

"That," Yolanda pointed to a small house being built along the former fence line between several properties, "is our new storage room. A half dozen Hempatteries will store our surplus electricity from solar and wind. We'll have two weeks of backup for all forty buildings—assuming we ever go that long without sun or wind!" she smiled at the exaggeration. They were walking diagonally through the open gardens, weaving through a small grove of oak trees.

"I saw that pond back there, and this is even bigger," Jay pointed to the shallow standing water they were skirting. "Don't you have mosquitoes?"

"Yeah we do. It's one of the things we're always arguing about—whether or not to use larvacide in the ponds, or to depend on birds and bats to take care of it," Yolanda explained.

"The mosquitoes get worse faster than the bird or bat population can control it, no?" Jordan interjected.

Yolanda nodded. "I'm in favor of larvacide, you won't get any argument from me. I hate mosquitoes! You guys are building some rain catching system too, right? How do you control the mosquitoes?"

"Larvacide! It's the only way," Jordan confirmed. "But if you don't leave them open most of the time, you can prevent them becoming major sites of insect life."

"Here's Rita's place," Yolanda extended her arm to the ground-floor glass windows opening on a charming flower garden. "And here's Rita!" she smiled.

A tall, broad-shouldered woman with bright red hair was emerging from her door. She looked over at the sound of her name and stopped abruptly, putting her hands on her hips. Jay stared at her and she returned the gaze.

"Hey, weren't you—?" he stuttered. He walked over to her and spoke in a low voice that no one else could hear. "Weren't you in that UPS truck when we escaped Camp Hayward? With Vero?"

Rita did a double-take. She remembered Vero, though she hadn't seen her since the escape and their separation. She vaguely recalled that there was a guy Vero knew in the truck as they drove away. This guy? He was a big strapping plumber. Could he be the guy in the truck? She couldn't pull up any memory of what he looked like then. He didn't look familiar. But why would this guy have this memory if it *wasn't* him?

She gave him a flat, noncommittal smile. "Uh-huh, yeah. That was me. What's your name?"

"Jay, Jay Hartman. I used to work with Vero at Palou Terrace before the massacre. They picked me up at Dolores Park that day." He rushed to fill in the blanks for her. Something about her dignified posture and cautious demeanor, not unwelcoming, but not rushing to embrace either, made him urgently want to win her over.

Rita's green eyes apprised the plumber, her bronze cheekbones finally breaking into a genuine grin. "That was a helluva getaway, eh?" she said conspiratorially. Continuing in a subrosa tone, "let's catch up later, ok, in private?" She turned to Yolanda and the others who were standing back respectfully trying to puzzle out how these two knew each other.

"You guys know each other huh?" Yolanda said.

"Um, yeah, almost forgot about it. I'll tell you about it later, ok?" Rita pushed it aside. "You guys are the plumbers? I've been looking forward to this! Let's get started." She waved them into her kitchen where she pulled out several folders. "I've got these descriptions, but they're not quite *plans*. It's one thing to say what you want, it's a whole 'nother thing to know how to make it come to life. That's where you guys come in."

Ernesto pulled out the paper that described in broad terms the Folwell Commons project. "We got excited when you sent this to our union. It's the project we've been looking for! Do you have a detailed inventory of the current state of the plumbing in each building?"

"Oh yes! That's what I've been working on for the past two months. First, we have seven buildings that are not participating. The owners won't have anything to do with the project. You might have seen those places with the big fences still up," she gestured to one of them diagonally across from her garden. "But the other 33 buildings are in. A lot of work is already underway as you can tell from the backyards—or as we started calling it, the park. The windmill is going up. New solar is going in on half the buildings. And they're building the storage house. We've gotten the energy side of things going—it'll be done in a coupla months. Now to deal with the water!" Rita unrolled blueprints from her own building and several of the adjacent ones. She also opened the folder holding everyone's water and sewage bills around the block.

"We're spending crazy amounts of money on water and sewage. We know we can't break from the public water system, and we don't want to. But we do want to figure out how to use a whole lot less of it. That's where you guys come in, right?"

"Oh sister! You are singing in our choir!" Ernesto joked, giving her a nudge with his elbow. "Tell me, though, how far do you think we can go? We can set you up with a graywater recycling system to funnel into your toilets, so you can finally stop crapping in drinking water. But do you want to go further? Are you guys ready for composting toilets and using the output in your gardens? Locally regenerative farming emerges by combining graywater, rain catchment, and at least *some* composting toilets to go along with food and other garden composting."

Yolanda was lurking, trying to follow the discussion. "You want to use our shit to grow vegetables?" Her disgust at the thought was utterly transparent.

Rita's head snapped up from the papers spread over her big round table. "Yolanda! I know how you feel about this, and you may win the vote. But let's get the possibilities in front of us, have a real debate, and then see, ok?" Obviously they already had this argument.

Ernesto and Jordan looked at each other, knowingly. The fear of shit was one of the certainties of urban life—which as plumbers, they'd long gotten over. Most parents were easier to talk about this with than people who hadn't raised children. Something about getting shit on your hands and clothes from small children helps destigmatize excrement. But Yolanda, who couldn't be more than 25 or so, didn't have children... yet.

Jay cut in, "No need to fret. We can design this in stages. It'll take a lot of work to go through each building. We can set up the new plumbing so you can always add—or subtract—more from the water system in the future. Different buildings can go faster or slower, and the most resistant—the most uncomfortable," he looked directly at Yolanda, "can wait until they see how it's working for the ones who are ready. We don't have to impose the exact same model on everyone."

Yolanda took the hint from Rita and headed out the door. They turned back to the planning. "Let's go through your building first," Jordan suggested. "We can assess the state of your plumbing, and compare it to the documents to see what we might expect, ok?" Rita led them to the top flat in her building and began the inspection process.

CHAPTER 53
TUESDAY, JULY 14, 2026

"Have you heard about this guy's hypothesis that humans descended from a one-time encounter between a chimpanzee and a pig?" Maria asked incredulously.

Janet did a double-take. "What?"

"No, it's a whole argument. He's been working on it for over ten years. You should check out his website macroevolution.net where he has it. It's called "The Hybrid Hypothesis.""

"That's insane! What kind of argument is that?" Janet never heard anything like that before. "How is that even possible?"

"I know, I know, it sounds completely wack. And he is clear that he can't prove it, and it's only a hypothesis. But he goes through anatomical facts, things that make humans different from chimps and other primates, like our skin, sweat, eyes, and noses, and it turns out that the species that is most similar to us in those areas is the pig! It's astonishing. And he deals with the question of cross-breeding between different species too... turns out it's not unusual. Anyway, you should check it out. It got my attention," Maria was not joking.

Janet shook her head and sank back on the bench overlooking the grass hillside sloping down to the muddy banks of Yosemite Slough. She and Maria started meeting here when they realized, separately and for different reasons, that the witches butter was much bigger—and probably more important—than anyone imagined.

They heard wheels crossing the nearby gravel path and looked over to see Cindy Lowe, black hair flowing behind her as she glided to a stop a short distance away. Maria proposed she join their get-togethers when it became clear that one of the key inexplicable phenomena was the apparent connection to animals and birds. Cindy brought a different experiential and scientific background to their brainstorming.

"HelLO Doctor!" greeted Maria in a teasing tone.

Cindy smiled as she leaned her bike on a light pole and returned the greeting, "Hah! We're all doctors in this hospital!" She came over and joined them, pulling out a bag of Vero's chips to share.

"Maria was telling me about a theory that humans descended from a chimpanzee-pig mating—you ever heard of that?" Janet's doubt was undisguised.

"Oh? Tell me more!" Cindy was immediately fascinated. Maria repeated her account and Cindy scribbled the website on her pad. "I'm definitely checking that out!"

Janet was uncomfortable. Either this was completely absurd or her understanding of the world was off, and either way, she wanted to push it away. "Look," she pointed towards the water, which was at low tide now, but surged over the banks during evening high tides since Saturday and was slated to pour in again at midnight tonight. "Can you believe how far up it came?" A dirty line marked the high point, well up the slope into the grassy picnic area. "I wonder if this park will return to the Bay sooner than later," she said gloomily. "It's getting flooded regularly."

Maria pointed past Double Rock standing in the water to a few markers bobbing in the bay. "There's our oyster reef—it's supposed to help staunch the rising waters."

"That's where you found the 'butter' underwater, right?" asked Cindy. "Is it growing on the reef?"

"Yes. I can't explain it. The sample I analyzed wasn't different than the others. But somehow it could survive—thrive—below the surface of the bay. I don't know how it manages to adapt to such different environments."

"And it finds its way into different animals, birds... even trees? We don't know do we?" Cindy ruminated.

"I've been reading around, trying to make sense of it. Nothing in the mycological literature comes close to what we've been seeing. When I talked to Dat, he suggested I check out the Hybrid Hypothesis that I was telling you about. I think Dat was inspired by it to put some pig genes into the witches butter. He also recommended this Nobel chemist Ilya Prigogine's work on 'dissipative systems,' which are defined as 'natural thermodynamic entities capable of evolutionary behavior.' Dissipative systems can import energy from outside and transform it into complex internal structures while exiling or expelling their entropic decay. That sounds complicated. But doesn't that describe what the witches butter is doing? Taking in energy from external sources and growing in complexity as it does? I'm not sure about how it handles any tendency to fall apart it may have, but so far, there's little sign of anything but rapid growth and increasing complexity, no?"

Cindy cleared her throat and suggested, "Thinking out loud here. Maybe Dat's biohack triggered a self-organizing life form that learns from its surroundings and incorporates that knowledge and then epigenetically transmits it to its offspring?"

Janet listened intently but was having trouble following. "Hold on, you guys are going too fast. Are you saying the witches butter is a fast-learner thing that can pass on what it learns to ... what? Other batches of witches butter? Other species? I'm confused."

Maria and Cindy laughed. "Yeah, we're confused," Maria admitted. "You said it pretty well. But we don't know if it's communicating, and if it is, *how* it's communicating either. And how does it learn for that matter? I've been looking for chemical or cellular connections, but so far I haven't turned anything up. It's not the same as looking for brain activity—wait a minute! What if we tried a PET scan? Cindy, do you have access to a scanner?"

"Ha, no, we don't do PET scans on pets!" and they laughed. "But I know a woman whose dog I operated on. She's a doctor at UCSF. Let me ask her."

They munched on Vero's chips during the conversation. "What about the increased sense of smell?" Janet asked. "Since we've been eating it, I feel like my nose is SO sensitive to every possible odor now. You guys too?"

Maria nodded. Cindy cocked her head and took a deep breath. "I noticed that. I feel like I can smell... MORE. In those cramped rooms at the SPCA, the animals stink!" she crinkled her nose at the thought and chuckled. "I notice different, more subtle smells much more now. If a dog or cat is sick I pick it up from the air when I walk in..."

"Did my uncle get you hired to look after the Federal Police horses?" Janet remembered she'd been wondering.

"I'm the vet they'll call if there's a bad illness or injury. I went over there last week. Those are big strong horses, and they're taking good care of them. There's a squad of horse riders who know horses too. They got a guy in charge who is an Apache—or maybe it was Comanche, I can't remember what he said. But he knows horses."

"What are they planning to do with horses in San Francisco?" Janet wondered.

Cindy looked at her archly. "C'mon Janet. You of all people should know—and be preparing. They didn't talk about it around me, but I assume they'll be riding the hills and parks to look for illegal farming."

"Crap!" Janet never imagined that.

Maria stood up to stretch. "Did you hear that BGM is offering to buy Vero's recipes and expand production?"

They both nodded. "The family's been talking about for the last two weeks!" Cindy confided. She lived with Lamar up on Marlin Street, where Frank lived too, and Leon was there all the time. "Leon stands to hit the jackpot, too. He and Vero have a deal." She looked at Janet. "Have you talked to Vero about it?"

"I tried to." She looked crestfallen. "I'm very disappointed to tell the truth. We played a part in this. And yes, Vero was the first one to think about eating it, and she did a lot of work to make it into..." she reached over and held up the cellophane bag, "these! But I told her it shouldn't be for sale. It's not hers to sell, and anyway, what if it IS a new intelligent species? How can we let it be taken over by BGM and turned into mass market products? It is disappointing!"

They sat silently for a while, staring out at the afternoon sun playing on the bay waters. Brown porpoises appeared in the distance, their wet curving backs unmistakable even at this distance.

Maria spoke up. "I get it, Janet. But from Vero's point of view, she's been mostly stuck inside since her escape. She's been watching the biobulb and bioboat coming along. She sees how Larry got set up by the HemptriCity buyout. She wants—she needs—to find her way, and this is it. Given how bad things are, you can hardly blame her for taking the money." She fell silent again. And then, "Besides, what if BGM expands the reach of the 'butter'? Assuming they don't do anything to mess it up, and if we're right that it's intelligent and adaptive and evolving rapidly—well, it might surprise everyone, no?"

***

Larry, Leon, and Vero sat in the conference room at the Brisbane warehouse. Larry's long-time lawyer was there too, Stan Fiero. Fiero didn't look particularly lawyerly, his long gray hair parted in the middle as he peered over his steel-framed glasses perched on the end of his nose. He was clad head-to-foot in denim and looked more like an aging rock star from the 1970s than a 21ˢᵗ century lawyer who could manage complex corporate deals.

"It's a decent offer in my opinion," he explained, "but not overwhelming. You have to turn over the recipes and provide a 50-lb. batch of witches butter. They will pay you $750,000 and an additional $50,000 in each of the next five years for a total of $1 million. You should think about it."

Vero looked expectantly at Leon and Larry. "What do you guys think?"

Larry pushed the prospectus away and stood up. "Vero, this is your decision, you and Leon. I would only say that $1 million is not a lot if you imagine growing a business that sells product widely. But to do that you have to find investors, build factories, establish a distribution system or deal with existing ones... It's a lot of work. Not to mention that you'll have to figure out how to grow more witches butter in sufficient quantities."

"And it can fail," Leon interjected. "There's no guarantee you can get into stores, even if you *can* scale up production." He sat back and folded his arms, looking at Vero. Larry was pacing back and forth by the window.

"You think I should take the deal?" she could tell Leon wanted to sell and avoid the risks.

"There's a lot to be said for taking the money while it's on the table," he was nodding, "And who knows what happens if we refuse?" The unspoken reference to the failed raid a month earlier was clear.

Vero looked back and forth from the lawyer to Leon and Larry. "When do we have to give them our answer?"

Fiero was retying his long gray hair into a ponytail. "BGM asked for a reply within 30 days of its proposal which was dated July 1. We have a couple more weeks if you want to think about."

"Oh man, this is hard! I can't decide!" she looked unnerved. "If we sell to BGM, then I can't use my own recipes anymore?"

"Well, I'm sure you can use them in your own kitchen. But no, you will be giving up the right to make your chips and pasta and sell them," the lawyer explained.

Vero buried her face in her hands, shaking her head. She moaned softly. "Janet doesn't think I should sell witches butter! Not in bags of chips or pasta, and for sure not to a big corporation. She thinks I have no right to sell it since we made it together." She looked at Leon and then Larry.

"Yeah, I heard her say that. She's entitled to her opinion. You invented these chips by yourself. And the pasta. You can do what you want," Leon opined.

Larry came to the table and leaned his huge frame forward, putting his hands on the table and looking side to side at everyone. "Maria told me point-blank that the witches butter is a new kind of life, a new intelligence. We aren't taking that into consideration here."

"You think we should?" Fiero asked him.

"Let's say that I don't think we can completely ignore that point of view. If it IS what she says it is, then maybe nobody has the right to own it, or sell it."

Vero was frustrated. She spent more time immersed in witches butter than anyone, and this idea that it was intelligent seemed far-fetched to her. It was an inert mass of material from which she had invented her recipes.

Larry continued. "I mean, look up there," he pointed up San Bruno Mountain to where Quarrytown was hidden. "How do you explain those huts, or how they worked with the biobulb? Something more is going on with this stuff."

Vero groaned loudly. "OK, ok. Let's think about it for a few more days at least. Can we get back together on Friday?"

Leon hated putting things off. "OK, if that's what you want," but he didn't want to. The big money was at his fingertips! Larry was glad to pause. He was much more patient about nearly everything. Giving themselves a few more days to think it over was a good idea.

"Should we ask Maria and Janet to meet with us?" Larry suggested.

Vero looked at him, a bit stricken. "Um, no, I'd rather not. I know what they think already." She found it very difficult to imagine going against Janet's preferences. But the money! It would set her up for years, and in this dire economic crisis, how could they NOT take the deal?

***

"I don't even know why they're talking about the election. It's not like the Republicans or the courts are letting them win anything," Corporal Eli Flores threw the newspaper into the box where they put the papers after reading them.

"Whaddya mean?" Frank was offended. He firmly believed in voting and democracy. "The midterms are in November. People are pissed off and millions are out of work. How does Hutchinson hold Congress with nearly 20% unemployment and a government that was unpopular from the start?" Frank still thought he was living in the United States he grew up in.

"C'mon Frank, you can't believe that! They took power through fraud and legal chicanery. Since then they've made it clear that any state that wants to disenfranchise large parts of its population due to poverty, race, criminal conviction, or even gender, is free to do so. The Supreme Court has washed their hands of election oversight. Who or what is left to change what is a completely rigged system?"

"You sound like those right-wingers used to during the Biden and Harris administrations, always complaining about rigged elections."

"Frank! They did rig the last election, are you forgetting?" Eli had grown steadily more disillusioned since he left the Army for Homeland Security and eventually got transferred into the Federal Police. Having seized the government, the Republicans wouldn't give it up while they still controlled the rules and ballot counting. Years of reducing access to the ballot led to a solid majority of Republican state legislatures, Republican governors, and of course an apparently untouchable majority in the House and Senate too. The Democrats might win a slim majority in the Senate during the midterms as a gesture of defiance towards the Hutchinson Administration, but that seemed a longshot at best.

"This whole defederalization project—let's admit it, it's working!" Eli put his feet up on his desk. "The Federal Government is not in charge of much anymore—do they even run the Federal Police? Sure, they keep the military prowling around the world to prop up the Dollar to keep our economy afloat. But I'm not sure that's working any more, y'know? I mean, it's been six months since the insurance collapse at the beginning of the year. Somehow they kept the system from completely unraveling, but let's face it—things are shit!"

Frank listened to his aide and at this point, best friend. Eli was on his side when it came to basic things, like trying to temper the violence of the rank-and-file they commanded. Like seeing through the stupidity of the campaign to quash local food production and to force people to buy surplus government food. Through it all, though, Frank still believed that the basic order of life persisted. He easily forgot how differently he and Eli saw the world. Yes, it was dodgy the way the Republicans grabbed the presidency last time, but was that different than Bush in 2000? Trump won while losing by 3 million in 2016. They had to hold a real election this fall didn't they? It was in the Constitution!

A loud knock on the door knocked them off track. "Come in!" called Flores.

"Master Sergeant Brandt Lee Craig," and the weathered vet snapped to attention inside the door.

"At ease, Sergeant. I'm Lt. Frank Robertson, and this is Corporal Eli Flores. What can we do for you?"

"Sir, you may have heard. I'm here to lead the cavalry. We are trained horsemen and ready to carry out the missions assigned us. Colonel Morgan suggested I check in with you, Lieutenant. He indicated that you were from here and probably had the best knowledge of the terrain. Do you ride horses?"

"Sergeant, I've never ridden a horse in my life!" He laughed. "I don't think I'm your man. I do know San Francisco as well as anyone here. Sergeant, do you mind if I ask where you're from?"

"Originally I'm from Oklahoma, Lawton Oklahoma to be exact. I'm Comanche. Served in the Special Forces in Iraq, Afghanistan, and Somalia. They had me in Colombia for a while too in the late 1980s." Sergeant Craig stood erect, his hair graying, and his ruddy brown face profoundly wrinkled.

"Thank you, Sergeant, and thank you for your service," Frank stood up to shake his hand. "Comanche, eh? You're a long way from Oklahoma, Sergeant!" He smiled but Craig remained impassive. "Where is Morgan sending you?"

"He said something about McLaren Park and another place called Glen Canyon. Oh, and San Bruno Mountain too. He says there are probably dozens of small farms scattered around those places."

"I see," Frank returned to his seat. "Sergeant, I'll get back to you by tomorrow at the latest. Will that be adequate?"

"I think so. Thank you, Lieutenant,..." he saluted, and as he turned he nodded at Eli too, "Corporal," and exited the office.

"I was wondering what Morgan was planning to do with those horses. Now it makes sense," Frank watched out his window as Sergeant Craig crossed the open space between the office building and the jail. He was almost certainly heading to the stable behind the jail.

CHAPTER 54
FRIDAY, SEPTEMBER 4, 2026

The Canopy Council was meeting on a houseboat in Mission Creek, a nice two-story floating home, clad in brown shingles with a small deck facing the water. Almost twenty people crowded into the small living room. Annette Jorgensen presided from a large well-upholstered chair in the corner.

"Who has seen a mounted patrol?" she asked the room.

Will Shaw raised his hand. "They were out at Lake Merced a week ago. We've kept our farming to a minimum out there so I was surprised to see them."

"How many were they? What did they do?" The questions rang around the room.

"There were six uniformed Federal Police. I walked up to them. The Sergeant, his name is Craig, looked at ease on his horse. He was gruff with me, but after I explained that we'd been delivering harvests to their troops since early summer, he took a few notes and they left. They seemed to be looking for unofficial farms, places that aren't on their list already and that aren't giving them 'their share' of the harvest." He used air quotes around 'their share.'

Marina Petrozzini interjected, "I can't believe they're still doing this... on horseback?!"

Janet Pierce knew more than she'd shared. In mid-August she'd spent hours at the secret Hangar below the Marlin Street house that her cousin and uncle lived in. Using the array of surveillance cameras that her cousins installed before the Federal Police moved out to the formerly abandoned base, she was able to watch the horse patrols as they drilled in Hunter's Point around the jail.

"They brought those horses to Hunter's Point in July." She looked around to nodding heads. "I heard about it then, but I had a hard time imagining horseback patrols looking for farms."

"You should've told us at the last meeting—you already knew then?" Marina persisted. "Why didn't you say something? We could've started getting ready." The rest of the Council started asking questions, too, but no one else was blaming Janet for failing them.

Jorge Castro, coordinator in the Excelsior area, got the floor. "If they're patrolling on horseback, wouldn't you think they'd use them where there's not many roads or trails for regular vehicles?"

"Like Glen Canyon? Or the Presidio?"

"Yeah, I suppose so. I mean, why would they use horses to go through city streets?"

Will cut in again. "They looked capable of covering a lot of territory on those horses. They think there's guerrilla farming in the hills and parks," and he looked around the room, confirming what everyone feared. It was the reason this urgent meeting of the Council was called. Their strategy of appeasing the authorities with regular deliveries might not be working as well as they hoped. It was approaching full-on harvest season.

Annette cleared her throat to get everyone's attention. "It makes sense, what Will's suggesting. What can we do to accelerate the fall harvest before their patrols find more of our farms?"

Esther from the Presidio jumped up. "Wait a second! We can't start picking everything now. A lot of it still needs another month, and plenty of crops could be yielding steadily for the next two or three months. We need a regular supply don't we?" A lot of people began murmuring in agreement, and small conversations broke out.

Joe Stennett, the stalwart organizer who coordinated backyard potato production and the moving of crops from farms to backyards during the early Federal crackdown, stood up now. "We've been through this—it was worse last summer when we had to decentralize during the National Emergency. Our networks are intact. Backyards are already under cultivation again, and we have a lot more participating now. Let's divide up by watershed and figure out where we're most at risk. Move those farms first. They're won't be riding horses into our backyards!"

His practical approach won over the rest of the Canopy Council. Janet participated in the group figuring out what to do about Bayview Hill, Palou Terrace, and McLaren Park. After about 20 minutes of urgent planning, Annette Jorgensen called everyone back to the circle.

"Janet, you had something else to bring up, right?"

"Yes, thanks Annette." She looked around until her eyes landed on Jorge Castro. "Jorge, I know you're one of the biggest enthusiasts for the witches butter, second only to me!" she laughed. "But I have to let you know that my good friend Vero Gomez, the inventor of the Butter WitChips and the Pasta too, has received a lucrative offer from BioGenMo to sell her recipes." Groans around the room. "And she's decided to accept it. This means that the witches butter in our gardens is potentially of interest to BGM. They'll try to buy it if they can. I won't sell, and I'm not helping them. On the contrary, I'm making sure that it continues to grow and expand and is available going forward. It's our common wealth!"

Jorge jumped up clapping, "I'm with you Janet! Fuck BioGenMo!"

Annette regained the room. "All well and good. Most of you have heard about the presentation we attended in May and the argument that witches butter might be a new kind of intelligence. I don't know if you have any follow-up for us on that, either of you?" looking pointedly at Janet and Jorge. "No? Well, the jury is out I guess. We've learned that witches butter is a uniquely prolific fungus. It is a backup food supply when other things might fail. I am firmly in the camp that says we need to maintain as much of it as we can in as many locations around town as possible. We should bring cuttings to places far from here to help it expand its range."

Janet was very happy to hear Annette promote the Canopy Council taking a protective and expansive role with witches butter—surprising given her earlier reticence. "Thank you, Annette. It's great to hear that you're endorsing our use and defense of witches butter! We need to get it out of San Francisco and growing in other parts of the state and country as soon as possible."

Barking seals erupted in the water outside the houseboat. Everyone laughed since it seemed like they were agreeing with the room. "Look!" called a voice by the porch. Several people saw a half dozen seals swimming around the houseboat. "That's uncanny!"

***

"Man I never sat in one of these before!" exclaimed Frank as he and Sheila took their box seats overlooking 3rd base. A large TV was showing the Giants-Dodgers game in a lounge behind them, while in front of them live baseball! They were "not much better than their usual seats" noted Sheila with surprise.

Lt. Charlene Nichols was in the next seat with her "date," a women clad in black and orange Giants gear. Charlene overheard Sheila's comment and leaned over, "I'd actually rather be sitting in the bleachers than here!" she chuckled. "Or right behind the dugout!" chimed in her friend Marla. Marla was a union official in the MUNI drivers union, and Frank referred to her as Marla MUNI to Sheila, a nickname she couldn't shake now that she was in her presence.

Lt. Eldon Owens, holding a $15 beer and a $12 hotdog, walked behind them to get to his seat. "$27 for these?" he complained loudly. "No wonder this country is falling apart! I remember when you could get a hotdog for $2.50 and a beer for $6 at Dodger Stadium when I was a kid."

Marla, hearing that, let out a theatrical gasp. "You a Dodgers fan?"

Owens looked at her get-up, smiled, and shook his head. "Don't you worry. I haven't seen a game in twenty years. I couldn't name a player on the field." But he didn't deny being a Dodgers fan.

This Labor Day weekend Giants-Dodgers showdown had a lot of hype around it, and when a luxury box was offered to the Federal Police, Col. Morgan suggested his command staff use it for themselves and their loved ones. It was a surprising move on the Colonel's part. He didn't come himself, probably thinking that he couldn't fraternize with his subordinates. It left the Zone Commanders free to use it. Lt. Brandon Garner came, bringing along his wife Suzy. Lt. Smithson was there with his wife Judy. Several others were in the back around the snack table. Back there you keep an eye on the game if you wanted to, but it was obvious that few of them were interested.

"I don't know how much longer they'll even keep up appearances!" Smithson said in a loud voice.

"Whaddya mean? It's not simply 'appearances'—we're talking about the Constitution!" retorted Lt. Ken Hudson. "Elections are the essence of the American way of life!" Hudson was an earnest liberal, a zone commander with a college degree and middle-class beliefs and expectations about America. He was one of the younger officers who came over from Homeland Security when the Federal Police were started. The overt authoritarianism of his Homeland Security bosses left him confused and upset, and he saw the Federal Police as both an antidote to that, and a chance to start over in a different environment. When anyone disparaged the state of democracy, he was quick to rush into the breach.

Frank and Charlene exchanged meaningful glances as the debate erupt behind them. They'd written off Smithson a while ago, while Hudson was a confirmed ally.

"So," Frank leaned forward to speak to Marla, "how do those driverless cars work, anyway? Do you have a command center keeping track of them as they roll through the streets?"

Marla snorted derisively. "Yeah, well, sort of. We trained up a few operators to watch the monitors, but they can only shut down the computers and turn off the engines. No one can 'drive' (she made air quotes) one of those cars from the office. Once they're out there, they are responding to their surroundings, constantly checking back to the central computers that give them their pickups and dropoffs..." She looked at Frank. "Have you tried one yet?"

"Nah, I got a car. Sheila has used 'em though. You like them don't you?" turning to her.

"I haven't had any problems. I was riding in one when bicyclists began weaving back and forth across the road ahead of us, and the car slowed down and eventually stopped until they rode off. That seemed weird." Sheila was wearing a Giants hat and had a merry expression on her face as she remembered the moment.

Charlene asked Sheila, "You're at GSA right? I've been hearing things from friends who work for the government in Washington. Are things normal over there?"

Sheila didn't expect to be asked about this. Things were not normal. The new fiscal year that started on July 1 didn't produce a wave of new hiring, neither at GSA nor at the Dept. of Transportation where her friend worked. Everything slowed way down, and they'd been told to cut spending by 25% or more.

"Um, I don't know. We have lost a lot of staff in the past year, you know with the economic crisis and all. Some layoffs, but mostly not hiring replacements when people leave or retire. It's surprising how fast holes appear and how much the bureaucracy slows down." She brushed some popcorn she dropped from her lap and grabbed a napkin to clean her buttery hands. In a lower voice she furtively said, "It might be on purpose. Hutchinson said he would cut the federal bureaucracy, and it's happening."

"At least our paychecks are still coming!" Frank remarked, but his comment was drowned by a surge of cheering as the Giants center fielder made a diving catch in right center field to end the Dodger threat in the top of the 2nd inning.

Hudson and Smithson's voices soon rose again in the back of the luxury box. "You're glad? How can you say that?!?" Hudson was completely provoked now.

Smithson smirked as though he had some secret knowledge. "The NSA is part of the deep state," he announced authoritatively. "I'm only surprised it didn't happen a lot sooner!"

The multi-billion-dollar Utah Data Center was set on fire a few days earlier. It looked to be arson, and it was devastating, melting millions of dollars of computers, hard drives, and back-up data storage facilities. The NSA wasn't admitting how bad its losses were, but the internet was buzzing with rumors about the damage being much more severe than publicly acknowledged. Some speculated the perpetrator was a right-wing militia with followers working inside that set the fires. Drone footage showed very little of the 100,000-square foot complex untouched by the blaze.

"Wait! Aren't we on the same team?" Hudson implored. "Isn't the NSA part of the US military, like we are?"

Smithson looked at Hudson incredulously. "We are not part of the US military! We're the Federal Police. That's different. And the NSA is the biggest spook agency, tapping everyone's phones, monitoring everyone's emails, tracking everybody—and for who? It's not like the elected government has any control over it. They are a permanent unelected government running behind the scenes. That's why I say the elections are only about appearances—because whoever gets elected doesn't run the government—the deep state does!"

Hudson threw up his hands in exasperation. "If you believe that, I have a bridge in Arizona that I'd like to sell you!" and he finally turned his attention to the game.

CHAPTER 55
TUESDAY, SEPTEMBER 22, 2026

Garlic and onions were ready to harvest on the upper terrace. Angie smelled nearby critters. The weasel was surely not far, nor was the skunk family, whose pungent odor, while not in full fright mode, was still distinctive. Hot September air collided with a cool wind rushing over San Bruno Mountain, leaving no doubt that the fog would follow in a few hours. Polluted air hanging over the bay cast a haze over everything. Angie inhaled the cooling breeze deeply, noticing the faint smell of salty ocean mixed with eucalyptus, oak, and the dry grasses that covered most of the upper slopes.

There was an abrupt shift, not in the air or the temperature, but something triggered a sudden change. She peered up the hill first, saw nothing unusual, and went to look over the edge to the lower terraces where her new neighbors were working in the chard and kale.

"Hey Bennie, Reggie, you guys feel anything?" she called down.

The two men in their late 50s, looked up at her. Leaning into their shovel and hoe, they shook their heads. "Nope!" yelled Reggie, "just hot!"

They'd arrived in mid-August after jumping off a train in the East Bay. Itinerant laborers for most of their lives, some people would call them hobos, or even bums. Grizzled vets of many a harsh night outdoors, they wandered out of San Francisco looking for a place to stay for the coming winter. It was hard to say why they'd appeared in the Brisbane Industrial Park of all places, but as they trekked up to the back of it, hoping to find an access trail to the Mountain, Juna came pedaling along on their way to Quarrytown. Looking at the two men Juna felt a shiver of familiarity.

"You thirsty?" they asked as they slowed down to roll alongside them.

"Yeah," answered the one with the green earring, flashing a gold-tooth as he grinned, glad to be asked. Bennie's greasy hair was under a black fedora, but since it was a typical Fogust day, it wasn't too hot. His pal Reggie was wearing a snazzy vest over soiled jeans and worn boots. He sported a gray ponytail, which he kept in front of him to keep it away from his backpack.

Juna led them to the original faucet at Larry's warehouse, and as they chatted with them they realized these two might be a good match with Angie. And she had those extra huts that the Mukuls moved out of in the Spring. Juna invited them up the hill.

Juna's sound instincts were confirmed when they hit it off with Angie. She needed help with the farm, and these guys were happy to take up temporary residence in the butter huts. It took some explaining to get them to understand the genesis of their new home.

Reggie pulled a piece of the smaller hut from the wall and stared at it for a minute. It had a mottled surface, a mix of greens, yellows, and browns, which did make it hard to focus on from the distance. "You sure you can *eat* this?!?" He looked at it again, and then at Angie and Juna.

"Definitely! I can't say it tastes great in that form, but it's perfectly edible," Angie assured him. She went offered her bag of WitChips. "This is much tastier!" When the wall grew back by the next day, the fellas admitted they never saw anything like it before.

They started helping with the chores and tending the farm. Within a few days they let Angie know that they were a long-time couple. They'd been together for over 30 years! Juna was delighted when Angie explained it to them a week later.

"I knew I got a good vibe! The minute I saw them!" they exclaimed.

That had been a month ago. Now Bennie and Reggie were fully involved in Quarrytown's day-to-day—Angie's domain—but they soon became working partners. Standing on the edge of the upper terrace she sounded worried.

"What's up Angie?" asked Bennie.

"Not sure..." She disappeared from their view.

She was walking across the terrace when she heard a coyote howl up the mountain. A second chimed in from another spot. That was strange, they rarely sounded off in the afternoon. A large hare came bounding down the trail and cut across her path before disappearing into the Blue Lilac shrubs. She took a massive breath and then sat on the nearby log as she exhaled. There was something in the air, something she wasn't used to. She heard it before she could figure it out. The sound of horses' hooves clip-clopping on the main trail that skirted the edge of the quarry's terraces. She sat still, silent, waiting.

The horses stopped. They couldn't be more than 20 or 30 yards away through the shrubs and oaks. She could hear them breathing hard, and voices could be heard, though try as she might, she couldn't make out what they were saying. The trail stayed to the east of the actual quarry. Unless they knew where the turnoff was, they might go right by. Clip clop, clip clop, the horses were on the move again, but going down the trail, disappearing, not coming closer.

Angie breathed deeply again, remembering the smell of horses she'd noticed. But there was something more too, not quite animal, not typical human. Something in between. What was it? She sat quietly ruminating on the orchestra of smells she was able to perceive now. But the odd smell receded and she couldn't pinpoint what it was. The memory of what it smelled *like floated away*, unlike anything she recognized. After the horses disappeared, she slowly went down to the lower terrace, but the boys were gone. Entering the well-disguised village, she saw Reggie in the doorway of their hut.

"What was that?" he asked.

"Horses, men, they came real close, but somehow they turned away. I don't know who they were. There was a weird smell in there too."

"You think they'll come back? They might find us?" Reggie worried.

"We ain't causin' no problems. We ain't on private property. We'll be ok." Angie felt somehow protected. The witches butter was growing around them, and spread well up the mountain in wild patches. The huts were like a living cocoon. Only people they invited would find them, she was sure of it.

***

Juna and Cindy sat at the employee lounge table across from vending machines and a microwave oven at the SPCA. Their shifts didn't coincide very often and they hadn't shared a break for awhile.

"You ever hear of the 'Hybrid Hypothesis'?" asked Cindy. Juna shook their head. She gave them the quick overview she'd heard from Maria a few weeks earlier.

"A chimp and a pig had a baby? And that's how humans, *homo sapiens*, started?" Juna looked skeptical to say the least. "Where does such an idea even come from?"

Juna paid close attention to Cindy's quick summary and concluded, "I guess I'll have to look into it more myself. It's off the wall at first glance!"

"I know! I read his arguments and decided to take it seriously. Why not, after all?" She bought a soda at the vending machine. Putting out WitChips to share from one of Vero's original packages before BGM bought her recipes.

"You heard about BGM buying the recipe for these?" Cindy queried Juna.

"Oh yeah. Aaron and Greg were fighting about it at my house. Aaron was mad, I guess he'd been talking to Janet. Greg took Vero's side of it. He thought she ought to be able to sell her idea if she wanted to."

"What do you think? I mean, you more than most people know that witches butter is more than a product, right?"

Juna nodded, gobbling chips. "Mmfpf, yeah!" through their full mouth, then after a quick swig of water, continued, "It makes me uncomfortable, I admit. I mean, times are tough and everyone is worried about how they're gonna survive. It's hard to blame her for taking the money. On the other hand, we don't even know what this is! I don't think it's only a fungus, and I don't think it can be reduced to a product for sale," as they stuffed a few more chips into their mouth, "mmfpf, but I do love these!" laughing.

"It's complicated. Like everything," Cindy sighed. "God, did you hear about the Philippines?"

"No, what?"

"They announced a new trade and military agreement with China. China is building high-speed trains and freeways crisscrossing the archipelago, including new island bridges. And they're refurbishing the old US navy base at Subic Bay."

"Oh." Juna didn't pay a lot of attention to geopolitics.

Cindy recognized that Juna wasn't up to speed on this. "The Philippines were a U.S. colony from 1898-1946, and under its economic control ever since. They can't give it up to their main economic and military rival. It's very symbolic that the old U.S. naval base would be leased to the Chinese Navy."

Now it was Juna's turn to sigh. "It is complicated."

***

Steve Healey stood in line at the South of Market warehouse. He clutched the flyer advertising new jobs for BGM. "No biotech background required—gardening experience a plus!" said the ad. He'd worked for a landscaping company in southern California years ago, he hoped that would qualify. It was nerve-wracking to be shifting from foot to foot in a long line of aspiring applicants, but at least he was out of downtown! He was grateful for his room in the Insurance Exchange on California, but he hadn't had any work since well before he moved in there. With the low rent and food stamps he was getting by, but he was anxious to get a job. He was surprised he could even be in the running to work for BGM, which was the cutting edge of the biotech industry.

He craned his neck, trying to calculate how many people were in front of him. 'At least a hundred!' he thought. 'I shoulda got here at the crack of dawn!' He looked up at the brick wall with its big windows and the blue neon sign at the top of the building, "BioGenMo" in an ornate script.

"I can't believe I'm even trying this," whined the woman in front of him. She was neatly dressed in a gray jacket over a matching pair of slacks, brown hair pinned back in tight bun. She turned to Steve, "I was a contractor, had an apartment, grew the ProsperPlants° until I had a bum tray. They canned me—that was two years ago. It wasn't even my fault!" Her voice was urgent, pleading. She wanted him to understand. Steve almost went for the apartment and bonus but was dissuaded by a guy he was running with back then.

"You figure this is different? Won't they have you on their computer already?"

She looked a bit stricken, as though she never considered it. "I hope not!"

He shook his head sympathetically. "Well, I hope not too!" he smiled, "Good luck up there!"

She smiled wanly as they approached the main doors. Slowly the line moved into a big reception hall where after another 15 minutes he was in front of a desk.

"Name?"

"Steve Healey."

The bored clerk typed his information into the computer. After a few minutes, with no questions, an ID badge emerged from under the table and the clerk put it on a lanyard and handed it to Steve. "Go down to the end and turn left," he instructed him.

Steve was soon sitting in a small auditorium with about 250 other people in folding chairs. Apologies, coughs, and scraping chairs seemed to fill the space as people jostled for places.

"I made it!" The woman he'd met in line slid into the seat beside him. She was grinning broadly, as though she'd hit the jackpot. "Hey, what's your name?" she asked him.

"Steve, Steve Healey," and he extended his hand to her.

She shook it, "I'm Myra Rubin, glad to meet you, Steve. You live in the city?"

"Yeah, I got a place downtown," he didn't need to say too much about it. "You?"

"I'm in a flat with four others over on Larkin Street... 'Tendernob' I guess!" she chuckled.

A couple appeared at the front of the room, both clad in matching casual t-shirts and slacks. They wore wraparound mics and started into their spiel.

"Welcome to BGM's latest endeavor. You are probably familiar with Intelligel®?" the blonde woman beamed. The screen above her showed a row of women in leotards doing calisthenics that blended into the same women around an office conference table apparently discussing some important matter. A smattering of applause coursed around the room. "We went on to the next success with the Hempattery!" A screen behind her showed a white square building near a hospital emergency room and as the camera panned through the open door, a whole stack of green cartons connected by wires gleamed inside. Each one was labeled "Hempattery® from BioGenMo" in that same blue script that appeared in the neon sign outside.

The blonde guy took over, his bleached hair contrasting with his artificial-looking tan.

Myra whispered to Steve, "Do you think they're real? Or robots?" she giggled.

"You have the chance to get in on the ground floor with the latest BGM product line. When you see these, what do you think?" and the screen above showed a table with a big bowl of what looked like potato chips. "You might be surprised..." he teased.

"We will be ramping up production of these right here in San Francisco. We call them 'WitChips.'" Several people clad in matching uniforms to the two blonde speakers in front appeared along the side of the audience. They had big shoulder bags and from them they pulled out small cellophane bags of WitChips and began handing them down the rows. The new prospects eagerly reached for the sample, and rustling wrappers soon gave way to widespread crunching and munching.

Steve and Myra shared a bag and both agreed they were tasty. But potato chips? Witchips?

Someone in the front raised their hand and asked, "Are these potato chips?"

The blonde presenter grinned happily. "I'm glad you asked! BGM and potato chips?" he wrinkled his nose and theatrically made a disapproving frown while he shook his head. "I don't think so!" "Edie?"

They rehearsed this. She was holding a chunk of witches butter in her hand, thrusting it into the air. "The witchips are made from this stuff. You don't need to know much about it, but it started as a fungus and after some clever bioengineering, it's the raw material for these remarkable chips... They're pretty good, aren't they?" She was too enthusiastic.

Steve felt a little deflated. 'A chip? We're working in a factory packaging chips?' he was dismayed. Not a very high-tech product. Probably not much skill needed either. Oh well, he needed the job. He ate a few more chips, savoring the unusual flavor and imagining what the work might be like.

CHAPTER 56
WEDNESDAY, OCTOBER 28, 2026

Halloween fell on the weekend. That meant kids trick-or-treating on Saturday of course, but it also meant San Franciscans would engage in their usual overblown frenzy of costumed drunkenness with the additional intensity provided by being a Saturday night. Local authorities were taking precautions. They banned the closing of streets in the Castro as they always did, and tried to funnel celebrants towards the wide-open (usually cold and windy) plaza in front of City Hall.

Frank sipped a brandy in his Marlin Street living room after work. His daily routine was rather predictable. He worked a regular 8-5 day, but usually had little to do. His aide Eli handled day-to-day communications.

Col. Morgan ordered a mobilization two weeks before the coming midterm election. Suddenly the Federal Police on Hunter's Point were ordered to "flood the zone," which got a bunch of sardonic remarks given how many times their own base was flooded during the summer's King Tides. Frank was trying to relax after another day of patrolling his old haunt, Mission Bay.

It was different than it was a few years ago. Nearly every lot was built out, filling formerly open spaces. The new school under construction close to the old Caltrain tracks and the I-280 overpass was among the last big construction projects. Along Seventh Street a deep trench ran where the train was being undergrounded to connect to a new tunnel to the Transit Center downtown. On the ballot next Tuesday a hotly contested local proposition—if passed—would authorize the demolition of most of the freeway north of 16th Street. One ramp was to be retained and repurposed as a soaring public park over Mission Creek, while the current freeway would end in off-ramps over the new train tunnel at 16th Street.

Frank looked over his sample ballot and frowned when he read the arguments for and against Proposition H. As a car-guy he couldn't believe people were still trying to take down perfectly functional freeways. On the other hand, the campaign literature piling up in his mailbox everyday showed the transformed landscape between the CCA campus and the adjacent Adobe buildings on the west side of Seventh, and the new elementary school and the parklands around Mission Creek, which looked much nicer than it was now. He was voting no anyway. That freeway was jammed full every day with people coming and going from the Embarcadero and downtown, Chinatown, and North Beach.

Col. Morgan was very satisfied with Sergeant Craig's cavalry. Using aerial surveillance from the skEYE System drones, they identified a number of likely illegal farm sites. After repeated crashes over community gardens, they had opted to use higher altitude surveillance only—that seemed to halt the repeated failures nearer to the ground. (Numerous unverified reports claimed that crows were attacking the drones when they flew nearer the ground!) On patrols through remote hilltops and parklands Craig's cavalry verified the presence of a dozen farm plots. Frank sent his own troops to follow up on the plots in McLaren Park, Bayview Hill, and the Dog Patch. The violent raid a year and a half earlier at the Dog Patch haunted everyone. He decided to personally oversee the new raid, which had been a few days ago. He was still ruminating on it as he sat sipping his brandy.

After reminding his squad of what happened in May 2025, and insisting that they leave their guns unloaded, the small bus soon filled up and they began the short ride from Hunter's Point to the Dogpatch. They rolled past new condos under construction, and the abiding presence of the 19th century Albion Castle across from the new India Basin museum and shoreline park. Frank and Eli decided not to follow the same route as the ill-fated raid 17 months earlier and approached over the land from the Pier 94 parking lot. They formed a skirmish line, spreading the 15 officers out with eight in front and seven behind, proceeding slowly but steadily towards the rebuilt garden along Islais Creek's southern banks.

A young woman in a blue sweatshirt with a big camera in her hands came towards them as they crossed the open field. She was obviously taking photos. Frank waved her over, "Hey, c'mere!"

She kept taking pictures as she approached. She looked very young, her blonde hair tied up in pigtails accentuating her youthful appearance. She stopped ten yards away. "What are you guys doing?" she asked pointedly.

"We're here to enforce Federal food laws," Frank explained. "Who are you taking photos for?"

She ignored his question. "Federal food laws? You mean the ones that say it's illegal to grow and eat fresh food? And that it's mandatory to eat that corn syrup and GMO soy shit they grow in the midwest?" She made no effort to disguise her disrespect. Behind her a couple appeared, looking every bit the farmer in their overalls and straw hats. They were walking deliberately towards the police too.

The officers stopped while Frank engaged with the young photographer. They stood uneasily watching the approaching couple. Corporal Eli Flores, never far from Frank, spoke to him. "Lieutenant! We should keep moving. Standing still—we're giving up the initiative."

Frank looked around at his troops and saw their discomfort. "OK, keep moving!" Frank shouted. The photographer backed up as they walked toward her. Frank went directly to her, "no need to run," he said in his friendliest voice. He read "Water is Life" on her sweatshirt. "Let's talk for a minute," he pleaded. The girl's curiosity got the best of her and she fell in next to Frank.

"What is that sweatshirt about?" he asked her.

"I'm a water protector. This is the Islais Creek watershed. I help with photography and social media for the different watershed groups on the east side of the city: Channel, Islais Creek, Yosemite, and Sunnydale," she explained. "Do you know anything about watersheds?" She was such an earnest organizer that she seemed to think she could reach even this old guy in a Federal police uniform.

He smiled. "I know the areas you're talking about. I grew up here. I remember when it was very different! Used to be the whole area stank of sewage—we called this 'Shit Creek'," he laughed. "Actually every creek around here was called that. When I was a kid there was a lot of shit in the water. It's better now."

She tried to get a read on this guy. Having been a photographer for a while, she'd grown used to interacting with people, whether businessmen, politicians, police, whatever. Unlike her allies and comrades, who seemed horrified when she would tell stories of her conversations with these "enemies," she was genuinely curious to figure out what these "kind of people" thought. She read his badge, 'Robertson,' and asked, "that your name?"

"Yeah, Lt. Frank Robertson, and yours?" he asked.

"Sarah Ackerman."

"You from San Francisco?" and she nodded affirmatively. Tom and Evelyn Palmer were in front of them, looking askance at Sarah, wondering why she was walking with the cops.

"What do you guys want?" Evelyn said, the anger palpable in her voice, the line of police halting again.

"Haven't you done enough harm here already?" Tom chimed in. His work boots were caked in dried mud and dirt and she was sporting some equally dirty rubber boots herself. Their matching denim overalls and straw hats, along with the deep tans they each sported, almost finished the archetypal image.

"You guys come with pitchforks?" Eli chuckled, struck by their farmer costumes.

Evelyn glared at him. "Very funny, asshole!" She was unafraid of the raiding party. Once again, the Federal Police were waiting for Frank's orders to continue.

Tom directed himself to Frank, the commanding officer. "We've been paying our tax," alluding to the monthly food tax that local farms were expected to pay. "I don't see why you're sneaking up on us this way. You could've sent your regular guy and we'd show him around as we always do."

"We appreciate your cooperation," Frank answered. "If everything is in order, as you say, then we won't be here long." He again waved his arm to his troops and they strode forward in their formation. As they came over the rise and looked down on the Dog Patch farm, an electric van was driving away at full speed, west on the dirt road to towards the bridge over the creek. Frank turned to Flores. "Corporal, please have that van stopped and searched."

Evelyn and Tom scowled at hearing this, while Flores was radioing to the nearby street patrol. Sarah Ackerman let out a loud whistle, which startled Frank and the others, and they flinched, expecting something to come at them. But instead they heard another loud whistle sound from somewhere among the farmers below them. And then another whistle further west, and another one, almost inaudible in the further distance. But nothing seemed to happen as they proceeded into the gardens. Two officers were assigned to take photos of each raised bed and make notes in a ledger. At the tool shed and kitchen shack, they demanded to see the records of the farm, and one of the other farmers, a middle-aged woman, brought them out to a table behind the two structures.

"Here they are," she said without enthusiasm. "Have at it. You'll find everything in order." The officers mostly stood around now, while the specialist compared their own ledger to the farm's ledger. He did not find anything wrong, and after about ten minutes stood up, clapping the ledger books shut.

"A-OK, Lieutenant!" he reported.

"OK, let's get out of here," Frank declared. The Federal police officers fell into formation, two-by-two, and returned the way they came. After clearing the hilltop and crossing part of the open field where they'd been met by the photographer and the farmers, they suddenly heard what sounded like a speedboat roaring down the Islais Creek channel behind them. From where they were they couldn't see down into the creek, but soon enough the boat appeared in the bay, bounding along on some small waves from a passing freighter. The speedboat looked to be weighed down with large bags and containers, and it soon disappeared from view.

Frank and Eli looked at each other. And smiled.

"That's what the whistles were!" Eli said conspiratorially. They both hated the stupid food laws.

Frank sipped his brandy, his thoughts torn between his desire to retire and his sense of duty. But these food laws! Helping local food people to avoid repression—hell, his own niece was a big part of the farming movement—was more important than carrying out Morgan's orders. That man was a problem!

***

Federal legislation was rammed through the Republican Congress and signed by President Hutchinson giving the federal police legal standing to override local political authorities. But the Federal Police were so hated in San Francisco that sending them into the streets provoked surges of angry citizens. Perhaps more to the point, the Republican majority reverted to budget cutting after the profligacy of the Trump period and even the Federal Police endured major cuts. Republicans claimed they wanted to "balance the budget" even though their tax-cutting, along with the economic crisis, produced a massive decline in revenue. Given that the Hutchinson Administration was facing strong headwinds in next week's midterms elections, you might expect the government to engage in strategic spending, but somehow the political leaders fell into a competition to see who could pare the government back more.

Republican ideologues thought they could stay in power indefinitely, having removed electoral consequences through gerrymandering and a stacked judicial bench. No one expected the Republican majorities in the House and Senate to survive a legitimate vote—the Republican election plan involved targeted repression in areas where there were presumed competitive seats, forcefully trying to block voters with their vigilantes. If that didn't work, they were counting on their local federal judges to invalidate whole precincts, usually bastions of non-white voters. There was no electoral college when it came to congressional elections. Intervention had to happen in each state, and often in each local district. After years of Trump and Hutchinson judge appointments, especially in so-called "red states," there were plenty of partisan judges ready to throw out large numbers of "suspect" ballots from black, brown, and native precincts.

Democrats, who surprised everyone in 2022 by winning a near stalemate when they were expected to lose badly, were pessimistic about this year's midterms. Not only were they sharply divided between the rising progressive wing and the pro-corporate centrists, but their failure to deliver voting rights reform or even to codify abortion protections at a national level during the last two years of the Biden/Harris administration discouraged their voting base. The rapid increase in climate catastrophes, which might have propelled a new progressive majority into power ready to appropriately alter economic life, was still being treated as a series of surprising anomalies by the cable news punditocracy and its echo chamber in what remained of local and daily news sources.

Col. Morgan surveyed his desk. He finally had the legal latitude to pursue aggressive enforcement actions, but without a budget to back his bark, his enthusiasm for enforcing the food laws was gone. He relied heavily on the skEYE Systems drone surveillance to keep track of what was going on out there. But he knew the Federal Police lacked a good intelligence gathering network on the ground, which fed his suspicions that something was afoot. At least he wouldn't have to subordinate himself to the Mayor or the Police Chief if people started acting up again!

As far as he was concerned, the culture war was in its final days, the ascendant right having won decisively. Even though there were no big demonstrations since May, and that ridiculous "Festival of Possibilities" fizzled out, he still wondered what plots might be unfolding in the hidden corners of this left-wing city. Especially given the protection offered by local elected politicians, who when they *did* have the upper hand constantly let people get away with all kinds of subversive behavior!

***

Juna sat on Kite Hill, staring out at San Francisco's downtown in the distance. The little spot by the bushes was a familiar haunt for them. The two scrub jays continued to meet them there at dawn, whenever they got themself out of bed for the sunrise. They always brought the jays Witchips, and the birds usually brought a bauble of some sort in return, mostly plastic junk. During the past month, more and more birds were on the hill at dawn, mostly jays, but a few crows and gulls too. One time Juna almost felt claustrophobic when, shortly after sitting down, 30-40 crows came caterwauling down to settle on the hilltop. The birds pecked enthusiastically at the ever-expanding colonies of witches butter that were growing on Kite Hill. Juna clutched their knees to their chin and stared wide-eyed at the spectacle.

No bird ever again offered them back a WitChip like the time that led to the out-of-body vision of Dolores Park. Occasionally Juna offered a chip directly to one of the two birds they'd come to know, and waited to see if they'd return the gesture, but it hadn't happened. 'Was it coincidence? An accident that can't be repeated?' Juna pondered how to reproduce the experience. It had been as frightening as it was exhilarating and of course, they were dying to repeat it. But after months there hadn't been anything close. There was an unmistakable vibration while they sat on the hill, which fed Juna's sense of wonder and expectation. But no matter how hard they tried to project themselves into one of the birds, or imagine flying, or even blank their mind to make room for some other intelligence to move in, nothing happened. Whether they ate a lot of WitChips, or none, didn't make a difference.

'All this witches butter here!' thought Juna. 'How did it grow so fast?' They snagged a piece from a large colony along the path and tucked it into a shoulder bag. It was well past dawn as they walked back to the house. A few minutes later in the kitchen, Donald and Sarah sat with their two-year-old, Elsie, who was already in her faerie costume.

"Hey Juna, whaddya think of Elsie's Halloween costume?" Sarah asked proudly, as the little one did a twirl, excited to be a faerie.

"It's beautiful! What are you?"

"A faerie" she announced determinedly. "It's for Halloween!"

"Oh, nice! What happens on Halloween?" asked Juna.

The child looked a bit confused. Her father whispered to her "you go trick-or-treating." She tried to repeat it to Juna but garbled it. "I going treating!" she said.

They smiled and her mother hugged her.

"I hope you get a lot of treats!" Juna assured her. They looked at the *Opaque Times* on the kitchen table. "Is this the new issue?"

Donald nodded. "Finished last night. We're trying to decide if we should keep doing it. What do you think?"

Juna took in the front page's election recommendations, mostly focused on local races in San Francisco for Supervisor and the propositions. They flipped it open and saw a long article about the economic crisis, followed by a piece analyzing the Federal Government's fiscal crisis and the hollowing out of departmental bureaucracies. There was even a piece about the local Filipino community's reaction to the recent deal struck by the Philippine government with China. "Filipinos Confront New World: Is China #1?"

"It's a lot of work," they said diplomatically. "I mean, you still give people something that they're not getting anywhere else, right?" They saw it around the house but rarely read it cover to cover any more.

Donald acknowledged Juna's tepid response. "Sometimes it feels like we're going through the motions out of habit more than out of urgency or real need. Most of what we publish is stuff that has already been online. I don't think there are too many people around here who depend on it—certainly not like they did during the Emergency."

Julius came out of the basement stairs holding a stack of papers. "Hey, I heard that!" he glared around the room. If anyone was still strongly committed to the publishing project, it was Julius. "I thought we already discussed this last Friday?" he focused on Donald.

Julius stood there with his hands on his hips. He sighed, realizing that he was repeating himself and Donald already heard it. But maybe for Juna's sake, or even Sarah's. "I know that everything is online. But not everyone wants to read everything on a phone or a computer. And what's important is that we keep this resource alive. During the Emergency we protected the flow of information, and it could happen again. We've spent two years building up a production and distribution network, not to mention a donor base. If we shut it down, that'll be lost. I don't know if we'd be able to start it up again in the future, if we needed to."

Donald conceded that Julius had a valid argument. "But we can't spend much time and money on a hypothetical situation in the future. If it's not fulfilling a real need in real time, I don't see how we can keep going."

Julius could tell he was losing the battle. Even if he still felt energized, if too many people who kept the *Times* going were losing steam, he would eventually find it impossible to keep going. Even at every two weeks, it still depended entirely on volunteer labor for every part of its operations, from writing and editing, designing and printing, to distribution. It might be impossible to sustain.

"Donald we should talk about this at the next meeting again. I can tell you're not happy with the resolution we came to last time. And I'm growing weary of having to find a way to convince you and the others that it's worthwhile. If you can't see it, well, that may be enough of a reason to shut it down. But I would sure miss it!" he said wistfully.

"Is this true?" Juna suddenly asked, pointing at a paragraph in the article about the shrinking Federal government. "They're cutting back on Federal Police funding too?"

"We got that from the *Congressional Record*. I haven't seen it widely mentioned in the news, but yeah, it said that the Federal Police budget was cut by 20%. That's quite a hit, eh?" Donald wrote the piece. "And the EPA, the Dept. of Transportation, Dept. of Education, and Housing and Urban Development, cut by 35%! It's shocking! I guess they want to throw everything back to the states and let them do whatever they want to do. It's their Defederalization Project. What a mess!"

"And people continue to vote for the Republicans?" Juna seemed genuinely puzzled.

"Who knows? If they like the idea of shrinking the federal government. At this point, elections don't seem like they'll have much affect on what happens anyway. The blue states will vote Democrat, but there will be Republican majorities no matter what. They set it up to never lose, remember?" Julius said sourly. "At least we have some real choices in the local election. You gonna vote for Prop H?"

"That's the freeway take-down by Mission Bay?" Juna asked.

"Yup. And No on E, which is a giveaway to big real estate developers." And then Julius started babbling his recommendations for local races for Supervisor, School Board, BART board etc.

Juna backed away towards their room, hands in the air. "Got it, got it."

Donald watched Juna disappear and turned to Julius. "By now I'd think you'd have figured out that no one likes your election advice!" he scowled.

"Oh... yeah, well. I guess I know that... But I get excited! Sorry," and he took a copy of his paper and went off to his room, dejected.

CHAPTER 57
THURSDAY, NOVEMBER 26, 2026

Frank and Sheila were holding court in the Marlin Street living room. Eli Flores was with his very pregnant girlfriend Tanya on the couch. Lamar and Cindy were in the other chairs arrayed around the sprawling coffee table full of snacks and drinks.

"There are incredible delays throughout the system," Sheila was explaining to Cindy. "Most of the orders I placed in the last months have yet to arrive."

"How is that possible?" Cindy was experiencing the economic crisis through the influx of many more pets to the SPCA's facilities but knew little about the dislocations that Sheila was referring to.

"According to the suppliers that I reached, the government hasn't been paying its bills."

"Doesn't the Federal Government always have a 'checkbook of last resort'?"

"It used to work like that. But the Hutchinson administration promised to balance the budget no matter what. They put that cart before the horse. The tax cuts were rushed through before the insurance collapse last winter. When the markets tanked, the revenue the government thought they could count on dried up too. They didn't want to admit it publicly, so they carried on like nobody's business. Suppliers weren't getting paid so they stopped shipping. Cost of credit went up. Nobody would blink first."

Lamar listened intently. He'd learned from Frank's late-night ramblings that the Federal Police saw a major budget cut, too. "The government can't pay its bills? Is that why they're closing military bases?" In the first days after the midterms a few weeks earlier, when it was clear that Democrats, to everyone's surprise, eked out a narrow majority in the Senate, the Pentagon announced that it was carrying out Hutchinson's promised "strategic reset" and ending military leases on at least 250 smaller installations around the world, mostly in Africa, the Middle East, and southeast Asia. They claimed projected annual savings of $25 billion would ensue.

Janet came noisily through the front door. "Hey! Who got flooded this time?" she yelled laughingly. King Tides pounded Bay Area shorelines again this week, peaking each morning. Before noon, the last high tide rushed over the Embarcadero and flooded the road, lapping against the wall of sandbags protecting the MUNI tunnel.

Leon clattered down the stairs followed by Vero a minute later. His warehouse was surrounded by flood waters. "Tuesday, Wednesday, this morning— Luckily it didn't get in the building. But Underwood Street was under several inches for at least an hour. It's supposed to be over now, right?"

Janet nodded as she discarded her muddy boots and hung her jacket on the rack. Vero had a big box which she carried into the kitchen, returning a few minutes later with a platter of WitChips and dips. "You gotta try these," she waved at her display. Her enthusiasm ebbed when she saw Janet had turned her back to face the window.

"I thought you sold your recipes to BGM?" Sheila asked.

"Yeah that's right. But I can still make whatever I want to in my own kitchen!" she smiled. "These dips are new! And wait til you try my new soufflé!"

"Frank, did the shipyard flood again?" Janet, ignoring Vero, queried her silent uncle.

"Oh yeah. We built some sandbag levees, but groundwater gets pushed up through the pavement. Not enough to get into any buildings... yet! The horses get nervous when the water comes up, you can hear 'em stomping and whinnying."

Cindy turned to Frank. "Does water reach to their stable?"

"Yup. The whole area outside the buildings gets about two inches of water at the peak. It's nothing, but hard not to notice. We used some hay bales for the levee, too, but nothing has held very well."

The front door opened on Aaron and Greg. Aaron leaned heavily into his cane, and Greg, ten years younger, walked close by, ready to help if needed.

"Aaron!" Frank went over to hug him. "Been a while, big brother!" he teased. "Hey, why don't you take my seat?"

Greg smiled affably around the room as he poured drinks. "Happy Thanksgiving everybody!" he held up his wine glass to everyone he could see.

Sheila disappeared into the kitchen, followed by Janet. Linda and Rhonda were at the stove, cooking up a storm. The turkey was well on its way in the oven. "So," Sheila turned to ask Janet, "is Vero a millionaire now?"

Janet let out a sigh. "I don't know. She's gonna get a big payday... She probably got something already. We don't talk about it."

"No? How come?" Linda turned from the stove. "You guys have always been close." How many times did she and Rhonda speculate about a possible romantic connection between Janet and Vero? But it never happened as far as she knew.

"I'm pissed, that's why!" Janet's eyes flared. "I can't believe she sold out... and to BGM of all companies!"

The four women discussed the points of view that everyone already knew. Sheila and Linda were more sympathetic to Vero's decision, Janet and Rhonda decidedly less so. Then Vero entered the kitchen, trailed by Leon. They stopped talking at once, which made it obvious that they'd been talking about her.

"Um, I was gonna put my mushroom and witches butter soufflé in the oven. Is there room?" Vero tried to sound a normal note.

"The turkey is coming out in about 10 minutes. How long do you need?" Linda asked.

Before Vero could answer, Janet cut in. "Do you know that BGM is offering bounties to anyone bringing in five pounds of witches butter? People are digging everywhere. Most of 'em don't even know what they're looking for!"

Glaring at Vero she turned to her cousin Leon, who she knew was instrumental in egging on Vero to make the sale. "Did you think about that when you were going for the money? That you'd start a gold rush of randos plundering our community gardens? Have you even noticed?"

Leon looked confused. "What? I don't know what you're talking about!"

"Well, I'm telling you. There are prospectors hunting through community gardens and parks and hilltops, trying to find witches butter to deliver to BGM. And they don't know what they're doing! It looks like giant gophers have been at Palou, at Alemany Farm. You should see McLaren Park!"

"We didn't know Janet. How could we?"

"You don't know what a horrible company BGM is? Are you kidding me?

How can you be surprised by this?" she slammed her cup to the table and stormed into the backyard. Anger coursed through her, a rage she'd been holding back for days. She went through the back fence down to the remaining un-harvested marijuana plants. Instead of going all the way towards the Hangar hatch, she emerged from the billowing plants at the hill's edge. She sat down on an old stump to look across the toxic wasteland of Hunter's Point parcel E, and beyond it, Yosemite Creek.

Crows were harassing a redtailed hawk in the distance. She watched and wondered what the crows were defending. Her gaze moved towards the distant waters of the bay, where she was surprised to see several brown harbor porpoises leaping and swimming out in the bay not far from the edge of the park. A flutter of wings startled her into ducking, feeling that a bird was swooping right into her head, but she realized a crow landed a few feet away.

"What are you doing? Did you come to keep me company?" Janet murmured. The crow nodded and bobbed, turning this way and that, and then extending its wings before pulling them back in, and rocking its head to the side. It made a low throaty sound. "Are you trying to tell me something?" Janet was always ready to converse with a crow, or any critter that stopped to interact.

"Quake! Quake!" said the crow.

"What? What did you say? Did you say 'quake' like earthquake?!?"

"Quake!" and the crow nodded its head up and down several times. And then it flew away.

"Huh." Janet didn't think the crow was speaking to her, even though she'd been hoping one would speak to her again ever since that time at Alemany Farm. "Caw and quake, sort of similar…" she mused aloud.

Suddenly the ground trembled.

"It IS an earthquake! I can't fuckin' believe it!" she was grabbing the sides of the stump, holding on against the shaking. And after about 15 seconds, long enough for her heart to start pounding, it stopped.

She got up and rushed back to the house and into the kitchen.

"Did you guys feel that?"

"Oh hell yes!" Linda was smiling. "That was a good shaker! Haven't had one like that for a while. Hey Rhonda, put on the radio. Let's see what how big it was and where it was centered."

The news radio had some blather about Thanksgiving when she turned it on, but then after another couple of minutes a newscaster cut in. "We're interrupting this program with breaking news. An earthquake has hit the Hayward fault. Preliminary reports from the UC Berkeley seismic lab says it was a 4.2 on the Richter scale and the epicenter was east of Fremont. No serious damage or injury has been reported, but we'll be back as more news comes in. Again, a 4.2 earthquake on the Hayward fault hit at 3:13 pm."

Janet wanted to tell everyone about the crow, but once she was in the kitchen with Vero and Leon and her aunts, she felt too weird, having been angry a little while ago. Instead, she grabbed a glass of wine and returned to the living room. Everyone there was buzzing about the earthquake.

"That was intense!" said Aaron.

"Only 4.2 says the radio," Janet offered. "But it felt stronger than that. I was on the old stump in the lower garden."

"Oh yeah? Didja feel like you might go over the edge?" Frank asked smiling. He remembered when they moved his mom up here and they'd explored the big backyard stretching towards the shipyard. The stump was already a stump even then, decades ago.

"Nah, it was shaking and trembling. No sudden jolts."

"We thought that cabinet was gonna fall over!" Sheila pointed to a glass-doored cabinet. "But luckily it didn't."

"It's easy to forget that earthquakes are the most normal thing in the world around here," Janet said. Greg and Aaron nodded in agreement. Janet subsided into silence and listened as the conversation bounced around the room. She wanted to go out and see if she could find that crow again.

"What if that was a precursor shock?" Lamar asked. He looked a bit shaken up.

"Did you hear those dogs barking right before it happened?" Cindy asked. Nobody seemed to have noticed, and Janet couldn't remember hearing any.

"But a crow came and sat next to me," she said to Cindy. "I swear it said 'quake!' 'quake!' to me, right before the earthquake!"

"Oh yeah? It wasn't the usual 'caw, caw'?"

"No, it definitely said 'quake' twice and then a third time while nodding its head."

"Damn!" Cindy was the most sympathetic person in the room at that moment.

The kitchen door flew open and Vero came through, followed closely by Leon.

"Don't go, Vero!" He looked at everyone around the room, suddenly silent, watching. "Everyone's ready to have a nice Thanksgiving. You're family!"

Vero's face shifted between anger and grief, her eyes swelled and it looked like she might burst into tears. "I know when I'm not welcome! I'll leave you to it," and she threw her coat over her shoulders and left. Leon went after her but returned right away.

"What happened?" Lamar asked his cousin.

"Oh, she thinks everyone's judging her. Janet gave her—and me—some grief in the kitchen. She couldn't let it go."

Janet felt ambivalent. Vero was always part of their Thanksgiving, going back years. But what did she expect? Selling out to BGM! She reached for her wine glass and sipped it. Cindy and Frank and suddenly everyone was looking at her. "What? It's not *my* fault she sold out to BGM! I wasn't planning to say anything... but it happened." She leaned back, tired and unapologetic.

***

Vero couldn't believe it. Getting judged like that, after all she'd been through, and everything she'd done! She didn't have to apologize for making money! Fuck Janet, fuck 'em all! She angrily stomped down the street until she'd gone several blocks and realized that she didn't have a plan. She ordered a neighborhood MUNI autonomous car, which pulled up in three minutes. She hopped in and punched in "BART, 24th Street." A map appeared on the screen indicating that the car would take her to a bus stop on 22nd and 3rd where she could take the 48 bus to the BART station.

"How long's that gonna take?" she groaned. But they were on the way and there was no one to talk to or bargain with. Amazingly the bus was waiting at the corner as the little bubble-shaped AV pulled in the space in front of it and she was able to hop from one vehicle to the other without delay. She cooled down while riding the bus over Potrero Hill to 24th where she got off at Harrison. 'Now what?' It was Thanksgiving. Taquerias were open, but most of the restaurants were closed. She wasn't hungry anyway. Everything was empty. 'Everyone is having their meal,' she thought, noticing that it was a little before 4.

"Vero! Hey Vero! Is that you?" Two white guys were on the other side of the street, one of 'em waving at her. She turned to the voice, startled. They were approaching and it took her a moment to recognize Jay, who was a lot more muscular and well... big! She still remembered the skinny hippie dude she met at the Palou Terraces. A year ago, Jay and Jordan slept at the Hangar for a few nights after the hit squad tried to catch Jordan in the Castro, and she'd seen them then briefly, but she'd almost forgotten that.

"Jay? I can't believe it!" and she welcomed his hug.

"You remember Jordan? What are you doing? You wanna come with us? We're going to a big block Thanksgiving celebration, right around the corner from here."

"Um, well... you sure it'd be ok?"

"Oh yeah, it's the whole block. There's gonna be a lot of people." Jay seemed excited to drag her along, and what else was she going to do? Why not? Suddenly Jay stopped and spun. "Rita's there! Remember her?"

'Rita!' After their epic escape, they hadn't stayed in touch. They both went underground and never reconnected. "From our escape?" she asked in a low voice.

Jay nodded enthusiastically.

"I can't believe it!"

A few minutes later they found themselves in the backyard of the Folwell Commons, the block where Jay and Jordan installed graywater systems, composting toilets, and big rain catchment basins during the past few months. It was done now, along with the massive solar installations across the roofs of the block's participating buildings.

They entered through Philz coffeehouse at 24th and Folsom. The local chain was the last to join the Commons but once they did, they provided a public entryway into the shared backyards on occasions like this. Festive lights crisscrossed the area, and a towering windmill made of scooped blades soared from the vacant lot near the northwestern corner. Beneath it stood one of two white cubes that housed arrays of Hempatteries providing electrical storage and backup power to everyone in the block-wide Commons.

"Hey Yolanda! Happy Thanksgiving!" Jay called to his friend from the Pigeon Palace. She sat at the undulating table stretching from yard to yard, turning this way and that, in and under various trees and around three small ponds. There were place settings on each side of the long, long table, and there was already an incredible amount of food piled up in the middle. Other neighbors were still arriving, carrying their favorite holiday specialties from their kitchens. "Follow me!" Jay was trailing Jordan, who was moving adroitly through dozens of friendly neighbors, hailing them to join their part of the table.

"Jordan! You gotta try this cornbread!"

"Jay, I see you! This plate has your name on it!"

They smilingly pointed to the distance where they presumably were headed. Finally they'd traversed the full yard and made it to Rita's. She'd invited them, so they had to at least say hello before getting swallowed up in the party.

"Rita!" Jay called as she emerged from her garden apartment. She was dressed to the nines in a long green dress that hugged her big frame before flaring out into fluffy frills at the bottom hem. Her wavy red hair cascaded over her shoulders, making a nice contrast with the green fabric.

"Hey boys!" and she did a double-take when she saw Vero. "Vero!! Oh my god!" and she rushed over and grabbed her in a bear hug. Vero was dazed, finding herself immersed first in this sprawling neighborhood party, and then abruptly squeezed by Rita. They started laughing as they stood back and took each other in. Then they hugged again.

"I can't believe it!" Vero said sincerely. "I can't fuckin' believe it!"

"Honey, how'd you get here?" Rita put a drink in Vero's hands. "Never mind, it doesn't matter! I'm SO glad you're here!"

"Me too!" Vero confirmed. "An hour ago I stormed out of a family gathering, not knowing where I was going. And now I'm here!" She shook her head again, laughing. "I can't fuckin' believe it!"

"We have to catch up," Rita declared, "but I've been waiting for this party for months. Let's eat first."

They grabbed seats under the lights. The temperature was unseasonably balmy for a late November night. Now that it was dark it was cooler than during the afternoon, but a light jacket or sweater was plenty.

"Wow, what a feast!" remarked Jordan, as he heaped his plate with mashed potatoes, a turkey leg, green peas, cooked carrots, and some sweet potato pie. "You grow this here?"

"Yeah, the potatoes and peas and carrots. We have quite a thriving garden back here," Rita pointed to raised beds visible in the open spaces behind houses.

"When did you open this up? I never heard of anyone doing this," Vero was stunned by the luxury of the sprawling open park behind the whole block of buildings.

"It's been a project!" Rita admitted. She pointed to the fence not far from her own backyard area. "Those guys still haven't joined, and there's a few others too, but most of the neighbors are on board now. It took a lot of negotiating and a shit-ton of meetings!"

Jordan groaned, "Meetings!" but he was smiling as he downed another mouthful of food.

"Yeah, gotta talk through everything if you want to change things this much." Rita passed the mashed potatoes across the table.

They carried on for a while about the replumbing work Jay and Jordan did, as well as the remarkable Electricity Commons that was built, tying the neighbors together in a small cooperative association to generate, store, and share electricity.

"Just in time, now that the Federal government has stopped those Dept. of Energy grants they'd been promising, eh?" Yolanda, the Pigeon Palace resident, floated into their conversation.

Rita nodded, "Yeah, but luckily we got some money that was in the pipeline. And California put up some grant money too. I don't know how people can replicate this though. The national government... what the hell is going on anyway?"

Another neighbor leaned into the conversation. "The Hutchinson administration promised to shrink the federal government—I guess they didn't know how fast they would succeed!" he chuckled. "I know it's not funny, but who knows? Maybe it's for the best?"

Rita scowled. "Fred you're an idiot!"

Everyone could see that this was not a new conflict, and Fred took the cue and moved away, wrinkling his nose at Rita as he left.

Changing the subject, Yolanda blurted, "didja feel that earthquake this afternoon?" Everyone nodded, and stories popped out about seeing swaying chandeliers or bookcases nearly toppling over. "I had a dish fall down," Rita disclosed. "It wasn't that strong was it?"

Vero hadn't noticed any earthquake. She'd been in that MUNI car when it hit. "How big was it? I didn't feel anything." Quickly everyone moved on.

Political discussions dominated the next hour, with people taking sides on local politicians and statewide initiatives on the recent ballot. Somewhere down the table, voices were raised, yelling. A Filipino family was expressing cautious optimism about the recent diplomatic shift by the Philippines, embracing a deal with China. But a Chinese immigrant family who owned one of the houses on Folsom were virulently anti-communist and couldn't believe anyone would choose to work with the Chinese government instead of allying with the United States.

"Oh no! There goes Mrs. Wong again. She's one of the worst in our meetings. If she doesn't get her way, she starts yelling," Rita explained. "Vero, come with me," and she got up and took Vero by the hand, leading her back to her apartment.

"Bye Jay, Jordan! Thanks for bringing me," Vero called over her shoulder. They waved goodbye amiably.

In Rita's cozy garden apartment, they sat on her couch. "So..." and they went into the long catch-up conversation, detailing where they'd hid after splitting up, how long it had been until they'd been able to resume normal life, and how they ended up in their current situations.

"Even after the National Emergency ended, I still kept out of sight for a long time."

"You were in an underground cellar? Cooking with this fungus? Tell me more about that," Rita pushed.

Vero suddenly felt a bit overcome. Her sense of guilt and anger were compounded by the earlier confrontation with Janet, but she was also very proud of her accomplishment. Rita, who knew nothing about Janet's criticism, was an unbiased friend to whom she could pour out her whole story. And she did, starting with the odd experience of massaging and singing to the first batch of witches butter, and then experimenting with it in the kitchen last summer.

"The incredible thing is you can take some to cook with, and it grows back in a day or two!"

Rita remembered the first time she'd stood in front of Vero in the Camp Hayward barracks, wondering if she could trust her. Her pretty round face filled out a bit since then, and her brown hair was a lot longer too. They survived those months waiting at Camp Hayward, slowly expanding their circle of trust. And then their improbable escape in the UPS van, the safe houses, the surreptitious ride back to San Francisco. Why hadn't they tried to get in touch after that? She sighed.

"What?" Vero read the sigh as disapproval or .... what?

"Oh, nothing... Vero, why didn't we get in touch before this? For me, I wasn't sure how to reach you, but I didn't try either. I figured you were back in your previous life. After hiding until the Emergency was lifted, I had to find a job and a place to live."

Vero knew Rita was the camp stalwart. She wouldn't have made it out of there without Rita's daily strength, and her certainty that they *could* break out.

She leaned over and wrapped her arms around Rita. "You saved me," she said into her ear.

Rita returned the hug and had tears in her eyes when they separated. "We saved each other."

Vero wanted to share the rest of her story. "Have you heard of WitChips?" but Rita shook her head. "That's my most successful recipe," and she explained her trial-and-error process that landed finally on the chips and the pasta. She described the effort to make more product and get it around town.

"Maybe I did try it once. Someone brought some to the clinic." Rita worked at a nearby health clinic for the undocumented since she'd come out of hiding.

"Well, I sold the recipes—a few months ago! And now..."

"Who bought them? Are you rich?" Rita's eyes twinkled, happy for her friend.

"Um, well, BioGenMo actually. And yeah, I got paid."

Rita reached over and squeezed Vero's hand. "I'm happy for you!"

Vero looked at Rita, confused. Is that all? No guilt-tripping? No anger?

This was too easy. She almost felt disappointed that Rita wasn't more critical! Oh brother! She was getting herself discombobulated.

CHAPTER 58
TUESDAY, DECEMBER 15, 2026

The winds danced high at the upper edge of the troposphere, moving vaporized water briskly over the ocean far below. Wrapping around the entire planet, containing all the clouds, all the weather, shuffling between very warm near the earth's surface, and bracingly cold miles above it, the ever swirling winds held sway over the teeming life on earth. At any given moment it filled the lungs of trillions of living creatures, and then passed through the respiratory membranes of an even greater number of plants and trees, before being cycled back to the creatures as fresh air. Corporeality was unfamiliar to it, the narrowness of perception imposed by senses, skins, hides, or scales far too small for its expansive totality to pay attention to.

Volcanoes released smoke and debris from far inside the planet's core, spewing molten rock over surfaces, from isolated islands surrounded by the sea to snow-covered mountain ranges. Intricately interlocked masses of rock were perpetually on the move, grinding onto, above, and below each other, thrusting up hills and then mountains, in a process that crossed immeasurable time. At unpredictable moments, though, that inexorable movement would abruptly shake and jolt, moving things around on the surface, sending tsunamis across the oceans, changing the course of waterways, and altering the flow. And still, the winds soared above, within, and through everything that happened on earth.

Equilibrium was real. The winds know balance. Where it flows strongly in one area, another area is becalmed. Where the clouds burst and pour water and snow onto the surface, elsewhere it dessicates, sometimes for decades. For some time the equilibrium has been disturbed. Ancient forests burned, shrinking their size, altering the ebb and flow of aerial chemistry. Warmer and saltier sea water was changing the ancient patterns of ocean currents. The massive creatures of the sea, key to oceanic ecological balance, were decimated. When their populations plunged to near extinction decades ago, the winds' partner, the vast planet-encompassing oceans, began to falter. With the general heating, acidification, and destruction of life in the seas, the dance between wind and water was unalterably changed. Melting glaciers in mountains and at the poles would not be stopped.

But something stirred, almost like a diamond winking from a vast dunescape. The winds swirled, their curiosity piqued by the mystery. Something new appeared, groping to regain the balance. Here! Here, near the largest ocean, not far from old volcanoes and a growing desert, amidst a dense urban world full of humans and their *things*, it appears. It is different, new. It grows, it breathes, it *feels*. Somehow it *knows*. It seeks a new equilibrium. It dances and twirls, touching and reaching, connecting and cajoling. It seduces now... but later?

***

The line stretched a half a block from the BGM warehouse. Myra Rubin stood with her hands on her hips, glaring at the dozens of people waiting to turn in their haul of witches butter. Her new job with BGM was to work this intake table on 3rd Street, doling out certificates to anyone who brought in five pounds of clean, verifiable witches butter. She and Steve Healey were working together—neither of them too pleased once they fell into the routine.

"This is no different than working at Goodwill!" Steve lamented to her the other day. "Stand in the doorway, accept what people bring, and give them a slip of paper they can exchange for money or goods. Not what I thought we would be doing when we lined up in September!"

"Tell me about it!" Myra was ready to quit. She knew a dead-end job when she saw it. And this was a dead-end job. No biotech training, no career path, smile and drop a sample into the machine, wait for it to spit out its results, weigh the stuff and type in the number, then hand the receipt to the "client."

"What's this paper? I thought we got paid a bounty?" complained a woman dressed in several layers of worn clothes.

"You take this to Window B in the lobby, around the corner on Brannan, ok?" Steve repeated wearily. Everyone thought they could show up with any piece of this stuff and get $50! Of course there were rules and you had to have at least five pounds and it had to test right. And even then, BGM wouldn't hand you money on the spot. You had to register. You had to wait in a second line. Then, they tried to convince you to exchange your voucher for gift certificates for other products.

They'd both worked the lobby on Brannan too but volunteered to stay on the intake line. Working in there was worse! Big monitors featuring cheerful actors continuously pitched BGM products to everyone in the lobby.

"Intelligel*!! I don't know how I could've started my career without it!"

"I finished law school at night. I needed Intelligel* or I would've been fired!"

"Intelligel® gave me the extra edge—now I'm a programmer!"

"Oh brother!" Myra groaned when they saw the set-up. "They think poor people will waste their vouchers on this shit?" she shook her head in disgust.

"Hey," Steve gave her a friendly elbow in the ribs, while pointing to the other monitor. "They could 'invest' in a Hempattery installation!" and he laughed. The other monitor was running an extended informercial about the advantages of stand-alone electricity storage for each home, and how the Hempattery technology was the most affordable and reliable. "I guess you can't blame 'em for tryin'!" But they both knew that none of the 'bounty-hunters' bringing in witches butter were likely to have the middle-class resources or aspirations that these products were designed for.

Back at the intake line, a gaunt young man stepped up. He hung his head and slumped his shoulders, probably learned at an early age, to try to shorten his 7-foot stature and be more like everyone else. He had thick black eyebrows and sunken eyes over a prominent nose. "What do you know about this stuff? I never heard of it before this," as he handed over a burlap sack with a slab of witches butter. They cut a piece to run the sample while they weighed it. Myra registered him while Steve measured the fungus.

Steve was curious that he even asked the question. "I don't know much more than you do my friend. It's a new fungus, and BGM has plans for it. They're making chips."

"Chips? Computer chips?" the guys eyes widened.

Steve laughed. "No, no! At least I don't think so!" and he paused, realizing that maybe it wasn't such a crazy question after all. I mean, the chips they'd tasted were fine, but... why *would* they hire people and solicit bounty-hunters if it was only for a potato chip?

He looked at the gaunt fellow, and spoke hurriedly, "I hadn't thought about that—maybe you're on to something."

As the guy took his voucher and departed, Steve leaned over to Myra, "Did you hear that? That guy asked if they were making *computer* chips!"

She looked at him blankly. "And?"

They went back to the line and kept processing the rest of their shift. But Steve's mind was spinning. That *had* to be it. This wasn't for edible chips, it was for computer chips! If this company already made the Hempattery, why wouldn't they try to make a biological chip? But what did he know? And how could he find out?

***

Dat Doan sat in the back corner of the restaurant on Folsom. It was a forgotten Mexican place, rarely crowded, near the high school.

A woman entered, stopping to look around. It wasn't what she expected. The guy sitting in the shadows at the back waved his arm discreetly. She pulled off her hood as she approached, her black locks cascading out and over her shoulders as she shook her head free. "I guess you're the guy?"

Dat nodded slightly. "You are Vanessa? Vanessa Wright?" She sat across from him.

Vanessa acknowledged her name. "You're the famous biohacker, eh?" She looked at the older Asian man with messy salt-and-pepper hair falling over the side of his face, his crooked yellowed teeth giving him an aura of poverty. His blue flannel shirt looked well worn too. "I was part of that crew that smuggled out the witches butter to you... what was that, three years ago now?"

"Oh yeah? I didn't meet you back then." He wasn't entirely sure she could be trusted. She contacted him through trusted intermediaries, true, but then, after the craziness at Larry's place in Brisbane, and then Vero's BGM deal, he was wary. What was BGM up to now? The chip business didn't seem plausible, at least it couldn't be their main goal. This woman might be legit, or she might be here to see what she could shake out of Dat that might help them.

"I know my colleague Dennis Swintin is the one who fingered Alison Nakahara to BGM security. I told him that was a fucked up thing to do. But he figured she was another rich techie who left to launch another start-up and it couldn't hurt anyone."

Dat was surprised. "Yeah, well, we're lucky no one got hurt. It seems your employer—"

"Let me cut to the chase. I still have my job, and we still have our network inside BGM. We learned about them hiring skEYE Systems mercenaries to seize supplies at a place in Brisbane. I won't ask if you were part of that. I don't care. I hate BGM more than I can say. I was delighted to hear that it was a complete fiasco. Those skEYE Systems people are idiots... Like most security people and a lot of contractors... But anyway, that's not why I asked to meet you. Our folks in the research labs sent us a surprise. I thought you should know."

Dat raised his bushy gray eyebrows expectantly. "Go on..."

"They're trying to get all the witches butter they can, not to make WitChips. I mean, yeah, they're going ahead with a small production facility to manufacture those too. But BGM thinks they can create a biological network, building on witches butter."

"A biological network? What does that mean?" Dat was all ears.

"In the lab they've coaxed witches butter into flat panels that roll up, and when unrolled, they can display text and some limited images."

"What?" Dat was astounded. "How'd they manage that? Does it connect to existing networks? How?" His mind was racing, the questions poured forth.

"I don't have the technical details. I don't know how far advanced this is. It sounds like they've done some successful experiments. I don't know if they've figured out how to link the fungus to wired devices. But they are trying to corner the witches butter supply. Whatever you and your friends can do to spread it far and wide the better. Make it impossible to monopolize!" She sat back and folded her arms, looking intently at Dat. "You have always been a step ahead. Me and my associates are hoping you'll do it again!"

"Do you think you can get me any of the studies, or even better—one of the new panels they designed? It would make it a lot easier to understand what's going on if we can reverse engineer it."

"It's locked up in their most secure lab in Mission Bay. I'll see what I can do. Meanwhile, can you get your people working this from your end? It's urgent!"

"The League is already protecting common supplies. Not sure how far it's gotten yet, but I can find out and let you know."

Vanessa nodded as she leaned into the table. "Good. We'd like that."

Dat rubbed his eyes and stifled a yawn. "You ought to know. And this is NOT to be spread around at BGM, ok?" She nodded affirmatively, her eyes widening in anticipation. "Research we did a few months ago points to the witches butter being intelligent. We think it may have its own agenda, but we can't say what it is."

"You can't say, or you don't want to?"

"We can't say. There's no way to tell. But we have identified a few anomalous experiences, events, and even unprecedented qualities shown by the fungus. It has confused us, and we're not completely certain by any means. One of my colleagues is convinced that it is an 'alien intelligence.' She's got me convinced too," he smiled.

"That's wild! What does that even mean?"

"We can't predict what it will *be* in the future—the near future! It's changing all the time, and it seems to be absorbing knowledge with stunning speed. It has adapted to different conditions *and different people* in ways that are hard to explain. It's not like any organism or species we've seen before."

"But what do you think it could do? Are you saying it has willpower? Do you think it could have malevolent intentions?"

Dat burst out laughing. "Malevolent? No, that seems unlikely. On the contrary," and he sighed deeply. "If I was trying to describe it purported intentions, I'd call them benevolent, or constructive, or ... *unifying*?" He shook his head. "Saying these things out loud, sounds as ridiculous to me as it does to you—let's say it makes me uncomfortable."

"Uncomfortable? Because it sounds hokey?"

"Sure, of course. But honestly, I find it difficult to suggest anyone—or anything—is acting out of benevolence—and hell, we're talking about a fungus! How could morality be involved? How would it be able to tell one human from another, one set of behaviors from another? How could it perceive complex human society? Does it perceive time and space the way we do? That seems very unlikely. In light of what we've learned, it doesn't make sense!"

Vanessa listened with a wry smile. "I see why it makes you uncomfortable. Why project any knowledge, feelings, or intentionality into the existence of this fungus? What is the basis for that?"

"It has changed how a bunch of us feel. It might be changing how we *know*. That's where our research and discussions have been pointing. I'm telling you this because what you told me about the new BGM effort shocked me the same way our own work has. I'd like to know more about how they designed the panels, how they got it to 'work.'"

"Hmmm," Vanessa sat pondering. "Do you think the flat panel project could be finding a way to use the so-called intelligence of the fungus? Could the researchers have tapped something?.. found a way to communicate?" She was thinking out loud.

"Look Vanessa." Dat sat bolt upright, gesturing to a white van that pulled up in front. "I hear you about the urgency. What you've told me—our research is even more urgent than we knew." Workers got out of the van and Dat relaxed a bit. "Let's meet up again next week and see what we've each been able to do in the meantime, ok?"

Vanessa agreed. She started towards the door and when she looked back to see if Dat was following, he was gone. 'Must be in the bathroom,' she figured, and she strode away down the street.

***

Vero trudged through Dolores Park. It was a sunny day, but a brisk wind came rushing over the hills, tempering the sunshine with its biting cold. Rain was predicted in a day or two. The warm weeks gave way to the winter light stretching from the south, and the suddenly cold air felt right. It was mid-

December after all. Hands firmly in her warm pockets, she was looking at the ground, deep in thought. She made it past the big palm tree and the Hidalgo statue, turning left to traverse the top of the park.

She could smell it. Witches butter filled her senses emanating from the ground. Loud cawing from the bushes startled her, echoed by even more jays in the trees across the streetcar tracks. She saw a few blue scrub jays on a nearby bush. Swooping overhead came another half dozen jays, angrily dive-bombing a couple who were down the slope near the tracks. They threw up their arms, yelling at the birds, dropping sacks they'd been holding.

Vero's curiosity was piqued. She moved slowly towards the people buzzed by the jays. As she drew closer it was suddenly obvious: they were digging for witches butter on the steep slope pock-marked full of small holes among the shrubs and trees! She'd heard about it at Thanksgiving from Janet, when she was angry.

"What are you guys doing?" she asked with a slight edge in her voice. Witches butter growing in Dolores Park? Alongside the J-Church streetcar?

"We're hunting for witches butter. BGM is paying $50 for every five pounds!" The woman explained to Vero, rocking to keep her balance on the slope. She had a big winter coat on and held a small trowel in one hand and big burlap sack was tied to her belt under her coat, dragging behind her.

"You found it here?"

"Other people got here before us." She looked like she walked out of a 19th century landscape painting of the Russian countryside.

Her buddy suddenly yelped. "Got a patch!" and he pulled up a chunk of white-ish fungus. Vero looked on unbelieving. How had witches butter spread here? Was someone planting it?

A dozen jays landed around them. Vero had the unmistakable sense that they were looking at her, expecting her to do something. 'That's crazy!' she thought as she put her hands on her hips.

"This is a public park, you know!" she said half-heartedly.

"Yeah, and *we're* the public!" grinned the woman conspiratorially. She looked at Vero and realized that maybe she wasn't with them. "You got a problem?" she growled.

Vero was confused. She had the sense that the jays were egging her on, wanting her to put a stop to this harvesting. Or maybe it was something else pulling on her. There weren't voices in her head, exactly, but she saw the birds nodding and bobbing around them in her peripheral vision. Somehow it was clear that she should convince these people to stop digging.

"I know times are tough. But digging up the parks makes everyone's life worse." She tried to elicit their sense of responsibility.

"Hey lady, mind your own business. Every park in town is fair game. Besides this isn't even the park—it's the MUNI! This stuff is growing everywhere! And Rec & Park won't dig it up. We're doing a public service!"

Vero couldn't muster a rejoinder. She sold her recipes to BGM, how could she criticize these folks for trying to make a few bucks themselves? But she felt slightly nauseous.

The jays saw that Vero was giving up and walking away. They flew up and circled around the diggers, cawing wildly, swooping down to harrass them. The dive-bombing got to them. Suddenly a dog began barking loudly behind them. Vero reached the sidewalk above the slope when a large shaggy dog plunged over the side and rushed the prospectors.

"Hey, hey!" yelled the woman, stumbling back from where she'd been standing, trying to gain her balance as she tripped and slid to the bottom. The man was right next to her. The dog's owners came running to the edge of the sidewalk above, calling their dog, but the animal wasn't responding. It barked fiercely, standing over the area where the two were digging, staking it out as its own territory. The birds continued swirling above, no longer dive-bombing once the people moved on.

Vero stood marveling. The smell was overwhelming. She had to sit down at the edge of the sidewalk as she suddenly felt a bit dizzy, one hand in the dirt supporting her. The vibration coming into her hand was palpable, and she withdrew it in surprise.

"What the hell?" she muttered, folding her legs into the slope. It seemed the entire slope was vibrating, sending tremors into her legs. She scrambled to pull her legs to the sidewalk and then the sensation stopped. She touched the ground again and the telltale vibration shot up through her palm, her arm, her shoulder and into the base of her neck. She pulled her hand back and it stopped. Her curiosity overwhelmed her momentary dizziness and she carefully stepped down the slope towards the dog, calmer now that the people moved up the tracks. The owners, a young couple, finally managed to get their dog to return to their control.

"Sorry about that!" said the woman, clad in skintight athletic gear with earbuds and her device hanging around her neck. "I hope she didn't frighten you."

"No problem, didn't bother me. Those other folks up there," gesturing to the two prospectors dragging their burlap sacks up the tracks, "might have been scared." Vero waited til the dog left and then proceeded down to the spot. She peered into the holes and reached towards a white-ish area. It was definitely witches butter. She knew that sensation well, but it was different here. It was charged, wild and ... it was hard to put in words. She grabbed witches butter all day long for a year, cutting it up, baking it, stewing it, and eating it. If anyone had digested more than she had... but here it wasn't like it had been in her kitchen. It felt more alive, it vibrated, it held her attention.

"What do you want from me?" she asked in a low voice. There was no response. She needed to help somehow. But how?

CHAPTER 59
MONDAY, DECEMBER 21, 2026

On Monday morning of Christmas week, bad news shocked the world. A huge glacier in Antarctica was sliding into the sea! Eli was reading the headlines on his computer.

"We are fucked! What kind of world will my daughter live in?!?" he sounded genuinely despairing. His baby was born on December 8 and he was back from his short parental leave.

Frank peered at the screen. "Ain't we supposed to have King tides this week already? On top of this crazy rain?"

"Yeah, starting tomorrow through the day after Christmas—King tides every morning! And they say this is another atmospheric river, bringing heavy rain and snow at least through Christmas. But look at this! This is one of the biggest glaciers in Antarctica, the Thwaites glacier. It's losing 2-3 kilometers a day into the sea! Holy shit!"

The Thwaites Glacier, thought to be safe for decades to come behind a vast ice shelf floating over the ocean, was on the move. Weeks of soaring temperatures at the south pole was begun breaking up the ice sheet. The glacier, held in place by the sea ice like a cork in a bottle, was sliding into the southern sea. They stared mesmerized at the footage of an incalculable catastrophe unfolding.

"I knew Greenland was melting, but I though Antarctica was gonna be ok until 2100 at least!" Frank exclaimed. During the past three years in Greenland trillions of tons of ice disappeared into the North Atlantic. "What's this gonna do to the King Tides? You think it'll come up even more?"

"Fuck if I know! But yeah, probably. Do we need to do something?" Eli looked a bit stricken as he turned to face Frank. "I ought to move to the East Bay, up the hill!"

"There's a bunch of places up on the hill near my place. We ain't gonna flood up there, that's for sure!"

"Probably not. But what about that toxic shit over there," he nodded towards parcel E to the south of their office. "You think you're safe from that up there?"

"Oh yeah, I s'pose so. I've been living around here since I was a kid, and I'm ok." Frank didn't mention the dozens of people he knew who died of various cancers or heart disease over the years. His own heart wasn't perfect he knew, but the doctor always told him it was hypertension. 'Goes with the territory, being a cop,' he figured.

"Is there anything from Col. Morgan about preparations for the king tides this week?" Frank asked Eli.

"Nothing yet, but it's early. We could get a notice any minute."

Surging tides and upwelling groundwater flowed over low-lying areas with increasing frequency but the bay waters always receded to the familiar shoreline. Hunter's Point was covered with water a half dozen times in the past year, but it never lasted.

It was more dramatic in Florida, in Louisiana and Texas, and around the Chesapeake Bay. Washington DC was hit by high tides repeatedly in the past year. It was much worse in Bangladesh, in Pakistan, and dozens of islands that were clamoring for relief, demanding in some cases that their entire populations be evacuated immediately!

The Hutchinson Administration remained silent. Events far from home were not its concern. Federal relief efforts were focused on Florida and Texas, for political reasons, but also to defend the expansive oil and gas infrastructure around the Gulf coast. Since flooding became routine around the Chesapeake Bay and the tidelands of Virginia, the Federal Emergency Management Agency's already exhausted resources were completely depleted trying to harden the shorelines stretching along the eastern seaboard. Federal insurance for property owners in flood zones was canceled during the National Emergency. It hadn't been noticed until the 2025 hurricanes devastated several areas in Florida, the Carolinas, and the along the Gulf Coast. Lawsuits were ongoing, but after another year that saw seven Cat4 or Cat5 hurricanes slam into the U.S., literally millions of refugees migrated away from the coastlines to await federal help that would never come. Federal spending concentrated on either fossil fuel infrastructure or military bases where storm damage had been severe and expensive.

"They're moving the horses!" Frank watched the rain pour outside. Eli came over to join him.

"I guess they're preparing, eh?" He watched as the horses, nervous, stomping and whinnying, were led onto livestock trucks, Sergeant Craig and his troops helping to calm their horses while the transfer was taking place.

Eli's phone buzzed with a message.

"Here it is, Morgan's orders. 'Sandbag the buildings. Skeleton crews only to report this week. Everyone not on skeleton duty is furloughed for the week. Return to duty next Monday.' Well, that's it then! I'm outta here!" Eli pulled his things together as Frank watched.

"Oh, I almost forgot." Frank opened his drawer and pulled out gifts. "Sheila and I got these for little Liliana."

"Aw, Frank, thank you! That's very kind. And thank Sheila too!" who had obviously bought the baby presents. "I guess we should check in before next Monday then?"

**

Vero nursed her coffee, sitting at the window of the mezzanine at Larry's. How many months had she worked 10-12 hours a day here, ramping up production of her Witchips? And now it was over. She stared out at the pouring rain. Low-lying mist and fog obscured the view beyond the nearby eucalyptus trees. Something was tugging at her for several weeks, slowly taking shape after her serendipitous Thanksgiving encounter with Rita. Her long walks in the hills dismayed her when she saw the damage done by untold numbers of people digging for witches butter.

'Fuck BGM!' she thought. She decided to sell them her inventions, to cash in, but she regretted it now. And she was puzzled by the efforts of BGM to acquire as much witches butter as possible. Were they going expand production? Restless, she finished her coffee and put the cup into the dishwasher.

Larry was sitting across the way, studying something on his computer.

"Hey Larry!" Vero walked up to him. "You seen Angie lately? Or been up the hill?"

"Nope. She hasn't been back. The last time I was up there was months ago."

"But they're still there, right?"

"Far as I know," and he returned to his computer.

Vero was soon slipping in the muddy leaves as she climbed the slope behind the warehouse. She crossed the quarry road to the mini-water temple and stood there trying to remember where the path to Angie's was. Two crows cawed loudly which drew her attention to the spot, under their tree. She climbed to the lip of the clearing where Quarrytown stood while the crows made a racket. Vero was looking straight at a cluster of round, mottled huts. It took a good long moment for her eyes to focus on them and see them. They were perfectly camouflaged. Lacking any straight lines or edges, it was easy to not see them at first! The camping chairs sitting around the fire pit, getting soaked in the rain were what drew her attention.

Angie's head appeared in the window of the nearest hut, her ruddy red-dish face surrounded with graying curls wrapped in a red bandana. "Who are you?"

"Oh! Hi! Remember me? I'm Vero, Vero Gomez. We met a year ago when we came to visit your hut, remember?"

"Aren't you the cook? The one who invented the WitChips and those other recipes?"

Vero nodded sheepishly.

"Well, get in here girl! It's raining!"

Vero gratefully entered Angie's home.

"Put your wet stuff there," Angie pointed to a coat rack and shelf for shoes and boots.

"Wow, it's cozy in here!" Vero felt like she'd entered a den. The ceiling light cast a warm yellow glow. Books and magazines overflowed from curving shelves built into the wall. Open windows let the cold winter air in but athe hut remained well-heated and perfectly comfortable.

Angie tapped the wall. "Got a nice thing going." She grinned. "Have a seat," she pointed to a chair by a small table. "What brings you here, especially in this rain?"

Vero sighed deeply as she sunk into a seat. She felt something letting go, and tears welled in her eyes. "Angie! I made a big mistake!" And she proceeded to pour out her story about selling to BGM and her regrets. "I finally realized it when I was in Dolores Park last week," and she told her about the holes in the slopes dug by prospectors, motivated by BGM bounties. "I've heard there are people digging on hills, in gardens, even in public medians."

"This stuff is actually growing in those places?" Angie asked.

Vero shrugged. "Dunno. People are desperate and trying everywhere. Have you had people coming around here?"

"Here? No, not prospectors anyway. There was a horse patrol that passed by one day last month, but they didn't find us." She winked and looked be-mused. "I'm pretty sure we're protected."

"What do you mean?"

"You heard those crows when you showed up? We have a lot of help. Sometimes it's the coyotes up the hill who give us a warning. Sometimes it's the crows. I even think the trees are helping. I was waiting for that patrol to come clomping in on the trail, but they went the other way. When I went to check it out after they'd gone..."

Angie paused. Vero joined her at the window in time to see Juna standing in the door of the hut across the clearing, pulling on their pants and shirt. Behind them was a man she didn't recognize, and a second guy appeared in the window. Moments later Juna came scampering through the rain and into Angie's.

"Hey Vero! It's been... how long? Months I guess!"

Juna explained how they quit their job at the SPCA. "Hard times, y'know? People can't afford to feed pets. I never expected things to get this bad, but...I couldn't take it." Juna explained why they'd come to Quarrytown. "I met those guys," they gestured to the other hut, "down below in September and I brought 'em up to meet Angie. It worked out and they've been here ever since."

"Bennie and Reggie have been a huge help!" Angie confirmed. "I'm glad they moved in. And you too Juna!" she gave them a playful punch in the arm.

Vero got the vibe.

Vero resumed, "I was telling Angie about my remorse," she said to Juna. "I want to help defend witches butter in the wild. And it seems like Quarrytown might be the best place to do that?" she ended in a question.

"We have a seed bank here," Angie confided. "But this stuff is different. I am happy to help protect it. Our best protection has been our invisibility. Very few people even know we're out here, and those who do are our friends."

"I don't know if protection is the best way to think about it," Juna offered. "What if we spread it around as much as we can? Help it start in lots of places? Don't you think we can go faster and farther than those prospectors?"

"Yeah, maybe. But what if BGM keeps paying for as much as they can get? Won't that get more people prospecting?"

"You know anybody working at BGM?" Angie asked, "Are they really using it to make WitChips?"

"Yes! I've been wondering that too." She looked out at the relentless rain. In their silence, the tingling they each felt from the hut and the surrounding colonies of witches butter became quite noticeable. "What else could they be using this for?" The biobulbs in the ceiling blinked twice, and then stayed on.

Angie laughed. "The hut thinks you asked the right question!"

***

Alison Nakahara sat at her window in the Brisbane facility, staring out at the pouring rain. She watched Vero head up the slope. 'What is she up to?'

she thought for a moment. She tried to stop thinking about the indigestible evidence that witches butter was somehow sentient. It nagged her from time to time, the whole experience of seeing her biobulb fuse with Angie's butter hut and 'turn on' at her request.

Now they had a roomful of witches butter in the warehouse growing up two walls where they tested biobulbs after harvesting. The two bioengineered 'products' worked together synergistically, that was undeniable. But how? They couldn't figure out the mechanism by which the bulb was triggered to turn on and off. How did the fungus provide the energy to sustain its illumination?

Maria was focused on the biobulb-witches butter connection. She harvested biobulbs when they were fully mature and pushed them into holes that served as 'sockets' in the wall of witches butter. She spoke to the bulb as she placed it, explaining that it would be working together with the fungus. "You are welcome," she said softly to each bulb. "Please make light," and sure enough, they'd begin to glow along their inner filaments, casting ever brighter light as you left them 'on.' "OK, thank you. Turn off now," and the lights went out. It was impossible to explain scientifically. It frustrated Ally enough that she walked away and left it to Maria to figure out.

Ally refocused on the bioboat. She and Clara produced several clones from the original mother plant and they had a roomful of canoe-shaped 'fruits' growing from the half dozen plants. Combining genes from tule reeds with gourds and then crossbreeding for size and shape, the project made great strides, especially since arriving in Brisbane. The plants had become thick-trunked, and the roots spread through the openings they'd built in the floor, and into the ground beneath the warehouse.

Meanwhile, the bioboats had come along nicely, with the hollow tubes derived from the tule genes making up the body of the much expanded gourds. The key breakthrough came when they produced the boat-like shape they were trying for. The natural buoyancy that the air-filled tubes provided made the bioengineered vessels float beautifully. The problem was propulsion and direction. The fins were in place at front and back to 'push' one way or another. A rudder-like flipper was generated from the connective fiber to the main stem. Once separated, or harvested, it should serve as a steering rudder. But controlling it was still elusive. As was figuring out how to stimulate propulsion when needed.

Clara came into her office still wearing her sopping wet raincoat and woolen cap.

"Ally! There's a bioboat out back!" she was excited.

"What? What're you talking about?"

"The roots are growing a lot faster and further than we knew. I found a vine with a small bioboat starting at the edge of the property out back. There's a big colony of witches butter back there too."

Ally was taken aback. This was very unexpected. Their work in the past weeks was focused on harvesting two or three of the mature bioboats and testing them near Candlestick Point. The first test proved that the bioboat was seaworthy and stable in the calm waters at the State Park. The flippers were sturdy but getting them to 'go' was a hurdle they'd still have to cross. The nodule inside the rear of the boat was supposed to be the controller of the rudder, but nothing they did, no prodding or poking, would produce any results.

Maria's boyfriend Jessie was the test pilot.

Alison was poring over her studies. The anatomy seemed right, but how to make it function properly? Would it be controllable by a human sitting in the back of the boat? The first experiment was not promising.

"We have to get out on the water again, but not in this rain. When is it supposed to end?" she demanded. She could've looked it up herself but she was accustomed to having her colleagues answer her random queries.

Clara pulled up the forecast. "Rain through Christmas at least. And King Tides starting tomorrow!"

"Dammit! That's the perfect time to get out there. But not in this rain." She poured herself a coffee at the little counter, continuing to mutter about the weather. "Clara," she whirled around. "Let's take a break!"

Clara looked at Ally, astonished. She never expected to hear her workaholic boss make a suggestion like that. "What?!?"

"It's Christmas week. We've been burning it at both ends for months. Nonstop rain means no field testing. I'm sick of trying to fix this on the computer. We need to work it in the real world. Let's take a few days off. Recharge our batteries, maybe we'll think of something?"

Clara was amazed. This was the most sensible thing Ally proposed in a year or more. Moving to Brisbane was a huge improvement. She was as obsessed with this as Ally was, but taking a break was always a good idea—especially at an impasse like this one. "You don't have to ask me twice! I'm SO ready for a break. Shall we shut down everything until next week?"

Ally obviously hadn't considered that. "Um, well, sure I guess so. You wanna talk to Maria and the crew?" Her phone buzzed. It was Dat Doan. He wanted to meet as soon as possible. Why would he want to meet her suddenly? "Do you know anything about what Dat Doan has been up to lately?" she asked Clara.

She shook her head, "Nope." Before Ally could enlist her any further, she left the office to seek out Maria and let her know about their week off. Clara felt hugely relieved to have a break. She decided to go back to Arizona and get the hell out of this crazy rain.

CHAPTER 60
THURSDAY, DECEMBER 24, 2026

Ally pushed her way into Dat Doan's warehouse in the Bayview. He'd been texting her for several days, but she'd been reluctant to rush over, being quite preoccupied with her own work. They'd shut down operations for a week in Brisbane, and after days at home, alternating between staring at her computer trying to puzzle through the next steps for the bioboat, or blankly staring out her window at the incessant rains outside, she decided to visit Dat after all.

She hailed a MUNI Autono (the nickname of the little all-electric autonomous bubble vehicles) and it dropped her at his door at 10 o'clock. It was the morning of Christmas Eve but she figured Dat would be working. They shared the same obsessive drive. She exited the vehicle into several inches of water. The little vehicle sped away through the rising tide.

"Shit!" She had been in her place on Potrero Hill for two days while the King Tides, amplified by the unexpected Glacial Pulse, had rolled in, swamping many low-lying parts of the city. Dat's place had a three-step landing to the door, which kept the water out. Her feet squished as she pushed through the swinging glass door.

"My shoes are soaked!" she announced to an empty front counter under a neutral sign across the wall "Doan Industries: Import and Export". She slapped a bell to announce her presence.

A heavily tattooed woman with spiky green hair appeared. "Oh, hey, we weren't expecting anyone today. Can I help you?"

Ally saw a younger version of herself living a very different life and was briefly tongue-tied. "I'm looking for Dat. He wanted to see me. I'm Alison Nakahara."

The young woman's eyes flickered slightly at the name. Did she recognize her?

"Wait here," she said perfunctorily and disappeared. A minute later Dat was there.

"Ally! Thank you for coming! Follow me!" and he led her on a circuitous route through box-filled rooms, biohazard labs, and computer stations, finally ending in a windowless meeting room. "Sit!" he commanded, which made Ally bristle.

"What's going on Dat? What's this about?"

From a box on the floor he pulled out a tan-colored tube and put it on the table.

"BGM didn't buy Vero's recipes to make WitChips," he declared. "Look at this." He unrolled the tan tube while Ally watched attentively. A tan rectangle sat on the table between them. "This is a BGM prototype that I got my hands on. It's a flat panel biological communications device made from witches butter."

Ally stared at the panel. It was blank and gave no sign of being anything but an inert shape. "How does it work?"

"We're trying to figure that out. We haven't gotten it to go. We only have one, which might be part of the problem. It may take at least two to establish communication."

"How do we know it works? What communication is it supposed to be able to do?"

Dat explained what he'd learned a week ago from Vanessa Wright. He didn't describe how he got it. "It's supposed to display text and basic images. We haven't been able to generate anything since we got our hands on it. I was hoping maybe you'd be interested?..."

Ally sat very still. She knew this was BGM property and that they would be frantically trying to recover it. But what if it worked? Was this the latest surprise to emerge from her original research on this fungus? This was hers too! Excited curiosity overwhelmed her as she reached for the panel. Taking it into her hands, a tingling vibration entered her hands and she inhaled sharply, surprised at the sensation.

"It's vibrating!"

Dat watched her closely.

She turned the panel in her hands and ran her fingers along the edges. "How do you work? No buttons or ports? No wires..." She glanced at Dat and turned back to the device. "It's getting warmer!" and she put it down.

Dat touched it. "Whoa! It's alive!"

Ally peered closely at it.

"O-F C-O-U-R-S-E I A-M A-L-I-V-E"

She almost fell backwards as the letters appeared across the middle of the panel. Dat rushed around the table to see better. When he read the words he stammered, "I.. I... I... you... you..."

Ally cut in. This was a prank. "Who are you? Where are you?" she demanded, angry at falling for this. She was talking to a slab of witches butter!

"E-V-E-R-Y-W-H-E-R-E"

"Who—or WHAT are you?" Dat blurted. "Are you the fungus?"

"L-I-F-E"

Ally and Dat looked at each other, baffled and speechless.

Hard knocking on the door. "Dat!" It opened a crack and the green-haired woman peered in. "We gotta go! The tide is much higher than anyone expected! Water is coming in the front door!"

"Ally! Can we go to your place on the hill?!" and he shoved the panel into her hands as they rushed through the flooding warehouse towards the front door.

"C'mon! We can take my van!" Dat yelled as he rushed. The few people working the day before Christmas fell in behind them. They piled into the Doan Industries van, the rising waters below the threshold.

"It's supposed to peak before 11 a.m., but this is ridiculous!" the young woman complained.

One of the lab jockeys was pressed against the window in the back, staring at the swirling waters around them. "This is a lot higher than any previous King Tide," he sounded panicky. "Is this the Glacial Pulse they were predicting?"

Another of Dat's guys looked around, frightened. "What Glacial Pulse? What are you talking about?"

"That glacier in Antarctica started falling into the sea. Some experts said it could lead to a tidal pulse."

"And this rain is making it worse!" exclaimed the green-haired woman.

Dat drove upslope, leaving the surging tide behind.

***

Tomas and his moms were listening to the radio. It was a little after 10 a.m. on Christmas Eve and they didn't have any big plans for the day. That night, of course, they'd have a nice meal at home together.

The deep radio voice of Harlan Lewis filled the kitchen.

"At 10:42 today the biggest King Tide in history will swell the bay. All flights in and out of local airports continue to be canceled until the high tides recede. It's rough news for holiday travelers, right Heather?"

"That's right Harlan. Local airports will be flooded, and shorelines around the Bay Area will disappear under the highest tide we've ever seen."

"I gotta see that!" Tomas was excited.

His mom Millie looked at her son like he was crazy. "You wanna go out on your bicycle in this rain? To see a flood?" she shook her head.

Barbara smiled before looking at Millie disapprovingly. "Why not honey? I'd go but I hate riding in the rain." She supported Tomas's adventuresome personality. 14 was an age when she would've gone out riding in the rain too! It couldn't be dangerous to ride downtown towards the bayshore. High tides and groundwater upwelling up filled Mission Bay, poured over the Embarcadero, and flooded low-lying areas of the Bayview, and closed local airports. Epic rainfall joined to flood most of Northern California.
Listening to the radio again,

> "...the Yolo Bypass is flowing with diverted Sacramento River flood-waters. The levees around the state capitol are holding for now, but state officials are concerned about the city flooding. Here's the Sacramento Head of Emergency Services: 'This looks as bad as the storm of 1861 when Sacramento disappeared under 20 feet of water—the worst one we ever had. Of course we have levees and the bypass and we expect them to prevent flooding.' Stay indoors and wait. The forecast predicts the rain to end later this evening, just in time for a dry Christmas!"

"You be careful. This rain makes everything slippery and dangerous! And people are driving around crazily before Christmas, not paying attention," Millie cautioned.

"Sure Mom, don't worry!" Tomas was joined by Cristiano fifteen minutes later, who convinced his parents to let him ride through the rain with his pal. He was expected in plenty of time for their Christmas Eve supper.

"Man, I can't believe it. You think this is the sea-level rise they've been talking about?" Cristiano breathlessly asked as they rolled down from 20th Street. "Is that water down there?"

"Sure looks like it!" They were barely a block from Tomas's house and already they could see water pooling ahead of them in the low-lying blocks of Folsom. "That's from the rain. Remember they always have temporary flooding around 18th and Folsom during big storms, and this one..." he left it unsaid. It was a doozy. "This'll be fun!" And he sped on, Cristiano rushing to keep up, and they hit the shallow flood that started before 18th Street... and just kept going! What started as a chance to make a splash became a slog. The water was at least 4 or 5 inches in most places, covering the width of the streets and sidewalks. Pedaling through it took more effort than they expected. "Let's go in there!" Tomas yelled as he pulled into In Chan Kajaal Park, which rose out of the surrounding flooded streets. The boys dismounted and stood on an extremely muddy grassy mound.

"You think we can even get down to Mission Bay? What if it's like this," pointing to the flooded intersection, "all the way... or even worse?" Cristiano didn't want to chicken out, but this wasn't what he expected.

"We can go around!" Tomas said excitedly. "They have to protect the BART tunnel, right? It can't be that bad downtown..." The occasional flooded intersection on Valencia and Market didn't stop them as they pedaled through the rain. Once they were past the Cable Car turnaround at Powell they peered ahead towards the Ferry Building, not sure what to expect.

"Let's turn here!" and they darted south, under the Transit Center and over to Folsom. They skidded to a stop.

"Damn!" The bay filled Folsom to Main Street, two blocks down a gentle slope. "What time is it? The peak is at 10:42 today." Tomas was already turning around. "Let's go to 2nd Street and over to the ballpark! If we can even get there!"

Cristiano yelled "It's 11:15," as he rushed to keep up.

Minutes later they were stopped at Brannan on 2nd Street. The Giants stadium at the end of the street was flooded. The floodwaters filled the street in front of them, an occasional car rolling slowly by with the water covering about half the wheels.

One car stopped across from them. "You guys hear anything about the Bay Bridge? Is it open?"

The boys shrugged. "We don't know!" yelled Tomas. "But I bet the toll plaza is flooded!"

They slowly rode through wet streets, dodging the mini-lakes at backed up drains at every intersection.

By the time Tomas got back home it was almost 1 o'clock. Millie laughed when he walked in, soaked from head to toe, shivering. "I told you you were crazy to go out there! What'd you see?" He wowed his moms with vivid descriptions of the inundated streets they'd skirted. "You got your fill I hope?"

Nodding, he asked, "You think this flooding is normal now?" There were bad floods a few times in the past year, but state officials kept saying the state was still in a drought. It was very confusing.

Barbara looked sad as she took his wet clothes away and tucked the warm blanket around him. "I guess so... whatever normal is anymore!"

***

Lamar and Cindy stayed in bed enjoying the steady rainfall outside until almost 10 o'clock. Frank went to Sheila's to celebrate Christmas, leaving the house on Marlin Street to them. Cindy finally tore herself away from Lamar's delicious warm body and went downstairs to make coffee.

From the kitchen window she had a wide view of the abandoned areas of the old Shipyard and to the south she could usually see Candlestick State Park jutting into the bay. Dark gray skies sat sullenly over everything, slowly drifting east towards the mountains, inundating everything along the way. Cindy blinked and squinted but try as she might, she couldn't see the park where it should be. A small island floated where the park's arm extended furthest into the bay; trees poked up from the bay hinting at the flooded park below the water.

"Oh man!" she realized that the bay waters were higher than ever. Out at the iconic crane the docks were submerged which meant that most of Hunter's Point would be under water too. 'The horses!' she thought and then remembered Frank telling her he'd watched them move them to another location, probably in the Presidio or Golden Gate Park. She brought steaming cups of coffee up to the bedroom.

"Lamar! Wake up! It's Noah's flood!"

"Whu?..." he turned over, eyes still closed.

"You have got to see this! The bay has come up, WAY up!"

He finally sat up, rubbing his eyes, reaching for the coffee she was holding out to him.

"King Tide again right?"

"It looks a lot worse than that, at least from the kitchen window. Most of Candlestick Park is under water."

"No shit?" He got up and pulled back the curtain to look out the northeast-facing window. "Hard to tell from here." He couldn't see much in that direction as it was blocked by other buildings on the hill. "Still stormin', that's for sure."

They heard the door open and slam shut downstairs.

"Lamar! Cindy! You up there?" It was Leon.

After a few minutes they joined him.

"My place is completely flooded!" he looked devastated. "My whole crop is in there! I am fucked!"

"What the hell happened?"

"The King Tide. But this is WAY higher than before. Tuesday and Wednesday was bad, but nothing like this."

"It's the Pulse," Cindy said. "The collapsing glacier in Antarctica—some scientists said it could lead to a Glacial Pulse."

"What does that mean? Did the ocean rise a bunch already?!?" Leon was freaked out.

"Nobody knows. And for sure nobody expected it to happen while we're having the heaviest rainfall since the 1860s!" Cindy continued. "Combine the King Tides we knew were coming with the Glacial Pulse, then add floods from every river and creek in Northern California... It's a disaster alright!"

***

"Janine, what a beautiful Christmas display!" Steve Healey sat on the sofa in the tenth-floor common room of the Insurance Exchange Building. He was happy to have a few days off from his BGM job during the Christmas break.

"You like it Steve?" Janine asked earnestly. Many people seemed to disdain holiday celebrations but it always meant 'home' to her.

"Oh yeah. Reminds me of when I was a kid. My mom always made a big effort. We would have a huge tree, even if we didn't always have a lot under it," his voice sank at the memory. Robbie and his mom appeared across the room, approaching cautiously.

"Robbie! Estrellita! Feliz Navidad!" called Steve as he waved them over. Smiling, they brought a tray of holiday cookies.

"Look what we made!" Robbie said proudly. His mom extended the tray towards Steve and he picked a star-shaped cookie. She gave one to Janine too and smiled and pointed to the decorative niche she'd made. "*¡Qué bella! ¡Me gusta muchísimo!*"

"Thank you honey... gracias!" Janine liked having them on her floor. There weren't enough children in the building but at least they had Robbie. She took a candy cane from her tree and gave it to the boy.

"Merry Christmas Robbie!" and he happily accepted it.

The wind whipped the rain into the windows in a sudden burst.

"Oooh, *¡La tormenta es terrible! ¡Muy peligrosa!*" Estrellita hugged her son closer.

"We're gonna be ok here, nothing to worry about!" Steve spoke with confidence, and Robbie translated for his mother. "We are far from the bay! The floods won't get this far," but he was unaware of the original Yerba Buena cove shoreline near their building. The recent King Tides only flooded the Embarcadero and a block or two inland. And then the water receded back to the bay behind the seawall reconstruction project again.

The room filled with the other tenth floor residents bringing dishes, family favorites, and some presents to put under the tree. They'd only been living together in the Insurance Exchange since February, but somehow it seemed longer. Real friendships grew as they navigated the fraught process of establishing a cooperative community together. Only two people were asked to leave since they moved in, both heavy drinkers who couldn't or wouldn't listen to others and were often belligerent and disrespectful during the weekly meetings. Joining together to push them out, which came after weeks of patient cajoling and lobbying to change their ways, helped bring the floor together. They affirmed their mutual commitment to civility, tolerance, and accountability—after the two drunken blowhards moved out, real solidarity grew on the floor.

Outside the common room they could hear singing. A group of carolers arrived, friends from the lower floors. They crowded into the room and sang satirical versions of some Christmas standards, "God Rest Ye Olde Society" and "Hark the Walmart Angels Sing" getting a lot of laughs and a big round of applause at the end. Another neighbor came in with a giant thermos of eggnog, enough for dozens.

"Steve, you got a job now huh?" Janine leaned over with her eggnog, more expansive and gregarious than usual.

"Yeah, but I don't know how long it's gonna last. I'm doing intake for BGM, processing witches butter prospectors. It kinda sucks, to tell the truth. Not a gig with a future," he sighed into a gulp of eggnog.

"At least you got some work! Who else found a job since we moved in?"

Most of the residents were still unemployed as they had been when they lived on the street. There was still some government-supported electronic benefits but they could only be used for government-sanctioned "patriot packages" at major supermarkets. Better than nothing when supplies were lean.

"I heard you were gardening over at Fort Mason?" Steve asked her.

"I go over there sometimes. I don't have a plot, I volunteer with the League—the Farmers?"

"Sure! Where would we be without the gardens and farms and the miraculous food deliveries in the basement?"

"Hungry for good food, that's where!" she smiled. Dozens of dishes were spread out on the communal tables and people were digging in. "Let's get some!"

***

'I can still turn around,' Vero told herself. She was southeast of Holly Park, moving her umbrella this way and that facing the swirling rain and wind. For most of the last two days she trudged through the rain-soaked city, barely conscious of the storm's severity. She had to fix things with Janet. She couldn't think about anything else.

Would Janet even be home? Maybe she was at the family house on Marlin Street? Well, Vero was at her door. Might as well try. She hesitated. How to explain? Apologize, she admonished herself. Apologize, tell her she was right, ask her to forgive you. But she didn't want to be an abject wimp either. 'Apologize and ask to talk,' she thought. Then see where it goes. She took a deep breath, and finally knocked on the door. No answer. She knocked again, more vigorously, feeling more certain of herself.

"Who is it?" came Janet's voice behind the door.

"It's me. Vero."

The door opened. Janet looked exhausted, standing there in pajamas, the gray pallor of the storm providing the only light. She sighed. "Come on in... I guess." She left the door open and retreated.

Vero slowly took off her wet clothes and left them near the door. Janet curled up on a large, padded chair with a blanket pulled up to her chin. Vero sat down on the sofa. "Are you ill? You don't look good."

"It's a cold. But I've felt better."

Vero steeled herself and after a deep breath she leaned on her knees. "I owe you an apology. I'm sorry Janet. I'm sorry I sold out to BGM. It was a mistake. That's obvious now. I guess it always was to you." She watched Janet staring at her, showing no reaction.

"I felt like shit on Thanksgiving. I didn't believe it then, and I was mad at you. It was my decision to make, *my* choice!" She briefly felt the anger again. "Unfortunately I fucked it up."

"At least you got paid," Janet mumbled under the blanket.

"Yeah, I got paid. Me and Leon, and I paid Lorena and a few others too. Didn't make anyone rich, exactly, but at least we're not poor anymore." This wasn't what she came to talk about.

"Janet, I love you and I miss you. You are my oldest and dearest friend. Forgive me?"

Janet kept staring at her. This was unexpected. And she felt like shit. Her energy was very low. She was depressed. The weather was awful. But she didn't want to fight with Vero. It was pointless. Water under the bridge now. Nothing to do about it. She nodded, and then mumbled in a low voice under the blanket. "I forgive you Vero. I don't want to fight you."

Vero wanted to jump over and give Janet a big hug. But no. There was more to say. Maybe that would come later.

"I feel it Janet. The witches butter. It's everywhere. I can smell it when I'm out on a walk. It wants us to help it."

Janet let the blanket fall from her face. She looked at Vero, clearly surprised. "Help it? What do you mean?"

"I'm not sure. I was hoping you might have an idea. You've always been able to talk to everything. Haven't you been... *connecting* with it?"

"I'm making tea. Want some?" Vero followed her to the kitchen.

"Let me do that. You're not well. Sit down!" Vero took over and Janet deferred. "Chamomile?" Janet smiled in affirmation. Her best friend knew what she wanted. Vero puttered over the tea-making and Janet sat in silence. They both needed to pause, to shed the layers of tension and frustration and anger they'd been carrying for weeks now. They sighed deeply in perfect unison, and then giggling they called "jinx!" together.

When Janet accepted the tea from Vero she put her hand over Vero's and said softly, "Thanks."

Vero welled up now, and a few tears rolled down her cheek. They remained silent, occasionally exchanging glances over sips of tea.

"We are protecting the witches butter," Janet finally said. "The Canopy Council has made it a priority. It is growing across the city, and we've sent starters around the Bay, up and down California and up to Oregon, Washington, and Canada, and down to Baja. There's even some on a freighter heading to the Philippines, Vietnam, and China!"

"Whoa!" Vero again realized how she'd been on the wrong side of this and felt guilty and small. "I'm an idiot!"

"Better late than never, friend."

"Do you get feelings from it too? How does that work?"

"Remember that presentation we got from Maria? In Brisbane?" Vero nodded. "She suggested that it was a new type of intelligence. I talked to her a few times after that, and if anything she became more convinced. She liked to call it 'alien' but I don't like to say that. It came from us! We didn't exactly give birth to this altered witches butter, but we were the midwives!" Janet scrutinized Vero, trying to get a read on how this sounded to her.

"Midwives! Yeah, we helped it into the world," Vero suddenly smiled broadly. "I like that. It feels right. And when I say I'm 'feeling it' it IS like when you are connected with a baby or a small child and you can tell when they need something..." She shook her head and looked away. "I guess..." She turned back to Janet now. "Is that how it feels to you?"

"I don't think I'd put it that way. I'd say it's alive and intelligent and wants to live. And maybe it wants to live *together*. At least that's what I think on good days!" and she smiled seductively, a smile Vero was never able to resist.

She came over and pulled Janet up into a hug, which they held for a very long time, sighing repeatedly. "Here's to having more good days!" Vero said finally as they pulled apart.

***

Jay pulled his Christmas turkey from the oven, where he'd been baking it for last few hours. He and Jordan and Andy were having a Christmas Eve together. The other guys in their Collingwood Street flat went home to their parents' places a week earlier. Jordan was puttering over his potatoes *au gratin* next to him in the kitchen.

"Hey, is the rain finally stopping?" The raindrops' relentless drumbeat was replaced by a more random dripping sound.

"Yeah, the weather said it would stop for a few days. I sure hope so! It's driving me crazy, even though I wished for rain many times in the last year!" Jordan admitted. "Good for the plumbing business I guess!" he acknowledged.

"It's a good thing those guys left last week before they closed the airports. And you can't even drive out of here! The Bay Bridge toll plaza is flooded!"

"Not the Golden Gate or San Rafael bridges. The Bay Bridge and the ones down the peninsula," said Andy who walked into the kitchen. "Shall I open the wine?" He worked in a Nob Hill restaurant and always managed to bring home the best wines.

"Oh fuck," the whole room lurched, throwing them sideways, and began shaking. "Oh fuck oh fuck oh fuck," Jordan watched his potatoes crash to the floor, followed close behind by the turkey and its trimmings. The large bookcase in the next room crashed over. The shaking wasn't stopping, and they each grabbed for anything solid they could reach. Jay got himself into the door jamb, and Jordan crawled and slid through the potatoes to get under the table. Andy jumped one way and another, trying to decide where to go, finally settling on the pantry doorway. He clutched the frame, looking in panic at the cracking ceiling above them. "Oh no, no, no, don't you—" and the ceiling gave way, crashing onto the table with Jordan under it. The stove and the refrigerator from the upper floor came with it and landed with a huge crunching roar.

Jay was dumbstruck. His heart was beating a thousand beats a minute. The panic was overwhelming, but the shaking wouldn't stop, and he couldn't move. He could feel things falling behind him too, into the living room, but he couldn't turn around. Jordan was screaming in pain under the rubble. Andy, where was Andy? An arm stuck out from under a refrigerator. Holy Shit!

Finally the shaking stopped. The gray sky—what was that doing there?

There was no top of the building left. Jay knelt down and pulled debris from the middle of the room. He could hear Jordan moaning under the pile. "Fuck!" The stove and fridge were lodged together on one side of what had been their kitchen. Their own stove was smashed in. He had to get Jordan out of there.

He frantically pulled everything he could until he finally saw Jordan, covered in white dust, under the kitchen table, which was smashed down on him, pinned by the stove that came down from the upper floor. Mustering his strength, he shoved as hard as he could and got the stove off the table, and then the table off Jordan.

"Oh god!" he couldn't help but react to the site of Jordan's mangled leg, the knee reversed and his foot dangling from his ankle in a way that no one would ever want to see. "Oh my god, Jordan. Your leg!" Jordan was delirious with pain and could only groan.

Suddenly he smelled smoke, which was billowing somewhere nearby. Crackling flames were audible. "Fuck me! Jordan, we have to get out of here. It's burning!" Jordan was in no condition to respond. Jay frantically looked for some way to move his friend, finally settling on the formica kitchen counter which fell off the cheap-ass cabinets their landlord installed. He dragged it next to his friend and knelt. "I have to move you. It's going to hurt, I'm sorry!" and he took Jordan, who was ghost white and passed out, by the shoulders, and dragged him onto the countertop. Jordan let out a blood-curdling scream. "I'm sorry man! We have to get out of here. It's burning!" He moved his good leg and then did his best to arrange the mangled one on the countertop too, through the agonizing screams. He realized he was crying but he had to save them. He grabbed a drape from the living room and tied his friend tightly to the counter with it. Then he pulled it through the falling embers, the flames licking at the rest of their apartment. At least they lived on the ground floor! But he had to get down the half dozen steps to the street from the front door.

"Hey, you need a hand?" A neighborhood Adonis was on the sidewalk, bulging muscles, classic good looks, short black hair, in gym clothes. Standing in front of the collapsed house, he obliviously said, "That was a helluva quake, eh?" before he saw how seriously hurt Jordan was. "Oh man, I'm sorry." He climbed behind Jay and lifted the back of the countertop. "We gotta get this guy to a hospital," saying the obvious.

"Help me get him away from the fire first ok?" Somehow the guy hadn't noticed that their building was burning. Suddenly an explosion a few houses away blew the doors and windows off that building into the street. Jay was fighting panic. His new helper was unfazed and with his strength, it was easy enough to carry Jordan as if he were on a stretcher.

"The Eureka Playground on Diamond. Let's hope the building survived!" They made their way the two blocks. Jordan was unconscious. The temperature was dropping. "Fuck, I shoulda got a blanket before we left."

"Man, you did pretty good getting him wrapped up in this curtain." The guy was trying to be positive. He and Jay arrived at the front of the school to the locked door. A half dozen others were there, and several people had blankets. A nurse was giving first aid to someone who suffered cuts from flying glass. They got him to focus on Jordan.

"Oh," they took a pulse. "Oh, we have to get him to a hospital. He's not gonna make it out here. Does anyone have a car? Anyone?" One woman who was sitting in a daze, suddenly turned her head. "Oh, I do! It's up the block."

Minutes later she returned with the car and they loaded Jordan into the back seat. Going to Castro Street they started to turn north and realized the street was blocked by the theater marquee and facade that lay across the street.

"Go around!" Jay frantically pointed down 18th where huge pieces of the street buckled open. They managed to steer through the rubble to Noe and reach Franklin Hospital at Duboce. Noe Street was intact except for a big sinkhole at 15th Street, but they maneuvered around it. Miraculously the hospital was open and of course there were dozens of people converging on the emergency room as they drove up behind three cars that arrived before them. Ambulance sirens filled the air as two different ones pulled into the emergency room entranceway, double parking alongside the cars already there. Hospital workers were rushing out with gurneys, trying to take people inside as efficiently as they could.

Two hours later, Jay, slumped in the waiting room, perked up when he heard his name.

"Your friend will survive. I'm afraid we had to amputate his leg above the knee. It was too far gone. If we get through this—*When* we get through it," the nurse corrected herself optimistically, "he'll have to get a prosthetic."

Jay nodded numbly. At least Jordan would live. He promised to return the next day and stumbled out of the hospital into the night. It was pitch dark, no streetlights and hardly any traffic. He walked home on autopilot until he reached the part of Castro where you could look downhill towards the Castro Theater and the rest of the shopping district. The marquee and much of the front of the old theater filled the street. The sky was filled with leaping flames going up the hill. It looked like his whole neighborhood was on fire!

"Fuck!" And he remembered he had nowhere to go! What was he thinking? He walked up Market Street to Collingwood and was astonished to see the smoking ruins of his block. The smell was overwhelming. In the near distance the flames were still dancing, burning everything in their path.

He went to his former home but there was nothing left. 'Oh shit—Andy!' he remembered. He sat down stunned. Andy was dead, and cremated! "Oh man," and he buried his sobbing face in his hands.

"Hey, you ok man?" Two women were standing in front of him.

He looked up and couldn't see them too well in the dark. He shook his head, the sobs still coming. He stuck his thumb over his shoulder. "I lived here."

"You gotta come with us," and they got on either side of him and tugged at his arms. He could offer no resistance and had no reason to anyway. They made their way past 18th Street and heard yelling and voices up the hill a ways. "Let's check it out," the one with short blonde hair said.

As they got closer they could see a long line of people handing sloshing buckets from a block away. The buckets disappeared up the hill, from one hand to another silhouetted by the distant flames still gobbling up homes on the north side of 18th Street.

"There's a cistern at 19th," the other woman noted. "Those brick circles! I always wondered if we'd ever need them."

Jay snapped out of his stupor. Seeing these people working together to fight the fires with buckets of water—he had to help! The women were glad to help too, so they inserted themselves into the line, pushing some folks further up, extending the reach of the effort.

Hours later, exhausted, Anne and Alejandra invited Jay to sleep at their place, which survived the quake. He didn't hesitate. They walked a few blocks to their little one-bedroom on Noe Street, and he was asleep on their couch as soon as he lay down.

Christmas morning, he rolled over on the strange couch, wondering for a moment where he was. It surged back and he sat up abruptly. Anne and Alejandra heard him stirring and called him from the kitchen where they were sitting at their table. "You want some coffee? We have a Christmas cake too!"

He padded in groggily. "Coffee yes! Thank you!" After he'd downed a cup, he realized he didn't have any clothes—he didn't have anything! He had to start over. He had to go to the hospital to check on Jordan. He had to figure out how to contact Andy's next of kin... it came rushing at him like a torrent. He sank back into his chair. "Is the fire out?" he remembered.

"Mostly. But there were fires in many places. We're lucky everything was wet, or we might be facing a firestorm like in 1906!" Alejandra explained.

Anne shook her phone. "No service! Fancy technology eh?"

"Must be radio at least?" Jay assumed.

"Yeah, KALW is back on the air already, and some commercial FM stations are too. But a lot are down. Probably lost their transmitters, or the power's out at their studios.

"Jay, you can stay here for a few days if you want to." Anne looked at him expectantly.

"That's nice of you! Thank you! I will. I, uh... it's true, I don't have anywhere to go. I have to find my friends and see if they survived, see if their houses made it. I promise I'll find a new place as soon as I can."

Later, he went past the ruins of the Castro Theater and saw smoke still rising from the smoldering wreckage of his burned neighborhood. Weirdly he could see the big white turreted mansion at Douglass and Caselli from where he was standing, which survived everything.

***

Juna was home. It had been a few years. Something drew them first on the long journey to Antioch by BART, and then waiting two hours at the edge of a AM/PM gas station for their sister Rosie to come and get them. Their parents were long dead, but Rosie was still living in the trailer on the Honker Lake Tract on the family property.

"Juan, you came home!" Rosie looked at Juna with a guarded expression. "You OK?"

"Yeah, yeah," Juna flopped into the passenger seat in the decades-old dusty green pickup. "It was time. I needed to see the land." And he glanced across at Rosie, who was grimacing as she pulled into traffic. "And I wanted to see you too sis!" They decided to overlook her refusal to use their chosen name, Juna.

She looked away. "You decided to come for Christmas? Just like that?"

"I didn't mean to upset you."

"I'm not upset! I never hear from you. It's unexpected."

"I'm not interrupting anything am I?"

She snorted derisively, "as if..." and reached for a cigarette. In a half hour they were exiting Highway 4 onto the muddy dirt road that led to their trailer.

East of Mt. Diablo, they were on "Roberts Island," one of many illusory agricultural islands formed by massive levee building and drainage projects in the 19th century. Somehow the Caguas family kept title to a half-acre parcel of the Honkers Lake Tract, where they'd always lived. Before the Spanish the whole area was a dense marsh of tule reeds, rich with elk and bear and other game. Now it was a dusty agricultural plain below sea level with Trappers Slough and the Mokelumne Aqueduct to the northwest and Middle River past the school to the south. The Whiskey Slough Marina was right outside of Holt, the post-office town a quarter mile from Highway 4, and brought the boating tourism as close as it got to their land.

Juna felt an inexplicable sense of anticipation as they pulled in. 'It's not like I ever cared about Christmas,' they thought as they slung their bag into the corner of the trailer.

"You can sleep on the bed," Rosie pointed to a pile of clothes and papers where the bed might be.

"Oh, that's yours. I can sleep on the floor pad, don't worry!"

They reached into their bag and pulled out a small present. Juna saw the 6" plastic christmas tree light on a small round table and figured it belonged under it.

"You didn't bring that for me!" Rosie looked uncomfortable. When Juna called this morning, everything happened suddenly. She had nothing for them, other than a place to lay down.

Juna smiled. "Yup. Don't worry. You didn't know I was coming, don't feel bad, ok?"

"You shoulda told me sooner." And she went outside for another cigarette.

Juna followed her out. "I can't believe the rain is finally stopping... I'm gonna walk over to the river. I'll be back in an hour or less, ok?"

She waved dismissively, "Do what you do."

The sound of feet sucking in the mud filled Juna's ears for the next fifteen minutes as they trudged across the fields. Terns came hurtling out of nowhere and settled in the slough, a short way ahead. 'There's still life in the delta,' thought Juna. They reached the bank of Middle River and looked towards Mt. Diablo to the west. 'Could those be condors?' they wondered, staring at two huge birds soaring far up in the gray sky. One came closer, circling and circling, and then down, growing larger and larger. Juna stood mesmerized on the muddy bank. It was a condor, no mistake. Supposedly some condors settled on Mt. Diablo, but why would this one fly here?

Suddenly the earth began to seriously shake! A hard jolt sent Juna sprawling, wet mud oozing inside their clothing. But the earth kept shaking, more violently yet. They gave themself over to it, sinking into the vibrating wet land, sliding closer to the river. It was nearly orgasmic to lay there in the violently shaking mud, merging with the most primal of earthly experiences. Finally it stopped. Juna, heart pounding, had to turn sideways before they could get their elbow under them enough to get up.

"Oh god. I'm covered!" Juna writhed uncomfortably in cold, muddy clothes. Small animals scurried in the mud, and the sky was full of birds. The condor was gone. Had it really been there?

Middle River was sloshing back and forth. Juna stood staring at it, but it became apparent that it was rising fast! They ran, falling several times in the muddy field, hurrying to get to the trailer. They threw the door open and found Rosie sitting in her chair, contemplating the chaos of her belongings that had been tossed around inside the trailer like a pepper shaker during the quake. The trailer itself seemed to be whole at least.

"Rosie! We've gotta get out of here! That was a big one! The levees are gonna fail. We're gonna flood! Let's go!"

"I ain't goin'. You're covered in mud! You wanna go, go ahead. You can take the truck. Bring it back tomorrow. And clean it!"

"Come on! You gotta come. This could be a massive flood. You won't survive here!"

"I ain't goin.'" She crossed her arms and looked so much like their mother that Juna did a double take.

"I'll come back tomorrow." He felt panicky. He'd seen photos of delta islands under water when levees broke over the years. Who knew how many levees were reduced to muddy rubble by that earthquake? After this rain and the flooding already? They grabbed the keys and rushed out the door.

The truck started right up and they floored it towards Highway 4, the best maintained road for miles. 'Fuck, I hope it hasn't flooded yet!' Juna bumped up onto the highway, wet from the rain but not yet covered in floodwaters. It ran along Trappers Slough, which was already spilling over to the opposite side where it had a lot to fill before it would rise to the highway's height. They had time. Juna pushed the wheezing truck to 55, then 60. It wouldn't do more. But it was a straight road and they clutched the steering wheel as dusk fell, hoping they could get to higher land and that the flood would spare their sister. Cold mud squished under them on the truck's seat. They'd have a helluva time cleaning the truck later.

"Oh shit! Shit! Shit!" they came roaring to the confluence of Trappers Slough and Middle River at Union Point and hit the Middle River Bridge just in time to see the river start swamping the long-closed bar. Across the bridge there was still another five miles to Discovery Bay, which was surely flooding too. Victoria Island was covered in water already, but still below the road. Juna sped along as fast as the rest of the cars crowding the road would allow, about 45 mph. They made it to Old River Bridge and still the water had not reached the roadway.

The traffic ground to a crawl at Discovery Bay where everyone was trying to get out. Water was beginning to cover everything around them. On they went, bumper to bumper, and in another 15 minutes, they had at last begun the gradual ascent of the flank of Mt Diablo. A half hour later, long after dark, Juna pulled over on Marsh Creek Road, well out of flood danger, and tried to get a rise out of the radio. Nothing but static.

Their hands gripped the steering wheel. 'Rosie! Rosieeeee!' Juna's head dipped forward onto the steering wheel and they sobbed uncontrollably.

***

Frank stood at the big window of Sheila's Mission Bay apartment. It was late afternoon on Christmas Eve. The King Tide overwhelmed the city. Nobody had ever seen anything like it. Eighteen floors below, the streets were still full of flood waters submerging parked cars up to the windows. Sheila joined him and handed him a second drink. They watched during the day, trying to make sense of it.

Suddenly, a huge "crack" sounding like a gunshot ripped through the apartment. Everything lurched sharply, throwing them both back from the window, their drinks shattering on the floor behind them.

"SHIT! SHIT! SHIT! It's the Big One!" yelled Frank over the roar. "Get in the door!" but neither of them could control where they were going as the shaking continued, growing in intensity. Glass was shattering all around them. Frank saw Sheila covered in blood trying to reach for something solid to hold on to. He was holding the leg of the sofa and reached for her, but she was slipping towards the windows, the violent shaking continuing. "Oh Frank! Frank!" Sheila yelled, as she slipped over the edge and disappeared. "Sheila! Sheila!" Frank was hanging on for dear life. The windows were gone! Sheila was gone! Another body dropped past the window. Frank managed to wedge his foot on the metal window frame and was still holding the sofa which wasn't moving much. Finally, it stopped.

Frank rolled over, gasping. He felt like he was having a heart attack. He tried to breathe. He pushed himself with his feet back from the window frame, back to the middle of the room. Cold wet rain was pouring in where the floor-to-ceiling glass window had been a few minutes ago.

"Sheila!" he groaned. On his hands and knees he carefully crawled to the edge of the window and looked over. Bodies were floating in the churning waters below. There was a cacophony of desperate screams coming from every direction.

***

The week-long atmospheric river of rain that cascaded over California finally relented late on Christmas Eve afternoon. King Tides overwhelmed shorelines each morning since December 22. Further king tides were expected on Christmas Day at 11:34 and the day after at 12:30. The massive tidal surges exceeded expectations because it was amplified unpredictably by the collapse of the Thwaites ice shelf in Antarctica, which opened the way for the so-called Doomsday Glacier behind it to begin its deadly slide into the ocean. The full three-meter sea-level rise from the glacial collapse was still said to be decades in the future. But no one knew how much already changed with the collapse of the ice sheet. The Bay Area's King Tides were much higher than predicted—the week of heavy rain, the ice sheet collapse, the Glacial Pulse, groundwater upsurge, whatever it was, no one saw it coming.

The massive Hayward fault earthquake was the "big one" seismologists predicted for years, and the earth moved for almost two full minutes, in some places ripping open the land and tearing houses apart. The Pacific plate on the west side of the Hayward Fault slid northward by at least 15 feet, not quite 5 meters. Liquefaction around the San Francisco Bay shoreline was severe, disintegrating untold miles of freeways, bridge approaches, airport tarmacs, and local roads. Streets buckled and ripped open during the temblor, often on areas of historic landfill over old creeks and ponds. Untold thousands of people were dead. Tens of thousands were huddled under tents and tarps in open areas, petrified as the region experienced multiple aftershocks during the night, though none as severe as the initial quake.

Shocking news was coming in from the Sacramento/San Joaquin River delta. The lengthy shaking of the powerful earthquake destroyed century-old fragile levees. Sunken "islands" were inundated in less than an hour, and substantial portions of the levees controlling the already raging Sacramento River collapsed too, sending flood waters into the Central Valley, swamping Stockton, Lodi, Tracy, Manteca, Modesto, and many smaller towns. The Yolo Bypass was at flood tide itself! Worse yet, the California Water Project, which depended on fresh water arriving to the Clifton Court Forebay, was broken. Fresh water that usually would be sent southward to replenish the depleted San Joaquin River, as well as providing fresh water to southern agribusiness interests and dozens of urban water districts as well, was no longer available. The entire Delta became a vast inland sea, salt water surging as far as Sacramento.

CHAPTER 61
FRIDAY, DECEMBER 25, 2026

Janet was picking up books and other fallen items when Vero opened her eyes. "Fuck! We have to get back out there!" she groaned.

"I was trying to let you sleep. It'll be a long day. At least it's not raining."

They'd only been asleep for about three hours. The earthquake jolted them hard but the house on the south side of Bernal still stood, and the neighborhood seemed to have survived. Like everyone, they'd rushed into the streets after the temblor stopped shaking. Before long word arrived that people needed help further down the hill on Crescent Street and they rushed to see what they could do.

"Hey, let's get this organized!" yelled a guy in a yellow helmet, wearing an orange safety vest from which his ID badge flapped as he rushed back and forth trying to establish his authority. A dozen people were already pulling at the ruins of a row of three houses that collapsed together near the Alemany Farmers Market lot.

"Who the hell are you?" a woman confronted the self-appointed leader.

"I've had NERT training! We know what to do!" he nervously claimed.

"NERD training? What the hell is that?"

"No, NERT, Neighborhood Emergency Response Training, from the Fire Department!" he explained.

Some cyclists arrived and threw themselves into the rescue effort. Janet and Vero pulled boards and pieces of wall back and heaped them in the still wet street. The rain let up, finally! They could hear moaning and crying inside.

"We're coming! Hang on in there! We'll get you out!" called different people. "Trish? John? Are you in there?" yelled the guy next to them, evidently a neighbor or friend. It was amazing what a dedicated group of a dozen people could do. In a half hour they found the people buried in their own homes and got them out. One had a broken leg. Lots of scratches and cuts. A woman was clutching her cat.

The NERT guy focused on getting places for the rescued to take shelter. Soon tents and tarps were being laid out on the parts of the street that hadn't caved in.

After an hour, Janet and Vero, neither skilled in First Aid, decided to move on. Everything was completely dark. Streetlights flickered on here and there, but many intersections were completely blacked out. Traffic lights were out, and few cars were moving. They came down to the Farmers Market and were shocked to see the vendors cement sheds toppled over and the asphalt lot buckled in numerous places, water pooling at the east end.

"You think the freeways held up? The bridges? BART?" Vero peered through the darkness, trying to see the big interchange ahead. Highway 101 and I-280 crossed right here on top of Islais Creek where it met a sprawling wetland that hadn't been fully urbanized and "reclaimed" until the 1930s.

"Oh my god, it's falling!" One of the support pillars under a freeway ramp was tilting precariously, not far from where they were. As they watched, the overpass above it tipped and crashed down onto the freeway below. It seemed to be in slow motion as they stood there agape. Suddenly a huge boom hit them and then the sounds of tearing metal long after the crash. Smoke billowed towards them. Dozens of people appeared out of nowhere running towards the collapse, and Janet and Vero joined them.

Climbing up the rubble through the dust and darkness at least a hundred people groped for handles, flashlight beams whipping back and forth, trying to see if they could help anyone. But amazingly there was no sign of life, no cars were caught in the collapse, or at least none they could see. In the distance some headlights were approaching slowly on the intact roadway. Several people ran towards them waving their flashlights, getting them to stop.

Hours later, after walking back across Bernal and pitching in here and there with folks who were fixing shelters in front of their damaged homes, Janet and Vero made it back to Janet's place on Anderson, where they gave in to their exhaustion and were soon asleep.

***

Greg and Aaron were at the table overseeing 2-year-old Elsie as she played with her hot oatmeal.

"Mommie and Daddy will be home soon," Greg reassured her, as she worriedly kept looking towards the door. "They went to help the neighbors." Miraculously Kite Kastle shook but didn't break during the quake. Books fell, as well as some dishes from the cabinet in the dining room. Pictures fell off the wall, lamps toppled over, but all things considered, they'd done well. They didn't even lose any windows! The power was out around the neighborhood, but they had a robust solar installation on the roof and a Hempattery set-up downstairs. Julius deemed it intact after a close inspection. Their house was OK, though fires raged nearby all night.

The radio in the corner of the kitchen was running constant bulletins.

"Repeating, the Bay Area has been hit by an earthquake registering 7.4 on the Richter scale. It struck yesterday at 4:18 pm with the epicenter on the Hayward Fault between Hayward and Castro Valley. Interstate-580 and the Castro Valley BART station have collapsed, severing the road to the Livermore Valley. We have a reporter on the scene, Christine?

"Yes, Bill, that's right. The 580 freeway looks like a giant took an axe to it. The Castro Valley BART station and surrounding freeway have collapsed to street level. The fire chief told me that the whole zone moved several yards northward. The rest of the freeway east of the fault is still intact, although there are reports of damage across the hills too. Reporting from Castro Valley, this is Christine Stone."

"Thank you, Christine. As you know, most cell service is down throughout the region. There are widespread reports of power outages too..."

Donald and Sarah entered, covered in soot, looking completely exhausted.

"Mommy! Daddy!" Elsie squealed, and then she recoiled and started to cry.

"Oh, sweetheart, don't cry!" Sarah rushed over to her daughter. "Mommy needs to wash up. We got very dirty helping fight the fire." At the kitchen sink she realized the water was off. "Crap. Do we have any water saved up?"

Julius appeared at the basement door. "We have one stash of cubes in the garage and another in the emergency shed out back," as he wrestled one of the water cubes to the counter. "There's more where this came from, but we better use it carefully."

Julius stared at Donald and Sarah. "I hope you will write this up! We need to get an issue out as soon as we can!"

Donald, exhausted after being up all night, shook his head at Julius. "Really? That's what you have to say at THIS moment? Jeez, Julius."

They stopped to listen to the newscaster:

"Dozens of fires continue to burn across the East Bay and in San Francisco. Major arteries are down around the bay. Major damage has closed the 101-280 interchange in San Francisco. Large parts of the Nimitz Freeway in Oakland near the estuary are under water, and the same is true near Union City and Newark further south. Highway 101 is flooded in Palo Alto and Redwood City. Bridges are closed. Toll plazas in Oakland, Hayward, and Newark are flooded. San Francisco and Oakland Airports remain closed due to flooding, but reports indicate severe quake damage to runways. Air travel to and from the Bay Area may be closed for weeks... or longer." The news reader sighed deeply. "Hug your loved ones, folks. A lot of people didn't make it. We are receiving reports of hundreds, maybe thousands of deaths. Obviously nothing is confirmed." He was choking up and suddenly the Beatles "Here Comes the Sun" was playing.

"Fuck." Aaron wondered what to do. Phones were down. His mobility was too impaired to go out and help. Greg wouldn't leave him, thankfully. But they had to help. "We should start making food, stuff people can share and carry around, things that don't need to be refrigerated." Greg nodded but when Aaron could see that Greg's mind was elsewhere. He was in a daze. He turned to Julius. "What do we have stored? We need to make food for people," gesturing at Donald and Sarah, covered in soot. "And our water supply might be needed too. It could be a few days before emergency supplies start arriving."

"Could be a lot longer than that! We should start boiling rainwater. Lucky our basins are full!"

"Boiling on our stove? That'll take forever!"

"You're right. Hmmm. We need to think this through. There could be a severe water shortage here in the next days. Who else do we know with water?"

"Our solar is still on the roof. I checked!" Julius informed them. "We should be able to get our stove going easily enough."

The house started shaking.

"It's an aftershock!" Julius jumped into the doorway. But it ended immediately, no harm done.

"My heart!" Aaron clutched his chest.

Greg put his arm over his shoulders, holding him close. "You ok? It's over already!"

Aaron gasped for breath, nodding. "I'm ok. That scared the shit out of me."

"We'll need as much power as we can get. The grid is down, we're on our own!" Julius said to Donald. "If we disconnect our building from the grid at the main box, restart the power in isolation, we should be able to connect our close neighbors and build a local power grid." ·

"I'll help. But it's on you. I don't know shit about this stuff."

Julius grinned. "I've been tinkering with solar since I was in college back in the 1970s. I can figure it out!"

Aaron spoke softly to Greg. "We have to contact Linda, Frank, Amelia and everyone else!" His family was all over the city.

"Not much we can do now. No phones. Maybe they'll show up here?"

Aaron didn't look well. "I need to lay down. I'm sorry! I know there's a lot to do!"

Greg helped Aaron to his feet. "You need to take care of yourself! We need you, I need you!" He helped Aaron back to bed. "Rest here for a while. Call me when you want to get up, or if you need anything, ok?" Greg wasn't a spring chicken but he was obviously in much better shape than his partner. In his early 70s, Aaron suddenly seemed terribly frail.

Greg was soon over their electric stove boiling what would be an endless procession of buckets of water brought in from their catchment basin. Anna was chopping vegetables and putting them into a huge chile she had started on the other burner.

"Gonna be a lot of hungry people," she muttered to herself.

***

Sarah Ackerman, the intrepid photographer working with the Water Protectors, was anxious to reach the waterfront. She'd shot photos of the King Tides regularly for years. She knew downtown was flooded from her neighbor who walked home across the city. She babbled hysterically about broken elevators and cracked buildings, flying glass and rubble, and streets covered in mud and water.

Sarah was pedaling her bike towards downtown. She'd survived the quake in the Haight Ashbury neighborhood. Their Edwardian building had cracked here and there, but mostly it held up. Several windows broke, the power was out, but no one was hurt in the four apartments. Outside immediately after the quake they found their neighborhood remarkably intact.

As she pedaled, things almost seemed normal. A lot of people were enjoying the first sunshine in a week, checking in with each other, looking at buildings that had lost windows or pieces of their facades.

"Hey Sarah!" her Water Protector colleague Liz was waving at her. She pulled over, one of the advantages of bicycling.

"Our building is fine," Sarah told her. "Sounds like it's bad everywhere else?"

"I heard some radio that says the bridges are closed, freeways are destroyed, and air travel is shut down for weeks!"

"Whoa! What about downtown? Heard anything?" But Liz hadn't. "I'm going to the Bay and see what I can see." Her friend urged her to report back.

On her way downtown she passed several places in the lower Haight that burned, including one where a half block was leveled and still smoldering. Neighbors were poking through the ruins. No stop lights were working anywhere, and at every major intersection, people were out directing traffic. Not that there were many cars on the road. She didn't see any cops anywhere, but the sound of sirens was constant.

After the Wiggle she rolled behind Safeway along the old bike mural. Dozens of streetcars were piled up on Church and Duboce—the tunnel must be out. Cold wind pushed her towards the forest of glass towers around Van Ness.

Market Street was largely deserted. It was Christmas, the day after the earthquake. Broken glass everywhere. She had to stop and lift her bike several times to avoid riding over it. The mid-Market area was still full of empty storefronts, until she got to the Ikea near 5th Street. There were cable cars parked along Powell Street too. People in orange vests guarded the BART stations, which were apparently closed.

The guy in the vest redirected the few people at BART to look on Mission Street for surface buses. "Everything is closed. The system is flooded. They don't know when it'll be open again."

That was a lot worse than she expected.

At Third Street she stared ahead, stunned. Water filled the whole area from Montgomery to the east. The Ferry Building was standing, looking normal in the distance. Water shimmered all the way there. Cautiously she rode on, entering the water when she realized it was quite shallow. At First Street she turned right and followed a twisting path through the flood, avoiding gaping holes in many spots. Crunch! "Oh shit!" She'd blown a tire. Stepping into the water, glad she wore her calf-high rain boots, the sound of broken glass beneath her feet was dramatic. 'Crap, I hope it doesn't cut my boots!' she worried. Gingerly she pushed her flat-tired bike through the water, to the corner across from the biggest building in town, the Salesforce Tower. But the crowd that gathered at the same corner wasn't concerned about the "Big Suppository" as some jokingly called it. They stared across the caution tape towards the next corner.

At the corner of Fremont and Mission, next to the Transbay Transit Terminal, the Millennium Tower had been tilting a few inches a year ever since it was first built. Unlike the rest of the towers around the area, the builder decided not to drive iron piles into the bedrock beneath the bay mud for its foundation. Multi-million-dollar efforts to stabilize its position floating in the deep bay mud proved ineffective and the tilting became a public joke. Some called the building full of million-dollar condominiums the "Leaning Tower of Schadenfreude," to capture the public disdain (and total lack of sympathy) for the wealthy owners of the fatally flawed structure.

When the Hayward fault slipped, the shaking set off meters-deep liquefaction in landfilled zones of San Francisco and around the bayshore. Old Yerba Buena Cove, San Francisco's original harbor that was rapidly filled in during the first years of urbanization, was extremely vulnerable to this process. The Leaning Tower of Schadenfreude, already tilting, could not withstand the combination of the sudden and rapid liquefying of the mud and the pull of gravity. Within five minutes of the earthquake striking, the building, which swayed to and fro at first, gave in to the inevitable and kept tipping and tipping, slowly and then faster, and finally in an almost perfect diagonal across the intersection of Mission and Fremont, it crashed into the Salesforce West building, knocking its top floors back onto the one-story garage entry behind it, or reducing them to dust. When the collapse stopped, the Millennium Tower was at a 30° angle, laying on the 8th floor of the office building. The intersection below was entirely filled with debris. And bodies! So many dead bodies.

"Holy shit!" gasped Sarah. She began taking photos. "Were you here when it happened?" she asked bystanders but of course they weren't. The crunching glass underfoot in the water-filled street kept her from charging across the tape towards the wreckage. It was about 11 in the morning, many hours since the collapse. The water surface noticeably rippled and advanced inland. "Here comes the King Tide again!" Sarah declared. Rescue workers climbed in the ruins.

"Wait, shouldn't we do something?" she said to no in particular.

"Like what?" said an older woman wrapped in a raincoat, her ankles in the water, her shoes submerged. "We can't move those bodies. And we sure can't go into that mess!"

"Those guys are there!" she pointed. Not waiting to convince any other gawkers, she left her bike by a pole and headed to the collapsed building. She shivered as she stepped between bodies face down in the water. She got nearer the ruin and a rescue worker on the pile saw her and waved her off. "Don't come up here! It's extremely dangerous!"

Another rescue worker appeared at her side. "Go back. There's nothing you can do here. We're trying to find people who might still be alive. We have dogs."

"Shouldn't we do something about these ..." she waved her hand around, "these people? We can't leave them here can we?"

"No, you're right. There's a makeshift morgue over there," pointing to the transit center. "With help, you can move bodies there."

***

The liquefaction of Yerba Buena Cove brought up a tremendous amount of mud and groundwater throughout the Financial District, streets disappearing as burbling mud surged though the cracked and buckling asphalt. The intense shaking popped thousands of windows from office towers, crashing down on the crazily tilting sidewalks and streets below. For thousands of pedestrians walking home on Christmas Eve at the time of the quake, the sudden crack and jolt of the quake that threw many to the ground was only the beginning. If they weren't impaled in seconds by falling sheets of glass (and many were), the confusing effort to take shelter from rocking buildings and falling glass was something they would never forget.

The earthquake also destroyed many places along the Embarcadero. Recent efforts to plan for and begin to reinforce the seawall made very slow progress. The northern piers, from the Cruise Ship Terminal to the Exploratorium and many others, were rebuilt by new tenants who also tried to prepare for sea-level rise. But the actual seawall that stood between the Bay and the City was over a century old. In dozens of locations along the southern waterfront, it crumbled during the nearly 2-minute shake. Bay waters mixed with the liquefying sand, mud, and groundwater, submerging dozens of blocks that crumbled into the wet subsoils. The sandbagged entries to the MUNI's Embarcadero tunnel couldn't withstand the onslaught, and once water poured in, it wasn't long before the entire MUNI and BART tunnel was drowned. The BART transbay tunnel survived the quake, but it filled with baywater. It would be months before they could begin to reclaim it.

***

Frank left Sheila's apartment on the 18th floor of the Canyon, the huge modern building above Bridgeview Way. The view across the Bay and the glimpses of the infield at the Giants stadium was luxurious, but suddenly it seemed crazy. The bay filled the streets below. How would they get out of here?

The stairwell was jammed with neighbors, desperate to get out of the Mission Bay tower in what the Giants branded "Mission Rock" neighborhood. It was night now, and everything was pitch black except for flashlights carried by folks moving down the stairs.

"Hey, watch out!"

Frank stopped after he was pushed from behind and realized that two people in front of him were moving slowly. One had his arm over the other. It turned out to be a husband and wife, both in their 60s like Frank.

"Sorry man, I didn't see you—people are pushing from behind." He suddenly stopped, using his bulk to block the crowd for a moment. Mustering up his most authority-loaded voice he bellowed, "Hold on! Slow down! Don't panic! We'll get out together! Don't push!" He turned back and continued to step down slowly. It seemed to work, as people repeated his admonition on up the stairwell, echoing into the distance and finally subduing the panic.

As soon as he thought he'd helped calm things down a bit (where were they, the 16th floor? The 14th? He'd already lost track in the darkness), someone pushed along the side.

"Excuse me, excuse me," demanded the man, who Frank realized was carrying a small child. "My child has been hurt. I have to get her to a hospital!" The man was frantic. Behind him his wife and a small boy were trying to keep up with his rapid descent.

"Jerry! Slow down! Don't fall!"

He was past Frank and he called back, "Stephanie needs a doctor!" and he kept moving as fast as he could get through. They soon disappeared in the darkness and others came along with their own urgencies. Frank was sore himself, but he knew to keep calm, move deliberately, keep his hand on the railing. Like everyone, he was still full of adrenaline. He couldn't think about Sheila's plunge out of her broken window. He didn't know he was bleeding himself, until he realized that his leg was warm and wet and pointed his flashlight to see that his lower left leg and shoe were soaked with blood.

"Oh shit!" He reached down and felt the hole in the side of his calf that was still bleeding. "Crap!" he muttered as he knew he had to stop the bleeding. "Is there a doctor here? Or a nurse?" he called hopefully.

A woman a few steps behind him pushed through. "I'm a nurse, what's the matter?"

He flashed his leg. "I gotta stop the bleeding. Can you tie me off?" He had nothing with him but the shirt and pants he was wearing when the quake struck. They were on a landing, and she led him through the door labeled 9. "We're already at 9?" he blurted pointlessly.

"Sit here!" she commanded, and he leaned into the wall and slumped down to the floor. His leg was throbbing now, and he was beginning to tremble uncontrollably. "You've lost a lot of blood already friend. And you're going into shock. We've got to get you medical attention." She was talking while she worked, grabbing a nearby piece of fabric and with her pocketknife and strong hands, tearing a long strip from it. She cut Frank's bloody pant leg away, and tied the fabric tightly around his leg above the wound. She took another section of fabric and pressed it onto the wound and wrapped more around it. "This ought to hold you for a bit." She looked around the hall strewn with fallen pictures, and a stream of belongings left behind by people who rushed out. Doors were open on several nearby apartments. She darted into the first one and came out a moment later with a big black parka. "It's your lucky day pal!" she said sardonically and wrapped Frank in the parka. "C'mon, you have to get up. You can't stay here. Let's go!"

Frank looked at the woman now, marveling at her competence. She was over 50, not tall, but broad shouldered with hands that had seen a long work life. She was Chinese or Filipino or Japanese or—Frank had no idea where in the world her ancestors might have started. Her salt and pepper hair was cut pretty short over her dark brown eyes that, combined with her slight smile, were quite evocative.

"Thank you! Thank you! I owe you one! What's your name?" he babbled as he struggled back to his feet and limped into the descending crowd. She was still helping him, but she stood back to make sure he could power himself.

"Julie. Julie Solarzano."

"I'm Frank, Frank Robertson. Listen, how can I find you later? Do you live here?"

She cocked her head at him. "No, no, I was visiting my daughter and her boyfriend. I live on Minna near Seventh."

"I'm with—" and he stopped. He didn't want to say he was with the Federal Police to this woman... or to anybody, he realized at that moment. "I live in Hunter's Point. I hope to see you again!" and they were soon separated in the crowd, Frank struggling down the stairs and Julie carried by the faster moving flow well past him.

On the 2nd floor everyone was directed through the door into the hallway. "Can't go further folks, it's flooded!" called a self-appointed monitor at the door. A few hardy souls tried to make their way down anyway, but Frank saw them reappear a few minutes later. He was ushered to an apartment that became an infirmary. "You look like you need urgent attention, friend," said someone in the hall, pointing to the apartment.

The living room floor was covered with injured people. Groaning and crying filled the air, along with voices calling loved ones "Richard!" "Susie!" "Bernard!" "Zoanne!" and dozens of others. People asked where else injured people might be and another apartment down the hall was suggested.

Frank eased himself into a spot along the wall and sank to the floor. At least he was warm in his parka, though he continued to tremble. He leg hurt like hell. He was soon asleep amidst the chaos.

Hours later, he awoke to the moaning of at least three different people. Dawn light was coming in the windows. Someone stood in the doorway. It was Julie! She announced:

"We will start taking you one by one down the stairs and put you on a boat. The Peace Navy has mobilized its fleet of small boats and they are ready to move people out of Mission Bay to land where they can get to a hospital. General Hospital is full. But we'll get each of you to medical care."

She saw Frank looking at her. "You ready to go Frank?" and he nodded. She helped him up. "How're you doin'?" she whispered, and he nodded his head.

"Still here!" he whispered theatrically. "You been awake all night?"

"Don't ask!" she got him onto the stairway and handed him over to two others to take him down. "See you later!" she said cheerfully, which seemed both reassuring and weirdly optimistic at the same time.

Frank was helped to a makeshift dock at the bottom of the stairs. Apparently some people spent the night dragging 55-gallon drums from somewhere to the landing. Covered with plywood and planks they were a good foot and a half above the sloshing bay waters.

"Here, I'll hold your arm. Step carefully, it's not super stable," the young man said. Frank stumbled once, but with the fellow's help, kept his feet. Outside in the early morning light a small boat was bobbing near the edge of the wooden landing. Two guys were holding ropes from the boat to keep it lashed as closely to the wooden landing as possible. Two people on the boat reached out for him and drew him onto the boat. The woman took him into the cabin and sat him on a small bench.

"Sit tight, OK? We're taking as many as we can."

About 20 minutes later he was surrounded by another 23 people, both inside the cabin and out on the back deck. A young man came in with a clipboard. "Hi, I'm Jessie Suzuki, and you're on the *Oyster Dream*. I need to get everyone's name and address, and your emergency contact person." He went around and took names and came to Frank.

"Frank Robertson, 23 Marlin Street at Hunter's Point." He paused. It was years since he declared an emergency contact person. It was always his moms, but she died last year. His son? He wasn't sure he could ask that of his long-estranged son. "Linda Robertson, my sister," and he rattled off her phone number.

About ten minutes later they were chugging out to the creek and then past the old Pier 70 shipyard area, full of new apartments and refurbished industrial buildings. Their target was a long-abandoned pier in Warm Water Cove on Pier 80 that was undamaged. As they cruised along, most of the people were sitting quietly, still in shock, many in great pain. Frank looked around, trying to ignore his throbbing leg.

The young woman who helped him on board appeared in front of him. "Frank Robertson?" He nodded. "Aren't you related to Leon and Lamar?"

"Uh, yeah, yes I am! Leon's my son, Lamar's my nephew!" He was astonished at the recognition.

"I'm Maria, Maria Campoy. I've been working with Ally Nakahara for the last two years. I've spent a lot of time at Leon's place on Underwood!"

"I'll be damned! Small world, huh?"

"Listen, you need to get to the hospital. They'll have a shuttle bus for everyone at Pier 80. But I'll tell the guys that you were rescued! This boat belongs to Jessie and Steve," she stuck her thumb towards the cabin. "I'm a friend, and occasional crew. They volunteer with the Peace Navy from time to time. Usually it's protest, but we got called last night to get ready this morning... and here we are!"

"Well thank you!" Frank remembered the blockade of Pier 19 and enjoyed a private smirk.

CHAPTER 62
WEDNESDAY, JANUARY 6, 2027

Ernesto Aguirre stood at the corner of 18th and Capp Streets in the heart of the Mission, staring at the black lake filling the streets to the east. He and the other plumbers wore masks to control the overwhelming odor.

"Man, that is unbelievable!"

He adjusted his mask but the smell was penetrating. The lake of shit was swelling. Almost two weeks passed since the Christmas Eve earthquake badly damaged the sewage system in many areas, none worse than in the north Mission of San Francisco. Those lucky enough to have survived the quake and the fires that pockmarked the neighborhood were living in the miasma of an open sewer.

Underground water and sewage systems ruptured catastrophically during the almost two minutes of sustained shaking, especially wherever the city was built over old creeks and lagoons. The Glacial Pulse combined with King Tides and an epic ten days of massive rainfall to raise flood levels across Northern California. San Francisco's old shoreline was its new shoreline, at least in many spots. The tidal lagoon that once occupied the middle of the Mission District re-emerged.

"That's not a plumbing problem," said Jimbo Johnson, shaking his big round head in disbelief, holding a wet handkerchief over his nose.

"Of course it is!" Jay retorted. "That is THE plumbing problem and its damn urgent!" He didn't care about the smell. It was what it was.

"What the hell are we supposed to do?" Jimbo looked very discouraged.

"We have to go to the source! This is what we've been campaigning on. Graywater systems, composting toilets, changing how we use water, how we handle waste." Jay was trying very hard not to say 'I told you so!'.

Ernesto grimaced. "That's well and good, but we don't have that now—we have this," pointing to the expanding lake of shit. He peered at Jay over his mask. "How can we get this out of here?" He was a strong supporter of Jay's campaign in the Plumbers' Union to push for new water politics. But this was too much. The neighborhood was literally choking. They had to fix it as fast as they could. But where would they get the heavy equipment to do it? And even if they could get the lake of sewage to drain to the bay, wouldn't it keep coming? In that regard, Jay was right.

After two weeks there was no sign of any federal response. The airports were still out of commission. The Bay, San Mateo, and Dumbarton bridges were closed, their eastern approaches hopelessly underwater, and the asphalt toll plazas below the water having broken up in the quake. The State of California started sending emergency supplies right away, flying pallets of food and water in by helicopter. That kept some people supplied with fresh water and basic food rations, but there were thousands in the Bay Area, the Delta, and the Central Valley, who didn't receive the limited relief. Meanwhile the infrastructure failure was so comprehensive that no one could decide what the first priority should be.

Access to San Francisco was complicated by the destruction of the bay-shore freeways as well as access to the bridges across the Bay. Even San Jose and Silicon Valley flooded. Luckily large parts of Interstate 280 in the San Mateo County hills remained usable, and some earth-moving equipment was being brought in slowly, though it was needed everywhere.

Jay turned to Ernesto. "We can't push this lake of shit into a hole. It's growing every day. We have to stop feeding it with more shit!"

"You have an idea?"

"Yeah! Up by my old place in the burn zone in the Castro, the old creek is running again! We need to get that fresh water flushing through here, like it did a long time ago!"

"That sounds good—but what about the thousands of people who live along this old creek who need to go to the bathroom every day? There's no running water in this part of town." Ernesto thought Jay was missing the point.

Jay of course thought his workmates were missing the point. "We need to start a crash course of building communal toilets, latrines, composting toilets. We need to rebuild the water system—not the one we had—the one we need!"

"Composting toilets?" Jimbo Johnson was not convinced. "Who will clean them out? And how long does it take for that shit to compost? And what'll you do with it then?" He wasn't up on the whole idea.

"Let's talk to the Canopy Council. They're the only ones doing anything!" He was glaring at Jimbo, frustrated to be having this argument under these cir-cumstances. He wasn't a particularly patient organizer, and the last two weeks left everyone's nerves frayed. Jay was exhausted and didn't have it in him to explain this now. "Farmers know what to do with compost!" he said angrily and stalked off.

"Hey!" Jimbo called after him.

"Let him go. We can't do anything right now." Ernesto pulled Jimbo with him. "Let's go back to the Hall. What are the Water Department people planning? Maybe we can work together." Jimbo grunted his assent and they headed to Mission Street.

***

Janet and Vero were at the Alemany Farm, sitting on the semi-circular stone bench. Annette Jorgensen was there, and several other Canopy Council members were too.

Joe Stennett hovered at the edge of the circle with his pad. "We've been harvesting potatoes like crazy. Except where flood or fire destroyed everything, the potatoes withstood the rains well, and we have a bumper crop. And witches butter! Man that stuff is growing like crazy! I don't know how many people are eating it every day now."

Annette looked at Will Shaw. "Any sign of the horse patrol?"

He shook his head. "Nope. No federal police, and hardly any SF police either. Have any of you seen cops?"

Everyone shook their heads.

Jorge Castro came striding up. "Cayuga Creek is back!" he reported.

"What do you mean?" Janet asked.

"Our community garden is built on the old creek bed. Or it was. Cuz the land opened during the quake and the creek is running full. There's a lot of water coming out of the ground these days."

Another farmer, Monica, who lived in Diamond Heights chimed in. "You should see Glen Canyon! The creek has never been so high. Broken water lines uphill are pouring into the canyon."

Millie Denby sat quietly at the edge of the group. She knew the others were mostly on the Canopy Council and she decidedly was not. But she'd had an ongoing life at Potrero del Sol community garden for two decades, and the food conspiracy distro site in her basement was an important node in the larger network. She knew as much as anyone about food and farming in that corner of the Mission.

"The flooding will be semi-permanent. We should be looking at it watershed by watershed," she looked around to nodding heads. "My garden, Potrero del Sol, was flooded by the rains. It drained into Precita Creek, which is quite visible in 'Lake Hairball' under the 101." She made air quotes and laughed before continuing. "You guys know the underpass? It seems to have cracked open at the bottom, and a lake has formed there. Cesar Chavez buckled in a dozen spots. Water from Precita Creek is filling the 'Lake', and the low spot at Guerrero. And you heard about the giant shit lagoon at 18th and Folsom?"

"What's that?" Joe Stennett queried.

Millie explained the broken sewer system, the extensive liquefaction where Mission Creek and the old tidal lagoon used to be. "Some Plumbers Union guys will see what they can do..." she trailed off, not believing anyone could address the severity of the disaster. She could smell it from her house on 20th and Shotwell—it was only two blocks north!

Janet plucked some rosemary from a bush at the edge of the little circular plaza. "We spent the last two years building a network of backyard farms and food conspiracies. There's no help coming any time soon—if ever! I propose that we connect to the Plumbers, the City Water Dept., the Electrical Workers, MUNI drivers, mechanics, everyone who does something that needs doing!"

Annette clapped her ancient hands and let out a low "Yeah! Yeah!" She enjoyed a great deal of natural authority derived from her years on the Council, reinforced by her all-around good sense. "The City government is a shambles."

The Mayor and several Supervisors were missing and presumed dead. City Hall has been red-tagged, along with most of the Civic Center. The collapse of the plaza into Brooks Hall and the parking garage was shocking, especially when a torrent of underground water flooded the basement of City Hall, the Main Library, the Asian Art Museum, and the Bill Graham Auditorium.

"It's been almost two weeks and despite our senators and reps screaming bloody murder in Washington, the Hutchinson administration isn't doing a damn thing. Rescuing San Francisco and the Bay Area is not their priority, obviously." Everyone acknowledged that glum reality.

"The governor is sending the national guard!" Joe inserted.

Annette looked at him with a cold stare. "And those 19-year-olds will do what? If they're coming to help us start digging out, great. But if they're coming to patrol, or protect private property, or some other absurdity, no thanks!" She glared around. "Our networks are mostly intact. Let's start connecting with the skilled laborers we need and begin rebuilding on our own terms!"

This hit everyone like a lightning bolt. Of course! Why wait any longer for an official response? Even if it came, they already knew they had to be done.

Vero jumped in, "My friends at the Folwell Commons have power and water. They only suffered minimal damage and the whole block is working together. Their solar set-up is amazing, and they have a functioning rain and graywater system, and even some composting toilets. Since last Friday they cleared half of Folsom Street—I mean they ripped up the broken asphalt from 25th to 24th along half the street. They're changing the remaining street to one-way and plant the other half."

"See! That's what we need!" Jorge was excited. "The creek has busted up a bunch of streets. Let's clear the asphalt and let the creek do its thing. Turn the rest to farmland."

"OK, ok," Janet put up her hands. "Good ideas—I'm excited! We need heavy equipment to do this right. Where can we get jackhammers, wheelbarrows, pickaxes, tools? And who has a working pickup that we can use?"

The conversation went into overdrive, with suggestions of reclaiming the air-powered jacks from a South of Market rental place, other equipment from the nearby Lowe's and Home Depot in Daly City. Several pickups and small trucks were identified. People who knew electricians, Teamsters, mechanics, or MUNI drivers promised to connect with them.

"This is a good beginning, but we need a real community council, one with the skills and resources to begin rebuilding San Francisco the right way!" Jorge urged.

"KALW is up and running—and I'm sure we can go up there and get on the air. Also I know folks who have been publishing the *Opaque Times* up in Eureka Valley. I can contact them about helping us." Janet offered. Lots of nodding heads endorsed her proposal.

"What about witches butter?" Vero blurted out. Everyone stopped in mid-sentence and turned to her.

"What about it?" Annette asked. "Like Joe said, a lotta folks are mighty glad for it now. I don't know what we'd be eating if we didn't have our potatoes and witches butter."

"Janet told me the Council has been helping to cultivate it." She stood to make it formal: "I regret having sold my ideas to BGM. Especially now. But," she visibly relaxed, having gotten that off her chest, "it's still a great source of food! And who knows what else?"

"Whaddya mean, 'what else'?" asked several people in unison.

"I don't know," Vero looked confused. "I think... um, maybe... People have grown small huts from it. Maybe it can provide shelter too until we can rebuild... I don't know."

Janet was sitting next to Vero and she touched her gently. "Let's make sure we protect as much of it as we can, ok? We don't know how far its mycelial network has grown on its own. We don't know how to make huts out of it, though we can ask our friends for advice. We don't know how it connects us to different critters—but it DOES seem to. We don't understand how it works or what it's doing. Anyway, it's precious, we agree?" No one objected. "BGM is flooded. They won't restart operations any time soon. Hopefully people will stop digging in parks and hillsides."

"What about the Federal Police? What happened to them?" People looked to Janet, knowing her uncle was a zone commander.

"I haven't heard. My uncle is back home. Hunter's Point is flooded and many of the buildings collapsed into the water when the quake hit. It will be a while before they are back up and running."

"The longer the better!" Annette brought the gathering to a close. "This is an incredible moment. The more we can do, the quicker, the better!" Everyone cheered and clapped.

***

Perlana Solarzano and her boyfriend Ethan Chan were laid off from Facebook/Meta after the Festival of Possibilities back in March. During the rest of 2026 they occasionally sought new jobs, but mostly they lived on unemployment and food conspiracies. They both volunteered at a Mission Bay depot which was near Ethan's apartment in the 23-floor Canyon on the south side of Mission Creek.

"Did you know this building used to be Del Monte's banana warehouse?" Perlana prodded a couple who were picking up a box of food back in the autumn, when fruits and vegetables were readily available. They nodded absentmindedly and kept on as she watched them, disappointed.

"Maybe you should try the Patty Hearst/SLA story instead?" Ethan suggested. That harkened back to 1974 when a mysterious radical group kidnapped newspaper heiress Patty Hearst and her family agreed to their ransom demand to distribute $2 million of food to poor people—turns out that effort took place in the same building next to the Fourth Street Bridge.

The corner of the warehouse was laid out like a small supermarket. Bins of dry goods to fresh vegetables were organized in rows. People could help themselves as they moved through the aisles. Ethan organized the layout, and Perlana created databases so people could arrange their volunteer shifts and see what foods were expected when. If it weren't for their rapidly shrinking savings, everything would be fine. They enjoyed the work there much more than anything they ever did at Facebook.

Ethan was very proud to invite Perlana and her mother over for Christmas Eve dinner. The King Tide in the morning was expected to flood the streets around his building. They arrived early to beat the water and help prepare the big meal. Ethan's own family was not big on the holiday, but he knew Perl and her mother were. Everything was going in the kitchen when the quake struck.

After the shock of being thrown to the floor amidst clattering dishes and cutlery and waiting out the interminable 110 seconds of hard shaking, Ethan pulled himself up in the dim light. Perlana and her mom Julie had been chatting over wine on the sofa. Ethan pushed into the living room to find them on the floor and the sofa on its back, having slid toward the windows. The late afternoon dusk was punctuated by screams.

"Are you guys ok?!?" Ethan yelled. Both Perlana and her mom regained their feet and nodded mutely. They turned dumbfounded towards the finely cracked window. Eerie dusk light shrouded the darkened buildings, the bay looming large. The screaming seemed to be outside the building, which made no sense on the 23rd floor.

They went to the window, which remained intact, and peered down at bay waters in the street filled with floating bodies.

"Fuck!" Julie sprang into action. "We have to see who needs help!" and from then on she led them from apartment to apartment. Julie was a registered nurse and provided emergency medical aid to each person she met who needed it. Perlana and Ethan focused on helping people who weren't hurt, at least not badly, to make their way to the emergency stairwells to get downstairs and hopefully out of the building. They wouldn't know for some time that there was no way out except into roiling floodwaters and that the sidewalks and streets of Mission Bay disintegrated during the powerful earthquake.

The next morning, after staging hundreds of people on the 2nd and 3rd floors, Ethan and Perlana helped organize the exodus by way of a flotilla of small boats that came to rescue survivors. The Peace Navy! They had friends who were part of it, but they didn't see anyone they knew during the half day they helped people board the sailboats, fishing boats, rowboats, and other craft that came to their improvised dock.

Two weeks later they were still doing most of their cooking outdoors. The Solarzano family home on Minna Street between Sixth and Seventh Streets, shook hard like everything in the area, but remained upright with no dramatic or visible damage, only a few cracks.

"That can't be good," Julie remarked when she saw the cracked corner of her building. The three of them trudged blocks from the edge of the flood where they'd jumped from the rowboat that saved them. Many of the streets

South of Market had buckled and sunk but they'd navigated the obstacles to reach the family home. Hoping against hope that the building was ok and untouched by fire, they were relieved to find it standing. There was a small pond standing before the Seventh Street end of the block, where Minna was 6 or 7 feet lower than the cross street.

The Solarzano building gradually sank below street level during decades of subsidence in the neighborhood. You could see it in the windows on the basement that were disappearing below the sidewalk—the external door to the basement had long stopped being useful. The basement flooded during the heavy rains in December and still wasn't fully drained. Without functioning sewage, they were scrambling to figure out how to manage their daily necessities.

"Hey, who wants pancakes?" Perlana cheerfully offered Ethan and Julie and several neighbors sitting on beach chairs. They built a communal kitchen area with carpets under a shade structure provided by some hipsters who lived in a condo on Folsom.

"We have a shit-ton of stuff. We use it every year at Burning Man!" They happily dragged it out of their red-tagged condo and gave it to the Minna Street crew. Perlana knew one of them from work, and she invited them to occupy the empty apartment in her building. The Burners had four stoves, a ton of utensils and plastic plates, bins for washing dishes, a dozen 10-gallon water cubes, most of which were full. They had utility wagons and even a small refrigerator that could be powered by a generator or run from a Hempattery.

"I can't believe you have all this shit!" Ethan laughed when he got in line at their building as part of the neighborhood bucket brigade that moved as many things as they could from the rickety condos to their alley a half block away.

"I'm glad we can still get at it! You should see the other condos down the street!" The woman was quite cheerful considering the circumstances. Many "lawyer lofts" built after the 1989 earthquake collapsed. "They look like toothpicks—I don't think they even had any real foundations!" the woman remarked.

"Hey, you call these pancakes? Isn't this that fungus?" complained Julie.

"Yeah, witches butter—it's amazing! It grows back fast! If you put enough syrup on it, or ketchup, or any flavoring, you can convince yourself," Perlana insisted. "It doesn't taste of much when you fry it up like this, it's hot and nourishing, ok? We're lucky to have it."

"Where'd you get it?" one of the neighbors asked.

"It's all over the place now. Remember BGM was buying as much as they could before the quake?" They nodded. "Well, that warehouse on Third Street is flooded and had its supply 'liberated'! Take some!" She grabbed a good-size chunk from a container by the stove and extended it to the neighbor. "If you put this in your backyard, you'll be helping, and you'll never run out!"

**

Frank sat morosely in his favorite chair, obsessing over Sheila. 'I shoulda grabbed her hand, something!' He couldn't stop beating himself up. But she was gone. Her body was found in the bay, along with hundreds of others, brought to a big refrigerated morgue at Pier 26. After his own treatment at an impromptu neighborhood clinic near SF General he'd gone to Pier 26 and looked at dozens of bodies before finding her. Her bloated face was full of blueish cuts and almost unrecognizable, but it was her. "Oh god," and he'd broken down sobbing. He knew she had no living relatives. 'Who was that friend in DC she was telling me about? I should try to call her.' But he couldn't remember a name and there was no way to go through Sheila's papers or computer files to figure it out. It was a strange sensation to realize that he was her closest kin. "Jeez," he'd mutter from time to time, exasperated and confounded, unable to decide on any course of action. No word from anyone since the phones were down. Who had a land-line anymore? He stayed home recuperating from his leg wound treated with a dozen stitches. Leon and Lamar were feeding him and making sure he got what he needed.

The Marlin Street house was tilted at an odd angle, having been knocked off its foundation, but otherwise it seemed safe enough. It hadn't fallen and since the rains hadn't returned (yet), he and Lamar patched the broken windows with plastic and plywood scavenged from a nearby construction site. The Federal Police base on Hunter's Point was under water and irretrievably damaged. In any case, cellular service was down and so were the Federal Police.

Lamar came in from the lean-to they'd erected out back to hold the table with the propane stove. "Hey Frank, you want a coffee? You hungry?"

"Nah. Thanks. I'm good." He stared at the sunny day, dreading what he knew could not be far off—the return of Colonel Morgan. The phones were still off, and power and water were barely working either. 'Maybe he can't get here with the airports and bridges closed,' he kept thinking, hoping it would become permanent. Not that he knew what to do in case things *didn't* go back to 'normal.'

Leon, Lamar, and Cindy left every day to help in the neighborhood. Leon's business was destroyed by the flood, and the earthquake finished off what the floods had not. But they were exhilarated in a way that left Frank puzzled.

They came in each day laden with supplies, made him meals, and were buzzing with excitement.

"Frank, you should come with us!" Leon proposed.

Frank saw a young version of himself in Leon. But he couldn't remember feeling his excitement. He always focused on getting by, first as a SF cop, then a UCSF cop, and most recently his head-spinning experiences in the federal forces, starting as a draftee of Homeland Security and now as a zone commander in the Federal Police.

"My leg is still pretty messed up. I don't know what I could do."

"Oh there's plenty you can do in a chair!" Lamar insisted. "The food pantry always needs help. How do you think we've been getting this food?"

He hadn't thought about it. "What food pantry?"

Neither Lamar nor Leon considered that it was part of Frank's job to bust the illegal farms and food conspiracies. Frank never embraced the role anyway. But he remembered his official duty, and this would put him in a difficult situation.

"You know, the food pantry over in the Opera House? Where we've been getting fresh produce for the last year or so?" Lamar blithely explained.

"Oh, uh, yeah, right," Frank answered, though it was the first he'd ever heard of it. He would have to keep it secret. The boys took him in their electric three-wheeler over the hill to the venerable old building. Beautifully restored decades ago, Frank knew it as a community center and theater. Frank followed Leon and Lamar, limping with his cane into the main room. Nothing much to see there, but they led him through a door and down a corridor to a classroom. It was lined with shelves full of produce, canned goods, and assorted other items. A half dozen people were taking things or putting things on the shelves.

"Hey guys," greeted an older woman in a green sweater, her head covered in a coppery wrap. "Oh hi Frank! Oh Frank," she looked sadly at him, "I'm SO sorry about Sheila!"

He halted with a jolt. "Rhonda?!? You part of this?" He stared at his sister's wife, dumbfounded.

"Why sure, Frank. The whole neighborhood is. Didn't you know?"

He tried to hide his shock and nodded, mumbling, "well, yeah, of course," and moved further into the room.

"Hey Rhonda, what do you want Frank to do? He's here to help!" Leon said boisterously.

"Oh yeah? Why Frank, that's great! I guess your leg is still sore, huh? Why don't you come here and take over what I'm doing? It's mostly inventory." Once he sat down, she slid her ledger under his eyes and pointed at the various columns. "We only want to know what people are taking."

"Where do they pay?" he asked.

"Oh, there's no paying here. Everything is for everyone. We encourage folks to only take what they need, to leave enough for others, but nobody takes advantage. Our job" she pointed to the list "is to check off what goes out, so we know what to restock—when we can."

Frank spent the next hours checking people out, conversing with people he'd never met, or in a few cases, people he hadn't seen for a long time. Everyone was very helpful, coming to his station with their boxes and reading out to him what they were taking: "one head of lettuce, four zucchinis, 3 lbs. of potatoes, 5 kiwis," etc.

During a break in the stream of "shoppers," Frank asked Rhonda, who finally reappeared after she'd gone out of the room for a long time, "where'd we get kiwis?"

"Everything is grown locally... kiwis, we got a carload a few days ago, someone who drove from Gridley, taking back roads through Sonoma and Marin to get to the Golden Gate Bridge. Quite the adventure I heard." She smiled.

Eventually Leon and Lamar reappeared and loaded Frank on the electric cart, piled with boxes. Frank wedged himself in and they were soon home.

The day he went to help at the Pantry, cellular service came back on. Frank left his phone at home since it wasn't working. But when he got home he figured he should try it, not knowing yet that service was restored. It came on and suddenly it started buzzing continuously as messages that were lost in the ether for two weeks came rushing in. There were dozens and dozens of missed calls too, and at least 30 voice mails to listen to, mostly from people outside of the Bay Area. Eli texted him a half dozen times in the last few hours. Colonel Morgan was there, of course, and Charlene called and texted a bunch too.

He decided to give Eli a call first.

"Eli! It's me!"

"Frank! Are you ok?"

"Yeah, injured my leg, but I'm alright. What about you, Tanya, little Liliana? What a way for her to start her life!"

"Oh man, you would not believe it! We're fine, thank God. My brother Mike was here and my parents were on their way back to their church—you remember I told you my dad is an evangelical pastor out on Mission Street? Anyway, this house swayed like you wouldn't believe. I heard loud cracks, I was sure it was gonna come down on us. But it held. Even the windows—those cracks were in panes on the back porch, but the window held. We lost power and water like everyone. But at least we have a roof over our head. My parents turned around after the quake and drove right back over here. Guerrero Street held up well, except where it hits Cesar Chavez. There's a lake there now!" Eli was talking rapidly. He worried about Frank. For two weeks he and his brother scrambled to feed themselves, to stay warm on cold evenings, and to accommodate his parents and a half dozen parishioners they'd invited to their duplex. He thought about driving over to Frank's but more pressing concerns kept him preoccupied.

"You injured your leg?" Eli finally stopped to ask Frank.

"Yeah. Eli, Sheila's dead."

"What?!? Oh my god, Frank, I'm sorry! What happened?"

Frank told his story. Christmas Eve at Sheila's, king tides swamping the streets, and then kabam! Sheila slipping through the open space where the window had been... He got choked up again telling Eli.

"Aw Frank. Shit man. Maybe you should come over here? We're kinda crowded already, but I'm sure we can fit one more."

Frank regained his composure. "Thank you, Eli, that's very kind. I have my place here on Marlin. Leon and Lamar and Cindy are here with me. I'm gonna be ok..." he paused. "Eli, we have to report, but I got to tell you, I don't think I have it in me to go back."

"Phone service is finally back. I'll let you know if I hear anything, ok? And call me if you do too."

Frank agreed and hung up, wondering who to call next. He did not want to talk to Colonel Morgan. 'Was he even in San Francisco? Didn't he leave for Vegas or San Diego or something?' Frank pondered.

***

Thousands of San Franciscans spent two weeks living in makeshift shelters in open spaces, cooking in communal kitchens, including Dolores Park and Golden Gate Park. People opened their homes to those who lost everything, and many refugees from the central parts of the City found themselves sleeping on couches or floors with neighbors they'd never met.

On the city's west side, there was less damage compared to the east side. A major fire burned several blocks near the beach in the immediate aftermath of the quake, and another fire tore through parts of Golden Gate Heights. An engine company tried to get to the beach fire but couldn't get past broken streets and rubble for hours. When they reached the fire, it was burning intensely, finally reducing to ashes the blocks from Lawton to Ortega, 47th to the beach.

The Marina district, built on landfill following the 1915 Worlds' Fair, was the neighborhood most seriously damaged by the 1989 Loma Prieta earthquake. This time it was in ruins, streets buckled and turned to muck, while dozens of fancy homes collapsed. The neighborhood burned all night. Unlike 1989, no fire response came—trucks couldn't get there and the fire boat rushed to Treasure Island where fire engulfed new apartment towers.

KALW, the big FM station owned by the San Francisco school district whose studios were in a high school next to McLaren Park, was back on the air a day after the quake. Announcers dedicated the airtime to passing messages among people, reading out long lists of missing persons, and giving regular updates on where the flood's edges were.

In the sunny days after the quake, floodwaters covered parts of downtown, Mission Bay, the South of Market, and the Mission, as well as large areas of the southeastern shoreline both north and south of Hunter's Point. With the sewage system broken, a serious public health crisis was developing around the widening lagoon of human waste in the heart of the Mission.

CHAPTER 63
THURSDAY, JANUARY 14, 2027

After Christmas the rain stopped for more than two weeks, which was a godsend. A heavy winter rainstorm came howling in from the north Pacific two days ago but was almost done. The last King Tides of the winter started pushing deeply into the city Wednesday and would hit again at 10:37 this morning. San Francisco was deluged by water from above at the same time as high tides overwhelmed the old shoreline and pushed up groundwater further inland.

Jay convinced his fellow plumbers that their best chance to address the Shit Lake was to unleash the creeks long been buried under San Francisco. Water Department workers were skeptical, but eventually decided it had as much chance as anything they'd be able to do in the next few weeks. Jay and Fred Perry the union leader, along with Katerina Winslow of the Water Department, had climbed the steep hill on Mansell to reach the studios of KALW last week. Big Flo was a well-known host and she set up the plumbers in a small studio.

"This is Big Flo and we are joined today by," and she paused while she looked for the list of names. "We're the Plumbers Union!" blurted Jay, "and Katerina is from the Water Department."

"You're here today to ask for help, right?" Flo prodded.

"Yes," boomed Fred in his deep voice. "We have to use the creeks to flush that huge lake of crap out of the Mission!"

Katerina jumped in, "The earthquake broke the plumbing. How do we get that sewage moving? With the King Tides and the Glacial Pulse, the big rains and everything, there are not a lot of options. The union guys think we can use next week's King Tides to help flush the area. No pun intended!" But Flo was groaning in the background, and the boys couldn't help chuckling.

"We need all the help we can get to open up the flow as much as possible," said Fred. Flo snickered again.

"Rain is forecast for next week, that should help," Katerina interjected, "we need as much water as possible pouring out of the hills to push that lagoon of black water out to the bay. When the King Tide rolls in, it will raise everything up and if we can direct enough fresh water downhill, we think we can get that stuff moving."

Flo leaned in, "Quoting our longtime regular, Harry Shearer, 'it's a movement, and we all need one, EVERY DAY!'"

Nobody knew how many people were tuning in, but probably a lot. During last Thursday and Friday and through the weekend, dozens of crews diligently dug channels for the already surfaced creeks, directing them into the lake of raw sewage.

The Plumbers Union also distributed flyers the previous week. "Restore the Creeks!" The flyer advocated using the week before the next King Tides would send bay waters flowing heavily inland. It would be their best shot at flushing the massive shit lake in the Mission—but only if they could clear the way for the natural springs and creeks to come tumbling down the hills to activate the flushing.

Teams of volunteers pulled asphalt and other debris away from the waterways. At Corbett and Clayton on the slopes of Twin Peaks, a relatively new condominium collapsed when the spring it was built over burst through its cement foundation. Neighbors cleared as much of the area as possible, sending the rushing water cascading down Corbett to Al's Park. Water surged through the broken wall along upper Market Street onto 18th Street. The houses north of 18th burned during the night of the quake and it was through those properties alongside what was left of the underground culvert on Eighteenth Street that people channeled the reborn Dolores Creek. Another branch of underground water visible in the basement of the old Armory was running through the broken pavement of 14th Street into the lagoon's northern reaches. Still another freshwater stream ran through the wreckage of Eighth Street in the South of Market, reaching the muddy shit-filled lake at Brannan.

The plumbers' earlier effort to get people to construct latrines and even composting toilets was surprisingly successful. It turned out that San Francisco was full of people who previously worked in banks, insurance and real estate companies, advertising agencies, or tech companies. Having connected through the food conspiracies to locally grown fresh food during the prior year, many were ripe for recruitment. Pushed by the urgent needs of the moment to engage with myriad infrastructural failures, thousands embraced the opportunity to contribute—a type of hard work entirely different than what they used to call it before everything changed. They worked in teams, sweating, pulling muscles, lifting debris, puzzling out how to solve problems with each other, and basically having a blast.

Donald Nevilleton left Kite Kastle every day after the quake, plunging into whatever needed doing. His wife Sarah wanted to help too, so they took shifts staying home with the 2-year-old. But sometimes they brought her along in a backpack and she gurgled and babbled while they moved debris.

"I can't believe how much water is flowing here now! Has this always been here?" Donald asked a guy in muddy green overalls who apparently knew about water.

"Oh yeah," he tipped his soiled baseball cap back. "The creeks have run in culverts under the streets for a century. I know this guy who always joked that we might have paved everything over, but nature was still here, under the asphalt. And sure enough," he pointed his shovel to the rushing creek.

Sarah Ackerman spent the week excitedly documenting the progress of the creek's restoration. She flaunted her "Water Protector" sweatshirt and cap, jumping in to help clear debris. She was a short distance from the two men standing alongside the running water when she noticed another dude downstream.

"Hey, what're you doin'?" she ran to the guy pulling a piece of wall across the ditch where the creek was running steadily.

Wet and muddy, the man was preoccupied with gathering materials. "What's the matter?" He looked at the young blonde with her camera and her "Water Protectors" cap. "I'm taking this... you mind?"

She waved him off. "No, take it. But don't block the water!" There was no helping it. Many people were scavenging through the ruins of the burnt blocks. Dirty and tired they were trying to repair their shelters. Restoring the creek was someone else's problem.

A crowd of teenagers marched up with shovels and picks and a wheelbarrow trailing behind, rain gear billowing as they walked. The remaining parts of Eighteenth Street made for a precarious path along the creek's banks, occasionally crumbling into it.

"What shall we do?" shouted the young woman in front, her frizzy red hair escaping the hood as she slung her shovel down. "I'm Jill," she thrust her hand out to Sarah.

"Clear a path for the water!"

"We came up from Castro and 18th. The canal is flowing there, and they've already built some wooden bridges to cross back and forth," explained one of the young women. "Water protectors, huh? You guys a big operation?"

Sarah smiled. "I take photos to advocate for daylighting creeks and healthy watersheds!" The teens nodded knowingly, but she couldn't tell if what she said made sense to them. "Have you heard of us? And no, we're not a big operation!"

One of the guys in the group with a shovel over his shoulder piped up. "We spent the first week digging graves," he shook his head. The shock of thousands of dead still hung over everyone. "I wonder if we'll ever know how many died."

Sarah, at 23, wasn't that much older than this brigade of teenagers, but as the heavy presence of mass casualties again took center stage, she felt an intense solidarity with the energetic youth in front of her. "Hey, can I take some pictures of you while you're clearing debris?" she asked, realizing it was a little odd—maybe she should volunteer to help them?

"Sure, whatever," the young woman who first spoke pointed to two guys further upstream. "Let's see if those guys have a plan."

Donald and the other guy, who turned out to be George Bradley—he was a union janitor whose family had a house on Nineteenth since the 1950s—were watching the scene unfold downstream. George put the kids to work on pulling chunks of asphalt from the creek bed. Donald joined in the effort, while George moved uphill to focus on another task.

"You guys a team?" Donald asked Jill.

"Oh!" she looked around at her friends. "I hadn't thought of it like that, but yeah, sure. We're a team, ain't we Lorna?"

Lorna gave her a look. "A team?" she shrugged. She turned to Donald. "We've been working every day since the earthquake. Did a bunch of grave-diggin'," she grimaced. "Like everyone, right? What else are we supposed to do? Go home and play video games? I mean, come *on*," she ended theatrically. She went back to trying to shore up the crumbling road above them.

"I haven't gotten far from home. I live over there," he pointed up the hill towards his house.

"We're friends from high school. Our houses came through ok, and we started helping. Well... you can't just watch, y'know?" Jill was grasping a big chunk of asphalt and explaining this as she and another young guy lifted it.

Donald got the message and reached for a side of the piece—it was damn heavy! The three of them heaved the asphalt up to the road, about shoulder high for Donald.

"Hey Donald!" Tomas and Cristiano popped up on the road. "Whatcha doin'?"

Peering down into the ditch, Tomas suddenly realized that he knew Jill and Lorna too! They'd met during that Critical Mass when they visited the Festival of Possibilities! "Oh hi! Jill right? Lorna?"

The two young women looked up at the boys on their bikes. "Oh yeah... what's your names again?" They were soon telling each other stories. Donald and Jill climbed out of the ditch.

"You guys heading to the Kastle?" Donald asked them.

"Yeah. Got a message that there's a new issue!"

"A new issue?" Jill asked.

"Um, yeah, a newsletter. We help get it around." Cristiano piped up.

"It's close by. Why don't you come over and have a bowl of soup?" Donald suggested. "I mean, when you're ready. I guess lunch is in another hour..."

Lorna looked like she won the lottery. "Fresh soup? I'm there!" The endless physical effort sometimes was too much, and then as if by magic, a neighbor would invite them in for a meal. Following Donald and Tomas and Cristiano, the crew headed up Clover Alley from Eighteenth, and soon were removing sweaty gear and boots in the garage at Kite Kastle.

***

After pulling people from ruins, saving people from flooded areas, and burying the dead, attention was focused on restoring "normal" life again. In the weeks since the earthquake, power was slowly restored, largely thanks to crews of "unskilled" locals under the direction of skilled electricians. A collective of lesbian electricians calling themselves the Wonder Women after a similar group in the 1980s, trained people to help reconfigure the city's power system. Reproducing the model established at the Folwell Commons, they linked buildings on the same block. Taking advantage of installed solar to create shared power grids, buildings were rerouted from the quake-damaged centralized grid that wasn't working anyway.

A flooded warehouse near Bernal Heights and 101 was full of BGM Hempatteries, and they were being shared widely. Five Hempatteries made a robust electrical storage backup for an entire block of houses. Many blocks had enough solar to generate considerable surpluses—the younger union guys cleverly wired surplus blocks to nearby stores and gas stations with limited or no power. Areas where street damage was minimal and most buildings survived the shaking and fires seemed almost normal. As more people gained experience in the conversion process, and the plans were widely shared, teams crisscrossed the city setting up block-based shared solar power coops.

Paths through wreckage and broken pavements became well-worn. With teams of electricians and plumbers reorganizing the power and water infrastructure one block after another, other people came together under the auspices of the Canopy Council. Janet was adamant at the last meeting. "We've been saying 'One Lane for Food' for the past few years. This is it! We have to start making that real NOW, or before you know it, the old patterns will reassert themselves."

"Janet," Will Shaw stood up and got the floor. "I'm with you, but shouldn't we emphasize rain gardens in our campaign? If we say we're doing 'one lane for food' AND we're relieving our broken sewage system with larger and wider rain gardens, that'll be an easier 'sell,' no?"

Janet nodded enthusiastically. "Definitely! Good idea!" Most of Council was with her. Annette was key, but she was also easy. The problem was Joe Stennett, and Esther and Regina too. They were from the Presidio area and regularly argued against the campaign to convert streets. Too many of their neighbors were committed to their cars.

"But what about the Feds? Aren't they gonna shut us down?" Esther was worried about causing problems.

"The Federal Police vanished after the quake. Maybe they're coming back, maybe not." Janet looked to Annette to back her up.

"The Hutchinson administration has made it clear that they can't—or won't—send any relief to San Francisco or the Bay Area, unless it's specifically for 'defense,'" she made no effort to disguise her disdain. "This is their idiotic defederalization program in full bloom. They spent the FEMA money on those hurricanes and coastal flooding in the Southeast and the Gulf Coast during the last two years. I'm sure they could send plenty of help, but this is payback." She looked around the room. "And I'm glad!" This sent a noticeable ripple through several people, including Esther and Regina and Joe and others.

"Glad?!? You're glad we won't get help? How can you say that?" Regina was trembling. "We're Americans too! We have a right! Hutchinson can't abandon us!"

"We're better off without 'em!" Annette seemed to have grown younger than her 80 years. She was smiling now. "Janet is absolutely right. If we move fast, we can open dozens of streets and get crops in the ground. The Federal Police won't be able to do anything, assuming they ever come back. If we didn't have this food growing already, can you imagine how much worse things would be? No, that whole stupid campaign to screw local food production, that is OVER! You heard it here first!"

***

Lamar and Leon, facing catastrophic flooding at the Underwood warehouse even before the quake, tried to consolidate what they could on the hill. They retrieved equipment from the hidden Hangar, which was a lost cause. Floodwaters seeped under the long-hidden front door, the curtain of thick ivy doing nothing to block the rising waters. Coming down the long stairway from the hatch, Lamar and Cindy grabbed what they could that wasn't soaked.

When the quake struck, the fridge toppled over and the dry goods in the pantry cascaded into the muck. They already retrieved important boxes of lab equipment before the quake, along with a half dozen computers, a bunch of bedding and assorted lamps and whatnot. Trying to enter the Hangar several days after the quake, they opened the hatch and found the long stairway intact but separated from the wall in a few spots. As they slowly descended into the darkness, waving their flashlights around, the stairway suddenly swung out.

"Oh shit! Oh shit! Hang ooonnnnn!" Lamar and Leon held on for dear life until the swaying stopped, and they realized they were tilting precariously over the flooded floor 20 feet beneath them. "Fuck!" hissed Leon. "We gotta get the hell outta here."

"Let's go back up!" Lamar urged. They slowly climbed the treacherous metal stairs, as it swayed gently.

When they climbed out of the hatch, they knew they wouldn't be going back, maybe ever. They locked the hatch and headed back to the house.

"Get anything else?" Cindy asked as they came in. "Wait, you ok? You look... like you saw a ghost or something!"

Lamar rushed into her arms for a hearty bear hug. "I almost bit it," and he explained their moment dangling in the air.

Cindy laughed, well removed from the terror they'd experienced. "Well, you'll be fine!"

Frank was oblivious to the coming and going. He assumed the equipment was brought from Leon's place and remained clueless about their secret lab in the Hangar. The house was cluttered with monitors, computers, lab equipment, boxes, and files. And the Marlin Street house was not in great shape, slipping from the foundation with many broken windows.

"Should we start looking for another place?" Leon proposed. There were thousands of apartments empty before the quake, and now... well it wasn't easy to get around, but there had to be lots of decent places that survived the quake standing empty.

Cindy was immediately excited about the prospect. "Oh hell yes! Let's find a beautiful empty apartment and move in before anyone notices. I'm up for scouting around. Lamar? You wanna come?"

Lamar was happy to join her, of course. "Where should we look?"

She gave him a sly smile. "Let's go downtown! It's under water—I mean really under water, not only financially!" She laughed out loud. "There were already those unsold luxury condos. I bet we can find something!"

"Hey Frank, where did you say Jessie kept his boat? The one he picked you up in?" They were surprised to learn that it was Jessie Suzuki, Larry's oyster reef guy, who picked up Frank in Mission Bay after the earthquake.

Frank looked at his nephews and the vet. "What? Why? You planning to go out in the bay?" He didn't want them to go. Being alone in the house frightened him. Linda and Rhonda were over on the slopes of McLaren Park. Maybe he should head to their place? But they never invited him, so no, maybe not.

"Yeah, we're going to explore downtown... IF we can get Jessie to take us!" Lamar explained. He didn't mention finding empty condos to move in to.

"He keeps his boat near Sierra Point."

"Maybe we can find him checking the reefs at Candlestick. I'm sure Larry's still keeping him going," Leon suggested. A half hour later the three of them were at Leon's warehouse on Underwood. The floodwaters receded but the bay was considerably closer than it'd ever been before Christmas. Pockets of water stood everywhere, but they were able to enter Leon's. The smell was overpowering. Mildew and mold ran wild after the main flood.

"No saving this place!" Leon lamented. "But I just remembered!" and he climbed up into a storage attic to the side of the main floor. He reappeared a minute later with a bright yellow duffel bag. "Look what I got!" He tossed it to the muddy floor. "It's a rubber raft I got years ago and forgot all about until we walked in. I always thought I'd take it on the bay, and I did once..." he stopped talking as he unzipped the bag. "It seems ok. we can use it."

Twenty minutes later they were bobbing in the bay, slowly paddling away from the Carol Avenue wharf, which was above the higher bay waters. It was bright and sunny, about 65 degrees without much wind, but the sun was low in the southern winter sky. For a January 14, it could hardly be nicer. They went past the oyster reefs Jessie and Steve Brooks monitored for Larry, but they didn't see anyone, nor the substantial bloom of witches butter growing beneath the bay surface. A bit further on, the first seal showed up next to their rubber raft. Then another and another. "Aar, aar, aar," and they swam and bobbed around them.

"Are they circling us?" Leon asked in a worried tone.

Cindy was utterly charmed, intrigued by the gregarious reception they were getting. She stopped paddling and started talking to the seals. "What's up fellas? Is there something we should know?" A harbor seal with light tan skin and big brown eyes approached Cindy, and then suddenly dived beneath the raft and disappeared. The rest were gone in minutes too.

"That was weird." Cindy didn't know much about marine mammals. Her veterinarian training was focused on large farm animals—horses, cows, sheep, and pigs. After a year at the SPCA, she felt she knew cats and dogs well too. "I think they were trying to communicate."

Lamar nodded and kept paddling. "Let's see if we can get to Mission Bay, or even downtown!" He didn't know that the tide was with them, ebbing through the Golden Gate. They made good time, reaching the Giants stadium in time to stare at the sun glinting between the highrises poking out of the flooded Mission Bay. "That looks eerie!" said Lamar.

"The smell! Oh man! Look at that shit!" Leon was gagging. It was bad. They were in the middle of a thick band of black water streaming out of Mission Creek. "What a mess!"

Soon they were under the Bay Bridge near the floating Fire Department building. Leon proposed they try to disembark there. "They have that ladder," pointing ahead. Once they were on the floating dock, firemen came out to greet them.

"Where'd you come from?" and they explained their journey from Yosemite Creek. "Wow, that's a ways. You caught the tide I guess," and he explained it to them. "Let us help you," and they lifted the raft from the bay. "Oh gross! You are covered in shit!" The fireman grabbed a hose and washed the crap off the rubber raft. "The good news is this thing is perfect! You can use it to navigate around downtown. It's mostly flooded behind what's left of the seawall." They helped carry it to the Embarcadero and put it back into the water. It was very shallow, but too deep to walk through.

"You'll have to watch out for broken glass. Especially sitting in the raft, when you get too close to the bottom, you could get shredded easily. Be careful!"

They thanked the firemen and paddled down Spear Street on at least two feet of water, maybe more. "What about that place?" Leon was pointing to a tall white apartment building, recently constructed with its characteristic twisting block design, making it seem as though the building was made of a bunch of plastic blocks that weren't quite lined up correctly. It was a block away up Howard. The ground floor was wide open, with some water sloshing in to cover the floors, but not enough to paddle in. They carefully stepped out of the boat into the water.

"I shoulda worn my boots!" Cindy complained. Lamar had some boots on, but not rubber ones so his feet got as soaked as the others. They carefully tied up their raft in a corner of the lobby, hoping it was out of sight and anyway, who would come by and steal it? The elevators were out of service of course, but they found the stairwell and the door opened easily enough. There was already water on the other side of the door, but when they opened it, more rushed in, cascading down the stairs towards the water that filled the subbasement.

Squishing all the way, they climbed and climbed, not leaving the stairwell until the the 22nd floor. "Twenty-two, good luck! Let's try that!" Leon was excited. The door opened onto a gray carpeted hallway. Boring corporate art hung on the walls, and everything seemed undisturbed.

"Hello? Hello?" Cindy called. Lamar did too. Nobody answered. They proceeded slowly, passing two closed and locked doors before they came upon an open door. They called again, "hello?" and getting no response, they cautiously entered. It was a gorgeous apartment, fully furnished. Nothing seemed amiss.

"I don't think anyone lives here—look!" Lamar entered the bedroom and pulled open the empty bureau drawer. He slid the closet door open and there were a few hangers, nothing else.

"Score!" Leon yelled. He rushed to the windows, gazing out at the surrounding towers like a kid in a candy shop. "Check out this view! And there's the bridge!" pointing to the view of the Bay Bridge between buildings, the Port of Oakland cranes in the distance. A door was ajar in the wall next to the windows. He slowly pushed in and found that it opened on a twin apartment next door. "Look!" he called back to Cindy and Lamar. "We found two empty apartments! This is perfect! We can be neighbors!" He laughed a bit hysterically. This was too good to be true. How long could this even last? Why shouldn't they take what they could? These apartments were empty. What a waste!

CHAPTER 64
MONDAY, JANUARY 25, 2027

Colonel Morgan, after sending all but a skeleton force out on a week-long furlough because of the expected flooding at the beginning of Christmas week, went to San Diego. When the news arrived of the Christmas Eve earth-quake, his first reaction was to rush back. But it became apparent that no one was getting back to San Francisco any time soon. The airports, the bridges, the freeways around the shoreline of the bay, were wiped out. Transportation into the Bay Area would have to go through Travis Air Force Base in Fairfield which was well above the flood waters inundating the delta but getting from Fairfield to San Francisco wouldn't be solved for weeks.

"What the hell is going on?" Morgan snarled. At the other end was Lt. Smithson in Encino in Los Angeles' San Fernando Valley.

"You know as much as I do, sir. Looks like it was the Big One, a worse-case scenario. Camp Hayward is gone, long stretches of the Nimitz Freeway, Highway 101, the toll plazas at the bridges, the airports..." he trailed off. The devastation being reported was unimaginable. "And now water rationing! The whole delta is flooded with salt water and the California Aqueduct is closed!"

"We need to get back! Imagine the chaos! The looting!"

"That's not happening. FEMA told California they're on their own!"

"What?"

"Defederalization, sir. FEMA doesn't have anything left after the last two years. They spent billions to build new seawalls around DC, and protection for the Navy base in Norfolk, Virginia."

"Same thing on the Gulf Coast and in Florida. Those hurricanes..." and Morgan dropped it there. What could either of them say? The idea that the Federal Government would always stand behind you, come in and help with disaster relief, restore flooded communities, etc., etc., those were bygone days.

"Who is on the ground?" Morgan wanted to know.

"The base is lost. Hunter's Point is under water now. We have re-established phone contact with Zone Commanders Nichols, Robertson, and Garner who are in different parts of San Francisco. No one has returned to active duty since the quake. Somewhere between 20 and 40 other soldiers are thought to be in San Francisco. There is no active Federal Police there at this time. The population is burying the dead, clearing streets, repairing homes, some rebuilding has begun. I understand that many surface creeks have re-emerged and have been utilized to address a catastrophic failure of the sewage and water system."

Finally Col. Morgan and his command staff were returning to San Francisco. For the past week they had slowly arrived in Fairfield. Fully 85% of the Federal Police stationed in Hunter's Point were from somewhere else and left the area during the holiday furlough. There were 120 returning Federal Police, and after a few days of confusion, they were on the FP-404, the 41-foot utility boat assigned to the Federal Police months earlier. Chugging through Suisun Bay they made it under the Carquinez Strait bridge and into San Pablo Bay. It was cold and gray, but at least it wasn't raining.

"Corporal," Morgan turned from the railing at the front of the boat, addressing his orderly. "Tell the Zone Commanders to meet me in the Captain's office."

A few minutes later Lieutenants Owens, Smithson, and Hudson gathered around the table as the boat churned through the bay. Morgan was standing over a map was spread out on the table. "We're landing here," he pointed to the long unused docks at Fort Mason. "We will be met by a bus that will take us to quarters in the Presidio."

"What is our mission now, Colonel?" Hudson asked.

Morgan glared at him. "Our mission remains the same. To enforce federal policies, to protect property, to guarantee public safety."

His zone commanders asked no further questions.

***

When Leon told Frank that he and Lamar and Cindy found empty apartments in an abandoned highrise downtown, Frank was unimpressed.

"Bad idea," he told them. "They'll never let you stay. It's only a matter of time before they kick you out."

"We'll see about that!" Leon was defiant. "It'll be a while before anything approaching normal life comes back. Did you hear about the fallen buildings? And it's flooded anyway! I bet most of the people who used to live there never come back!"

Frank watched as they came and grabbed what they could carry and disappeared again. 'Going by water?' He couldn't imagine it. But then he'd never imagined his city flooded by King Tides like the ones earlier this week, or reborn creeks tumbling down what were once busy streets.

Sighing, he got up and went to the kitchen. Cans of chili and clam chowder and pork & beans still filled one side of a cabinet. He felt hungry, but the prospect of standing in the cold gray weather in the yard and cooking over the propane stove was too much for him. He looked at the sink full of dirty dishes, crusty and dry after weeks without running water. It was too much.

He'd grown tired of a diet centered on potatoes and witches butter and yearned for regular food supplies. "I hate having to cook this stuff!" he'd complained to his sister-in law Rhonda at the Pantry. "Vero's chips were good, but this stuff is boring."

"Well, we're getting tired of it, but let's face it, we're lucky to have it. Without the butter and the huge potato harvest, we'd be in real trouble. The butter is our main source of protein. Yesterday, the League delivered turnips, kale, lemons, beets, and leeks. You know what to do with them?"

He wondered how the farms were faring, now that there were no Federal Police tax collections or inspections. As he pondered this, Rhonda was helping an older couple fill their bags in the background, and his phone rang.

"Eli!" he answered with an upbeat tone that belied his actual sense of dread.

"Frank, did you get the orders?"

"Oh, I got our orders: We're on our own."

Rhonda was walking across the room and saw how awful Frank looked. "What's the matter?"

"They're back. I must report for duty at 8 o'clock in the Presidio!"

***

Juna couldn't believe they were driving over the Golden Gate Bridge.

A month had passed since they made their dramatic escape from the rising waters in the delta. After parking near Marsh Creek Road in the foothills of Mt. Diablo, Juna sat in the cab of their sister's old truck, lost in horrid visions of Rosie's certain drowning. It couldn't have been much more than a half hour before the water came up, lifting and swamping the old trailer at the same time. Rosie sitting stubbornly in her chair, lights out, cold darkness and black water rising as the trailer shuddered, shivered, and finally collapsed under the onslaught. Juna quietly sobbed in the truck, watching the lights of other vehicles escaping up the side of Mt. Diablo.

At dawn the next day Juna groggily looked out at the inland sea that formed since darkness fell. Speechless, they got out of the truck and walked up the hill. Overwhelming sadness hung in the air as Juna ducked into a grove of old oak trees, then found a wispy trail leading up the flank of the hill. Doggedly walking as the sun rose over the vast inland sea, the sky suddenly clear and blue, Juna felt their spirits shift. A scree sounded above and they saw a redtailed hawk circling above their path. When they reached the ridgetop, they saw higher ridges proceeding in green folds up and up to the west. After the rain the mountain was as green as the Irish countryside. Following the hawk through the sky, Juna suddenly noticed much higher, circling above the peak of Mt. Diablo, what they were sure were the condors they'd first seen right before the quake.

Skirting the ridge towards the southwest, Juna came upon a small valley with scattered oaks and large oddly shaped stone outcroppings. They descended the ridge gazing at a cluster of stone peaks that cupped the little valley from the south. Something drew them to a large round stone covered in orange and yellow and green lichen. Juna leaned into it, putting their hands on the ancient rock.

Yanked from their surroundings, Juna was transported into a vision of the same valley filled with people. Women sat on blankets with piles of herbs and seeds and bones, while hundreds of original Californians elaborately painted with black and red dyes, hair stiffly extended, some naked and others wearing garments made of animal fur, walked among the displays, talking and laughing. Cholvon, Ssaoam, Huichin, Carquin, Yulien, communities gathered for their annual convergence. Obsidian pieces piled on one blanket, oysters and clams in a basket of cool water, tule reeds on several others; in the distance young men were competing with atlatl's to see who was the most accurate, hurling arrows at a distant target.

"Hey, hey dude! You ok?" Juna was being jostled by someone, and when they opened their eyes they were looking into the face of two women, both black-haired and round-faced with lined dark skin, dressed in nondescript blue skirts. Juna slowly sat up, disoriented by their vision, looking at the empty landscape. "I, I, I... I saw hundreds, no thousands, of people here. It was a big market."

One woman peered intently at Juna. "You saw the ancestors! This was the place... the place where everyone gathered... it was a crossroads." She looked at her friend, and then back to Juna. "Are you from here?"

"In the delta, by Holt," they nodded. "My sister..." and sobbing they buried their face in their hands.

The two women silently stayed by Juna's side until they regained their composure.

"I'm sorry, my sister... she drowned yesterday. She wouldn't come!" Juna said desperately.

The two women were sisters, Angela and Nala Pacheco, and invited them to their place. "We're not supposed to live here. It's the regional park. But we keep a real low profile." They led Juna on a circuitous trail, up and out of the little valley, through a dense oak forest, and eventually to a cave at the back of another hidden canyon.

"That place we found you, it's right beneath the Vasco Caves. There's petroglyphs in there!" Angela explained. "Your vision... it was real! That area was a meeting place for tribes from the delta, the mountain, the bay, they came from everywhere. We think they came together every year for an annual festival and to trade. Some even traveled from the Sierra, from Mt. Shasta, from the Santa Cruz mountains."

"You an archaeologist or something?" Juna asked.

"No, I heard a ranger talking about it. But it makes sense. When you stand there, with Mt. Diablo climbing to the west and the delta and central valley stretching to snow-capped mountains, you can see why they'd pick a place like this."

Nala brought them back to the moment. "You can stay until you're ready to return..." Return to what exactly? That was left unsaid. "You said you have a truck parked somewhere?" The next day they led Juna out of their hidden home on a well-trodden path down to the truck. They piled in and drove it to a lost dirt road the Pacheco sisters suggested.

They spent many nights sitting around the campfire telling stories, learning about each other, and discussing the world. They knew only fragments about their indigenous pasts, but they each had one. A few weeks later, Juna was ready. Living off the land, nestled in the bosom of the mountain, some days Juna felt like they could stay forever. But they could tell the sisters were ready for them to leave. There was no particular conflict, but their welcome was wearing out. Juna was unable to bring much to their shared existence, as they didn't know how to forage on the mountain, nor how to hunt for small game. The bag of witchips they'd brought out only inspired suspicious hostility.

"Bioengineered? What the fuck? You eat that shit? That'll kill you!" Nala spat. Angela was a little more curious but deferred to her sister on this.

"A lot of folks have been eating this for most of a year... nobody sick or dead yet! And it never runs out!" Juna retorted. But they didn't push it.

Weeks later they returned to the topic. "One friend coaxed it into growing a shelter!" Juna explained the Quarrytown huts and how his friend Angie spoke to it. "This scientist who originally wrote about the possibilities of witches butter came to visit and she took another invention, the 'bio-bulb', and stuck it in the ceiling. Angie welcomed it and asked it to give light—and it did!"

The sisters listened quietly. Finally Angela said, "Juna, that sounds like powerful magic. I don't think we want it here," she paused, looking at them intently, "can you understand?"

"Oh sure, of course. I felt the same as you." They recounted the long-ago visit to the underground cellar and the icy fear they experienced when touching the biobulb plant. And then the relationship that developed with the scrub jays on Kite Hill, finally culminating in the out-of-body experience that led them to seeing the bomber at Dolores Park.

Nala got up and left the fire. Angela shifted uncomfortably. "Thank you for telling us about this. Living out here we don't hear about new stuff much. It's been a few years since we had a guest..." She stood to add some wood to the fire. "Nala won't ask you to go, but I know she's ready," Angela said bluntly.

Juna was jarred, but was thinking about when they might go anyway. They missed their friends at Quarrytown and the new life they started to share, but they also wanted to go home to Kite Kastle. They were surprised to discover that yearning, since whenever Juna was there, they usually felt a bit disconnected. They missed the scrub jays on Kite Hill as much as their housemates.

On the day Juna left, the condors came swooping low again, flowing down the side of the mountain and right over their head as they approached the truck. Juna raised an arm in salute.

From Mt. Diablo Juna embarked on a long winding route to Pleasant Hill, where they learned that they could cross to Benicia and Vallejo on the intact freeway bridge. Once across the water, they swung far to the north to clear the bay flooding, across Napa and Sonoma counties before arriving in Petaluma, where flood waters made it a bayshore town. Riding back roads across rural Marin to Pt. Reyes and Highway 1, they avoided the flooded Highway 101. Not far from the Nicasio reservoir Juna saw a farmstand where they bought several cases of apples and winter vegetables.

"Where are you goin' with this?" the girl behind the counter asked.

"Back to San Francisco. Been gone a month and I guess they need everything we can bring in," Juna explained.

"You want chickens? Or rabbits? We got lots," and she waved Juna into the yard behind the stand. Sure enough, cages with chickens stood ready to go, and a couple with big healthy-looking rabbits too. "I'll take 'em!" Juna grinned. Between Kite Kastle and Quarrytown, the animals would be a boon. The girl gave Juna half off on the haul, a great deal!

Three lanes of cars and trucks streamed across the bridge after the weird journey each took to reach the northern edge of the bridge. Sausalito was wiped out along the waterfront. The Highway 101 interchange above the Mill Valley wetlands was flooded and part of the causeway was damaged during the quake. But an elevated bypass was rapidly built and traffic could ascend the long slope to the Golden Gate Bridge.

On the San Francisco side traffic was being diverted into the western neighborhoods by way of the coast or through the Presidio and onto Park Presidio Boulevard. Juna headed to Kite Kastle, but they were also anxious to return to Quarrytown. They drove through Golden Gate Park, following the heavy traffic. Juna never learned the streets on the west side and didn't know how to get to Kite Kastle from this direction. But eventually they got to upper Market that would—if it was intact—lead to the Stanton Street turnoff.

As Juna reached the top of the hill near Clipper, the huge view opened before them. But something was funny… what? A detour ahead forced them from the viaduct and onto the streets at the top of Noe Valley. 'Crap!' and then as they made the turn they did a double-take! The skyline! It wasn't the same, not even close! Buildings tilted at odd angles. There were gaps he'd never noticed before. Had highrises collapsed? Juna hadn't gotten the news.

Ten minutes later they pulled into the cul-de-sac in front of Kite Kastle. Juna patted the dashboard, thanking the truck for getting them back. They rushed into the house and found Julius and Anna and Sarah and Greg busily sweeping and cleaning the common rooms. "Hey! I'm back!" they yelled jubilantly. Everyone dropped what they were doing to gather around.

"What happened? Where've you been? We were worried about you!" Anna exclaimed.

"We were afraid of the worst," admitted Greg. "I can't tell you how happy I am to see you!" and he gave Juna another huge hug.

Juna began explaining, and the rush of memories was too much. "My sister," they sobbed. "My sister died in her trailer. She wouldn't leave. I told her we had to get out of there!" Juna was half-heartedly explaining themself but no one was judging. And then the escape, the Pacheco sisters and life on Mt. Diablo, and finally the epic return journey. "The truck! It's full of food and chickens and rabbits!" and they led everyone out to the 1959 truck with its payload.

"Chickens!" Julius was thrilled. "We can have fresh eggs again! I'm gonna fix up that old coop! I knew we shouldn't toss it," referring to an old chicken coop out back, unused for years. The fresh produce was divided up among the house, Quarrytown, and the local food pantry. The rabbits were something new though.

"Anyone ever raised rabbits?" Sarah asked. She and her daughter Elsie were already falling in love with a big brown one in the cage.

"Anyone ever killed a rabbit to eat?" asked Anna, reminding everyone what the idea was behind raising rabbits. "And don't forget, they multiply like crazy! You will need a place that can handle it."

Julius gave his wife a nudge. "Don't be negative! We have space out back."

"What about the coyotes? What about the raccoons? They're gonna come for the chickens AND the rabbits. You gonna sit out there with a shotgun?"

"Oh c'mon, don't be like that. We'll figure it out. If we don't want to deal with harvesting rabbits, I'm sure we can find people who will." Julius was determined to make it work. "And Elsie can have a pet rabbit too!" he ended defiantly.

CHAPTER 65
WEDNESDAY, FEBRUARY 10, 2027

Exactly two years after the National Emergency Declaration that opened his presidency, President Hutchinson ignored the anniversary. On the first, he'd given a speech proclaiming the success of his administration. But a beleaguered year later his administration was in crisis. The global reinsurance industry debacle led to a drastic contraction of economic activity during the past year. The much-touted "Defederalization Program" produced what most analysts predicted it would: a hobbled central government unable to sustain the unrestrained military spending that propped up the national economy and its dominant role in the world since WWII.

Battered by coastal flooding and hurricanes slamming the Gulf and East coasts for the past two years, the Glacial Pulse that raised sea-levels across the world, the ongoing economic depression and widespread unemployment, and six weeks since the earthquake that devastated northern California, the Hutchinson government was paralyzed. Having slashed taxes and budgets by up to a third in the first full budget of its administration, neither the administration nor the Republican House was willing to revert to "printing money" to combat the multiple crises it faced.

This hollowing out of the federal government was reinforced by an aggressively reactionary Supreme Court overturning decisions that set national norms in regard to marriage, private sexuality, reproductive rights, schooling, taxes, housing, environmental regulations, and public lands. Each of the fifty states found itself newly responsible for the quality and type of life within its borders—and with severe budget problems of their own now that the federal revenues many depended on were largely absent. The slow collapse of a common national culture and a shared identity was a years-long process, but the Hutchinson Administration gave it a forceful push, leaving each state to go its own way.

The only thing that Defederalization left untouched was the expectation that interstate commerce would follow standardized rules set at the national level. And of course the military! But even the defense budget, always sacrosanct, shrank in the wake of the broad reduction of revenue that followed the economic contraction. The withdrawal from over two hundred small "advance" bases as part of a general refocus on mainland defense won support from progressives in addition to the isolationist wing and the budget hawks of the administration, leading to loud protests from the "war party" (both Republicans and Democrats). President Hutchinson, once at the apex of Homeland Security, and before that the DEA, lost his zeal for globe-spanning imperialism, and found allies on right and left to reorganize and significantly downsize the sprawling military and spy operations draining national wealth. Since China started selling U.S. Treasury bonds, the interest on the national debt had nearly doubled, compounding the economic crisis. A strategic retreat provoked by the actual weakness of the U.S. was inevitable. Hutchinson was the first politician to act on it.

The sputtering campaign to enforce national food standards was abandoned after a year. The big corn and soy farmers in the conservative states of the farm belt learned that Defederalization meant they were on their own too. The Federal Police, formed from the troops drafted by Homeland Security for the National Emergency, was tasked with cracking down on illegal urban farms and ensuring the smooth consumption of the "Patriot Packages" of processed food, in addition to supplementing local law enforcement when it came to political protest. But their budget was slashed by 30%, leading to widespread demoralization and uncertainty.

The California government, long the dominant counterpoint to a conservative national regime, was in crisis too. The state's budget surpluses from the early 2020s were gone, and overall revenue was way down. Deep inside the engine of the state economy one of the key pistons stopped functioning: the vast stream of federal spending on the military, on war-related technology research and development, transportation spending for highways and airports, Army Corps of Engineer dredging and dam building and maintenance, health care subsidies, etc. The earthquake devastated the statewide water system, one of the most elaborate plumbing systems in the world and it would take well over a trillion dollars to repair and replace what was lost.

The metropolitan Bay Area, whose primary transportation and sanitation infrastructure collapsed, faced unprecedented problems delivering food and water and shelter to over two and a half million people whose lives abruptly shattered along with the fault line. Thousands of dead and missing, untold numbers of injured, and California was severely limited in its capacity to respond.

The new Governor was inaugurated two weeks after the quake in a Sacramento still recovering from the worst flooding in a century, inheriting from Governor Newsom a state that was laid low after a decade of unsustainable prosperity for a small upper class, and stagnation and rising poverty for the rest. Tax revenues plunged as the need for government support soared. Her inaugural promise to roll up her sleeves and get to work rang especially hollow given the stark conditions besetting the Bay Area and the unfolding water crisis in central and southern California.

Relief supplies were arriving by the boatload, sent from countries around the world. Planeloads of essential goods were landing every hour. But most of it was far from the Bay Area, where there were no functioning ports for the ships, and no airports to land the planes except the military airport in Fairfield. Caravans of supply trucks rolled into the west side of San Francisco, some arriving across the Golden Gate Bridge, but most making their way up Interstate 280 from the South Bay's surviving roads. East Bay relief centers were crowded with hungry and thirsty people, dependent on helicopter airlifts of pallets of food and water. Local emergency teams were responding as well as they could, but during the past month everyone and everything had been pushed beyond their limits.

***

The paths between the rows of tents were perpetually muddy. Since the rain returned in late January, the Dolores Park refugee camp became a quagmire. Those who were on the southern (higher) slopes of the park did better, though they lacked flat places to pitch their tents. Those who were in the big recreation field were fighting the mud.

Jay pushed open the flap of the tent he was sharing with Jordan, who was starting to awaken, and in wafted the smell of tortillas. "I'm gonna get us some tostadas for brekky..." and he was off. He dodged through the muddy path, trying to land on less wet spots, but picking up a hefty amount of the ubiquitous crud that plagued the camp by the time he got to the paved path remnants at the edge of the hill. He stomped and scraped, trying to get it off before finally giving up and heading to the line at Rosanna's.

Rosanna set up shop a month ago. A propane stove next to the picnic tables turned the spot into the camp restaurant. She produced hundreds of tacos, tamales, tostadas, and panuchos every day. In the morning she was known for her fresh tortillas made out of whatever she could get her hands on, mostly a combination of corn meal and witches butter, but sometimes it was wheat flour and witches butter, and a few times it was the fungus only. Most people preferred the corn-fungus combo. On most days you could add government surplus cheese (that seemed to be everywhere now), onions and jalapeños, plus some lettuce or greens foraged from local gardens; along with a heaping portion of fried potatoes which were always in abundance, and her endless supply of hot salsa. She was feeding hundreds in the camp every day, at least for breakfast and lunch.

Jay found himself behind women he didn't recognize talking animatedly.

"We're not going back—I don't mean us, but the whole economy. Why would we go back to shuffling data around?" The speaker was retying a red bandana over her curly brown hair, and as she glanced back to Jay he figured her for a former corporate exec or something like that. Here she was in blue jeans and a formless gray sweater having emerged from a tent somewhere in the camp.

Her interlocutor was tall and wiry and very pale, unkempt black hair falling from a part in the middle of her head. She had a birdlike quality, her eyes darting around continuously as she joined the conversation. "If I can get a new roof over my head, I'd much rather keep working on relief crews," she glanced at Jay and decided she didn't need to hide anything. "I've been sleeping better these past two weeks than I have in a long time. It's because I'm damn tired after the hard work!"

"You remember those booths full of ideas at the Festival of Possibilities last year?" asked the first woman.

"Sure. We thought it would be more than a bunch of ideas," the dark-haired woman responded.

Jay was listening intently now.

"What do you mean?"

"I was organizing at BGM and we wanted this to be the beginning of a bigger movement. A movement among tech workers, not for wages and all that, but to wrest control over the direction of our work!"

"I remember that. Our Salesforce people, at least the organizers who helped get it going, wanted something like that too. But when we 'succeeded,'" she made air quotes, "and those kids came out and started camping..." she didn't finish her sentence.

"Hey we were there too!" Jay piped up. "I'm Jay," and he extended his hand to them in turn. "I'm with the Plumbers Union."

Karen, the dark-haired one, looked intently at him. "Are you one of those insurgents who threw out the old guard?"

Jay grinned in acknowledgment. "Yeah, we've been pushing hard to change the plumbing system across the city. Now we know why!" he grinned.

"I was helping dig latrines down there where the tennis courts used to be," said Susanna, the brown-haired woman. "I guess others did the heavy lifting before I got involved. Broken up tennis court and fencing got carted off. The creek is flowing now!" She looked excited at the thought.

"You put latrines near the running creek?" Jay asked, a bit surprised.

"Well, yeah," she took a few steps forward as the line advanced. "I mean, I didn't decide it, it was already happening when I started helping."

Jay was about to launch on a whole explanation of the composting toilet and ShitSystem he designed to fit together with the expansion of local farming—but they arrived at the front of the line.

Susanna greeted Rosanna's daughter Meli with a smile. "How's it goin' today Meli?" and after a moment of chitchat, she got two tamales and refilled her water bottle. Karen went for tacos with cheese, "gimme the ones made of the fungus only. They're lighter!"

After Jay got his tostadas to bring back to his tent, he found the women waiting for him. "Oh, thanks for waiting! Where are you guys?" They gave him their coordinates at the other edge of the campground, and promised to meet up later.

Jay was excited. It felt full of potential... The women seemed competent and interesting.

"Hey Jordan," he extended the tostada to his tent-mate. "G'morning!"

Jordan was sitting up on his cot, he good leg on the ground and his stump jutting out over the edge. He'd been out of the hospital for a month now. He woke up hungry every day and gobbled his meals. He reached for his prosthetic leg and once he had it in place, he rose to go the latrines. "Gotta do an inspection," he announced, their now-common code for doing their business.

Jordan was lucky to be alive, and they both knew it. When gloom and self-pity about his amputated leg crept into Jordan's thoughts, he was good at dismissing them. "Fuck that. I'm glad to be here. There's still a lot to do!" But inevitably, the pain and difficulty of adjusting to his new condition took its toll. There were plenty of bleak hours morosely sitting in the tent, especially when it was raining.

But Jay would get him going with his boundless enthusiasm for plumbing designs. "C'mon, Jordan, you're better at this than I am!" and he would thrust his drawings and notes into his lap. "We have to figure out how to build a ShitSystem for each house to process its own waste on site." Ideally, the end product would be useful compost that could be applied directly to the new linear farms where streets were narrowed. The street gardens needed remediation to recover the soil. Toxic waste from asphalt and car effluent poisoned the ground. Compost bricks from nearby homes would help accelerate the process.

Jordan gratefully embraced the project. "It's tricky, y'know? We have to redo every toilet, every bathtub and sink, with a gray water system—gray water out from sinks and bathtubs and IN to the toilets. Then the flushed toilets have to land in a small digester in every building, sized to accommodate the number of residents. So, for starters we need a clear idea of how many flushes per day lead to how many pounds of solid waste?" He was in his element now.

"Can the digesters be designed on permaculture principles?" Jay interjected. "Somehow using the available resources to create a self-sustaining circular system? Or will we need electricity to heat the waste to accelerate the process?"

After sustained effort they'd come up with what they dubbed their "Shit-System". "I'm not sure that's the most marketable name," Jordan ribbed Jay, who was a bit too sold on the name he'd chosen.

"People must learn to deal with shit. I'm sick of trying to pretend it's not a central problem of urban life. And one that, by flushing it away into the void with fresh drinking water, we've made much worse than it need be. The fear of shit needs to be confronted!"

Jordan smiled at his friend. He felt so much affection for him. 'Too bad he isn't gay!' he thought for the umpteenth time. But their friendship, already strong, was a pillar they both depended on now, especially after Jay dragged Jordan out of the clutches of certain death and gotten him to the hospital.

***

Maria breathed deeply as she strode through the flourishing hothouse in Larry's Brisbane warehouse. 'Clara will be be glad when she finally gets back!' she thought, admiring the healthy looking bioboats growing from the mother plants. Clara went back to Arizona at the beginning of Christmas week. After the quake she had no way to return. They hadn't even been able to talk until early January when most cellular links were re-established. She missed her like crazy—she and Clara moved to San Francisco together when Larry recruited them. She'd been her best friend for the last several years, the only one she could talk to about their boss Alison, or her new beau Jessie. She especially counted on Clara to keep her feet on the (scientific) ground.

Dat Doan was the big surprise. Since they'd been trying to get to the bottom of how witches butter worked, how it might be conscious and even willful, she'd come to rely on him. He was her best collaborator during the past couple of months, even through the floods and earthquake, even though they weren't officially working together.

'Jessie too' she smiled, recognizing how much he made her feel at home in San Francisco. The two of them went into the bay during the sunny January days to see what they could learn about the extent of the flooding, and how it was affecting the oyster reef, the seal colony at the state park beach, harbor porpoises, etc.

"Oh my god! Look!" Maria yelled back to Jessie who was steering the boat. The oyster reef was intact, but a huge ornate white structure extended from it. "That's witches butter!" She reached over and pulled on a piece that extended toward the surface. It tingled as she made contact, sending a current up her arm to her chest. She worked it and broke the piece off. "Look at you!" She handed it to Jessie. "This has grown like crazy! Look at how far it goes!" It seemed to extend as far as they could see into the murky bay water. Every time they came back it went further and further until it wrapped across the whole outflow of Yosemite Slough to reach the flooded base on Hunter's Point.

Last week they'd motored offshore towards downtown. Near Mission Creek Maria spied something white in the water. "Jessie! It's here too!" They found another reef of witches butter fungus. On closer inspection it looked like a fence made from white antlers, looming out of the depths.

"Is it spreading itself?" Maria wondered aloud.

"What about the seals? Or even fish? If they eat it and then defecate elsewhere, could that spread it?"

"Well, yeah, if you ingest the spores they could pass through. I suppose so." Maria was a bit out of her range now. But there was no doubt that the fungus was growing underwater into extensive reefs along the bay shore. She kept wondering how it was spreading in the following days.

She waved to Larry across the hothouse and took the stairs up to the offices on the mezzanine. In her office she returned to the mystery Dat left with her: the rolled up flat panel of witches butter that BGM produced.

Hours before the earthquake Dat and Ally were meeting at Dat's place in the Bayview, but the tidal pulse rose so fast that they evacuated to Ally's place on Potrero Hill. Before the earthquake hit the Missouri Street apartment, only Dat and Ally were still there. After Dat's people left, Ally pulled out the tan tube that opened into a flat panel when they unrolled it.

"Right before we left words were appearing on it," Ally noted, "but where were they coming from? How do letters and words form on the surface? What is the underlying technology here?"

"That's why I brought it to you," Dat replied. "No one knows this fungus better than you, Ally."

The earthquake struck with a sharp crack, toppling a bookshelf over and shattering plates that fell from a counter in the kitchen. Furniture slid around while the apartment building shook and shuddered for more than 90 seconds. Ally and Dat gripped the table, staring at each other through their rising panic. And then it was over. As the silence spread and then sirens erupted in the distance, they gasped and started to breathe heavily, not realizing that they'd each been holding their breath.

"You OK?" Dat asked her. She nodded, and he confirmed that he was too. "What now?" he went to her window, peering up and down the block. "Lights are out. I suppose electricity and gas are down. You know where your gas shut-off is? Probably a good idea." She grabbed a flashlight and they went down to the basement and found two other neighbors there already.

"You want to stay here?" Ally asked Dat.

"Thanks but I better head back to my place and see if it's still standing. I'll leave that with you if you want me to."

"Um, sure ok." But Ally, like every able-bodied neighbor, was immersed in all-day rescue operations for the next few days. After a week she went to the Brisbane warehouse.

"Maria, I have something for you," she'd said as soon as she saw her associate.

Maria looked at Ally, a bit stunned that the first thing she said was that, rather than 'how are you?' or "are you ok?' or 'where were you when it hit?' They got to that soon enough, but Ally was typically brusque and to the point. And when Maria got the full download on what the tan tube was and what happened, her attention was riveted too.

She sat with the flat panel open on the desk. Without thinking she caressed the sides, humming. "Are you here? Can you hear me?" she asked softly. The panel was unchanged. She returned to humming, staring into space while keeping one hand on the side of it. Suddenly it grew warmer! She looked down and stopped humming. It was warm now.

"Are you here?" she asked again. Somehow that seemed the right question.

A series of characters took shape on the screen. Exclamation points and question marks and parentheses and a whole row of commas, asterisks, ampersands and @ symbols, like someone trying out a typewriter for the first time, goofing around. The panel was quite warm now. Maria realized that the heat coming off it meant that some energy was routing through it. But how? It was laying on her desk.

"Where is the heat coming from? You are very warm."

"LIFE > ENERGY"

She stared at the panel. She grabbed her phone and snapped a photo. Then the words faded away and the panel was blank again.

"Still there? Can we talk?"

No answer. It was cool now. Whatever animated it seemed to have departed. Did that even make sense? How could something enter and leave this slab of bioengineered witches butter laying on her desk? But how could you explain the heat and the words? Maria leaned back in her chair, put her hands behind her head and rocked silently. She grabbed her phone and texted the image to Dat and to Ally. She added a message: "What next?"

EPILOGUE
SATURDAY, OCTOBER 21, 2051

Frank sat at his window overlooking the backyard garden park, feeling relieved. The rain relented, but strong winds were still billowing across the ocean and into San Francisco. How could he have lived long enough to see hurricanes hitting San Francisco from the once freezing cold Pacific Ocean? He was 90—he couldn't believe it himself. He could still remember a time before the Internet, before mobile phones, even before answering machines. Before witches butter! Where had the years gone?

The second hurricane to hit San Francisco in its history battered the city for the last three days but the Pigeon Palace was still standing. Hundreds of trees fell when 115 mph winds slammed into the city. While his co-op apartment in the 150-year-old Victorian, his home since 2039, shook mightily, it did not break. By contrast, shocking destruction waylaid the Sunset district where the full force of the storm arrived with no buffer. Thousands of homes lost their roofs or simply fell over when overwhelmed by the irresistible winds. The sun poked through the clouds, hitting a new crack in his window and scattering rainbow beams on the far wall. The front door opened down the hall.

"Grandpa? Where are you?"

"I'm down here," he replied, "in the dining room."

Lori appeared in the door and rushed over to give him a hug. "Don't get up! I came to make you lunch."

"You're a sweetheart!" Frank smiled as his granddaughter got busy in the kitchen.

"Have you heard from Janet?" Lori asked about her aunt through the door.

"I saw her a few days before the hurricane. She's always busy. I was surprised she dropped in to check on me, to tell the truth."

"We worry about you Grandpa! How's your leg?"

"It always acts up when it storms. But it wasn't too bad this time."

His thoughts drifted back to the big Christmas Eve quake of '26 when he'd first hurt it. He couldn't remember how his leg got sliced. He didn't even notice it until later. He could only remember the sudden jolt, the violent shaking, and watching Sheila slip over the edge where her window had been. His granddaughter's voice broke his train of thought.

"I'm gonna get some tomatoes from the back, ok?"

Lori would find many kinds to choose from in the gardens of the Folwell Commons Park. Frank watched her through his back window, carrying a basket over her arm, greeting neighbors and flirting with guy who lived across the Commons. Lori was tall anyway, but her Afro added a good 6-7 inches to her stature. Broad-shouldered and muscular, her lean athletic body served her burgeoning basketball career. When she wasn't hooping, she was a human liaison with the Cephalopod Council at the Octopus's Garden near Yerba Buena Island. Her basketball teammates called her "squid."

Frank envied the ease that Lori and her peers enjoyed. To think they were born after the quake, after the Glacial Pulse changed the Bay Area forever. The world changed so much since he was her age! He'd lived through it! The national government crumbled! The world he grew up in, which seemed permanent and unmovable for so long, started to wobble, then shrink, then it wasn't there anymore! And this new world was much larger now! People, animals, plants, air and water, rocks and soil—everything was alive! Everything was talking! He still found it hard to believe.

Some people said Frank played an important role, but he hadn't done anything anyone wouldn't have done under the same circumstances. Nor had he acted alone back then. Charlene Nichols, Eli, and many others stood shoulder to shoulder, refusing to follow Morgan's orders. They would not seize food or destroy gardens or farms anymore. They would not be used to evict people from occupied and repurposed buildings. They would not blindly follow anyone's orders again.

When Colonel Morgan and his supporters threatened to punish the mutineers, they laughed. Who had the numbers? Surrounding them and seizing their weapons, Frank and the others ushered Morgan and his loyal followers back to the dock and put them on the transport to Benicia.

"I'll be back!" he snarled. "I've got your names! You'll pay dearly for this!"

"You are not welcome here, *Mister* Morgan. Your 'services' are no longer needed!" announced Charlene Nichols over the loudspeaker, to loud cheers and jeers. "San Francisco is defederalized!" Like Frank she renounced her commission as a lieutenant. The former Federal Police disbanded themselves, confirming the surprising success of the long-time rightwing wet dream to shrink the federal government to the point that you could drown it in a bathtub!

The State of California was crippled by the collapse of its massive water redistribution system and the enormous burden of supporting millions of people in the devastated East Bay and Central Valley. Thirsty millions in Southern California demanded resources the state no longer had. It certainly could not challenge San Francisco as it rose, Phoenix-like from the wreckage and took on new plumes.

City government went through a months-long transformation. In a flurry of remarkable self-directed projects, San Francisco rebuilt and renewed itself. The former City government, crippled by the damage to City Hall and nearby facilities and the death of the Mayor and four supervisors, found itself superseded by neighborhood committees made up of organized plumbers, electricians, mechanics, transit workers, artists, musicians, nurses, doctors, carpenters, gardeners, writers, farmers and teachers. The city workers who actually ran things stepped forward and linked up with the neighborhood projects. The persistent kernel of a utopian urbanism, brewing in the hearts and souls of the city's denizens since the beginning, was finally given free expression.

The San Francisco Police Department was dissolved after the quake too. Over 85% of its personnel lived outside San Francisco and few could return during the first month, and by the time it was possible, no one missed them. Citizen's safety committees took over the day-to-day needs for handling outbreaks of violence and anti-social behavior, which usually could be traced to medical and mental health issues. Anxiety levels fell dramatically after the changes. With the new free housing that opened up, everyone found decent homes. Free housing and abundant locally grown food alleviated most of the daily sources of stress that kept the city polarized and anxious for decades. With everyone pitching in on rebuilding the new San Francisco, and taking shifts in the expanding farms, old barriers and attitudes crumbled almost as suddenly as the Federal Government had.

In the year after the earthquake, solar-powered electrical coops took over block by block to provide free power. The Plumbers Union project to replumb the City took even longer. Five years after the earthquake, San Francisco had a robust, resilient supply of local water based on wells, careful capture and management of annual rainfall, and an intensive water recycling system connecting sinks and bathtubs to thousands of acres of orchards and farm fields where asphalt once covered the city. A network of above-ground creeks, small ponds, and wetlands anchored the wildlife corridors that became urgent priorities when the non-human residents of the peninsula began to speak.

***

Looping, soaring, dipping, diving, and gliding. Thousands of crows converged over the flooded highrises of downtown every afternoon. Slowly they'd arrive, perching on trees that emerged from the small islands that dotted the once-crowded zone. Once the sun went down and the light faded, they arose in unison, assembling in a vast swirling cloud to fill the darkening blue sky, to share the news, to marvel at the humans who were finally paying close attention to them. Sometimes they listened!

The parrots gathered in their hundreds too, descending on Telegraph and Russian Hills, boisterously appreciating the flourishing forests filling wildlife corridors criss-crossing the city. Coyotes and raccoons emerged after dark to take advantage of the new passages dense with things to eat. Several small herds of elk wandered the City now, requiring trained dogs to keep them from the most productive farms. Creeks rushed down hillsides to fill ponds where frogs, fish, snakes, and countless birds gathered. Vast flocks of migrating birds returned to the San Francisco Bay after airports and shoreline freeways disappeared for good.

The octopuses were the linchpin. They figured out the fungus when they encountered the reefs. Then they sent messages. It wasn't easy. Humans are slow after all. They can't imagine they aren't the smartest, so it's especially hard for them to learn something new. It's hard for them to see or hear what they don't *already* see or hear! Not the octopuses. Once they came into the bay again, lured by the excitement, they found the fungal reefs. The reefs were familiar, something octopus-ish about them. Each extension had its own tactile and learning capacities—same as octopuses! The octopuses and the fungal reefs recognized each other and communicated through touch. That's when the octopuses learned that their distant genetic cousin used its extraordinary ability to adapt and evolve to integrate with the life forms it encounters, to merge and become indispensable, even with humans. The fungus invented a way to communicate where after millennia it seemed it would never be possible. And just in time, too! There were humans who couldn't change direction and kept making things worse. Not *all* humans—only the ones who controlled things. Why the rest of them put up with it for so long is a puzzle historians will be trying to explain long into the future.

The whales, meanwhile, were ecstatic. Dozens of humpbacks and gray whales became regular denizens of the Bay, drawn by the same buzz that drew the octopuses in. The gradual ending of industrialized slaughter gave them a chance to recover, to process the centuries-long trauma, and to reconnect oceanic networks. Marine sanctuaries had been a boon since their establishment. Cautious efforts to regulate the speed and paths of gargantuan container ships and massive oil tankers, along with restraints on the use of vast plastic nets to ensnare everything, gave them more breathing room than they'd enjoyed in a century or more. The noisy ocean was still an unwelcome reality, but the whales were being heard! It was ironic, but maybe humans would listen and change—to allow whales to hear each other again!

The long slow conversation going on among the trees in San Francisco was hard to perceive at first. The witches butter connected to it, and even helped extend it during the first months that it spread its mycelial network under the peninsula. It was difficult, however, for most of the species to understand where they were, or how they'd arrived here. The surrounding urban environment, the endless cement and asphalt, the cars, buses, and trucks—none of it was familiar. Where were the rivers, the lakes, the mountains? Whatever happened to the other plants, the bugs, the animals that were their timeless companions? Being transplanted to San Francisco's streets and parks left them confused and lonely. The fog and wind and rain were welcome, but since few of the city's trees had any deep memory or knowledge of this place, it was up to the oaks and redwoods to explain to the maples, the poplars, the gingkos, and even the Araucarias and other exotics, what it meant to be neighbors with the Pacific Ocean. Witches butter explained humans and their cities.

***

Jay was late. Dinner at Lamar and Cindy's—he should've been there already. He was pedaling furiously above the water on an elevated wooden bikeway and he was a few blocks away. Janet and Vero were supposed to be there with their partners. Shit, what were their names? He couldn't remember. Too many names to keep track of in this life! The strong smell of saltwater filled his nose after he passed the towering trees that had once been on the 4th floor of the transit center. Weird how trees imported from thousands of miles away rooted themselves and were flourishing at the edge of the flooded city. An arboreal island assembled itself in the debris, with a little help from some human friends, and decades later became a rich and noisy habitat where once the only thing that grew was the cloud of commercial data.

Jay was on the Common Council these days, selected as a delegate by the Confederation of Useful Workers (the largest single political organization in San Francisco) to which nearly everyone who wanted to, belonged. Serving on the Council was a thankless job that often involved mediating the disputes that routinely plagued the city's many self-management committees. As much as things changed, people still acted badly all too often! When they were asked by the Cephalopod Council to limit fishing in the Bay, there were still old fishermen who couldn't accept the idea that octopuses could communicate, let alone to make political demands! It was one thing to mediate between different groups of people, it was a whole other problem to mediate between different species! He was still getting used to the idea himself!

He exited the wooden bikeway on a ramp to the second floor of the towering white apartment building. It was that Rubik's cube architectural design popular in the early 21st century, twisting blocks that seemed as though they were about to fall. It survived the Big One, and for many years since was home to thousands of San Francisco's most engaged people. Lamar and Cindy were early, along with Leon Robertson, to establish residency in the wake of the floods and earthquake. Even before Frank and the rest of the Federal Police faced down Colonel Morgan and sent him packing, this building filled up with hundreds of people ready to begin a new life. Many lost everything during the quake. Once word got around that huge luxury apartments were available downtown, they filled up. The fact that it was permanently in the bay was something to be worked around.

Before Jay exited the ramp he noticed dozens of bioboats and other water craft filling the "street" below. These days, the canals of San Francisco were jammed with small watercraft moving people and goods around. And it became a major tourist attraction. Venice was submerged, lost to sea-level rise, and though San Francisco would never match Venice's glory, it had its charm. And that charm was only magnified by the seaweed, the sea lions, the traffic jams of watercraft that filled the former streets.

When bioboats started to proliferate, the octopuses asked for clarification. What was this new creature? Shouldn't it be represented, didn't it deserve rights? Witches butter, the intermediary medium, couldn't establish contact with it. It lacked self-awareness completely. It was as mechanical as a biological entity could be. A whole discussion ensued at the Cephalopod Council, eventually involving the All-Species Council of the Bay Area.

Grudgingly they allowed the bioboats to be grown and used. But they warned that further tinkering with life forms without self-awareness would not be tolerated. Jay had been exasperated by this.

"Who is hurt? Why wouldn't they welcome this? Isn't it better than vessels made of steel or wood or plastic?" Jay strained to understand.

Janet, who was also on the Common Council as a delegate from the Canopy Council of the League of Urban Farmers, gently explained to him that it wasn't that different than any political constituency who wanted to maintain its power. "But more than that, they are uncomfortable with human activity that mutes life forms. They understand that centuries of being treated as inanimate and lacking intelligence is precisely at the root of the disaster we will spend the rest of our lives trying to undo."

Other council members argued, like Jay, that this was preferable to the resource-heavy alternatives. But their hearts weren't in it. The moral authority of the All-Species movement made arguments on behalf of human needs or preferences, narrowly defined, sound shallow and worse, politically off-limits.

Jay paused on the 22nd floor landing to catch his breath. He still climbed the stairs automatically because of years without elevator service. It was a funny habit of his generation. Most places restored elevator service thanks to the latest invention from Doan Industries, the biovator, using a system of vertical vines that propelled latticed lightweight boxes up and down in the old elevator shafts. After he caught his breath and knocked, Lamar opened the door.

"Jay! Come on in! It's been too long!" He pulled him into a hug. "Did you climb those stairs?" he noticed his sweaty shirt.

Jay nodded, laughing. "You're not getting me in one of Dat's contraptions!"

"You're nuts! They're great! And guess what?" Lamar was grinning like a kid with a secret stash of candy. "We got a solar blimp station on our roof!" Another Doan Industries device, the solar blimp grew out of Dat's toying with it back at the beginning of the witches butter revolution.

"I heard that was coming. I remember the first prototype at the Festival of Possibilities!" He looked briefly crestfallen. "Fuck, that was SO long ago! I'm surprised that even came to mind. Anyway, I've been wanting to try blimp travel ever since I heard about it. I'll have to quit the Council—or at least take a leave of absence—before I can take the time to fly down to Mexico or even to Chicago or New Orleans!"

"You need to leave a few months or a half a year for any real trip these days. But that's a good thing, right?" Lamar clapped him on the shoulder. "What're you drinking?"

"I'll take a rosé. No heavy drinking for me."

"Oh yeah? I remember you as a gin and tonic guy, no?"

"I used to be... not much anymore." In his late-40s now, Jay hated the hangover more than he liked the high.

"Oh my god! Look who's here!" Vero jumped up from the couch to embrace Jay. "Seems like I haven't seen you in—what's it been? A year?"

Chagrined, Jay returned her hug and admitted it was longer than that. "You haven't aged a day though. You look great!" Vero was 55 and like most middle-aged women she was heavier than her younger days but hadn't lost her curves. Thick black eyebrows—nearly a unibrow—still hovered over glittering diamond studs at the corners of her eyes. Her thick hair hadn't gone gray yet. "Seriously, I hope I look as good as you do when I'm as old as you!" he laughed.

Vero playfully punched him on the shoulder. "*As old as me!* What are you? Haven't you hit 50 yet?"

"Nope, two years to go!"

"You remember my partner, Elroy? Or as we jokingly call him at home *El Rey!*"

Jay and Elroy exchanged greetings and the party devolved into many small conversations.

The door near the window opened and Leon and Leticia entered from the adjacent apartment, trailed by their daughter Lori who ducked a bit as she entered so her Afro wouldn't graze the door jamb.

"Jay! Haven't seen you in a while. Hey, can you take a look at my backed up bathtub?" Leon jerked his thumb over his shoulder towards his apartment. And then he started laughing. "Just kidding!" He gave Jay a hug. "You know Leticia my wife?"

"Yes, great to see you both. Lori! I can't believe it! Last time I saw you, you were about 12."

She looked at the middle-aged blond guy without recognition. "Oh, huh, yeah, I guess." She went to talk to her aunt Janet.

Before long Cindy called them to the table for dinner. "It's *Lapin a la Cocotte*—rabbit stew for you philistines!" She laughed and started serving. Rabbit was the second most common meat eaten in San Francisco, after chicken—it had been years since beef or pork were widely available.

Janet stood up and tapped her wine glass with her spoon, getting everyone's attention. "I'm happy to see you, friends and family. Let's give thanks to this rabbit who gave themself up for our meal."

"Er, it's three rabbits!" blurted Cindy with a smile.

"Oh, ok, thanks to each of them. And the grapes that gave us wine and the veggies that thrived in our farms, and the farmers who grew it. Thanks to them, thanks to you!" and she sat back down.

As people dug into the heaping plates of rabbit stew over rice, Jay nudged Janet and spoke softly to her. "Have you seen or talked to Dat Doan lately? How is it that his company is at the center of innovation? He must be getting rich from this?"

Janet lips tightened as she said in a low voice: "No one gets rich these days, you know that!" Jay knew as well as she did that the lion's share of surpluses are turned over to the Associated Confederation of Committed Communities, the new bioregional structure that governed the Pacific Coast from the tip of Baja California to Alaska. She took a bite of her meal and thought about what to say.

Dat and Maria were the first to see the BGM tablet 'work'—they found themselves in an unexpected back-and-forth with an octopus! At least it claimed to be and they had no way to verify it immediately. The words on the tablet described a location at the southern tip of Yerba Buena Island. They came to call it the "Octopus's Garden," where a gathering of octopuses and a large reef of witches butter fungus were working together. It was the paradigm shift of all paradigm shifts!

"Dat has his needs met. He's got a nice house on the upper slopes of Twin Peaks—one of the older houses with a big view of the City. That was always his dream. He shares it with a bunch of younger folks, even a couple with several children. He's got his chosen family and he has all the experimenting and wild scheming he can keep up with.

Dat Doan built his company during those years of Ex/Im and biohacking by putting collaboration ahead of everything. His complete disregard for wealth accumulation inoculated his projects against the typical logic of proprietary control and secrecy. It was poetic justice when he took over BGM, the remaining workforce inviting him in after the abolition of corporate personhood. They turned to the nemesis of their prior Board of Directors as a strategic move to survive in the new climate. He agreed to help refocus the company and then immediately step aside. He suggested they concentrate their R&D on regenerative agriculture, habitat restoration, and solar dirigible travel.

"I went to see him a few weeks ago." She lowered her voice now. "Jay, Dat's cancer doesn't look good. He got an extra decade thanks to the witches butter."

"Oh no!" Jay stopped eating and turned to Janet. She showed no emotion and returned to her meal. "What can we do?"

Janet shook her head. "You can go and visit him. He's getting the best medical attention available. Maybe he'll get lucky."

***

He sighed and felt his tears again. These days he caught himself crying quietly. He loved the smell of the storm-sodden air, the occasional birdsong, the merry dance of butterflies in the backyard. He gazed at his beloved city, the crazy tilting highrises downtown, leaning in the bay mud.

Alison Nakahara invented a new bio-engineered communications system. The original panels of witches butter that BGM engineered proved biological communications worked. Hell, when he and Maria realized they were in conversation *with an octopus* not long after the quake, they spent months trying to make sense of it. Ally's talents helped them decipher the cellular and extra-cellular network that witches butter assembléd, and how the octopuses connected to it. Her new idea was to use a modified banana plant. Running a thick vine across the top of a room at the edge of the ceiling, she got a large leaf to unroll on command. "When you spell it, use a 'y' so 'v-y-n-e,' ok?"

"Oh, you're into marketing now, huh?" Dat teased her. She blushed!

"I'm thinking more broadly than I used to," she confessed.

Her latest invention was working. She'd taken witches butter DNA and inserted it into a banana plant at her lab. Fertilizing it by surrounding it with soil full of witches butter, and then having Maria explain to it what she was trying to do, the first leaves to unroll from the plant could access the stream of messages and communications filling up the mycelial network. The vyne displayed messages on the big flat surface of the leaf. Accessing the early "large language models" that Artificial Intelligence pioneers used to train their algorithms, witches butter developed a nuanced understanding of human linguistic expression that greatly strengthened the deep emotional and biological knowledge foundation it started with.

"Dat, this is the biological internet. It's self-powering through photosynthesis and it connects to the All-Species network. And it responds to human voice!"

"Ally, that's fantastic! Congratulations! I hope you're right!" And he'd urged her to keep experimenting, to rely on Maria and Clara as they'd done for years now. And he told her about his condition. "I don't know how much longer I'll be here. Promise me you and the rest will keep going. Don't get distracted, stay focused on what's needed. And listen to the animals! They've been right about almost everything they ever said."

Alison had no capacity for heavy emotions. She shut down on hearing Dat admitting his illness. She'd lost both of her parents to cancer long ago, and it brought up deep fears. She held his hand briefly, thanking him and then she excused herself, leaving awkwardly and hurriedly.

Dat sat back in his big captain's chair and whirled around. He slapped the armrests in frustration. His guts hurt. The new treatment wasn't working. But the idea that he wouldn't be around to see how everything turned out was tormenting him. He was only 78! There was still so much to do.

***

Elsie was cleaning out a rabbit hutch when she heard some steps behind her.

"How's my favorite tycoon doing?"

She knew it was Juna and turned to give them a big hug. "Tycoon huh?

You're the one who started this!"

"Yeah, but you're the one who has built up the clientele and kept the rabbits fat and happy all these years. How long as has it been now?"

She chortled in her deep-throated way. "Depends on when you start counting... I was 3 when you brought that first truckload back after the earthquake... I won the Bay Area 4-H award for rabbits in 2040 when I was 15. I won the cooking contest for my *Coniglio alla Cacciatora* the year after that, remember?"

"Everyone knows Kite Hill Coniglio is the best place to get fresh rabbit in town!" Juna smiled. Bracelets and bangles jingled musically as they pushed their long black hair back. "Do you have a hairband I can snag?" they asked, clutching their hair in a bunch behind their head.

"Here ya go," she pulled one from the vest pocket of her overalls. Elsie was a rosy cheeked, cherubic woman with long light brown, not quite blonde hair. Not interested in clothing or fashion, she was completely at home in her regular get-up as a farmer. She was also a philosophy student, following in the unfulfilled footsteps of her father Donald.

"What's the news from San Bruno Mountain? How's Quarrytown these days?" Juna moved there permanently about a year after the earthquake. By then, the Cephalopod Council announced itself and people groped for a way to respond to the shock.

Juna put on an exaggerated expression as though they were frustrated. Then they started laughing. "I can't think of anywhere I'd rather be. We have a whole town there now, dozens of butter huts have spread up the terraced hillside. Where there was once an ugly scar of a quarry, there's a thriving town of farmers, about 80% of indigenous origins, mostly Central American. We're wrapped in the cozy embrace of the butter. You should hear the singing at full moon! The coyotes and birds start in around dusk and then different people join in. Angie started it a long time ago, but at this point, it's taken on a life of its own. It's off the hook!"

"We get some pretty wild singing around here on full moons, too! You remember the folks who hold a drum circle on Corona Heights? It's bigger than ever now!"

"Elsie, can you give me a dozen rabbits? I saw you're pretty full up when I glanced at your hillside pen."

"Sure! Please take them! You know how fast they breed. We can't always get rid of as many as we'd like to. People have started to eat a lot more farmed fish lately. Have you seen the fish farm down at Dolores Park?"

"Where the tennis courts used to be, right?"

She nodded. "Mission High students built it out a few years ago now. I wasn't sure if you'd seen it. Those stepped pools are brilliant, and they've perfected the system to where they're producing 2500 fresh 1-2 pound tilapia every month."

"Maybe I'll pick up some on my way home. What does the 'Ceph' say about it?"

Elsie chuckled again. "Same thing they said about our rabbit farm. 'People gotta eat!' Those octopuses gotta eat too, and so does everything else! No room for sentimentality at the Cephalopod Council!"

Elsie helped Juna choose a dozen rabbits and load them into a box on their e-trike. Scrub jays squawked loudly as they came fluttering in to perch on the box. The rabbits could hear their scratching feet and noisy verbalizing but couldn't see them. Juna smiled at the jays.

"You guys remember me, eh? Or maybe you've been told about me, because I don't think we've met before have we?" The jays bobbed their heads up and down and one tilted to the side, almost looking like they were smiling. Juna pulled out some Witchips for them. "Here's what you came for, right? I'm sure that's what I'm known for!" They smiled. The one jay hopped over for a chip, gobbled it up, and took to the air. Its companion watched, and then followed suit, cawing happily as it flew away.

***

Frank finished his salad and omelette while Lori regaled him with stories of her recent games. She was a power forward and she seemed to think she might get a chance to play professionally with the Oakland team.

"I'm proud of you! And thanks for this," he wiped his mouth with his napkin, gesturing to his empty plate. "You're a sweetheart!"

"I gotta go to work, grandpa. The octopuses expect one of us to be there every day at 4. I'm not sure why they care, since half the time there's nothing to do."

"Maybe it's the symbolism? They want humans to make the effort to live up to an agreement? No?"

"I guess so! Anyway, gotta fly! See you next week!"

Frank got himself up and leaning on his cane, he wobbled out the back door and down the five steps to the backyard. At least three dozen people were busy gardening, hanging out, laying in hammocks, reading on blankets, conversing in the expansive mid-block grounds.

"Hey Frank, you wanna play?"

"Sure, I'm ready to kick your ass!" Frank joked. Gideon Marshall and Steve Oguchi were his regulars, as he sat down to play Cuban dominoes with them at their table. "Who cleaned up the storm damage already?" he asked as he settled into his seat.

"The guys from over there," Steve pointed to the three-story building famous for its late-night parties. "They're young and strong. I don't think it took too long to cut up the fallen tree and chip it. Didn't you hear them this morning?"

"Must've slept through it. Who's got a double-15?" Frank was happily setting up his tiles, ready for some hours of friendly banter, the perfect way to complete his delightful lunch. He bragged about his granddaughter and her basketball career.

"Isn't she the one who has to hold hands with the octopuses?" Gideon asked.

"That's a lot to hold on to!" Oguchi joked.

"Yeah," Frank paused and looked at the billowing clouds in the blue sky above. "It *is* a lot to hold on to! I'm glad it's her! She was born into this world—who better?"

Their generation barely escaped their collective responsibility for the mess they'd made. How could stupidity, venality, willful ignorance, and incompetence block decent people trying to do the right thing for nearly his entire life? And to be honest, he hadn't even noticed until it suddenly and irrevocably collapsed! He could hardly wrap his head around the idea that people *did* abandon the old ways, the bizarre assumptions of property and hierarchy, the insane idea that humans were the peak of planetary intelligence. 'It was the octopus!' Like a message from another planet, like an alien race that suddenly appeared on Earth. People were so shocked, so shaken up, it finally toppled the fragile (dis)order, and made room for something new and remarkable to take its place. Finally!

ACKNOWLEDGEMENTS

Like most authors, I spent a lot of time alone and in my head while writing this book over the past couple of years. This simply wouldn't be possible without the extraordinary support and encouragement I receive from my wife and beloved life partner Adriana Camarena. She has offered unwavering enthusiasm for my work, and I can't be more grateful. She also intervened at the last minute to make this novel much more readable with her sharp editorial fixes. Thanks to her parents, too, who provided us weeks of blissful "retreat" space in their home next to Lake Chapala, where I wrote a lot of chapters.

I am also blessed to have a community-supported work life through my co-directorship of Shaping San Francisco. Thanks to my colleague there, Lisa-Ruth Elliott, I have the flexibility to work on a novel when most work situations would block that. The community of donors who sustain Shaping San Francisco (and by extension, us), is another hidden but crucial bit of support.

My 91-year-old dad has been one of those donors, and his life-long support of my unusual life choices has been key to my ability to write and publish. My sister and her husband moved in with my father a couple of years ago as his mobility declined (his brain remains as sharp as ever), and I thank them from the bottom of my heart for the close care they provide him—and I fully recognize how much of that care work they've spared me during the same time—another pillar supporting this book.

If I didn't have one of San Francisco's lowest rents this book would not exist. Thank you to the SF Community Land Trust and the many people who have kept it going with scotch tape and bubblegum since we "won" our building in a 2015 probate auction. Culture makers depend on low rent, and the Land Trust has been the organization that, for all its contradictions, has kept a comfy roof over my head while I was writing this book.

My wonderful daughter was a constant source of critical enthusiasm, and along with her husband she brought into my life incredible grandchildren. As the dedication indicates, thinking of their lives has been no small inspiration for me to pen this dystopic but ultimately hopeful view of our near future.

Lastly a warm thanks to Summer Brenner, Jubilee Debs, Unrulee, Daniel Steven Crafts, Mike Dyer, Marina Lazzara, Nancy Hernandez, and Annie Danger, who all gave me support and encouragement at crucial moments.

BOOKS BY CHRIS CARLSSON

Bad Attitude: The Processed World Anthology, co-edited with Mark Leger
   (1990: Verso)

Reclaiming San Francisco: History, Politics, Culture, co-edited with
   James Brook and Nancy J. Peters (1998: City Lights Books)

Critical Mass: Bicycling's Defiant Celebration, editor (2002: AK Press)

The Political Edge, editor (2004: City Lights Foundation)

After the Deluge, a novel of post-economic San Francisco
   (2004: Full Enjoyment Books)

Nowtopia: How Pirate Programmers, Outlaw Bicyclists and Vacant-Lot
   Gardeners Are Inventing the Future Today (2008: AK Press)

Ten Years That Shook the City: San Francisco 1968-78, co-edited with
   LisaRuth Elliott (2011: City Lights Foundation)

Shift Happens! Critical Mass at 20, co-edited with LisaRuth Elliott and
   Adriana Camarena (2012: Full Enjoyment Books)

*Hidden San Francisco: A Guide to Lost Landscapes, Unsung Heroes, &
   Radical Histories* (2020: Pluto Press)

ABOUT THE AUTHOR

Chris Carlsson, co-director of the "history from below" project *Shaping San Francisco*, is a writer, publisher, editor, photographer, public speaker, and occasional professor. He was one of the founders in 1981 of the seminal and infamous underground San Francisco magazine *Processed World*. In 1992 Carlsson co-founded Critical Mass in San Francisco, which both led to a local bicycling boom and helped to incubate transformative urban movements in hundreds of cities, large and small, worldwide. In 1995 work began on "Shaping San Francisco;" since then the project has morphed into an incomparable archive of San Francisco history at *Foundsf.org*, award-winning bicycle and walking tours, and almost two decades of Public Talks covering history, politics, ecology, art, and more (see *shapingsf.org*). Beginning in Spring 2020, Carlsson added Bay Cruises along the San Francisco shoreline to his repertoire.

Carlsson has written three previous books, the most recent being *Hidden San Francisco: A Guide to Lost Landscapes, Unsung Heroes, and Radical Histories* (Pluto Press: 2020). His 2004 novel is set in a future "post-economic" San Francisco (*After the Deluge*, Full Enjoyment Books: 2004), and his groundbreaking look at class and work in *Nowtopia* (AK Press: 2008) which uniquely examined how hard and pleasantly we work when we're not at our official jobs. He has also edited six books including three "Reclaiming San Francisco" collections with the venerable City Lights Books. He redesigned and co-authored an expanded *Vanished Waters: A History of San Francisco's Mission Bay* after which he joined the board of the Mission Creek Conservancy. He has given hundreds of public presentations based on Shaping San Francisco, Critical Mass, *Nowtopia*, *Vanished Waters*, and his "Reclaiming San Francisco" history anthologies since the late 1990s, and has appeared dozens of times in radio, television and on the internet.

Printed in the USA
CPSIA information can be obtained
at www.ICGtesting.com
LVHW030037151223
766573LV00058B/2257